John Edwin Sandys

Isocrates

Ad demonicum et Panegyricus

John Edwin Sandys

Isocrates

Ad demonicum et Panegyricus

ISBN/EAN: 9783741179648

Manufactured in Europe, USA, Canada, Australia, Japa

Cover: Foto ©Andreas Hilbeck / pixelio.de

Manufactured and distributed by brebook publishing software
(www.brebook.com)

John Edwin Sandys

Isocrates

ISOCRATES

EDITED BY

J. EDWIN SANDYS, B.A.

FELLOW AND LECTURER OF ST JOHN'S COLLEGE
AND LECTURER AT JESUS COLLEGE, CAMBRIDGE.

AD DEMONICUM

ET

PANEGYRICUS.

RIVINGTONS:
London, Oxford, and Cambridge.
1868

Cambridge:

PRINTED BY C. J. CLAY, M.A.
AT THE UNIVERSITY PRESS.

TO

STEUART ADOLPHUS PEARS, D.D.

HEAD MASTER OF REPTON SCHOOL,

THIS VOLUME

IS GRATEFULLY DEDICATED

BY

HIS FORMER PUPIL

THE EDITOR

PREFACE.

In the Lent and Easter terms of this year, I was called upon, in the course of College routine, to give lectures on the *ad Demonicum* and *Panegyricus* of Isocrates, a subject which had been selected for one of the minor University Examinations. The present volume is the result of those lectures. Owing to the fact that there was no edition with English notes of sufficient fulness and accuracy to be worth recommending as a text-book for use in the lecture-room, I was compelled to endeavour to supply the deficiency from independent sources, supplemented by the best continental editions, and during the last three months the rough memoranda thus collected for immediate use, have been prepared for the press and amplified to an extent which I scarcely contemplated when I began the task. The names of the continental editions which I have consulted will be found in their proper place, and my special obligations to my predecessors have been fully acknowledged in the notes, wherever such obligations have been really worth recording. One who is late in the field must expect to be frequently anticipated, especially in illustrative passages gathered from the range of ordinary classical authors, and an attempt to state every instance of this kind is not only hopeless, but in many cases unsatisfactory. For instance, I have in several of the notes found myself giving credit to one editor for a valuable collection of references which he himself had borrowed without acknowledgment from a previous editor. I have endeavoured to verify all these borrowed references, and in all cases, in which I have not done so, have given the name of the person who is

responsible for the accuracy of the statement. But the field is
still unexhausted, and even in the case of ordinary authors,
the industrious reapers of Germany have left many gleanings
'for the stranger' to gather.

The quotations from Isocrates himself are naturally frequent.
The general rule that every author is his own best interpreter
is particularly applicable in the case of Isocrates. No author
takes such delight in quoting from himself, and besides the
three great instances in which he quotes whole pages from
his previous writings, we have many shorter passages in which,
owing partly to a certain poverty of invention, partly to the
fact that the same theme often haunted him for years together,
partly to a self-complacent feeling that what he had once
expressed well could not easily be expressed better, he repro-
duces the same thoughts with only slight varieties of diction.
In such cases the blending of identity and variety is often
instructive; and for the purposes of explanation and textual
criticism are sometimes particularly important.

The real difficulties that arise in Isocrates are generally the
result of rhetorical exaggeration : but, for the rest, there is
perhaps no Attic author who is equal to him in simplicity of
constructions, in purity of language and transparency of style.
It is this that renders him peculiarly suitable as a stepping-stone
to the less easy prose of the other Attic orators, and of Aristotle,
Plato, and Thucydides; it is this that has made him as favorite
a subject in the schools of Germany as he was in our English
schools during the sixteenth and seventeenth centuries[1].

[1] See Roger Ascham's *Scholemaster*, passim. It was under Ascham's
tuition that Queen Elizabeth, in the 14th year of her age, translated the *ad
Nicoclem* and the *Nicocles* of Isocrates, (on the duties of kings and of subjects).
In the 20th year of her reign, Ashton drew up the Bailiffs' and Burgesses'
ordinances for Shrewsbury School, in which the head master is instructed to
teach 'for Greke...Isocrates ad Demonicum and Xenophon his Cyrus' (No.
34. in Baker's *Hist. of St. John's Coll.* p. 413. ed. Mayor). One of the
most popular school editions of the *ad Demonicum* and the *ad Nicoclem* was

With regard to the first of the selections included in this volume, I venture to think that (quite apart from the subject matter, which will be interesting or not according to the temperament of the reader) it will be found a useful study in the choice of words, that it will enable beginners to lay the foundation of a good Greek vocabulary, and be not entirely unprofitable to those who are more than beginners.

The second of these selections may be made equally useful for educational purposes, and has during the last year been satisfactorily tested in the Fifth form of Shrewsbury School. The many points of historical and literary interest which are there either incidentally or fully dwelt upon (e. g. the Persian wars, the Athenian and the Spartan supremacies, the influence of the Homeric poems, the mysteries of Eleusis, and the tribunals of Athens)—these, and similar subjects which arise immediately out of the text, if thoroughly studied once for all, will equip the learner with a variety of information, which will render his progress in harder authors more rapid and satisfactory.

The number of books of reference quoted in this edition has been reduced as far as possible: I have assumed the possession of a good Grammar, Lexicon, History, and Classical Dictionary, and have seldom travelled into the province of such books of reference, except where the statements contained in them appear to require either correction or expansion. On points of syntax, I have in accordance with the plan of this series given references to Madvig's Greek Syntax; but occasionally where a subject has been somewhat inadequately treated there, I have added or substituted a

that of 1677, published under the *imprimatur* of the Vice-Chancellor of Oxford, and the commendations of Ralph Cudworth (the celebrated Master of Christ's), and other Cambridge men. 'Librum *Georgii Sylvani* Pannonii... grato ac libenti animo testimoniis nostris ornamus, omnibusque Ludorum Literariorum magistris commendatum habemus.'

reference either to Donaldson's *Greek Grammar*, or Jelf's edition of Kühner, or lastly, to an excellent book, better known in America than in England, Goodwin's *Syntax of the Moods and Tenses of the Greek Verb* (3rd ed. Cambridge, U. S.). Frequent references have also been given to Veitch's Greek Verbs, irregular and defective, and to other accessible books; but, as a general rule, the information contained in books, that are out of the reach of ordinary readers and are not likely to be contained even in the best of school-libraries, has been incorporated into the notes, with a short indication of the source from which it is derived.

It was originally my intention to prefix to this volume a dissertation on the life, character and writings of Isocrates : this intention has, for various reasons, been abandoned. The plain facts that are known about him may be found either in Smith's Dictionaries, in Westermann's *Geschichte der Beredtsamkeit*, or in the Index to Benseler's edition in the Teubner series. A list of some of the *Subsidia* which bear more or less directly on the subject will be found on a subsequent page.

In conclusion, I have to return my thanks to all who have in any way helped me in carrying this little volume through the press; amongst others, to Professor Cowell, who has revised and supplemented one or two notes that touch on questions of Comparative Philology; to the Rev. R. Shilleto, who has allowed me to submit some of the pages to his criticism, and has added one or two remarks of his own ; to Mr. A. S. Wilkins, who has aided me in correcting the proofs of a majority of the notes ; and especially to the Rev. J. E. B. Mayor, who, besides other help and encouragement, has liberally given part of his valuable time to revising the whole of the notes.

J. E S.

St. John's Coll. Cambridge,
Sept. 30, 1868.

ON THE STYLE OF ISOCRATES.

LANGUAGE is the 'dress of thought,' or 'the incarnation of thought:' and all that is immediately connected with the visible form in which thought is clothed or embodied, so far as regards the individual words, the order of their arrangement, the relation of one sentence to another and the combined influence of all the sentences on the full development of an author's meaning, may be considered the natural subject of every attempt to state the characteristics of an author's style. It is on this principle that I propose in the few following pages to treat briefly and summarily of the style of Isocrates, with special reference to the words, the sentences, and the general effect of his writings.

The vocabulary of Isocrates belongs to the purest Attic dialect, unalloyed by the admixture of archaic and foreign elements; poetical, metaphorical and uncommon expressions are used with judgment and caution, and the words in general are chosen with discrimination and placed in effective positions, with a special view to perspicuity, variety and harmony[1].

The harmony of individual words is closely connected with the relation subsisting between each word and the word immediately preceding or succeeding it. If a word ends with a vowel and the next begins with a vowel, the result is a *hiatus*, which can either be removed entirely by the elision of one of the two vowels or by the introduction of a consonant between them, or can be modified by allowing the two vowel sounds to

---

[1] As an instance of a naturalised foreign word we have σατράπηι (*Paneg.* § 152), of a poetic word, οὐρανομήκηι (*de Perm.* § 134). Among the metaphorical expressions we find ἐδωρεύειν (*Paneg.* 131), ἴχνος τῆς ἐκείνου πραότητοι (*Hel.* 37), ἐξοκείλας (*Epp.* II. 13). Some of the rare words are quoted on p. xxxiv *init.*

blend with one another. Isocrates generally does his best to
avoid *hiatus* altogether, a fact which is not only expressly
stated by ancient authorities but is also partially confirmed by
the evidence of the best manuscripts[1].

The structure of his sentences demands a more explicit
statement than is necessary in the case of his vocabulary; and
it may help us to a clearer view of this part of our subject, if
we dwell for a moment on the two-fold Aristotelian division of
style, with reference to the internal structure of sentences and
their relation to one another.

The first is the λέξις εἰρομένη (the jointed style) or, as it
is called by a later authority writing from a different point of
view, the λέξις διηρημένη (the disjointed style), in which 'the
sentences and clauses are strung together, εἰρόμενα,—hang
from one another like the links of a chain or the joints of a
reed..., with no other connexion than that which is supplied
by the σύνδεσμοι or connecting particles[2].' The author quoted
by Aristotle as an illustration of this style is Herodotus—an
author in whom thought follows upon thought, clause upon
clause, sentence upon sentence—each simply connected and
yet disconnected with its immediate sequel: in a style, in short,
which, in our own literature, may best be paralleled by the
Voiage and Travaile of Sir John Maundevile or any well-told
story of fairy-land,

'He flows, and, as he flows, for ever will flow on.'

The second division is the λέξις κατεστραμμένη, ἡ ἐν περιόδοις λέξις (the compact, condensed, concentrated, comprehensive periodic style). The difference between the two styles
may be easily illustrated by a variety of similes; to adopt
one of these, which has the advantage of antiquity, the first
resembles a number of stones lying near one another, loose,
scattered and uncombined: the second resembles the same

---

[1] Dionys. Halic. *de vi Demosth.* c. 4, *judic. de Isocr.* c. 2; Cicero, *Orat.*
44; Plut. *Moral.* 350 E, Ἰσοκράτης ὁ φοβούμενος φωνῆεν φωνήεντι συγκροῦσαι;
Hermog. περὶ Ἰδεῶν a (*Rhet. Gr.* II. 338, Spengel), v. p. xxxv, and p. 128 n.

[2] Mr Cope's Introduction to Aristotle's *Rhetoric*, p. 306—316.

stones when bound compactly in the self-supporting cohesion of a vaulted dome[1].

This latter is the style of all the more artistic Greek writers and of Isocrates in particular. A rhetorician by profession, he devoted many years of a prodigiously long life to the cultivation of this 'periodic style';—casting and recasting his clauses, moulding and remoulding his sentences;—at one time elaborating moral maxims to be drilled into his readers with the double point of a polished antithesis; at another, writing clear sensible and ingenious speeches, to be delivered by his clients before the law-courts or the general assemblies of Athens[2]; but never so well pleased with himself as when dealing with grand questions of public policy[3], or dwelling in satirical, contemptuous and patronising terms on his more or less illustrious contemporaries[4], or lastly, dilating with supreme complacency on himself, his many pupils and his so-called philosophy[5].

As might be expected, from the variety of his subject matter, the style of his sentences is also varied within certain limits. In his treatise addressed to Nicocles, the sentences are thrown into a short and concentrated form; in his forensic speeches, the sentences are sometimes expressed very briefly[6], but more frequently in a slightly expanded shape, and it is mainly in his more ambitious and in some respects less successful efforts, that the sentences assume their greatest length. This length, however, in no single instance detracts from the clearness of his meaning, for notwithstanding the

---

[1] Demetrius περὶ Ἑρμηνείας c. 13, Mr Cope *l. c.* p. 310, and De Quincey, Vol. x. *on Style*, p. 188.

[2] *Aegineticus* (a speech which well deserves Dobree's eulogy: '*nitidissima oratio*'), *de Bigis* (in defence of the son of Alcibiades), *Plataicus* (p. 105. n.) &c.—An edition of these speeches is still a *desideratum*.

[3] *Panegyricus, de Pace.*

[4] Esp. in the speech *contra Sophistas*, the *Helenae Encomium*, the *Busiris*, and the *Panathenaicus*, § 7 sqq. See p. 160. n.

[5] Esp. *De Permutatione*, written, as Isocr. says, ὥσπερ εἰκὼν τῆς ἐμῆς διανοίας καὶ τῶν ἄλλων τῶν βεβιωμένων. v. p. 48. n.

[6] *Trapeziticus* and *Amartyrus.*

variety of subordinate clauses interwoven into the expanding fabric, notwithstanding the complex contrasts between particle and counter particle, and the long suspense in which the attention is held by his ascending periods, nevertheless his careful choice of words, and his scrupulously distinct arrangement of the various parts, combine in producing an unmistakeable transparency which pervades the sentence to the very end.

The consideration of the sentences of Isocrates naturally leads us to a statement of some of the artificial devices with which he endeavours to give precision and embellishment to his language. His frequent, not to say excessive, use of these artifices is mainly due to the general influence of the 'Sicilian school' of Rhetoric and to the instructions of Gorgias in particular. The names they have received from the Greek writers on Rhetoric are very numerous and sometimes confusing, but the following table contains all that are absolutely necessary for our present purpose :

     (i) ἀντίθεσις   = a parallelism in sense,
     (ii) παρίσωσις = a parallelism in structure,
     (iii) παρομοίωσις = a parallelism in sound.

The last of these is subdivided into three species :

     1. ὁμοιοκάταρκτον,
     2. ὁμοιοτέλευτον,
     3. παρονομασία[1].

By ἀντίθεσις is meant 'the opposition either of words or sense, or both, in two corresponding clauses of a sentence ;' e. g. contrast of words alone : διδότω γὰρ ὁ πλούσιος καὶ εὐδαίμων τῷ πένητι καὶ ἐνδεῖ: of sense alone, ἐγὼ μὲν τοῦτον νοσοῦντα ἐθεράπευσα, οὗτος δ' ἐμοὶ μεγίστων κακῶν αἴτιος γέγονεν ;

---

[1] For the varied meanings of these and similar terms, v. the passages quoted s. vv. either in Ernesti's *Lex. Technolog. Graec.* or in the *Index Rhetoricus* of Spengel's *Rhetores Graeci*. The simple classification adopted in the text is due to Mr Cope (*Journ. of Cl. and S. Philol.* No. VII. 69—72).—For examples, v. Index to this vol.

and of both words and sense, *οὐ γὰρ δίκαιον τοῦτον μὲν τὰ ἐμὰ ἔχοντα πλουτεῖν, ἐμὲ δὲ τὰ ὄντα προϊέμενον οὕτω πτωχεύειν*[1].

By *παρίσωσις* is meant a 'general correspondence or equality in the forms of two sentences and includes *ἰσόκωλα*, which are sentences in which the two members are of the same length;' *e.g.* Isocr. *Helen.* § 17 (where the words, syllables and even the very accents correspond):

τοῦ μὲν ἐπίπονον καὶ φιλοκίνδυνον τὸν βίον κατέστησε,
τῆς δὲ περίβλεπτον καὶ περιμάχητον τὴν φύσιν ἐποίησε[2].

By *παρομοίωσις* (or *παρήχησις*) is meant parallelism in sound between words that are brought together in the same sentence. This includes the three varieties of *ὁμοιοκάταρκτον*, *ὁμοιοτέλευτον*, and *παρονομασία*. The first of these three terms may be used to denote similarity in the beginnings of words; the second, similarity in the endings; and the third, a general similarity of sound or form pervading the whole of the words.

The above figures have their origin in natural principles. Contrast of thought naturally expresses itself in contrast of words, hence the origin of *ἀντίθεσις*. The same principle extended to clauses and sentences gives us the origin of *παρίσωσις*; and lastly, the power of association, which causes one uttered sound to suggest another similar sound, leads to the development of *παρομοίωσις*. All these figures of form have their natural uses; and are unconsciously used by numbers who have never heard of Gorgias and the 'Sicilian school;' it is the *conscious* and deli-

---

[1] Anaximenes 'Ρητορ. πρὸς 'Αλέξανδρον, c. 26 (t. 212. *Rhet. Gr.* ed. Spengel). For striking instances of forced antithesis, v. Thuc. II. 40. 4 and v. 95, both of which exemplify Pascal's comparison, 'Ceux qui font des antithèses en forçant les mots sont comme ceux qui font de fausses fenêtres pour la symétrie.'

[2] *εἰ δὲ τὸ παράδειγμα τοῦτο καὶ ὁμοιοτέλευτόν ἐστιν, οὐδὲν διαφέρει· πολλοὶ γὰρ λόγοι καὶ ἐκ δύο καὶ ἐκ πλειόνων σχημάτων σύγκεινται.* Alexander περὶ σχημάτων, II. 26.—Lyly's *Euphues* will supply the reader with as many English instances as he pleases of all the figures mentioned in the text, *e.g.* 'either by wit to obtain some conquest, or by shame to abide some conflict' (which is an instance of *παρίσωσις*, *ὁμοιοκάταρκτον* and (false) *ἀντίθεσις*).

berate use of them that is now claiming our attention. In the earlier writings of Isocrates these artistic devices have received one of their fullest exemplifications, but although often very effective, they are not unfrequently the result of manifest effort, and are spoiled by their painfully elaborate and artificial character. It is satisfactory however to notice that in his old age, he abjures to a great extent the excessive use of these artificial ornaments. In the *Panathenaicus*, a speech published in the ninety-fourth year of his age, he tells us that in the days of his youth he made it his principle to write orations on matters of public interest to Athens and to Greece, orations 'fraught with many a parallelism in sense and in structure and with the other figures that light up rhetorical compositions and extort applause from the audience,' but that such a fashion of speaking was ill suited to his grey hairs[1].

In conclusion, we must consider the style of Isocrates in relation to the constituent parts of his compositions and to the general effect thereby produced. There can be no dispute as to the excellence of his arrangement of these constituent parts; sometimes this appears in a careful and formal division of his orations into the four great sections of prelude, statement, proof, and peroration[2]; at other times, in a scrupulous observance of the wholesome (but not very original) rule which he is said to have laid down in his *Art of Rhetoric*; 'in narration, the first and the second and the remaining parts must be stated in due order; we must not before the first point is finished pass on to another and then from the very end revert to the first; and similarly in the case of each particular point, the ideas must be rounded off and complete in themselves[3];' sometimes on the other hand he prefers, in the case of two separate narratives, which have several points in common, to interweave the relation

---

[1] *Panath.* § 1—3.

[2] 'Isocrates primus in quatuor partes orationem divisit, προοίμιον, διήγησιν, πίστεις, ἐπίλογον. v. Dionys. Halic. pp. 480—496.' Baiter and Sauppe, *Orat. Attici*, II. 224.

[3] Baiter and Sauppe, *ib.* 225.

of the one with that of the other, taking care at the same time that no real obscurity shall arise from the apparent complication[1].

His speeches have generally 'one leading idea, of suitable importance, fertile in its consequences, and capable of evoking not only thought but feeling; in these leading thoughts he seizes certain points opposed to one another, such as the old and the new times, or the power of the Greeks and that of the Barbarians; and expanding the leading idea in a regular series of sequences and conclusions, he introduces at every step in the composition the propositions which contradict it in its details, and in this way unfolds an abundance of variations always pervaded and marked by a recurrence of the original subject; so that, although there is great variety, the whole may be comprehended at one glance[2].'

The general effect of each of his writings (so far as it can be broadly stated without entering into detail on all their diversified subjects) is exactly what might be expected from the facts that have been already stated. At the end of our perusal we feel that it is the graceful rhetorician and not the vehement orator, the dexterous fencer and not the bold man of battle, that has engaged our attention: that we have been listening only to the thin, clear echoes of a silver chime, and not to the thunders of a Pericles or a Demosthenes.

Isocrates in his sententiousness, his prosiness, and self-laudation, as well as in his length of years, is emphatically the Nestor of the 'Attic orators';

> Nestor the leader of the Pylian host,
> The smooth-tongued chief, from whose persuasive lips
> Sweeter than honey flowed the stream of speech.
> Two generations of the sons of men
> For him were past and gone, who with himself

[1] v. p. 78. n.
[2] Müller's *Gk. Literature*, c. xxxvi.

Were born and bred on Pylos' lovely shore,
And o'er the third he now held royal sway.'

Born in the era of Pericles, Isocrates reached the era of Philip.
The year of his birth was 436 B.C., eight years after that of
Xenophon and Aristophanes, and eight years before that of
Plato. He survived all three, and had only two years more
been added to his days, he would have lived a whole century
and seen Alexander ascend the throne of Macedon. As it
was, he died in the year 338 B.C. shortly after the battle of
Chaeroneia[1]. He was buried in the sepulchre of his family
and near his tomb was placed a tablet representing his
various instructors, and among them stood Gorgias, (with
Isocrates beside him), while the tomb itself was surmounted
with a lofty pillar, which was crowned with a Siren as an
emblem of his style[2].

[1] The traditionary story, which attributes his death to the grief and
disappointment caused by the news of that battle, is probably untrue. It is
recorded by Pausanias (*Attic.* 18), Lucian (Μακρόβια, 23), and Pseudo-Plutarch, and is familiarised by Milton's allusion to the 'Dishonest victory...
fatal to liberty' which 'killed with report that old man eloquent;' but the
3rd letter (the genuineness of which can hardly be doubted) contains a
special congratulation to Philip, which must refer to this very victory.
Isocrates was very weak at the time when he wrote the letter (παντάπασιν
ἀπειρηκώs) and probably died not long after. (v. *Blass* quoted on p. xxx.)

[2] Philostrat. *vit. Soph.* 1. 17, ἡ σειρὴν ἡ ἐφεστηκυῖα τῷ Ἰσοκράτους τοῦ
σοφιστοῦ σήματι...πειθὼ κατηγορεῖ τοῦ ἀνδρός κ.τ.λ. Pseudo-Plutarch *vit.*
x. *orat.* εἰσιν τριάκοντα πηχῶν, ἐφ' οὗ σειρὴν πηχῶν ἑπτὰ συμβολικῶs, ὃι νῦν
οὐ σώζεται.

A SELECTION OF PASSAGES BEARING ON THE STYLE OF ISOCRATES.
(Only the shortest, the most interesting, or the least accessible, are here
printed).

ΣΩΚΡΑΤΗΣ   Νέος ἔτι, ὦ Φαῖδρε, Ἰσοκράτης· ὃ μέντοι μαντεύομαι κατ'
αὐτοῦ, λέγειν ἐθέλω.

ΦΑΙΔΡΟΣ   Τὸ ποῖον δή;

Σω.   Δοκεῖ μοι ἀμείνων ἢ κατὰ τοὺς περὶ Λυσίαν εἶναι λόγους τὰ τῆς
φύσεως, ἔτι τε ἤθει γενικωτέρῳ κεκρᾶσθαι· ὥστε οὐδὲν ἂν γένοιτο θαυμαστὸν
προϊούσης τῆς ἡλικίας εἰ περὶ αὐτούς τε τοὺς λόγους, οἷς νῦν ἐπιχειρεῖ, πλέον
ἢ παίδων διενέγκοι τῶν πώποτε ἁψαμένων λόγων, εἴτε * εἰ αὐτῷ μὴ ἀποχρήσαι
ταῦτα, ἐπὶ μείζω [δέ] τις αὐτὸν ἄγοι ὁρμὴ θειοτέρα. φύσει γάρ, ὦ φίλε, ἔνεστί
τις φιλοσοφία τῇ τοῦ ἀνδρὸς διανοίᾳ.

* mss. ἔτι τε...μείζω δέ.

PLATO, *Phaedrus*, p. 279.

For Aristotle's quotations see Index to this volume.

Ὁμοιοτέλευτα et ἰσοκατάληκτα et πάρισα et ὁμοιόπτωτα ceteraque huius-
modi scitamenta, quae isti apirocali, qui se Isocratios videri volunt, in con-
locandis verbis inmodice faciunt et rancide, quam sint insubida et inertia et
puerilia, facetissime hercle significat in quinto saturarum Lucilius.   (148—
103 B.C).

...Hoc 'nolue'-(ris) et 'debueris' te
Si minus delectat, quod ἄτεχνον et Eisocratium est
Ὀχληρόνque simul totum ac συμμειρακιῶδεs,
Non operam perdo.

AUL. GELLIUS, *Noct. Attic.* XVIII. 8.

Suavitatem Isocrates, subtilitatem Lysias, acumen Hyperides, sonitum
Aeschines, vim Demosthenes habuit.   Quis eorum non egregius? tamen
quis cuiusquam nisi sui similis.

CICERO, *De Oratore*, III. viii. 28.   v. ib. II. iii. 10 (pater eloquentiae);
xlii. 94; and III. xliv. 175.—*Orator*, xii. 38; xlii. 40—42; xliv. 149
—151; li. 172; and lii. 174—176.—*Brutus*, viii. 32—34, and *Epp.
ad Atticum*, II. 1. 1 (Isocrati μυροθήκιον).

Ὁ δ' Ἰσοκρατικὸς (sc. λόγοι) κομψεύεται μέν, ἀλλὰ μετὰ σεμνότητος, καὶ
πανηγυρικώτερός ἐστι μᾶλλον, ἢ δικανικώτερος.   ἔχει δὲ τὸν κόσμον μετ' ἐνερ-
γείας, καὶ κομψικὸν ἐστι μετὰ τοῦ ἀνυστικοῦ καὶ χρήσιμον οὐ μὴν ἀγων-
ιστικόν· περιγράφων δὲ τὴν ἀπαγγελίαν ταῖς περιόδοις, καὶ ὅλως μεσότητα

σωφρονίζων λιτότητι, τὸ δὲ λιτὸν ἐξαίρων. καὶ αὐτοῦ μάλιστα ζηλωτέον τήν τε
τῶν ὀνομάτων συνέχειαν, καὶ τὸ τῆς ὅλης ἰδέας ἐπιδεικτικόν.

DIONYSIUS of Halicarnassus. (ob. B.C. 7).
τῶν ἀρχαίων κρίσις V. 2.

...πέφυκε γὰρ ἡ Λυσίου λέξις ἔχειν τὸ χάρισ, ἡ δ' Ἰσοκράτους βούλεται.
de Isocrate judicium, 3.

ἀναγνώσεων μᾶλλον οἰκειότερά ἐστιν ἢ ῥήσεων.
ib. 3.

δουλεύει ἡ διάνοια πολλάκις τῷ ῥυθμῷ τῆς λέξεως καὶ τοῦ κομψοῦ λείπεται
τὸ ἀληθινόν.
ib. 12.

Clarissimus ille praeceptor Isocrates, quem non magis libri bene dixisse,
quam discipuli bene docuisse testantur.

QUINTILIAN (40—118 A.D.), Inst. Or. II. 8. 11.

(After characterizing Demosthenes, Aeschines, Hyperides and Lysias)
Isocrates in diverso genere dicendi nitidus et comptus et palaestrae quam
pugnae magis accommodatus omnes dicendi Veneres sectatus est, nec
immerito; auditoriis enim se non iudiciis comparat; in inventione facilis,
honesti studiosus, in compositione adeo diligens, ut cura eius reprehen-
datur.
ib. X. 1. 79.

Nam mihi videtur M. Tullius, cum se totum ad imitationem Graecorum
contulisset, effinxisse vim Demosthenis, copiam Platonis, iucunditatem Isocratis. Nec vero quod in quoque optimum fuit, studio consecutus est
tantum; sed plurimas vel potius omnes ex se ipso virtutes extulit immortalis
ingenii beatissima ubertas.

ib. X. 1. 108.   v. also IX. 4. 35—36; 3. 74, XII. 10. 49.

πολὺ τὸ καθαρὸν τῆς λέξεως παρ' Ἰσοκράτει.

HERMOGENES (fl. 2nd cent. A.D.), περὶ ἰδεῶν, a (Rhetores Graeci,
II. pp. 277 and 283, ed. Spengel.).

...ὁ δὲ Ἰσοκράτης μὴ οὖσαν φύσει παρίωσιν ἐβιάσατο ἂν γενέσθαι, διὰ τὸ
μᾶλλον αὐτῷ ἐδλλους μᾶλλον καὶ ἐπιμελείας ἢ πιθανότητος καὶ ἀληθείας.
ib. p. 334. cf. ib. p. 338 fin. and p. 412.

οὐκ ἀχρεῖον δὲ οὐδὲ τῶν Ἰσοκράτους παραγγελμάτων ἐντρέπεσθαι, μὴ τραχύ-
νειν τὸν λόγον τῇ παραθέσει καὶ συμπλοκῇ τῶν καλουμένων φωνηέντων, ἃ τὴν
κρᾶσιν οὐκ ἀνέχεται καὶ τὸν λόγον οὐχ ὁμοίως συνυφαίνειν ἔοικεν, οὔτε λεῖόν τε
καὶ ἀνταίστως εἰς τὴν ἀκοὴν παρίησιν, ἀλλ' ἐπιλαμβάνεται τοῦ πνεύματος καὶ
ἐπίσχει τὸ πνεῦμα τῆς φωνῆς.

LONGINUS (fl. 3rd cent. A.D.), Ars Rhetorica, ap. Rhetores Gr. 1. 306,
ed. Spengel.

ON THE TEXT OF ISOCRATES.

THE text of Isocrates is perhaps in a sounder condition than
that of any Greek author. Wolf and Coray effected all that
the aid of inferior MSS allowed, but a new era in Isocratean
criticism began with Bekker's discovery of the *codex Urbinas*.
The other MSS are supposed to have been transcribed from
earlier copies that had been annotated with interlinear and
marginal explanations taken down by pupils in the lecture-
rooms of ancient expositors of Isocrates[1]. These explanations
were carelessly copied into the text, but the *codex Urbinas*
enabled Bekker to remove the interpolations and to restore the
true readings in a great number of passages. It must not be
however supposed that this famous MS is infallible; although
possibly the best of all Greek MSS, it is after all only the
best among the bad, and those who are likely to be carried
away by the characteristic enthusiasm and poetic diction of the
Zurich editors[2] may have their attention drawn with advantage to the following blunders, a few of which I quote (from
the *Panegyricus* alone):—§ 29 ἡδίστους τὰς ἐλπίδας (for ἡδίους),
§ 103 τῆς ἡμετέρας εὐδαιμονίας (for ἡγεμονίας), § 142 Κοίνωνος for
Κόνωνος, § 157 ἐν τῇ τελευτῇ τῶν μυστηρίων (for ἐν τῇ τελετῇ),
and § 176 τὰ τοὺς ἑταίρους ἐλαττοῦντα (for ἑτέρους). But these
and similar mistakes are too obvious to mislead the critic, or
in any great degree to impair the value of its readings. The
cod. Urb. must therefore be the basis of every edition of

[1] v. Baiter and Sauppe, praef. ii.
[2] 'I. Bekkerus limpidum fontem, cuius memoria interciderat, feliciter
invenit, atque solerti opera effecit, ut dictionis isocrateae pellucidae undae
per alveum suum latum magis quam profundum placide queant decurrere.'
ib. i.

xxii ON THE TEXT

Isocrates.—The next place must be assigned to the *cod. Am-brosianus,* which sometimes alone preserves the true reading; and, when it agrees with the *cod. Urb.* the combined authority is almost irresistible.

The principle of the Zurich editors is to follow the MSS as closely as possible, even where the usage of Isocrates would suggest another reading; the principle advocated by Benseler in the Teubner edition of 1851 is to follow the usage of Isocrates, even when the MSS are against him. In Benseler's preface the following canons are laid down:

(1) *Ubi in Isocratis scriptis hiatus restat, ibi locus est corruptus, aut non Isocrateus.*

(2) *Ad aequabilitatem membrorum et antithetorum studium debet attendere, qui Isocratis verba est restiturus.*

(3) *Isocr. se non minus in elegendis quam in conneãendis verbis diligentissimum praestitit scriptorem.*

(4) *Isocr. dialeão usitata cum iudicio quidem sed constanter usus est.*

(5) *Isocr. orationes suas ad unam speciem confirmavit easdemque sententias iisdem verbis expressas saepius repetiit.*

(6) *Isocr. sua bene excogitavit et disposuit.*

In accordance with these canons supplemented by the authority of the best MSS he published an edition of the text in 1851. The respect due to a veteran editor whose familiarity with his author was shown as far back as the year 1829, ought not perhaps to prevent us from venturing for a moment to doubt the soundness of his application of these principles. All of his canons are useful, as an indication of the general usage of the author, but it does not follow that every single passage must be corrected to suit those general principles. The first is perhaps the least satisfactory of all and must be accepted with considerable reserve, but the others are more trustworthy, and their application, if conducted with caution, may be of great service in settling the text.

The text of the present edition is mainly based on that of the Zurich editors supplemented by Benseler's editions. My

first intention was simply to reprint the text of the Teubner
series; but it was not long before I found that many of its
readings were untenable; I have therefore resorted, in many
cases, to the safer readings of the Zurich editors—a course
which has been amply justified by Benseler's new edition of the
Panegyricus and the Philippus (in 1854). The edition contains
a German translation and very copious notes, mainly on the
subject-matter and on the errors of previous translators. In
this excellent edition, which, I regret to say, did not reach me
until more than half the Panegyricus was in type, the editor
has himself, in at least twenty instances, deserted his former
readings.

The following account of the more important MSS is necessary to explain the details of the table of readings. It is
copied from Baiter's preface to the Panegyricus—which is now
out of print—and is supplemented with extracts from the
preface of the Zurich editors.

I. *Codicum Isocrateorum* duas familias distinxit Bekkerus, quae cum aliis
rebus inter se differunt, tum Antidosi aut integra aut mutila. Ex hoc
genere unus nominandus est antiquissimus

Cod. Vaticanus 65 (Λ), membranaceus, forma quadrata, foliis 304 versuum vicenorum binorum. ἐτελειώθη ἡ βίβλος αὕτη παρὰ Θεοδώρου ὑπάτου
καὶ βασιλικοῦ νοταρίου γραφεῖσα οἰκείᾳ χειρὶ μηνὶ ἀπριλλίῳ...ἐτ. ς.φοα. (i. e.
6571 A. M. Const. = 1063 p. Chr. n.) Continet omnes orationes [sed ejus
quae est ad Demonicum partem majorem manus alia multo recentior sup-
plevit]. In margine leguntur scholia pauca et exigui momenti, tum ab
eadem manu scripta tum a seriori. Epistolae desunt. Hoc codice, ex
Italia in bibliothecam Parisiensem Imperialem translato, postea suae sedi
restituto, primum usus est Coray, qui eum totum excussit; praesto erat
etiam Bekkero, qui Callimacheam et Nicianam cum eo contulit.

Alterius generis adhuc innotuerunt quattuor; quorum praestantissimus
est

Cod. Urbinas 111 (Γ), "membranaceus, forma quadrata, foliis 420, pa-
ginis versuum 24 et sub finem 26, a duabus scriptus manibus, quarum
prima ad follum 316 r. pertinet, margine a pluribus corrigentium variasque
lectiones apponentium oppleta. neque iis se finibus continuit correctorum
temeritas, sed textum quoque adorta effecit ut multis locis, quid ab initio
scriptum fuerit, dignosci non possit. nocuit etiam mador, quo factum est
ut subinde folia foliis adhaerescerent. insunt orationes 19, desunt Callimacheam et Nicianam." Haec Bekkerus, qui nihil de aetate codicis annotavit.

In fine Busiridis subscribitur: βούσιρις ΗΒΗΩΙΔΔΔΔ. Διωνύσιος ἅμα τοῖς ἑταίροις Θεοδώρου καὶ εὐσταθίου. Insunt etiam epistolae [ix]. Hunc codicem totum excussit Bekkerus, eumque editioni suae quasi fundamentum subjecit. [Urbinatis tanta est bonitas, ut non solum Isocratis ceteris codicibus omnibus, sed etiam aliorum scriptorum graecorum libris manu scriptis plerisque antistet milibus trecentis.]

Cod. Vaticanus 936 (Δ), "bombycinus, forma et ipse quadrata, foliis 234, quorum 184—222 Themistio data sunt. Themistium excipiunt Isocratis epistolae. communem hujus cum Urbinate originem arguit communis in extrema Antidosi lacuna, desunt et quae Urbinati desunt, et de Bigis oratio." Cum hoc Bekkerus contulit Evagoram, Helenam, Sophistas, Antidosin. [Insunt orationes xviii, et Epistolae ix, desunt Callimachea, Niciana, de Bigis.]

Cod. Laurentianus (Θ), ['papyraceus, in 4, saeculi XIII. madore et tineis multis locis male redactus' Bandini ap. BS.] "foliis 145; Aristotelem habet De Mundo, Isocratis orationes undecim (Hel. Evag. Bus. Paneg. Areop. Plat. Archid. Soph. Phil. Panath. Antid.), Polemonis de Callimacho et Cynaegiro declamationes, Theophrasti characteres primos." Cum hoc Bekkerus contulit dumtaxat Archidamum; ex Antidosi varias lectiones indicaverat Mustoxydes, cui scriptus videtur seculo XII. In Archidamo parvi momenti est, multo majoris in Antidosi, ubi interdum solus veram Isocratis manum servavit.

Cod. Ambrosianus (E), bombycinus, saeculi XIV. ut videtur Mustoxydi. Fuerat Michaëlis Sophiani; Mediolanum adductus est ex insula Chio a. 1606. Perhibebatur continere Panathenaicum ceteris auctiorem (vid. Colomesius Opusc. p. 36 sqq.), quod tamen negant et Mustoxydes et Angelus Maius. Error natus videtur e permutatione duarum orationum, Panathenaici et Antidoseos. [Continet orationes xxii. Epistolae novem in ΓΔΕ leguntur hoc ordine: 1. ad Dionysium. 2. ad Archidamum. 3. ad Iasonis liberos. 4. ad Timotheum. 5. secunda ad Philippum. 6. prima ad Philippum. 7. ad Alexandrum. 8. ad Antipatrum. 9. ad Mytilenaeorum magistratus.] Ex hoc codice primum integra edita est Antidosis, praeter quam hucusque cum eo collatae sunt quattuor orationes [Archid., Socialis, Trapez., Paneg.]. [Baiterus a. 1831 excussit reliqua.]

Copiae victorianae (Vict.), lectionis varietas a P. Victorio in exemplari suo editionis Aldinae margini annotata.

Cod. Scaphusianus (Z), chartaceus, sec. XV. a Graeca manu eleganter scriptus...In oratione ad Demonicum est optimae notae et aliquot locis ipsi Urbinati anteponendus.

TABLE OF VARIOUS READINGS.

The following table represents, so far as I am aware, all the discrepancies between the text of Baiter and Sauppe (in the Zurich edition of the *Oratores Attici*, 1839) and the text of Benseler (in the Teubner series, 1851).

Vulg. denotes the readings of Coray's ed. so far as they are based on MSS; in *Paneg.* §§ 52—99 Ambr. 1, Ambr. 2, are used to distinguish between the Ambrosian MS in the *Paneg.* and the same MS in the corresponding passage of the *Or. de Pcrm.* (v. p. 72. n.) The MSS are only quoted where necessary. When nothing is said to the contrary, the text of BS has MS authority.

AD DEMONICUM.

	Baiter and Sauppe.	Benseler.
§ 4	λόγον Urb.	λόγον μόνον Vulg.
6	ἐλυμήνατο Scaph. and Urb. (marg.)	ἔβλαψε Urb.
9	ὑφίστατο Urb. (corr.) and Scaph.	ὑπέμενεν Urb. *prima manu*
10	γένει Scaph.	τῷ γένει Urb.
11	δοκεῖς (*conj.* Bekker)	δοκοίης
13	νόμοις	ὅρκοις Urb. Scaph.
19	μόνον τῶν κτημάτων	μόνον τῶν χρημάτων Urb. Scaph.
	τὰς κατὰ γῆν	κατὰ γῆν Scaph.
26	τοῖς φίλοις συνάχθεσθαι	συνάχθεσθαι Ambr. Scaph.
29	βελτίω	βέλτιστα Ambr. Scaph.
34	γνῶσιν Urb. [γνώμην Vulg.]	διάνοιαι (Priscian)
35	ὑπὲρ σεαυτοῦ Urb.	ὑπὲρ τῶν σεαυτοῦ Scaph.
37	οἷά περ Vulg. [οἷ ἂν *conj.* Schn.]	οἷα Urb. Scaph. and Ambr. *prima manu*
38	ἢ δέ ['in Urb. fuit τὸ vel τὰ' Bekk.]	ἢ δέ
47	ἐλυπήθημεν	ἐλυπήθησαν Urb. Scaph.
	δι' αὐτὰ τὰ Scaph.	διὰ τὰ Urb.
	ἕνεκεν Urb.	ἕνεκα Vulg.
49	φήσομεν	φήσωμεν Urb.
	χρωμένους	χρωμένοις Urb. ('vitiose.' Strange)

PANEGYRICUS.

In the right-hand column *t.* denotes Benseler's reading in the Teubner Series (1851), *tr.* that of Benseler's revised text published in (1854). The asterisk denotes that Benseler has deserted his former reading and returned to that of Baiter and Sauppe.

	Baiter and Sauppe.	Benseler.
1	ἑαυτῶν MSS.	αὑτῶν
2	ἐπὶ δὲ	ἐπὶ δ'
4	τοῖς ἄλλοις μηδὲν πώποτε	*t.* μηδὲν πώποτε τοῖς ἄλλοις *tr.* [πώποτε μηδὲν τοῖς ἄλλοις Urb.]

	Baiter and Sauppe.	*Benseler.*
14	μηδὲν Urb. pr.	τῶν ἄλλων μηδὲν Ambr. Vict.
17	τῇ πόλῃ	τῇ πόλεε Urb. (corr.) and Ambr.
	αὑταῖς (conj.)	l. αὑταῖς tr. MSS.
18	δυσπείστωι	δυσπείστωι l.
		δυσπίστωι tr. Urb. Ambr.
19	φιλονικίας Urb.	φιλονικίας l. Urb.
		φιλονεικίας tr. Ambr.
23	ἀμφισβητοῦνται Urb.	+ περὶ αὐτῶν Ambr.
28	δούσης δωρεὰς διττὰς Ambr.	δούσης δωρεὰς διττὰς l. Ambr.
		– διττὰς tr. Urb.
29	ὠφελίας Urb.	ὠφελείας Ambr.
33	ὁμολογουμένους MSS.	ὁμολογουμένους l. ὁμολογουμένως tr. (conj. Wolf. 'Quod malim.' Baiter)
35	καλῶς	καλῶς καλῶς Urb. Ambr.
	°θεῶν Urb.	τῶν θεῶν Ambr.
41	δὲ ἀσφαλεστάτην	δ' ἀσφαλεστάτην
43	σπεισαμένους πρὸς ἀλλήλους	σπεισαμένους Urb.
44	°εὐτυχίας MSS.	εὐεξίας (conj. Bekker)
45	ἔτι δὲ ἀγῶσαι	ἔτι δ' ἀγῶσαι
51	ὑποθέμενος Urb.	ὑποθέμενος ἐρεῖν Ambr.
56	ἑαυτῶν Urb. Ambr. 1 and 2	αὐτῶν
57	αὐτοῦ Urb. Ambr. 2, Laur.	αὐτῶν Ambr. 1
59	°βιάσασθαι MSS.	βιάσασθαι (conj. Morus)
60	ἔσχε Ambr. 1 and 2, Laur.	ἔσχεν Urb.
	ἐπειδὴ δὲ εἰς	ἐπειδὴ δ' εἰς
62	°εἰσβαλεῖν Urb. Ambr. 1, and Laur.	εἰσβάλλειν Ambr. 2 ('quod malim propter καθιστάναι... διδόναι... ἀξιοῖν.' Baiter)
	διατελοῦσι MSS.	διατελοῦσιν
65	Πελοπορνησίους Urb. Ambr. 1	Πελοποννησίων Ambr. 2 and Laur.
66	ἐπὶ δὲ τῶν μεγίστων Urb. Ambr. 1 and Laur.	+ στὰς Ambr. 2 and Vat. Δ de Perm.
70	τοσοῦτον Urb. Ambr. 2, and Laur.	+ διὰ τὴν τότε στράτειαν Ambr. 1
73	με ἀγνοεῖν	μ' ἀγνοεῖν
	τοῖν πολέοιν Urb.	τοῦν πόλεοιν τούτοιν Laur. (τοῖν πολέοιν ταύταιν Ambr. 1, and ταῖν πολίοιν τούτοιν Vict.)
74	μικρὰ δέ τινα [μικρὰ δὲ Ambr. 2, Laur.]	l. μικρὰ δέ τι tr. Urb. Ambr. 1. [lg. μικρὰ δ' ἔτι J. E. S.]
76	τοιαῦτα τυγχάνοι (αὐτὰ τυγχάνοι Urb. Ambr. 2, and αὐτὰ τυγχάνει Ambr. 1)	τυγχάνοι τοιαῦτα Laur.
78	τοὺς νόμους Urb. Ambr. 1	τοὺς μὲν νόμους Ambr. 2, Laur.
83	σύμπασαν Ἑλλάδα Urb. Ambr. 1 and 2	Ἑλλάδα σύμπασαν (Ἑλλάδα πᾶσαν Laur.)
	°ἔμελλον MSS.	ἤμελλον ['In 7 passages in Isocr. all MSS. have ἔμελλ-, in 12 Urb. has ἤμελλ-.' Strange ap. Jahn's *Jahrb.*]
84	τελευτήσειεν Urb. Ambr. 1 and 2	τελευτήσειαν Laur.

	Baiter and Sauppe.	*Bensder.*
86	°κινδυνεύειν Urb.	κινδυνεύσειν Ambr. 1 and 2, Laur.
	ἔφθησαν Urb. Ambr. 2 and Laur.	ἔφθασαν Ambr. 1
87	°τὴν τῶν βαρβάρων MSS.	τὴν βαρβάρων t.
93	°τῶν δ' ἄλλων Ambr. 2 and Laur. (τῶν δὲ ἄλλων Ambr. 1)	τῶν ἄλλων Urb.
97	καὶ οὐδὲ MSS.	καὶ μηδὲ ap. Dionys. Halic.
	°ἐμέλλησαν Urb.	ἐμελέτησαν Ambr. 1
98	ναυμαχήσαντες Urb. et al.	συνναυμαχήσαντες Laur.
105	δεινὸν ἡγούμενοι Vulg. (coll. ad *Nicocl.* 24, *Areop.* 64) [Urb. *prim. man.* δεινοί]	δεινὸν οἰόμενοι Urb. corr. et Ambr.
107	διετέλεσαν (*conj.* Bekker)	διετέλεσαν t. διετελέσαμεν *tr.* Urb. Ambr.
	μεγίστην, καὶ κεκτημένοι Urb. σύμπαντες οἱ ἄλλοι – (ἄλλοι σύμπαντες Ambr.)	μεγίστην, κεκτημένοι Ambr. σύμπαντες Urb.
108	ὑποκειμένη Urb.	t. ὑποκειμένη δὲ *tr.* Ambr.
	°οἱ ('placet ὅσα' Sauppe)	ὅσα ('vel εἶναι vel ὅσοι habere videtur Urbinas' Bekker)
110	δεκαδαρχιῶν Urb.	δεκαρχιῶν Ambr. Viél.
	°διαλυμηνάμενα Urb. Ambr. Viél.	λυμηνάμενοι t.
111	°ἐπίας Ambr. ('fort. verum est ἐπί' Sauppe)	ἐπὶ Urb.
	°καὶ φονίας MSS.	[καὶ φονίας]
113	°ἐφίκοντο; ἢ MSS.	ἐφίκοιντ' ἢ
	τὰς ἑαυτῶν πόλεις Urb. Ambr.	τὰς αὑτῶν πόλεις
110	ἀναγεγραμμένας Urb.	γεγραμμένας Ambr. Viél.
122	ὧν ἄξιον	t. ὧν ἂν ἄξιον *tr.* [ἂν ἄξιον Ambr. ἀνάξιον Urb.]
125	πρότερον μὲν τοῖς MSS.	πρότερον μὲν τοὺς μὲν (*conj.* Baiter)
	συγκαθιστᾶσι MSS.	συγκαθιστᾶσιν
130	ἔστι δὲ οὐχ	ἔστι δ' οὐχ
	τοιαῦτα λέγονται Urb. Ambr.	λοιδοροῦνται — Vulg. coll. *de Pace* § 71
	λοιδοροῦνται Urb. Ambr.	τοιαῦτα πράττονται —
135	ἡμᾶς τε οἰκείων	ἡμᾶς τ' οἰκείων
139	°μεγάλας τὰς ῥοπὰς Urb. Ambr.	μεγάλας ῥοπὰς
144	ἐπῆρχε Urb.	ἐπῆρξε Ambr.
	δὲ Ἀταρνέα	δ' Ἀταρνέα
	δὲ ὀλίγῳ	δ' ὀλίγῳ
145	°τὸν βασιλέως Urb. Ambr. Viél.	τὸν τοῦ βασιλέως
146	φαυλότητα ἐν MSS.	φαυλότητας ἐν (*conj.*)
147	°ἐπιβουλῇ MSS. except. Urb.	ἐπιβουλὴν Urb.
149	ἀπώλοντο	ἀπώλοντο
153	ὑπὲρ αὐτῶν	ὑπὲρ αὐτῶν t.—ὑπὲρ αὐτῶν MSS. *tr.*
156	ἐκηρύσσαντο	ἐκηρύσαντ'
158	τῶν δ' ἐπὶ	τοὺς δ' ἐπὶ Urb. Ambr.
160	ὃν οὐκ ἀφετέον Urb. *prima manu.*	οὐ σαφέστερον οὐδέν· ὃν οὐκ ἀφετέον Ambr. et Urb. *sec. manu.*

	Baiter and Sauppe.	*Benseler.*
161	°ἐχθρῶν τῶν ἐκείνου	ἐχθρῶν ἐκείνου Urb.
	°οὐδὲ Ambr.	οὐδ' εἰς al. MSS.
163	ἐὰν MSS.	ἂν
	ἀποκλίνειεν Urb. Ambr.	ἀποκλίνειαν Vict.
165	ἐκεῖνοι μὲν οὖν	ἐκεῖνοι μὲν l. Urb. et Ambr.—ἐκεῖνοι μὲν [οὖν] li.
171	°ἐξεστηκόσι MSS.	ἐξεστῶσι l.
173	ὠφελίας Urb.	ὠφελείας Ambr. Vict.
176	°ἃ χρῆν Urb. Ambr.	ἃ 'χρῆν l.
178	δὲ ἄρτι	δ' ἄρτι
179	°πρὸς ἀνθρώπους Urb. Ambr.	πρὸς τοὺς ἀνθρώπους
183	πολλαχῇ [πολλαχοῦ Urb.]	πολλαχῇ l. πολλαχῇ li. Ambr.
187	ἐν τε τῷ παρόντι	+ καιρῷ
189	μεγάλα Urb. Ambr. Vict.	μεγάλ'
	αὐτοί τε	αὐτοί τ'

LIST OF EDITIONS.

The following are the editions of Isocrates so far as they are known to the present editor.

(1) The *editio princeps*, Demetrius Chalcondylas, Milan, 1493. It commences with the life of Isocr. as told by Pseudo-Plutarch, Philostratus, and Dionysius of Halicarnassus. The Epistles are omitted and the volume closes with a device indicating the name of the printer :—Ulric Scinczenzeller. (2) The *Aldine* ed., Venice, 1513 &c. (3) The ed. of *Jerome Wolf*. 'Ισοκράτους ἅπαντα· Isocratis scripta Graeco-Latina, postremo recognita, annotationibus novis et eruditis illustrata..., Hieronymo Wolfio Oetingensi interprete et auctore.. Basileae ex officina Oporiniana. 1570 fol. [edd. pr. 1548, 1551].—This ed. contains the first modern *commentary* on Isocr. The text with lat. trans. occupies more than 600 pages; the notes, which are sometimes prolix and irrelevant, but often good, occupy more than 700. (4) *Henry Stephens*, Paris, 1593 fol. with 7 *diatribae.* (5) *William Battie* (fellow of King's Coll. Cambr.) 1729. (6) *Athanasius Auger*, Paris, 1782. (7) *Gulielmus Lange*, Halis, 1803. (8) *Coray*, 'Ισοκράτους λόγοι καὶ ἐπιστολαὶ μετὰ σχολίων παλαιῶν οἷ προσετέθησαν σημειώσεις...παιδείας ἕνεκα τῶν τῆς 'Ελλάδα φωνῆς διδασκομένων 'Ελλήνων. [Paris, 1807—8]. (9) *Bekker*, Oxford, 1822, Berlin, 1823. (10) *W. Dindorf*, Leipsig, 1825. (11) *W. S. Dobson*, London, 1828. (12) *Baiter and Sauppe*, Zurich, 1839. (13) *Baiter*, Paris (Didot) 1846. (14) *Benseler*, Leipsig, 1851 (and with new *title-page*, 1856).

In the above list (4), (5), (6), (13), have little besides a Lat. translation, (11) is a useful (but uneven) variorum ed., (12) and (14) are now the best for textual criticism, (3) and (8) for exegesis.

(II)   The best Commentaries on *ad Demonicum* and *Panegyricus:*—

(1)   Opuscula Graecorum veterum sententiosa et moralia; collegit...et illustravit *Io. Conrad Orelli.* Tomus II. pp. 18—42, 522—569, Isocratis quae fertur Admonitio ad Demonicum. Lipsiae, 1821. (2) ed. *J. G. Strangius* 1831. (3) Isokrates ausgewählte Reden, Fur den Schulgebrauch erklärt von *Dr Otto Schneider.* I. Bändchen *Demonicus, Euagoras, Areopagiticus.* Teubner, Leipsig, 1859. II. Bändchen *Panegyricus, Philippus,* 1860. (4) *Paneg.* recens. et illustr. *S. F. N. Morus* ed. 3 auctior, Lipsiae, 1804. (5) *Paneg.* cum brevi annot. crit. ed. *Pinzger*, Leipsig, 1815. (6) Isocr. orat. commentariis instructae ab *I. H. Bremi (Paneg., Archid., de Pace, Trapezit.*), Gothae, 1831. (7) *Paneg.* cum *Mori* suisque annotationibus

edidit *F. A. G. Spohn:* ed. altera emendatio et auctior: curavit *I. G. Baiterus.* Lipsiae, 1831. [Out of print.] (8) Isokrates' Panegyrikos und Philippos. Berichtigt, übersetzt und erklärt von *Dr Gustav Eduard Benseler.* Engelmann, Leipsig, 1854. (9) Ausgewählte Reden des Isokrates, Panegyricus und Areopagiticus, erklärt von *Dr R. Rauchenstein.* Weidmann (Reimer), Berlin [1849, 1855], 1864.

The commentaries to which the present editor is particularly indebted are (3), (7), (8) and (9).

III.   Subsklia. *Harpocrationis lex.* in X oratores Att. ex recens. G. Dindorf. Oxon. 1853.

Schirach, G. B. Diss. II. de vita et genere scribendi Isocr. Halae Magd. 1768. Pp. 30, pp. 58.

Mitchell, T. (Coll. Sidn. Cantab. Soc.) Index Graec. Isoc. Oxon. 1828.

Dobree, P. P. Adversaria I. pp. 263—283. Cambridge, 1831, 2.

Strange, J. G. Bemerkungen zu den Reden des Isocr. Jahn's neue Jahrbücher für Philologie. Suppl. III. 439 sqq. 562 sqq. 1824.

Pfund, J. G. de Isocr. vita et scriptis. Berolini, 1833. pp. 24.

Stallbaum, G. Isocrates ad ill. Phaedr. Plat. origines, Lipsiae, 1850. p. 21.

Vischer, W. zu Isokr. Paneg. § 106, Schneidewin's *Philologus,* 1855. 243—9.

Spengel, L. Isokrates u. Platon. München, 1856,

Schröder, H. P. Quaestiones Isocr. duae. (1) Socrates sitne in Isocr. praeceptoribus numerandus. (2) Isocr. qualis fuerit homo. Trajecti ad Rhenum, 1859. pp. 200.

Le discours d'Isocrate sur lui-même, intitulé, sur l'Antidosis, traduit en Francais...par *Auguste Cartelier,* revu et publié avec le texte, une introduction [D'Isocrate en général, pp. ciii] et des notes, par *Ernest Havet,* [pp. 257] Paris, 1862.

Blass, F. Isokrates' dritter Brief und die gewöhnliche Erzählung von seinem Tode. Rheinisches Museum, 1865. 109—116.

Thompson, Dr. W. H. Plato, *Phaedr.* London, 1868. Appendix II. on the Philosophy of Isocrates, and his relation to the Socratic schools. pp. 170—183.

INTRODUCTION.

AD DEMONICUM.

THE treatise which bears this name chiefly consists of a series of moral maxims addressed to one Demonicus. After a brief introduction (§§ 1—12), the writer commences a series of practical precepts of a very diversified nature, as may be seen at a glance from the summary of §§ 13—43 in the following commentary. At the end of these precepts, the writer concludes with an epilogue consisting partly of expressions of hope that the fair promise of the boyhood of Demonicus may be fulfilled in his advancing youth, partly of appeals to the need of cultivating self-denial and industry, and to the lasting happiness which crowns a virtuous life.

Of the personality of Demonicus nothing is known except what is stated in the treatise or may be easily deduced therefrom. We find that he was still young (§ 44), and that he had recently lost his father Hipponicus, whose character was well known and admired by the writer (§§ 2, 9—11). He is recommended to do all honour to kings, to obey their laws, and to ensure their good will (§ 36). He therefore must have lived in a monarchical state, but could not himself have belonged to the royal family[1].

---

[1] Hence he could hardly have been king of Cyprus as stated by Constantinus Porphyrogenitus (Emp. of East, 911—959 A.D.), nor son of Evagoras king of Cyprus as stated by Tzetzes (Byzantine Grammarian, flourished 12th century, A.D.)

θανόντος Εὐαγόρου δὲ, γράφει πρὸς παῖδα τούτου,
οὗ κλῆσις ἦν Δημόνικος, πολλὰς τὰς παραινέσεις.

Doubts have often been raised as to the authorship of the treatise. It is found in all the best manuscripts of Isocrates, it is quoted as his by a critic of the first century B.C. and a rhetorician of the second century A.D., but its genuineness has nevertheless been sharply attacked. The anonymous writer of the argument (v. p. 1 *infra*) states that certain persons held it spurious (in common with the *ad Nicoclem* and *Nicocles*) because of its 'feebleness of diction' (τὸ ἀσθενὲς τῆς φράσεως); and, in more recent times, the assault has been renewed by Henry Stephens[1], and in the present century by Coray and Benseler.

Stephens opens his case by stating that scarcely a hundredth part of the readers of Isocrates can be aware that there are three writers of that name, (1) the Athenian orator, (2) his pupil, Isocrates, born at Apollonia in Pontus ('Απολλωνιά-της), and (3) a friend and contemporary of Dionysius of Halicarnassus. He then quotes a number of words and phrases, which, he asserts, could not have proceeded from Isocrates the Athenian[2]; disposes of a passage in the Greek lexicographer Harpocration, which appears to be in favour of the claims of the second Isocrates[3], and concludes that the third Isocrates was the real author.

The greatest of all the objections to this view is the high probability that the third Isocrates never existed: his existence depends entirely on a misunderstanding of the following passage of Dionysius[4]:

Ἰσοκράτης μὲν ὁ σὸς ἑταῖρος καὶ ἐμός, ὦ Ἐχέκρατες, εἴπερ ἄλλο τι, φησὶ χρῆναι προσεῖναι τοῖς σπουδαίοις ἀνθρώποις (ἐν τῇ παραινέσει τῇ πρὸς Ἱππονίκου) καὶ τὴν φιλοπροσηγορίαν, ὅπερ ἐστὶ τὸ προσφωνεῖν τοὺς ἀπαντῶντας, ὡς αὐτός φησι (v. § 20). If there is

---

[1] In Isocr. *diatribae.* 1593.

[2] Some of these have been removed with the help of better MSS than those which were known in Stephens' time : *e.g.* ἀκμὴν (in § 3) : the others (so far as they are worth mentioning) will be discussed under the head of Benseler's objections.

[3] See p. 20 n.

[4] *Ars Rhet.* v. 1.

sufficient reason to believe that by the words 'your companion and mine' any other than a contemporary of Dionysius is meant, the conclusion drawn by Stephens is invalid; and such a reason is found in the fact that Dionysius was an admirer of the Athenian Isocrates, the 'Attic orator,' whom he frequently mentions, and on whose style he wrote an appreciative treatise still extant. It would be perfectly natural for him, in writing to Echecrates, to speak of that Isocrates as their common friend in exactly the same way as Cicero, in writing to Atticus, speaks of Theophrastus, the pupil and successor of Aristotle as '*Amicus meus*[1].'

2. Coray's main objections are two. The first is that some of the maxims appear more suited to a writer living under a monarchical government than to an Athenian. This point is answered elsewhere (§ 36, n. on Lange). The second relates to the antithetical form of the treatise. 'If,' says Coray, 'you except the favorite ἀντίθετα of Isocrates, it contains nothing characteristic of him. And even of these ἀντίθετα, the writer makes an excessive use.' Coray therefore admits that it contains one strongly marked characteristic of Isocrates. We shall enquire presently whether it does not contain more than one.

3. Benseler's attack is supported by stronger arguments than those above quoted. His reasons (so far as they are deduced from internal evidence) are shortly summed up on p. iv. of his preface to the Teubner edition. These will now be taken seriatim, and an attempt will be made to answer each.

(a) 'It contains expressions which are either rare or foreign to the usage of Isocrates.'

§ 20, φιλοπροσήγορος. This is undoubtedly a rare word, but it occurs in exactly the context where we should expect it. The writer wishes for a more general word than εὐπροσήγορος, and therefore uses φιλοπροσήγορος, and proceeds to point out the distinction between εὐπροσηγορία and φιλοπροσηγορία. The mere rarity of the word cannot go for much

[1] *Epp. ad Att.* ii. 16.

when the undisputed writings contain such words as τεφθρεία (*Hel.* § 4); φθόη (*Aegin.* § 11); τύρβη (*de Perm.* § 30); ἐπικήρως (*Busir.* § 49); ἐνδελεχίστατος (*de Perm.* § 84); κατασκελετευθεῖσαν (*ib.* § 268); and διασπαριφᾶσθαι (*Areop.* § 12).

§ 4, τὰ τῶν τρόπων ἤθη. Benseler finds fault with the pleonasm. But similar pleonasms are found in the acknowledged writings of Isocrates, and this fulness of expression enables the writer to keep up a more perfect parallelism with the words of the corresponding clause, τὴν δεινότητα τὴν ἐν τοῖς λόγοις.

§ 49, ἐλαττουμένους. See note, p. 39.

§ 15, κόσμος pro εὐκοσμία. Isocrates uses κόσμος in the sense 'ornament' and also in the sense 'heavens'. There is surely no great objection to his using κόσμος in the sense 'propriety'; but as a matter of fact the translation 'ornament' will suit the passage sufficiently well (see n.), although μέγιστον σεαυτῷ πρέπειν κόσμον would, it is admitted, be a more obvious form of expression.

ib. κρατεῖσθαι pro κατέχεσθαι. This meaning of κρατεῖσθαι ('to be held fast, kept in check') probably does not occur in Isocrates, but I am unable to see any conclusive reason against the possibility of his using the word in this sense.

§ 3, συγγράφειν. The force of Benseler's objection to this word is not easily seen. In another passage (*Paneg.* § 177) συγγράφεσθαι is used, but in a different sense.

§ 16, σύν. This preposition is never used by Isocrates'. The fact is curious; but his frequent use of it in compounds may help to deprive the objection of part of its force.

(β) 'Difference of dialect,' § 7. θαρσαλέως. (See note.) This is the Ionic and *early* Attic form, and is the MS reading. We cannot fairly alter the reading, but it is worth while to notice that in *de Perm.* § 121, two good MSS (*Urb.* and *Vat.*) read θαρσήσουσι (which Bekker adopts).

§ 24, θέλε (see note). §§ 16, 44, συνειδήσεις, εἰδήσεις. These

---

¹ 'Obiter moneo, quod satis mirum est, Isocratem ipsa praepositione σὺν prorsus abstinuisse, praeter unum locum *ad Dem.* § 16.' Baiter, praef. ad *Paneg.* p. xvi.

are more Ionic than Attic (see p. 16 n.). We shall return to some of these details presently.

(γ) ‘Union of positive and comparative’ (v. p. 37 n.).

(δ) ‘Bad arrangement of precepts’ (v. p. 13 n.).

We have still to consider a point which Benseler considers of the highest importance. The *Ep. ad Dem.* contains a number of instances of hiatus. These are, §20, λόγῳ εὐπροσήγορος, 38, δύνασθαι, ἀνέχου...τὸ ἴσον...ὠφελεῖ, ἡ. 49, παντὶ ἐλαττούμενος. 40, σώματι εἶναι, and 14 others. *e.g.* § 7, δὲ εὐγενείους, § 24, μήτε ἄπειρος, § 11, σὲ ὥσπερ. Some of these can be readily defended by the pause between one word and the next (cf. *Paneg.* 74, παραλελεῖφθαι ὅμως) many of them can be removed by elision. Now in other parts of Isocrates, when similar instances of *hiatus* occur, Benseler either (very properly) places a mark of elision, or promptly inverts the order of a word or two, and does away with the obnoxious collocation. The *Ep. ad Dem.* he leaves helpless, and then points to the so-called flaws as a proof of its spuriousness. If a general avoidance of *hiatus* is, as must be admitted, a characteristic of the Athenian Isocrates, it is easy to quote passages in the *Ep. ad Dem.* in which the writer appears to prefer the rarer of two equally possible expressions when it enables him to avoid *hiatus*: *e.g.* § 3, ἔργον ἐπιχειρεῖν instead of ἔργῳ ἐπιχειρεῖν, and § 4, τοσούτῳ μᾶλλον... ὅσον οἱ instead of τοσαύτῃ μᾶλλον...ὅσῳ οἱ.

It is perhaps worth while to dwell for a moment on the three selected authorities on which Benseler relies for the support of his first canon (on the *hiatus*).

The first passage comes from Dionysius and may be found quoted on p. 128 of this edition. In a note on that page, it is suggested that the words of Dionysius in themselves are not conclusive; and it may here be added that in another passage of the same author we have a glimpse of the method by which he arrived at his statement. He quotes a few sections from the *Areopagiticus*, and states that there is not a single *hiatus* in the passage; and that he does not *think* there is one in the whole of the speech. The statement of Dionysius appears to be founded on a loose examination of passages like that which he quotes and at the very best is inconclusive. Besides, it is this very critic that cites the *Ep. ad Dem.* without expressing the slightest doubt as to its authorship.

The second passage comes from Hermogenes (2nd cent. A.D.) who says of the style of Isocrates, οὐ μόνον τὰ κῶλα συνέχεται τοῖς συμφώνοις ἀλλὰ καὶ πᾶς ὁ λόγος· τοσοῦτον αὐτῷ τῆς εὐφωνίας καὶ τοῦ κάλλους μεμέληκε. This is more definite; but the weight of the opinion of Hermogenes is for Benseler's purposes seriously impaired by the fact that the same Rhetorician elsewhere quotes the *Ep. ad Demonicum* as the genuine production of Isocrates the Athenian.

The statement of this rhetorician of the second century was in all probability derived ultimately from the lost treatise either written by Isocrates himself, or (more probably) drawn up by one of his pupils as a summary of his rules of Rhetoric. A quotation from this forms the third of Benseler's select authorities on the hiatus : the words are

δεῖ τῇ μὲν λέξει τὰ φωνήεντα μὴ συνεμπίπτειν.

If we could be certain in the first place that this rule was intended to apply to *all* kinds of composition, and, in the second, that Isocrates could never break through his own rule, this passage would be conclusive. To suppose that he intended the rule to be universal—to apply to an ordinary letter of advice as much as to highly elaborated orations, is, I cannot but think, unreasonable. Again, in the same set of rules gathered from the τέχνη we have a rule that prose is to be rhythmical, but never metrical. This rule is certainly violated in a passage which has not (as far as I can tell) been noticed by the continental editors (v. p. 149). If he could break his rule about metre, he could also break his rule about *hiatus*.

If we now pass to the internal evidence in favour of the genuineness, we find the same discrimination in the choice of words, and the same love of parallelisms in structure, sound and sense, that mark his undisputed writings in general.

But of all those writings, the one that deserves particularly to be compared with it is the hortatory discourse addressed to Nicocles on the duties of kings. The natural coincidences in thought and expression are sufficiently numerous to indicate identity of authorship, but without being of such an artificial nature as to betray the hand of a mere imitator of style of the treatise *ad Nicoclem*. Fortunately for the last treatise, and that on the duties of subjects (the *Nicocles*), almost half of the former and a long passage of the latter are quoted by Isocrates himself in the speech *de Permutatione* (§§ 73, 253); otherwise their genuineness would doubtless have been denied by the critics; the *ad Nicoclem* was actually attacked by Stephens, before the lost portion of the *de Perm.*, which contained the quotation, was discovered by Mustoxydes. The subject-matter is often distinctly characteristic of Isocrates; the precept μά-λιστα μὲν πειρῶ ζῆν κατ' ἀσφάλειαν (§ 43) is exactly what might be expected from one who never fought a single battle, and whose whole life was based on the principle ἐκτὸς κινδύνων καὶ ἀγώνων καρποῦσθαι τὴν σοφίαν[1]. The precept on 'wine-parties,' (§ 32 n.), and the frequent reminiscences of Theognis (v. § 7 n.), not to mention other details, point in the same direction.

Thus far for the internal evidence on the two sides of the question: we now proceed to a summary statement of the external evidence, and in so doing we may fairly premise that wherever the name of Isocrates stands by itself, the Athenian and not his pupil of Apollonia is to be understood.

The external evidence against the genuineness consists of a passage in the Lexicon of Harpocration. He quotes and explains the words ἐνακτὸς ὅρκος, and gives as one of his authorities, 'Isocrates of Apollonia, in the exhortations addressed to Demonicus.'

In favour of the genuineness we have another passage in the same lexicon, where the words διόπερ ἡμεῖς—παραίνεσιν γράψαντες are quoted, followed by the words Ἰσοκράτης παραινέσεσιν.

Secondly, Dionysius Halic., in a passage already quoted,

[1] Plato, *Euthyd.* 305 E.

speaks of his friend Isocrates as inculcating the duty of 'affability,' ἐν τῇ παραινέσει τῇ πρὸς Ἱππονίκου (v. § 20).

Thirdly, Hermogenes (περὶ μεθόδου δεινότητος 25 = *Rhetores Graeci*, II. 477, ed. Spengel), in speaking of various methods of inoffensive self-laudation, quotes instances from Demosthenes and Isocrates. The instance from the latter is thus introduced, ὁ Ἰσοκράτης ἐν τῷ πρώτῳ λόγῳ τῶν παραινεσίων τὸ πρῶτον προοίμιον ἑαυτοῦ ἔπαινον κατεσκεύασε, and then follows a short exposition of the first two sections.

Fourthly, it is contained in all the best MSS.

It would be easy to prolong this introduction by an examination into the credibility of each of the above points of external evidence; but it will be sufficient to state in brief that the self-contradicted evidence of Harpocration cannot be held sufficient in itself to counteract the strong external and internal evidence in favour of the genuineness. In the absence of undisputed remains of Isocr. the younger, we are unable to form any definite opinion on his style. In the case of other pupils of Isocrates, *e.g.* Theopompus, Ephorus, Lycurgus and Hyperides, we have more than enough remaining, to prove the distinct individuality of their manner of writing and to shew their general independence of their former master. Is it probable, we may ask, that Isocrates the younger wrote in a style, that has little, if any thing, to distinguish it from that of his master's treatise *ad Nicoclem* ?

Those who believe in the genuineness of the *ad Dem.* are bound to give a satisfactory or at least a plausible account of the circumstances under which it may have been written. In accordance with this bounden duty, we would venture to assign it to the period of his life which he spent in the Island of Chios. His departure for that island is generally assigned to the year 404 B.C., or according to a more probable calculation (into the details of which it is unnecessary to enter), to the year 393 B.C[1]. Chios was an Ionian island and the Chians spoke one of the four forms of the Ionic dialect[2].

---

[1] Rauchenstein ed. *Paneg.* p. 8.   [2] Hdt. 1. 142.

To this local influence, in some shape or other, we may possibly assign his use of the Ionic forms θαρσαλέως and εἰδήσεις[1].—Isocrates had lost his patrimony in the Peloponnesian war: in § 19 he tells us that 'wealth passeth away but wisdom alone is immortal.'—To repair his losses, he opened a school in Chios; hence the schoolmaster's tone that is apparent in such precepts as those of § 18, ἐὰν ᾖς φιλομαθὴς ἔσει πολυμαθής κ.τ.λ. and of § 40; he had only nine pupils, hence the words αἰσχρὸν τοὺς νεωτέρους μηδὲ τὰς κατὰ γῆν πορείας ὑπομένειν ἐπὶ τῷ βελτίω καταστῆσαι τὴν αὐτῶν διάνοιαν (§ 19). The monarchical state where Demonicus was living may probably have been Cyprus, and the *Ep. ad Dem.* would in that case be the precursor of the three Cyprian treatises of Isocrates, the *ad Nicoclem*, the *Nicocles* and the *Evagoras.*

We know nothing of the nature of Isocrates' original acquaintance with Demonicus or his father Hipponicus. That the name of Hipponicus occurs in the family of Isocrates is only the erroneous assertion of one of the writers in Smith's *Biographical Dictionary* (art. Callias and Hipponicus), who after telling us that Hipparete (daughter of the Hipponicus who fell at Delium) was the wife of Alcibiades, which is true, proceeds to state that 'another daughter of Hipponicus was married to Theodorus and became the mother of Isocrates the orator,' which is false. The error arose from a misunderstanding of Isocr. *de Bigis* § 31, where Alcibiades the younger, *not* Isocrates, is the speaker.

But apart from all debated questions of the personality of the sender and the receiver of this letter, we may find a point of some slight interest in its subject-matter. We have numberless instances of similar practical precepts in ancient and modern literature. The *de Officiis* of Cicero (in the first cent. B.C.), the distichs of varied dates that bear the name of Dionysius Cato, the writings of the three great Stoics of the first two centuries A.D., Seneca the courtier, Epictetus the slave, and Marcus Aurelius Antoninus, the emperor; the admonitions of

[1] Hdt. VII. 234, Hippocrates VII. 476, VIII. 430 (ap. Veitch. *Gk. Vbs.*).

the Emperor Basil (the Macedonian) to his son Leon (in the ninth century[1]); and in more recent times, the 'wise saws' of Shakspeare's Polonius, the Church-Porch of George Herbert, and the 'Christian morals' of Sir Thomas Browne, are among the many examples that might be quoted; but the treatise now under consideration has a value that is independent of all these, inasmuch as it embodies the current maxims of the popular morality of Greece;—maxims originally enshrined in the verses of the 'Gnomic poets[2]' and in the proverbial philosophy of the 'seven sages' of the sixth century. The precepts here recorded are founded in many cases on a shrewd and cautious observation of the ways of the world and therefore appeal too frequently to a cold and calculating self-interest, and to a regard for outward appearances; they are sometimes dashed with a gloom that reminds us of the elegies of Theognis, the exiled aristocrat of Megara. On the whole, however, they form a tolerably brilliant and far from inattractive specimen of the ordinary principles of Grecian Ethics.

PANEGYRICUS.

THE *Panegyricus* is perhaps the most celebrated of all the writings of Isocrates. Dionysius applies to it the epithet περι-βόητος[3], and Philostratus calls it κάλλιστος λόγων (*vit. Soph.* 1. 17). It consists of an appeal to the Greeks in general, to join in an expedition against Persia, under the united command of Athens and Sparta; but at the time when the speech was written, Athens had lost her supremacy and Sparta was the leading power in Greece: the orator is therefore compelled to enter upon an elaborate proof that the supremacy belongs by right to Athens: he accordingly dwells with patriotic zeal on the le-

---

[1] In *Exhort.* 66 the Emperor recommends his son to read the writings of Solomon and of Isocrates, and also the book of Ecclesiasticus.

[2] *ad Nicocl.* §§ 3, 43; Aeschin. III. § 135; Plato, *Protag.* 326.—On the ἀντίθεσις of Hippias, v. *ib. Hip. maj.* 286.

[3] *De Isocr. jud.* 14.

gendary and historic fame and the great public services of his
country; he speaks of her as the avenger of the oppressed, as
the champion of Greece against the Barbarians in general, as
the victor in the battles of Marathon, Artemisium and Salamis.
He closes the first great division of his speech by contrasting
the beneficent and disinterested rule of Athens with the cruel
and selfish dominion of Sparta, and thence deduces the propriety of restoring the supremacy to the state which claimed it
as a hereditary right, and had ratified the claim by the high
purposes to which in former days she had dedicated her authority. In the second part of the speech, he points out the critical
necessity of undertaking the expedition, and after dwelling on
the ignominious peace of Antalcidas, on the inherent weakness
of Persia, the immemorial enmity between the Greeks and the
Barbarians, he insists, in conclusion, that every motive whether
of gain or glory, of justice or revenge, declares that the time
for decisive action has arrived.

The name of *Panegyricus* is given to the speech by
Isocrates himself[1], and implies that it was written for recitation
at one of the great festal assemblies or πανηγύρεις, such as the
Panathenaic festival at Athens or the Panhellenic festival at
Olympia. That it was ever publicly recited by the author at
the latter festival, as Philostratus'[2] tells us, is extremely im-
probable. The strong language, in which he speaks of the
Lacedaemonians, would in itself have been fatal to his chances
of obtaining a hearing, to say nothing of the fact that his well-
known timidity and his weakness of voice must have prevented
him from making the attempt. At the very most, it is possible
that it was recited for him by another; but the principal way,
in which it became known to the Grecian world, was doubtless
the multiplication of copies of the original speech which were
either circulated at the πανήγυρις or sent to the leading men
in the various Grecian states[3]. In after years it was frequently

---

[1] *Phil.* § 9, 84, *Epp.* III. 6, *de Perm.* § 172.

[2] ὁ πανηγυρικὸς...λόγος, ὃν διῆλθεν 'Ολυμπίασι.

[3] *Phil.* § 11, (ὁ λόγος) ὁ πρότερον ἐκδοθείς.

quoted by Aristotle and imitated by the pupils of the ' orator,'
some of whom must have heard a great part of the speech in
the ordinary course of his instructions in rhetoric, and, if the
analogy of subsequent writings[1] is worth anything, may have
even ventured to criticise it and to propose alterations, during
the great length of time which the writer devoted to its
elaborate preparation. The actual number of years spent upon
it is variously stated. Quintilian[2] mentions ten years as the
lowest number recorded by his predecessors, Plutarch[3] makes it
'almost 3 Olympiads,' and the writer of the treatise *on the Sublime*,
sometimes ascribed to Longinus, in the course of a criticism on
Timaeus, the celebrated Sicilian historian (the pupil of one of
the disciples of Isocrates), records a frigid comparison instituted
by the historian between Isocrates and Alexander, praising the
latter for ' conquering the whole of Asia in a shorter time than
Isocrates took in writing the Panegyricus and advocating an
expedition against Persia.' ' On this principle,' says the critic,
' the Lacedaemonians were evidently far inferior in spirit to
Isocrates. The former spent thirty years over the conquest of
Messene, the latter only ten over the composition of the
Panegyricus.' The criticism is itself open to criticism ; it is
only quoted here to shew that the period of ten years is
recognised by more than one ancient authority.

The internal evidence of the speech is in favour of this
statement ; the peace of Antalcidas (387 B.C.) is never alluded
to in the first part of the oration. This appears to have been
written independently of that event ; in the second part however we have numerous allusions to it, expressed in indignant
terms which imply that it had only recently been negociated.
The exact date of the publication is determined by the

---

[1] *Phil.* §§ 17—23, and *Panath.* § 200, 'Επηεώρθοιτ τὸν λόγον...μετὰ
μειρακίων τριῶν ἢ τεττάρων τῶν εἰθισμένων μοι συνδιατρίβειν· ἐπειδὴ δὲ διεξι-
οῦσιν ἡμῖν ἐδόκει καλῶς ἔχειν καὶ προσδεῖσθαι τελευτῆς μόνον, ἔδοξέ μοι μετα-
πέμψασθαί τινα τῶν ἐμοὶ πεπλησιακότων,...ἵν' εἴ τι παρέλαθεν ἡμᾶς ψεῦδος
εἰρημένον, ἐκεῖνος κατιδὼν δηλώσειεν ἡμῖν.

[2] X. 4. 4.

[3] *Mor.* 350 E.

historical allusions in § 126. From that section, it appears
that the publication took place during the siege of Phlius and
Olynthus, but before the capture of these places. The siege of
Olynthus began in 382 B.C., that of Phlius in the early part of
380; hence we conclude that the speech was not published
before 380 B.C. Again the siege of Phlius after a duration of
20 months, terminated in the latter part of 379 B.C. almost
coincidently with the capture of Olynthus. Hence the speech
could not have been published after 379; and if we take into
consideration the great probability that it was published during
an Olympic πανήγυρις, we obtain the latter part of the summer
of 380 as a tolerably accurate approximation to the date of the
first appearance of the speech[1].

It is hardly necessary to add that the *Panegyricus* failed in
bringing about a practical result. It brought him rhetorical
fame and was destined to be the subject of quotation, imita-
tion and plagiarism[2]; but it is only an idle rumour (recorded by
Aelian[3] in the 3rd cent. A.D.) that ascribes to its influence the
expedition against Persia projected by Philip and accomplished
by Alexander. At its publication the former was only an
infant, and about a quarter of a century elapsed before the
birth of the latter; but Isocrates never entirely deserted his
favorite project. The idea of a Persian war, originally taken up
as a grand theme for rhetorical display, pursued him throughout
the whole of his subsequent life; he recurs to it in a letter[4]
written to Archidamus, king of Sparta, and also in a pamphlet[5]
addressed to Philip of Macedon, which forms a signal instance
of the blindness of its author to the real character of that
monarch, and places him in sharp contrast to the vigorously
patriotic policy of Demosthenes; and lastly, when the battle of

---

[1] The attempts to reconcile this date with the confused chronology of
§ 141, have not hitherto been successful.
[2] *Phil.* § 84, 91.
[3] *Var. Hist.* XIII. 11. Cf. Isocr. *Epp.* III. 3.
[4] *Epp.* IX. 19.
[5] The *Philippus*.

xliv INTRODUCTION. PANEGYRICUS.

Chaeroneia had virtually crushed the freedom and indepen-,
dence of Greece, the aged rhetorician, after a lapse of more
than 40 years from the publication of the *Panegyricus*, writes
a feeble letter to Philip, which closes with almost the last,
if not the very last, words he ever wrote,—words of hope that
the great project would still be accomplished : χάριν δ' ἔχω τῷ
γήρᾳ ταύτην μόνην, ὅτι προήγαγα εἰς τοῦτό μου τὸν βίον, ὥσθ' ἃ
νέος ὢν διενοούμην, καὶ γράφειν ἐπεχείρουν ἔν τε τῷ πανηγυρικῷ λόγῳ
καὶ τῷ πρὸς σὲ πεμφθέντι, ταῦτα νῦν τὰ μὲν ἤδη γιγνόμενα διὰ τῶν
σῶν ἐφορῶ πράξεων, τὰ δ' ἐλπίζω γενήσεσθαι.

ERRATA in the notes.

p. 1. col. 1. l. 4, *for* Mystodoxes *read* Mustoxydes
p. 12. col. 1. l. 13, dele the words in parenthesis
p. 16. col. 1. l. 7, dele 'only' and v. *Paneg.* § 179
p. 78. col. 1. l. 1, dele the first sentence and v. table of various readings

ΙΣΟΚΡΑΤΟΥΣ ΠΡΟΣ ΔΗΜΟΝΙΚΟΝ.

ΥΠΟΘΕΣΙΣ ΑΝΩΝΥΜΟΥ ΓΡΑΜΜΑΤΙΚΟΥ[1].

Ἔγραψε πολλοὺς λόγους, ὧν εἰσὶν αἱ παραινέσεις, εἰ καί τινες ἠβουλήθησαν αὐτὰς εἰπεῖν μὴ εἶναι αὐτοῦ διὰ τὸ ἀσθενὲς τῆς φράσεως, ἃς πρῶτον εἰκότως ἀναγινώσκομεν, οὐχ ὡς βελτίονας οὔσας τῶν ἄλλων λόγων· καὶ γὰρ καὶ ὁ πανηγυρικὸς αὐτῶν προέχει καὶ ἄλλοι πολλοί· ἀλλ' ὅτι περὶ ἠθῶν διαλαμβάνουσιν[2]. ἀναγκαῖον δὲ τὰ ἤθη πρὸ τῶν λόγων κοσμῆσαι, ὥσπερ ὁ γεωργὸς ὀφείλει, πρὸ τῶν σπερμάτων καὶ ἧς μέλλει καταβάλλειν φυτείας, ἐκκόπτειν ἀπὸ τῶν χωρίων τὰ λυμαινόμενα τούτοις, οἷον ἄγρωστιν καὶ τὰ τούτοις παραπλήσια· δι' ὅ, ὡς καὶ πρὸς παῖδας ταῦτα γράφων, ἠναγκάσθη ταπεινοτέρᾳ χρήσασθαι τῇ φράσει· ὥστε αὐτοῦ ἂν εἴησαν καὶ αἱ παραινέσεις. ἄξιον δὲ ζητῆσαι, διὰ ποίαν αἰτίαν οὕτως αὐτὰς ἀνα-

---

[1] ΥΠΟΘΕΣΙΣ.] This argument was written by an unknown grammarian, and was first published in 1817 by Andreas Mystodoxes (a learned Greek) from two MSS. in the Medicean Library at Florence. Its date is approximately determined by the fact that, in another argument, the same grammarian adds to a short notice of Nicocles, king of the Cyprian Salamis, the words τῆς νῦν Κωσταντίου καλουμένης. The name Constantia could not have been given to Salamis *before* 306 A.D. (the date of the accession of Constantine I.), and its earliest mention occurs in connection with Epiphanius, who is called Bishop of Constantia in 367. Hence we conclude that this argument was not written before the fourth cent. A.D. It contains many departures from Classical usage, some of which will be stated in the following notes.

[2] διαλαμβάνουσιν] = '*disserunt,*' '*exponunt;*' a meaning peculiar to late Greek. Schaefer (on *Gregorius Corinthus de dial.* p. 7) illustrates this meaning by quotations from Maximus Planudes (14th cent. A.D.) and Eudocia (Empress, 1059—1071 A.D.).

γινώσκομεν κατὰ τάξιν, πρῶτον τὴν πρὸς Δημόνικον, ἔπειτα τὴν
πρὸς Νικοκλέα, καὶ μὴ ἀδιαφόρως, ὥσπερ ἐν τοῖς ἄλλοις αὐτοῦ λόγοις. λέγομεν, ὅτι Ἰσοκράτης βουλόμενος κοινωφελὴς γενέσθαι, φορτικὸν δὲ ἡγούμενος τὸ πρὸς πάντας γράφειν τὰς συμβουλάς, ἦλθεν
ὡς τούτους γράφειν. τὸ δὲ ἀληθὲς πᾶσι παραινεῖ διὰ τῶν τριῶν
παραινέσεων, ὥσπερ καὶ ὁ Ἡσίοδος[1], ὡς πρὸς τὸν ἀδελφὸν λέγων,
ἐργάζευ νήπιε Πέρση, πᾶσι παραινεῖ. οὕτω καὶ ὁ Ἰσοκράτης.
τάττει οὖν πρῶτον τὸν πρὸς Δημόνικον, ὡς πρὸς ἰδιώτας πρῶτον
διαλεγόμενος, εἶτα βασιλεύειν διδάσκων ἐν τῷ πρὸς Νικοκλέα· πρῶτον γάρ τις ἰδιώτης γενόμενος ὕστερον ἔρχεται ἐπὶ τὴν βασιλείαν.
εἶτα λέγει ἐν τῷ πρὸς Νικοκλέα ἢ συμμαχικῷ, πῶς δεῖ καὶ τὸν
ἰδιώτην βασιλεύεσθαι.—Ἀνάγονται δὲ αἱ παραινέσεις ὑπὸ τὸ συμ-
βουλευτικὸν[2] εἶδος, κέκληνται δὲ παραινέσεις παρὰ τὸν αἶνον, ὅ
ἐστι τὴν συμβουλήν, ὡς καὶ Ἡσίοδος[3]· νῦν δὲ αἶνον βασιλεῦσι
στάσιν[4] δὲ οὐκ ἐπιδέχονται· σὺ γὰρ ἔχουσι τὸν ἀντιλέγοντα. καιρὸς
μὲν ἤδη, ὡς εἴπομεν, ἐπ᾽ αὐτὰς λοιπὸν χωρεῖν τῶν λόγων τὰς ἐξη-
γήσεις. ἀλλ᾽ ἐπειδὴ ἀναγκαῖον πρὸ αὐτῶν τῶν ἐξηγήσεων προηγεῖ-
σθαι τὰς ὑποθέσεις καὶ τοὺς σκοποὺς τῶν λόγων, δεικτέον πρῶτον
τοῦ λόγου τὴν ὑπόθεσιν. Ἱππόνικός τις, ὡς ἔχει ὁ παλὺς λόγος,
Κύπριος μὲν ἦν τῷ γένει, Ἰσοκράτους δὲ φίλος τοῦ σοφιστοῦ· οὗτος
τελευτήσας κατέλειψ[5] παῖδα, ὀνόματι Δημόνικον. τοῦτον Ἰσοκράτης
ὁρῶν παῖδα ὄντα καὶ πολλῆς ἐπιμελείας λόγων δεόμενον, γράφει
αὐτῷ ὑποθήκας, ὅπως δεῖ ζῆν αὐτὸν διδάξαι βουλόμενος ὥσπερ ἦν
εἶχε πρὸς τὸν πατέρα εὔνοιαν παραπέμψαι καὶ μέχρι τοῦ παιδός,
ὡς καὶ ἐν αὐτῇ τῇ ἀρχῇ τοῦ λόγου προοιμιάζεται. συμβουλεύει οὖν
αὐτῷ, γράψας δι᾽ ἐπιστολῆς· οὐ γὰρ ἐδύνατο καταλεῖψαι[6] Ἀθήνας

---

[1] Ἡσίοδος.] 'Works and Days,'
395.
[2] συμβουλευτικόν.] Cf. *Paneg.*
§ 11, ἐπιδεικτικῶς. n.
[3] Ἡσίοδος.] 'Works and Days,'
200.
[4] στάσιν.] Lit. 'they do not admit of an issue.' στάσις (= *status,
constitutio causae*) is a technical
term, used frequently by late writers
on Rhetoric to indicate the 'issue
joined by two contending parties.'
The grammarians generally take
great pains to define, in their Introductions, the στάσις of each succes-

sive speech or treatise that comes
under their notice. Our grammarian has just told us that the treatise
addressed to Demonicus is one of
those that falls under the 'deliberative class' of writings: he feels that
the reader will expect to be told, as
usual, the issue joined therein; and
accordingly informs him, with some
naïveté, that there is none, οὐ γὰρ
ἔχουσι τὸν ἀντιλέγοντα.
[5] κατέλειψι ... καταλεῖψαι.] In
Classical Gk. κατέλιπεν and καταλιπεῖν.

διὰ τοὺς μαθητάς. τινὲς δὲ ἐπιχειροῦσι λέγειν τὸν λόγον, ἐπιστολὴ πρὸς Δημόνικον. καὶ ἡ μὲν φαινομένη ὑπόθεσις αὕτη. εἰρήκαμεν δὲ ἐν τοῖς ἄνω, ὡς ὅτι* κοινωφελεῖς αὐτοῦ βούλεται ποιήσασθαι τὰς παραινέσεις καὶ συμβουλεῦσαι, πῶς δεῖ ζῆν τὸν ἰδιώτην. καὶ τοῦτο ποιεῖ διὰ τοῦ Δημονίκου, καὶ τὸ πῶς δεῖ βασιλεύειν προβαλλόμενος τὸν Νικοκλέα. φεύγων δὲ τὸ φορτικὸν οὐ φανερῶς ἐπιφέρει τοῖς ἑαυτοῦ λόγοις τὸν ἴδιον σκοπόν. ἄρχεται δὲ ἀπὸ θείων, εἶτα εἰς γονέας μεταβαίνει, εἶτα φίλους καὶ οἶκον καὶ πατρίδα, τήν τε δίαιταν καὶ τὴν περὶ τὸ σῶμα καὶ τὴν περὶ ψυχήν. χωρητέον οὖν λοιπὸν καὶ ἐπὶ τὸ προοίμιον, παρὰ τὸν οἶμον, ὅ ἐστιν ὁδόν. Ἡσίοδος⁹·

μακρός τε καὶ ὄρθιος οἶμος ἐπ' αὐτήν.

ὁδὸς δὲ τοῦ λόγου οἱ ἀγῶνες καὶ αἱ πράξεις.

---

* ὡς ὅτι] (=Eng. 'how that'). This pleonasm is used elsewhere by the writer of this argument, and is (like ὡς-οἷον, οἷον-ὡς) a character-istic of late Greek.

⁹ 'Ησίοδος.] ' Works and Days,' 288.

(α΄.) Ἐν πολλοῖς μὲν, ὦ Δημόνικε, πολὺ διεστώσας εὑ- 2
ρήσομεν τάς τε τῶν σπουδαίων γνώμας καὶ τὰς τῶν φαύλων
διανοίας, πολὺ δὲ μεγίστην διαφορὰν εἰλήφασιν ἐν ταῖς
πρὸς ἀλλήλους συνηθείαις· οἱ μὲν γὰρ τοὺς φίλους παρόντας
μόνον τιμῶσιν, οἱ δὲ καὶ μακρὰν ἀπόντας ἀγαπῶσι, καὶ τὰς
μὲν τῶν φαύλων συνηθείας ὀλίγος χρόνος διέλυσε, τὰς δὲ ḫ

§§ 1—12. *A general introduction,
stating the object of the letter.*
1, 2. *Time and space cannot
sever the friendships of good men: I
therefore send you this letter as a sure
proof of my goodwill towards you and
yours, and as a token of my intimacy
with your late father, Hipponicus.* 3.
*Every thing, on your side and mine,
favours my project.* 4. *I propose
therefore to exhort you,* not *to mere
intellectual excellence, but to moral
excellence,* 5—7 *a possession which is
more grand and enduring than
beauty, wealth, strength, and noble
birth.* 9—12. *You have a pattern
of moral excellence in your departed
father, on whose character I hope to
dwell at length on a future occasion.
To aid you in copying that pattern,
I now send you a few brief and suggestive maxims.*

1. τῶν σπουδαίων)(τῶν φαύλων.]
The 'good' and the 'bad,' those
who live with an earnest object, a
'moral attention' (σπουδή), and
those who do not. It is unnecessary
to give these words a semi-political
sense, as Schneider does, comparing
the well-known usage of ἀγαθός,
ἐσθλός, ἄριστοι, καλοὶ κἀγαθοί, βέλτιστοι, *boni, optimi, optimates* (the
aristocracy), and κακοί, δειλοί, *mali*
(the commons). Cf. § 48.
γνώμας...διανοίας.] 'judgments'
...'thoughts.' The distinction is not
imaginary; the former implies real
knowledge (γνῶσις), the latter mere
opinion and nothing more. Cf. Isocr.

Nicocles, § 16, μᾶλλόν ἐστιν ἑνὸς ἀνδρὸς
γνώμῃ προσέχειν τὸν νοῦν μᾶλλον ἢ
ταυτοδαπαῖς διανοίαις ζητεῖν ἀρέ-
σκειν. In § 45 a partial distinction
is kept up between γνώμη and διάνοια, διάνοια almost =νοῦς in § 32,
and is placed in simple contrast to
σῶμα in Isocr. *Philippus*, § 63, ἀφορμὴν οὐδεμίαν ἔχων (Conon) πλὴν τὸ
σῶμα καὶ τὴν διάνοιαν ἤλπισε Λακεδαιμονίους καταπολεμήσειν.—One of
the clearest definitions of διάνοια, in
contrast to δόξα and φαντασία, may
be found in Plato, *Sophista*, p. 263 E,
when the Eleatic Stranger says, οὐκοῦν διάνοια μὲν καὶ λόγος ταὐτόν,
πλὴν ὁ μὲν ἐντὸς τῆι ψυχῆι πρὸς
αὑτὴν διάλογος ἄνευ φωνῆς γιγνόμενος
τοῦτ᾽ αὐτὸ ἡμῖν ἐπωνομάσθη διάνοια
...τὸ δέ γ᾽ ἀπ᾽ ἐκείνης ῥεῦμα διὰ τοῦ
στόματος ἰὸν μετὰ φθόγγου εἴρηται
λόγος, κ.τ.λ.
μεγίστην διαφορὰν εἰλήφασιν]
=μέγιστα διαφέρουσιν. The article
τὴν placed after μεγίστην would
perhaps improve the sense, but MS.
authority is against it. Schn. inserts
it on the ground that the last syllable of μεγίστην led to its accidental
omission.
συνηθείας...φιλίας.] 'Intimacies
...friendships.' The generic term
συνήθεια includes the specific term
φιλία, but, being the weaker word,
is appropriately applied in this passage to the acquaintanceship of bad
men, the nobler word φιλία being
reserved for the good alone, on the
principle laid down by Laelius in

5

ΠΡΟΣ ΔΗΜΟΝΙΚΟΝ.

—2]

τῶν σπουδαίων φιλίας οὐδ' ἂν ὁ πᾶς αἰὼν ἐξαλείψειεν.
2 ἡγούμενος οὖν πρέπειν τοὺς δόξης ὀρεγομένους καὶ παιδείας
ἀντιποιουμένους τῶν σπουδαίων ἀλλὰ μὴ τῶν φαύλων εἶναι
μιμητὰς, ἀπέσταλκά σοι τόνδε τὸν λόγον δῶρον, τεκμήριον
μὲν τῆς πρὸς ὑμᾶς εὐνοίας, σημεῖον δὲ τῆς πρὸς Ἱππόνικον
συνηθείας· πρέπει γὰρ τοὺς παῖδας ὥσπερ τῆς οὐσίας οὕτω

Cicero, *De amicitia,* § 18, *Hoc primum sentio, nisi in bonis amicitiam esse non posse.*

διλύσει.] 'Is wont to sever'—the aorist, *not* of instantaneous action, but of frequency, or, as it is sometimes called, the Gnomic aorist, expressing 'that which has often happened, and consequently (in cases singly occurring) is *wont* to happen.' Madvig, *Gk. Syntax,* § 111 a. Cf. § 6, *infra,* ἀνήλωσεν, κ.τ.λ. n.

2 ἀλλὰ μή...] 'The good, *and* not the bad.' ἀλλά often introduces a negation in direct opposition to a previous affirmation, and in such cases '*and*' is often a better translation than 'but.' Cf. § 21, δι' ὧν εὐδοκιμήσεις ἀλλὰ μὴ δι' ὧν εὐπορήσεις.

τεκμήριον...σημεῖον.] 'An infallible proof...a token.' In Aristotle σημεῖον is the name given to 'proof' in the general, whether fallible or not: and the *genus* σημεῖον is subdivided into two *species,* τεκμήριον and σημεῖον. Arist. *Rhet.* I. 2, τῶν δὲ σημείων...τὸ μὲν ἀναγκαῖον τεκμήριον, τὸ δὲ μὴ ἀναγκαῖον ἀνώνυμόν ἐστι κατὰ τὴν διαφοράν. ἀναγκαῖα μὲν οὖν λέγω ἐξ ὧν γίνεται συλλογισμός. Also II. 25, τὰ δὲ τεκμήρια καὶ τεκμηριώδη ἐνθυμήματα κατὰ μὲν τὸ ἀσυλλόγιστον οὐκ ἔσται λῦσαι... λείπεται δ' ὡς οὐχ ὑπάρχει τὸ λεγόμενον δεικνύναι.

The double meaning of σημεῖον, as the name of a *species* as well as of a *genus,* is by no means unparalleled. The same phenomenon may be noticed in the two meanings of δῶρον [(1) a gift in general, (2) a bribe)(δωρεά=an honourable gift] and of σύλλογος [(1) an assembly in

general, (2) an assembly differing from the ἐκκλησία].

πρὸς ὑμᾶς.] 'To you and yours.' ὑμᾶς may possibly have been preferred to σέ, to avoid the *Hiatus* (see Introduction on the *Style* of Isocr.). It is not however equivalent in meaning to σέ, but has its plural sense. The two passages adduced (by Coray) to prove that the plural of 2nd person may be used for the singular will not bear examination: the first is Isocr. *Phil.* § 32, γνοίη δ' ἄν ὡς οὐδεμιᾶς σοι προσήκει τούτων ὀλιγωρεῖν, ἢν ἀνενέγκῃς αὐτῶν τὰς πράξεις ἐπὶ τοὺς σοὺς προγόνους· εὑρήσεις γὰρ ἑκάστῃ πολλὴν φιλίαν πρὸς ὑμᾶς καὶ μεγάλας εὐεργεσίας ὑπαρχούσας. Ἄργος μὲν γάρ ἐστί σοι πατρίς, ἧς δίκαιον τοσαύτην σε ποιεῖσθαι πρόνοιαν, ὅσην περ τῶν γονέων τῶν σαυτοῦ· Θηβαῖοι δὲ τὸν ἀρχηγὸν τοῦ γένους ὑμῶν τιμῶσι. The pl. pron. in both cases evidently refers to Philip and the royal family. The same explanation will apply to the second passage (Isocr. *Ep. ad Phil.* III. 5, τῇ βασιλείας τῆς ἐξ ἀρχῆς ὑμῖν ὑπαρχούσης). A stronger passage might have been quoted from *Panath.* § 237, ἵνα τῷ τε πλήθει τῷ τῶν πολιτῶν χαρίσῃ καὶ παρὰ τοῖς εὐνοϊκῶς πρὸς ὑμᾶς διακειμένοις εὐδοκιμήσῃς, but even there it is easy to explain ὑμᾶς as =τοὺς πολίτας. In Latin the usage is quite as strict: and the passage in Ovid, *Fasti,* I. 9 (*Invenies illic et festa domestica vobis; Saepe tibi pater et saepe legendus avus*), is no exception to the rule. The use of ἡμεῖς for ἐγώ is another matter. v. § 5. n.

Ἱππόνικον.] v. *Introduction.*

3 καὶ τῆς φιλίας τῆς πατρικῆς κληρονομεῖν. (Β΄.) Ὁρῶ δὲ c
καὶ τὴν τύχην ἡμῖν συλλαμβάνουσαν καὶ τὸν παρόντα καιρὸν συναγωνιζόμενον· σὺ μὲν γὰρ παιδείας ἐπιθυμεῖς, ἐγὼ
δὲ παιδεύειν ἄλλους ἐπιχειρῶ, καὶ σοὶ μὲν ἀκμὴ φιλοσοφεῖν,
4 ἐγὼ δὲ τοὺς φιλοσοφοῦντας ἐπανορθῶ. Ὅσοι μὲν οὖν πρὸς
τοὺς ἑαυτῶν φίλους τοὺς προτρεπτικοὺς λόγους συγγράφου-
σι, καλὸν μὲν ἔργον ἐπιχειροῦσιν, οὐ μὴν περί γε τὸ κρά-

τῆς φιλίας τῆς πατρικῆς.] πα-
τρικός, πάτριοι, and πατρῷοι are
often hard to distinguish from one
another. Hermann's distinction, 'πάτρια sunt, quae sunt patris, πατρῷα
quae veniunt a patre, πατρικά, qua-
lia sunt patris,' will not answer in
every case. The use of πατρικῆς in
the present passage may, however,
be partially explained by referring
to Bekker's Anecdota, I. p. 2971
πατρῷα λέγουσιν οἱ ῥήτορες χρήματα
καὶ κτήματα καὶ τόπους, πάτρια δὲ
τὰ ἰδῃ καὶ τὰ νόμιμα (Cf. Isocr. Fa-
nœg. §§ 18, 25, 31, &c.) καὶ τὰ
μυστήρια καὶ τὰς ἑορτάς, πατρικὸν δὲ
φίλον ἢ ἐχθρόν (Cf. Paneg. § 184,
Trapez. § 43, ξένοι πατρικοί, Aegin.
§ 50, φιλίαν...παλαιὰν καὶ πατρικήν).

3. καιρόν.] καιρός, the opportuni-
ty, crisis, emergency; not derived
from κείρω, to clip, to cut, but connected with the Sanskrit word kâla
= the right time, from kâr = to do.
Hesychius (Alexandrine Grammarian, fl. 380 A.D.) states that καρός
was another form of καιρός. καιρός,
then, means the 'time for doing,'
' the fit time.'

συναγωνιζόμενον.] Cf. Isocr. Evagoras, § 59, τὴ τύχην αὐτῷ συναγω-
νιζομένην.

ἐπανορθῶ.] This is the only compound of ὀρθόω which doubles the
augment. The augmented tenses
always take the double augment;
e.g. ἐπηνωρθώσαντο, Paneg. § 165,
ἐπηνώρθωσαν, Lysias, Orat. Funé-
bris, § 70, and ἐπηνώρθουν, Isocr.
Panath. § 200. The other compounds, such as διορθόω, κατορθόω,
συγκατορθόω make διώρθωσα, κατώρ-
θωσα, and (Isocr. Phil. § 151) συγκατ-

ώρθωσα. (v. Veitch, Greek Verbs,
sub voc.)

4. τοὺς προτρεπτικοὺς λόγους.] i.e.
Discourses inviting the reader to
intellectual pursuits, e.g. to the cultivation of oratorical power—τὴν
δεινότητα τὴν ἐν τοῖς λόγοις inf.
The λόγος προτρεπτικὸς πρὸς τέχνας
of Galen (Physician, Philologist, and
Philosopher, A.D. 130—200) and the
λ. π. πρὸς φιλοσοφίαν of Iamblichus
(Neoplatonist, fl. 300 A.D.) are
quoted as examples by Conrad
Orelli.—The Letter to Demonicus
is not a λόγος προτρεπτικὸς but a
λόγος παραινετικός. cf. § 5, παραδελη-
σιν (παραίνεσιν. The article τοὺς
shews that the writer had in his
mind certain well-known exhortations composed by contemporary
Sophists.—Isocrates (of Apollonia),
a pupil of Isocrates, wrote a λόγος
προτρεπτικὸς which is mentioned
by Suidas with the names of four
other writings of his (1) Ἀμφικτυ-
ονικός, (2) περὶ τοῦ τάφου μὴ παι-
ῆσαι Φιλίππῳ, (3) περὶ τοῦ μετοικι-
σθῆναι, (4) περὶ τῆς ἑαυτοῦ πολιτείας.
The present passage is enough to
prove that, if Suidas is speaking ac-
curately, the λόγος προτρεπτικὸς of
Isocr. the younger is not identical
with the λόγος παραινετικὸς πρὸς
Δημόνικον.

ἔργον ἐπιχειροῦσιν.] The verb
ἐπιχειρεῖν has three different constructions, 1. with the infinitive, e.g.
§ 3, παιδεύειν ἄλλους ἐπιχειρῶ. 2.
with the dative, Paneg. § 132, ἔργοις
ἐπιχειρεῖν. 3. with the accus., as
here. Of these 1. and 2. are extremely common, 3. is somewhat
rare. Other instances may be found

τιστον τῆς φιλοσοφίας διατρίβουσιν ὅσοι δὲ τοῖς νεωτέροις d
εἰσηγοῦνται, μὴ δι' ὧν τὴν δεινότητα τὴν ἐν τοῖς λόγοις
ἀσκήσουσιν, ἀλλ' ὅπως τὰ τῶν τρόπων ἤθη σπουδαῖοι πεφυ- 3
κέναι δόξουσι, τοσούτῳ μᾶλλον ἐκείνων τοὺς ἀκούοντας ὠφε-
λοῦσιν, ὅσον οἱ μὲν ἐπὶ λόγον μόνον παρακαλοῦσιν, οἱ δὲ
τὸν τρόπον αὐτῶν ἐπανορθοῦσι.

5   Διόπερ ἡμεῖς οὐ παράκλησιν εὑρόντες ἀλλὰ παραίνεσιν
γράψαντες μέλλομέν σοι συμβουλεύειν, ὧν χρὴ τοὺς νεωτέ-

in Plat. *Legg.* v. p. 739 E, ἦν (sc. πολιτείαν)...ἐπικεχειρήκαμεν, and *Crito*, p. 45 C, οὐδὲ δίκαιόν μοι δοκεῖ ἐπιχειρεῖν πρᾶγμα. In the passage before us ἔργῳ ἐπιχ. is avoided because it would involve a *Hiatus*, v. § 2, πρὸς ὑμᾶς. n.

τῆς φιλοσοφίας.] On the meaning of φιλοσοφία, φιλόσοφος, φιλοσοφεῖν in Isocr. see *Paneg.* § 6. n.

ὅσοι.........μή.] Madv. *Syntax*, § 703 (*b*).

τὰ τῶν τρόπων ἤθη.] The morals of their characters—a somewhat pleonastic expression, found however in Plat. *Legg.* VI. p. 773 E, χρήμασί τε καὶ τρόπων ἤθεσι. ib. XI. p. 930 A, τρόπων ἤθη, and elsewhere. The fact that Isocrates does not use the expr. was alleged as early as the time of Henr. Stephens as an argument against the genuineness of the *Ep. ad Dem.* Similar pleonasms may however be found in his universally acknowledged writings, *e.g. Phil.* § 67, τῆς ἐξ ἀρχῆς γενέσεως (of the birth of Cyrus I.).—τὴν τῶν ἔργων πρᾶξιν (Plat. *Menex.* 237 B.) is *not* a pleonasm, as it must mean 'the *manner* in which the deeds were done.'

τοσούτῳ...ὅσον.] τοσοῦτον...ὅσον and τοσούτῳ...ὅσῳ are very common formulæ. τοσούτῳ...ὅσον is less usual, but is here and elsewhere (Isocr. *De Pace*, §§ 47, 143) preferred, because ὅσῳ οἱ μὲν would violate the rule of the *Hiatus*, v. § 2, πρὸς ὑμᾶς. n.

5. ἡμεῖς]=ἐγώ. Isocrates constantly uses the 1st pers. pl. instead

of sing. especially when a *Hiatus* is thereby avoided. Cf. *Phil.* § 105, ἡμῶν, εἰ...τολμῷμεν. ib. § 151, ἡμῖν ἀντεῖπαν...ἐμῷ. *Busiris*, § 32... τοσούτῳ πλέον ἡμῶν ἀπέχει τοῦ πιστὰ λέγειν, ὅσον (cf. last note) ἐγὼ μὲν οὐδένας αὐτὸν αἰτιῶμαι τῶν ἀδυνάτων κ.τ.λ. and at least 15 other passages. Sometimes the simple love of variety is enough to make him use the pl. *e.g. Paneg.* § 14. ἡμῖν . διατριφθέντων...βεβίωκα, n. cf. *Paneg.* § 47. n. quot. The use of 'nos' for 'ego' is not uncommon in Latin (Cic. *Catil.* I. IX. 22) and sometimes leads to anomalous collocations. Cf. Terent. *Eunuchus*, IV. 3. 7 (=I. 649), *absente nobis.* Catull. 106, 5, *insperanti ipsa refers te nobis.* Ovid. *Heroid.* 5. 45, *nostros vidisti flentis ocellos.*

ὧν...τίνων...ποίοις... τῶν.] Lit. ' we are about to advise you on those objects, after which the young ought to strive, and what deeds they ought to avoid, &c.' ὧν, &c. = ταῦτα, ὧν. The change from ὧν to τίνων is to be noticed. On τίνων...ποίοις...τῶν for ὧντινων....ὁποίοις....ὅσων, see Madvig. *Synt.* § 198 b. A similar variation of structure may be noticed in Thuc. I. 137. Θεμιστοκλῆς φράζει τῷ ναυκλήρῳ ὅστις ἐστὶ καὶ δι' ἃ φεύγει (*q. d.* narrat quis sit et quam ob rem fugit). In Isocr. *ad Nicocl.* § 2, ὁρίσαι, ποίων ἐπιτηδευμάτων ὀρεγόμενοι καὶ τίνων ἔργων ἀπεχόμενοι ἄριστ' ἂν τὴν πόλιν διοικοῖεν, the *sense* is almost the same, but the *structure* more uniform.

8   ΙΣΟΚΡΑΤΟΥΣ   [§§ 6

ρους ὀρέγεσθαι καὶ τίνων ἔργων ἀπέχεσθαι καὶ ποίοις τισὶν
ἀνθρώποις ὁμιλεῖν καὶ πῶς τὸν ἑαυτῶν βίον οἰκονομεῖν.
ὅσοι γὰρ τοῦ βίου ταύτην τὴν ὁδὸν ἐπορεύθησαν, οὗτοι μόνοι b
τῆς ἀρετῆς ἐφικέσθαι γνησίως ἠδυνήθησαν, ἧς οὐδὲν κτῆμα
6 σεμνότερον οὐδὲ βεβαιότερόν ἐστι. κάλλος μὲν γὰρ ἢ χρόνος ἀνήλωσεν ἢ νόσος ἐμάρανε, πλοῦτος δὲ κακίας μᾶλλον
ἢ καλοκαγαθίας ὑπηρέτης ἐστίν, ἐξουσίαν μὲν τῇ ῥαθυμίᾳ
παρασκευάζων, ἐπὶ δὲ τὰς ἡδονὰς τοὺς νέους παρακαλῶν·
ῥώμη δὲ μετὰ μὲν φρονήσεως ὠφέλησεν, ἄνευ δὲ ταύτης
πλείω τοὺς ἔχοντας ἐλυμήνατο, καὶ τὰ μὲν σώματα τῶν
ἀσκούντων ἐκόσμησε, ταῖς δὲ τῆς ψυχῆς ἐπιμελείαις ἐπε-
7 σκότησεν. ἡ δὲ τῆς ἀρετῆς κτῆσις οἷς ἂν ἀκιβδήλως ταῖς c

βίον οἰκονομεῖν.] οἰκονομεῖν (οἰ-
κονόμος—οἶκος, νέμω) here and in § 46
merges the full meaning of οἶκος
in the secondary and metaphorical
sense given to the whole word. Cf.
Arist. *Aves*, 1232, μηλοσφαγεῖν τε
βουθύται ἐπ' ἰσχάραις...Hom. *Il.*
IV. 3, νέκταρ ἐῳνοχόει, Plato, *Protag.*
340 A, τὸν Σκάμανδρον πολιορκούμενον ὑπὸ τοῦ 'Αχιλλέως. Cic. *Verr.*
V. § 47, navem aedificatam. Virg.
Aen. II. 16, equum...aedificant.
Exodus xxxviii. 8, *looking-glasses of
brass*, &c.

ὅσοι γὰρ...ἐστι.] Trans. 'For as
many as have traversed this path of
life, these only are, in genuine wise,
enabled to arrive at virtue—that
grandest and most enduring of all
possessions,' lit. 'than which no
possession is, &c.'

ἠδυνήθησαν.] Cf. *Paneg.* § 102 n.

6. **κάλλος...παρακαλῶν.**] 'For,
as for beauty, time may waste or
disease may wither it; while wealth
is the vassal (or 'minister') of vice
rather than of true nobility, assur-
ing licence to idleness and alluring
young men to pleasure.'

**ἀνήλωσεν....ἐμάρανε....ἐστίν....
ὠφέλησεν...ἐλυμήνατο...ἐκόσμησε.**]
Gnomic aorists, here, as sometimes
elsewhere, coupled with the present
tense: see the instances given in
Madv. *Synt.* § 111 a. cf. § 33, πρὸτ-

τουσιν...προσείημίωσε, § 47, ἐλυτή-
θησαν...ἔχομεν, *Paneg.* § 46, διελύθησαν...ἐστίν and, as an instance of
more complex interweaving of aorist
and present, Eurip. *Fragm.* 833
(Dind.), χωρεῖ δ' ὀπίσω τὰ μὲν ἐκ
γαίας | φύντ' εἰς γαῖαν, τὰ δ' ἀπ'
αἰθερίου | βλαστόντα γονῆς εἰς οὐρά-
νιον | πόλον ἦλθε πάλιν· θνήσκει
δ' οὐδὲν | τῶν γιγνομένων, διακρινό-
μενον δ' | ἄλλο πρὸς ἄλλου | μορφὴν
ἰδίαν ἀπέδειξε.

παρασκευάζων......παρακαλῶν.]
ὁμοιοκάταρκτα, see Introduct. on
Style of Isocr. Cf. § 42, περι-
χαρῆς...περίλυπος. *Paneg.* § 14, καταγελᾶν...καταφρονεῖν.

ῥώμη...ἐπεσκότησεν.] 'Strength
united with prudence, is helpful,
but, without it, does more harm
(than good) to its possessors, and,
while it adorns the bodies of the
athletes, it nevertheless casts a cloud
over the culture of the soul.'

οἱ ἀσκοῦντες.] *i.e.* 'those who
go into training,' ἀσκεῖν lit. 'to
practise,' gen. with acc. of the thing
practised. Hippocrates (*The Father
of Medicine*, 460—357 B.C.) uses
the expression οἱ ἀσκέοντες absolutely, of gymnasts. v. § 12, ἐπὶ
τοὺς ἀνταγωνιστὰς ἀσκεῖν.

7. **ἀκιβδήλως.**] 'Like true metal,'
'without alloy,' (α–κίβδηλος. κίβδος
=alloy). The word is doubtless sug-

διανοίαις συναυξηθῇ, μόνη μὲν συγγηράσκει, πλούτου δὲ
κρείττων, χρησιμωτέρα δ᾽ εὐγενείας ἐστὶ, τὰ μὲν τοῖς ἄλλοις
ἀδύνατα δυνατὰ καθιστᾶσα, τὰ δὲ τῷ πλήθει φοβερὰ θαρσαλέως ὑπομένουσα, καὶ τὸν μὲν ὄκνον ψόγον, τὸν δὲ πόνον
8 ἔπαινον ἡγουμένη. ῥάδιον δὲ τοῦτο καταμαθεῖν ἔστιν ἔκ τε
τῶν Ἡρακλέους ἄθλων καὶ τῶν Θησέως ἔργων, οἷς ἡ τῶν d
τρόπων ἀρετὴ τηλικοῦτον εὐδοξίας χαρακτῆρα τοῖς ἔργοις

gested by the immediate context:
πλούτοι...πλούτου. Cf. Dem. adv.
Lept. ad fin. Θαυμάζω δ᾽ ἔγωγε, εἰ
τοῖς μὲν τὸ νόμισμα διαφθείρουσιν
θάνατος παρ᾽ ὑμῖν ἐστιν ἡ ζημία, τοῖς
δ᾽ ὅλην τὴν πόλιν κίβδηλον καὶ ἄπιστον ποιοῦσιν λόγον δώσετε. The
metaphor occurs often (v. § 25. n.)
in the παραινέσεις of Theognis (the
elegiac poet of Megara, c. 570—c.
490 B.C.) whose maxims of moral
advice to his friend Cyrnus will
often be quoted in the succeeding
notes.

συγγηράσκει...πλούτου.] An allusion to § 6, κάλλος ἢ χρόνος ἀνήλωσεν ἢ νόσος ἐμάρανε, πλούτου δὲ κ.τ.λ.

πλούτου κρείττων, χρησιμωτέρα
εὐγενείας.] Of the four terms quoted
the first corresponds to the fourth,
and the second to the third. Two
of them are as near as possible to
each other, the other two as far as
possible from each other. This figure
of speech is usually called a Chiasmus (after the letter χῖ. ᗮⅩᗮ 1 and
4 are connected by one branch of
the letter, 2 and 3 by the other).
Cf. § 38, δικαίαν πενίαν ἢ πλοῦτον
ἄδικον. Panrg. § 95, καλῶς δυσθα-
νεῖν ἢ ζῆν αἰσχρῶς. Nicocl. § 7, περὶ
τῶν δικαίων καὶ τῶν ἀδίκων καὶ τῶν
αἰσχρῶν καὶ τῶν καλῶν. Plat. Sympos.
196 B, ἔρως οὔτ᾽ ἀδικεῖ οὔτ᾽ ἀδικεῖται
οὔθ᾽ ὑπὸ θεοῦ οὔτε θεόν. Theaet.
173 D, νόμους δὲ καὶ ψηφίσματα λεγόμενα ἢ γεγραμμένα οὔτε ὁρῶσιν οὔτε
ἀκούουσι. Cic. Phil. II. § 95, Vivus
eripuit, reddit mortuus. Liv. VIII. 6,
fin. Milites militibus, centurionibus
centuriones, tribuni tribunis compa-

res collegaeque. The usual English
arrangement of such sentences is also
frequently found in Gk. and Lat.
(e.g. § 33, fin.) The pliancy of the
latter languages often however allows
Chiasmus to be used with telling effect.—Cf. Panrg. § 54. n.

ἀδύνατα)(δυνατά.....φοβερά)(θαρσαλέως.] Obs. the collocation.

θαρσαλέως.] θαρσεῖν, θαρσαλέος are
used by the earlier writers, Thucydides, &c.; θαρρεῖν, θαρραλέος by
Plato and the later Attic writers.
The latter forms (according to Baiter
and Sauppe on Isocr. de Perm. § 121)
occur 16 times in Isocr., the former
never except in this passage: see
Introd. on the genuineness of the
Ep. ad Dem.

8. ῥάδιον...συνεγράφεσαν.] 'Now
it is easy to discern this from the
labours of Hercules and the exploits of Theseus, for whom the excellence of their character imprinted
so deep a stamp of glory on their
exploits, that not even eternity itself
can engender oblivion of the achievements of those heroes.' Cf. Phil.
§ 144, τὴν Ἡρακλέους ὑπερβολὴν
καὶ τὴν Θησέως ἀρετήν. See also
§ 50. n. The exploits of Theseus
are recounted at length by Isocr.
Helenae Encomium, §§ 18—38 (περὶ
τῆς Ἑλένης Ἰσοκράτη ἔγραψεν ὅτι
σπουδαία εἴπερ Θησεὺς ἱέρωσεν, Arist.
Rhet. II. 23).—The legend of Theseus is well told by Prof. Kingsley
in his Greek Fairy Tales, and more
briefly by Mr Cox in his Tales of
Ancient Greece, p. 159.

ἐπέβαλεν, ὥστε μηδὲ τὸν ἅπαντα χρόνον δύνασθαι λήθην
ἐμποιῆσαι τῶν ἐκείνοις πεπραγμένων.

9 (γ΄.) Οὐ μὴν ἀλλὰ καὶ τὰς τοῦ πατρὸς προαιρέσεις ἀνα-
μνησθεὶς οἰκεῖον καὶ καλὸν ἕξεις παράδειγμα τῶν ὑπ᾽ ἐμοῦ
σοι λεγομένων. οὐ γὰρ ὀλιγωρῶν τῆς ἀρετῆς οὐδὲ ῥαθυμῶν
διετέλεσε τὸν βίον, ἀλλὰ τὸ μὲν σῶμα τοῖς πόνοις ἐγύμναζε,
10 τῇ δὲ ψυχῇ τοὺς κινδύνους ὑφίστατο. οὐδὲ τὸν πλοῦτον c
παρακαίρως ἠγάπα, ἀλλ᾽ ἀπέλαυε μὲν τῶν παρόντων ἀγαθῶν ὡς θνητός, ἐπεμελεῖτο δὲ τῶν ὑπαρχόντων ὡς ἀθάνα-
τος. οὐδὲ ταπεινῶς διῴκει τὸν αὑτοῦ βίον, ἀλλὰ φιλόκαλος
ἦν καὶ μεγαλοπρεπὴς καὶ τοῖς φίλοις κοινός, καὶ μᾶλλον 4
ἐθαύμαζε τοὺς περὶ αὑτὸν σπουδάζοντας ἢ τοὺς γένει προσή-
κοντας· ἡγεῖτο γὰρ εἶναι πρὸς ἑταιρίαν πολλῷ κρείττω φύ-
11 σιν νόμου καὶ τρόπον γένους καὶ προαίρεσιν ἀνάγκης. ἐπιλίποι δ᾽ ἂν ἡμᾶς ὁ πᾶς χρόνος, εἰ πάσας τὰς ἐκείνου πράξεις

9. οὐ μὴν ἀλλὰ καὶ.] sc. οὐ μὴν
(ἐκ τῶν Ἡρ· ἄθλων καὶ τῶν Θησ.
ἔργων τοῦτό σοι καταμαθεῖν ἐστίν)
ἀλλὰ καί... 'not indeed..., but...'
or 'not but that,' or 'nevertheless.'
Trans. 'nevertheless, by remember-
ing the principles of your *father*, you
will have in your home a noble example (a fine home-example) of that
which I am telling you.' Cf. *Phil.*
§ 113 (speaking of Hercules as a
worthy pattern for his descendant
Philip) μὴ δεῖν ἀλλοτρίοις χρῆσθαι
παραδείγμασιν ἀλλ᾽ οἰκεῖον ὑπάρχειν.

ὑφίστατο.] The reading ὑφίστατο
is adopted by Baiter and Sauppe on
the authority of the Codex Scaphu-
siensis and of the Codex Urbinas.
The original reading however of
Cod. Urb. was ὑπέμενεν, and this
was subsequently altered into ὑφίστατο. Benseler accepts ὑπέμενεν.
The difference in sense is perfectly
immaterial.

ἀπέλαυε...ἀθάνατος.] Imitated (?)
by Lucian, *ap. Antholog. Pal.* x. 26,
ὡς νεθνηξόμενος τῶν σῶν ἀγαθῶν ἀπό-
λαυε, | ὡς δὲ βιωσόμενος φείδεο σῶν
κτεάνων. | ἔστι δ᾽ ἀνὴρ σοφὸς οὗτος,

ὃς ἄμφω ταῦτα νοήσας | φειδοῖ καὶ
δαπάνῃ μέτρον ἐφηρμόσατο.| The first
two lines are quoted in the margin
of one of the MSS. collated by
Auger.

10. μεγαλοπρεπής.] Cf. Arist. *Eth.*
II. 7. 6, 'In respect of wealth...the
mean state is called munificence (μι-
γαλοπρέπεια)...the *excess* is called
want-of-taste (ἀπειροκαλία) or vulgar-
profusion (βαναυσία), the *defect* pal-
triness (μικροπρέπεια)'. v. also *Eth.*
IV. (2) = 4.

τοὺς γένει προσήκοντας.] Bens.
reads τῷ γένει· BS. γένει. The art.
is exceptional and one good MS.
(Cod. Scaph.) omits it. As instances
of the usual form may be quoted, Eur.
Med. 1304, οἱ προσήκοντες γένει. Lycurg. *Leocr.* § 138, τοῖς μήτε γένει
μήτε φιλίᾳ μηδὲν προσήκουσι. Isocr.
Aegin. § 33, γένει μὲν φασι προσήκειν.

ἡγεῖτο...ἀνάγκης.] 'For, in point
of companionship, he deemed nature
far more sovereign than convention,
character than kindred, principle
than compulsion.' On φύσις χρόνος,
cf. *Paneg.* § 105, n.

11. ἐπιλίποι...] Cf. Lysias, *Or.
Funebr.* § 1, πᾶσιν ἀνθρώποις ὁ πᾶς

καταριθμησαίμεθα. ἀλλὰ τὸ μὲν ἀκριβὲς αὐτῶν ἐν ἑτέροις
καιροῖς δηλώσομεν, δεῖγμα δὲ τῆς Ἱππονίκου φύσεως νῦν
ἐξενηνόχαμεν, πρὸς ὃν δεῖ ζῆν σ' ὥσπερ πρὸς παράδειγμα, b
νόμου μὲν τὸν ἐκείνου τρόπον ἡγησάμενον, μιμητὴν δὲ καὶ
ζηλωτὴν τῆς πατρῴας ἀρετῆς γιγνόμενον· αἰσχρὸν γὰρ τοὺς
μὲν γραφεῖς ἀπεικάζειν τὰ καλὰ τῶν ζῴων, τοὺς δὲ παῖδας

χρόνος οὐχ ἱκανὸς λόγων ἴσον παρα-
σκευάσαι ταῖς τούτων ἔργοις. Isocr.
Archidamus, § 81 and *De Pace*, § 56,
ἐπιλίποι δ' ἄν με τὸ λοιπὸν μέρος τῆς
ἡμέρας εἰ...Cicero, *pro Caelio*, § 29,
*dies me deficiat, si, quae dici possunt,
coner exprimere.*

ἐν ἑτέροις καιροῖς δηλώσομεν.]
The promise, as far as we are aware,
remained unfulfilled. Had it been
accomplished we should have had a
laudatory biography of Hipponicus,
rivalling that of Evagoras.

δεῖγμα...παράδειγμα.] The sound
and the sense of these words may be
represented by 'sample' and 'example'. A similar *lusus verborum*
may be found in Thuc. II. 62. 3, μὴ
φρονήματι μόνον ἀλλὰ καὶ καταφρο-
νήματι. Dem. *Fals. Leg.* § 122, p.
378, σύλλογοι καὶ λόγοι παντοδαποί,
(ap. Spengel. *Rhetores Graeci*, III. 36).
Instances of the collocation of ἐκφέ-
ρειν and δεῖγμα may be found in
Plat. *Legg.* VII. 788 c.   Isocr. *De
perm.* § 54. ὥσπερ δὲ τῶν καρπῶν,
ἐξενεγκεῖν ἑκάστου δεῖγμα παράσχο-
μαι. al.—The term δεῖγμα is frequently used of the 'samples' exhibited by the ἔμπορος or wholesale
dealer. Cf. Aristobulus ap. Plutarch.
Dem. 23, ὥσπερ τοὺς ἐμπόρους ὁρῶμεν, ὅταν ἐν τρυβλίῳ δεῖγμα περι-
φέρωσι, δι' ὀλίγων πυρῶν τοὺς πολλοὺς πιπράσκοντας...... Hierocles,
Ἀστεῖα 9, σχολαστικὸς οἰκίαν πωλῶν
λίθον ἀπ' αὐτῆς εἰς δεῖγμα περιέφερε.
Cf. Isocr. *Epp.* 8. § 6, ἅπαντες γὰρ
ὥσπερ δείγματι τοῖς τοιούτοις χρώμενοι καὶ τοὺς ἄλλους τοὺς συμπολιτευο-
μένους ὁμοίους εἶναι τούτοις νομίζουσιν.

νόμου...ἡγησάμενον.] Cf. § 36,
ἰσχυρότατον μέντοι νόμον ἡγοῦ τὸν
ἐκείνων τρόπον. n.

πατρῴας.] v. § 1, τῆς φιλίας τῆς
πατρικῆ. n.

αἰσχρὸν...γονέων.] Trans. 'For it
is shameful, if, *while* painters por-
tray those living beings that are
beautiful, children nevertheless refuse to imitate those parents who are
good.' The particles μὲν and δὲ
make the two clauses of the sentence
co-ordinate with one another, but the
English idiom requires the first clause
to be made *subordinate* to the second.
See Madvig, *Synt.* § 189 a and cf.
§ 19, τοὺς μὲν ἐμπόρους... and Isocr.
Archidam. § 54, πῶς οὐκ αἰσχρὸν τότε
μὲν ἕκαστον ἡμῶν ἱκανὸν εἶναι τὰς
ἀλλοτρίας πόλεις διαφυλάττειν, νυνὶ
δὲ πάντας μήτε δύνασθαι μήτε τολ-
μᾶσθαι τὴν ἡμετέραν αὐτῶν διασῴ-
ζειν.   On τὰ καλὰ τῶν ζῴων cf.,
§ 10, n.   This comparison between
artists and children, like many other
comparisons, will hardly bear examination: if the former were in the
habit of painting *only* beautiful ani-
mals, the illustration would be more
satisfactory.

γραφεῖς.] In Isocr. the acc. pl.
of words ending in -εύς is generally
-έας, *e.g.* γονέας, *Paneg.* § 111, ἱππέας,
ib. § 148, συγγραφέας, *Mantitea*,
Πλαταιέας, Φωκέας, βασιλέας. In
16 passages the above forms are
supported by all the MSS.   However *ad Nicocl.* § 31 supplies an instance in which the contracted form
-εῖς is recognised by the Urbino MS.
and one of the Vatican MSS., and
there is good authority for χαλκιδεῖς
in *de Perm.* § 113.   In the passage
before us γραφεῖς is supported by
the best MSS., and the same is the
case with γονεῖς in §§ 14, 16 (v. Baiter, *Exc.* II. a. ap. Bremi, *Isocr.* p.

12 μὴ μιμεῖσθαι τοὺς σπουδαίους τῶν γονέων. ἡγοῦ δὲ μηδενὶ
τῶν ἀθλητῶν οὕτω προσήκειν ἐπὶ τοὺς ἀνταγωνιστὰς ἀσκεῖν,
ὡς σοὶ σκοπεῖν, ὅπως ἐφάμιλλος γενήσει τοῖς τοῦ πατρὸς
ἐπιτηδεύμασιν. οὕτω δὲ τὴν γνώμην οὐ δυνατὸν διατεθῆναι c
τὸν μὴ πολλῶν καὶ καλῶν ἀκουσμάτων πεπληρωμένον· τὰ
μὲν γὰρ σώματα τοῖς συμμέτροις πόνοις, ἡ δὲ ψυχὴ τοῖς
σπουδαίοις λόγοις αὔξεσθαι πέφυκε. διόπερ ἐγώ σοι πειράσομαι συντόμως ὑποθέσθαι, δι᾽ ὧν ἄν μοι δοκεῖς ἐπιτηδεύ-

---

100). On the whole, then, the form
-έαν seems to prevail in Isocr. On
the other hand, definite traces of -εῖν
are found in the acknowledged
writings, and therefore the fact that
the latter form occurs in the *Ep. ad
Dem.* is in itself, perhaps, no proof
of the spuriousness of that *Ep.*
Lastly, it is perfectly possible that
the original reading may have been
altered from γραφέας and γονέας into
the contracted form now presented
by the MSS. (Cf. Introd. on Gen.
of *ad Dem.*)—Speaking of Attic
writers in general the following is a
fair statement: 'forma soluta etsi
Atticis usitatissima est, tamen etiam
contracta, si momentum huius rei
codices fidei probatae faciant, apud
scriptores optimos invenitur.' Weber Dem. *in Aristocratem*, § 189.

12. οὕτω...πέφυκε.] Translate:
'Now this disposition of mind is impossible in the case of one who is not
fraught with many noble maxims,
for, by the laws of nature, just as
bodies grow by means of moderate
exercise, even so the soul grows by
means of sober precepts.'—ἄκουσμα,
lit. a maxim uttered and *heard;*
often, as here and in § 19, a maxim
written and *read.* (The modern Eng.
use of the word 'lecture' may be
an exact contrast to this transition
of meaning.) The *general* meaning
'maxim,' apart from all direct idea
of *oral* precept, is to be found also
in Plat. (?) *Ep.* 2, p. 314 A, εὐλαβοῦ
μέντοι μή ποτε ἐκπέσῃ ταῦτα εἰς ἀνθρώπους ἀπαιδεύτους· σχεδὸν γάρ...
οὐκ ἔστι τούτων πρὸς τοὺς πολλοὺς

καταγελαστότερα ἀκούσματα, κ.τ.λ.
q. v.

τὰ μὲν...ἡ δέ.] Lit. 'the bodies
on the one hand'...'the soul on the
other,' i. e. '*As* the bodies...*so* like-
wise the soul...' This use of μέν...δέ
is very common in comparisons.
Cf. § 25, τὸ μὲν γὰρ χρυσίον... The
similitudines of Demophilus (a collection of Pythagorean precepts) are
constantly expressed in this form:
e.g. sim. 14, λιμὴν μὲν πλοίῳ ὅρμος,
βίῳ δὲ φιλία. Cf. also the saying
attributed to Socrates (Orelli, *Opusc.*
Mor. L. 30), κοσμητέον ἱερὸν μὲν ἀναθήμασι, τὴν δὲ ψυχὴν μαθήμασιν.

αὔξεσθαι.] Isocr. (like Plat. and
Aristoph.) uses both of the forms
αὐξάνομαι (*Paneg.* § 104) and αὔξο-
μαι (*Phil.* § 38). Eurip. uses the
former once (*Med.* 918), the latter
often.

αὔξεσθαι πέφυκε.] i. e. 'tis their
nature to increase. *Philip.* 35, ἅπαντες πλείω πεφύκαμεν ἐξαμαρτάνειν ἢ
κατορθοῦν. Soph. *Phil.* 80, ἔξοιδα
καὶ φύσει σε μὴ πεφυκότα | τοιαῦτα
φωνεῖν μηδὲ τεχνᾶσθαι κακά.

δι᾽ ὧν ἄν μοι δοκεῖς...ἐπιβοῦναι.]
ἄν belongs to ἐπιδοῦναι, cf. *Epp.* 8.
§ 9, οὕτω δ᾽ ἄν μοι δοκεῖτε (MSS. δοκοίητε) κάλλιστα βουλεύσασθαι. Madv.
Synt. § 173, R. 1.—The MSS. have
δοκοίητε and this reading is adopted
by Benseler. Cobet (*nov. lect.* p.
367) says:—'*optativus debetur cor-
rectori semidocto, qui Atticae consue-
tudinis immemor aut ignarus, ἄν
cum verbo finito conjungendum esse
putavit, quum esset cum ἐπιδοῦναι ab
Isocrate conjunctum, idque Bekkerus*

μάτων πλεῖστον πρὸς ἀρετὴν ἐπιδοῦναι καὶ παρὰ τοῖς ἄλλοις
ἅπασιν ἀνθρώποις εὐδοκιμῆσαι.

13   (δ΄.)   Πρῶτον μὲν οὖν εὐσέβει τὰ πρὸς τοὺς θεοὺς μὴ d

senserat, sed doceijn ab illis servatum
est, quibus codicis Urbinatis auctori-
tas potior est quam sana ratio et
dicendi usus.'

§§ 13—43. *The Prologue having
ended, the following sections contain
a series of miscellaneous moral
maxims, distributed as follows:*

§ 13. *Duty towards Heaven.* 14.
*Duty towards parents. Of Bodily
exercise.* 15. *Of Laughter and Rashness of Speech. The virtues which
grace a young man's character.* 16.
*The force of conscience. Summary
of duty towards Heaven, parents,
friends, and laws.* 17. *Of pleasures.
Of calumny.* 18, 19. *Of acquiring
knowledge.* 20. *Of conversation.*
21. *Of self-training and self-control.*
22. *Of keeping secrets.* 23. *Of oaths.*
24—27. *On the choice of friends, on
tests of friendship, on the treatment
due to friends.* 27, 28. *On dress;
on use of wealth.* 29. *Contentment
and ambition. Consideration for the
unfortunate. On doing good to good
men.* 30. *On flatterers and false
friends.* 31. *On sociability.* 32. *Of
wine and of munificence.* 33. *Of
knowledge, ignorance, friendship.*
34. *Of counsel and execution.* 35.
*Of circumspection in choosing coun-
sellors.* 36. *Of imitating and obey-
ing kings.* 37. *Of public service and
its responsibilities.* 38, 39. *Of justice and injustice.* 40. *Of the exercise of mind and body.* 41. *Of speech
and silence.* 42. *Of moderation and
reserve. And lastly,* 43. *Of security
in life, and honour in death.*

13 sqq. The above summary will
be sufficient to shew the extent to
which a methodical arrangement is
adopted by the writer: the thread
that joins one maxim to another is
often very slender, and the order in
which they are set down is sometimes perfectly capricious. Benseler
(*Praef.* p. iv.) appeals to the ' *mala*

praeceptorum dispositio' as an argument against the genuineness of the
Ep. It is easy, however, to answer
that (1) The other λόγοι παραινετικοί, which are now universally accepted, are almost as unmethodical
in arrangement; and (2) Isocr. himself, when about to quote a long
passage from one of them, draws, to
the following effect, a special distinction between the style of the
Ep. ad Nicocl. and that of his other
works (*De Perm.* §§ 67, 68). 'You
have now heard part of two of my
writings (*i. e.* extracts from *Paneg.*
and *De Pace*); but I wish to go
through some small portion of a
third also, that you may see still
more clearly that virtue and justice
are the aim of all my writings. The
writing, which is now to be brought
before you, is addressed to Nicocles,
of Cyprus, who was king at the
time; and gives him advice on the
right method of governing his subjects, but it is not in the same style
as the writings which have just been
read to you. In the former, that
which I say is always in compact
and close harmony with the previous
context; in the latter, the reverse is
the case; for it is by separating each
sentence from that which has gone
before, and by dividing the whole
into "chapters," that I there attempt
briefly to state each point of my advice, &c.'

εὐσέβει.] In commands the *aor.
imp.* is used when the action required is single and transient; the *present imp.* whenever the command is
lasting in its obligation; many instances of the latter may be found
in the subsequent §§. Madv. *Synt.*
§ 141.

εὐσέβει...ἡμῶνον.] For the general sense of this and the following
§ we may compare the beginning of
the *Aurei Versus* of Pseudo-Pytha-

μόνον θύων ἀλλὰ καὶ τοῖς ὅρκοις ἐμμένων· ἐκεῖνο μὲν γὰρ
τῆς τῶν χρημάτων εὐπορίας σημεῖον, τοῦτο δὲ τῆς τῶν τρόπων καλοκαγαθίας τεκμήριον. τίμα τὸ δαιμόνιον ἀεὶ μὲν,
μάλιστα δὲ μετὰ τῆς πόλεως· οὕτω γὰρ δόξεις ἅμα τε τοῖς
θεοῖς θύειν καὶ τοῖς ὅρκοις ἐμμένειν.

14   Τοιοῦτος γίγνου περὶ τοὺς γονεῖς, οἵους ἂν εὔξαιο περὶ ϲ
σεαυτὸν γενέσθαι τοὺς ἑαυτοῦ παῖδας.

'Άσκει τῶν περὶ τὸ σῶμα γυμνασίων μὴ τὰ πρὸς τὴν ῥώ-

goras: ἀθανάτους μὲν πρῶτα θεούς,
νόμῳ ὡς διάκειται, | τίμα καὶ σέβου
ὅρκον...τούς τε γονεῖς τίμα, τούς τ᾽
ἄγχιστ᾽ ἐκγεγαῶτας. Cf. Theognis,
171.

σημεῖον)(τεκμήριον.] § 2. n.

τίμα...ἐμμένειν.] *i. e.* 'Do honour
to Heaven on *all* occasions, but
especially in the rites of public worship; for thus men will see that you
are not only sacrificing to the gods,
but are also likely to be true to your
oaths.' Benseler (*Praef.* xliii.) explains as follows: *Qui deos publice
colit, pium et religiosum se ostendit et
talem qui etiam iusiurandum sit
conservaturus;* and this explanation
is less forced than that given by
Schneider, who supposes that the
words τοῖς ὅρκοις ἐμμένειν refer to
some oath like that taken by *Athenian* citizens, τὰ ἱερὰ τὰ πάτρια τι-
μήσω.

Isocr. appears to inculcate, besides
a general worship of Heaven, an
especial attention to *public* worship
and the religion of the state, on the
low ground that a reputation for
honesty is thus acquired.—Plato, in
a curious passage at the end of
Legg. IX. p. 909 D, suggests the abo-
lition of purely private acts of worship, ἔστω γὰρ νόμος ὅδε τοῖς ξύμπασι
κείμενον ἁπλοῦν 'Ἱερὰ μηδὲ εἰς ἐν
ἰδίαις οἰκίαις ἐκτήσθω· θύειν δ᾽ ὅταν
ἐπὶ νοῦν ἴῃ τινί, πρὸς τὰ δημόσια ἴτω
θύσων.

14. γονεῖς.] Cf. γραφεῖ, § 11 n.
The father of Dem. was dead: the
word γονεῖς must therefore be taken
in a general sense. Cf. Isaeus, *de*

Cironis hæredit. § 32, 'The law en-
joins men to support their parents
(γονέας); by parents are meant the
mother, the father, the grandfather,
the grandmother, and their mother
and father, if they be still alive.'

ἑαυτοῦ.] The reflexive pron. of
the 3rd pers. is here used instead of
that of the 2nd pers. ἑαυτοῦ for
σεαυτοῦ (which is the reading of
some MSS.). Cf. § 21, ἑαυτὸν and
αὑτὸν=σαυτόν. For instances of
αὑτοῦ=ἐμαυτοῦ cf. Isocr. *Aegin.*
§ 23, ἐπειρώμην...στέρεσθαι...τῶν
ἐμαυτοῦ, πρὸς δὲ τούτοις ὁρῶν τὴν
μητέρα τὴν αὑτοῦ καὶ τὴν ἀδελφὴν
ἐκ τῆς πατρίδος ἐκπεπτωκυίας. *Phil.*
§ 129, πρὸς τὴν πατρίδα τὴν αὑτοῦ
(=ἐμαυτοῦ), ib. § 149, πρὸς αὑτὸν=
πρὸς σαυτόν.—Pors. ad Eur. *Or.* 626,
says 'hoc pronomen omnium perso-
narum commune est.' For examples
of this usage in Aesch. and Soph.
see Mr Jebb's note on Soph. *Elet.*
285. A similar usage may be noticed
in σφεῖς and the *reflex. poss. pron.*
δι, σφέτερος (v. Lidd. and Scott).

ἄσκει...δυνάμενος.] 'Of bodily
exercises, practise *not* those that
conduce to strength, but rather those
that conduce to health: and this
point you may gain, if you cease
from your exertions, while still able
to continue them' (*i. e.* if you rest
from your exercise before you are
exhausted). Cf. Pseudo-Pythag.
Aur. Vers. 32, οὐδ᾽ ὑγιείης τῆς περὶ
σῶμ᾽ ἀμέλειαν ἔχειν χρή | ἀλλὰ ποτοῦ
τε μέτρον καὶ σίτου γυμνασίων τε |
ποιεῖσθαι· μέτρον δὲ λέγω τόδ᾽ ὃ μή
σ᾽ ἀνιήσει, and Celsus, I. 2 (quoted

μὴν ἀλλὰ τὰ πρὸς τὴν ὑγίειαν· τούτου δ' ἂν ἐπιτύχοις, εἰ
λήγοις τῶν πόνων ἔτι πονεῖν δυνάμενος.

15   Μήτε γέλωτα προπετῆ στέργε μήτε λόγον μετὰ θράσους 5
ἀποδέχου· τὸ μὲν γὰρ ἀνόητον, τὸ δὲ μανικόν. Ἃ ποιεῖν
αἰσχρόν, ταῦτα νόμιζε μηδὲ λέγειν εἶναι καλόν. Ἔθιζε σεαυτὸν εἶναι μὴ σκυθρωπὸν ἀλλὰ σύννουν· δι' ἐκεῖνο μὲν γὰρ
αὐθάδης, διὰ δὲ τοῦτο φρόνιμος εἶναι δόξεις. Ἡγοῦ μάλιστα
σεαυτῷ πρέπειν κόσμον, αἰσχύνην δικαιοσύνην σωφροσύνην· b
τούτοις γὰρ ἅπασι δοκεῖ κρατεῖσθαι τὸ τῶν νεωτέρων ἦθος.

by Facciolati), 'exercitationis ple-
rumque finis esse debet sudor; aut
certe lassitudo quae citra fatigatio-
nem sit.'

15. μήτε...μανικόν.] 'Love not
headlong laughter, and embrace not
rashness of speech; for the latter is
folly, the former madness.' μανικὸν
is a stronger word than ἀνόητον. Cf.
the gradation in Isocr. *Panath.*
§ 157, εἰς τοῦτ' ἦλθεν οὐκ ἀνοίας ἀλλὰ
μανίας. τὸ μὲν refers to λόγον, κ.τ.λ.,
and τὸ δὲ to γέλωτα, κ.τ.λ. The
sense gained by translating τὸ μέν,
'the former,' τὸ δέ, 'the latter,'
though much may be said for it, is,
perhaps, less forcible. It is perfectly
natural to describe wild and giddy
laughter as a characteristic of madness, and rashness of speech as a
sign of senselessness.—Cf. Epictetus,
Manuale, cap. 33, 4, γέλων μὴ πολὺν
ἔστω· μηδὲ ἐπὶ πολλοῖς, μηδὲ ἀνειμέ-
νον. Geo. Herbert, *Church Porch*,
'*Laugh not too much: the wittie man
laughs least;*' and Lord Chester-
field's *Letters*, 112, *Frequent and loud
laughter is the characteristic of folly
and ill-manners: it is the manner
in which the mob express their silly
joy at silly things; and they call it
being merry...I am neither of a me-
lancholy, nor a cynical disposition;
and am as willing, and as apt to be
pleased as any body; but I am sure
that, since I have had the full use of
my reason, nobody has ever heard
me laugh.* v. also *Let.* 134.

μήτε...ἀποδέχου] does not mean

'Do not welcome rashness of speech
in *others*,' but 'do not embrace it
yourself.'—'Facile intelligitur, De-
monico praecipi quid ipsi faciundum,
quidve fugiendum sit,' Wolf. If,
however, the expression refers to
the way in which Demonicus is to
treat the rash speeches of others,
then μήτε...στέργε must also be
taken in a similar sense.

ἃ ποιεῖν...καλόν.] Hence probably the line in Publius Syrus, n.
793, '*Quod facere turpe est, dicere
honestum ne puta.*'

ἔθιζε...ἦθος.] 'Accustom yourself
not to be sullen, but meditative; for
owing to the former men will think
you stubborn, owing to the latter,
sensible. Consider that the ornament which best becomes you, is
modesty, justice and self-restraint;
for by all these things the character
of young men appears to be controlled.'

σκυθρωπόν.] For this and a
variety of other words expressive of
sullen sternness read the speech of
Hercules in Eur. *Alc.* 773—802.

αὐθάδης.] In the *Eudemian
Ethics*, iii. 7, the αὐθάδης is described as μηδὲν πρὸς ἕτερον ζῶν, ἀλλὰ
καταφρονητικός. In the *Magna
Moralia*, 29, Aristotle reminds us of
the derivation of the word (αὐτός,
and ἥδομαι)—lit. 'self-pleasing,'
'self-willed,' 'stubborn.'

κόσμον.] The ordinary punctuation is thus: ἡγοῦ μ.σ.τ. κόσμον,
αἰσχύνην, δικαιοσύνην, σωφροσύνην.

16   Μηδέποτε μηδὲν αἰσχρὸν ποιήσας ἔλπιζε λήσειν· καὶ
γὰρ ἂν τοὺς ἄλλους λάθῃς, σεαυτῷ συνειδήσεις.

Τοὺς μὲν θεοὺς φοβοῦ, τοὺς δὲ γονεῖς τίμα, τοὺς δὲ
φίλους αἰσχύνου, τοῖς δὲ νόμοις πείθου.

Τὰς ἡδονὰς θήρευε τὰς μετὰ δόξης· τέρψις γὰρ σὺν τῷ c
καλῷ μὲν ἄριστον, ἄνευ δὲ τούτου κάκιστον.

17   Εὐλαβοῦ τὰς διαβολάς, κἂν ψευδεῖς ὦσιν· οἱ γὰρ πολλοὶ τὴν μὲν ἀλήθειαν ἀγνοοῦσι, πρὸς δὲ τὴν δόξαν ἀποβλέ-
πουσιν. Ἅπαντα δόκει ποιεῖν ὡς μηδένα λήσων· καὶ γὰρ
ἂν παραυτίκα κρύψῃς, ὕστερον ὀφθήσει. μάλιστα δ' ἂν εὐ-

This must mean ‘consider that propriety, sense of shame, uprightness
and self-mastery especially become
you.’ To this punctuation and
translation there are two objections,
(1) Isocrates never uses κόσμοι as a
synonym of εὐκοσμία, but only in the
sense of ‘ornament.’ (2) Even on
the assumption that κόσμοι may be
translated ‘propriety’ in Isocr., we
then have an awkward sequence of
words consisting of three specific
terms immediately following the
generic term in which they are included,—a collocation as unnatural,
in an enumeration, as ‘flowers,
roses, violets and blue-bells,’ or
any similar series.—For these reasons I prefer placing (with Schn.) a
comma after κόσμον alone, and
taking it in close conjunction with
πρέπειν, lit. ‘become you, as an
ornament.’

πραπεῖσθαι.] Here = κατέχεσθαι,
contineri.

16. μηδέποτε μηδέν.] Here the
negatives strengthen and do not
destroy one another. Cf. Plato
Parm. 166 A, τἄλλα τῶν μὴ ὄντων
οὐδενὶ οὐδαμῇ οὐδαμῶς οὐδεμίαν κοι-
νωνίαν ἔχει. v. also Madv. Syn.
§ 209 b. The same idiom is not uncommon in Chaucer and Shaksp.
e. g. Cantrb. Tales, Prolog. 70, He
never yit no vilonye ne sayde In al
his lyf, unto no maner wight.

συνειδήσεις.] Future of σύνοιδα,
rarely used in Attic Gk. In § 44

we find εἰδήσεις, but in Isocr. Sophist.
§ 3, we have the common fut. of
οἶδα. ἅ τε πρακτέον ἐστὶν εἴσονται
καὶ διὰ ταύτης τῆς ἐπιστήμης εὐδαί-
μονες γενήσονται. εἰδήσω is more
Ionic than Att. but is found also in
Aristot. Magn. Mor. i, 1, 3. 18.
(Veitch, Gk. Verbs, p. 187-8). Benseler quotes συνειδήσεις and εἰδήσεις as departures from Isocratean
usage and as tending to prove the
spuriousness of this Ep. It is however highly probable that the rarer
forms may have been designedly
chosen with a view to securing
ὁμοιοτέλευτον or the ‘jingle of like
endings’ λήσειν—συνειδήσεις· εὑρή-
σεις—εἰδήσεις, just as in the passage
quoted from Sophist. § 3, the common form εἴσονται corresponds in
sound to γενήσονται.

τέρψις...ἄριστον.] Cf. Eur. Hipp.
109, τερπνὸν ἐκ κυναγίας τράπεζα
πλήρης. and Madv. Syn. § 1 b, R. 3.

17. διαβολάς.] In pass. sense,
‘Beware of calumnies’ (against yourself) not ‘Beware of calumniating
others.’

κρύψῃς.] Must be translated in
its true transitive sense, which it
always keeps in prose writers. The
two passages (Soph. El. 826. Eur.
Phœn. 1117) sometimes quoted from
the poets to prove that κρύπτειν may
be intrans. are easily explained: see
Mr Jebb’s n. on Soph. El. l. c.

μάλιστα...ἐπιτιμήῃς.] Possibly
borrowed from Thales, of whom

δοκιμοίης, εἰ φαίνοιο ταῦτα μὴ πράττων, ἃ τοῖς ἄλλοις ἂν
πράττουσιν ἐπιτιμῴης.

13   Ἐὰν ᾖς φιλομαθής, ἔσει πολυμαθής. Ἃ μὲν ἐπίστασαι,
ταῦτα διαφύλαττε ταῖς μελέταις, ἃ δὲ μὴ μεμάθηκας, προσλάμβανε ταῖς ἐπιστήμαις· ὁμοίως γὰρ αἰσχρὸν ἀκούσαντα
χρήσιμον λόγον μὴ μαθεῖν καὶ διδόμενόν τι ἀγαθὸν παρὰ
τῶν φίλων μὴ λαβεῖν. Καταναλίσκε τὴν ἐν τῷ βίῳ σχολὴν c
εἰς τὴν τῶν λόγων φιληκοΐαν· οὕτω γὰρ τὰ τοῖς ἄλλοις χα-
19 λεπῶς εὑρημένα συμβήσεταί σοι ῥᾳδίως μανθάνειν. Ἡγοῦ
τῶν ἀκουσμάτων πολλὰ πολλῶν εἶναι χρημάτων κρεῖττω·
τὰ μὲν γὰρ ταχέως ἀπολείπει, τὰ δὲ πάντα τὸν χρόνον
παραμένει· σοφία γὰρ μόνον τῶν κτημάτων ἀθάνατον. Μὴ 6
κατόκνει μακρὰν ὁδὸν πορεύεσθαι πρὸς τοὺς διδάσκειν τι
χρήσιμον ἐπαγγελλομένους· αἰσχρὸν γὰρ τοὺς μὲν ἐμπόρους

Diogenes Laert. I. § 36, says:
Θαλῆ, ἐρωτηθεὶς τῶν ἂν ἄριστα καὶ
δικαιότατα βιώσαιμεν, ἐὰν, ἔφη, ἃ
τοῖς ἄλλοις ἐπιτιμῶμεν αὐτοὶ μὴ δρῶ-
μεν. Cf. Nicocl. § 61, περὶ ὧν ἂν ἐν
τοῖς λόγοις κατηγορῆτε, μηδὲν τούτων
ἐν τοῖς ἔργοις ἐπιτηδεύετε.

18. **ἐὰν—πολυμαθής.**] i. e. 'If
learning you love, most learned you'll
be.' 'Isocrates....did cause to be
written, at the entrie of his schole, in
golden letters, this golden sentence,
ἐὰν ᾖ φιλομαθής, ἔσῃ πολυμαθής,
which excellentlie said in Greke, is
thus rudelie in Englishe, if thou
lovest learning, thou shalt attayne to
moch learning.' Ascham's Scholemaster, p. 24 (ed. Mayor). I can
find no trace of authority for
Ascham's 'ethical narrative': the
story, however graceful, is probably
untrue, otherwise it might throw
some light on the vexed question
of the authorship of this Ep.—At
Shrewsbury school, the words may
be seen over one of the entrances,
inscribed 'in golden letters,' and
further illustrated by a pair of quaint
symbolical statues, representing φιλομαθής and πολυμαθής respectively.

τρ. ταῖς ἐπιστήμαις.] 'Add to
your knowledge': ἐπιστήμαις, dat.
after προσλάμβανε and not (like μελέ-
ται) an instrumental dative, as some
take it.   The parallelism or παρίσωσις of the sentence is, I admit, slightly in favour of making the
2nd dative identical in construction
with the 1st : τ. ἐπιστήμαις would
then mean 'by learning,' 'by application.'   But the meaning of
ἐπιστήμαις is fixed by the previous
verb ἐπίστασαι and must here=
'knowledge.'—If the parallelism
had to be kept up at all hazards,
we should have to adopt the conjecture of Wyttenbach (ap. Schneid.)
προσλάμβανε ταῖς ἐπιμελείαις.

19. **πολλὰ πολλῶν.**] The collocation is intentional, and is also
found in other artistic writers. Cf
e.g. Demosth. adv. Lept. § 78. p.
480, ἀπὸ πολλῶν πολλά (τρόπαια).
Isocr. de perm. 217, τιμῆι ἕνεκα
φημὶ τάσδαι πάντα πράττειν. Plato
Mενεx. p. 249 c, πᾶσαν πάντων
παρὰ πάντα ἐπιμέλειαν ποιουμένη.

κτημάτων.] Al. χρημάτων, v.
Table of var. readings.

μὴ κατόκνει—διάνοιαν.]   Cf.
Theognis, 71, ἀλλὰ μετ' ἐσθλὸν ἰὼν
βούλευσαι, πολλὰ μογῆσαι | καὶ μακρὴν
ποσσὶν Κύρν' ὁδὸν ἐκτελέσαι.

αἰσχρόν...μὲν....δὲ.] Cf. § 11,
αἰσχρὸν...γονέων. n.

τηλικαῦτα πελάγη διαπερᾶν ἕνεκα τοῦ πλείω ποιῆσαι
τὴν ὑπάρχουσαν οὐσίαν, τοὺς δὲ νεωτέρους μηδὲ τὰς κατὰ
γῆν πορείας ὑπομένειν ἐπὶ τῷ βελτίω καταστῆσαι τὴν αὐτῶν
διάνοιαν.

20   Τῷ μὲν τρόπῳ γίγνου φιλοπροσήγορος, τῷ δὲ λόγῳ εὐπροσήγορος. ἔστι δὲ φιλοπροσηγορίας μὲν τὸ προσφωνεῖν ᴸ
τοὺς ἀπαντῶντας, εὐπροσηγορίας δὲ τὸ τοῖς λόγοις αὐτοῖς
οἰκείως ἐντυγχάνειν. Ἡδέως μὲν ἔχε πρὸς ἅπαντας, χρῶ δὲ
τοῖς βελτίστοις· οὕτω γὰρ τοῖς μὲν οὐκ ἀπεχθὴς ἔσει, τοῖς
δὲ φίλος γενήσει. Τὰς ἐντεύξεις μὴ ποιοῦ πυκνὰς τοῖς αὐτοῖς, μηδὲ μακρὰς περὶ τῶν αὐτῶν. πλησμονὴ γὰρ ἁπάντων.

21   Γύμναζε σεαυτὸν πόνοις ἑκουσίοις, ὅπως ἂν δύνῃ καὶ
τοὺς ἀκουσίους ὑπομένειν. Ὧν ὧν κρατεῖσθαι τὴν ψυχὴν ᶜ
αἰσχρὸν, τούτων ἐγκράτειαν ἄσκει πάντων, κέρδους, ὀργῆς,
ἡδονῆς, λύπης. ἔσει δὲ τοιοῦτος, ἐὰν κέρδη μὲν εἶναι νομί-
ζῃς, δι᾽ ὧν εὐδοκιμήσεις, ἀλλὰ μὴ δι᾽ ὧν εὐπορήσεις· τῇ

20. τῷ—εὐπροσήγορος.] 'Be
courteous in character and affable
in speech.' The word εὐπροσήγορος
is perfectly common; φιλοπροσήγορος is found in Plutarch. *Moral.*
p. 9. extr. (quoted by Schneid.) ἐν-
τευκτικοὺς τοὺς παῖδας εἶναι παρασ-
κευαστέον καὶ φιλοπροσηγόρους. φιλοπροσηγορία (*comitas*) and εὐπροσηγορία (*affabilitas*) appear, however,
to be used in this passage alone.
In formation, the last two words
are unexceptional, and, although
Denseler would class them among
the 'verba rara et ab Isocratis usu
aliena,' there seems little reason to
doubt the possibility of their having
been actually used by Isocrates.—
In λόγῳ εὐπροσήγορος the *hiatus* has
not been, as usual, avoided. See
Introd. on style of Isocr.

21. γύμναζε—ὑπομένειν.] The
thought and expression seem to be
borrowed from Democritus (Stobaeus, *Florilegium* 29) οἱ ἑκούσιοι
πόνοι τὴν τῶν ἀκουσίων ὑπομονὴν
ἐλαφροτέραν κατασκευάζουσι.

ὑφ᾽ ὧν—εὐπορήσεις.] 'Practise

self-mastery in all those passions,
to be over-mastered by which is disgraceful to the soul, viz. lucre, anger,
pleasure and pain. Such a character you will be, if, as things *lucrative*,
you deem those which will increase
your reputation and *not* those which
will increase your resources.'—τοιοῦτος = ἐγκρατὴς implied in ἐγκράτεια,
see *Pang.* § 110. n.

ἐγκράτειαν κ. τ. λ.] Aristot.
Eth. VII. 1. 7. ἀκρατεῖς λέγονται,
καὶ θυμοῦ καὶ τιμῆς καὶ κέρδους.
On the difference between ἐγκρατὴς
and ἀκρατὴς cf. Aristot. *Eth.* VII.
1. 6. 'The man of imperfect self-
control (ὁ ἀκρατὴς) does things at
the prompting of his passions, although he knows that they are
wrong, while the man of self-control
(ὁ ἐγκρατής), knowing his lusts to be
wrong, refuses, by the influence of
reason, to follow their suggestions.'
σωφροσύνη = perfected self-mastery,
ἐγκράτεια = self-control, ἀκρασία =
imperfect self-control, ἀκολασία =
utter absence of self-control.

εὐδοκιμήσεις ... εὐπορήσεις.] An

δ' ὀργῇ παραπλησίως ἔχῃς πρὸς τοὺς ἁμαρτάνοντας, ὥσπερ
ἂν πρὸς ἑαυτὸν ἁμαρτάνοντα καὶ τοὺς ἄλλους ἔχειν ἀξιώ-
σειας· ἐν δὲ τοῖς τερπνοῖς, ἐὰν αἰσχρὸν ὑπολάβῃς τῶν μὲν
οἰκετῶν ἄρχειν, ταῖς δ' ἡδοναῖς δουλεύειν· ἐν δὲ τοῖς πονηροῖς, ἐὰν τὰς τῶν ἄλλων ἀτυχίας ἐπιβλέπῃς καὶ αὐτὸν ὡς
ἄνθρωπος ὢν ὑπομιμνήσκῃς.

22 Μᾶλλον τήρει τὰς τῶν λόγων ἢ τὰς τῶν χρημάτων πα-
ρακαταθήκας· δεῖ γὰρ τοὺς ἀγαθοὺς ἄνδρας τρόπον ὅρκου
πιστότερον φαίνεσθαι παρεχομένους. Προσήκειν ἡγοῦ τοῖς

instance of παρομοίωσις, exemplify-
ing both ὁμοιοκάταρκτον and ὁμοιοτέλευτον.

πρὸς ἑαυτόν.] See § 14, ἑαυτοῦ. n.

ἐν τοῖς πονηροῖς.] The four terms,
κίρδουν, ὀργῇ, ἡδονῇ, λύπῃ, are
taken up *seriatim* in the long sentence immediately following them.
In that sentence the four corresponding terms are, κίρδη, τῇ ὀργῇ, ἐν τοῖς
τερπνοῖς, ἐν τοῖς πονηροῖς respectively. Therefore ἐν τοῖς πονηροῖς = ἐν
τοῖς λυπηροῖς (which is the actual
reading of some MSS., arising probably from a marginal explanation),
'in painful things.'—The word πονη-
ρός, like μοχθρός, has two senses:
(1) that of physical distress (as here),
(2) that of moral depravity (as in
§ 21). Cf. Aristoph. *Plut.* 220:

A. ὅσοι δίκαιοί οὐσιν οὐκ ἦν
ἄλφιτα.

B. πασαὶ πονηροὶ γ' εἶπαι ἡμῖν
ξυμμάχουι.

'In Greek, the words πονηρὸς, κακὸς
and κακότηι, δειλὸι, δύστηνοι, μέ-
λιοι, σχέτλιοι, ταλαίπωροι, τλήμων,
are all employed, by the poets principally, in this double sense. In
Latin we have *miser* and *tristis*; in
French *misérable*; in Italian *tristo*;
and in English *wretch* and *wretched*,
unhappy and *sad*, as *a sad fellow*, *a
sad dog*.' From Mr Cope's n. on
Plato, *Gorgias*, p. 505 A.

αὐ. ἐν ἀνθ. ὢν ὑπ.] Schneider
quotes Menander, *Fragm.* 101, ἄν-
θρωπου ὢν τοῦτ' ἴσθι καὶ μέμνησο' ἀεί.

ἐὰν αὐτὸν ὑπομιμνήσκῃς = ἐὰν μνη-
σθῇς, and after 'verbs of knowledge

and experience' (such as οἶδα, μέμνημαι, ἐπίσταμαι), if the subject of
the leading verb should also be its
object, the participle is put in the
nominative and referred to the subject; e.g. ἴσθι ἀνόητοι ὤν. The
peculiarity of ὡς ἄνθρωπος ὢν may
be stated in one of two ways, either
ὤν is used where εἰ might have been
expected [Cf. Thuc. IV. 37, γνούς δὲ
ὁ Κλέων καὶ Δημοσθένηι, ὅτι, εἰ καὶ
ὁποσοσοῦν μᾶλλον ἐνδώσουσιν οἱ Λακεδαιμόνιοι, διαφθαρησομένους αὐτοὺς ὑπὸ τῆς σφετέραι στρατιᾶι,
ἔπαυσαν τὴν μάχην], or (which is
preferable) ὡς is somewhat irregu-
larly prefixed to the participle. In
the latter case, cf. Xen. *Anab.* I. 3,
15, ὡς μὲν στρατηγήσοντα ἐμὲ...μη-
δεὶς ὑμῶν λεγέτω. Soph. *Phil.* 253,
ὡς μηδὲν εἰδότ' ἴσθι μ' ὧν ἀνιστορεῖς.
Madv. *Synt.* § 178 a, R. 3 and 5,
also § 181, and Goodwin's *Gk. Moods
and Tenses*, § 113. n. 10.

On αὐτὸν = σαυτόν, see § 14, ἑαυτοῦ. n.

22. λόγων...παρακατ.] Cf. Anax-
andrides (ap. Stob. *Flor.* XLI. 2),
ὅστις λόγων παρακαταθήκην γὰρ λα-
βὼν (fort. leg. παραλαβών) | ἐξεῖπεν
ἄδικόν ἐστιν ἢ ἀκρατὴς ἄγαν.

τρόπον ὅρκου π.] Cf. the account
of Xenocrates in Cic. *pro Balbo*,
V. § 12, 'Athenis aiunt, quum qui-
dam apud eos, qui sancte graviterque
vixisset, et testimonium dixisset, ut
(ut mos Graecorum est) jurandi
caussa ad aras accederet, una voce
omnes judices, ne is juraret, recla-
masse.'

πονηροῖς ἀπιστεῖν, ὥσπερ τοῖς χρηστοῖς πιστεύειν. Περὶ
τῶν ἀπορρήτων μηδενὶ λέγε, πλὴν ἐὰν ὁμοίως συμφέρῃ τὰς ε
πράξεις σιωπᾶσθαι σοί τε τῷ λέγοντι κἀκείνοις τοῖς ἀκούου-
23 σιν. Ὅρκον ἐπακτὸν προσδέχου διὰ δύο προφάσεις, ἢ σεαυτὸν αἰτίας αἰσχρᾶς ἀπολύων, ἢ φίλους ἐκ μεγάλων κινδύνων διασώζων. ἕνεκα δὲ χρημάτων μηδένα θεῶν ὀμόσῃς,
μηδ᾽ ἂν εὐορκεῖν μέλλῃς· δόξεις γὰρ τοῖς μὲν ἐπιορκεῖν, 7
τοῖς δὲ φιλοχρημάτως ἔχειν.

24   Μηδένα φίλον ποιοῦ, πρὶν ἂν ἐξετάσῃς, πῶς κέχρηται
τοῖς πρότερον φίλοις· ἔλπιζε γὰρ αὐτὸν καὶ περὶ σὲ γενέ-

περὶ τ. ἀπορρήτων.] 'About secrets, speak to no one, except it be
equally advantageous, to you that
speak and to those that hear, that
the actions be kept secret;' i. e. do
not tell a secret to a person who has
a greater *interest* than yourself in
divulging it, '*nemini arcana tua
credas nisi illi, de quo certus sis,
profrii commodi causa ea esse cela-
turum.*' Lange proposes to insert
μὴ before σιωπᾶσθαι, and translates,
'*nisi res illas non taceri,* i. e. vul-
gari, *atque expediat tibi, qui evulgas,
ac aliis qui istas audiant.*' The
sense thus obtained is good in itself,
but the insertion of μὴ has no MS.
authority.

23. ὅρκον ἐπακτόν.] 'Accept an
imposed oath for two reasons only,
either to free yourself from a shameful charge, or to rescue your friends
from great perils.' Harpocration
(fl. during or after 1st cent. A.D.)
explains the phrase thus: ἐπακτος
ὅρκος· ὃν αὐτός τις ἑκὼν αὑτῷ ἐπάγε-
ται, τουτέστιν αἰρεῖται. Λυσίας ἐν
τῷ πρὸς Χαιρέστρατον καὶ Ἰσοκράτης
Ἀπολλωνίδης [see *Introd. to Ep. ad
Dem.*] ἐν ταῖς πρὸς Δημόνικον παραι-
νέσεσι. ἔστι δὲ ὅρκου τρία εἴδη. ἀπό-
μοτος καὶ κατώμοτος καὶ ὁ καλούμενος
ἐπακτός. εἶναι δὲ τούτων οὐχ ἁπλοῦν·
δεῖ γὰρ τὸν προτεινόμενον ὑπὸ τοῦ
ὁρκίζοντος αὐταῖς ὑφ᾽ ἑαυτου ἀντιφωνεῖν
τὸν ὀρκιζόμενον. The first part of
this explanation does not suit the
passage before us: ἐπακτὸς ὅρκος

ought to mean 'an oath imposed
from without,' 'an involuntary oath,'
not 'an oath which a person wil-
lingly takes upon himself.' The
latter part of the explanation contains a trace of the true meaning of
the phrase: mention is there made
of a species of ὅρκος ἐπ., in which
the oath was tendered (προτεινόμενον) and dictated by one party (ὁ
ὁρκίζων) and accepted *verbatim* by
the other (ὁ ὁρκιζόμενος). Suidas
(fl. 11th cent. A.D.) quotes Harpocration, and adds the words: ἄλλοι
δὲ τοὐναντίον, ὁ ἀλλαχόθεν ἐπιφερό-
μενος, ἀλλ᾽ οὐκ αὐθαίρετος.

πρόφασις] = 'plea,' 'reason,'
'ground' (cf. Thuc. VI. 6, τῇ ἀλη-
θεστάτῃ προφάσει), but far oftener,
in bad sense, = 'pretext,' 'pretence,'
'excuse.'

ἕνεκα—ἔχειν.] St Basil the Great
(329—379 A.D.) *ad adolesc.* cap. V.
(VII.) says of Cllnias, the Pythagorean, ἐξὸν δὲ ὅρκου τριῶν ταλάντων
ζημίαν ἀποφυγεῖν, ὁ δὲ ἀπέτισε μᾶλλον ἢ ὤμοσε, καὶ ταῦτα εὐορκεῖν μέλ-
λων. Epictet. *Manuale,* c. xxxiii. 5,
ὅρκον παραίτησαι, εἰ μὲν οἶόν τε, εἰς
ἅπαν· εἰ δὲ μὴ, ἐκ τῶν ἐνόντων.

24 πῶς κέχρηται...] Cf. Epi-
charmus, *Frag.* 129 (ap. Cic. *ad
Quint.* III. I, 23), γνῶθι πῶς ἄλλῳ
κέχρηται.

καὶ περὶ σὲ...καὶ περὶ ἐκ.] The
second καὶ cannot be translated except by emphasizing ἐκείνους. 'For
you must expect him to shew the

σθαι τοιοῦτον, οἷος καὶ περὶ ἐκείνους γέγονε. Βραδέως μὲν
φίλος γίγνου, γενόμενος δὲ πειρῶ διαμένειν. ὁμοίως γὰρ
αἰσχρὸν μηδένα φίλον ἔχειν καὶ πολλοὺς ἑταίρους μεταλλάττειν. Μήτε μετὰ βλάβης πειρῶ τῶν φίλων μήτ' ἄπειρος b
εἶναι τῶν ἑταίρων θέλε. τοῦτο δὲ ποιήσεις, ἐὰν μὴ δεόμε-
25 νος τὸ δεῖσθαι προσποιῇ. Περὶ τῶν ῥητῶν ὡς ἀπορρήτων
ἀνακοινοῦ· μὴ τυχὼν μὲν γὰρ οὐδὲν βλαβήσει, τυχὼν δὲ
μᾶλλον αὐτῶν τὸν τρόπον ἐπιστήσει. Δοκίμαζε τοὺς φίλους
ἔκ τε τῆς περὶ τὸν βίον ἀτυχίας καὶ τῆς ἐν τοῖς κινδύνοις

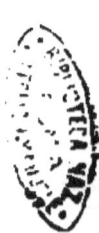

same character in dealing with you
also, as he has shewn in dealing
with *them*.' Cf. Isocr. *De Perm.*
§253, οὐκοῦν χρὴ καὶ περὶ τῶν λόγων
τὴν αὐτὴν ἔχειν διάνοιαν ἥνπερ καὶ
περὶ τῶν ἄλλων. Thuc. VI. 13, τοῖς
δὲ 'Εγεσταίοις ἰδίᾳ εἰπεῖν, ἐπειδὴ ἄνευ
'Αθηναίων καὶ ξυνῆψαν...πόλεμον,
μετὰ σφῶν αὐτῶν καὶ καταλύεσθαι.
Plato, *Lysis*, 211 A, ὅπερ καὶ ἐμοὶ
λέγεις, εἶπέ καὶ Μενεξένῳ. Gk.
usage also admits of the omission
of either καὶ, *e.g.* we might have had (as
in Eng.) (1) ἐλπίζε αὐτὸν καὶ περὶ σὲ
γεν. τοι., οἷος περὶ ἐκείνους γέγονεν,
or, still more idiomatically, (2) ἐλπίζε αὐτὸν περὶ σὲ γεν. τοι., οἷοι καὶ
περὶ ἐκείνους γέγονεν.

βραδέως...] A maxim possibly
borrowed from Solon (ap. Diogen.
Laert. I. § 60), φίλους μὴ ταχὺ κτῶ,
οὓς δ' ἂν κτήσῃ μὴ ἀποδοκίμαζε.
Cf. Theognis 1143.

ὁμοίως—μεταλλάττειν.] *i.e.* 'it is
as disgraceful to have many comrades
and to be constantly changing them
as to have no true friend whatever.'
Hesiod (*Works and Days*, 715), μηδὲ πολύξεινον μηδ' ἄξεινον καλέεσθαι.
The weaker word ἑταῖροι is here
naturally used when speaking of
fitful and changing friendships, and
in the very next sentence the difference between φίλοι and ἑταῖροι is still
partially kept up. 'Try not your
friends to your own hurt, but be not
willing to abstain altogether from
trying your comrades.'

θέλε] The form θέλω is used by
the Attic Tragedians; the form

ἐθέλω by Hom., Hes., Theogn., and
Pindar; Herodotus has both. 'In
Attic prose θέλω is not frequent, and
pretty much confined to the pres.
θέλω, Antiphon, 3, 8, 3, θέλεις, Xen.
Hell. 3, 4, 5, &c.; subj. θέλω, Thuc.
5, 35, &c.; opt. θέλοιμι, Thuc. 6,
34; imper. θέλε, Isocr. 1, 24; θέλων,
Xen. *Cyr.* 4, 5, 19; θέλειν, Pl. *Rep.*
391... ἐθέλω is far more frequent and
is used after both vowels and consonants.' (Veitch, *Greek Verbs*, s.v.).
—Benseler, in an exhaustive note
(on Isoc. *Areop.* § 41), after giving
more than 200 references to the Attic
orators, makes this generalisation:
'Patebit ex his, quae nunc attuli,
ἐθέλειν in oratoribus semper esse
adhibitum consonante antecedente,
interdum etiam vocali antecedente,
quamquam tum θέλειν saepius legi-
tur.'—Of Isocr. in particular he
says, 'θέλειν tantummodo scripsit,
si praecedens verbum in vocalem
exit...θέλε exhibetur uno tantum in
loco ab omn. Codd. *ad Demon.* §
24.' Schneider defends θέλε in this
passage, on the ground that the laws
of Gk. euphony may have led Isocr.
to prefer it to ἐθέλε.

τὸ δεῖσθαι προσποιῇ.] Bekker
and Dindorf read ἐὰν μὴ δεόμενος
του, δεῖσθαι προσποιῇ, but the MS.
reading is supported by *Epp.* II. 21,
προσποιήσομαι τὸ βέλτιον φρονεῖν.

25. δοκίμαζε κ.τ.λ.] Cf. Ennius
(ap. Cic. *de Amic.* 17. 64), *amicus
certus in re incerta cernitur.*

τὸ μὲν γὰρ χρυσίον.] On this
use of μὲν...δὲ, v. § 12. The com-

κοινωνίας· τὸ μὲν γὰρ χρυσίον ἐν τῷ πυρὶ βασανίζομεν,
τοὺς δὲ φίλους ἐν ταῖς ἀτυχίαις διαγιγνώσκομεν. Οὕτως c
ἄριστα χρήσει τοῖς φίλοις, ἐὰν μὴ προσμένῃς τὰς παρ' ἐκείνων δεήσεις, ἀλλ' αὐτεπάγγελτος αὐτοῖς ἐν τοῖς καιροῖς
26 βοηθῇς. Ὁμοίως αἰσχρὰν εἶναι νόμιζε τῶν ἐχθρῶν νικᾶσθαι
ταῖς κακοποιίαις καὶ τῶν φίλων ἡττᾶσθαι ταῖς εὐεργεσίαις.
Ἀποδέχου τῶν ἑταίρων μὴ μόνον τοὺς ἐπὶ τοῖς κακοῖς
δυσχεραίνοντας, ἀλλὰ καὶ τοὺς ἐπὶ τοῖς ἀγαθοῖς μὴ φθονοῦν-
τας· πολλοὶ γὰρ ἀτυχοῦσι μὲν συνάχθονται, καλῶς δὲ d
πράττουσι φθονοῦσι. Τῶν ἀπόντων φίλων μέμνησο πρὸς
τοὺς παρόντας, ἵνα δοκῇς μηδὲ τούτων ἀπόντων ὀλιγωρεῖν.

parison between testing gold in the fire and testing friendship in misfortune is common, *e. g.* Menander, *Fragm.* 143, χρυσὸν μὲν αἴθων ἐξελέγχθαι πυρί [ἢ δ' ἐν φιλίαις εὔνοια καιρῷ κρίνεται. Ovid, *Trist.* I. 5, 25. Scilicet ut fulvum spectatur in ignibus aurum, Tempore sic duro est inspicienda fides. Menand. *Monost.* 276, κρίνει φίλους ὁ καιρός, ὡς χρυσὸν τὸ πῦρ. Also Theognis, 78, 415 sqq., 1105.

χρυσίον = χρυσὸς εἰργασμένος: similarly ἀργύριον = ἄργυρος εἰργασμένος.

26. τῶν ἐχθρῶν.....εὐεργεσίαις.] A good example of ἀντίθεσις and παρίσωσις.—For the genitive after νικᾶσθαι, and ἡττᾶσθαι, cf. Eur. *Med.* 315, σιγησόμεσθα, κρεισσόνων νικώμενοι, and *Ion,* 1117, τὸ μὴ δίκαιον τῆς δίκης ἡσσώμενον. This gen. is really a gen. of *comparison.* 'The gen. stands with some verbs derived from a comparative, and expressing a comparison (*e. g.* πλεονεκτεῖν, ἐλασσοῦσθαι, ὑστερεῖν, ἡσσᾶσθαι), together with one or two others, which without being so derived, have a similar signification' (περιγίγνεσθαι, περιεῖναι, λείπεσθαι, νικᾶσθαι). Madv. *Synt.* §64.
Isocr. assumes that it is disgraceful to be overcome by our enemies in doing injury, and states that it is equally disgraceful to be outdone by our friends in kindly offices. The

point assumed is a common maxim of popular pagan morality, *e. g.* in Aristot. *Rhet.* I. 6, 26, one of the 'things that are choice-worthy' (τὰ προαιρετά) is πράττειν...καὶ τὰ τοῖς ἐχθροῖς κακὰ καὶ τὰ τοῖς φίλοις ἀγαθά. Cf. Xenoph. *Mem.* II. 6, 35, ἀνδρὸς ἀρετὴν εἶναι νικᾶν τοὺς μὲν φίλους εὖ ποιοῦντα, τοὺς δ' ἐχθροὺς κακῶς. Also Pindar, *Pyth.* II. 83 (= 154), and *Isth.* III. 66 (= 81).—To shew that this opinion met with some noble exceptions, we may refer to the words of Socrates (ap. Plat. *Rep.* I. 335), 'If any one states that it is just to render to every man his due, and if he means by this, that what is due from a just man is injury to his enemies and assistance to his friends, the statement is that of an unwise man : for the doctrine is really untrue, because it has been shewn that in no case is it just to injure anybody;' and of Diogenes (ap. Plutarch *de cap. ex inimicis utilitate,* 4 = p. 88 b) τῶν ἀμυνούμαι τὸν ἐχθρόν; αὐτὸς καλὸς κἀγαθὸς γενόμενος. This is not the place for a comparison between pagan and Christian ethics, but the above passages are very suggestive in relation to Matthew v. 44, &c. Cf. § 29, τοὺς ἀγαθοὺς εὖ ποίει. n.

καλῶς πρ. φθονοῦσι.] Cf. Aesch. *Ag.* 832, παύροις γὰρ ἀνδρῶν ἐστι συγγενὲς τόδε [φίλον τὸν εὐτυχοῦντ' ἄνευ φθόνου σέβειν.

27 Εἶναι βούλου τὰ περὶ τὴν ἐσθῆτα φιλόκαλος, ἀλλὰ μὴ καλλωπιστής. ἔστι δὲ φιλοκάλου μὲν τὸ μεγαλοπρεπές, καλλωπιστοῦ δὲ τὸ περίεργον.

Ἀγάπα τῶν ὑπαρχόντων ἀγαθῶν μὴ τὴν ὑπερβάλλου- c σαν κτῆσιν ἀλλὰ τὴν μετρίαν ἀπόλαυσιν. Καταφρόνει τῶν περὶ τὸν πλοῦτον σπουδαζόντων μέν, χρῆσθαι δὲ τοῖς ὑπάρ- χουσι μὴ δυναμένων· παραπλήσιον γὰρ οἱ τοιοῦτοι πάσχου- σιν, ὥσπερ ἂν εἴ τις ἵππον κτήσαιτο καλὸν κακῶς ἱππεύειν 8 28 ἐπιστάμενος. Πειρῶ τὸν πλοῦτον χρήματα καὶ κτήματα κατασκευάζειν· ἔστι δὲ χρήματα μὲν τοῖς ἀπολαύειν ἐπιστα- μένοις, κτήματα δὲ τοῖς κτᾶσθαι δυναμένοις. Τίμα τὴν ὑπάρχουσαν οὐσίαν δυοῖν ἕνεκεν, τοῦ τε ζημίαν μεγάλην ἐκτῖσαι δύνασθαι, καὶ τοῦ φίλῳ σπουδαίῳ δυστυχοῦντι βοηθῆσαι· πρὸς δὲ τὸν ἄλλον βίον μηδὲν ὑπερβαλλόντως b ἀλλὰ μετρίως αὐτὴν ἀγάπα.

27. εἶναι κ.τ.λ.] *i.e.* 'In mat- ters of dress, resolve to be tasteful, and not foppish. Now the tasteful man is marked by dignified grace, the fop by exquisite embellishment.' τὸ μεγαλοπρεπὲς is difficult to ren- der adequately; it here implies a kind of 'becoming dignity' caused by the blending of the grand and the graceful. George Herbert's line, 'In clothes cheap *handsomeness* doth bear the bell,' might possibly help us. In most other passages, 'magnificence' will fairly translate it. For the sense, cf. Shak. *Ham- let,* I. iii. *Costly thy habit as thy purse can buy, But not express'd in fancy; rich, not gaudy: For the ap- parel oft proclaims the man.*

28. παρῷ κ.τ.λ.] 'Endeavour to build up wealth, both for use and for acquisition: now wealth is a thing of *use* to those who know how to enjoy it; a thing of *acquisition* to those who are able to acquire it.' κτῆμα generally = that which one *possesses* (κέκτηται, obtinet), but here apparently means that which one acquires (κτᾶται, acquirit μ.

χρήματα κ. κτήματα.] Cf. *ad*

Nicol. § 16, κτησαμένου...χρησαμέ- νους. Areop. § 35, κτήσεις...χρήσεις. Curius ap. Cic. *ad Fam.* VII. 29, 1, *sum enim* χρήσει μὲν tuus, κτήσει δὲ *Attici nostri*, and especially Aristot. *Rhet.* I. 5, ὅλως τὸ πλουτεῖν ἐστὶν ἐν τῷ χρῆσθαι μᾶλλον ἢ ἐν τῷ κεκτῆ- σθαι.

κτᾶσθαι.] This is the reading of the MSS., the common reading of the *old* editions was χρῆσθαι, a reading which has the merit of im- proving a truism, and giving a sense similar to the old precept, 'Get to live; Then live and use it, else it is not true That thou hast gotten.'

τίμα...] 'Prize your present pro- perty for two reasons,—that you may be able both to pay off a heavy fine, and to succour an honest friend in his misfortune.'

ἀγάπα.] 'Esteem,' 'regard.' ἀγα- πᾶν is probably connected in de- rivation with the root of ἀγαμαι, and stands in the same relation to φιλεῖν as *diligere* does to *amare*. (On στοργή, ἔρως, φιλεῖν, ἀγαπᾶν, see Mr Cope's article, *Journ. of Philology,* I. 1, p. 88—93.)

29 Στέργε μὲν τὰ παρόντα, ζήτει δὲ τὰ βέλτιστα.

Μηδενὶ συμφορὰν ὀνειδίσῃς· κοινὴ γὰρ ἡ τύχη καὶ τὸ μέλλον ἄδρατον.

Τοὺς ἀγαθοὺς εὖ ποίει· καλὸς γὰρ θησαυρὸς παρ' ἀνδρὶ σπουδαίῳ χάρις ὀφειλομένη. Τοὺς κακοὺς εὖ ποιῶν ὅμοια πείσει τοῖς τὰς ἀλλοτρίας κύνας σιτίζουσιν· ἐκεῖναί ϲ τε γὰρ τοὺς διδόντας ὥσπερ τοὺς τυχόντας ὑλακτοῦσιν, οἵ τε κακοὶ τοὺς ὠφελοῦντας ὥσπερ τοὺς βλάπτοντας ἀδικοῦ-
30 σιν. Μίσει τοὺς κολακεύοντας ὥσπερ τοὺς ἐξαπατῶντας·

29. στέργε.] στέργειν (as well as αἰνεῖν and ἀγαπᾶν) has often, as here, the meaning 'acquiesce in,' 'tolerate,' 'put up with,' 'be content with.' Elsewhere, in Isocr., the construction is different from that of the present passage: e.g. De pace, § 6, στέργειν τοῖς παροῦσι, and § 23, οὐ στέργοντας ἐφ' οἷς ἂν ἔχωμεν ἀλλ' ἀεὶ τοῦ πλείονος ὀρεγομένους. The acc., however, is found in Hdt. IX. 17, οὕτω δὴ ἐστέρξαν τὰ παρεόντα, Eur. Phorn. 1685, τἀμ' ἐγὼ στέρξω καὶ, and Dem. Callic. § 22, τὴν τύχην στέργειν, and is here used probably to keep up the parallelism with the acc. τὰ βέλτιστα.

μηδενὶ συμ. ὀν.] = Nemini calamitatem exprobraveris, 'Reproach no man with his misfortune.' Obs. the difference between the Eng. and the Gk. and Latin idioms. Cf. Theognis, 117, χρήματ' ἔχων πενίην μ' ὠνείδισας, ἀλλὰ τὰ μέν μοι | ἐστι, τὰ δ' ἀλλ' ἕξω θεοῦσιν ἐπευξάμενος. Dem. Androt. p. 612, § 61, τὰς ἰδίας συμφορὰς ὀνειδίζειν καὶ προφέρειν ἑκάστῳ, and Isocr. Paneg. § 107.

κοινὴ...ἄδρατον.] These epithets are placed expressly at the beginning and end of the sentence, to bring out a stronger emphasis. Cf. also § 7, πλούτου κρείττων. n.

τοὺς ἀγαθοὺς εὖ ποίει, κ.τ.λ.]= 'Bonis benefacito' (Dion. Catonis Distich. i. 36). The limitation is curious. Equally low is the moral tone of the following lines from Theognis, 105 sqq. δειλοὺς δ' εὖ ἕρ-

δοντι ματαιοτάτη χάρις ἐστίν,| ἴσον γὰρ σπείρειν πόντον ἁλὸς πολιῆς· | οὔτε γὰρ ἂν πόντον σπείρων, βαθὺ λήϊον ἀμῷς, | οὔτε κακοὺς εὖ δρῶν, εὖ πάλιν ἀντιλάβοις, κ.τ.λ. Cf. § 26. n.

καλὸς...ὀφειλομένη.] For the sentiment and the words cf. Agapetus (Deacon of Ch. of St Sophia, 527 A.D.), ad Justinian. adhortat. c. 7, μόνος τῇ εὐτοίᾳ ὁ θησαυρὸς μόνιμός ἐστι τοῖς κεκτημένοις αὐτόν, τῶν γὰρ ἀγαθῶν ἔργων αἱ χάριτες ἐπὶ τοὺς ποιοῦντας ἐπαναστρέφουσιν.

τοὺς τυχόντας ὑλακτοῦσιν.] Aristotle (Eth. vii. 6, 1), speaking of anger, used the same homely illustration, ἔοικε γὰρ ὁ θυμὸς ἀκούειν μέν τι τοῦ λόγου, παρακούειν δέ, καθάπερ...οἱ κύνες, πρὶν σκέψασθαι εἰ φίλοι, ἂν μόνον ψοφήσῃ, ὑλακτοῦσιν. [Philippians iii. 2, βλέπετε τοὺς κύνας, βλέπετε τοὺς κακοὺς ἐργάτας.]

Obs. the use of τε in ἐκεῖναί τε...οἵ τε κακοί, 'both—and,' i.e. 'just as' —'so.' See § 32 for the same use of τε in a partial comparison.

30. μίσει...ἐξαπατῶντας.] Trans. 'Abhor flatterers as you would abhor deceivers, for both alike, when trusted, do wrong to those that trusted them. If you welcome those friends who are ready to be complaisant, to your greatest injury; you will, throughout your life, be destitute of those who are ready to incur your hatred for your highest good.' A little difficulty has sometimes been felt about the meaning of this sentence: e.g. Rodolphus Agricola

ἀμφότεροι γὰρ πιστευθέντες τοὺς πιστεύσαντας ἀδικοῦσιν.
Ἐὰν ἀποδέχῃ τῶν φίλων τοὺς πρὸς τὸ φαυλότατον χαριζομένους, οὐχ ἕξεις ἐν τῷ βίῳ τοὺς πρὸς τὸ βέλτιστον ἀπεχθανομένους. Γίγνου πρὸς τοὺς πλησιάζοντας ὁμιλητικός, ἀλλὰ d
μὴ σεμνός· τὸν μὲν γὰρ τῶν ὑπεροπτικῶν ὄγκον μόλις ἂν
οἱ δοῦλοι καρτερήσειαν, τὸν δὲ τῶν ὁμιλητικῶν τρόπον

(one of the earliest translators of this *Ep.*) renders the last clause '*qui tibi ad ea quae sunt optima, assistant.*' It is just possible (as suggested by Wolf) that he read παρισταμένους, but no one has seriously proposed to alter the MS. reading ἀπεχθανομένους. The sentence is, I believe, perfectly coherent and intelligible. The mention of 'flatterers,' and the warning against them, naturally lead the writer to an admonition respecting false friends. He tells Demonicus that if he chooses for his companions men who are ready to cringe to him and gratify him for his apparent advantage, but real hurt, he will, through life, miss the '*faithful wounds*' inflicted by those who for his real good are ready, if necessary, to be his apparent enemies. [Proverbs xxvii. 6; xxviii. 23.] See § 45.

πιστευθέντες.] πιστεύω in the act. 'governs' a dat. of the person and acc. of the thing (πιστεύω τινί τι), and is only *indirectly* transitive; and, strictly speaking, only a *direct* transitive can be converted into a true passive. The use of the passive, therefore, in πιστευθεὶς is noteworthy; and at the first blush of the matter would seem to imply the existence of such a formula as πιστεύω τινά τι, which does not really exist. The same peculiarity may be noticed in Isocr. *de Bigis*, § 26, ἐπιστεύθησαν (οἱ Ἀλκμαιωνίδαι), *de Pace*, § 76, πιστευόμενος (τὸν δῆμον), Dem. *in Aristocr.* 622, § 4, τῶν πολιτευομένων καὶ πιστευομένων, *in Conon*, 1269, § 40, and elsewhere. The same is the case with *other* verbs which are not directly trans.

A list of more than twenty such Greek verbs (*e. g.* ἐπιβουλεύεσθαι, καταγελασθῆναι, κατηγορεῖσθαι, ὑπερέχεσθαι, φθονεῖσθαι, ἀπειλεῖσθαι) is given by Mr Cope, *Journ. of Philol.* 1. i. 93—96. To these may be added παρανεῖν, which in the act. is intransitive (although Lidd. and Scott, by a curious inadvertence, quote Dem. *in Con.* 1257, 13, to prove that it may be trans. in act., ταύτην [*i. e.* τὴν ὥραν] ἂν ἤδη ἐπαρώνουν οὗτοι...εἰς τοὺς παῖδας). For the pass. v. Dem. *in Con.* 1258, 7, παρωνουμένων ὑπὸ τουτωΐ, and *De Fals. Leg.* 403, § 220. Similarly we have παρανομεῖν εἴς τινα, and παρανομεῖσθαι. The instances of this peculiarity in Latin are mostly poetical (Ovid. *A. A.* III. 679, *persuasus eris*; *Amor.* II. 6, 61, *Colligor...placuisse*), and mainly confined to the perf. pass. part. (*e. g.* regnatus, triumphatus, bacchatus). Tacitus, whose diction is often poetical, uses the passives *triumpharetur*, *regnantur* and *ministrantur* (Dräger, *Syntax u. Stil des Tacitus*, § 26).

χαριζομένους.] Cf. Dem. *in Aristocr.* 664, § 134, ἐστὶ γὰρ φίλων ἀγαθῶν οὐ τοιαῦτα χαρίζεσθαι τοῖς εὔνοις ἐξ ὧν κάκεινος καὶ σφίσιν αὐτοῖς ἔσται τις βλάβη. ἀλλ' ὃ μὲν ἂν μέλλῃ συνοίσειν ἀμφοῖν, συμπράττειν, ὃ δ' ἂν αὐτὸς ἀμείνω ἐκείνου προορᾷ, πρὸς τὸ καλῶς ἔχον τίθεσθαι καὶ μὴ τὴν ἤδη χάριν τοῦ μετὰ ταῦτα χρόνου παντὸς περὶ πλείονος ἡγεῖσθαι.

ἀπεχθανομένους.] The exact opposite to χαριζομένους, *e. g.* Isocr. *Epp.* 9, 12, δεξαίμην ἂν δικαίως ἐπιτιμήσας ἀπεχθέσθαι μᾶλλον ἢ παρὰ τὸ προσῆκον ἐπαινέσας χαρίσασθαι.

31 ἅπαντες ἡδέως ὑποφέρουσιν. ὁμιλητικὸς δ' ἔσει μὴ δύσερις
ὢν μηδὲ δυσάρεστος μηδὲ πρὸς πάντας φιλόνικος, μηδὲ
πρὸς τὰς τῶν πλησιαζόντων ὀργὰς τραχέως ἀπαντῶν, μηδ' c
ἃν ἀδίκως ὀργιζόμενοι τυγχάνωσιν, ἀλλὰ θυμουμένοις μὲν
αὐτοῖς εἴκων, πεπαυμένοις δὲ τῆς ὀργῆς ἐπιπλήττων· μηδὲ
παρὰ τὰ γελοῖα σπουδάζων, μηδὲ παρὰ τὰ σπουδαῖα τοῖς
γελοίοις χαίρων (τὸ γὰρ ἄκαιρον πανταχοῦ λυπηρόν)· μηδὲ
τὰς χάριτας ἀχαρίστως χαριζόμενος, ὅπερ πάσχουσιν οἱ
πολλοί, ποιοῦντες μὲν, ἀηδῶς δὲ τοῖς φίλοις ὑπουργοῦντες·
μηδὲ φιλαίτιος ὢν, βαρὺ γάρ, μηδὲ φιλεπιτιμητής, παρο- 9
ξυντικὼν γάρ.

32   Μάλιστα μὲν εὐλαβοῦ τὰς ἐν τοῖς πότοις συνουσίας·
ἐὰν δέ ποτέ σοι συμπέσῃ καιρός, ἐξανίστασο πρὸ μέθης.
ὅταν γὰρ ὁ νοῦς ὑπ' οἴνου διαφθαρῇ, ταὐτὰ πάσχει τοῖς ἄρ-

31. φιλόνικος.] Derived from φίλος
and νίκη [φιλόνεικος (Plat. Protag.
336 E, &c.) is really a separate
word, derived from νεῖκος]. Cf.
Aristot. Rhet. II. 12, 6, φιλότιμοι
μὲν εἰσι, μᾶλλον δὲ φιλόνικοι· ὑπερο-
χῆι γὰρ ἐπιθυμεῖ ἡ νεότης, ἡ δὲ νίκη
ὑπεροχή τις. Plat. Rep. IX. 581 E,
&c. The two words are constantly
interchanged in MSS.
    χάριτας ἀχαρίστως χαριζόμε-
νος.] Cf. Eur. Erechth. (Fragm.
353, 1), τὰς χάριτας ὅστις εὐγενῶς
χαρίζεται | ἥδιστον ἐν βροτοῖσιν· οἳ
δὲ δρῶσι μέν, | χρόνῳ δὲ πολλῷ
δρῶσι, δυσγενέστεροι.
    An accusative of the notion con-
tained in a verb may stand with a
verb which governs a proper object-
accusative. This acc. has generally,
as here, the same root as the verb,
and must be defined by an adj.,
pron., adverb, or attributive clause;
e.g. Dem. de Cor. § 239, πεινᾶι χα-
ρίζει χάριτας Hor. Carm. III. 29, 50,
ludum insolentem ludere. See Madv.
Gk. Syn. § 26 a, b; Mr Mayor's note
on Cic. Philip. II. § 42; and, for the
fullest account, Lobeck, Paralipom.
(p. 501—538, de figura etymologica).
    32. μάλιστα μέν—μέθης.] 'If pos-
sible, avoid drinking-parties alloge-

ther; but if ever such an occasion
befal you, rise up from your place
before you are drunk.' Herbert,
Ch. Porch, 'Stay at the third cup;
or forego the place, Wine above all
things doth God's stamp deface.' The
form of the precept is borrowed
from Theognis, 484, μὴ τὸν οἶνον
ὑπερβάλλῃς, | ἀλλ' ἢ πρὶν μεθύων
ὑπανίστασο...ἢ παρεὼν μὴ πῖνε.
    τὰς ἐν τοῖς πότοις συνουσίας. lit.
'meetings consisting of (or involving) carousals.' The precept is characteristic of Isocr. Cf. his indignant
remarks, de Perm. §§ 285-7. 'The
most promising of our young men
pass their youth in drinking-parties
(ἐν πότοις καὶ συνουσίαις) and idle
amusements, while you (men of
Athens) disregard all anxiety for their
improvement. Those, again, who
have inferior gifts of nature, spend
the day in such vices as, in former
times, not even a slave of any de-
cency would have dared to practise;
for some of them may be seen drink-
ing in taverns, and others cooling
their wine at the fountain of Ennea-
crunus, &c.'
    ὅταν—διανοίας.] 'For when the
mind is enfeebled by wine, it is in
the same condition as chariots that

μασι τοῖς τοὺς ἡνιόχους ἀποβαλοῦσιν· ἐκεῖνά τε γὰρ ἀπά-
κτως φέρεται διαμαρτόντα τῶν εὐθυνούντων, ἥ τε ψυχὴ b
πολλὰ σφάλλεται διαφθαρείσης τῆς διανοίας.

Ἀθάνατα μὲν φρόνει τῷ μεγαλόψυχος εἶναι, θνητὰ δὲ
τῷ συμμέτρως τῶν ὑπαρχόντων ἀπολαύειν.

33   Ἡγοῦ τὴν παιδείαν τοσούτῳ μεῖζον ἀγαθὸν εἶναι τῆς
ἀπαιδευσίας, ὅσῳ τὰ μὲν ἄλλα μοχθηρὰ πάντες κερδαίνον-
τες πράττουσιν, αὕτη δὲ μόνη καὶ προσεζημίωσε τοῖς ἔχον-
τας· πολλάκις γὰρ ὧν τοῖς λόγοις ἐλύπησαν, τούτων τοῖς
ἔργοις τὴν τιμωρίαν ἔδοσαν.

Οὓς ἂν βούλῃ ποιήσασθαι φίλους, ἀγαθόν τι λέγε περὶ c
αὐτῶν πρὸς τοὺς ἀπαγγέλλοντας· ἀρχὴ γὰρ φιλίας μὲν ἔπαινος, ἔχθρας δὲ ψόγος.

34   Βουλευόμενος παραδείγματα ποιοῦ τὰ παρεληλυθότα τῶν

have lost (*not* 'thrown away') their
drivers; for just as *they* are borne
along without control, when they
have missed those who should guide
them (*fut. part.*), even thus is the
soul oft overthrown, when the intellect is enfeebled.' The comparison of the ψυχὴ to the ἅρματα may
remind us of the famous *mythus* in
Plato, *Phaedrus*, p. 247—257, where
the ψυχὴ is elaborately compared to
the 'combined efficacy of a pair of
winged steeds and a charioteer'
(ξυμφύτῳ δυνάμει ὑποπτέρου ζεύγους
τε καὶ ἡνιόχου). One horse is of
generous breed, the other the reverse, corresponding, doubtless, to
the 'passionate' and 'appetent'
principles, τὸ θυμικὸν and τὸ ἐπιθυ-
μητικόν; while the charioteer answers to the 'reasoning' principle,
τὸ λογιστικόν. The comparison in
the text is roughly drawn, and is
merely incidental.—The word σφάλλεται (lit. 'stumbles') is designedly
chosen from the language of the
'race-course,' to maintain metaphorically the general sense of the
simile.

τῆς διανοίας here = τοῦ νοῦ, which
is avoided, apparently for rhythmical reasons. At the beginning of

the sentence the writer refuses to
use ἡ διάνοια instead of ὁ νοῦς, probably because ἡ διάνοια ὑπ' οἴνου
would involve a *hiatus*.

ὑπ' οἴνου is Schneider's emendation
of ὑπὸ οἴνου, which is found in MSS.

ἀθάνατα—ἀπολαύειν.] Cf. § 9. n.
The nom. μεγαλόψυχος is used, because the 'subject' of εἶναι is the
same as the subject of φρόνει, otherwise an acc. would have been required. Cf. Thuc. IV. 28, Κλέων
οὐκ ἔφη αὐτὸς ἀλλ' ἐκεῖνον (Νικίαν)
στρατηγεῖν. Madv. *Syn.* § 160.

33. πράττουσιν...προσεζημίωσε.]
On the interchange of pres. and aor.
see § 6. n. By αὕτη is meant ἡ παι-
δευσία.

ἂν...ἐλύπησαν, τούτων.] *i. e.* τοῖς
ἔργοις τὴν τιμωρίαν ἔδοσαν τούτων,
ἃ τοῖς λόγοις ἐλύπησαν. 'Vengeance for the pain which they have
inflicted' (Madv. *Syn.* § 27 a).—At-
traction takes place, as here, even
when the demonstrative is expressed
after the relative clause. Cf. Xen.
Mem. II. 1, 25, οἷς (for ἅ) ἂν οἱ ἄλλοι
ἐργάζωνται, τούτοις σὺ χρήσῃ. Madv.
Syn. § 103.

34. βουλευόμενος, κ.τ.λ.] *i. e.*
'when deliberating make the past an
example for the future.' *Respice,*

μελλόντων· τὸ γὰρ ἀφανὲς ἐκ τοῦ φανεροῦ ταχίστην ἔχει τὴν διάγνωσιν. Βουλεύου μὲν βραδέως, ἐπιτέλει δὲ ταχέως τὰ δόξαντα. Ἡγοῦ κράτιστον εἶναι παρὰ μὲν τῶν θεῶν εὐτυχίαν, παρὰ δ' ἡμῶν αὐτῶν εὐβουλίαν. Περὶ ὧν ἂν d αἰσχύνῃ παρρησιάσασθαι, βούλῃ δέ τισι τῶν φίλων ἀνακοινώσασθαι, χρῶ τοῖς λόγοις ὡς περὶ ἀλλοτρίου τοῦ πράγματος· οὕτω γὰρ τὴν ἐκείνων τε διάνοιαν αἰσθήσει καὶ σεαυ-
35 τὸν οὐ καταφανῆ ποιήσεις. Ὅταν ὑπὲρ τῶν σεαυτοῦ μέλλῃς τινὶ συμβούλῳ χρῆσθαι, σκόπει πρῶτον πῶς τὰ ἑαυτοῦ διῴκησεν ὁ γὰρ κακῶς διανοηθεὶς περὶ τῶν οἰκείων οὐδέποτε καλῶς βουλεύσεται περὶ τῶν ἀλλοτρίων. Οὕτω δ' ἂν μά- c λιστα βουλεύεσθαι παροξυνθείης, εἰ τὰς συμφορὰς τὰς ἐκ τῆς ἀβουλίας ἐπιβλέψειας· καὶ γὰρ τῆς ὑγιείας πλείστην ἐπιμέλειαν ἔχομεν, ὅταν τὰς λύπας τὰς ἐκ τῆς ἀρρωστίας ἀναμνησθῶμεν.

aspice, prospice. Cf. Isocr. ad Nicol. § 35, ἂν τὰ παρεληλυθότα μνημονεύῃς, ἄμεινον περὶ τῶν μελλόντων βουλεύσει. These passages are, I believe, the groundwork of a more elaborate sentiment, attributed to Isocr. by Stobaeus (Flor. I. 45), Ἰσοκράτης εἶπεν ὅτι τὸν χρηστὸν καὶ ἀγαθὸν ἄνδρα δεῖ τῶν μὲν προγεγενημένων μεμνῆσθαι, τὰ δὲ ἐνεστῶτα πράττειν, περὶ δὲ τῶν μελλόντων φυλάττεσθαι. Almost the same words are elsewhere ascribed to Bias (Orelli, Opusc. Mor. I. 182).

τὸ γὰρ ἀφανὲς κ.τ.λ.] From Cleobulus (?) quoted by Stob. Flor. III. 31, τὰ ἀφανῆ τοῖς φανεροῖς τεκμαίρου.

βουλ. βραδέως κ.τ.λ.] Cf. the maxim of Bias (Stob. Flor. III. 30), βραδέως ἐγχείρει τοῖς πραττομένοις, ἐγχειρήσας δὲ πράττε βεβαίως.

παρὰ τῶν θεῶν εὐτ.] Some of the MSS. have τοῦ θεοῦ, an alteration which involves a hiatus, and is probably due to Christian transcribers who were naturally sensitive on the point of polytheism. Similarly § 16, τὸν μὲν θεὸν φοβοῦ for τοὺς μὲν θεούς, § 45, τῷ θεῷ for

τοῖς θεοῖς.

περὶ ἀλλοτρ. τοῦ πρ.] τοῦ πράγματος=ὃ ἂν αἰσχύνῃ παρρησιάσασθαι; and ἀλλοτρίου has a predicative force. Schneider's correction ἀλλοτρίου του (=τινὸς) πράγματος is ingenious but unnecessary.

35. ὅταν—ἀλλοτρίων.] It was on a similar principle that the discord of the Milesians was pacified by the Parians (Hdt. V. 28, 29). The Parians explored the district, noted down the names of those whose private property was most carefully cultivated, and proposed that the public affairs of Miletus should be entrusted to them, δοκέειν γὰρ ἔφασαν καὶ τῶν δημοσίων οὕτω δὴ σφέας ἐπιμελήσεσθαι, ὥσπερ τῶν σφετέρων.

οὕτω δ'—ἀναμνησθῶμεν.] Imitated by Agapetus (fl. 527 A.D. ad Justinian, adhort. 25), βουλεύου μὲν τὰ πρακτέα βραδέως, ἐπιτέλει δὲ τὰ ἐμβληθέντα σπουδαίως. ἐπεὶ λίαν ἐστὶ σφαλερὸν τὸ ἐν τοῖς πράγμασιν ἀπερίσκεπτον. εἰ γὰρ τὰ ἐξ ἀβουλίας τις ἐννοήσει κακά, τότε γνώσεται καλῶς τῆς εὐβουλίας τὰ χρήσιμα, ὡς καὶ ὑγιείας τὴν χάριν, μετὰ τὴν πεῖραν τῆς νόσου.

36   Μιμοῦ τὰ τῶν βασιλέων ἤθη καὶ δίωκε τὰ ἐκείνων ἐπι- 10
τηδεύματα· δόξεις γὰρ αὐτοὺς ἀποδέχεσθαι καὶ ζηλοῦν,
ὥστε σοι συμβήσεται παρά τε τῷ πλήθει μᾶλλον εὐδοκιμεῖν
καὶ τὴν παρ' ἐκείνων εὔνοιαν βεβαιοτέραν ἔχειν. Πείθου
μὲν καὶ τοῖς νόμοις τοῖς ὑπὸ τῶν βασιλέων κειμένοις, ἰσχυ-

36. μιμοῦ τὰ τῶν βασιλέων ἤθη.]
Lange appeals emphatically to this
precept to prove that Isocrates the
Athenian could not have written
this *Ep.* It is hard to see any reason why the acknowledged writer of
the treatise addressed to Nicocles,
the Cyprian king, and of the speech
on the duties of his subjects, both of
which are saturated with maxims
suited to a monarchy, could not have
written the passage now before us.
The writer immediately afterwards
admits the propriety of courting the
populace, if one is living under a
democracy, and expresses himself
in language which is perfectly proper
for an Athenian citizen of moderate
views. His position with reference
to the treatise *ad Nicoclem* is clearly
brought out in a slightly coloured
passage, written for Athenian readers, *de Perm.* § 70, φανήσομαι πρὸς
αὐτὸν ἐλευθέρως καὶ τῆς πόλεως ἀξίως
διειλεγμένος...ὅπου δὲ βασιλεῖ διαλεγόμενος ὑπὲρ τοῦ δήμου τοὺς λόγους
ἐποιησάμην, ἦπου τοῖς ἐν δημοκρατίᾳ
πολιτευομένοις σφόδρ' ἂν παρακελευ-
σαίμην τὸ πλῆθος θεραπεύειν.

βεβαιοτέραν.] Cobet (*var. lect.*
p.155) quotes this passage and says,
'quia non dicitur ἔχω βέβαιόν τι sed
βεβαίως, necessarium est βεβαιότερον
(adv. compar.). *contra rectissime dicitur* ἔχειν τινὰ βέβαιον φίλον, σύμμα-
χον, ἐραστήν.' A real difference,
however, may be noticed between
such phrases as κτήματα βεβαίως ἔχω
and κτήματα βέβαια ἔχω. Both these
formulae of expression are necessary,
and actually exist in passages which
are too numerous to be rashly
altered. Schneider quotes Thuc. i.
32, τὴν χάριν βέβαιον ἕξουσι. Dem.
Olynth. II. 10, δύναμιν βεβαίαν κτήσασθαι. Paneg. § 173, εἰρήνην βε-

βαίαν ἀγαγεῖν, as instances of the
second formula; and Plut. *Mor.* p.
93 B, μηδένω μίαν φιλίαν κεκτημένοι
βεβαίαν. Isocr. *Archid.* § 39, βεβαίως τὴν εἰρήνην ἄξομεν, as examples of the first. Both the forms
are in use, and, in their proper
places, are equally correct: it is
therefore unnecessary, in this case,
to follow Cobet, who is often too
dogmatic. Much however, with regard to Attic usage, &c., may be
learnt from his *variae* and his *notae
lectiones*, as the very next note may
help to testify.

ὑπὸ τῶν βασιλέων κειμένοις.]
κεῖμαι is the only proper perf. pass.
of τίθημι. τίθεμαι is *pass.* in form,
and *mid.* in sense. The instances
of the use of τίθεμαι as a *pass.*,
though common in Lucian and late
writers, are (in classical Greek) very
few and precarious. Cobet (*var. lect.*
p. 311), says, 'Athenienses, et antea
Iones omnes, pro τίθεμαι constanter
κεῖμαι dicebant. τιθέναι νόμον et ὁ
νόμος κεῖται, περιτιθέναι στέφανον τῇ
κεφαλῇ et ὁ στέφανος τῇ κεφαλῇ
περίκειται, προστιθέναι νεκρὸν et ὁ νε-
κρὸς πρόκειται, sic..ἀνακεῖται τὰ ἀνα-
θήματα, τὸ σύνθημα σύγκειται, εὖ
διακεῖσθαι et εὖ διατιθέναι et in ceteris
omnibus, quod quis non sexcenties
inter legendum vidit? Nonnunquam
ὑπὸ additur, ut in Isaeo Oral. III.
32, εἴτις ἤδει τοῦθ' ὑπὸ τοῦ πατρὸς
κείμενον (nomen a patre impositum).'
The latter part of this lucid statement is illustrated by the use of
ὑπὸ in the present passage, and the
general principle is clearly seen
in Plato, *Theaet.* p. 177 D, ἃ ἂν
θῆται πόλις δόξαντα αὐτῇ, ταῦτα καὶ
ἔστι δίκαια τῇ θεμένῃ, ἕως περ ἂν
κέηται. τίθημι in short is a defective vb. and borrows κεῖμαι as its

ρότατον μέντοι νόμον ἡγοῦ τὸν ἐκείνων τρόπον. ὥσπερ γὰρ
τὸν ἐν δημοκρατίᾳ πολιτευόμενον τὸ πλῆθος δεῖ θεραπεύειν,
οὕτω καὶ τὸν ἐν μοναρχίᾳ κατοικοῦντα τὸν βασιλέα προσή- b
κει θαυμάζειν.

37   Εἰς ἀρχὴν κατασταθεὶς μηδενὶ χρῶ πονηρῷ πρὸς τὰς
διοικήσεις· ὧν γὰρ ἂν ἐκεῖνος ἁμάρτῃ, σοὶ τὰς αἰτίας ἀναθήσουσιν. Ἐκ τῶν κοινῶν ἐπιμελειῶν ἀπαλλάττου μὴ
πλουσιώτερος ἀλλ' ἐνδοξότερος· πολλῶν γὰρ χρημάτων c
κρείττων ὁ παρὰ τοῦ πλήθους ἔπαινος.

   Μηδενὶ πονηρῷ πράγματι μήτε παρίστασο μήτε συνη-
γόρει· δόξεις γὰρ καὶ αὐτὸς τοιαῦτα πράττειν, οἷ' ἂν τοῖς
ἄλλοις πράττουσι βοηθῇς.

38   Παρασκεύαζε σεαυτὸν πλεονεκτεῖν μὲν δύνασθαι, ἀνέχου

---

perf. pass. The same principle is
widely spread in the case of other
defective verbs. Lists are given, in
ordinary school grammars, of many
of these, e.g. αἱρέω, λαμβάνω, φέρω,
but the verb τύπτω is in the same
grammars conjugated in full, without any warning that τύπτω (= ver-
bero or vulnero), ἔτυπτον, τυπτήσω
(= verberabo), τύπτομαι (= vapulo
or vulneror), and ἐτυπτόμην (pass.)
are the only parts used by writers of
Attic prose. The aor. act. is really
ἔπραξα, pass. ἐπλήγην [e.g. Lysias,
iv. (περὶ τραύματος) § 15, τύτερον
ἐπλήγην ἢ ἐτάραξα;] and amongst
other parts that are borrowed we
have πέπληγα, πέπληγμαι, πεπλή-
ξομαι, πληγήσομαι (Cobet, var. lect.
330—343, and Veitch, Gk. verbs).
The speech of Dem. in Conon,
in a case of 'assault and battery,'
forms a good study on this point.
We there find the forms τύ-
πτειν, ἔτυπτον, τυπτόμενον (with the
verbal τυπτητέος), also πατάξαντι,
πατάξαι, ἐπλήγην (= vulneratus
sum) and πληγὰς ἐνέτεινα ἐμοί (i. q.
ναρμίανι), but in the Argument to
the speech, written by a late Scholiast, we have τετυπτῆσθαι, instead
of the usual phrase πληγὰς εἰληφέναι.
νόμον...τρόπον.] Cf. § 11, νόμων

τὸν ἐκείνου τρόπον ἡγησάμενος. The
contrast of the two words νόμον...
τρόπον is possibly suggested by their
'assonance.' In both, the two vowels
correspond, and the final consonants coincide. (Cf. Aristoph. Nub.
394, and Mr Green's note.)
   ὥσπερ—θαυμάζειν.] Obs. the
highly artificial parallelism of this
sentence.
   37. εἰς ἀρχὴν—ἀναθήσουσιν.] A
precept almost identical with this in
expression is elsewhere wrongly
attributed to Bias (ap. Orelli Opusc.
Mor. I. 162). Cf. Cic. ad Quint.
fratr. I. 1, § 10.
   ἐκ τῶν κοινῶν κ.τ.λ.] A noteworthy example of this was Cato's
honest discharge of his dishonest
mission to Cyprus, B.C. 58—56
(Plut. Cato, 34—39).
   οἷ' ἂν.] v. Table of var. readings.
   38. πλεονεκτεῖν.] (Cf. πλεονεκτοῦ-
σι, § 39) = 'to gain an advantage,' a
vox media = lit. 'to have or claim
more than another,' sometimes used
in a comparatively good sense, e.g.
Plato, Gorg. 491 A (περὶ τίνων ὁ κρείττων τε καὶ φρονιμώτερος πλέον
ἔχων δικαίως πλεονεκτεῖ;) = 'has a
right to a larger share;' but almost always in a bad sense, 'to be
greedy and grasping,') (ἰσομοιρῆσαι,

δὲ τὸ ἴσον ἔχων, ἵνα δοκῇς ὀρέγεσθαι τῆς δικαιοσύνης μὴ δι'
39 ἀσθένειαν ἀλλὰ δι' ἐπιείκειαν. Μᾶλλον ἀποδέχου δικαίαν
πενίαν ἢ πλοῦτον ἄδικον· τοσούτῳ γὰρ κρείττων δικαιοσύνη d
χρημάτων, ὅσῳ τὰ μὲν ζῶντας μόνον ὠφελεῖ, ἡ δὲ καὶ τε-
λευτήσασι δόξαν παρασκευάζει, κἀκείνων μὲν τοῖς φαύλοις
μέτεστι, τούτου δὲ τοῖς μοχθηροῖς ἀδύνατον μεταλαβεῖν.
Μηδένα ζῆλου τῶν ἐξ ἀδικίας κερδαινόντων, ἀλλὰ μᾶλλον
ἀποδέχου τοὺς μετὰ δικαιοσύνης ζημιωθέντας· οἱ γὰρ δίκαιοι

Paneg. § 17. n.). Isocr. himself
raises a protest against this low
meaning οἱ πλεονεκτεῖν, πλεονεξία,
πλεονεκτικόι, in an interesting passage, _de Perm._ §§ 281—284. The
passage is too long to quote _in ex-
tenso_, the following extracts may
suffice: εἰ τις ὑπολαμβάνει τοὺς
ἀποστεροῦντας ἢ παραλογιζομένους
ἢ κακόν τι ποιοῦντας πλεονεκτεῖν, οὐκ
ὀρθῶς ἔγνωκεν'...οὐδὲ τοῖς ὀνόμασιν
ἐπεί τινες ἔτι χρῶνται κατὰ φύσιν,
ἀλλὰ μεταφέρουσιν ἀπὸ τῶν καλλίστων πραγμάτων ἐπὶ τὰ φαυλότατα
τῶν ἐπιτηδευμάτων...τοὺς δὲ ταῖς κα-
κοηθείαις καὶ ταῖς κακουργίαις χρωμένους, καὶ μικρὰ μὲν λαμβάνοντας,
πονηρὰν δὲ δόξαν κτωμένους, πλεο-
νεκτικοὺς νομίζουσιν, ἀλλ' οὐ τοὺς
ὁσιωτάτους καὶ δικαιοτάτους, οἱ περὶ
τῶν ἀγαθῶν ἀλλ' οὐ τῶν κακῶν πλεο-
νεκτοῦσι.

ἵνα δοκῇς—ἐπιείκειαν.] Lit. 'that
men may see that you are aiming at
justice, _not_ because of weakness, but
because of equity,' _i.e._ if you act
justly, when too weak to commit injustice, men will not give you credit
for your justice. You must be
strong enough to overpower others,
and if you are then content with
what you have, men will believe in
your really equitable character.—μὴ
δι' ἀσθενείας. Cf. Aristotle's libel on
humanity (_Rhet._ ii. 5, 8), ὡς ἐπὶ τὸ
πολὺ ἀδικοῦσιν οἱ ἄνθρωποι, ὅταν
δύνωνται. The best comment, however, on this maxim is contained in
a fine fragment of Philemon (one of
the dramatists of the New Comedy,

fl. 300 B. C.) beginning thus: ἀνὴρ
δίκαιός ἐστιν οὐχ ὁ μὴ ἀδικῶν—ἀλλ'
ὅστις ἀδικεῖν δυνάμενος μὴ βούλεται,
κ.τ.λ.

39. **μᾶλλον—μεταλαβεῖν.**] Cf. Theognis, 144 sqq. βούλεο δ' εὐσεβέων ὀλί-
γοις σὺν χρήμασιν οἰκεῖν | ἢ πλουτεῖν
ἀδίκως χρήματα πασσάμενος...χρή-
ματα μὲν δαίμων καὶ παγκάκῳ
ἀνδρὶ δίδωσιν, κ.τ.λ.

Coray wishes to insert καὶ before
τοῖς φαύλοις; this is unnecessary,
although Isocr., in a similar passage, _ad Nicol._ § 31, has τὰ μὲν
(χρήματα) καὶ φαύλοις πάρεστι.

δικαίαν πενίαν)(πλοῦτον ἄδικον.]
For the inverse parallelism or Chiasmus see § 7. n.

ἡ δὲ.] v. Table of var. readings.

τούτου.] _Neut._ although it refers
to fem. δικαιοσύνη. Similarly, in
contrasting ἀρετή and χρήματα,
Solon, fr. 16 (ap. Schn.), says, οὐ δια-
μειψόμεθα | τῆς ἀρετῆς τὸν πλοῦτον,
ἐπεὶ τὸ μὲν ἔμπεδον αἰεί, | χρήματα
δ' ἀνθρώπων ἄλλοτε ἄλλος ἔχει. See
further, Madv. _Syn._ § 99 a.

μοχθηροῖς.] On the two meanings
of μοχθηρός, &c. see § 21, ἐν τοῖς
πονηροῖς. n.

κερδαινόντων)(ζημιωθέντας.]
'Gainers ')(' losers.' These words
are constantly opposed to one another: and so also are the corresponding nouns κέρδος and ζημία. Cf. the
warning in Isocr. _Nicol._ § 50, μὴ τὸ
μὲν λαβεῖν κέρδος εἶναι νομίζετε, τὸ δ'
ἀναλῶσαι ζημίαν, and esp. Plato.
Hipparchus, 226 E, κέρδος δὲ λέγεις
ἐναντίον τῇ ζημίᾳ; Ἔγωγε.

τῶν ἀδίκων εἰ μηδὲν ἄλλο πλεονεκτοῦσιν, ἀλλ᾽ οὖν ἐλπίσι
γε σπουδαίαις ὑπερέχουσιν.

40 Πάντων μὲν ἐπιμελοῦ τῶν περὶ τὸν βίον, μάλιστα δὲ
τὴν σαυτοῦ φρόνησιν ἄσκει· μέγιστον γὰρ ἐν ἐλαχίστῳ νοῦς
ἀγαθὸς ἐν ἀνθρώπου σώματι. Πειρῶ τῷ μὲν σώματι εἶναι 11
φιλόπονος, τῇ δὲ ψυχῇ φιλόσοφος, ἵνα τῷ μὲν ἐπιτελεῖν
δύνῃ τὰ δόξαντα, τῇ δὲ προορᾶν ἐπίστῃ τὰ συμφέροντα.

41 Πᾶν ὅ τι ἂν μέλλῃς ἐρεῖν, πρότερον ἐπισκόπει τῇ γνώμῃ·
πολλοῖς γὰρ ἡ γλῶττα προτρέχει τῆς διανοίας. δύο ποιοῦ b
καιροὺς τοῦ λέγειν, ἢ περὶ ὧν οἶσθα σαφῶς, ἢ περὶ ὧν ἀναγ-

ἀλλ᾽ οὖν—ὑπερέχουσιν.] 'At any
rate in good *hopes* they surpass
them.' By ἐλπίδες σπουδαῖαι, Isocr.
means not only good hopes in the
present life, but especially hopes of
happiness in an after-world. Cf.
Paneg. § 28. n.
This passage is the foundation of
an apophthegm attributed to Isocr.
(*Apoph.* 8, ed. Bens.), ἐρωτηθεὶς, τίνι
οἱ φιλόσοφοι τῶν ἀμαθῶν διαφέρουσιν, εἶπεν, 'ὡς οἱ εὐσεβεῖς τῶν ἀσε-
βῶν, ἐλπίσιν ἀγαθαῖς.' A similar
saying is assigned to Chilo (Diog.
Laert. 1. § 69), ἐρωτηθεὶς τίνι διαφέρουσιν οἱ πεπαιδευμένοι τῶν ἀπαιδεύ-
των, ἔφη, ἐλπίσιν ἀγαθαῖς.
40. μέγιστον—σώματι.] 'The
greatest thing in the smallest com-
pass is a good mind in a man's body.'
Stobaeus (*Flor.* III. 56) quotes the
following apophthegm, Περίανδρος
ἐρωτηθεὶς, τί μέγιστον ἐν ἐλαχίστῳ,
εἶπε, φρένες ἀγαθαὶ ἐν σώματι ἀνθρώπου. The saying has the air of a
late fabrication; but, if genuine, is
doubtless the source of the present
passage.
πειρῶ — συμφέροντα.] 'Endeavour in your body to love labour,
and in your mind to love wisdom;
that you may have power to carry
out your will with the former, and
knowledge to foresee your interests
with the latter.' The natural order
of the last two clauses is inverted;
it would be more natural to speak
of foresight (προορᾶν) first, and ac-

complishment (ἐπιτελεῖν) second.
But Isocr. prefers sacrificing this
order to the desire of bringing the
importance of cultivating the mind
into a position of slightly stronger
emphasis.
τῷ σώματι φιλόπονος...ἵνα κ.τ.λ.]
Cf. Milton (*Apol. for Smectym-
nuus*), speaking of himself, '*With
useful and generous labours preserving the bodies health and hardinesse,
to render lightsome, cleare and not
lumpish, obedience to the minde, &c.*'
σώματι εἶναι.] Another reading
is σῶμα εἶναι, but the reading in the
text has far better authority. Observe the *hiatus* (which might be
avoided by transposing φιλόπονοι
and εἶναι) and cf. § 49, ποσεῖ ἐλαττουμένους. Benseler (in 1832, ed.
Areop. p. 396) says of these two
instances, 'corrigenda esse cense-
rem, nisi cum Baitero statuerem,
hanc orationem non esse ab Isocrate
ita, uti eam nunc habemus, profec-
tam.'
41. ἡ γλῶττα προτρέχει τῆς διανοίας.] Borrowed from Chilo (quoted
by Stob. *Flor.* III. 79, and Diog.
Laert. I. 70), ἡ γλῶσσά σου μὴ προ-
τρεχέτω τοῦ νοῦ. For the metaphor
προτρέχει cf. the saying of Socrates,
κρεῖττόν ἐστι τῷ ποδὶ ὀλισθάνειν ἢ τῇ
γλώσσῃ (Orelli, *Opusc. Mor.* I. 26),
and Hom. *Il.* III. 213, ἐπιτροχάδην
ἀγόρευεν.
λέγειν...εἰπεῖν.] The meaning of
the two words is almost identical.

καλὸν εἰπεῖν. ἐν τούτοις γὰρ μόνοις ὁ λόγος τῆς σιγῆς κρείττων, ἐν δὲ τοῖς ἄλλοις ἄμεινον σιγᾶν ἢ λέγειν.

42 Νόμιζε μηδὲν εἶναι τῶν ἀνθρωπίνων βέβαιον· οὕτω γὰρ
οὔτ' εὐτυχῶν ἔσει περιχαρὴς οὔτε δυστυχῶν περίλυπος.
Χαῖρε μὲν ἐπὶ τοῖς συμβαίνουσι τῶν ἀγαθῶν, λυποῦ δὲ μετρίως ἐπὶ τοῖς γιγνομένοις τῶν κακῶν, γίγνου δὲ τοῖς ἄλλοις
μηδ' ἐν ἑτέροις ὢν κατάδηλος· ἄτοπον γὰρ τὴν μὲν οὐσίαν ἐν

Isocr. constantly uses them for variety of expression. Cf. *Paneg.* §§ 10, 11, *de Perm.* § 272, ἔχω μὲν εἰπεῖν, ὅπω δὲ λέγειν. §§ 292, 293, δεινοὶ λέγειν, followed soon after by δεινοὶ εἰπεῖν (the latter formula being somewhat rare, but found in Dem. *in Androt.* § 31, *adv. Lept.* § 150, *de Symmor.* § 8). *Panath.* § 262, ἀπλήστως διακείμενος…πρὸς τὸ λέγειν καὶ πόλλ' ἂν εἰπεῖν ἔχων, &c. Cf. also Dem. *Phil.* II. § 11, ταῦθ' ἃ πάντες μὲν ἀεὶ γλίχονται λέγειν, ἀξίως δ' οὐδεὶς εἰπεῖν δεδύνηται.

σιγῆς κρείττων.] For the form of the precept cf. Eurip. ἢ λέγε τι σιγῆς κρεῖττον ἢ σιγὴν ἔχε. Stobaeus (*Flor.* 34, 6) quotes this passage with the var. σιωπῆς. A distinction, however, may generally be drawn between σιγή and σιωπή, parallel to that which usually subsists between σιγᾶν (=silere, to remain silent) and σιωπᾶν (=tacere, to become silent). Isocr. is telling Dem. when he is to keep silence; not, when he is to cease talking.

42. μηδὲν—βέβαιον.] The sentiment is too common to need much illustration. Menander has the line βέβαιον οὐδέν ἐστιν ἐν θνητῷ βίῳ, and Marcus Antoninus (the Stoic Emperor) has an epigrammatic but gloomy passage to the same effect (*Comm.* II. 17). The greater part of this section is imitated by Basil I. (Emperor of the East, A.D. 867—886), who was familiar with the writings of Isocr. (v. *Introd. ad Dem.*): ἴσθι τέκνον ἐμὸν ὡς οὐδὲν ὁ βίος οὗτος ἔχει τὸ στάσιμον οὐδὲ τὸ βέβαιον ἢ ἀμετάβλητον. ἄλλοτε γὰρ

ἄλλως ἀμείβει τὰ πράγματα καὶ τροχοῦ δίκην κυλιομένου τὰ μὲν ἄνω φέρεται κάτω, τὰ δὲ κάτω φέρεται ἄνω. διὸ μήτε εὐτυχίαις ἐπαίρου μήτε ἐν ταῖς δυστυχίαις καταφέρου, ἀλλ' ἴσω κατ' ἀμφω σταθερὸς καὶ ἀμετάντητος. (*Exhort. ad Leon. filium,* 38.)

εὐτυχῶν)(δυστυχῶν.] An instance of ἀντίθεσις and ὁμοιοτέλευτον, just as περιχαρὴς)(περίλυπος is an instance of ἀντίθεσις and ὁμοιοκατάρκτον. v. *Introd. on Style.*

γίγνου…κατάδηλος.] i.e. Whether in sorrow or in joy, in neither case betray your feelings to other persons. Lit. 'Do not become conspicuous as being in *either* state.' The sense is not 'make it manifest that you are in neither condition.' ὢν comes in constr. not before, but after κατάδηλος. Cf. Plato, *Apol.* p. 23, κατάδηλοι γίγνονται προσποιούμενοι μὲν εἰδέναι, εἰδότες δὲ οὐδέν. Madv. *Synt.* § 177 b.—Cf. Theognis, 1159, ὁ μὲν ἐσθλὸν | τολμᾷ ἔχων τὸ κακόν, οὐκ ἐπίδηλος ὅμως.—For μηδ' ἐν ἑτέροις cf. Dem. *adv. Callip.* § 2, μηδὲ μεθ' ἑτέρων τὴν γνώμην γενόμενοι.

ἄτοπον γάρ…] In the speech written for the king of Cyprus we have an *apparently* contradictory precept (*Nicocl.* § 52), μηδὲν ἀποκρύπτεσθε μηθ' ὧν πέπραχθε μηθ' ὧν ποιεῖτε μηθ' ὧν μέλλετε πράττειν. There the king is telling his subjects to conceal nothing from *him*; here the case is different. Even if the discrepancy were real, Isocr. is not the man to be constantly consistent with himself; witness the passage

ταῖς οἰκίαις ἀποκρύπτειν, τὴν δὲ διάνοιαν φανερὰν ἔχοντα
43 περιπατεῖν. Μᾶλλον εὐλαβοῦ ψόγον ἢ κίνδυνον· δεῖ γὰρ c
εἶναι φοβερὰν τοῖς μὲν φαύλοις τὴν τοῦ βίου τελευτήν, τοῖς
δὲ σπουδαίοις τὴν ἐν τῷ ζῆν ἀδοξίαν. Μάλιστα μὲν πειρῶ
ζῆν κατὰ τὴν ἀσφάλειαν· ἐὰν δέ ποτέ σοι συμβῇ κινδυνεύειν, ζήτει τὴν ἐκ τοῦ πολέμου σωτηρίαν μετὰ καλῆς δόξης,
ἀλλὰ μὴ μετ' αἰσχρᾶς φήμης· τὸ μὲν γὰρ τελευτῆσαι πάντων ἡ πεπρωμένη κατέκρινε, τὸ δὲ καλῶς ἀποθανεῖν ἴδιον d
τοῖς σπουδαίοις ἀπένειμεν.

44 (ε΄.) Καὶ μὴ θαυμάσῃς, εἰ πολλὰ τῶν εἰρημένων οὐ

from *Panath.* § 172, quoted *Paneg.*
§ 58. n.
   ταῖς οἰκίαις.] Pl. preferred, possibly because ἐν τῇ οἰκίᾳ ἀποκρ.,
which is more natural, would contain a *hiatus.*
   43. **τοῖς μὲν φαύλοις κ.τ.λ.**]
Observe the parallelism. For φαύλοις)(σπουδαίοις see § 1. n.
   μάλιστα μὲν...ἐὰν δὲ ποτε.] Cf.
§ 32. For the sense cf. ad *Nicocl.*
§ 36, μάλιστα μὲν πειρῶ τὴν ἀσφάλειαν καὶ σαυτῷ καὶ τῇ πόλει διαφυ-
λάττειν· ἢν δ' ἀναγκασθῇς κινδυνεύειν,
αἱροῦ τεθνάναι καλῶς μᾶλλον ἢ ζῆν
αἰσχρῶς.
   ἀλλὰ μή.] Cf. § 2 n. *Paneg.* § 40,
μετὰ λόγου καὶ μὴ μετὰ βίας. n.
   τελευτῆσαι ... ἀποθανεῖν.] Used
partly for variety: further, καλῶς
τελευτῆσαι βίον would involve *hiatus,* and the use of ἀποθανεῖν avoids
it.
   §§ 44–52. *We now reach the
Epilogue. Its general sense may be
summed up as follows.*
   § 44. *Many of these precepts are,
I am well aware, unsuitable to your
present age: but you will one day
have hard work to find a faithful
counsellor, and this treatise will then
serve as a store-house of moral
maxims.* 45. *I trust I shall not be
disappointed in my present opinion
of you.* 46. *Strive to do well, for
this will yield a harvest of enduring
delight.* 47. *Let your motto be,
'pains now, pleasures anon,' and*

*not 'pleasure now and pain here-
after.'* 48, 49. *Remember that the
bad may do as they please; the good
cannot neglect virtue, and that because they have many to rebuke them,
if they are inconsistent. Much is
expected of you; be not traitor to your
high privileges.* 50. *You may tell
the manner in which Heaven regards
the good and the bad, from the legends
of the virtue of Hercules and the vice
of Tantalus—from the boon of im-
mortality conferred on the first and
the sore punishment inflicted on the
second.* 51. *With such instances before us, we should eagerly strive after
true nobility, and not only remain
steadfast to the precepts here given, but
read the best writings of others also.*
52. *Like the bee, we must range everywhere and gather precious stores from
every quarter; for, even after all is
done, 'tis hard enough to over-master
the failings of humanity.*
   44. **εἰ...οὐ...πρέπει.**] μή is more
common after θαυμάζω εἰ..., e.g.
Isocr. *de Pace,* § 12, θαυμάζω δὲ
τῶν τε πρεσβυτέρων εἰ μηκέτι μνημο-
νεύουσι καὶ τῶν νεωτέρων, εἰ μηδενὸς
ἀκηκόασι, κ.τ.λ. *Aeginet.* § 26, οὐκ
ἐκεῖνον ἄξιον θαυμάζειν εἰ μὴ παρ-
έμεινεν. In the present passage the
meaning of εἰ...οὐ πρέπει is very
nearly = that of ὅτι...οὐ πρέπει. The
sentence εἰ...πρέπει is not a conditional, but an object-sentence, and
therefore οὐ is perfectly natural.
The writer is *certain* that the pre-

πρέπει σοι πρὸς τὴν νῦν παροῦσαν ἡλικίαν· οὐδὲ γὰρ ἐμὲ
τοῦτο διέλαθεν· ἀλλὰ προειλόμην διὰ τῆς αὐτῆς πραγμα-
τείας ἅμα τοῦ τε παρόντος βίου συμβουλίαν ἐξενεγκεῖν καὶ
τοῦ μέλλοντος χρόνου παράγγελμα καταλιπεῖν. τὴν μὲν
γὰρ τούτων χρείαν ῥᾳδίως εἰδήσεις, τὸν δὲ μετ᾽ εὐνοίας συμ-
βουλεύοντα χαλεπῶς εὑρήσεις. ὅπως οὖν μὴ παρ᾽ ἑτέρου c
τὰ λοιπὰ ζητῆς, ἀλλ᾽ ἐντεῦθεν ὥσπερ ἐκ ταμιείου προφέρῃς,
ᾠήθην δεῖν μηδὲν παραλιπεῖν ὧν ἔχω σοι συμβουλεύειν.

45   Πολλὴν δ᾽ ἂν τοῖς θεοῖς χάριν σχοίην, εἰ μὴ διαμάρτοιμι
τῆς δόξης ἧς ἔχων περὶ σοῦ τυγχάνω. τῶν μὲν γὰρ ἄλλων 12
τοὺς πλείστους εὑρήσομεν, ὥσπερ τῶν σιτίων τοῖς ἡδίστοις
μᾶλλον ἢ τοῖς ὑγιεινοτάτοις χαίροντας, οὕτω καὶ τῶν φίλων
τοῖς συνεξαμαρτάνουσι πλησιάζοντας, ἀλλ᾽ οὐ τοῖς νουθε-
τοῦσι. σὲ δὲ νομίζω τοὐναντίον τούτων ἐγνωκέναι, τεκμηρίῳ

cepts are not suitable, and therefore does not use μή. v. Madv. *Synt.* § 194 c.

ἀλλὰ προειλόμην κ.τ.λ.] *i.e.* 'but I deliberately preferred, by means of the same treatise, not only to bring forward advice for your present life, but also to leave you instructions for the time to come.' πραγματεία is best translated 'treatise' in this passage. Strictly speaking, the meaning of the word here lies between 'treatise' and 'business,' just as in *Philip.* § 7, διαδο-θέντος τοῦ λόγου...ὅντος δ᾽ οὖν ἐμοῦ περὶ τὴν πραγματείαν ταύτην, ἐφθητε ποιησάμενοι τὴν εἰρήνην πρὶν ἐξεργασθῆναι τὸν λόγον. παράγγελμα is often used as a military term = 'marching-orders,' or 'watchword,' either of which senses would help to illustrate this passage.

τὴν μὲν γάρ τ. χρείαν κ.τ.λ.] 'For you will easily know your need of such precepts; but you will have difficulty in finding one who is ready to counsel you with good-will.' χρεία here means either (1) 'use,' 'advantage,' or (2) 'need,' 'necessity.' Wolf prefers, (1) [= πῶς καὶ πότε χρὴ τούτοις χρῆσθαι], but (2) harmonizes better with the latter half

of the sentence. On εἰδήσεις] εὑρή-σεις cf. § 16, συνειδήσεις. n.

ᾠήθην.] After ᾠήθην, a principal verb of past time, the opt. would be more regular than the subj. But when the sentence is 'so put as not to form part of a representation belonging to the past,' the subj. is often preferred. Madv. *Synt.* § 131 b. (*e. g.* Dem. *in Conon.* § 17, οἱ νόμοι καὶ τὰς ἀναγκαίας προφάσεις ὅπως μὴ μείζους γίγνωνται προσδόντο). See also esp. Goodwin's *Gk. Moods and Tenses,* § 44, 2.

ὥσπερ ἐκ ταμιείου.] ἡ μεταφορὰ ...ἀπὸ τῶν ἐδωδίμων. (Coray.)

45. ὥσπερ τῶν σιτίων τοῖς ἡδί-στοις κ.τ.λ.] Cf. § 35. ad *Nicocl.* § 45.

συνεξαμαρτάνοντες)(νουθετοῦν-τες.] A similar contrast may be observed in the general meaning of § 30, πρὸς τὸ φαυλότατον χαριζομέ-νους)(πρὸς τὸ βέλτιστον ἀπεχθανομέ-νους. ad *Nicocl.* § 42, συνεξαμαρτά-νουσιν)(ἀποτρέπουσιν. This meaning of νουθετεῖν, 'to admonish a person for his good,' is well brought out in *Panvg.* § 130. For the sense cf. also ad *Nicocl.* § 28, πιστεύε ἡγοῦ μὴ τοὺς ὅσαν ὅτι ἂν λέγῃς ἢ ποιῇς ἐπαι-νοῦντας ἀλλὰ τοὺς τοῖς ἁμαρτανομένοις ἐπιτιμῶντας, and *Panath.* §§ 271-2.

χρώμενος τῇ περὶ τὴν ἄλλην παιδείαν φιλοπονίᾳ· τὸν γὰρ
αὐτῷ τὰ βέλτιστα πράττειν ἐπιτάττοντα, τοῦτον εἰκὸς καὶ
τῶν ἄλλων τοὺς ἐπὶ τὴν ἀρετὴν παρακαλοῦντας ἀποδέ- b
46 χεσθαι. Μάλιστα δ' ἂν παροξυνθείης ὀρέγεσθαι τῶν καλῶν
ἔργων, εἰ καταμάθοις, ὅτι καὶ τὰς ἡδονὰς ἐκ τούτων μάλιστα
γνησίως ἔχομεν. ἐν μὲν γὰρ τῷ ῥαθυμεῖν καὶ τὰς πλησμονὰς ἀγαπᾶν εὐθὺς αἱ λῦπαι ταῖς ἡδοναῖς παραπεπήγασι, τὸ
δὲ περὶ τὴν ἀρετὴν φιλοπονεῖν καὶ σωφρόνως τὸν αὑτοῦ
βίον οἰκονομεῖν ἀεὶ τὰς τέρψεις εἰλικρινεῖς καὶ βεβαιοτέρας

φιλοπονίᾳ.] One of the apo-
phthegms of Isocr. (ap. Benseler, 11.
177) is recorded as follows: ἰδὼν
μανίαν φιλοπονοῦντα, ἔφη, κάλλιστον ὄψον τῷ γήρατι (= Att. γῆρᾳ)
ἀρτύεις.

παρακαλοῦντας.] This is not the
fut. part. (= παρακαλέσοντας) but the
pres. According to Benseler the
only instance in Isocr. of the 'Attic
future' of verbs in έω is διατελοῦμεν
(Archid. § 87), which is the reading
of the Codex Urbinas; the Ambrosian and Laurentine MSS. having
διατελέσομεν, which Benseler adopts.
Another instance occurs in Trapes.
(a speech which Bens. rejects), § 56,
συκοφαντήσων καὶ...ἐγκαλῶν. (Rost
ap. Bremi Isocr. p. 206.) Just as in
this last passage ἐγκαλῶν is almost
certainly fut. because συκοφαντήσων
is fut., similarly παρακαλοῦντας is
almost certainly pres. because ἐπιτάττοντα is pres. The uniformity
of the sentence is thus preserved.—
For this pres. part. in the sense of
'ready or likely to do a thing,' cf.
§ 30, χαριζομένους and ἀπεχθανομέ-
νους, § 33, ἀπαγγέλλεται, § 44,
συμβουλεύσντα.

46. μάλιστα κ.τ.λ.] 'Now, you
would especially be incited to reach
forward to good deeds, if you clearly
saw that the pleasures which we win
from these sources are won in a
specially genuine manner (or most
genuinely)'.

μ δ' ἂν παροξυνθείης...εἰ καταμάθοις. For this common form of a
conditional sentence see Madv. Synt.

§ 135, and Mr Thring's Manual
of Mood Constr. p. 17. The following lines from Soph. Elect. will
supply easy instances of various
hypothetical sentences, 376-7, 394,
413, 430, 547-8, 554, 557, 583, 604.

ἐν μὲν γάρ κ.τ.λ.] 'For while,
in the case of idleness and love of
surfeit, pains are planted by the
very side of pleasures, yet the loving
labour spent on virtue, and the pru-
dent conduct of one's life, ever
yield delights that are pure and
more lasting.' παραπεπήγασιν, are
'bound up with.' (Lidd. and Sc.).
The pleasure is no sooner over than
pain follows at once (εὐθύς).

For the sense and expression
Schn. quotes Sextus Empiricus (a
sceptic of the first half of the 3rd
cent. A. D.), Hypotyp. § 24, πάσῃ
ἡδονῇ παραπέπηγεν ἀλγηδών.— In
the Phaedo of Plato, p. 60 B, Socrates speaks to this effect: 'How
strange is the nature of pleasure
(τὸ ἡδύ) in regard to that which
seems to be its very opposite—pain
(τὸ λυπηρόν); in that the two are
unwilling to be present to a man
at once, but if he pursue the one
and take it, he is pretty nearly compelled to take the other also, as if
the two, distinct as they are, were
yet, at one end, closely knit together
(ὥσπερ ἐκ μιᾶς κορυφῆς συνημμένω
δύ' ὄντε, i. e. 'twin and yet twain').
Menander (fragm. of Plocium) has
ἀλλ' ἐγγὺς ἀγαθοῦ παρατέθεικε καὶ
κακόν.

βίον οἰκονομεῖν.] Cf. § 5. n.

47 ἀποδίδωσι· κἀκεῖ μὲν πρότερον ἡσθέντες ὕστερον ἐλυπήθη- c

εἰλικρινέ͡ς.] The deriv. of this word (like that of *sincerus*) is much disputed. It is either from (1) ἕλη, εἵλη='the sun's warmth' or 'sunlight' [ἕλη· ἡλίου ἀλέα ἢ αὐγή. Timaeus, *Lex. Platon.*], and κρίνω; or from (2) εἵλω, to roll, and κρίνω, to discern. (1) gives the meaning, 'held up and judged by the sunlight,' 'transparent,' hence 'sincere,' 'truthful.' (2) produces the sense *volubili agitatione secretum*, 'discerned by rolling or sifting,' hence 'sifted,' 'separated,' 'pure.' Or again, if we take the word εἵλη or ἕλη (=*gres, turma*), which is connected with εἵλω (*volvo*), we obtain a modification of (2). The primary meaning will then be 'parcelled off by itself' (εἰλαδόν, *Dadôn, turmatim, gregatim*), 'distinct,' hence 'unsullied.' (1) is supported by Ruhnken and Hemsterhuis (ap. Timaei *Lex.* v. ὑπ' αὐγάς), and is still the popular deriv. (2) was proposed by Valckenaer, who is followed by Stallbaum (Plat. *Phaedo*, 66 A. n.), and others. (1) is poetic and elegant, but, I venture to think, untrue and indefensible. It is fair to state that the objection sometimes brought against (1), on the ground that εἵλη, ἕλη always mean the 'warmth' and not the 'light' of the sun, is considerably modified by the quotation, given above, from Timaeus. (2) In either of its forms is preferable, because the idea of 'separated,' 'unmixed,' 'pure,' is more consistent with the explanations of Hesychius and Suidas (=καθαρόs, ἄδολοs, ἀμιγήs); and still further, because that idea is more suitable to most passages in which the word is used, and esp. to the following: Plato, *Phaedo*, 66 A, αὐτῇ καθ' αὑτὴν εἰλικρινεῖ τῇ διανοίᾳ. 81 C, ψυχὴν αὐτὴν καθ' αὑτὴν εἰλ. Symp. 211 E, αὐτὸ τὸ καλὸν ἰδεῖν εἰλικρινές, καθαρόν, ἄμικτον. Xen. Cyrop. 8, 5, 14, διὰ τὸ εἰλικρινῆ εἶναι ἕκαστα τὰ φῦλα (cf. φυλοκρι-

νεῖν). To these, which have been quoted by others, I may add Plutarch *de EI in Delphis*, p. 393 C, τὸ δὲ ἓν εἰλικρινὲς καὶ καθαρόν· ἕτερον γὰρ μίξει πρὸς ἕτερον ὁ μιασμός... οὐκοῦν ἔν τε καὶ ἄκρατον δεῖ τῷ ἀφθάρτῳ καὶ καθαρῷ προσήκει. If der. (1) is adopted, the rough breathing will be necessary; if (2), the word will be written, as in the text, without the aspirate. (See further, Trench, *Synon.* § 86, and Wordsworth, Ellicott, and Lightfoot on *Philippians*, 1. 10).

εἰλικρινὲς κ. βεβαιοτέρας.] Obs. comparative coupled with positive. Bens. cites this collocation as part of his proof of the spuriousness of the Ep. ad Dem. Schn. points out, in reply, the propriety of the combination, on the ground that delight derived from pleasures is to a certain degree 'lasting' (βεβαία)[?], but not 'pure and unmixed' (εἰλικρινής); we may therefore say with perfect correctness that the delights derived from virtue are εἰλικρινεῖς καὶ βεβαιότεραι. He then quotes Hom. *Od.* VIII. 187, δίσκον μείζονα καὶ πάχιστον, Plato, *de Legg.* 1. p. 649 D, εὐτελῆ τε καὶ ἀσυνετώτερα, Tacitus, *Agricola*, 1, *apud priores agere digna memoratu* pronum magisque in aperto *erat.* &c.

ἀποδίδωσι.] 'Yields a harvest,' 'yields a return,' lit. 'gives back.' In Aristot. *Rhet.* II. 7, 5, among the reasons, which shew the absence of real gratitude, we have ὅτι ἀπέδωκαν ἀλλ' οὐκ ἔδωκαν (they merely gave *back* a favour). Lidd. and Scott quote the passage in the text with this explanation, 'ἀπ. τοα, c. Adj. to *render* or *make* so and so, like ἀποδέδειμαι.' In all the passages of Isocr. that have come before me, it bears the meaning 'restore,' 'return,' 'repay;' (except *Callimach.* § 6, where εἰς τὴν βουλὴν ἀνέδωσαν must mean 'they brought the matter before the Council,' *detulerunt.*) The sense gained by translating ἀπο-

σαν, ἐνταῦθα δὲ μετὰ τὰς λύπας τὰς ἡδονὰς ἔχομεν. ἐν
πᾶσι δὲ τοῖς ἔργοις οὐχ οὕτω τῆς ἀρχῆς μνημονεύομεν, ὡς
τῆς τελευτῆς αἴσθησιν λαμβάνομεν· τὰ γὰρ πλεῖστα τῶν
περὶ τὸν βίον οὐ διὰ τὰ πράγματα ποιοῦμεν, ἀλλὰ τῶν ἀπο-
48 βαινόντων ἕνεκα διαπονούμεν. (ς'.) Ἐνθυμοῦ δὲ, ὅτι τοῖς
μὲν φαύλοις ἐνδέχεται τὰ τυχόντα πράττειν· εὐθὺς γὰρ τοῦ
βίου τοιαύτην πεποίηνται τὴν ὑπόθεσιν· τοῖς δὲ σπουδαίοις d
οὐχ οἷόντε τῆς ἀρετῆς ἀμελεῖν διὰ τὸ πολλοὺς ἔχειν τοὺς
ἐπιπλήττοντας. πάντες γὰρ μισοῦσιν οὐχ οὕτω τοὺς ἐξαμαρτάνοντας ὡς τοὺς ἐπιεικεῖς μὲν φήσαντας εἶναι, μηδὲν δὲ
49 τῶν τυχόντων διαφέροντας, εἰκότως· ὅπου γὰρ τοὺς τῷ λόγῳ
μόνον ψευδομένοις ἀποδοκιμάζομεν, ἢ πού γε τοὺς τῷ βίῳ

δίδωσι κ.τ.λ. as above, is rather more
satisfactory, as it brings out the idea
of *recompense* which pervades the
whole context. In any case *ώ. κ.
βεβ.* will be the predicate.

Ὀλυσήθησαν.] This is the reading
of the Cod. Urbinas and Cod. Sca-
phusiensis, and is followed by Benseler. Bekker, Dindorf, and Baiter-
and-Sauppe prefer ἐλυσήθημεν. The
writer could hardly be so depreciatory to himself and Dem., as to
include both among those who lived
in 'idleness and love of surfeit,'
and yet this must be involved in
the use of ἐλυσήθημεν, unless it is
meant for a vague plural, including
'men in general.' The MS. authority for ἐλυσήθησαν is stronger, the
sense produced is better; and lastly,
the 1st pers. pl., which is found in
some MSS., is easily accounted for
by a desire to assimilate ἐλυσ. with
ἔχομεν.

To illustrate the change of person, cf. *Panег.* § 39, δείξομεν...ἰδί.
δαξεν, and on the transition from
aor. to present cf. § 6. n. The nom.
to ἐλυσήθησαν is οἱ ῥαθυμοῦντες καὶ
τὰς πλησμονὰς ἀγαπῶντες, or any
similar idea implied in the words
ἐν τῷ ῥαθυμεῖν, κ.τ.λ.

κἀκεῖ μὲν—ἡδονὰς ἔχομεν.] For
the general meaning the lines of Geo.
Herbert (imitated possibly from

Musonius ap. Gellium, *Noct. Attic.*
XVI. 1) will suffice: *If thou do
ill; the joy fades, not the pains:
If well; the pain doth fade, the joy
remains.*

48. φαύλοις)(σπουδαίοις.] These
words appear to bear a semi-social
meaning in this passage, contrasting
the vulgar and the respectable.
This sense is borne out by § 49,
χρήματα...δόξαν...φίλοιν. v. § 1. n.

εὐθὺς γάρ...ὑπόθεσιν.] Similarly
Archid. § 90, οὐχ ὁμοίως ἅπασι βου-
λευτέον, ἀλλ' ὡς ἂν ἐξ ἀρχῆς ἕκαστοι
τοῦ βίου ποιήσωνται τὴν ὑπόθεσιν.

49. ὅπου γάρ—ἢ πού γε.] 'For
whereas we count reprobate those
who are false even in word alone;
why surely, we cannot deny (lit.
'can we deny?') that *those* are bad
who fall behind-hand during the
whole of their life.'

For ὅπου δὲ...ἢ πού cf. *de Perm.*
§ 70 (quoted § 36. n. 1), *de Perm.*
§ 33, ὅπου γάρ...ἢ πού σφόδρ' ἂν,
Epp. 2, 15. εἰ γάρ...ἢ πού σε γε
προσήκει. *de Pace*, § 24, ὅπου γὰρ
Ἀθηνόδωρος καὶ Καλλίστρατος...οἷοί
σοι πόλεις οἷοί τε γεγόνασιν, ἢ πού
βουληθέντες ἡμεῖς πολλοὺς ἂν τόπους
τοιούτους κατασχεῖν δυνηθείημεν. ἢ
πού implies assurance blended with
real or ironical doubt; ἢ πού in
such sentences is often interroga-
tive.

παντὶ ἐλαττουμένους οὐ φαύλους εἶναι φήσωμεν; δικαίως δ'
ἂν τοὺς τοιούτους ὑπολάβοιμεν μὴ μόνον εἰς αὐτοὺς ἁμαρτάνειν, ἀλλὰ καὶ τῆς τύχης εἶναι προδότας· ἡ μὲν γὰρ αὐτοῖς ε
χρήματα καὶ δόξαν καὶ φίλους ἐνεχείρισεν, οἱ δὲ σφᾶς αὑ-
50 τοὺς ἀναξίους τῆς ὑπαρχούσης εὐδαιμονίας κατέστησαν. Εἰ 13
δὲ δεῖ θνητὸν ὄντα τῆς τῶν θεῶν στοχάσασθαι διανοίας,
ἡγοῦμαι κἀκείνους ἐπὶ τοῖς οἰκειοτάτοις μάλιστα δηλῶσαι,
πῶς ἔχουσι πρὸς τοὺς φαύλους καὶ τοὺς σπουδαίους τῶν ἀνθρώπων. Ζεὺς γὰρ Ἡρακλέα καὶ Τάνταλον γεννήσας, ὡς

ἐλαττουμένους.] Bens. (Praef. iv.)
says that the sense 'inferiores ea
quam de se praebuerant opinione,'
i.e. 'falling short of previous expec-
tations' is foreign to Isocr. However, in de Perm. § 281, he has these
words: εἴ τις ὑπολαμβάνει τοὺς ἀπο-
στεροῦνται ἢ παρὰ λογιζομένους ἢ
κακόν τε τοιοῦντας πλεονεκτεῖν,
οὐκ ὀρθῶς ἔγνωκεν· οὐδένεν γὰρ ἐν
ἅπαντι τῷ βίῳ μᾶλλον ἐλαττοῦνται
τῶν τοιούτων, οὐδ' ἐν πλείοσιν ἀπο-
ρίαις εἰσίν, ... οὐδ' ὅλως ἀθλιώτεροι
τυγχάνουσιν ὄντες. Here (as also in
Panath. § 243) there is a contrast between πλεονεκτεῖν (in its good sense,
v. § 27. n.) and ἐλαττοῦσθαι, between
'gaining advantage,' and 'losing advantage;' 'honourably improving
one's position,' and 'dishonourably
impairing it;' and this meaning is
readily applicable to the present passage. οἱ ἐλαττούμενοι = here, 'those
who give up their advantages, χρήματα, δόξας, φίλους,' and, by an easy
transition, 'those who fall behind-
hand,' or, in homelier phrase, 'drop
off.'
On the hiatus in παντὶ ἐλαττ. it
may be observed that, in the passage quoted above from de Perm.,
the hiatus is avoided. Isocr. appears
to have been somewhat less sensitive on such points, in his 'moral
writings' (λόγοι παραινετικοί) and
'forensic speeches written for clients'
(λ. δικανικοί), than in speeches like
the Paneg. and de Pace (which are
λ. συμβουλευτικοί), or the Helenae

Encomium and the Busiris (λ. ἐπιδεικτικοί). v. Paneg. § 143. n.
οὐ φ. εἶναι φήσωμεν.] On this
use of οὐ cf. Plato, Prot. 352 D,
πολλούς φασι γιγνώσκοντας τὰ βέλτιστα οὐκ ἐθέλειν πράττειν. Madv.
Synt. § 205 (b). For φήσωμεν (the
subj. dubitativus) see Madv. Synt.
§ 121. [φήσωμεν, Cod. Urbinas foll.
by Benseler; φήσομεν is adopted by
Bekk. and BS.] 'οὐ malim abesse.'
Baiter.
50. τοὺς φαύλους τῶν ἀνθρώπων.]
'Those men who are bad.' τῶν
ἀνθ. a species of partitive genitive,
Madv. Synt § 50. A favourite construction, not only in the Ep. ad
Dem. (e.g. § 11, τὰ καλὰ τῶν ἔργων...
τοὺς σπουδαίους τῶν γονέων, § 42,
ἐπὶ τοῖς συμβαίνουσι τῶν ἀγαθῶν,
&c.) but also in the acknowledged
writings of Isocr. (e.g. Areop. § 47,
τὰς ἐπιεικεῖς τῶν φύσεων, de Pace,
§ 109, &c.).
Ἡρακλέα...ἀρετήν.] In Philip.
§ 109, 110, Isocr. speaks of the
mental excellence (τῶν τῇ ψυχῇ
προσόντων ἀγαθῶν) of Hercules as a
tempting subject for encomium, 'a
theme fraught with many praiseworthy deeds and languishing for
lack of a worthy panegyrist;' and
in § 144 he characterizes Hercules,
Tantalus, and others, in the following terms: τὸν Τάνταλον πλοῦτον·
τὴν Πέλοπος ἀρχήν· τὴν Εὐρυσθέως
δύναμιν· τὴν Ἡρακλέους ὑπερβολήν·
τὴν Θησέως ἀρετήν.—The stories of
Hercules and Tantalus are well and

οἱ μῦθοι λέγουσι καὶ πάντες πιστεύουσι, τὸν μὲν διὰ τὴν
ἀρετὴν ἀθάνατον ἐποίησε, τὸν δὲ διὰ τὴν κακίαν ταῖς μεγί-
51 σταις τιμωρίαις ἐκόλασεν. οἷς δεῖ παραδείγμασι χρωμένους
ὀρέγεσθαι τῆς καλοκαγαθίας, καὶ μὴ μόνον τοῖς ὑφ᾽ ἡμῶν b
εἰρημένοις ἐμμένειν, ἀλλὰ καὶ τῶν ποιητῶν τὰ βέλτιστα

briefly told by Mr G. W. Cox, *Tales
of Ancient Greece*, pp. 66—77.

ὡς οἱ μῦθοι λέγ. κ.τ.λ.] Cf. *Paneg.* § 28, καὶ γὰρ εἰ μυθώδης ὁ λόγος
γέγονεν, ὅμως αὐτῷ καὶ νῦν ῥηθῆναι
προσήκει. n. Isocr. argues from mythical narratives whenever they suit
his subject, but applies to them no
principles of historical criticism.
Grote's *H. G.* new ed. i. p. 335. n.

51. χρωμένους.] Bens. retains χρω-
μένοις, which is said to be the reading of the Urb. MS. Δεῖ would then
be followed by a very rare construction, the dat. with the inf. Instances
of this construction are Eur. *Hipp.*
940, θεοῖσι προσβαλεῖν χθονὶ | ἄλλην
δεήσει γαῖαν, and Xen. *Anab.* III.
4, 35, δεῖ ἰσχύσαι τὸν ἵππον Πέρσῃ
ἀνδρὶ καὶ χαλινῶσαι δεῖ καὶ θωρα-
κισθέντα ἀναβῆναι ἐπὶ τὸν ἵππον.
The *usual* formula is δεῖ με τοιεῖν
τι and not δεῖ μοι ποιεῖν τι. For
this reason, and also because the
presence of the dat. is accounted for
by the immediate juxtaposition of
οἷς...παραδείγμασι, which may have
led the copyist wrong, it seems safer
to adopt the other reading χρωμένους. (Partly from Schn.)

ὀρέγεσθαι.] Lit. 'to reach after.'
A frequent word in Isocr. Thus we
have it followed by δόξης § 5, τῶν καλῶν ἔργων § 46, τῆς δικαιοσύνης § 38;
also *ad Nicol.* § 2, τοίων ἐπιτηδευμάτων ὀρεγόμενοι, κ.τ.λ.; *de Pace*,
§§ 13, 62, and 144, ἄξιον οὖν ὀρέγεσθαι τῆς τοιαύτης ἡγεμονίας. (In
one passage we find him using a
rarer word, ὀριγνᾶσθαι. *Epp.* 6, 9,
τοίας δόξης ὀριγνᾶσθαι.) ὀρέγεσθαι
(like στοχάζω, τυγχάνω, κ.τ.λ.)
almost invariably takes the gen.
(Madv. *Synt.* § 57 a).

ὑφ᾽ ἡμῶν εἰρ.] Not ὑπ᾽ ἐμοῦ εἰ-
ρημέναι. Cf. § 5, ἡμεῖς. n.

τῶν ποιητῶν...καὶ τῶν ἄλλων
σοφιστῶν.] These words by themselves can be translated in two distinctly different ways: (1) 'of the
poets...and of the other sophists,'
and (2) 'of the poets...and of the
sophists besides.' (1) makes the
ποιητής a *species* of the *genus* σοφιστής. (2) regards the poet and the
sophist as perfectly independent of
one another. With regard to the
present passage, the following points
are all that I can urge in defence of
(1). (a) We are told by Diog.
Laert. (I. § 12), that not only οἱ
σοφοί, but οἱ ποιηταί also, were called
σοφισταί. καθὰ καὶ Κρατῖνος ἐν
Ἀρχιλόχῳ τοὺς περὶ Ὅμηρον κ. Ἡσί-
οδον ἐπαινῶν, οὕτως καλεῖ. (b) The
same writer (I. § 40) says that all
the 'seven wise men' [notably So-
lon] 'attempted poetry' (ἐπιθέσθαι
ποιητικῇ).—That (1) is wrong and
(2) right is, I think, decided by the
following passages: *Paneg.* § 82,
μηδένα...μήτε τῶν ποιητῶν μήτε τῶν
σοφιστῶν. (see n.). *ad Nicol.* § 13,
μήτε τῶν ποιητῶν τῶν εὐδοκιμούν-
των μήτε τῶν σοφιστῶν μηδενὸς
οἷον δεῖ ἀπείρων ἔχειν, ἀλλὰ τῶν
μὲν ἀκροατὴς γίγνου, τῶν δὲ μαθητής. Xen. *Memorab.* IV. 2, 1,
γράμματα πολλὰ συνειλεγμένα ποιητῶν τε καὶ σοφιστῶν τῶν εὐδοκιμω-
τάτων.

For this use of ἄλλος cf. *Paneg.*
§ 26, τῇ ἄλλῃ κατασκευῇ, *Philip.*
§ 148, καὶ γὰρ ἐκείνων μᾶλλον ἀγαν-
ται τὴν ἧτταν τὴν ἐν Θερμοπύλαις ἢ
τὰς ἄλλας νίκας, Plato, *Gorg.*
473 C, τελετῶν καὶ τῶν ἄλλων ξένων,
Eur. *Ion*, 161 (after speaking of an
eagle), ὅδε τοὺς θυμέλας ἄλλος ἐρέσ-
σει κύκνος (*i. e.* 'another bird, a
swan,' 'a swan besides'). Just as in
these passages, so in that before us,

μανθάνειν, καὶ τῶν ἄλλων σοφιστῶν, εἴ τι χρήσιμον εἰρή-
52 κασιν, ἀναγιγνώσκειν. ὥσπερ γὰρ τὴν μέλιτταν ὁρῶμεν ἐφ'
ἅπαντα μὲν τὰ βλαστήματα καθιζάνουσαν, ἀφ' ἑκάστου δὲ
τὰ βέλτιστα λαμβάνουσαν, οὕτω δεῖ καὶ τοὺς παιδείας ὀρεγομένους μηδενὸς μὲν ἀπείρως ἔχειν, πανταχόθεν δὲ τὰ χρήσιμα συλλέγειν. μόλις γὰρ ἄν τις ἐκ ταύτης τῆς ἐπιμελείας c
τὰς τῆς φύσεως ἁμαρτίας ἐπικρατήσειεν.

the noun may be taken to be in a kind of apposition to the case of ἄλλοι that is used, so that τῶν ἄλλων σοφιστῶν = 'of the other class of persons, I mean the sophists.'

τῶν ἄλ. σοφ. εἴ-τι-χρήσιμον-εἰρήκασιν almost = τῶν ἄλ. σοφ. τὰ χρήσιμα, 'all the useful maxims of the sophists besides.' Cf. de Perm. § 105, οὐ δίκαιόν ἐστι μετέχειν, εἴ τι Τιμόθεοι πράντων μὴ κατώρθωσεν.

By the σοφισταί in the text are meant not only the celebrated teachers of the fifth cent. B.C., who laid claim to wisdom and taught it for money, but also such men as Solon, Chilo, Pittacus, Bias, Periander, Cleobulus, Thales (τῶν ἑπτὰ σοφιστῶν, de Perm. § 235), the seven wise men of Greece, whose traditionary or recorded maxims have in many cases been imitated by the writer of this Ep. Xen. Memorab. I. 6, 14, τοὺς θησαυροὺς τῶν πάλαι σοφῶν ἀνδρῶν οὓς ἐκεῖνοι κατέλιπον ἐν βιβλίοις γράφοντες. On the sophists see further, Pang. § 3-n., and § 82. n.

The poets referred to are probably those who left behind them moral and didactic poems; e.g. Hesiod, Theognis, Phocylides. These poets were too much neglected, says Isocr. ad Nicol. § 43, σημεῖον δ' ἄν τις ποιήσαιτο τὴν Ἡσιόδου καὶ Θεόγνιδος καὶ Φωκυλίδου ποίησιν· καὶ γὰρ τούτους φασὶ μὲν ἀρίστους γεγενῆσθαι συμβούλους τῷ βίῳ τῷ τῶν ἀνθρώπων,

ταῦτα δὲ λέγοντες αἱροῦνται συνδιατρίβειν ταῖς ἀλλήλων ἀνοίαις μᾶλλον ἢ ταῖς ἐκείνων ὑποθήκαις, κ.τ.λ. The gnomes, or 'brief sententious precepts' of the leading tragedians are also doubtless alluded to. ad Nicol. § 44, τῶν προεχόντων ποιητῶν τὰς καλουμένας γνώμας. Milton, Par. Reg. iv. 261 sqq.

ὥσπερ τὴν μέλιτταν κ.τ.λ.] The comparison is common; e.g. Lucretius, III. 11, Floriferis ut apes in saltibus omnia libant, Omnia nos itidem depascimur aurea dicta, cet. Seneca, Ep. 84, 5, Apes debemus imitari et quaecumque ex diversa lectione congessimus, separare, deinde adhibita ingenii nostri cura et facultate, in unum saporem varia illa libamenta confundere. Plutarch (περὶ τοῦ ἀκούειν, 41 F), δεῖ μιμεῖσθαι μὴ τὰς στρεφηλόκους ἀλλὰ τὰς μελίσσας, κ.τ.λ. and an elegant passage in St Basil the Great, (exhorting Christian youth to the study of human learning), ad adolesc. cap. lii. (v.), κατὰ πᾶσαν δὴ οὖν τῶν μελιττῶν τὴν εἰκόνα τῶν λόγων ὑμῖν μεθεκτέον, κ.τ.λ. q.v.

καθιζάνουσαν ‖ λαμβάνουσαν.] An instance of παρομοίωσις, to secure which a rare form καθιζανούσαν (found only in Aesch. Eum. 39), is used instead of a commoner word, e.g. καθιζομένην (v. Veitch, Gk. Vbs. s.v. ἱζάνω).

μόλις] = vix, et vix tamen. See paraphrase at § 44- n. 1.

ΙΣΟΚΡΑΤΟΥΣ ΠΑΝΗΓΥΡΙΚΟΣ.

ΥΠΟΘΕΣΙΣ ΙΣΟΚΡΑΤΟΥΣ.

Ὁ λόγος κατ᾽ ἐκείνους ἐγράφη τοὺς χρόνους, ὅτε Λακεδαιμόνιοι μὲν ἦρχον τῶν Ἑλλήνων, ἡμεῖς δὲ ταπεινῶς ἐπράττομεν. ἔστι δὲ τοὺς μὲν Ἕλληνας παρακαλῶν ἐπὶ τὴν τῶν βαρβάρων στρατείαν, Λακεδαιμονίοις δὲ περὶ τῆς ἡγεμονίας ἀμφισβητῶν. τοιαύτην δὲ τὴν ὑπόθεσιν ποιησάμενος ἀποφαίνω τὴν πόλιν ἁπάντων τῶν ὑπαρχόντων τοῖς Ἕλλησιν ἀγαθῶν αἰτίαν γεγενημένην. ἀφορισάμενος δὲ τὸν λόγον τὸν περὶ τῶν τοιούτων εὐεργεσιῶν καὶ βουλόμενος τὴν ἡγεμονίαν ἔτι σαφέστερον ἀποφαίνειν ὡς ἔστι τῆς πόλεως, ἐνθένδε ποθὲν ἐπιχειρῶ διδάσκειν περὶ τούτων, ὡς τῇ πόλει τιμᾶσθαι προσήκει πολὺ μᾶλλον ἐκ τῶν περὶ τὸν πόλεμον κινδύνων ἢ τῶν ἄλλων εὐεργεσιῶν.

[The above summary was written by Isocr. himself. (*De Perm.* §§ 57, 58. v. *Panig.* § 51. n.)].

(α΄.) Πολλάκις ἐθαύμασα τῶν τὰς πανηγύρεις συνα- 41
γαγόντων καὶ τοὺς γυμνικοὺς ἀγῶνας καταστησάντων, ὅτι

§§ 1—14. *Exordium.* 1, 2. Although the founders of these general assemblies have wrongly assigned the highest honours to physical and not to intellectual excellence, 3, 4, I nevertheless propose to address you on this occasion with a view to promote the unity of Greece, and to induce her to make war against Persia. Many have attempted this theme already; but have not treated it in an adequate manner. 5, 6. The times of crisis have not yet passed by, and the need of such an exhortation as I propose is still as imperative as ever. 7—10.

Further, the power of oratory is such that it can treat the same facts in many various ways; I may therefore fairly endeavour to outrival my predecessors, and, by this spirit of competition, aid in advancing the art of oratory. 11, 12. I address myself, not to those who wish me to descend to their low standard of rhetoric, but rather to those who will try me by the highest criterion, and will despise me if I express myself in an unworthy manner.

πολλάκις ἐθαύμασα κ.τ.λ.] Aristot. *Rhet.* III. 14, 2, alludes to this

τὰς μὲν τῶν σωμάτων εὐτυχίας οὕτω μεγάλων δωρεῶν
ἠξίωσαν, τοῖς δ' ὑπὲρ τῶν κοινῶν ἰδίᾳ πονήσασι καὶ τὰς
αὑτῶν ψυχὰς οὕτω παρασκευάσασιν ὥστε καὶ τοὺς ἄλλους
2 ὠφελεῖν δύνασθαι, τούτοις δ' οὐδεμίαν τιμὴν ἀπένειμαν ὧν b
εἰκὸς ἦν αὐτοὺς μᾶλλον ποιήσασθαι πρόνοιαν· τῶν μὲν γὰρ
ἀθλητῶν δὶς τοσαύτην ῥώμην λαβόντων οὐδὲν ἂν πλέον
γένοιτο τοῖς ἄλλοις, ἑνὸς δ' ἀνδρὸς εὖ φρονήσαντος ἅπαντες
ἂν ἀπολαύσειαν οἱ βουλόμενοι κοινωνεῖν τῆς ἐκείνου δια-
3 νοίας. οὐ μὴν ἐπὶ τούτοις ἀθυμήσας εἱλόμην ῥαθυμεῖν, ἀλλ'

exordium : λέγεται δὲ τὰ τῶν ἐπιδει-
κτικῶν προοίμια ἐξ ἐπαίνου ἢ ψόγου·
οἷαν Γοργίας μὲν ἐν τῷ Ὀλυμπικῷ
λόγῳ 'ὑπὸ πολλῶν ἄξιοι θαυμάζεσθαι,
ὦ ἄνδρες Ἕλληνες'· ἐπαινεῖ τοὺς τὰς
πανηγύρεις συνάγοντας· Ἰσοκράτης δὲ
ψέγει, ὅτι τὰς μὲν τῶν σωμάτων ἀρετὰς δωρεαῖς ἐτίμησαν, ταῖς δ' εὖ φρο-
νούσιν οὐδὲν ἄθλον ἐποίησαν, and in
III. 9, he quotes πολλάκις...καταστη-
σάντων as an instance of διῃρημένη
λέξιν.

θαύματα τῶν....συνάγ....ὅτι...]
One of the common constructions
of θαυμάζω is the gen. of the person
and the acc. of the thing. θαυμ.
τινός τι (e.g. Soph. Phil. 1362, καὶ
σοῦ δ' ἔγωγε θαυμάσαι ἔχω τόδε), but
this acc. of the thing appears often
as here in the form of an explanatory sentence, stating the cause of
wonder introduced by such a word
as ὅτι, ὅπου, ὅπως, or εἰ, e.g. Isocr.
Nicocl. § 3, θαυμάζω τῶν ταύτην τὴν
γνώμην ἐχόντων ὅπως οὐ καὶ τὸν
πλοῦτον κακῶς λέγουσω. Philip. § 42,
θαυμάζω τῶν ἡγουμένων ἀδύνατον
εἶναι πραχθῆναί τι τούτων, εἰ μήτ'
αὐτοὶ τυγχάνουσι, κ.τ.λ., and Paneg.
§ 170.

πανηγύρεις] Alludes to the Panhellenic assemblies at the Olympic,
Pythian, Nemean, and Isthmian
games, and also to special assemblies like the Attic festival of the
Panathenaea. Contests both of physical and intellectual prowess were
instituted on these occasions, but
the former kind of excellence was

naturally more popular, and met
with greater encouragement than the
latter. In the Panathenaic oration,
§ 135, Isocr. speaks (in his old age)
with some little scorn of 'those who
in the general assemblies indulge in
vituperation; or, if they refrain from
such madness, bestow praise on the
most trifling objects, and on the most
lawless men.' During some of these
intellectual contests the greater part
of the audience went to sleep (Panath. § 263, ἐν τοῖς ὄχλοις τοῖς πανη-
γυρικοῖς, ἐν οἷς πλείους εἰσὶν οἱ καθεύ-
δοντες τῶν ἀκροωμένων), v. § 45. n.

τὰς μὲν τῶν σωμάτων κ.τ.λ.] Cf.
Epp. § 5, θαυμάζω δ' ὅσοι τῶν
πόλεων μείζονων δωρεῶν ἀξιοῦσι τοὺς
ἐν τοῖς γυμνικοῖς ἀγῶσι κατορθοῦντας
μᾶλλον ἢ τοὺς τῇ φρονήσει καὶ τῇ
φιλοσοφίᾳ τι τῶν χρησίμων εὑρίσκον-
ται, κ.τ.λ.

δωρεῶν.] On δωρεά)(δῶρα cf. ad
Dem. § 2. n.

τούτοις δ'] = 'to these men, I
say.' δέ in apodosis: this usage is,
in Attic prose, frequently found after
demonstrative adverbs and pro-
nouns, cf. § 98, ἃ δ' ἐστὶν ἴδια...ταῦτα
δέ, § 176, ἃ δέ...ταῦτα δέ, Areop.
§ 47, παρ' οἷς μὲν γάρ...παρὰ τούτοις
μέν...ὅπου δέ...ἐνταῦθα δέ... Thuc.
II. 46, ἆθλα γὰρ οἷς κεῖται ἀρετῆς
μέγιστα, τοῖς δὲ καὶ ἄνδρες ἄριστοι
πολιτεύουσι. See also Madv. Synt.
§ 188, R. 6 (where, for the misprint
Isocr. Paneg. 71, read Isocr. de Perm.
71).

ἱκανὸν νομίσας ἆθλον ἔσεσθαί μοι τὴν δόξαν τὴν ἀπ᾿ αὐτοῦ
τοῦ λόγου γενησομένην ἥκω συμβουλεύσων περί τε τοῦ
πολέμου τοῦ πρὸς τοὺς βαρβάρους καὶ τῆς ὁμονοίας τῆς
πρὸς ἡμᾶς αὐτούς, οὐκ ἀγνοῶν, ὅτι πολλοὶ τῶν προσποιη- c

3. **βάρβαροι.**] Constantly contrasted with Ἕλληνες, and meaning those who could not speak Greek. The word is onomatopoeic, the sound answers to the sense (cf. βαββάζω, βαμβαλίζω, Heb. 'Babel,' Eng. 'babble,' and Sanskrit, 'varvara' =jabberer), and represents the apparently incoherent and rapid utterance of those whose language the hearer cannot understand. Cf. e.g. Aesch. Ag. 1051 [1 Corinth. xiv. 11, ἐὰν οὖν μὴ εἰδῶ τὴν δύναμιν τῆς φωνῆς, ἔσομαι τῷ λαλοῦντι βάρβαρος· καὶ ὁ λαλῶν ἐν ἐμοὶ βάρβαρος].

τῶν πρ. εἶναι σοφιστῶν.] Alludes especially to Gorgias and his λόγος Ὀλυμπικός, the subject of which was similar to that of the Paneg. of Isocr. (Philostrat. Epist. 13).

The word σοφιστής is one of a large class of words derived from verbs ending in -ίζω. Cf. γραμματιστής, καλλωπιστής, ἀνδραποδιστής, Λακωνιστής. These, and similar words, generally denote an assumed character or profession. Σοφός=a really wise man; σοφιστής=one who lays claim to wisdom, 'a professor' of wisdom; hence (as this claim might often be unwarranted)=a mere professor of wisdom, who had no real right to the name.

The usage of the word in Isocr. is indicated by the following passages: Hel. § 9, τοὺς ἀμφισβητοῦντας τοῦ φρονεῖν καὶ φάσκοντας εἶναι σοφιστὰς οὐκ ἐν τοῖς ἠμελημένοις ὑπὸ τῶν ἄλλων, ἀλλ᾿ ἐν οἷς ἅπαντες εἰσὶν ἀνταγωνισταί, προσῆκει διαφέρειν καὶ κρείττους εἶναι τῶν ἰδιωτῶν, Panath. § 5 (Isocr. speaking of himself), ὑπὸ τῶν σοφ. τῶν ἀδοκίμων καὶ πονηρῶν διαβαλλομένους, de Perm. § 313 (speaking of the Athenians of former days), τοὺς καλουμένους σοφιστὰς ἐθαύμαζον·...Σόλωνα τὸν πρῶτον τῶν πολιτῶν λαβόντα τὴν ἐπωνυ-

μίαν ταύτην, ib. § 235, Σόλων μὲν τῶν ἑπτὰ σοφιστῶν ἐκλήθη καὶ ταύτην ἔσχε τὴν ἐπωνυμίαν τὴν νῦν ἀτιμαζομένην καὶ κρινομένην παρ᾿ ὑμῖν, Περικλῆς δὲ δυοῖν (Anaxagoras and Damon) ἐγένετο μαθητής, ib. § 268, Empedocles, Ion, Alcmaeon, Parmenides, Melissus, and Gorgias, are mentioned as παλαιοὶ σοφισταί. The fragment κατὰ τῶν σοφιστῶν teems with indignation against those who laid claim to the title of σοφιστής without deserving it. The name carried an obnoxious meaning, and was therefore little used by those who had the best right to it. Isocr. shews some hesitation in applying the term directly to himself, but in several passages of the speech, de Permutatione, e.g. § 155, 157, he virtually acknowledges himself as such, and defends his profession. On the whole, then, we may conclude that in Isocr. the word is used in a twofold sense, to indicate (1) those who had a real claim to the title of wise men, (2) those who had not. The use of the word in a good sense prevailed until the time of Aristophanes; thus Herodotus gives this name to the 'seven wise men,' and to Pythagoras (I. 29, IV. 95). And Cratinus (the comic poet, 519—422 B.C.) gave the name to the poets of the school of Homer and Hesiod (v. ad Dem. § 51. n.). Not till the exhibition of the 'Clouds' of Aristophanes (in 423) was the name (so far as we can tell) used as a term of reproach, a meaning which it constantly bears in the pages of Plato, who applies it to Protagoras, Gorgias, Polus, Hippias, Prodicus, Thrasymachus, and others.

An estimate of the character of these sophists is beyond the limits of an ordinary note. It will be enough to refer to the famous 67th chapter

σαμένων εἶναι σοφιστῶν ἐπὶ τοῦτον τὸν λόγον ὥρμησαν, 4²
4 ἀλλ᾽ ἅμα μὲν ἐλπίζων τοσοῦτον διοίσειν ὥστε τοῖς ἄλλοις
μηδὲν πώποτε δοκεῖν εἰρῆσθαι περὶ αὐτῶν, ἅμα δὲ προ-
κρίνας τούτους καλλίστους εἶναι τῶν λόγων, οἵτινες περὶ
μεγίστων τυγχάνουσιν ὄντες καὶ τούς τε λέγοντας μάλιστ᾽
ἐπιδεικνύουσι καὶ τοὺς ἀκούοντας πλεῖστ᾽ ὠφελοῦσιν· ὧν εἷς
5 οὗτός ἐστιν. ἔπειτ᾽ οὐδ᾽ οἱ καιροί πω παρεληλύθασιν ὥστ᾽
ἤδη μάτην εἶναι τὸ μεμνῆσθαι περὶ τούτων. τότε γὰρ χρὴ
παύεσθαι λέγοντας, ὅταν ἢ τὰ πράγματα λάβῃ τέλος καὶ b

of Mr Grote's *Hist. of Greece*, with
the masterly criticisms of Mr Cope
(*Journ. of Class. and Sacred Philology*, Nos. 2, 5, 7, 9), and to quote
the following incisive statement of
the contrast between Mr Grote's
view and the popular representation
of the sophists. 'According to the
common notion, they were a sect;
according to him, they were a class
or profession. According to the
common view, they were the propa-
gators of demoralizing doctrines,
and of what from them are termed
"sophistical" argumentations. According to Mr Grote, they were the
regular teachers of Greek morality,
neither above nor below the standard
of the age. According to the common view, Socrates was the great
opponent of the Sophists, and Plato
his natural successor in the same
combat. According to Mr Grote,
Socrates was the great representative of the Sophists, distinguished
from them only by his higher emi-
nence, and by the peculiarity of his
life and teaching. *Quarterly Review*, No. 175.

4. ὥστε τοῖς ἄλλοις κ.τ.λ.] These
words may be best taken as follows:
ὥστε δοκεῖν μηδὲν πώποτ᾽ εἰρῆσθαι
τοῖς·ἄλλοις περὶ αὐτῶν, joining τοῖς
ἄλλοις not with δοκεῖν but with
εἰρῆσθαι. For the dat. of the agent
after a pass. verb, cf. Eur. *Hec.* 236,
σοὶ μὲν εἰρῆσθαι χρεών, | ἡμᾶς δ᾽ ἀκοῦ-
σαι, &c.—v. Jelf (Kühner), § 611 a.
τοῖς ἄλλοις=πολλοῖς τῶν πρωτ. εἶναι
σοφιστῶν. περὶ αὐτῶν = περὶ τοῦ

πολέμου...καὶ τῆς ὁμονοίας.
The above interpretation is supported by the general tone of the
context: also cf. § 12, οἷον παρὰ τοῖς
ἄλλοις οὐχ εὑρήσετε. Schn. however
explains τοῖς ἄλλοις of the audience
and takes it with δοκεῖν, on the
ground that the other sense would
more naturally be expressed thus:
τοσ. τῶν ἄλλων δι., ὥστε μηδὲν κ.τ.λ.

ὧν εἷς οὗτός ἐστιν.] Obs. the very
short clause terminating the long
sentence consisting of §§ 3, 4. For
a still more striking instance cf. the
exordium of the Panathenaic speech,
where an elaborate sentence of 17
lines closes with the words νῦν δ᾽ οὐδ᾽
ὁπωσοῦν τοῖς τοιούτοιν.

5. ἔπειτ᾽ οὐδ᾽ οἱ καιροί...] i.e. 'In
the next place, the times of crisis
have not yet passed away, so as
to render it vain to make mention
of these subjects.' Καιροί frequently
in pl.='times of crisis,' 'times of
emergency.' (On the deriv. cf. ad
Dem. § 2).—ὥστ᾽ ἤδη κ.τ.λ. lit. 'So
that to make mention of them is by
this time in vain.' τὸ μεμνῆσθαι is
the subj.—μάτην εἶναι is here used
where μάταιον εἶναι might have been
expected. Cf. § 16, πόρρω...ἐστί, *Archid.* § 42, ἀρχαῖα καὶ πόρρω, Plato
Protag. 325 B, σκέψαι ὡς θαυμασίως
γίγνονται οἱ ἀγαθοί (='think what
strange people you make of your
virtuous men'). Cic. *ad Att.* 1. 7,
apud matrem recte est.

λέγοντας, ὅταν.] The old reading was λέγοντα ὅταν. To remove
the *hiatus*, Wolf proposed λέγονται,

μηκέτι δέῃ βουλεύεσθαι περὶ αὐτῶν, ἢ τὸν λόγον ἴδῃ τις
ἔχοντα πέρας, ὥστε μηδεμίαν λελεῖφθαι τοῖς ἄλλοις ὑπερ-
6 βολήν. ἕως δ' ἂν τὰ μὲν ὁμοίως ὥσπερ πρότερον φέρηται,
τὰ δ' εἰρημένα φαύλως ἔχοντα τυγχάνῃ, πῶς οὐ χρὴ σκοπεῖν
καὶ φιλοσοφεῖν τοῦτον τὸν λόγον, ὃς ἦν κατορθωθῇ, καὶ τοῦ
πολέμου τοῦ πρὸς ἀλλήλους καὶ τῆς ταραχῆς τῆς παρούσης c
7 καὶ τῶν μεγίστων κακῶν ἡμᾶς ἀπαλλάξει; πρὸς δὲ τούτοις,
εἰ μὲν μηδαμῶς ἄλλως οἷόν τ' ἦν δηλοῦν τὰς αὐτὰς πράξεις
ἀλλ' ἢ διὰ μιᾶς ἰδέας, εἶχεν ἄν τις ὑπολαβεῖν, ὡς περίεργον

a reading which has since been confirmed by the Cod. Urbinas and
Cod. Ambrosianus and is now universally accepted.—The two clauses
ἢ τὰ πράγματα κ.τ.λ, ἢ τὸν λόγον
κ.τ.λ. are completely parallel with
one another : thus λαμβάνειν τέλος
and ἔχειν πέρας are almost identical
in meaning, and are used only for
the sake of variety in expression.
Cf. λέγειν and εἰπεῖν, §§ 10, 11.

περὶ αὐτῶν.] The rule, by which
the hiatus is avoided in Isocrates, is
not universal, and this is one of the
exceptions. For other cases see
§ 143. n.—In Comic verse περὶ is
often allowed to stand before a vowel,
which either begins the next word,
or (as in περιιδεῖν) is part of the same
word. In Tragic verse this license
is not allowed. Cf. Porson on Eur.
Med. 284.

6. ἕως δ' ἂν κ.τ.λ.] '...But so
long as the events take their course
in like manner as before, and the
things said of them are all the time
poorly expressed, is it not certainly
our duty to scan and to study this
theme of oratory, which, if rightly
established, will rescue us from our
mutual warfare, from our present
confusion, and from the greatest ca-
lamities?'

πῶς οὐ χρή.] Lit. 'how is it not
right?' not in the sense 'in what special respect is it wrong?' but 'how
can it help being right?' The literal
translation is seldom adequate.

σκοπεῖν καὶ φιλοσοφεῖν.] φιλ. is
often applied by Isocr. to the me-

thodical and earnest pursuit of any
object (esp. oratory, cf. § 186, ποιήσει
καὶ φιλοσοφήσει, § 10. n.), *de Perm.*
121, τοῦτ' ἐφιλοσόφει καὶ τοῦτ' ἔ-
πραττεν ὅπως μηδεμία τῶν πόλεων αὐτῶν φοβήσεται, *de Pace*, 5, μελετᾶν
καὶ φιλοσοφεῖν, 116, φιλοσοφήσετε
καὶ σκέψεσθε, *Epp.* 7, 3, ζητεῖν καὶ
φιλοσοφεῖν, *Panath.* 11, φιλοσοφεῖν
καὶ ποιεῖν καὶ γράφειν ἃ διανοηθείην.
In the curious speech written by
Lysias ὑπὲρ τοῦ ἀδυνάτου (§ 10), his
disabled client says, πάντας οἶμαι τοὺς
ἔχοντάς τι δυστύχημα τοιοῦτο μαστεύ-
ειν τινὰ ζητεῖν καὶ τοῦτο φιλοσοφεῖν
ὅπως ὡς ἀλυπότατα μεταχειριοῦνται
τὸ συμβεβηκὸς πάθος. In all these
passages, the context precludes 'philosophy' in the highest sense of
the term.—The two verbs σκοπεῖν κ.
φιλ. mean almost the same as φιλο-
σόφωι σκοπεῖν. Cf. *de Pace*, 128,
διεξιέναι καὶ θρηνεῖν, Dem. *Aristocr.*
ἐπαινῶν καὶ διεξιὼν τὸν Κερσοβλέπτην.

κατορθωθῇ.] κατορθοῦν is used in
two senses, which must be carefully
distinguished. (1) 'to succeed' (intrans.), (2) 'to do a thing on right
principles' (trans. as here). Wherever the idea of success is sharply
contrasted with the idea of failure,
κατορθοῦν is generally used; when
there is no such contrast, κατορθοῦ-
σθαι, e.g. *Phil.* 35, *Areop.* 72, κατορθοῦν)(ἐξαμαρτάνειν, *Phil.* 68, *Archid.*
5, κ.)(διαμαρτάνειν, ib. 48, μὴ κ.)(πι-
κρῶ, and below, §§ 48, 69, 97, 124.
Arist. *Eth.* II. 6. 13, 14.

7. ἀλλ' ἤ...] = except. This
formula occurs only after an actual

ἐστι τὸν αὐτὸν τρόπον ἐκείνοις λέγοντα πάλιν ἐνοχλεῖν τοῖς
8 ἀκούουσιν· ἐπειδὴ δ᾽ οἱ λόγοι τοιαύτην ἔχουσι τὴν φύσιν,
ὥσθ᾽ οἷόν τ᾽ εἶναι περὶ τῶν αὐτῶν πολλαχῶς ἐξηγήσασθαι,
καὶ τά τε μεγάλα ταπεινὰ ποιῆσαι καὶ τοῖς μικροῖς μέγεθος d
περιθεῖναι, καὶ τά τε παλαιὰ καινῶς διελθεῖν καὶ περὶ τῶν
νεωστὶ γεγενημένων ἀρχαίως εἰπεῖν, οὐκέτι φευκτέον ταῦτ᾽
ἐστι, περὶ ὧν ἕτεροι πρότερον εἰρήκασιν, ἀλλ᾽ ἄμεινον ἐκεί-

or implied negative. It is doubtful whether it stands for (1) ἀλλὰ ἤ or (2) ἄλλο ἤ. Of these explanations (1) is adopted by Riddell (*Digest of Platonic Idioms*, § 148, ἀλλὰ states flatly the exception to the preceding negative; ἤ allows the negative statement to revive, subject to this exception (lion alone), (2) by Madvig, *Synt.* § 91, 2.—In this passage, where ἄλλως occurs in the first part of the sentence, (1) seems preferable. The construction may then be explained as a blending of two methods of expression, 1. μηδαμῶς ἄλλως...ἀλλὰ διὰ μιᾶς ἰδέας, and 2. μηδαμῶς ἄλλως...ἢ διὰ μιᾶς ἰδέας. In passages where ἄλλως, ἄλλως, &c. do *not* precede the formula, (2) is a satisfactory explanation.—See also Jelf (Kühner), *Gk. Gram.* § 773, 1—3.

8. Trans. 'but, whereas such is the nature of oratory that it is possible to describe the same things in many ways, not only to make great things humble and to crown little things with greatness, but also to relate things olden in a style that is new, and to speak of events that have lately happened in a style that is antique, we must no longer shrink from a subject, on which others have spoken before, but endeavour to speak better than they.'

οἱ λόγοι κ.τ.λ.] In the *Phaedrus* of Plato (written before the *Paneg.*) occurs the following passage, p. 267 A, Τισίαν δὲ Γοργίαν τε ἐάσομεν εὕδειν, οἳ πρὸ τῶν ἀληθῶν τὰ εἰκότα εἶδον ὡς τιμητέα μᾶλλον, τά τε αὖ σμικρὰ μεγάλα καὶ τὰ μεγάλα σμικρὰ φαίνεσθαι ποιοῦσι διὰ ῥώμην λόγου, καινά τε ἀρχαίως τά τ᾽ ἐναντία καινῶς,

συντομίαν τε λόγων καὶ ἄπειρα μήκη περὶ πάντων ἀνεῦρον; Hence it is probable that Isocr. is quoting a current formula in which Gorgias, Tisias, or some other sophist may have expressed his views on the power of oratory. That formula is here simply corroborated and sanctioned, and there is therefore no reason for placing implicit trust in those writers who cite the following apophthegm, apparently as an original remark of Isocr., ἐρομένου τινὸς αὐτόν, τί ῥητορική, εἶπεν, τά τε μικρὰ μεγάλα, τὰ δὲ μεγάλα μικρὰ ποιεῖν (*Pseudo-plutarch*, 838 F, *Hermogenes*, III. p. 363, Walz). Longinus(?), *de Sublim.* § 38, quotes the passage before us almost *verbatim* and criticises it, as follows: ὁ γοῦν Ἰσοκράτης, οὐκ οἶδ᾽ ὅπως, παιδὸς πρᾶγμα ἔπαθεν, διὰ τὴν τοῦ πάντα αὐξητικῶς ἐθέλειν λέγειν φιλοτιμίαν... οὐκοῦν, φησί τις, Ἰσόκρατες, οὕτω μέλλεις καὶ τὰ περὶ Λακεδαιμονίων καὶ Ἀθηναίων ἐναλλάττειν; σχεδὸν γὰρ τὸ τῶν λόγων ἐγκώμιον ἀπιστίας τῆς καθ᾽ αὑτοῦ τοῖς ἀκούουσι παράγγελμα καὶ προοίμιον ἐξέθηκε.

τὰ παλαιά.] (παλαι) 'things that have long been,' opp. to τὰ νεωστὶ γεγενημένα.—ἀρχαίως]καινῶς, 'in an antique or old-fashioned style')('in a novel style.' παλαιὸς=vetus; ἀρχαῖος=antiquus.

ἀρχαίως ἔνιοι μέν φασι σημαίνειν ἀρχαιοτρόπως, τουτέστιν ἀρχαιότεροι ὀνόμασι χρῆσθαι (Harpocration).

ἄμεινον — φευκτέον.] In the speech, *de Perm.* § 61, Isocr., speaking of the *Paneg.*, flatters himself that he has succeeded in this attempt to outrival his competitors, 'so that those who on former occasions wrote

9 νων εἰπεῖν πειρατέον. αἱ μὲν γὰρ πράξεις αἱ προγεγενη-
μέναι κοιναὶ πᾶσιν ἡμῖν κατελείφθησαν, τὸ δ᾽ ἐν καιρῷ
ταύταις καταχρήσασθαι καὶ τὰ προσήκοντα περὶ ἑκάστης
ἐνθυμηθῆναι καὶ τοῖς ὀνόμασιν εὖ διαθέσθαι τῶν εὖ φρο-
10 νούντων ἴδιόν ἐστιν. ἡγοῦμαι δ᾽ οὕτως ἂν μεγίστην ἐπίδοσιν
λαμβάνειν καὶ τὰς ἄλλας τέχνας καὶ τὴν περὶ τοὺς λόγους c
φιλοσοφίαν, εἴ τις θαυμάζοι καὶ τιμῴη μὴ τοὺς πρώτους τῶν
ἔργων ἀρχομένους, ἀλλὰ τοὺς ἄρισθ᾽ ἕκαστον αὐτῶν ἐξεργ-
αζομένους, μηδὲ τοὺς περὶ τούτων ζητοῦντας λέγειν, περὶ 43
ὧν μηδεὶς πρότερον εἴρηκεν, ἀλλὰ τοὺς οὕτως ἐπισταμένους
εἰπεῖν, ὡς οὐδεὶς ἂν ἄλλος δύναιτο.

11   (β΄.) Καίτοι τινὲς ἐπιτιμῶσι τῶν λόγων τοῖς ὑπὲρ τοὺς
ἰδιώτας ἔχουσι καὶ λίαν ἀπηκριβωμένοις, καὶ τοσοῦτον διη-

on this subject have destroyed all their speeches, in very shame for what they had said.'

9. τὰ πρ....ἐνθυμηθῆναι...διαθέσθαι.] ἐνθυμηθῆναι κ.τ.λ. corresponds in general sense to the technical term *inventio*, διαθέσθαι, κ.τ.λ. to *dispositio*. Cf. Cic. *Orator*, XIV. § 43, *Tria videnda sunt oratori, quid dicat* (=inventio) *et quo quidque loco* (=dispositio) *et quomodo* (=elocutio).

10. φιλοσοφίαν.] In Isocr. the word φιλοσοφία is used in a peculiar sense. It indicates a combination of ἡ πολιτικὴ and ἡ ῥητορική, in which the latter generally predominates. The words φιλοσοφία, φιλοσοφεῖν, φιλόσοφος are scattered broadcast over most of his writings, especially the speech *de Perm.* The following passages will indicate their meaning. *Hel.* § 66, χρὴ...τοὺς φιλοσόφους πειρᾶσθαι τι λέγειν περὶ αὐτῆς (='Ελένης). *Evag.* § 8, αἱ περὶ τὴν φ. ὄντες (identical with οἱ περὶ τοὺς λόγους in § 10). *Phil.* § 84, ὁ λόγος ὁ πανηγυρικός, ὁ τοὺς ἄλλους τοὺς περὶ τὴν φ. διατρίβοντας εὐπορωτέρους ποιήσας, ἐμοὶ πολλὴν ἀπορίαν παρέσχηκεν. *de Perm.* passim, especially § 270—280, τὴν καλουμένην ὑπό τινων φ. οὐκ εἶναι φημί, κ.τ.λ. § 195. § 50,

τῆς ἐμῆς εἴτε βούλεσθε καλεῖν δυνάμεων εἴτε φιλοσοφίας εἴτε διατριβῆς. *Panath.* § 209, τοσοῦτον ἀπολελειμμένοι τῆς κοινῆς παιδείας καὶ φιλοσοφίας εἰσὶν (οἱ Λακεδαιμόνιοι) ὥστ᾽ οὐδὲ γράμματα μανθάνουσιν.—See also Mr Cope's article in *J. of Class. and Sacr. Philol.* (No. 5, p. 150. n.) and Dr Thompson's ed. of the *Phaedrus* (Appendix II. On the Philosophy of Isocr.); *ad Dem.* § 4, *Paneg.* § 47. n.

λέγων...εἰπεῖν.] Cf. end of § 11, and *ad Dem.* § 41. n.

11. καίτοι, κ.τ.λ.] Trans. 'And yet there are some who find fault with those speeches which are beyond the range of ordinary hearers, and are excessively elaborated; and so far have they gone wrong that they examine speeches wrought in a surpassing manner by the same standard as the contests concerning private contracts, just as if both kinds of speeches ought to be alike, and not rather, in the latter case, framed in the language of plainness, in the former case, in the language of display; or as if they themselves saw clearly the true mean,' and he that knows how to speak with elaboration could not also express himself with simplicity.'

ὑπὲρ τ. ἰδ. ἔχουσι.] These words

μαρτήκασιν, ὥστε τοὺς πρὸς ὑπερβολὴν πεποιημένους πρὸς
τοὺς ἀγῶνας τοὺς περὶ τῶν ἰδίων συμβολαίων σκοποῦσιν,
ὥσπερ ὁμοίως δέον ἀμφοτέρους ἔχειν, ἀλλ' οὐ τοὺς μὲν
ἀφελῶς, τοὺς δ' ἐπιδεικτικῶς, ἡ σφᾶς μὲν διορῶντας τὰς b

are not to be taken as an instance
of *tmesis*, as if they were equivalent
to τοῖς ὑπερέχουσι τοὺς ἰδιώτας. This
formula would require the gen., and
it is therefore better to take ἔχουσι
absolutely. Coray's scholium is
brief and satisfactory; τοῖς ἰδεῖν
ὑπὲρ τοὺς ἰδιώτας. τοῖς μὴ ἰδιωτικῶς
ἔχουσιν, καθὰ λέγεται καλῶς ἡ κακῶς
ἔχειν· οὐ γὰρ ἐστι κατὰ τμῆσιν τὸ
λεγόμενον ... ὥς τινες (Morus and
Spohn) ὑπέλαβον.

11. Ἰδιώτας.] Cf. § 44. n.

πρὸς τοὺς ἀγ. ...σκοποῦσι.] For
this use of πρὸς (implying the standard of reference by which anything
is estimated) cf. § 76, οὐδὲ πρὸς ἀργύριον τὴν εὐδαιμονίαν ἔκρινον, Dem.
Lept. § 13, τὸ λυσιτελέστατον πρὸς
ἀργύριον σκοποῦσι.

περὶ τῶν ἰδίων συμβολαίων.] For
equally scornful allusions to forensic
speeches cf. *Panath.* § 11, where
Isocr. says of himself, ἐπὶ τὸ φιλοσοφεῖν καὶ ποιεῖν καὶ γράφειν, ἃ
διανοηθείην, κατέφυγον, οὐ περὶ μικρῶν τὴν προαίρεσιν ποιούμενος, οὐδὲ
περὶ τῶν ἰδίων συμβολαίων οὐδὲ
περὶ ὧν ἄλλοι τινὲς ληρούσιν, ἀλλὰ
περὶ τῶν Ἑλληνικῶν καὶ βασιλικῶν
καὶ πολιτικῶν πραγμάτων, δι' ἃ προσήκειν ᾤμην μοι τοσούτῳ μᾶλλον
τιμᾶσθαι τὸ ἐπὶ τὸ βῆμα παριόντων,
ὅσῳ περ περὶ μειζόνων καὶ καλλιόνων
ἢ 'κεῖνοι τοὺς λόγους ἐποιούμην. ὧν
οὐδὲ ἡμῖν ἀποβέβηκεν, and *de Perm.*
§ 2, 3, ἐγὼ γὰρ εἰδὼς ἐνίους τῶν σοφιστῶν βλασφημοῦντας περὶ τῆς ἐμῆς
διατριβῆς καὶ λέγοντας, ὡς ἐστι περὶ
δικογραφίας, καὶ παραπλήσιον ποιοῦνται, ὥσπερ ἂν εἴ τις Φειδίαν τὸν τὸ
τῆ' Ἀθηνᾶς ἕδος ἐργασάμενον τολμῴη
καλεῖν κοροπλάθον, ἢ Ζεῦξιν καὶ Παρ-
ράσιον τὴν αὐτὴν ἔχειν φαίη τέχνην
τοῖς τὰ πινάκια γράφουσιν, ὅμως οὐδὲ
πώποτε τὴν μικρολογίαν ταύτην ἠμυ-
νάμην αὐτῶν, ἡγούμενος τὰς μὲν ἐπὶ-

των φλυαρίας οὐδεμίαν δύναμιν ἔχειν,
αὐτὸν δὲ πᾶσι τοῦτο πεποιηκέναι φα-
νερόν, ὅτι προήρημαι καὶ λέγειν καὶ
γράφειν οὐ περὶ τῶν ἰδίων συμβολαίων
ἀλλ' ὑπὲρ τηλικούτων τὸ μέγεθος καὶ
τοιούτων πραγμάτων, ὑπὲρ ὧν οὐδεὶς
ἂν ἄλλος ἐπιχειρήσειε πλὴν τῶν ἐμοὶ
πεπλησιακότων ἢ τῶν τούτοις μιμεῖσθαι βουλομένων.

A curious commentary on these
passages is contained in the acknowledged fact that the forensic speeches
of Isocr. are, in many respects, the
best that he wrote.

ὥσπερ...] = *quasi, quasi vero*. The
ironical force of this word extends
not only over its own clause, but
also over the whole of the latter
part of the sentence, σφᾶς μὲν διορῶντας—εἰπεῖν. For the *acc. absolute*
after ὥσπερ cf. § 63, ὥσπερ...ὄντας,
and see Madv. *Synt.* § 181. The
Latin idiom corresponding to ὥσπερ
...ἀλλ' οὐ... may be seen in Cic. *pro
Rosc. Am.* § 92, Quasi nunc id aga-
tur, quis ex tanta multitudine occi-
derit, ac non (= ac non potius) hoc
quaeratur, &c.

ἀφελῶς.] The old reading was
ἀσφαλῶς, which implied a distinction between the cautious and solid
style of forensic oratory, and the
ornate language of speeches in which
display was the main object. This
sense is not quite satisfactory, as the
context demands a more decided contrast to that surpassing elaboration
of the λόγοι ἐπιδεικτικοί, which is involved in the words πρὸς ὑπερβολὴν
πεποιημένοι and ἀκριβῶς λέγειν. This
contrast is supplied by ἀφελῶς,
'plainly,' 'simply,' an emendation
first proposed by Valckenaer, and
supported strongly by Cobet (*nov.
lat.* 135, 6), who gives instances
of a similar confusion in MSS. between ἀσφάλεια and ἀφέλεια, and is

μετριότητας, τὸν δ' ἀκριβῶς ἐπιστάμενον λέγειν ἁπλῶς
12 οὐκ ἂν δυνάμενον εἰπεῖν. οὗτοι μὲν οὖν οὐ λελήθασιν, ὅτι

lastly confirmed by Hirschig (*Annot. crit. in comic.* p. 38, quoted by Schn.), who cites a scholium on *Antop.* § 46, where these words are quoted with ἀφελῶν and not ἀσφαλῶν. Bens. and BS retain ἀσφαλῶς.

ἐπιδεικτικόν.] The Greek writers on Rhetoric divided all orations into three classes: (1) 'deliberative or hortative,' (2) 'forensic or judicial,' (3) 'declamatory or show-speeches' (see esp. Arist. *Rhet.* I. 3, ἐξ ἀνάγκης ἂν εἴη τρία γένη τῶν λόγων τῶν ῥητορικῶν, συμβουλευτικόν, δικανικόν, ἐπιδεικτικόν. συμβουλῆι δὲ τὸ μὲν προτροπή, τὸ δὲ ἀποτροπή.. δίκης δὲ τὸ μὲν κατηγορία, τὸ δὲ ἀπολογία...ἐπιδεικτικοῦ δὲ τὸ μὲν ἔπαινος, τὸ δὲ ψόγος).

μετριότητας.] 'The mean.' [*Das rechte maass.* Morus, Schn., Rauchenst. &c.] Isocr. is speaking in bitter scorn and irony of his inappreciative critics. 'As if *they*, forsooth, saw clearly the true mean,—as if *they* were competent judges whether a speech was excessively elaborated, or excessively plain, and as if one who, like Isocrates, could speak with highly artificial grace could not also, if need were, condescend to speak with artless simplicity.' This, I believe, is the general meaning of the passage. μετριότητες is here used in the good sense. Cf. Thuc. II. 35, ἃ χαλεπὸν τὸ μετρίως εἰπεῖν, κ.τ.λ., Isocr. *ad Nicocl.* § 33, κράτιστον μὲν γάρ τῆς ἀρμῆς τῶν καιρῶν τυγχάνειν, ἐπειδὴ δὲ δυσκαταμάθητοί εἰσιν, ἐλλείπειν αἱροῦ καὶ μὴ πλεονάζειν· al γάρ μετριότητες μᾶλλον ἐν ταῖς ἐνδείαις ἢ ἐν ταῖς ὑπερβολαῖς ἔνεισιν, Antop. § 4, σωφροσύνη κ. πολλή μετριότης, de Perm. § 296, φωνῆι κουφότητα καὶ μετριότητα κ. τὴν ἄλλην εὐτραπελίαν, Epp. 3, § 4, πρὸς ἄλλο τι τῶν δεόντων ἀπλήστως ἔχειν οὐ καλὸν, al γάρ μετριότητες παρὰ τοῖς πολλοῖς (*i. e.* 'the majority of mankind') εὐδοκιμοῦσι, κ.τ.λ. These are, to the best of my belief, all the pas-

sages in which Isocr. uses the word; and, in every case, it is used in a good sense. The version of Wieland, (*Mittelmässigkeit*) and that of a recent editor, 'while they themselves see through the *moderate effusions*,' are therefore, I think, contrary to the usage of our author.

Observe the use of the plural μετριότητας. The fundamental idea of an abstract term is inconsistent with the pl. number; but a frequent departure from this rule is a leading characteristic of Isocr. The following are the principal instances: μετριότητες, χαλεπότητες, καινότητες, ἰσότητες, ταπεινότητες, λαμπρότητες, πραότητες, σεμνότητες, ἀληθείαι, αὐθάδειαι, ἐπιφάνειαι, ἔνδειαι, ἀργίαι, πενίαι, πλοῦτα, and φιλανθρωπίαι. For the comparatively rare use of the pl. abstr. in other authors, see Jelf (Kühner), *Gk. Gr.* § 355. Cf. Zumpt, *Lat. Gr.* § 61.

ἀκριβῶς (ἀπλῶς.] Elaborately)(simply. The sense 'loosely,' 'superficially,' given to ἀπλῶς in this passage in Lidd. and Sc. does not suit the context. Cf. *Phil.* § 28, ἀπλῶς)(ταῖς περὶ τὴν λέξιν εὐρυθμίαις κ. ποικιλίαις, § 46, μήτε κατὰ τ' ἄσιν ἀπλῶν μήτε λίαν ἀκριβῶν. Antop. § 41.

ἐπιστάμενον λέγειν ‖ δυνάμενον εἰπεῖν.] λέγειν and εἰπεῖν are almost convertible terms in Isocr., and no contrast between 'arguing acutely and *speaking* with simplicity' is here intended. In § 10 we have just had ἐπιστάμενον εἰπεῖν, and the collocations δυνάμενος λέγειν and δυνάμενος εἰπεῖν are both used several times in Isocr. without any appreciable distinction. *Ad Dem.* § 41. n.

εἰπεῖν is necessary to complete the parallelism of the sentence, in spite of the severe dictum of Cobet (*nov. lect.* 136): 'ne haec insulsa et pueriliter dicta et composita videantur, expunge ultimum vocabulum εἰπεῖν, quod nemo nostrum, nedum Isocrates, in tali re unquam addidisset.'

τούτους ἐπαινοῦσιν, ὧν ἐγγὺς αὐτοὶ τυγχάνουσιν ὄντες.
ἐμοὶ δ' οὐδὲν πρὸς τοὺς τοιούτους, ἀλλὰ πρὸς ἐκείνους ἐστί,
τοὺς οὐδὲν ἀποδεξομένους τῶν εἰκῇ λεγομένων, ἀλλὰ δυσχε-
ρανοῦντας, καὶ ζητήσοντας ἰδεῖν τι τοιοῦτον ἐν τοῖς ἐμοῖς,
οἷον παρὰ τοῖς ἄλλοις οὐχ εὑρήσουσιν. πρὸς οὓς ἔτι μικρὸν c
ὑπὲρ ἐμαυτοῦ θρασυνάμενος, ἤδη περὶ τοῦ πράγματος ποιή-
13 σομαι τοὺς λόγους. τοὺς μὲν γὰρ ἄλλους ἐν τοῖς προοιμίοις
ὁρῶ καταπραΰνοντας τοὺς ἀκροατὰς καὶ προφασιζομένους
ὑπὲρ τῶν μελλόντων ῥηθήσεσθαι, καὶ λέγοντας τοὺς μὲν ὡς
ἐξ ὑπογυίου γέγονεν αὐτοῖς ἡ παρασκευή, τοὺς δ' ὡς χαλεπόν ἐστιν ἴσους τοὺς λόγους τῷ μεγέθει τῶν ἔργων ἐξευρεῖν.
14 ἐγὼ δ' ἢν μὴ καὶ τοῦ πράγματος ἀξίως εἴπω καὶ τῆς δόξης d

The best commentary on τὸν δ' ἀκριβῶς—εἰπεῖν is Isocr. de Perm. § 49.

12. οὐ λελήθασιν, κ.τ.λ.] =δῆλοί εἰσιν ἐπαινοῦντες ταύτους τοὺς λόγους (or τοὺς ἀνθρώπους) ὧν, κ.τ.λ. For οὐ λελ. ὅτι see Madv. Synt. § 177, R. 2.

ἐμοὶ δ'—λόγους.] 'But *I* have nothing to do with such critics as these, but rather with those who will accept nothing that is said at random, but will fret beneath it, and expect to see something in *my* speeches of such a character as they will not find elsewhere (lit. among other *persons*). To *these* I shall make bold to say somewhat more on my own behalf, and then proceed to direct my words to the actual subject. I see other orators in the exordium of their speeches endeavouring to conciliate their audience ..and alleging, in some cases, that their preparation has been off-hand, in others, that it is difficult to find words equivalent to the magnitude of the deeds; but as for *myself*, if I speak not in a manner that is worthy, both of my subject and of my reputation, and of the time, not only which has been spent by me over my speech' [*i. e.* 10(?) years, see Introd. to *Paneg.*], 'but also the whole duration of my past life' [§§

years], 'I appeal to you to have no pardon for me but to deride and despise me.'

13. ῥηθήσεσθαι.] The distinction between the usage of the *fut.* and 3 *fut.* of *εἴρω* (in Attic writers) is this: the former is used chiefly in the forms ῥηθήσεσθαι, ῥηθήσόμενος, the latter is probably confined to the 3 p. sing. εἰρήσεται.—Veitch, *Gk. Verbs*, p. 205.

ἐξ ὑπογυίου]=ἐκ τοῦ παραχρῆμα. Cf. ἐκ χειρός, offhand (Polybius) ἐξ ἀ-προσδοκήτου, ἐξ ἑτοίμου, and (in § 147) ἐκ τοῦ φανεροῦ. Jelf (Kühner), *Gk. Gr.* § 523.—Cf. Plato, *Menex.* 235 c. ἐξ ὑπογυίου παντάπασιν ἡ αἵρεσις γέγονεν, ὥστε ἴσως ἀναγκασθήσεται ὁ λέγων ὥσπερ αὐτοσχεδιάζειν.—In *Evag.* § 81, we find τὸ ὑπογυιότα-τον)(τὸ παλαιόν, *Plataic.* § 17, τὸν πόλεμον τὸν ὑπογυιότατον (most recent), and *Epp.* 6, § 3, ὑπογυίου μοι τῆς τελευτῆς οὔσης (=at hand).

ὡς χαλεπόν κ.τ.λ.] Isocr. elsewhere uses this very plea himself: *Panath.* § 36—38, οὐκ ἀγνοῶ δ' ἡλίκος ὢν (an. aet. 94) ὅσον ἔργον ἐπίσταμαι τὸ μέγεθος, ἀλλ' ἀκριβῶς εἰδὼς καὶ πολλάκις εἰρηκώς, ὅτι τὰ μὲν μικρὰ τῶν πραγμάτων ῥάδιον τοῖς λόγοις αὐξῆσαι, τοῖς δ' ὑπερβάλλουσι τῶν ἔργων καὶ τῷ μεγέθει καὶ τῷ κάλλει χαλεπὸν ἐξισῶσαι τοὺς ἐπαίνους, κ.τ.λ.

τῆς ἐμαυτοῦ καὶ τοῦ χρόνου, μὴ μόνον τοῦ περὶ τὸν λόγον
ἡμῖν διατριφθέντος ἀλλὰ καὶ σύμπαντος οὗ βεβίωκα, παρα-
κελεύομαι μηδεμίαν συγγνώμην ἔχειν ἀλλὰ καταγελᾶν καὶ
καταφρονεῖν· οὐδὲν γὰρ ὅ τι τῶν τοιούτων οὐκ ἄξιός εἰμι
πάσχειν, εἴπερ μηδὲν τῶν ἄλλων διαφέρων οὕτω μεγάλας
ποιοῦμαι τὰς ὑποσχέσεις.

15 Περὶ μὲν οὖν τῶν ἰδίων ταῦτά μοι προειρήσθω. περὶ δὲ c
τῶν κοινῶν, ὅσοι μὲν εὐθὺς ἐπελθόντες διδάσκουσιν ὡς χρὴ
διαλυσαμένους τὰς πρὸς ἡμᾶς αὐτοὺς ἔχθρας ἐπὶ τὸν βάρβαρον τραπέσθαι, καὶ διεξέρχονται τάς τε συμφορὰς τὰς
ἐκ τοῦ πολέμου τοῦ πρὸς ἀλλήλους ἡμῖν γεγενημένας καὶ
τὰς ὠφελείας τὰς ἐκ τῆς στρατείας τῆς ἐπ' ἐκεῖνον ἐσομένας,
ἀληθῆ μὲν λέγουσιν, οὐ μὴν ἐντεῦθεν ποιοῦνται τὴν ἀρχήν, 44
16 ὅθεν ἂν μάλιστα συστῆσαι ταῦτα δυνηθεῖεν. τῶν γὰρ Ἑλλήνων οἱ μὲν ὑφ' ἡμῖν, οἱ δ' ὑπὸ Λακεδαιμονίοις εἰσίν· αἱ
γὰρ πολιτεῖαι, δι' ὧν οἰκοῦσι τὰς πόλεις, οὕτω τοὺς πλείστους αὐτῶν διειλήφασιν. ὅστις οὖν οἴεται τοὺς ἄλλους

κοινῇ τι πράξειν ἀγαθὸν, πρὶν ἂν τοὺς προεστῶτας αὐτῶν
διαλλάξῃ, λίαν ἁπλῶς ἔχει καὶ πόρρω τῶν πραγμάτων
17 ἐστίν. ἀλλὰ δεῖ τὸν μὴ μόνον ἐπίδειξιν ποιούμενον ἀλλὰ b
καὶ διαπράξασθαί τι βουλόμενον ἐκείνους τοὺς λόγους ζητεῖν, οἵτινες τὼ πόλεε τούτω πείσουσιν ἰσομοιρῆσαι πρὸς
ἀλλήλας καὶ τάς θ' ἡγεμονίας διελέσθαι, καὶ τὰς πλεονεξίας,
ἃς νῦν παρὰ τῶν Ἑλλήνων ἐπιθυμοῦσιν αὐταῖς γίγνεσθαι,
18 ταύτας παρὰ τῶν βαρβάρων ποιήσασθαι. (γ΄.) Τὴν μὲν
οὖν ἡμετέραν πόλιν ῥᾴδιον ἐπὶ ταῦτα προαγαγεῖν, Λακε- c
δαιμόνιοι δὲ νῦν μὲν ἔτι δυσπείστως ἔχουσι· παρειλήφασι
γὰρ ψευδῆ λόγον, ὡς ἔστιν αὐτοῖς ἡγεῖσθαι πάτριον· ἢν δ'
ἐπιδείξῃ τις αὐτοῖς ταύτην τὴν τιμὴν ἡμετέραν οὖσαν μᾶλλον ἢ 'κείνων, τάχ' ἂν ἐάσαντες τὸ διακριβοῦσθαι περὶ
τούτων ἐπὶ τὸ συμφέρον ἔλθοιεν.

or implied negative (e.g. Soph.
Ant. 175, ἀμήχανον... ἐκμαθεῖν,
πρὶν ἂν...φανῇ). The exceptions
to this rule are as follows: Simonides
of Amorgos (fl. 660 B.C.), φθάνει
δὲ τὸν μὲν γῆρας ἄζηλον λαβόν | πρὶν
τέρμ' ἵκηται, and Herodot. VII. 10, ὁ
δὲ ἀδικέει, ἀνατιθέμενος πρὶν ἢ ἀτρε-
κέως ἐκμάθῃ ['ubi si quis διαβάλλων
ἀδικέει, nihil aliud esse quam οὐ
δίκαιός ἐστι διαβάλλειν putaverit, nec
me neque sensum obsequentem habe-
bit.' From Mr. Shilleto's note on
Dem. Fals. Leg. § 235]. In the
present passage also the rule appears to be disregarded: at the
same time it is quite open, to any
who care to maintain the rule, to
take the clause λίαν ἁπλῶς ἔχει,
κ.τ.λ., as equivalent to a negative,
e.g. = οὔτε φρονίμως ἔχει οὔτ' ἐγγὺς
τῶν πραγμάτων ἐστίν. In this case
the sense would be: 'whoever thinks
that, &c., is not a sensible and practical man, until he has reconciled
Athens and Sparta.' The other
transl. is however preferable.

17. τὼ πόλεε τούτω.] These
forms of the fem. dual are supported by the highest MS. authority
here and elsewhere in Isocr. (e.g. de
Pace, § 116). Similarly in §§ 73, 75,

139 we have ταῖν (not ταῖς) πολέοιν.
The statement (in Wordsworth's Gk.
Gr. &c.) that ὁ and οὗτοι sometimes have no separate fem.-form
of the dual, is likely to mislead: the
fact is that the reverse is nearer the
truth, the forms τά and ταύτά being
extremely rare. Cobet (var. lect.
p. 70) goes so far as to say 'in pro-
nominibus, adjectivis, participiis,
una atque eadem forma est triplici
generi communis, τώ, ὤ, αὐτώ, τούτω, ἀλλήλω, τώ χεῖρε, τώ γυναῖκε
cet. τὼ Ἐλευσινίω θεώ.' In participiis
res manifesta est:' (Hom. Il. IX.
455, πληγέντε; Hesiod, Works and
Days, 197, τρωλευόντε; Plato, Phaedr.
237 D. δύο τινὲ ἰδέα ἄρχοντε καὶ
ἄγοντε, οἷν ἑπόμεθα).

ἰσομοιρῆσαι...πλεονεξίας.] Phil.
§ 39. πλεονεκτεῖν)(ἰσομοιρῆσαι. In
Phil. § 9 Isocr. quotes τὰς πλεονεξίας—ποιήσασθαι.

18. δυσπείστως ἔχουσι] almost
= δύσπειστοί εἰσι, which may have
been avoided propter hiatum.

ἢ 'κείνων.] κεῖνος is never found in
Isocr. except after ἤ. In such cases
as the present it is better to prefix
a coronis, to indicate prodelision,
than to write ἢ ἐκείνων or ἢ κείνων.

19 Ἐχρῆν μὲν οὖν καὶ τοῖς ἄλλοις ἐντεῦθεν ἄρχεσθαι καὶ
μὴ πρότερον περὶ τῶν ὁμολογουμένων συμβουλεύειν, πρὶν
περὶ τῶν ἀμφισβητουμένων ἡμᾶς ἐδίδαξαν· ἐμοὶ δ' οὖν
ἀμφοτέρων ἕνεκα προσήκει περὶ ταῦτα ποιήσασθαι τὴν d
πλείστην διατριβήν, μάλιστα μὲν ἵνα προὔργου τι γένηται
καὶ παυσάμενοι τῆς πρὸς ἡμᾶς αὐτοὺς φιλονικίας κοινῇ τοῖς
20 βαρβάροις πολεμήσωμεν, εἰ δὲ τοῦτ' ἐστὶν ἀδύνατον, ἵνα
δηλώσω τοὺς ἐμποδὼν ὄντας τῇ τῶν Ἑλλήνων εὐδαιμονίᾳ,
καὶ πᾶσι γένηται φανερὸν, ὅτι καὶ πρότερον ἡ πόλις ἡμῶν
δικαίως τῆς θαλάττης ἦρξε, καὶ νῦν οὐκ ἀδίκως ἀμφισβητεῖ
21 τῆς ἡγεμονίας. τοῦτο μὲν γὰρ εἰ δεῖ τούτοις ἐφ' ἑκάστῳ e
τιμᾶσθαι τῶν ἔργων τοὺς ἐμπειροτάτους ὄντας καὶ μεγίστην
δύναμιν ἔχοντας, ἀναμφισβητήτως ἡμῖν προσήκει τὴν ἡγεμονίαν ἀπολαβεῖν, ἥνπερ πρότερον ἐτυγχάνομεν ἔχοντες·
οὐδεὶς γὰρ ἂν ἑτέραν πόλιν ἐπιδείξειε τοσοῦτον ἐν τῷ πολέμῳ τῷ κατὰ γῆν ὑπερέχουσαν, ὅσον τὴν ἡμετέραν ἐν 15
22 τοῖς κινδύνοις τοῖς κατὰ θάλατταν διαφέρουσαν. τοῦτο δ'
εἴ τινες ταύτην μὲν μὴ νομίζουσι δικαίαν εἶναι τὴν κρίσιν
ἀλλὰ πολλὰς τὰς μεταβολὰς γίγνεσθαι, τὰς γὰρ δυναστείας
οὐδέποτε τοῖς αὐτοῖς παραμένειν, ἀξιοῦσι δὲ τὴν ἡγεμονίαν
ἔχειν ὥσπερ ἄλλο τι γέρας ἢ τοὺς πρώτους τυχόντας ταύτης ·

19. ἐχρῆν.] After consonants
Isoc. uses ἐχρῆν, after vowels χρῆν
or 'χρῆν. In one passage only
(Aegin. § 3) χρῆν (altered by Bens.
into ἐχρῆν, vulg. χρῆ) is found at
the beginning of a sentence. (Bena.
Praef. xlii.)

πρὶν...ἐδίδαξαν.] Madv. Synt. §
154. R. 1. and Goodwin's Gk. Moods
and Tenses, § 67. 1.

προὔργου τι.] lit. 'something to
the purpose,' 'that some progress
may be made.' Suidas, προὔργου· πρὸ
ἔργου, σύμφερον, πλέον. Ἰσοκράτης
φησὶν, ἵνα προὔργου τι γένηται, ἀντὶ
τοῦ πλέον. Isoc. uses the comp. of
προὔργου in § 133 and elsewhere.

φιλονικία.] A different word from
φιλονεικία, although L. and S. suppose the former to be only a MS. corruption of the latter. φιλονικία is often praiseworthy (vincendi studium);

φιλονεικία always the reverse (certa-
tionem significat cum vituperatione
quadam. Baiter).—ad Dem. § 31. n.

§§ 21—27. The supremacy is due
to Athens on every ground, whether
we look to her antiquity, her power,
her grandeur, or her general services
to Greece.

21. οὐδεὶς γὰρ κ.τ.λ.] Obs.
the parallelism of the whole of this
sentence.—διέφερον would have been
equally correct but less idiomatic:
διαφέρουσαν is preferred for the sake
of the παρομοίωσις with ὑπερέχουσαν. For the constr. v. Madv. Synt.
§ 20. R. 3.

22. δυναστείας] = ἡγεμονίας. cf.
§ 65 and (Dem.) Phil. IV. § 53. εἰς
τοσαύτας δυναστείας διῃρημένων τῶν
Ἑλληνικῶν πραγμάτων.

παραμένειν.] Madv. Synt. § 163, a.

τῆς τιμῆς ἢ τοὺς πλείστων ἀγαθῶν αἰτίους τοῖς Ἕλλησιν
23 ὄντας, ἡγοῦμαι καὶ τούτους εἶναι μεθ' ἡμῶν· ὅσῳ γὰρ ἄν b
τις πορρωτέρωθεν σκοπῇ περὶ τούτων ἀμφοτέρων, τοσούτῳ πλέον ἀπολείψομεν τοὺς ἀμφισβητοῦντας περὶ αὐτῶν.
(δ'.) Ὁμολογεῖται μὲν γὰρ τὴν πόλιν ἡμῶν ἀρχαιοτάτην
εἶναι καὶ μεγίστην καὶ παρὰ πᾶσιν ἀνθρώποις ὀνομαστο-
τάτην· οὕτω δὲ καλῆς τῆς ὑποθέσεως οὔσης, ἐπὶ τοῖς ἐχο-
24 μένοις τούτων ἔτι μᾶλλον ἡμᾶς προσήκει τιμᾶσθαι. ταύτην
γὰρ οἰκοῦμεν οὐχ ἑτέρους ἐκβαλόντες οὐδ' ἐρήμην καταλα- c
βόντες οὐδ' ἐκ πολλῶν ἐθνῶν μιγάδες συλλεγέντες, ἀλλ'
οὕτω καλῶς καὶ γνησίως γεγόναμεν, ὥστ' ἐξ ἧσπερ ἔφυμεν,
ταύτην ἔχοντες ἅπαντα τὸν χρόνον διατελοῦμεν, αὐτόχθονες

μεθ' ἡμῶν.] 'On our side,' *not* 'among us'. Cf. §§ 53, 140.

23. πορρωτέρωθεν.] 'From a greater distance.' This word has been missed by L. and S.; and another lexicographer quotes only Theophrastus, *de Sudoribus*, § 4. It occurs however in three passages of Isocr. besides the present; viz. *Archid.* § 16, *Panath.* § 120, *de Bigis*, § 4.

πόλιν...ἀρχαιοτάτην.] In Herod. VI. 106, on the eve of Marathon, the courier Pheidippides gives this message to Sparta: 'Men of Lacedaemon, the Athenians beseech you to hasten to their aid and not allow *the most ancient city* in all Greece to fall into bondage at the hands of barbarians.'

μεγίστην.] Cf. *de Perm.* § 299, καὶ φασιν...μόνην εἶναι ταύτην πόλιν τὰς δ' ἄλλας κώμας καὶ δικαίως ἂν αὐτὴν ἄστυ τῆς Ἑλλάδος προσαγορεύεσθαι καὶ διὰ τὸ μέγεθος καὶ διὰ τὰς εὐπορίας, κ.τ.λ.

περὶ αὐτῶν.] See tab. of var. readings.

24. ταύτην—προσήκει.] 'As for this city, which we now inhabit, we did not expel others from it, we did not find it deserted; we are no motley crowd collected out of many nations, but are sprung from such noble and genuine birth, that we continue for all time to hold this land from which we were born, being sons of its very soil, and being able to call our city by the same names as our nearest relations; for we alone of all the Greeks have the right to call the same country our foster-nurse, our fatherland, and our mother also.'

οὐχ ἑτέρους ἐκβαλόντες.] A passing blow at the Spartans.

οὐδ' ἐκ πολλῶν ἐθνῶν μιγάδες κ.τ.λ.] Cf. *Panath.* § 124, 5, ὄντας μήτε μιγάδας μήτ' ἐπήλυδας ἀλλὰ μόνους αὐτόχθονας τῶν Ἑλλήνων καὶ ταύτην ἔχοντες τὴν χώραν τροφόν, ἐξ ἧσπερ ἔφυσαν ἡμῖν καὶ στέργοντες αὐτὴν ὁμοίως ὥσπερ οἱ βέλτιστοι τοὺς πατέρας κ. τὰς μητέρας τὰς αὐτῶν, and *de Pace*, § 49. Contrast with this the state of Athens under the Emp. Tiberius, when Cn. Piso speaks of its inhabitants as 'non Athenienses tot cladibus extinctos, sed colluviem illam nationum.' (Tac. *Ann.* II. 55.).

αὐτόχθονες.] 'Aborigines.' A similar claim was asserted by the Arcadians and the Cynurians (Hdt. VIII. 73). As an emblem of being αὐτόχθονες and γηγενεῖς, the older Athenians used to wear grasshopper hair-pins, a custom which Thucydides (I. 6) describes as having lately ceased.—The sentiment of this and the next sentence are frequent rhe-

ὄντες καὶ τῶν ὀνομάτων τοῖς αὐτοῖς οἷσπερ τοὺς οἰκειοτά-
25 τους τὴν πόλιν ἔχοντες προσειπεῖν· μόνοις γὰρ ἡμῖν τῶν
Ἑλλήνων τὴν αὐτὴν τροφὸν καὶ πατρίδα καὶ μητέρα καλέ-
σαι προσήκει. καίτοι χρὴ τοὺς εὐλόγως μέγα φρονοῦντας
καὶ περὶ τῆς ἡγεμονίας δικαίως ἀμφισβητοῦντας καὶ τῶν d
πατρίων πολλάκις μεμνημένους, τοιαύτην τὴν ἀρχὴν τοῦ
γένους ἔχοντας φαίνεσθαι.

26 (εʹ.) Τὰ μὲν οὖν ἐξ ἀρχῆς ὑπάρξαντα καὶ παρὰ τῆς
τύχης δωρηθέντα τηλικαῦθ᾽ ἡμῖν τὸ μέγεθός ἐστιν· ὅσων
δὲ τοῖς ἄλλοις ἀγαθῶν αἴτιοι γεγόναμεν, οὕτως ἂν κάλλιστ᾽
ἐξετάσαιμεν, εἰ τόν τε χρόνον ἀπ᾽ ἀρχῆς καὶ τὰς πράξεις

torical common-places; e. g. Plato,
Menexenus (see § 7₆. n.), p. 237 B,
αὐτόχθονας κ. τῷ ὄντι ἐν πατρίδι
οἰκοῦντας κ. ζῶντας κ. τρεφομένους
οὐχ ὑπὸ μητρυιᾶς ὡς ἄλλοι ἀλλ᾽ ὑπὸ
μητρὸς τῆς χώρας ἐν ᾗ ᾤκουν, Lysias (?)
Or. Funebr. § 17, οὐ γὰρ ὥσπερ οἱ
πολλοὶ πανταχόθεν συνειλεγμένοι
κ. ἑτέρους ἐκβαλόντες τὴν ἀλλοτρίαν
ᾤκησαν ἀλλ᾽ αὐτόχθονες ὄντες τὴν
αὐτὴν ἐκέκτηντο μητέρα κ. πατρίδα.
(Demosth.) *Or. Funebr.* § 4. Hyperid. *Or. Funebr.* Col. 5 (with Prof. C.
Babington's n.), and Cic. *pro Flacco*,
§ 62, *Atheniensium urbs vetustate ea
est, ut ipsa ex sese suos cives genuisse
dicatur, ut eorum eadem terra* parens,
altrix, patria *dicatur.*

τοὺς οἰκειοτάτους.] Sc. προσαγορεύομεν. Cf. Eur. *Med.* 1153, φίλους
νομίζουσ᾽ οὕσπερ ἂν πόσις σέθεν, sc.
νομίζῃ.

προσειπεῖν.] As this aorist has
no present of its own, it borrows
προσαγορεύω. The parts of προσαγορεύω itself are far from common;
in Plato, *Theaet.* 147, we have προσαγορεύομεν, in Aesch. *P.V.* 834, προσ-
ηγορεύθης ἡ Διὸς κλεινὴ δάμαρ, and
in two fragments of Comic writers,
προσηγορεύθη. In Dem. *Boeot.* § 1
and Aristot. *Pol.* 7, 16, 18, we find
the subj. προσαγορευθῇ, and, lastly,
in Plat. *Phaedo*, 104 A, προσαγορευ-
τέον. Cobet (*var. lect.* p. 35—39)
maintains that by *classical* writers
the verb ἀγορεύω is used in the pres.

and impf. only, and that the real
tenses and derivatives in use are
ἐρῶ, εἶπον, εἴρηκα, εἴρημαι, ἐρρήθην,
ῥηθήσομαι· ῥῆσις, ῥητός, ῥητέον. This
statement will apply very fairly to
ἀγορεύω when compounded with
ἀπό, διά, ἐκ, κατά, σύν, ὑπό, πρό, but
in the case of προσαγορεύω (as Cobet
himself confesses) the existence of
parts directly formed is established
beyond a doubt by the passages above
quoted, esp. Aesch. *l.c.* (where προσηγορεύθη cannot possibly be altered
into προσερρήθη).—The speech of
Aeschines, *adv. Ctesiph.* shews the
usage of ἀναγορεύω. The parts there
used are ἀναγορεύς, ἀνειπεῖν, ἀπαρρη-
θῆναι, ὁ κῆρυξ ἀνεῖπε, followed by καὶ
πάλιν ὁ αὐτὸς κῆρυξ ἀνηγόρευε (?),
ἀνερεῖ and ἀναρρήσει. On the whole
then, it is better in Greek composition to use the forms -ερῶ, -εῖπον,
-εἴρηκα, -εἴρημαι, -ἐρρήθην, -ῥημα, -ῥη-
σις, -ῥητέος, but at the same time to
abstain from accepting dogmatic
views on the impossibility of the
existence of forms derived from ἀγορεύω. (Partly from Cobet *l.c.* and
Veitch, *Gk. Verbs*, s. v. ἀγορεύω.)

26. τηλικαῦτα...τὸ μέγεθος.] This
is a more accurate and more common expression than that of § 33,
τοσαύτην τὸ μέγεθος. The *regular*
usage of τοσοῦτος and τηλικοῦτος
may best be learnt from *de Perm.*
§ 257, τοσούτων τὸ πλῆθος κ. τηλικούτων τὸ μέγεθος ἀγαθῶν.

τὰς τῆς πόλεως ἐφεξῆς διέλθοιμεν· εὑρήσομεν γὰρ αὐτὴν e
οὐ μόνον τῶν πρὸς τὸν πόλεμον κινδύνων ἀλλὰ καὶ τῆς
27 ἄλλης κατασκευῆς, ἐν ᾗ κατοικοῦμεν καὶ μεθ᾽ ἧς πολιτευό-
μεθα καὶ δι᾽ ἣν ζῆν δυνάμεθα, σχεδὸν ἁπάσης αἰτίαν οὖσαν.
ἀνάγκη δὲ προαιρεῖσθαι τῶν εὐεργεσιῶν μὴ τὰς διὰ μικρότητα διαλαθούσας καὶ κατασιωπηθείσας, ἀλλὰ τὰς διὰ τὸ 46
μέγεθος ὑπὸ πάντων ἀνθρώπων καὶ πάλαι καὶ νῦν καὶ
πανταχοῦ καὶ λεγομένας καὶ μνημονευομένας.

28　　(ϛ´.) Πρῶτον μὲν τοίνυν, οὗ πρῶτον ἡ φύσις ἡμῶν ἐδε-

εὑρήσομεν — οὖσαν.] *i. e.* 'we shall find that, not only for the perils of war, but also for nearly the whole of that established order wherein we dwell, and wherewith we enjoy our constitutions, and whereby we are able to live, it is to *Athens* that we owe our gratitude.'

αἰτίαν governs not only τῶν κινδύνων but also τῆς κατασκευῆς, and, if translated literally, would involve a blunder in English, the same in kind but more heinous in degree, than the original blunder into which Isocr. has fallen. He does not mean that Athens 'caused' the perils of war, but that she was the champion of deliverance from those perils: the only defence that can be suggested for this abuse of language is the fact that αἰτίας is quite appropriate to the nearer word κατασκευῆς, however inappropriate to the more distant word κινδύνων. If a formal explanation is required, we must say that some word suitable to κινδύνων must be understood from the word αἰτίας, but, in any case, whether the error is deliberate or accidental, it is none the less a violation of Aristotle's wholesome warning 'against coupling a word with two others which can only with propriety be applied to one of them; as when ἰδεῖν is used in construction with ψόφον as well as χρῶμα, instead of αἰσθάνεσθαι, which is common to both.' (*Rhet.* III L 5, Mr Cope's *Intrad.* p. 295). The technical name given to this figure is *Zeugma*; the

author who, perhaps, uses it most frequently is Tacitus; *e. g. Ann.* II. 10, *quod arduum sibi* (sc. sumpsit), *cetera legatis permisit.* (Dräger, *Syntax u. Stil des Tac.* § 239, 4.) Cf. § 80, σωτῆρει ἀλλὰ μὴ λυμεῶνες ἀποκαλεῖσθαι. n. [Hirschig places κινδύνων in brackets.]

τῇ ἄλλῃ κατασκευῇ, 'the established order *besides*.' Cf. *ad Dem.* § 51, τῶν ἄλλων σοφιστῶν. n.

27. ἀνάγκη κ.τ.λ.] Trans. 'But of all benefactions we must needs prefer, *not* those which, by reason of their little-ness, fell into oblivion and silence, but those which, by reason of their greatness, are, of old time and in the present day and in every place, both rehearsed and remembered by all the world.'

§§ 28—50. *The arts of Peace, in which Athens has conferred signal blessings on the Grecian world.*

28, 29. *Her liberality with regard to the fruits of the earth, and the Eleusinian mysteries.* 30, 31. *The legend of that liberality is ancient, and therefore (?) credible; and is further confirmed by the annual offering of the First-fruits, and* (32, 33) *by antecedent probability.* 34—37. *Colonisation.* 38—40. *Legislation and good government.* 41. *Hospitality.* 42. *The establishment of a central emporium.* 43—46. *The attractions and advantages of Athens, her games and festivals; and lastly,* 47—50. *her practical philosophy and her oratory.*

28. πρῶτον μέν.] The δέ that

ήθη, δια τῆς πόλεως τῆς ἡμετέρας ἐπορίσθη· καὶ γὰρ εἰ
μυθώδης ὁ λόγος γέγονεν, ὅμως αὐτῷ καὶ νῦν ῥηθῆναι
προσήκει. Δήμητρος γὰρ ἀφικομένης εἰς τὴν χώραν, ὅτ'
ἐπλανήθη τῆς Κόρης ἁρπασθείσης, καὶ πρὸς τοὺς προγόνους ἡμῶν εὐμενῶς διατεθείσης ἐκ τῶν εὐεργεσιῶν, ἃς οὐχ b
οἷόν τ' ἄλλοις ἢ τοῖς μεμυημένοις ἀκούειν, καὶ δούσης δωρεὰς διττάς, αἵπερ μέγισται τυγχάνουσιν οὖσαι, τούς τε
καρποὺς, οἳ τοῦ μὴ θηριωδῶς ζῆν ἡμῖς αἴτιοι γεγόνασι, καὶ
τὴν τελετὴν, ἧς οἱ μετασχόντες περί τε τῆς τοῦ βίου τε-

corresponds to this μέν may be found in § 34, where it is resumed in the words περὶ μὲν οὖν, κ.τ.λ., followed by περὶ δὲ τοὺς αὐτοὺς χρόνους, κ.τ.λ.

καὶ γάρ εἰ μυθώδης...] Isocr. is not such an implicit believer in mythology as is sometimes asserted (e. g. Grote's *H. G.* I. p. 335, new ed. The passage there quoted from *Philip.* § 33, is, in the best MS. φασίν, οἷσπερ [not οἷς περὶ] τῶν παλαιῶν πιστεύομεν); cf. *Panath.* § 1, νεώτεροι μὲν ὦν προηρούμην γράφειν τῶν λόγων οὐ τοὺς μυθώδεις οὐδὲ τοὺς τερατείας καὶ ψευδολογίας μεστούς, κ.τ.λ., *Evag.* § 66, εἰ τοὺς μύθους ἀφέντες τὴν ἀλήθειαν σκοπῶμεν...He here tells the story of Demeter with a passing apology, as if conscious of its appropriateness rather than of its truth. An apology similar to this, but implying less reserve, may be noticed in Lycurgus, *adv. Leocratem*, § 95, where he introduces a graceful tale of filial affection, with the words εἰ γὰρ καὶ μυθωδέστερόν ἐστιν, ἀλλ' ἁρμόσει καὶ ὑμῖν ἅπασι τοῖς νεωτέροις ἀκοῦσαι.

The legend of Demeter and Persephone (ἡ Κόρη, cf. *Evag.* § 13) is tastefully told by the writer of the Homeric Hymn *ad Cererem*, by Ovid, *Fasti*, IV. 393—620, and more elaborately by Claudian (4th cent. A.D.), *De raptu Proserpinae libri*, III. It is briefly mentioned by Cicero (*in Verrem*, IV. § 107), whose knowledge of Sicily enables him to give an interesting account of the

traditionary scene of Demeter's bereavement. It may be found in a modern form in Harry Cornwall's poems, and in the *Tales of Ancient Greece* (by Mr Cox), p. 30 sqq. and especially p. 402—8.

καρπούς.] Cf. Plato, *Menex.* 237 E, μόνη γάρ (ἥδε ἡ γῆ)...καὶ πρώτη τροφὴν ἀνθρωπείαν ἤνεγκε τὸν τῶν πυρῶν καὶ κριθῶν καρπόν, κ.τ.λ., (Dem.) *Or. Funebr.* § 5, and Lucret. VI. 1, *Primae frugiparos fetus mortalibus aegris Dididerunt quondam praeclaro nomine Athenae Et recreaverunt vitam legesque rogarunt.*

τοῦ μὴ θηριωδῶς κ.τ.λ.] For the expression cf. *Nicocl.* § 6, ἐγγενόμενος δ' ἡμῖν τοῦ πείθειν ἀλλήλους καὶ δηλοῦν πρὸς ἡμᾶς αὐτοὺς, περὶ ὧν ἂν βουληθῶμεν, οὐ μόνον τοῦ θηριωδῶς ζῆν ἀπηλλάγημεν ἀλλὰ κ.τ.λ., Ovid, *Fasti*, II. 291, *vita feris similis*, &c.

τελετὴν—ἔχουσιν.] 'And that mystic initiation, the partakers of which have hopes that are more pleasant, concerning both the end of their life and all eternity.' The connection between the mysteries of Eleusis and the great mystery of Death is frequently insisted on, e.g. Homeric Hymn *ad Cerer.* 480, ὄλβιος, ὃς τάδ' ὄπωπεν ἐπιχθονίων ἀνθρώπων | ὃς δ' ἀτελὴς ἱερῶν ὅς τ' ἄμμορος, οὔποθ' ὁμοίων | αἶσαν ἔχει φθίμενός περ ὑπὸ ζόφῳ εὐρώεντι. Pindar, *fragm.* 102, ὄλβιος ὅστις ἰδὼν ἐκεῖνα (sc. τὰ μυστήρια) | εἶσιν ὑπὸ χθόνα· οἶδεν μὲν βιότου τελευτάν | οἶδεν δὲ διόσδοτον ἀρχάν.

λευτῆς καὶ τοῦ σύμπαντος αἰῶνος ἡδίους τὰς ἐλπίδας ἔχου-

Soph. *Fragm.* 719 Dind. (ap. Plutarch. *Mor.* p. 21 b) ὡς τρισόλβιοι | κεῖνοι βροτῶν οἳ ταῦτα δερχθέντες τέλη | μόλωσ' ἐς Ἀιδου· τοῖσδε γὰρ μόνοις ἐκεῖ | ζῆν ἐστι, τοῖς δ' ἄλλοισι πάντ' ἔχει κακά. Other passages might be quoted, but the most interesting is perhaps the passage cited by Stobaeus, *Flor.* 120, 26, from Themistius (?) (philosopher and rhetorician, fl. 350—390 A.D.). Part of it (τότε δὲ πάσχει—ἐμμένοντα) may be translated as follows: 'Then, in the moment of death, the soul is affected in like manner, as in the initiation into the Great Mysteries. Therefore it is that name answers to name, as well as thing to thing—τελευτᾶν to die, τελεῖσθαι to be initiated. At first, there are wanderings and weary coursings to and fro, and, until the consummation, a strange and doubtful marching through the gloom; and then, at the very verge of that consummation, there comes a blending of every horror,—'tis all shivering, trembling, sweating, and affrightment; and after this, a wondrous light bursts forth; and the pure meadows and open plains give their welcome, with minstrelsy and dances and the solemnity of hallowed sounds and saintly visions, wherein he who is now all-perfect and initiated obtains freedom and release at last. He ranges here and there engarlanded, he revels in the sacred mysteries, he shares the companionship of pure and holy men; and anon he looks on earth and contemplates the uninitiated and unpurified crowd of the living—all trampled down and huddled together in the depth of mire and mist, and abiding in their miseries through fear of death and through disbelief in the good things yonder.' In all the above passages (quoted by Lobeck, &c.) the mysteries are viewed in their relation to death, just as in the passage of Isocr. before us. It is however worth noticing (with Lobeck, *Aglaophamus*,

1. p. 70) that Isocr. himself elsewhere attributes the same reward of pleasant hopes to *all* who live in justice and piety, *de Pace*, § 34, ὁρῶ γὰρ...τοὺς μετ' εὐσεβείας καὶ δικαιοσύνης ζῶντας ἔν τε τοῖς παροῦσι χρόνοις ἀσφαλῶς διάγοντας καὶ περὶ τοῦ σύμπαντος αἰῶνος ἡδίους τοὺς ἐλπίδας ἔχοντας.

With regard to the nature and object of the Eleusinian mysteries much controversy has been waged. Whether they came from Egypt, and taught the doctrine of a future state (as Warburton believed)—whether they formed the relic of a revealed religion and remained as a protest against the Polytheism of Greece (as Faber conjectured)—whether they had a semi-sacramental import—whether they formed a kind of aristocracy of religion which incidentally became a safety valve for a dangerous scepticism — all these questions and others have been the subject of deep debate. A less ambitious view is that stated by Gibbon, who apprehended that in the mysteries there was no hidden meaning to conceal, and therefore nothing for modern ingenuity to discover; by De Quincey, who characterizes them 'as a gigantic hoax, the great and illustrious humbug of ancient history;' and by Lobeck, whose masterly book has demolished many of the baseless theories that have been built on the Orphic, Samothracian, and Eleusinian mysteries. For more or less full accounts of the general subject or the special ceremonies attending initiation see *Dict. Antiq.* s.v. *Eleusinia*; Warburton's *Divine Legation*, Bk. II. c. 4; G. S. Faber's *Origin of Pagan Idolatry*, Bk. V. c. 6; Gibbon, *Misc. Works*, II. p. 500; De Quincey, *On Secret Societies*; Lobeck's *Aglaoph.* I. 1—228; Appendix to Kennedy's Trans. of Demosth. *Lept. &c.* p. 287—297; Grote, *H. G.* I. p. 359, new ed.; Milman's *Hist. of Chris.* I. 1; and *Journal of Philology*, I. p. 9.

29 σιν, οὕτως ἡ πόλις ἡμῶν οὐ μόνον θεοφιλῶς ἀλλὰ καὶ φιλαν-
θρώπως ἔσχεν, ὥστε κυρία γενομένη τοσούτων ἀγαθῶν οὐκ c
ἐφθόνησε τοῖς ἄλλοις, ἀλλ' ὧν ἔλαβεν ἅπασι μετέδωκεν.
καὶ τὰ μὲν ἔτι καὶ νῦν καθ' ἕκαστον τὸν ἐνιαυτὸν δείκνυμεν,
τῶν δὲ συλλήβδην τάς τε χρείας καὶ τὰς ἐργασίας καὶ τὰς
30 ὠφελείας τὰς ἀπ' αὐτῶν γιγνομένας ἐδίδαξεν. καὶ τούτοις
ἀπιστεῖν μικρῶν ἔτι προστεθέντων οὐδεὶς ἂν ἀξιώσειεν.
(ζ.) Πρῶτον μὲν γὰρ ἐξ ὧν ἄν τις καταφρονήσειε τῶν λεγομένων ὡς ἀρχαίων ὄντων, ἐκ τῶν αὐτῶν τούτων εἰκότως d
ἂν καὶ τὰς πράξεις γεγενῆσθαι νομίσειεν· διὰ γὰρ τὸ πολλοὺς εἰρηκέναι καὶ πάντας ἀκηκοέναι προσήκει μὴ καινὰ
μὲν, πιστὰ δὲ δοκεῖν εἶναι τὰ λεγόμενα περὶ αὐτῶν. ἔπειτ'
οὐ μόνον ἐνταῦθα καταφυγεῖν ἔχομεν, ὅτι τὸν λόγον καὶ τὴν
φήμην ἐκ πολλοῦ παρειλήφαμεν, ἀλλὰ καὶ σημείοις μεί-
31 ζοσιν ἢ τούτοις ἔστιν ἡμῖν χρήσασθαι περὶ αὐτῶν. αἱ μὲν
γὰρ πλεῖσται τῶν πόλεων ὑπόμνημα τῆς παλαιᾶς εὐερ- c
γεσίας ἀπαρχὰς τοῦ σίτου καθ' ἕκαστον τὸν ἐνιαυτὸν ὡς
ἡμᾶς ἀποπέμπουσι, ταῖς δ' ἐκλειπούσαις πολλάκις ἡ Πυθία
προσέταξεν ἀποφέρειν τὰ μέρη τῶν καρπῶν καὶ ποιεῖν πρὸς
τὴν πόλιν τὴν ἡμετέραν τὰ πάτρια. καίτοι περὶ τίνων χρὴ 47
μᾶλλον πιστεύειν ἢ περὶ ὧν ὅ τε θεὸς ἀναιρεῖ καὶ πολλοῖς

29. **θεοφιλῶς......φιλανθρώπως.**]
Obs. the formation of these two
compounds and distinguish carefully
between θεοφιλής (= beloved of God)
and φιλόθεος (= loving God).

οὐκ ἐφθόνησεν κ.τ.λ.] Cf. Plat.
Menex. 238 A. τούτου δὲ τοῦ καρποῦ
οὐκ ἐφθόνησεν ἀλλ' ἔνειμε καὶ τοῖς
ἄλλοις. Cic. *pro Flacco*, § 62, *Ad-
sunt Athenienses unde humanitas,
doctrina, religio, fruges, iura, leges
ortae, atque in omnes terras distri-
butae putantur.*

τὰ μέν...] Sc. τῶν ἀγαθῶν, referring especially to the Eleusinian
mysteries.

καθ' ἕκ. τ. ἐν. δείκνυμεν.] The
great mysteries were celebrated every
year in Boëdromion (August) and
lasted nine days.—δείκνυμι is a word
frequently used of these mysteries.

cf. e.g. Xen. *Hell.* VI. 3, 6 (quoted
by Lobeck, *Aglaoph.* p. 51). Λέγεται Τριπτόλεμοι... τὰ Δήμητρος καὶ
Κόρης ἄρρητα ἱερὰ πρώτοις ξένοις
δεῖξαι Ἡρακλεῖ τε καὶ Διοσκόροιν.—
v. § 157. n.

31. **αἱ μὲν γὰρ πλεῖσται κ.τ.λ.**]
All. to the Proërosia, a sacrifice of-
fered to Demeter at the time of
seed-sowing. See *Dict. of Antiq.* s.v.
Schn. quotes the following *scholium*
on Aristoph. *Plut.* 1054, οἱ μὲν φασιν
ὅτι λιμοῦ, οἱ δὲ καὶ ὅτι λοιμοῦ πάσαν
τὴν γῆν κατασχόντος, ὁ θεὸς εἶπε
προηρόσιαν τῇ Δηοῖ ὑπὲρ ἀπάντων
θῦσαι θυσίαν Ἀθηναίοις. οὗ ἕνεκα
χαριστήρια πανταχόθεν ἐπέμποντο
Ἀθήναις τῶν καρπῶν τὰς ἀπαρχάς.
Cf. Lycurg. *Fragm.* XV. 9 (115.
oratt. Attici).

τῶν Ἑλλήνων συνδοκεῖ, καὶ τά τε πάλαι ῥηθέντα τοῖς παρ-
οῦσιν ἔργοις συμμαρτυρεῖ καὶ τὰ νῦν γιγνόμενα τοῖς ὑπ'
32 ἐκείνων εἰρημένοις ὁμολογεῖ;   (η'.) Χωρὶς δὲ τούτων, ἢν
ἅπαντα ταῦτ' ἐάσαντες ἀπὸ τῆς ἀρχῆς σκοπῶμεν, εὑρήσομεν, ὅτι τὸν βίον οἱ πρῶτοι φανέντες ἐπὶ γῆς οὐκ εὐθὺς
οὕτως ὥσπερ νῦν ἔχοντα κατέλαβον, ἀλλὰ κατὰ μικρὸν
αὐτοὶ συνεπορίσαντο. τίνας οὖν χρὴ μᾶλλον νομίζειν ἢ b
δωρεὰν παρὰ τῶν θεῶν λαβεῖν ἢ ζητοῦντας αὐτοὺς ἐντυ-
33 χεῖν; οὐ τοὺς ὑπὸ πάντων ὁμολογουμένους καὶ πρώτους
γενομένους καὶ πρός τε τὰς τέχνας εὐφυεστάτους ὄντας
καὶ πρὸς τὰ τῶν θεῶν εὐσεβέστατα διακειμένους; καὶ
μὴν ὅσης προσήκει τιμῆς τυγχάνειν τοὺς τηλικούτων ἀγαθῶν αἰτίους, περίεργον διδάσκειν. οὐδεὶς γὰρ ἂν δύναιτο
δωρεὰν τοσαύτην τὸ μέγεθος εὑρεῖν, ἥτις ἴση τοῖς πεπραγ-
μένοις ἐστίν.

34   (θ'.) Περὶ μὲν οὖν τοῦ μεγίστου τῶν εὐεργετημάτων καὶ c

τά τε πάλαι κ.τ.λ.] Obs. the
varied antithesis of this sentence.

31. τὸν βίον κ.τ.λ.] Cf. the
long description given by Lucretius
(v. 780—1457) of the gradual growth
of the infant world (*mundi novitas*)
and its inhabitants.   οὐκ εὐθὺς ἀλλὰ
κατὰ μικρόν may be paralleled by
Lucretius' adverb *minutatim* (used
several times in the above passage)
and especially by ll. 1452, 3, '*usus
et impigrae simul experientia mentis
Paulatim docuit pedetemtim progre-
dientis.*'

33. ὁμολογουμένους.] ὁμολογεῖσθαι generally takes the inf. and not
the participle. The former construction is always found in Isocr. except
in this passage; hence Wolf proposed
to read ὁμολογουμένως, an adverb
frequently used by our author, and
this reading is approved by Baiter,
who quotes especially Andoc. I.
§ 149, παρὰ πάντων ὁμολογουμένων.
The participial constr. is found in
Lysias, (περὶ τραύματος, § 7, νῦν δ'
ὁμολογούμεθα πρὶν παῖδας κ. αὐλη-
τρίδας κ. μετ' οἴνου ἐλθόντες) : Isaeus,
de Philoct. hered. § 49, οὗτοι ὁμολογου-

μένη οὖσα δούλη κ. ἅπαντα τὸν χρόνον
αἰσχρῶς βιοῦσα and *ib.* § 46. [Chief-
ly from Weber (Dem. *Aristocr.* § 74.
n.) who says '*ὁμολογεῖσθαι non raro
in participio exhibitum, sed saepe in
libris per ὁμολογουμένων obliteratum*].
In the present passage I prefer (with
DS Bens. Schn. and others) accepting the MS reading ὁμολογουμένους
which must then be construed with
the three participles γενομένους, ὄντας, διακειμένους. Trans. 'those
who are by all acknowledged both
to have been the first to exist and
to be, &c.'

34—37. These §§ refer to the me-
morable Ionic Emigration which is
commonly assigned to 1044 B.C. The
Abantes of Euboea, the Cadmeans
and Minyae of Boeotia, the Phocians
and the Athenians are said to have
taken part in this expedition. In the
current legend, the honour of plant-
ing the Asiatic Ionian cities is assigned to two sons of Codrus, Androclus
the founder of Ephesus and Neleus
of Miletus. These two towns—the
greatest of the ten continental Ionic
cities—are both described as found-

62 ΙΣΟΚΡΑΤΟΥΣ [§§ 34

πρώτου γενομένου καὶ πᾶσι κοινοτάτου ταῦτ᾽ εἰπεῖν ἔχομεν.
περὶ δὲ τοὺς αὐτοὺς χρόνους ὁρῶσα τοὺς μὲν βαρβάρους τὴν
πλείστην τῆς χώρας κατέχοντας, τοὺς δ᾽ Ἕλληνας εἰς μικρὸν τόπον κατακεκλειμένους καὶ διὰ σπανιότητα τῆς γῆς
ἐπιβουλεύοντάς τε σφίσιν αὐτοῖς καὶ στρατείας ἐπ᾽ ἀλλήλους ποιουμένους, καὶ τοὺς μὲν δι᾽ ἔνδειαν τῶν καθ᾽ ἡμέραν, d
35 τοὺς δὲ διὰ τὸν πόλεμον ἀπολλυμένους, οὐδὲ ταῦθ᾽ οὕτως
ἔχοντα περιεῖδεν, ἀλλ᾽ ἡγεμόνας εἰς τὰς πόλεις ἐξέπεμψεν,
οἳ παραλαβόντες τοὺς μάλιστα βίου δεομένους, στρατηγοὶ
καταστάντες αὐτῶν καὶ πολέμῳ κρατήσαντες τοὺς βαρβάρους, πολλὰς μὲν ἐφ᾽ ἑκατέρας τῆς ἠπείρου πόλεις ἔκτισαν,
ἁπάσας δὲ τὰς νήσους κατῴκισαν, ἀμφοτέρους δὲ καὶ τοὺς

ed directly from Athens. (See Grote's
Hist. of Gr. P. 11. c. 13.) The peo-
pling of the Cyclades (ἀνδσαι τὰς
νήσους), especially of Naxos, Ceos,
Siphnos, Seriphos, was also ascribed
to the Ionic migration. This great
movement took place under the
general auspices of Athens, and
was the means of providing a liveli-
hood for many distressed and dis-
contented exiles from the Pelopon-
nesus. (Thuc. I. 2, 6, καὶ ἐς Ἰωνίαν
ὕστερον, ὡς οὐχ ἱκανῆς οὔσης τῆς Ἀττικῆς, ἀποικίας ἐξέπεμψαν.)
περὶ δὲ κ.τ.λ.] The following
words form the frame-work of the
sentence : ὁρῶσα τοὺς μὲν βαρβάρους
...τοὺς δ᾽ Ἕλληνας...(τοὺς μὲν...τοὺς
δὲ...), οὐδὲ ταῦτα περιεῖδεν, ἀλλ᾽ ἡγεμόνας ἐξέπεμψεν, οἱ παραλαβόντες
κ.τ.λ., πολλὰς μὲν πόλεις ἔκτισαν,
ἁπάσας δὲ τὰς νήσους κατῴκισαν,
τὴν πλείστην τῆς χώρας.] Cf.
§ 132, τὴν πλείστην αὐτῆς, *Evag.*
§ 41, τὸν πλεῖστον τοῦ χρόνου, Jelf
(Kühner), *Gk. Gr.* § 442 C.
σφίσιν αὐτοῖς.] Almost = ἀλλή-
λοις. Isocr. frequently uses a *reflexive*
instead of a *reciprocal* pronoun. It
is often found with the reciprocal in
the immediate context, and is sometimes adopted only to secure an even
balance of clauses (παρίσωσις). Cf.
§§ 15, 43, ἡμᾶς αὐτούς...ἀλλήλοις,
§ 85, ἀλλήλους...σφᾶς αὐτούς, §§ 3,

106, 131, 166, 173, 174. For other
authors, cf. Dem. *Phil.* I. § 10, ἢ
βούλεσθε....περιιόντες αὐτῶν (= 'one
another') πυνθάνεσθαι 'λέγεταί τι
καινόν;' *De Cor.* § 19, Xen. *Mem.*
III. 5, 16, φθονοῦσιν ἑαυτοῖς μᾶλλον
ἢ τοῖς ἄλλοις ἀνθρώποις, cet.—Suidas,
Lexic., ἑαυτοὺς ἀντὶ τοῦ ἀλλήλους οἱ
Ἀττικοὶ λέγουσιν.—v. Jelf (Kühner),
Gk. Gr. § 654, 3.
35. ἐφ᾽ ἑκατέρας τῆς ἠπείρου.]
'On both continents,' *i.e.* Europe and
Asia. Similar phrases may be found
in *Panath.* §§ 44, 166; cf. § 179. n.
The allusion to the Asiatic Colonies
has been already explained ; by the
cities built in Europe, Isocr. possibly means the colonies founded by
Miletus on the W. shore of the
Euxine. These colonies would, as
usual, regard *Athens* as their mother-
state. At the same time, it is probable that Isocr. may be referring
by an inaccurate anticipation to the
later colonies of Thurii and Amphi-
polis, founded by Athens in the fifth
century.
ἀμφοτέρους.—ἱστόρισαν.] Arist.
(*Rhet.* III. 9, 7) quotes this sentence as an instance of ἀντικειμένη
λέξις, 'in which the parts are ba-
lanced, contrasted, set over against
one another...The antithesis may be
conveyed in two ways : either by
balancing opposite by opposite in

36 ἀκολουθήσαντας καὶ τοὺς ὑπομείναντας ἔσωσαν· τοῖς μὲν
γὰρ ἱκανὴν τὴν οἴκοι χώραν κατέλιπον, τοῖς δὲ πλείω τῆς c
ὑπαρχούσης ἐπόρισαν· ἅπαντα γὰρ περιεβάλοντο τὸν τόπον, ἐν νῦν τυγχάνομεν κατέχοντες. ὥστε καὶ τοῖς ὕστερον
βουληθεῖσιν ἀποικίσαι τινάς, καὶ μιμήσασθαι τὴν πόλιν τὴν
ἡμετέραν, πολλὴν ῥᾳστώνην ἐποίησαν· οὐ γὰρ αὑτοὺς ἔδει
κτωμένους χώραν διακινδυνεύειν, ἀλλ᾽ εἰς τὴν ὑφ᾽ ἡμῶν 48
37 ἀφορισθεῖσαν, εἰς ταύτην οἰκεῖν ἰόντας. καίτοι τίς ἂν ταύτης ἡγεμονίαν ἐπιδείξειεν ἢ πατριωτέραν τῆς πρότερον γενομένης πρὶν τὰς πλείστας οἰκισθῆναι τῶν Ἑλληνίδων
πόλεων, ἢ μᾶλλον συμφέρουσαν τῆς τοὺς μὲν βαρβάρους
ἀναστάτους ποιησάσης, τοὺς δ᾽ Ἕλληνας εἰς τοσαύτην εὐ-
πορίαν προαγαγούσης ;
38   (ι΄.) Οὐ τοίνυν, ἐπειδὴ τὰ μέγιστα συνδιέπραξε, τῶν

the two contrasted members ; or by
uniting two opposites as it were
under the *vinculum* of a single word,
as two opposite substantives or participles by a verb' (*paraphr. of l. c.
from* Mr Cope's *Introd.* p. 314);
ἐναντία, ὑπομονὴ, ἀκολούθησις· ἱκα-
νόν, πλείω.

36. τοῖς ὕστερον κ.τ.λ.] alludes
to the Dorian emigration and *not* to
the Aeolic, which *preceded* the Ionic.
v. Grote's *Hist. of Greece*, Pt. I. c.
18, Pt. II. c. 13, 14, 15.

ἀφορισθεῖσαν.] Rauchenstein
adopts ὁρισθεῖσαν (cf. *supr.* ἐνθρι-
σαν), the ingenious emendation of
Halbertsma and Meyler. Bens. and
Schn. retain the MS reading, which
is perfectly intelligible.

ταύτης ἡγεμονίαν κ.τ.λ.] ταύτης
is emphatic. The more usual construction would have been either
ταύτης τῆς ἡγεμονίας, or ἡγεμονίαν...
ἢ πατριωτέραν ταύτης τῆς κ.τ.λ. For
a very similar sentence cf. *Areop.*
§ 27, καίτοι πῶς ἂν τις εὕροι ταύτηι
βεβαιοτέραν ἢ δικαιοτέραν δημοκρατίας τῆς...καθιστάσης.

ἀναστάτους ποιησάσης.] The
word ἀνάστατος is used by Isocr. in
at least 30 passages, which may be
classified under four heads. It is
applied (1) to a 'city' (='ruined,'

'dismantled') in *Pang.* §§ 98, 117,
126, 181, and about 15 passages in
other writings; (2) to 'inhabitants'
(='driven from house and home'),
e.g. βάρβαροι as here, and ὅμοροι
§ 108 œl.; (3) to 'districts' (='devastated'), §§ 141, 161, 169; (4) to 'house-
holds' ('made desolate'). Cf. esp.
Archid. § 66 (a passage of peculiarly
varied vocabulary) : οὐδεμία γάρ ἐστι
τῶν πόλεων ἀκέραιος, οὐδ᾽ ἥτις οὐχ
ὅμόρους ἔχει τοὺς κακῶς ποιήσοντας,
ὥστε τετμῆσθαι μὲν τὰς χώρας, πε-
πορθῆσθαι δὲ τὰς πόλεις, ἀναστάτους
δὲ γεγενῆσθαι τοὺς οἴκους τοὺς ἰδίους,
ἀνεστράφθαι δὲ τὰς πολιτείας καὶ
καταλελύσθαι τοὺς νόμους. (Partly
from Bens. *Areop.* § 6. n.)

38. οὐ τοίνυν—λοιπῶν.] Trans.
'and after she had aided in accom-
plishing the greatest things, she did
not proceed to neglect the rest, but
she made such a beginning of her
benefactions (namely, the supply of
sustenance to those in need), as is
right for those to make, who in-
tend, in other good things also, to
exercise a good control; and consi-
dering that existence, based on these
conditions only, falls short of being
worthy of the desire of life, she
therefore paid such heed to the re-
mainder also, that, &c.'

ἄλλων ὠλιγώρησεν, ἀλλ' ἀρχὴν μὲν ταύτην ἐποιήσατο b
τῶν εὐεργεσιῶν, τροφὴν τοῖς δεομένοις εὑρεῖν, ἥνπερ χρὴ
τοὺς μέλλοντας καὶ περὶ τῶν ἄλλων καλῶν καλῶς διοική-
σειν, ἡγουμένη δὲ τὸν βίον τὸν ἐπὶ τούτοις μόνον οὔπω
τοῦ ζῆν ἐπιθυμεῖν ἀξίως ἔχειν οὕτως ἐπεμελήθη καὶ τῶν
λοιπῶν, ὥστε τῶν παρόντων τοῖς ἀνθρώποις ἀγαθῶν, ὅσα
μὴ παρὰ θεῶν ἔχομεν, ἀλλὰ δι' ἀλλήλους ἡμῖν γέγονε,
μηδὲν μὲν ἄνευ τῆς πόλεως τῆς ἡμετέρας εἶναι, τὰ δὲ
39 πλεῖστα διὰ ταύτην γεγενῆσθαι. παραλαβοῦσα γὰρ τοὺς c
Ἕλληνας ἀνόμως ζῶντας καὶ σποράδην οἰκοῦντας, καὶ τοὺς
μὲν ὑπὸ δυναστειῶν ὑβριζομένους, τοὺς δὲ δι' ἀναρχίαν
ἀπολλυμένους, καὶ τούτων τῶν κακῶν αὐτοὺς ἀπήλλαξε,
τῶν μὲν κυρία γενομένη, τοῖς δ' αὐτὴν παράδειγμα
ποιήσασα· πρώτη γὰρ καὶ νόμους ἔθετο καὶ πολιτείαν
40 κατεστήσατο. δῆλον δ' ἐκεῖθεν· οἱ γὰρ ἐν ἀρχῇ περὶ

εὑρεῖν.] 'Non video satis, qui locus hic sit infinitivo: itaque malim
εὑρῶσα.' Morus. But the sequence
εὑροῦσα, ἥνπερ could not, I think, have
been written by Isocr. (propter hiatum); and the Inf. can be explained
as an inf. in apposition to ἀρχὴν τ.
τῶν εὐεργ. Cf. Evag. § 28, λαβὼν
ταύτην ἀφορμὴν, ἀμύνεσθαι κ. μὴ
προτέρους ὑπάρχειν, Hel. § 10, νομί-
ζων ὀφείλειν τοῦτον τὸν ἔρανον, μηδενὸς ἀποστῆναι (quoted by Coray and
Spohn), and Plato, Apol. p. 21 λ,
ὄνομα δὲ τοῦτο λέγεσθαι (sc. ἐμέ),
σοφὸν εἶναι. Madv. Synt. § 190.

ἥνπερ χρή.] Ba. ποιήσασθαι. The
antecedent of ἥνπερ is ἀρχὴν.

καλῶν καλῶς.] This is a very
common collocation. Cf. Aristoph.
Ach. 253, τὸ κανοῦν καλὴ καλῶς
οἴσεις, also κακὸν κακῶς (e.g. Aesch.
Pers. 1035, δόσιν κακὰν κακῶν κακοῖς), λαμπρὸν λαμπρῶς, πάντες πάντως, and in Lat. misero misere (Lucr.
III. 898), often in Plautus, e.g. doc-
tum docte, bonus bonis bene feceris:
and, for one of many English instances, Shak. Rich. III. v. 1, Bloody
and guilty guiltily awake. (Partly
from Lobeck, Paralip. p. 58.)

ΗΣ omit καλῶν.—Bens. (with

Codd. Urb. and Ambros.) inserts
it.

39. σποράδην.] One of the many
adverbs in -δην. Cf. φοράδην, λογά-
δην, σύρδην, φύρδω, βάδην, ἀριστίνδην. For the phraseology cf. Hel.
§ 35 (of Theseus), τὴν πόλιν σποράδην κ. κατὰ κώμας οἰκοῦσαν εἰς ταὐτὸν
συνήγαγε, and Thuc. II. 15.

νόμους ἔθετο.] Observe the regular usage: (ἡ πόλις) ἔθετο τὸν νόμον·
(ὁ νομοθέτης) ἔθηκε τὸν νόμον· ὁ νόμος
ἐτέθη. Cf. ad Dem. § 36, κειμένους, n.
and de Perm. § 83, νόμους τιθέναι...
τῶν κειμένων.

40. ἐν ἀρχῇ.] 'In the beginning,'
'in the earliest times.' In Dobree's
Adversaria, Vol. I. p. 265, we find
the brief confession, Non intelligo.
In a case where Dobree is doubtful, no one can afford to be over-
confident, but the passage apparently
refers to the traditionary and mythical antiquity of various Athenian
courts of homicide and especially of
the Areopagus. The ancient glories
of that tribunal are mentioned by
Demosthenes (Aristocr. § 65) as follows: 'There are many institutions
among us of a character not to be
found elsewhere, but one there is,

τῶν φονικῶν ἐγκαλέσαντες καὶ βουληθέντες μετὰ λόγου d
καὶ μὴ μετὰ βίας διαλύσασθαι τὰ πρὸς ἀλλήλους ἐν τοῖς
νόμοις τοῖς ἡμετέροις τὰς κρίσεις ἐποιήσαντο περὶ αὑτῶν.
καὶ μὲν δὴ καὶ τῶν τεχνῶν τάς τε πρὸς τἀναγκαῖα τοῦ

the most peculiar of all, and the most highly venerable, the court of Areopagus; respecting which we have more glorious traditions and myths, and more honourable testimonies of our own, than we have of any other tribunal; of which it is proper you should hear one or two by way of sample (δείγματος ἕνεκα). In ancient times, as we are informed by tradition, the Gods in this tribunal alone deigned both to demand and to render justice for murder, and to sit in judgment upon disputes between each other; so says the legend: Poseidon demanded justice of Ares on behalf of his son Halirrhothius, and the twelve Gods sat in judgment between the Furies and Orestes.' (Mainly from C. R. Kennedy).—In § 81 Dem. speaks of the 5 courts in which homicide was tried (τὸ ἐν Ἀρείῳ πάγῳ, τὸ ἐπὶ Παλλαδίῳ, τὸ ἐπὶ Δελφινίῳ, τὸ ἐπὶ Πρυτανείῳ, τὸ ἐν Φρεαττοῖ) as δικαστήρια, ἃ θεοὶ κατέδειξαν (see Pancg. § 47. n.) καὶ μετὰ ταῦτα ἄνθρωποι χρῶνται πάντα τὸν χρόνον, and in § 70 he speaks of the founders of the Areop. as οἱ ταῦτα ἐξ ἀρχῆς τὰ νόμιμα διαθέντες, οἵτινές ποτ᾿ ἦσαν, εἴθ᾿ ἥρωες εἴτε θεοί. According to Aeschylus (Eum. 682, πρῶτας δίκας κρίνοντες αἵματος χυτοῦ) the first trial for homicide held at Athens was that of Orestes; but Hellanicus, a contemporary of Aeschylus, states that the Areop. had awarded sentence to many other heroes and even gods before him. The sanctity of that court made its verdicts respected throughout Greece, and before the first Messenian war the Messenians proposed to refer the points at issue to its decision, on the ground that, from of old, it had had jurisdiction in cases of homicide.

(Pausanias, IV. 5. § 1, ὅτι δίκας τὰς φονικὰς...ἐδόκει δικάζειν ἐκ παλαιοῦ.) (On the Areop., besides the *locus classicus* quoted from Dem., cf. Isocr. *Areop.* §§ 37—45, and Aesch. *Eum. passim*, with Müller's dissertation, §§ 64—73). For an allusion to the general claim asserted by Isocr. cf. Aelian (fl. c. 250 A. D.), *varia historia*, III. § 38, δίκας τε δοῦναι καὶ λαβεῖν εὗρον Ἀθηναῖοι πρῶτοι.

μετὰ λόγου καὶ μή.] ἀλλὰ μή would have been more idiomatic (cf. *ad Dem.* § 2. n.), but this is avoided *propter hiatum.*

ἐν τοῖς νόμοις.] Cf. Thuc. I. 77, παρ᾿ ἡμῖν αὐτοῖς ἐν τοῖς ὁμοίοις νόμοις ποιήσαντες τὰς κρίσεις.

τῶν τεχνῶν κ.τ.λ.] Pliny, *Nat. Hist.* VII. 194 sqq. (quoted by Schn.) gives a long list of Athenian discoveries in art: 'Brick-kilns (*lateriae*) and houses were first set up at Athens by the brothers Euryalus and Hyperbius; silver was discovered by Erichthonius of Athens; potteries (*figlinae*) invented by Coroebus; carpentry (*fabrica materiaria*), including the saw, the axe, the plummet, the gimlet, as well as glue and isinglass (*ichthyocolla*) by Daedalus; the culture of the vine and of trees by Eumolpus of Athens; olive-oil and oil-mills, as well as honey, by Aristaeus of Athens; the use of the hoe and the plough by Buzyges (= Βουζύγης) of Athens; &c. &c.

Aelian, *var. hist.* III. § 38, states that to Athens the world was beholden for the olive and the fig; for administration of justice; for athletics and chariot-driving; and a well-known passage in Milton, *Par. Reg.* IV. 240, speaks of '*Athens, the eye of Greece,* mother of arts *and eloquence.*'

βίου χρησίμας καὶ τὰς πρὸς ἡδονὴν μεμηχανημένας, τὰς
μὲν εὑροῦσα, τὰς δὲ δοκιμάσασα χρῆσθαι τοῖς ἄλλοις
41 παρέδωκεν. (ια'.) Τὴν τοίνυν ἄλλην διοίκησιν οὕτω φιλο-
ξένως κατεσκευάσατο καὶ πρὸς ἅπαντας οἰκείως ὥστε καὶ c
τοῖς χρημάτων δεομένοις καὶ τοῖς ἀπολαῦσαι τῶν ὑπαρχόντων ἐπιθυμοῦσιν ἀμφοτέροις ἁρμόττειν, καὶ μήτε τοῖς
εὐδαιμονοῦσι μήτε τοῖς δυστυχοῦσιν ἐν ταῖς αὐτῶν ἀχρή-
στως ἔχειν, ἀλλ' ἑκατέροις αὐτῶν εἶναι παρ' ἡμῖν, τοῖς
μὲν ἡδίστας διατριβάς, τοῖς δ' ἀσφαλεστάτην καταφυγήν.
42 ἔτι δὲ τὴν χώραν οὐκ αὐτάρκη κεκτημένων ἑκάστων, ἀλλὰ 49
τὰ μὲν ἐλλείπουσαν, τὰ δὲ πλείω τῶν ἱκανῶν φέρουσαν,
καὶ πολλῆς ἀπορίας οὔσης τὰ μὲν ὅπου χρὴ διαθέσθαι,
τὰ δ' ὁπόθεν εἰσαγαγέσθαι, καὶ ταύταις ταῖς συμφοραῖς
ἐπήμυνεν ἐμπόριον γὰρ ἐν μέσῳ τῆς Ἑλλάδος τὸν Πειραιᾶ
κατεσκευάσατο, τοσαύτην ἔχονθ' ὑπερβολὴν, ὥσθ' ἃ παρὰ
τῶν ἄλλων ἐν παρ' ἑκάστων χαλεπόν ἐστι λαβεῖν, ταῦθ'
ἅπαντα παρ' αὐτῆς ῥάδιον εἶναι πορίσασθαι.   b

τὰς μὲν εὑροῦσα κ.τ.λ.] In
Panath. § 102, Isocr. tells us of one
of his pupils, who had the assurance
to claim a similar merit for Lacedaemon (ὅτι τὰ κάλλιστα τῶν ἐπιτηδευμάτων εὑρόντες αὐτοί τε χρῶνται
κ. τοῖς ἄλλοις κατέδειξαν); he de-
nounces the claim as ἀσεβῆ καὶ
ψευδῆ καὶ πολλῶν ἐναντιώσεων με-
στόν, and proceeds to confute it at
length, § 204 sqq.
41. τοῖς χρημάτων δεομένοις—
τοῖς δυστυχοῦσιν.] Obs. the Chiasmus, or inverted parallelism (v. *ad
Dem.* § 7. n.).
ἡδίστας διατριβάς.] Aelian *var.
hist.* XII. § 46, records a saying of
Isocrates, part of which may be
quoted to illustrate this passage, τὴν
Ἀθηναίων πόλιν ἐπιδημῆσαι μὲν
εἶναι ἡδίστην, καὶ κατά γε τοῦτο
τασῶν τῶν κατὰ τὴν Ἑλλάδα δια-
φέρειν· ἐνοικῆσαι δὲ ἀσφαλῆ μηκέτι
εἶναι.
διατριβή = 'pastime;' διατρίβειν
with or without χρόνον = *terere* or
conterere tempus. The same idea

may be noticed in Shak. *Taming
of Shrew*, I. 2, fin. *Please ye we may*
contrive *this afternoon, And quaff
carouses*. And in Churchyard's *Wor-
thiness of Wales*, p. 110, *With ewe
and lambe, with goats and kids they
play, With greatest toils* to rub out
weary day.
41. διαθέσθαι]='to dispose of,'
'to distribute,' 'to sell.' Cf. Xen.
de Rep. Ath. II, 11, τὸν δὲ πλοῦτον
μόνοι οἷοί τ' εἰσιν ἔχειν (οἱ Ἀθηναῖοι)...
εἰ γάρ τις πόλις πλουτεῖ ξύλοις ναυπη-
γησίμοις, ποῖ διαθήσεται ἐὰν μὴ πείσῃ
τὸν ἄρχοντα τῆς θαλάττης; Sim. δια-
θέσθε = 'disposal,' Isocr. *Busiris*,
§ 14, τῇ τῶν ὄντων διαθέσει καὶ τῇ
τῶν ἐλλειπόντων κομιδῇ.
Πειραιᾶ.] On the Peiraeeus, the
great port of Athens, see Leake's
Athens, I. § 9. The particular part
of the Peiraeeus where the merchan-
dise of many nations was exhibited,
was called the Δεῖγμα or exchange.
ἃ—πορίσασθαι.] Obs. the elaborate parallelism, ἃ ‖ ταῦθ', παρὰ τῶν
ἄλλων ‖ παρ' αὐτῆς, ἐν ‖ ἅπαντα, χα-

43   (ιβ΄.) Τῶν τοίνυν τὰς πανηγύρεις καταστησάντων δικαίως ἐπαινουμένων, ὅτι τοιοῦτον ἔθος ἡμῖν παρέδοσαν,
ὥστε σπεισαμένους καὶ τὰς ἔχθρας τὰς ἐνεστηκυίας διαλυσαμένους, συνελθεῖν εἰς ταὐτόν, καὶ μετὰ ταῦτ' εὐχὰς καὶ
θυσίας κοινὰς ποιησαμένους ἀναμνησθῆναι μὲν τῆς συγγενείας τῆς πρὸς ἀλλήλους ὑπαρχούσης, εὐμενεστέρως δ'
εἰς τὸν λοιπὸν χρόνον διατεθῆναι πρὸς ἡμᾶς αὐτούς, καὶ τάς c
44 τε παλαιὰς ξενίας ἀνανεώσασθαι καὶ καινὰς ἑτέρας ποιήσασθαι, καὶ μήτε τοῖς ἰδιώταις μήτε τοῖς διενεγκοῦσι τὴν
φύσιν ἀργὸν εἶναι τὴν διατριβήν, ἀλλ' ἀθροισθέντων τῶν
Ἑλλήνων ἐγγενέσθαι τοῖς μὲν ἐπιδείξασθαι τὰς αὐτῶν

λετὸν)(ῥᾴδιον, and λαβεῖν ἢ περίσα-
σθαι. For an equally elaborate sentence, v. Dem. *Lept.* § 26, παρὰ
μὲν γὰρ τὰς ἐπὶ τῶν χορηγιῶν δαπά-
νας ἡμέρας μέρος μικρὸν ἢ χάρις τοῖς
θεωμένοις ἡμῶν, παρὰ δὲ τὰς τῶν εἰς
τὸν πόλεμον παρασκευῶν ἀφθονίας
πάντα τὸν χρόνον ἡ σωτηρία πάσῃ
τῇ πόλει.

43. τῶν τοίνυν—ἀνελείφθη.]
This long sentence can easily be
unravelled by noticing that it commences with a gen. absolute, in-
troducing the reason why those who
first instituted general assemblies
are well worthy of praise. This
is followed by an exhaustive summary of the characteristics of πανηγύρεις, introduced with ὥστε and
not concluded until near the end of
§ 44; after this summary is finished,
Isocr. gathers up all the threads of
the sentence in the clause τοσούτων
τοίνυν ἀγαθῶν—γεγνομένων (which
throws us back to τοίνυν at the beginning of § 43), and then concludes
with the principal vb. contained in
οὐδ' ἐν τούτοις ἡ π. ἡμ. ἀπελείφθη.

πρὸς ἡμᾶς αὐτούς]=ἀλλήλους, cf.
§ 34, σφίσιν αὐτοῖς, n.

44. ἰδιώταις.] The term ἰδιώτης
(= a non-professional man, an ama-
teur) is essentially *negative*, and its
exact meaning has constantly to be
determined from the context. The
only English word that in any de-

gree covers the same ground is the
word 'layman,' in contrast to 'law-
yer,' 'physician,' 'artist,' 'poet,' as
well as to 'clergyman.' The following passages may help to indicate the various points of negative
contrast in which the ἰδιώτης may
be placed : *Nicocl.* § 17, πρότερον ἰδιώ-
ται γίγνονται πρὶν αἰσθέσθαι τι τῶν
τῆς πόλεως καὶ λαβεῖν ἐμπειρίαν αὐτῶν, *ib.* § 35, τοῖς ἰδιώταις καὶ τοῖς
τυράννοις. *De perm.* § 69, τὰς ἰδιώτας καὶ τοὺς δυνάστας. *Paneg.* § 11,
ἰδιώτας = 'ordinary hearers')('true
critics.' Thuc. II. 48, ἰατρὸς καὶ
ἰδιώτης. Plato, *Protag.* 327 C, op.
to αὐλητής, *de leg.* p. 800 A, op.
to ποιητής, and (for a more general
instance) *Sophist.* 221 C, op. to τῷδ
τέχνην ἔχων.

In the present passage the contrast is drawn between the ordinary
man and professional gymnast. Cf.
Plato *Legg.* VIII. 839 E, εἰ τὸ σῶμα
ἔχων καὶ μὴ ἰδιωτικῶς ἢ φαύλως.

The word 'idiot' occasionally retains in old English the meaning of
ἰδιώτης. This is partly to be ascribed to the influence of the Latin
Vulgate. Cf. Wiclif's Trans. of
1 Cor. xiv. 16 (and 23), *Who fillith
the place of an idiot ; hou schal he
seie amen on thi blessinge?* Jeremy
Taylor, '*Humility is a duty in great
ones, as well as in idiots.*' (See further, Trench, *Select Glossary*, s. v.)

εὐτυχίας, τοῖς δὲ θεάσασθαι τούτους πρὸς ἀλλήλους ἀγωνι-
ζομένους, καὶ μηδετέροις ἀθύμως διάγειν, ἀλλ᾽ ἑκατέρους
ἔχειν, ἐφ᾽ οἷς φιλοτιμηθῶσιν, οἱ μὲν ὅταν ἴδωσι τοὺς d
ἀθλητὰς αὐτῶν ἕνεκα πονοῦντας, οἱ δ᾽ ὅταν ἐνθυμηθῶσιν,
ὅτι πάντες ἐπὶ τὴν σφετέραν θεωρίαν ἥκουσι,—τοσούτων
τοίνυν ἀγαθῶν διὰ τὰς συνόδους ἡμῖν γιγνομένων οὐδ᾽ ἐν
45 τούτοις ἡ πόλις ἡμῶν ἀπελείφθη. καὶ γὰρ θεάματα πλεῖστα
καὶ κάλλιστα κέκτηται, τὰ μὲν ταῖς δαπάναις ὑπερβάλ-
λοντα, τὰ δὲ κατὰ τὰς τέχνας εὐδοκιμοῦντα, τὰ δ᾽ ἀμφοτέροις τούτοις διαφέροντα, καὶ τὸ πλῆθος τῶν εἰσαφικνουμέ- c
νων ὡς ἡμᾶς τοσοῦτόν ἐστιν, ὥστ᾽ εἴ τι ἐν τῷ πλησιάζειν
ἀλλήλοις ἀγαθόν ἐστι, καὶ τοῦθ᾽ ὑπ᾽ αὐτῆς περιειλῆφθαι.
πρὸς δὲ τούτοις καὶ φιλίας εἰρεῖν πιστοτάτας καὶ συνου-

οἱ μὲν ... οἱ δ᾽.] We might have
expected either (1) τοὺς μὲν ... τοὺς
δὲ (in app. to ἐκατέρους), or (2)
ὅταν οἱ μὲν ἴδωσι ... οἱ δ᾽ ἐνθυμηθῶσι,
but Isocr. here prefers blending the
order of (1) with the *construction* of
(2).
αὐτῶν.] The *reflex. pron.* does
not refer to *τοσούτας*, but to the
subject of ἴδωσι. 'On their behalf,'
i.e. on behalf of the spectators; not
only to amuse those who were either
unable or unwilling to join in the
athletic contests, but also to be the
representative champions, whose
victory (as Pindar is constantly telling us) threw a reflected glory on
the various cities to which the spectators belonged.
σφετέραν θεωρίαν.] *poss. pron.*
in the same sense as the *objective*
genitive. Madv. *Synt.* § 67. b.
45. καὶ γὰρ θεάματα κ.τ.λ.] A
rapid enumeration of the leading attractions of Athenian πανηγύρεις, esp.
of the *Panathenca*, and the *Dionysia*,
with their shows, their dances, their
processions and their gymnastic and
intellectual contests.
The word θεάματα refers not
merely (as explained by Schn., who
lays perhaps too much stress on
κέκτηται) to the Parthenon, the
Poecile, the public buildings, and

similar 'sights,' but also to the
'spectacles,' the games, the magni-
ficent processions, and the general
amusements which characterized
the πανηγύρεις. The special 'sights'
of the πανηγύρεις, besides those
mentioned in the rest of this §,
included the exhibition of mena-
geries of bears and lions, as attested
by Isocr. *de Perm.* § 213, καθ᾽ ἕκαστον τὸν ἐνιαυτὸν θεωροῦντες ἐν ταῖς
θαύμασι [corrected by Dr. Thompson (*Journ. of Class. and Sacr. Phil.*
no. xi. p. 151) into θεάμασι. May
not the vulg., which is retained by
Bens., be defended by the immediate context θαυμάσεις τὰς πραότη-
τας ... τῶν θηρίων?] τοὺς μὲν λέοντας
πραότερον διακειμένους ... τὰς δ᾽ ἄρ-
κτους καλινδουμένας καὶ παλαιούσας καὶ
μιμουμένας τὰς ἡμετέρας ἐπιστήμας.
τὸ δὲ πλῆθος κ.τ.λ.] Cf. Dem.
Mid. § 217, ἐν πανηγύρει ... τοὺς ἐπι-
δημήσαντας ἅπαντας τῶν 'Ελλήνων.
See Becker's *Charicles*, scene x.
πρὸς δὲ τούτοις κ.τ.λ.] *i.e.* 'And
in addition to this, it is *our* city that
provides the best opportunities for
forming the most trustworthy friendships and meeting with the most
varied kinds of intercourse; and also
for beholding contests, not only of
speed and might, but also of speech
and mind, and of all other things

σίαις ἐντυχεῖν παντοδαπωτάταις μάλιστα παρ' ἡμῖν ἐστιν,
ἔτι δ' ἀγῶνας ἰδεῖν, μὴ μόνον τάχους καὶ ῥώμης, ἀλλὰ καὶ 50
λόγων καὶ γνώμης καὶ τῶν ἄλλων ἔργων ἁπάντων, καὶ
46 τούτων ἆθλα μέγιστα. πρὸς γὰρ οἷς αὐτὴ τίθησι, καὶ τοὺς
ἄλλους διδόναι συναναπείθει· τὰ γὰρ ὑφ' ἡμῶν κριθέντα
τοσαύτην λαμβάνει δόξαν ὥστε παρὰ πᾶσιν ἀνθρώποις
ἀγαπᾶσθαι. χωρὶς δὲ τούτων αἱ μὲν ἄλλαι πανηγύρεις
διὰ πολλοῦ χρόνου συλλεγεῖσαι ταχέως διελύθησαν, ἡ δ' b
ἡμετέρα πόλις ἅπαντα τὸν αἰῶνα τοῖς ἀφικνουμένοις πανή-
γυρίς ἐστιν.

47 (νζ'.) Φιλοσοφίαν τοίνυν, ἣ πάντα ταῦτα συνεξεῦρε καὶ
συγκατεσκεύασε, καὶ πρός τε τὰς πράξεις ἡμᾶς ἐπαίδευσε
καὶ πρὸς ἀλλήλους ἐπράϋνε, καὶ τῶν συμφορῶν τάς τε δι'
ἀμαθίαν καὶ τὰς ἐξ ἀνάγκης γιγνομένας διεῖλε, καὶ τὰς μὲν
φυλάξασθαι, τὰς δὲ καλῶς ἐνεγκεῖν ἐδίδαξεν, ἡ πόλις ἡμῶν

besides, with the grandest prizes for
them all.'
παντοδαπωτάταις.] Cf. de Perm.
§ 295, γυμνάσια πλεῖστα καὶ παντο-
δαπώτατα. This is the reading of
the best MSS. The superlative of
this word is often altered by transcribers into the positive: 'sciendum
librarios adjectivi παντοδαποῖς gradui
superlativo adeo se ubique locorum
gessisse inimicos, vix usquam ut nullis
librorum dissensionibus compareat.'
Dindorf (ap. Bens. Praef. xv.)
ῥώμης]||[γνώμης.] Obs. the παρο-
νομασία. Cf. Agathon (tragedian;
died 400 B. C.) ap. Stob. flor. 54, 41
γνώμη δὲ κρεῖσσόν ἐστιν ἢ ῥώμη χερῶν,
Epigram on Demosthenes (died 322
B.C.) ap. Plut. vit. Dem. § 30, εἴπερ
ἴσην ῥώμην γνώμῃ, Δημόσθενες, εἶχες,
οὔποτ' ἂν Ἑλλήνων ἦρξεν Ἄρης Μακε-
δών (Oh! had thy might and mind
been one, Greece had ne'er bowed
to Macedon).—v. also the fragm. of
Gorgias in DS oratores Att. II. p. 129.
This affectation is common in Isocr.
e.g. § 186, ῥήμην καὶ μνήμην, Antop.
§ 35, στήσεις...χρήσεις.
The contrast between 'physical'
and 'intellectual' contests is usually

expressed by the phrases ἀγῶνες γυ-
μνικαί)(μουσικαί or more frequently
μουσικῆς, Arist. Plut. 1160, Plat.
Menex. 249 B and C.
On these contests see Dict. Antiq.
art. Panathenaea, Dionysia. The
intellectual amusements included
rhetorical disputations, like the Paneg. and Panathenaic speeches of
Isocr.

46. αἱ μὲν ἄλλαι κ.τ.λ.] e.g. the
Olympic and Pythian games, held
once only in four years.
διελύθησαν...ἐστί.] Cf. ad Dem.
§ 6, ἀνήλωσεν...ἐστίν.

47. φιλοσοφίαν—ἐντίμους ὄντας.] The principal verbs are κατέδειξε ... ἐτίμησεν. The following
words form the skeleton of the sentence: φιλοσοφίαν (ἣ κ.τ.λ.) ἡ πόλις
κατέδειξε καὶ λόγους ἐτίμησεν, (ὧν
κ.τ.λ.) συνειδυῖα μὲν, ὅτι κ.τ.λ., ὁρῶσα
δὲ κ.τ.λ.

φιλοσοφίας.] i.e. 'practical philosophy.' de Perm. § 266, φιλοσοφίαν
οὐκ οἶμαι δεῖν προσαγορεύειν τὴν μηδὲν ἐν τῷ παρόντι μήτε πρὸς τὸ λέγειν
μήτε πρὸς τὸ πράττειν ὠφελοῦσαν.
v. 9. § n.

κατέδειξε, καὶ λόγους ἐτίμησεν, ὧν πάντες μὲν ἐπιθυμοῦσι, c
48 τοῖς δ' ἐπισταμένοις φθονοῦσι, συνειδυῖα μὲν ὅτι τοῦτο
μόνον ἐξ ἁπάντων τῶν ζῴων ἴδιον ἔφυμεν ἔχοντες, καὶ διότι
τούτῳ πλεονεκτήσαντες καὶ τοῖς ἄλλοις ἅπασιν αὐτῶν διη-
νέγκαμεν, ὁρῶσα δὲ περὶ μὲν τὰς ἄλλας πράξεις οὕτω ταρα-
χώδεις οὔσας τὰς τύχας ὥστε πολλάκις ἐν αὐταῖς καὶ τοὺς
φρονίμους ἀτυχεῖν καὶ τοὺς ἀνοήτους κατορθοῦν, τῶν δὲ
λόγων τῶν καλῶς καὶ τεχνικῶς ἐχόντων οὐ μετὸν τοῖς φαύ-
49 λοις, ἀλλὰ ψυχῆς εὖ φρονούσης ἔργον ὄντας, καὶ τούς τε d
σοφοὺς καὶ τοὺς ἀμαθεῖς δοκοῦντας εἶναι ταύτῃ πλεῖστον
ἀλλήλων διαφέροντας, ἔτι δὲ τοὺς εὐθὺς ἐξ ἀρχῆς ἐλευθέρως
τεθραμμένους ἐκ μὲν ἀνδρίας καὶ πλούτου καὶ τῶν τοιούτων
ἀγαθῶν οὐ γιγνωσκομένους, ἐκ δὲ τῶν λεγομένων μάλιστα
καταφανεῖς γιγνομένους, καὶ τοῦτο σύμβολον τῆς παιδεύσεως ἡμῶν ἑκάστου πιστότατον ἀποδεδειγμένον, καὶ τοὺς
λόγῳ καλῶς χρωμένους οὐ μόνον ἐν ταῖς αὐτῶν δυναμένους, e
50 ἀλλὰ καὶ παρὰ τοῖς ἄλλοις ἐντίμους ὄντας. τοσοῦτον δ'
ἀπολέλοιπεν ἡ πόλις ἡμῶν περὶ τὸ φρονεῖν καὶ λέγειν τοὺς
ἄλλους ἀνθρώπους, ὥσθ' οἱ ταύτης μαθηταὶ τῶν ἄλλων

κατέδειξε.] ' *Hac vi docendi, seu
instituendi, frequentissimum.* Dem.
Aristocr. § 11, ὁ τὰς ἀγωνστάτας τελε-
τὰς καταδείξας 'Ορφεύ.' Weber on
Dem. *Aristocr.* § 81 (quoted in § 40,
ἐν ἀρχῇ. n.).

πάντες.....φθονοῦσι.] Isocr. frequently speaks of his envious rivals,
e.g. Phil. § 11...ὁρῶν ὅτι χαλεπόν
ἐστι περὶ τὴν αὐτὴν ὑπόθεσιν δύο λόγους ἀνεκτὸν εἰπεῖν, ἄλλως τε κἂν ὁ
πρότερον ἐκδοθεὶς (sc. ὁ πανηγυρικὸς)
οὕτως ᾖ γεγραμμένος ὥστε τοὺς βα-
σκαίνοντας ἡμᾶς (cf. *ad Dem.* § 5.
n.) μιμεῖσθαι καὶ θαυμάζειν αὐτὸν μᾶλλον τῶν καθ' ὑπερβολὴν ἐπαινούντων.

48. **τοῦτο μόνον κ.τ.λ.**] Cf. *Nicocl.* §§ 6, 7.—On ῥῷον v. Cobet,
nov. lect. 284.

καὶ διότι.] This is the reading
of Codd. Urb. Ambr. Vict. and is
adopted by Bcos. as well as BS.—
Becker and Dindf. read καὶ ὅτι. It
is only when a *hiatus* is avoided by
the use of διότι instead of ὅτι, that

Isocr. prefers the former, *e.g. Plataic.* § 23, φανερὸν εἶναι διότι, and
esp. *Lochit.* § 7, ἐνθυμουμένους ὅτι...
καὶ διότι κ.τ.λ.—The word is constantly used by Isocr. in the same
sense as ὅτι, and yet Henr. Stephens
appealed to this very use of διότι in
the old editions of *Ep. ad Dem.* § 48,
to prove its spuriousness.

πολλάκις—κατορθοῦν.] Quoted
by Arist. *Rhet.* III. 9, as an instance
of ἀντικειμένη λέξις (v. § 35, ἀμφοτέρους—ἐφόρισαν. n.)

ἀτυχεῖν)(**κατορθοῦν.**] v. § 6, κατορθωθῇ. n.

ψυχῆς εὖ φρονούσης.] For the
sense cf. Quintil. *Inst. orat.* procem.
*Oratorem instituimus illum perfec-
tum, qui esse nisi vir bonus non
potest.*

50. **οἱ ταύτης μαθηταὶ κ.τ.λ.**]
Cf. *de Perm.* §§ 295–6, esp. ἀπας-
τας τοὺς λέγειν ὄντας δεινοὺς τῆς
πόλεως εἶναι μαθητάς, Thuc. II. 41,
ξυνελὼν λέγω τὴν πᾶσαν πόλιν τῆς

διδάσκαλοι γεγόνασι, καὶ τὸ τῶν Ἑλλήνων ὄνομα πεποίηκε 51
μηκέτι τοῦ γένους ἀλλὰ τῆς διανοίας δοκεῖν εἶναι, καὶ μᾶλλον Ἕλληνας καλεῖσθαι τοὺς τῆς παιδεύσεως τῆς ἡμετέρας
ἢ τοὺς τῆς κοινῆς φύσεως μετέχοντας.

51   (ιδʹ.) Ἵνα δὲ μὴ δοκῶ περὶ τὰ μέρη διατρίβειν ὑπὲρ
ὅλων τῶν πραγμάτων ὑποθέμενος μηδʹ ἐκ τούτων ἐγκωμιάζειν τὴν πόλιν ἀπορῶν τὰ πρὸς τὸν πόλεμον αὐτὴν ἐπαι-

Ἑλλάδος παιδεύσιν εἶναι, and Plato, *Protag.* 337 D, (IIippias *loq.*) τῆς Ἑλλάδος εἰς αὐτὸ τὸ πρυτανεῖον τῆς σοφίας.

τὸ τῶν Ἑλλήνων ὄνομα.] τῶν Ἑλλ. is the gen. of definition, used instead of a noun in apposition. In Eng. we can say either 'the name of Greeks,' or less frequently 'the name Greeks.' In Gk. both forms are found; (1) Isocr. *Archid.* § 110, τὸ τῆς Σπάρτης ὄνομα, and (2) Plat. *Rep.* p. 369 C, ταύτῃ τῇ ξυνοικίᾳ ἐθέμεθα πόλιν ὄνομα (quoted by Schn.). Similarly in Lat. the words *vox, nomen, verbum* often take a gen. of definition, *e.g.* Cic. *de fin.* II. 2, *hæc vox voluptatis* (= this word 'pleasure'), II. 24, *nomen amicitiae* (= the name 'friendship'), and Tac. *Germ.* 2, *vocabulum Germaniae* (= the term G.)— v. Zumpt, *Lat. Gr.* § 425 and Mr Mayor on Cic. *Phil.* II. § 78, *causam amoris.* n.

§§ 51—98. *The deeds of War, for which Athens deserves the supremacy.*

I. 51—65. *Wars with Greeks.*

II. 66—70. *Wars with Barbarians of the mythical period.*

III. 71—98. *Wars with Barbarians of historical times.*

I. *Wars with Greeks.* 51—53. *Athens—the disinterested champion of the oppressed.* 54—60. *Her character and power displayed in reference to the appeal of Adrastus and of the Heraclidae.* 61. *The help given to the Heraclidae formed the foundation of the prosperity of Sparta.* 62. *The ingratitude of that state towards her deliverer.* 63. *Even omitting that consideration, it cannot be an ancestral institution for the supre-* macy to belong to the Spartans, rather than to the Athenians; to an invading nation, rather than to aboriginal inhabitants; to those who were suppliants, rather than to those who befriended them. 64, 65. *In brief, Argos, Thebes, Lacedaemon, were then, as now, the greatest states of Greece, excepting Athens. We were either the champions or the victors of each of these states; and therefore we have the clearest claim to the supremacy.*

51. ὑποθέμενος.] sc. ἐρεῖν. v. table of var. readings.

ἐγκωμιάζειν......ἐπαινεῖν.] 'Eulogize'...'praise.' According to Aristot. *Rhet.* I. 9, 33, 34, and elsewhere, there is a real distinction between ἔπαινος and ἐγκώμιον. The former is 'the expression of moral approbation, and therefore is referred principally to motives and character: the object of the latter is facts, acts realized; the virtue is included by implication, but is here secondary and non-essential' (Mr Cope's *Introd.* p. 215). The object of ἔπαινος is πράξεις, the object of ἐγκώμιον is πράγματα, ἔργα. This distinction is a favourite topic with Greek Rhetoricians in general (see Index to Spengel's *Rhet. Graec.*), and Isocr. partially recognises it in the present passage. As a general rule however he uses the words convertibly, *e. g. Paneg.* § 186, *Archid.* § 100, *Helen.* §§ 14, 15, *Philip.* §§ 146, 147. In all these passages the two words and their corresponding verbs are apparently used indiscriminately. Cf. Plat. *Protag.* 326 A, πολλαὶ διέξοδοι κ. ἔπαινοι κ. ἐγκώμια παλαιῶν ἀνδρῶν ἀγαθῶν.

νεῖν, ταῦτα μὲν εἰρήσθω μοι πρὸς τοὺς ἐπὶ τοῖς τοιού- b
τοις φιλοτιμουμένους· ἡγοῦμαι δὲ τοῖς προγόνοις ἡμῶν οὐχ
ἧττον ἐκ τῶν κινδύνων τιμᾶσθαι προσήκειν ἢ τῶν ἄλλων
52 εὐεργεσιῶν. οὐ γὰρ μικροὺς οὐδ' ὀλίγους οὐδ' ἀφανεῖς ἀγῶνας
ὑπέμειναν, ἀλλὰ πολλοὺς καὶ δεινοὺς καὶ μεγάλους, τοὺς μὲν
ὑπὲρ τῆς αὑτῶν χώρας, τοὺς δ' ὑπὲρ τῆς τῶν ἄλλων ἐλευ-
θερίας· ἅπαντα γὰρ τὸν χρόνον διετέλεσαν κοινὴν τὴν πόλιν c
παρέχοντες καὶ τοῖς ἀδικουμένοις ἀεὶ τῶν Ἑλλήνων ἐπαμύ-
53 νουσαν. διὸ δὴ καὶ κατηγοροῦσί τινες ἡμῶν ὡς οὐκ ὀρθῶς
βουλευομένων, ὅτι τοὺς ἀσθενεστέρους εἰθίσμεθα θεραπεύειν,
ὥσπερ οὐ μετὰ τῶν ἐπαινεῖν βουλομένων ἡμᾶς τοὺς λόγους
ὄντας τοὺς τοιούτους. οὐ γὰρ ἀγνοοῦντες, ὅσον διαφέρουσιν
αἱ μείζους τῶν συμμαχιῶν πρὸς τὴν ἀσφάλειαν, οὕτως ἐβου-
λευόμεθα περὶ αὐτῶν, ἀλλὰ πολὺ τῶν ἄλλων ἀκριβέστερον d
εἰδότες τὰ συμβαίνοντ' ἐκ τῶν τοιούτων, ὅμως ᾑρούμεθα τοῖς
ἀσθενεστέροις καὶ παρὰ τὸ συμφέρον βοηθεῖν μᾶλλον ἢ τοῖς
κρείττοσι τοῦ λυσιτελοῦντος ἕνεκα συναδικεῖν.
54   (ιέ.) Γνοίη δ' ἄν τις καὶ τὸν τρόπον καὶ τὴν ῥώμην τὴν

ἡγοῦμαι κ.τ.λ.] All the following
sections, ending with § 99, are quoted
by Isocr. himself, with some slight
variations, which will be occasionally noticed, in the speech *de Perm.*
§ 59, ἀρξάμενοι ἀπὸ τῆς παραγραφῆς
[sc. ἀπὸ τῆς γραμμῆς ἣν μεχρὶ νῦν πα-
ράγραφον καλοῦμεν. Harpocr. Lex.]
ἀνάγνωθι τὰ περὶ τῆς ἡγεμονίας αὐτοῖς. The long quotation is introduced by a short summary of the
drift of the *Paneg.*, which is quoted
on p. 42.

52. μικροὺς...ὀλίγους...ἀφανεῖς.]
Correspond roughly to μεγάλους...
πολλούς...δεινοί. The inverted parallelism is only partially preserved.
τοῖς ἀδικ. ἀεὶ κ.τ.λ.] i.e. 'Champion of those of the Greeks who, *in
each successive instance*, are the victims of injustice.' For this common
use of ἀεί (=from time to time), cf.
Dem. *Lept.* 463 A, τοὺς ἀεὶ (in each
successive year) λειτουργοῦντας, and
Plato, *Phaedrus*, 242 B, ἀεὶ δὲ μ'

ἐπίσχει [sc. τὸ δαιμόνιον] ὃ ἂν μέλλω
πράττειν (v. Dr Thompson's n.).

53. τοὺς ἀσθ...θεραπεύειν.] Cf.
Plat. *Menex.* 244 E, εἴ τις βούλοιτο
τῆς πόλεως κατηγορῆσαι δικαίως,
τοῦτ' ἂν μόνον λέγων ὀρθῶς ἂν κατη-
γοροῖ, ὡς ἀεὶ λίαν φιλοικτίρμων ἐστὶ
καὶ τοῦ ἥττονος θεραπίς, and Dem.
Lept. 456, § 3. As instances in which
Athens helped the weak against the
strong, we have her support of the
Heraclidae against Argos (§ 54 sqq.),
the Ionians against Darius (500 B.C.),
the Corcyraeans against Corinth
(432), and the Egestaeans against
Syracuse (415).

ὥσπερ κ.τ.λ.] v. § 11, ὥσπερ. n.

54. ῥώμην.] In the corresponding
passage of *de Perm.* the vulg. reading is γνώμην, which Havet (p. 200)
wrongly calls 'bien préférable, d'a-
près la suite des idées.' The reading adopted in the text is not only
supported by MSS., but is in accordance with the sense of § 57.

τῆς πόλεως ἐκ τῶν ἱκετειῶν, ἃς ἤδη τινὲς ἡμῖν ἐποιήσαντο.
τὰς μὲν οὖν ἢ νεωστὶ γεγενημένας ἢ περὶ μικρῶν ἐλθούσας
παραλείψω· πολὺ δὲ πρὸ τῶν Τρωϊκῶν, ἐκεῖθεν γὰρ δίκαιον
τὰς πίστεις λαμβάνειν τοὺς ὑπὲρ τῶν πατρίων ἀμφισβη- c
τοῦντας, ἦλθον οἵ θ' Ἡρακλέους παῖδες καὶ μικρὸν πρὸ
55 τούτων Ἄδραστος ὁ Ταλαοῦ, βασιλεὺς ὢν Ἄργους, οὗτος
μὲν ἐκ τῆς στρατείας τῆς ἐπὶ Θήβας δεδυστυχηκὼς, καὶ 52
τοὺς ὑπὸ τῇ Καδμείᾳ τελευτήσαντας αὐτὸς μὲν οὐ δυνάμενος
ἀνελέσθαι, τὴν δὲ πόλιν ἀξιῶν βοηθεῖν ταῖς κοιναῖς τύχαις

ἱκετειῶν ἅς...] ὧν, attracted into
the same case as ἱκετειῶν, would
have been more idiomatic, but ἅς is
equally correct. Compare Dem.
Aristocr. § 215. περὶ τῶν νόμων ὧν
παραγεγράμμεθα with Andros. § 34.
περὶ τῶν νόμων οὓς παρεγραψάμεθα.

οἵ θ' Ἡρακλέους παῖδες καὶ...
'Ἄδραστος...οὗτος μὲν...οἱ θ' Ἡρακλέους παῖδες.] Obs. the inverted
parallelism or *Chiasmus*, a figure of
speech which is applied not merely
to single words (cf. *ad Dem.* § 7, n.),
but also (as here) to whole clauses.
This artistic arrangement allows the
stronger point to be mentioned first,
the weaker second; then follows an
expansion of the second point, and,
lastly, an effective exposition of the
first.

The more obvious arrangement is
adopted, when there is no sufficient
object to be gained in departing
from it (e.g. § 58). The Scholiast
on Isocrates, *Archid.* § 42, &c., singularly enough, calls this inartistic
sequence of clauses by the name
of τετράκωλος περίοδος χιαστή, a
name which ought to be applied
only to cases of 'inverted parallelism.'

On the Heraclidae and Adrastus
see *Class. Dict.*; Isocr. *Philip.* § 33,
34; Lysias (?) *Or. Funebr.* § 7—16;
Plato, *Menex.* 239 B, &c.

55. τὴν δὲ πόλιν κ.τ.λ.] Cf. Lysias (?) *Or. Funebr.* § 9. πατρίου τιμῆς ἀτυχήσαντες κ. Ἑλληνικοῦ νόμου
στερηθέντες κ. ἐοιρῇ ἢ ἐλπίδος ἡμαρ-

τηκότες. The resemblance between
this speech and the Funeral Oration
of Lysias is, perhaps, too close to
be merely accidental. The genuineness of the speech ascribed to Lysias, is often disputed. It is accepted by Fr. Schlegel, Stallbaum,
and Ottfried Müller (*Hist. Gk. Lit.*
chap. xxxv. § 3); and rejected by
Valckenaer, F.A. Wolf, and Dobree
(*adv.* t. init.) The argument from the
difference of style and from the fact
that Lysias (not being an Athenian
citizen) could not have *delivered* the
oration is not, I think, in itself conclusive. If Lysias wrote the oration
at all, he must have written it before
378 B.C. and probably soon after
394 B.C.; in which case Isocr. may
have read it before publishing the
Paneg. in 380 B.C. If this be true,
I can propose nothing save the hypothesis of a common source to save
Isocr. from the charge of having,
in this and several other passages
(§ 86—98), borrowed from Lysias.
On the whole, however, I confess
that the general argument for the
spuriousness of the Funeral Oration
is too strong to be lightly set
aside.—We are expressly told of
this resemblance by Pseudo-Plutarch
(*Isocr.* p. 239) and the rhetorician
Theon (*Progymn.* I. 155, Walz.)
εὕροις δ' ἂν καὶ παρὰ Ἰσοκράτει ἐν τῷ
Πανηγυρικῷ τὰ ἐν τῷ Λυσίου ἐπι-
ταφίῳ καὶ τῷ [Γοργίου conj. l'fund]
Ὀλυμπικῷ.

καὶ μὴ περιορᾶν τοὺς ἐν τοῖς πολέμοις ἀπιθνήσκοντας ἀτά-
φους γιγνομένους μηδὲ παλαιὸν ἔθος καὶ πάτριον νόμον
56 καταλυόμενον, οἱ δ' Ἡρακλέους παῖδες φεύγοντες τὴν Εὐρυσθέως ἔχθραν, καὶ τὰς μὲν ἄλλας πόλεις ὑπερορῶντες ὡς
οὐκ ἂν δυναμένας βοηθῆσαι ταῖς αὐτῶν συμφοραῖς, τὴν δ' b
ἡμετέραν ἱκανὴν νομίζοντες εἶναι μόνην ἀποδοῦναι χάριν
ὑπὲρ ὧν ὁ πατὴρ αὐτῶν ἅπαντας ἀνθρώπους εὐεργέτησεν.
57 ἐκ δὴ τούτων ῥᾴδιον κατιδεῖν, ὅτι καὶ κατ' ἐκεῖνον τὸν χρόνον ἡ πόλις ἡμῶν ἡγεμονικῶς εἶχε· τίς γὰρ ἂν ἱκετεύειν
τολμήσειεν ἢ τοὺς ἥττους αὐτοῦ ἢ τοὺς ὑφ' ἑτέροις ὄντας,
παραλιπὼν τοὺς μείζω δύναμιν ἔχοντας, ἄλλως τε καὶ περὶ
πραγμάτων οὐκ ἰδίων ἀλλὰ κοινῶν καὶ περὶ ὧν οὐδένας c

ἀποθνήσκονται.] On the usage of
θνήσκω (common in Tragic verse)
and ἀποθνήσκειν (frequent in Comedy
and Attic prose) see Veitch, *Gk.
Verbs*, 273—277. The simple form
τέθνηκα is used (in prose and verse)
as the pf. of both verbs. Cobet,
nov. lect. p. 29, 'Constanter ἀπο-
θνήσκω, ἀποθανοῦμαι, ἀποθανεῖν po-
pulus dicebat, relinquens θνήσκω,...
θανοῦμαι, καταθανοῦμαι, θανεῖν, κατθα-
νεῖν Tragicis, qui populares illas
formas numquam usurpabant: at
omnes pariter dicebant τέθνηκα, τεθνάναι, τεθνεώς quae forma numquam
componitur.'

57 τίς .... τολμήσειεν .... αὐτοῦ.]
The reading of cod. Urb. (followed by
BS) is αὐτοῦ, that of the cod. Ambr.
(followed by Bens.) αὐτῶν. The
reading adopted by Bens· may possibly be the original reading, and
(besides avoiding a hiatus) accounts
for the MS. variation αὐτοῦ, which
Bens. would probably attribute to a
desire to assimilate the pronoun to
its supposed antecedent τίς. According to his earlier view αὐτῶν =
Θηβαίων· according to his later view
it is a partitive genitive, referring
partially to τὰς ἄλλας πόλεις, and
meaning, 'unter ihnen, den Hellenen;' and this is perhaps a reasonable explanation. The sense gained
by retaining αὐτῶν is simple but

very weak. Havet (p. 101) refers
αὐτῶν (*sic*) to the plural idea involved in the word τίς, and thinks
that the slight harshness of this
construction led to variations in the
MSS., *e.g.* τίνες...τολμήσειαν...αὐ-
τῶν and τίς....τολμήσειεν.... αὐτοῦ.
Schn. cuts the knot by reading ἄλλων, and Rauchenstein says of αὐτοῦ 'es ist wegen des Hiatus und
wegen des Sinnes mehr als ver-
dächtig' and prints τοὺς ἥττους [αὐ-
τοῦ]. If a still bolder treatment
of the passage is necessary, it is
worth while to draw attention to
the suspicious reiteration, Η ΤΟΥΣ·
ΗΤΤΟΥΣ· Η ΤΟΥΣ· and to suggest
that Η ΤΟΥΣ ΗΤΤΟΥΣ ΑΥΤΟΥ Η
may be a corruption of ΗΓΟΥΝ
ΗΤΤΟΥΣ ΑΥΤΩΝ, a marginal explanation of τοὺς ὑφ' ἑτέροις ὄντας.
(For equally puerile explanations
see the Scholia, printed in Corny's
ed. I. p. 440—448.) The original
reading on this hypothesis will be
τίς γὰρ ἂν ἱκετεύειν τολμήσειε τοὺς
ὑφ' ἑτέροις ὄντας, παραλιπὼν τοὺς
μείζω δύναμιν ἔχοντας;

οὐδένας.] The pl. of οὐδείς is not
very common. For another instance
see *de Perm.* § 281 (quoted on p.
39). Ast's *Lex.* supplies only four
instances in Plato.

ἄλλους εἰκὸς ἦν ἐπιμεληθῆναι πλὴν τοὺς προεστάναι τῶν
58 Ἑλλήνων ἀξιοῦντας. ἔπειτ' οὐδὲ ψευσθέντες φαίνονται
τῶν ἐλπίδων, δι' ἃς κατέφυγον ἐπὶ τοὺς προγόνους ἡμῶν.
ἀνελόμενοι γὰρ πόλεμον ὑπὲρ μὲν τῶν τελευτησάντων πρὸς
Θηβαίους, ὑπὲρ δὲ τῶν παίδων τῶν Ἡρακλέους πρὸς τὴν
Εὐρυσθέως δύναμιν, τοὺς μὲν ἐπιστρατεύσαντες ἠνάγκασαν d
ἀποδοῦναι θάψαι τοὺς νεκροὺς τοῖς προσήκουσι, Πελοπον-
νησίων δὲ τοῖς μετ' Εὐρυσθέως εἰς τὴν χώραν ἡμῶν εἰσβα-
λόντας ἐπεξελθόντες ἐνίκησαν μαχόμενοι κἀκεῖνον τῆς ὕ-
59 βρεως ἔπαυσαν. θαυμαζόμενοι δὲ καὶ διὰ τὰς ἄλλας πράξεις
ἐκ τούτων τῶν ἔργων ἔτι μᾶλλον εὐδοκίμησαν. οὐ γὰρ παρὰ
μικρὸν ἐποίησαν ἀλλὰ τοσοῦτον τὰς τύχας ἑκατέρων μετήλ-
λαξαν, ὥσθ' ὁ μὲν ἱκετεύειν ἡμᾶς ἀξιώσας βίᾳ τῶν ἐχθρῶν e
ἅπανθ' ὅσων ἐδεήθη διαπραξάμενος, ἀπῆλθεν, Εὐρυσθεὺς δὲ
βιάσασθαι προσδοκήσας αὐτὸς αἰχμάλωτος γενόμενος ἱκέτης
60 ἠναγκάσθη καταστῆναι, καὶ τῷ μὲν ὑπερενεγκόντι τὴν ἀν-
θρωπίνην φύσιν, ὃς ἐκ Διὸς μὲν γεγονώς, ἔτι δὲ θνητὸς ὢν
θεοῦ ῥώμην ἔσχε, τούτῳ μὲν ἐπιτάττων καὶ λυμαινόμενος

---

58. ἐπιστρατεύσαντες ἠνάγκασαν κ.τ.λ.] In *Panath.* § 168—171,
Isocr. gives a very different account.
Here, he speaks of armed force;
there, of an embassy (ὁ δῆμος ἔπεμψε
πρεσβείαν). He is perfectly conscious of the discrepancy, and meets
the objection as follows: οὐδένα
νομίζω τῶν ταῦτα συνειδὼς ἂν δυνηθῆναι τοσαύτης ἀμαθίας εἶναι καὶ φθόνου
μεστὸν, ὅστις οὐκ ἂν ἐπαινέσειέ με καὶ
σωφρονεῖν ἡγήσαιτο τότε μὲν ἐκείνως,
νῦν δ' οὕτω διαλεχθέντα περὶ αὐτῶν.
περὶ μὲν οὖν τούτων οἶδ' ὅτι καλῶς
γέγραφα καὶ συμφερόντως. The start-
ling serenity of this passage is remarkable, even in a speech which
has been recently characterized as a
'wonderful effusion of senile self-
complacency.' (Dr Thompson's
Phaedrus, p. 177.)

ἀποδοῦναι θάψαι.] Madv. *Synt.*
§ 148 b, Goodwin's *Gk. Moods and
Tenses,* § 97.

The account of this event, given

by the Atheniaus in Herodot. (IX.
27) is as follows: 'When the Ar-
gives led their troops with Polynices
against Thebes, and were slain and
refused burial, it is our boast that
we went out against the Cadmeians,
recovered the bodies, and buried
them at Eleusis in our own territory.' (From Rawlinson).

60 τῷ μὲν...τούτῳ μέν.] The first
μέν (followed by a parenthetical μέν
and δέ) is immediately resumed in the
words τούτῳ μέν. Evag. § 23, ὅσα
μέν...ταῦτα μέν κ.τ.λ. Areop. § 47,
παρ' οἷς μέν...παρὰ τούτοις μὲν ὅσα
δέ...ἐνταῦθα δέ. See Madv. *Synt.*
§ 188, 4 and Buttmann's *Midias,*
Exc. xii. § 3.

ἐπιτάττων κ. λυμαινόμενος.] The
first of these words governs the dat.,
the second almost always the acc.
In two passages of Isocr. (*de perm.*
§ 119, *Nicocl.* § 18), λυμαίνεσθαι, governs the dat. but in the present instance τούτῳ is governed by ἐπιτάτ-

ἅπαντα τὸν χρόνον διετέλεσεν, ἐπειδὴ δ' εἰς ἡμᾶς ἐξήμαρτεν, 53
εἰς τοσαύτην κατέστη μεταβολήν, ὥστ' ἐπὶ τοῖς παισὶ τοῖς
ἐκείνου γενόμενος ἐπονειδίστως τὸν βίον ἐτελεύτησεν.

61   (ιϛ'.) Πολλῶν δ' ὑπαρχουσῶν ἡμῖν εὐεργεσιῶν εἰς τὴν
πόλιν τὴν Λακεδαιμονίων περὶ ταύτης μόνης μοι συμβέβη-
κεν εἰπεῖν· ἀφορμὴν γὰρ λαβόντες τὴν δι' ἡμῶν αὐτοῖς γενομένην σωτηρίαν οἱ πρόγονοι μὲν τῶν νῦν ἐν Λακεδαίμονι
βασιλευόντων, ἔκγονοι δ' Ἡρακλέους, κατῆλθον μὲν εἰς Πε- b
λοπόννησον, κατέσχον δ' Ἄργος καὶ Λακεδαίμονα καὶ Μεσ-
σήνην, οἰκισταὶ δὲ Σπάρτης ἐγένοντο, καὶ τῶν παρόντων
62 ἀγαθῶν αὐτοῖς ἁπάντων ἀρχηγοὶ κατέστησαν. ὧν ἐχρῆν
ἐκείνους μεμνημένους μηδέποτ' εἰς τὴν χώραν ταύτην εἰσβάλλειν, ἐξ ἧς ὁρμηθέντες τοσαύτην εὐδαιμονίαν κατεκτή-
σαντο, μηδ' εἰς κινδύνους καθιστάναι τὴν πόλιν ὑπὲρ τῶν
παίδων τῶν Ἡρακλέους προκινδυνεύσασαν, μηδὲ τοῖς μὲν c
ἀπ' ἐκείνου γεγονόσι διδόναι τὴν βασιλείαν, τὴν δὲ τῷ γένει
63 τῆς σωτηρίας αἰτίαν οὖσαν δουλεύειν αὐτοῖς ἀξιοῦν. εἰ δὲ
δεῖ τὰς χάριτας καὶ τὰς ἐπιεικείας ἀνελόντας ἐπὶ τὴν ὑπόθεσιν πάλιν ἐπανελθεῖν καὶ τὸν ἀκριβέστατον τῶν λόγων
εἰπεῖν, οὐ δή που πάτριόν ἐστιν ἡγεῖσθαι τοὺς ἐπήλυδας
τῶν αὐτοχθόνων, οὐδὲ τοὺς εὖ παθόντας τῶν εὖ ποιησάντων, d
64 οὐδὲ τοὺς ἱκέτας γενομένους τῶν ὑποδεξαμένων.   (ιζ'.) Ἔτι
δὲ συντομώτερον ἔχω δηλῶσαι περὶ αὐτῶν. τῶν μὲν γὰρ
Ἑλληνίδων πόλεων χωρὶς τῆς ἡμετέρας Ἄργος καὶ Θῆβαι
καὶ Λακεδαίμων καὶ τότ' ἦσαν μέγισται καὶ νῦν ἔτι διατε-

τῶν, and the second participle serves
simply as a quasi-adverb to define the
first, cf. § 6, σκοπεῖν κ. φιλοσοφεῖν, n.
61. κατῆλθον.] 'Returned.' This
word (like κατιέναι, and κάθοδος,) is
frequently used of 'return from ex-
ile. The passage usually quoted
to illustrate this meaning is Aristoph.
Ran. 1152—1169, where Aeschylus
recites from his Choephorae, the line
ἥκω γὰρ εἰς γῆν τήνδε καὶ κατέρχο-
μαι. Euripides accuses his rival of
tautology; and Aesch. defends himself as follows: ἐλθεῖν μὲν εἰς γῆν
ἔσθ' ὅτῳ μετῇ πάτρας | χωρὶς γὰρ

ἄλλης συμφορᾶς ἐλήλυθεν | φεύγων
δ' ἀνὴρ ἥκει τε καὶ κατέρχεται.
κατῆλθον...κατέσχον...κατέστη-
σαν...κατεκτήσαντο...καθιστάναι.]
The reiteration of κατά in these
compounds is probably intentional.
61 εἰσβάλλειν.] e.g. in the Peloponnesian war.
τοῖς ἀπ' ἐκείνου—τὴν βασιλείαν.]
The constitution of Lacedaemon
consisted, in part, of two hereditary
kings, descended from Eurysthenes
and Procles, the twin sons of Aris-
todemus, the great-great-grandson
of Hercules.

λοῦσιν. φαίνονται δ' ἡμῶν οἱ πρόγονοι τοσοῦτον ἁπάντων
διενεγκόντες, [ὥσθ'] ὑπὲρ μὲν 'Αργείων δυστυχησάντων Θη-
65 βαίοις, ὅτε μέγιστον ἐφρόνησαν, ἐπιτάττοντες, ὑπὲρ δὲ τῶν
παίδων τῶν 'Ηρακλέους 'Αργείους καὶ τοὺς ἄλλους Πελο- c
ποννησίους μάχῃ κρατήσαντες, ἐκ δὲ τῶν πρὸς Εὐρυσθέα
κινδίνων τοὺς οἰκιστὰς καὶ τοὺς ἡγεμόνας τοὺς Λακεδαιμονίων διασώσαντες, ὥστε περὶ μὲν τῆς ἐν τοῖς "Ελλησι δυναστείας οὐκ οἶδ' ὅπως ἄν τις σαφέστερον ἐπιδεῖξαι δυνηθείη.

66 (ιη'.) Δοκεῖ δέ μοι καὶ περὶ τῶν πρὸς τοὺς βαρβάρους 54
τῇ πόλει πεπραγμένων προσήκειν εἰπεῖν, ἄλλως τ' ἐπειδὴ
καὶ τὸν λόγον κατεστησάμην περὶ τῆς ἡγεμονίας τῆς ἐπ'
ἐκείνους· ἅπαντας μὲν οὖν ἐξαριθμῶν τοὺς κινδύνους λίαν

64. φαίνονται ... τοσοῦτον ... διενεγκόντες, ὥστε ... ἐπιτάττοντες ...
κρατήσαντες ... διασώσαντες, ὥστε
κ.τ.λ.] The irregularity of this
sentence has been often noticed. Its
peculiarity consists in the recurrence
of ὥστε near the close, as well as
near the beginning of the sentence.
This eccentricity may be treated in
one of two ways, (1) by the excision
of the first ὥστε, (2) by allowing
both to stand, and attempting to
explain them. The first of these
methods is adopted by Coray, Morus, Auger and Rauchenstein; the
second by Wolf, Spohn, Baiter and
Schneider. If we adopt (2), two
courses are open; either (a) to place
a full stop at διασώσαντες, in which
case ἐπιτάττοντες, κρατήσαντες, διασώσαντες would have to be explained as 'attracted' to the participle
διενεγκόντες. cf. Isaeus de Astyph.
hered. § 16, (quoted by Spohn) ἐπι-
δείξω γὰρ ὑμῖν ἐχθιστον ἁπάντων
ὄντα 'Αστύφιλον Κλέωνι, καὶ οὗτος
σφόδρα καὶ δικαίως μισοῦντα τοῦτον,
ὥστε πολὺ ἂν θᾶττον διαθέμενον μηδένα ποτὲ τῶν ἑαυτοῦ οἰκείων διαλε-
χθῆναι Κλέωνι, μᾶλλον ἢ τὸν τούτου
υἱὸν ποιησάμενον, or (β) to suppose
that the writer allows the sentence
to carry him away for a short time
until he recovers himself by repeating the first ὥστε, which enables

him to gather up the sense and to
conclude the whole sentence in a
regular manner. The meaning
would then be: 'Our ancestors are
proved to have excelled all of these
to so great a degree, that, (in as
much as they laid down the law for
the Thebans, &c. &c.), that, I say,
so far as regards their supremacy
among the Greeks, I know not how
one can display a clearer argument
than this.' If the first ὥστε must
be retained, I prefer proposing (β)
to adopting (a). Other suggestions
might easily be recorded, but after
a careful consideration of all the
explanations of the double ὥστε, I
feel convinced that Isocrates is very
unlikely to have adopted such an
awkward construction. I prefer,
therefore, to place ὥστε in brackets
and to attribute its existence in the
MSS to a desire, on the part of the
copyists, to supply an immediate
correlative to τοσοῦτον, instead of
waiting for the distant ὥστε, which
is its real correlative.

11. §§ 66—70. Wars with Barbarians of the Mythical period, especially the Thracians and the Scythians.

66. ἄλλως τ' ἐπειδὴ καὶ.] ἄλλως
τε καὶ ἐπειδὴ is more common but
less forcible. καὶ emphasizes τὸν
λόγον.

ἂν μακρολογοίην· ἐπὶ δὲ τῶν μεγίστων στὰς τὸν αὐτὸν τρόπον ὅνπερ ὀλίγῳ πρότερον πειράσομαι καὶ περὶ τούτων

67 διελθεῖν. ἔστι γὰρ ἀρχικώτατα μὲν τῶν γενῶν καὶ μεγίστας b
δυναστείας ἔχοντα Σκύθαι καὶ Θρᾷκες καὶ Πέρσαι, τυγχάνουσι δ᾽ οὗτοι μὲν ἅπαντες ἡμῖν ἐπιβουλεύσαντες, ἡ δὲ πόλις πρὸς ἅπαντας τούτους διακινδυνεύσασα· καίτοι τί λοιπὸν ἔσται τοῖς ἀντιλέγουσιν, ἢν ἐπιδειχθῶσι τῶν μὲν Ἑλλήνων οἱ μὴ δυνάμενοι τυγχάνειν τῶν δικαίων ἡμᾶς ἱκετεύειν
ἀξιοῦντες, τῶν δὲ βαρβάρων οἱ βουλόμενοι καταδουλώσα-
σθαι τοὺς Ἕλληνας ἐφ᾽ ἡμᾶς πρώτους ἰόντες;   c

68 (ιθ᾽.) Ἐπιφανέστατος μὲν οὖν τῶν πολέμων ὁ Περσι-
κὸς γέγονεν, οὐ μὴν ἐλάττω τεκμήρια τὰ παλαιὰ τῶν ἔργων
ἐστὶ τοῖς περὶ τῶν πατρίων ἀμφισβητοῦσιν. ἔτι γὰρ ταπεινῆς οὔσης τῆς Ἑλλάδος ἦλθον εἰς τὴν χώραν ἡμῶν
Θρᾷκες μὲν μετ᾽ Εὐμόλπου τοῦ Ποσειδῶνος, Σκύθαι δὲ μετ᾽

ἐπὶ δὲ τῶν μεγίστων στάς.] The
codd. Urb. and Ambr. I omit στάς,
the codd. Vat. and Ambr. 2, and (in
the twin passage in the speech *De
permutatione*) the cod. Laur. insert
it. The word may possibly have
fallen out in consequence of the
similarity of the preceding syllable
-στων, and, as Benseler suggests, is
necessary to keep up the parallelism with the previous participle ἐξαριθμῶν.

68. τοῖς περὶ τῶν πατρίων ἀμφ.]
'To those who are contending for
ancestral rights.' The expression τὰ
πάτρια *includes* and especially refers
to the supremacy. Dr Thompson
(*Journ. of Class. and Sacr. Phil.*
Vol. IV. p. 150) proposes an excellent emendation, περὶ τῶν πρωτείων
ἀμφ., which would have the same
meaning as περὶ τῆς ἡγεμονίας ἀμφ.
in §§ 70, 25, 57, 71, and 166; and
may be supported by Antep. § 6,
ἐπρωτεύσαμεν τῶν Ἑλλήνων. The
common reading may perhaps be
defended by § 54, τοὺς ὑπὲρ τῶν πατρίων ἀμφισβητοῦντας (unless, indeed, we emend that passage also),
and by § 37, ἡγεμονίαν πατριωτέραν.

The Lacedaemonians held that the
supremacy was their hereditary
right, one of their national institutions (§ 18, πάτριον); and Isocr. is
here asserting that in the dispute
for hereditary institutions, including
the supremacy, the old achievements
of Athens with regard to the Thracians and Scythians form an argument at least as convincing as any
that could be deduced from her prowess in the Persian War.

ἔτι γὰρ—χρόνον κ.τ.λ.] This
passage and § 54, ἦλθον—δεδυστυχη-
κώς, are quoted by Theon (Rhetori-
clau, fl. 315 A. D.), *Progymn.* I. p.
201, Walz, with the following introductory remark: διήγησιν δὲ δι-
ηγήσει συμπλέκειν ἐστίν, ὅταν δύο
διηγήσεις ἢ καὶ πλείους ἅμα διηγεῖσθαι
ἐπιχειροῦμεν, τοῦτο δὲ μάλα ἐπετή-
δευσαν αἱ ἀπὸ Ἰσοκράτους καὶ αὐτὸς
ὁ Ἰσοκράτη ἐν τῷ πανηγυρικῷ.

Θρᾷκες...Σκύθαι.] On the invasion of the Scythians see *Class.
Dict.*, and cf. *Panath.* § 193 and
Plato, *Menex.* 239 B. Müller (*Hist. of
Gk. Lit.* chap. III. § 8) holds that the
ante-historical Thracians (mentioned
in the text) and the Thracians of a

Ἀμαζόνων τῶν Ἄρεως θυγατέρων, οὐ κατὰ τὸν αὐτὸν χρόνον, ἀλλὰ καθ᾽ ὃν ἑκάτεροι τῆς Εὐρώπης ἐπῆρχον, μισοῦντες
μὲν ἅπαν τὸ τῶν Ἑλλήνων γένος, ἰδίᾳ δὲ πρὸς ἡμᾶς ἐγκλή- d
ματα ποιησάμενοι, νομίζοντες ἐκ τούτου τοῦ τρόπου πρὸς
69 μίαν μὲν πόλιν κινδυνεύσειν, ἁπασῶν δ᾽ ἅμα κρατήσειν. οὐ
μὴν κατώρθωσαν, ἀλλὰ πρὸς μόνους τοὺς προγόνους τοὺς
ἡμετέρους συμβαλόντες ὁμοίως διεφθάρησαν, ὥσπερ ἂν εἰ
πρὸς ἅπαντας ἀνθρώπους ἐπολέμησαν. δῆλον δὲ τὸ μέγεθος
τῶν κακῶν τῶν γενομένων ἐκείνοις· οὐ γὰρ ἄν ποθ᾽ οἱ λόγοι
περὶ αὐτῶν τοσοῦτον χρόνον διέμειναν, εἰ μὴ καὶ τὰ πρα-
70 χθέντα πολὺ τῶν ἄλλων διήνεγκεν. λέγεται δ᾽ οὖν περὶ μὲν e
Ἀμαζόνων, ὡς τῶν μὲν ἐλθουσῶν οὐδεμία πάλιν ἀπῆλθεν,
αἱ δ᾽ ὑπολειφθεῖσαι διὰ τὴν ἐνθάδε συμφορὰν ἐκ τῆς ἀρχῆς
ἐξεβλήθησαν, περὶ δὲ Θρᾳκῶν, ὅτι τὸν ἄλλον χρόνον ὅμοροι
προσοικοῦντες ἡμῖν τοσοῦτον διὰ τὴν τότε στρατείαν διέλι- 55

later period were distinctly different
races. Isocr. seems to identify them,
when he speaks of the broad inter-
val between the original abodes of
the invaders (Eleusis (?), Helicon,
and Parnassus) and the district to
which they retreated. Several other
writers attach great importance to
this invasion; *e. g.* in Xen. *Mem.*
III. 5, 9, it appears as a coalition
against Athens of the powers of
Europe. On the Amazons cf. Aesch.
Eum. 685—690 and Lysias (?) *Or.
Funebr.* § 4, Ἀμάζονες Ἄρεως μὲν
τὸ παλαιὸν ἦσαν θυγατέρες, οἰκοῦσαι
δὲ παρὰ Θερμώδοντα ποταμὸν κ.τ.λ.
with Taylor's *Lect. Lysiacae,* c. 4.

Εὐμόλπου τοῦ Ποσειδῶνος.] Isocr.
(*Panath.* § 193) states that Eumolpus
assailed Erechtheus in vindication of
the claims of Poseidon to be the
tutelary deity of Athens. See also
§ 157, Εὐμολπίδαι n.

69. κατώρθωσαν...διεφθάρησαν.]
See § 6, κατορθωθῇ. n. On the con-
jugation of compounds of ὀρθῶ see
ad Dem. § 3, ἐπανορθῶ. n.

ὥσπερ ἄν.] Sc. διεφθάρησαν. The
formula ὥσπερ ἄν εἰ (or ὡσπερανεί)
is often elliptical; *e. g.* Plato, *Gorg.*
479 A, φοβούμενοι ὥσπερ ἂν εἰ ταῖς

('fearing like a child'), *i. e.* φοβούμενοι ὥσπερ ἂν φοβηθῇ εἰ ταῖς θ.
(Goodwin's *Gk. Moods and Tenses,*
§ 42.)

διέμειναν — διήνεγκεν.] An instance of παρομοίωσις.

70. διὰ τὴν ἐνθάδε συμφοράν.]
The very same words are found in
a similar context in Lysias (?) *Or.
Funebr.* § 6.

ἐξεβλήθησαν.] ἐξέπεσαν is frequently used instead of the aor.
pass. of ἐκβάλλω. *De Bigis,* § 12,
ὑπὸ τῶν τριάκοντ᾽ ἐκπεσόντες, and,
immediately afterwards, κατελθεῖν
εἰς τὴν πατρίδα, τιμωρήσασθαι δὲ
τοὺς ἐκβαλόντας.

τὸν ἄλλον—κατοικισθῆναι.] *i. e.*
'Although in former times they
dwelt beside us, on our very borders,
nevertheless, by reason of that expedition, they left an intervening
space so broad, that in the district
between their land and ours many
nations and all kinds of races and
great cities have been established.'

τὸν ἄλλον χρόνον.] Referring to
future time. Dem. *Lept.* 462, ἕξειν
ὑπῆρχε τὸν γοῦν ἄλλον χρόνον.

τὴν τότε στρατείαν.] Lit. 'the
then expedition.' This Greek idiom

πον ὥστ᾽ ἐν τῷ μεταξὺ τῆς χώρας ἔθνη πολλὰ καὶ γένη
παντοδαπὰ καὶ πόλεις μεγάλας κατοικισθῆναι.

71 (κ´.) Καλὰ μὲν οὖν καὶ ταῦτα, καὶ πρέποντα τοῖς περὶ
τῆς ἡγεμονίας ἀμφισβητοῦσιν, ἀδελφὰ δὲ τῶν εἰρημένων καὶ
τοιαῦθ᾽ οἷά περ εἰκὸς τοὺς ἐκ τοιούτων γεγονότας, οἱ πρὸς
Δαρεῖον καὶ Ξέρξην πολεμήσαντες ἔπραξαν. μεγίστου γὰρ
πολέμου συστάντος ἐκείνου, καὶ πλείστων κινδύνων εἰς τὸν b

is very convenient, and is becoming more and more common in English. Similarly Shakspeare uses 'sometime' in at least seven passages, e.g. *Hamlet*, I. 2, *Our sometime sister, now our queen.*

ἐν τῷ μεταξὺ τῆς χώρας.] The bare transl. *'in dem Zwischenraume,'* 'in the intervening country,' is, as Schneider notices, not very accurate. This would require ἐν τῇ μεταξὺ χώρᾳ. Nor, again, is it possible to refer τῆς χώρας to Attica and the district to which these Thracians retired. It is very easy to be hypercritical on such a point as this. The essential meaning of the passage is the same in any case, but (if strict accuracy is required) τῆς χώρας is the land of the Thracians: ἐν τῷ μεταξὺ τῆς χώρας means 'in the interval between the land of the Thracians and our own land.' This idiom (by which the more remote extremity is omitted) Schneider illustrates by quoting Aristoph. *Av.* 187, ἀλλ᾽ ἐν μέσῳ δήπουθεν ἀήρ ἐστι γῆς. (The air, I ween, is 'twixt the earth and heaven.) A still more appropriate passage may be found in Eur. *Hec.* 435 sqq. ὦ φῶς᾽ προσειπεῖν γὰρ σὸν ὄνομ᾽ ἔξεστί μοι, | μέτεστι δ᾽ οὐδὲν πλὴν ὅσον χρόνον ξίφους | μεταξὺ βαίνω καὶ πυρᾶς Ἀχιλλέως. (O Light! I can address thee by thy name; But cannot share thee, save the while I walk 'Twixt this, and slaughter at Achilles' pyre.) v. Aristoph. *Ach.* 434, Soph. *O. C.* 291, and Halliwell's *Dict. of Archaic and Provincial Words*, where, it is stated that in English, 'between' is 'sometimes used elliptically, *this time* being understood.'

III. §§ 71—99. *The Persian Wars.*
71, 72. *In fighting against Darius and Xerxes, Athens conquered her allies and her enemies alike. She was thus held worthy of the prize of valour; and soon after, gained the undisputed empire of the sea.* 73, 74. *The Lacedaemonians, I admit, were in those times of crisis the causes of many benefits, but Athens outrivalled Lacedaemon. I may be permitted to dwell on this point, that so we may remind ourselves of the valour of our ancestors and our hostility to the Barbarians. And yet I am well aware how hard it is to speak on subjects which have long since been pre-occupied and, for the most part, exhausted by our most able citizens in their funeral orations; nevertheless, in as much as they bear on my object, I must not hesitate to make mention of them.*

71. ἀδελφὰ τῶν εἰρημένων.] The adj. ἀδελφός, 'twin with,' 'akin to,' 'answering to,' is common in Plato. In Isocr. *Hel.* § 23, we have ἐξ ἀδελφῶν...γεγονότες...ἀδελφὰς καὶ τὰς ἐπιθυμίας ἔσχον. Lysias (?) *Or. Funebr.* § 119.

οἱ πρὸς Δαρεῖον κ. Ξέρξην κ.τ.λ.] On the Persian wars, to which full allusion is made in the following sections, either the histories of Thirlwall or Grote, or 'The Tale of the Great Persian War' (by Mr Cox), may be read with advantage. In the following notes only the discrepancies between Isocr. and others will be dwelt upon, and the rhetorical exaggerations checked by occasional reference to historical authorities.

αὐτὸν χρόνον συμπεσόντων, καὶ τῶν μὲν πολεμίων ἀνυποστάτων οἰομένων εἶναι διὰ τὸ πλῆθος, τῶν δὲ συμμάχων
72 ἀνυπέρβλητον ἡγουμένων ἔχειν τὴν ἀρετήν, ἀμφοτέρων κρατήσαντες ὡς ἑκατέρων προσῆκεν, καὶ πρὸς ἅπαντας τοὺς κινδύνους διενεγκόντες, εὐθὺς μὲν τῶν ἀριστείων ἠξιώθησαν, οὐ
πολλῷ δ᾽ ὕστερον τὴν ἀρχὴν τῆς θαλάττης ἔλαβον, δόντων
μὲν τῶν ἄλλων Ἑλλήνων, οὐκ ἀμφισβητούντων δὲ τῶν νῦν
ἡμᾶς ἀφαιρεῖσθαι ζητούντων.   c

73   (κα΄.) Καὶ μηδεὶς οἰέσθω μ᾽ ἀγνοεῖν, ὅτι καὶ Λακεδαιμόνιοι περὶ τοὺς καιροὺς τούτους πολλῶν ἀγαθῶν αἴτιοι τοῖς
Ἕλλησι κατέστησαν· ἀλλὰ διὰ τοῦτο καὶ μᾶλλον ἐπαινεῖν
ἔχω τὴν πόλιν, ὅτι τοιούτων ἀνταγωνιστῶν τυχοῦσα τοσοῦτον αὐτῶν διήνεγκεν. βούλομαι δ᾽ ὀλίγῳ μακρότερα περὶ
τοῖν πολέοιν εἰπεῖν καὶ μὴ ταχὺ λίαν παραδραμεῖν, ἵν᾽ ἀμφοτέρων ἡμῖν ὑπομνήματα γένηται, τῆς τε τῶν προγόνων d
74 ἀρετῆς καὶ τῆς πρὸς τοὺς βαρβάρους ἔχθρας. καίτοι μ᾽ οὐ
λέληθεν, ὅτι χαλεπόν ἐστιν ὕστατον ἐπελθόντα λέγειν περὶ
πραγμάτων πάλαι προκατειλημμένων καὶ περὶ ὧν οἱ μάλιστα δυνηθέντες τῶν πολιτῶν εἰπεῖν ἐπὶ τοῖς δημοσίᾳ θα-

---

ἀνυποστάτων ... ἀνυπέρβλητον.]
Obs. παρομοίωσις.

72. ἀμφοτέρων—προσῆκεν.] Imitated by Lycurgus, *adv. Leocr.* § 70
(330 B.C.).

εὐθὺς—ἔλαβον.] Quoted by Arist.
Rhet. III. 9 as an instance of ἀντικειμένη λέξις (v. § 35, ἀμφοτέρους,
n.).

On δόντων κ.τ.λ. cf. *Areop.* § 17.

73. τοῖν πολέοιν.] v. § 17. n.

74. ὕστατον.] To be taken
with ἐπελθόντα λέγειν and not with
λέγειν alone, as Schn. proposes.

λέγειν ... εἰπεῖν ... εἴρηκα.] On
λέγειν || εἰπεῖν see *ad Dem.* § 41.
n.—εἴρηκα is used as the pf. of both
verbs.

χαλεπόν — προκατειλημμένων.]
Cf. *de Perm.* § 83. The thought is
very common, but has never been
so well expressed as by Choerilus of
Samos (ed. Näke, p. 104), ἆ μάκαρ
ὅστις ἔην κεῖνον χρόνον ἴδρις ἀοιδῆς |

Μουσάων θεράπων, ὅτ᾽ ἀκήρατος ἦν
ἔτι λειμών. [νῦν δ᾽ ὅτε πάντα δέδα-
σται ἔχουσι δὲ πείρατα τέχναι, | ὕστα-
τοι ὥστε δρόμου καταλειπόμεθ᾽, οὐδέ
τοι ἔστιν | πάντη παπταίνοντα νεο-
ζυγὲς ἅρμα πελάσσαι.

ἐπὶ τοῖς δημοσίᾳ θαπτομένοις.]
The funeral orations, delivered from
time to time in honour of those
Athenians who fell in battle, probably took their origin from the
Persian wars (v. Grote, *H. G.* IV.
170, new ed.), and the events of
those wars entered largely into their
composition. Ar. *Rhet.* II. 22. 6.
Dionys. Halic. *Ars Rhet.* VI. gives
a receipt for the composition of an
Oratio Funebris.

Dem. *Lept.* p. 499, § 141, μόνοι
τῶν ἁπάντων ἀνθρώπων ἐπὶ τοῖς τε-
λευτήσασι δημοσίᾳ ταφὰς ποιεῖσθε καὶ
λόγους ἐπιταφίους ἐν οἷς κοσμεῖτε τὰ
τῶν ἀγαθῶν ἀνδρῶν ἔργα.

The following is a list of all the

πτομένοις πολλάκις εἰρήκασιν· ἀνάγκη γὰρ τὰ μὲν μέγιστ'
αὐτῶν ἤδη κατακεχρῆσθαι, μικρὰ δέ τινα παραλελεῖφθαι.
ὅμως δ' ἐκ τῶν ὑπολοίπων, ἐπειδὴ συμφέρει τοῖς πράγμασιν, c·
οὐκ ὀκνητέον μνησθῆναι περὶ αὐτῶν.

75 (κβ.) Πλείστων μὲν οὖν ἀγαθῶν αἰτίους καὶ μεγίστων

known early specimens of this kind of Attic oratory, (1) The speech of *Pericles* in honour of those who fell before Samos (440 B.C.). Only one or two fragments of this are preserved.

(2) The speech of *Pericles* in the first year of the Peloponnesian war (431 B.C.), the substance of which is preserved in Thuc. II. 35—46.

(3) The oration composed by *Gorgias* the Sophist of Leontini, and published, if not actually delivered, in Athens (after 427 B.C.). According to Philostratus (*vit. Soph.* p. 493) it was intended to arouse the Athenians against Persia, and dwelt at length on the trophies of the Persian wars, ὑπὲρ ὁμονοίας μὲν τῆς πρὸς Ἕλληνας οὐδὲν διῆλθεν (cf. § 16. *fin.*), ἐπιστρέψει δὲ τοῖς τῶν Μηδικῶν τροπαίων ἑταίρας (cf. § 138. n.)

(4) The speech bearing the name of *Lysias*, ostensibly commemorating those who died in the Corinthian war (B.C. 394), and dwelling mainly on Mythical times and on the Persian wars. v. § 55. n.

(5) The *Menexenus* of *Plato* (the genuineness of which has been disputed on insufficient grounds); it consists almost entirely of a funeral oration which Socrates (who died 399 B.C.) pretends to have heard recited by Aspasia. The clue to the whole speech is contained in the brief introductory dialogue, in which Socrates comically exaggerates the effect produced on himself by such speeches, in a vein of irony which is perfectly appreciated by Menexenus: 235 c, ἀεὶ σὺ προσπαίζεις, ὦ Σώκρατες, τοὺς ῥήτορας. It was probably composed not long after the peace of Antalcidas (387 B.C., see

esp. § 115. n.), and it is easy to trace many conscious or unconscious coincidences of subject and expression in the *Menexenus* and the *Panegyricus*.—v. Cic. *Orat.* 44, § 151.

(6) The speech wrongly ascribed to *Demosthenes*, purporting to be delivered after the battle of Chaeronea (338 B.C.). Cf. Dem. *de Cor.* 320, § 285.

(7) The funeral oration of *Hyperides* in honour of those who fell in the Lamian War (322 B.C.). The greater part of it was discovered in Egypt in 1856; and was first edited by Prof. C. Babington (with a learned, and in the main correct, *appendix on the funeral orations of the Greeks*).

On the ceremonies of the public funerals see esp. Thuc. II. 34, or Grote's *H. G.* IV. 171, 266, new ed. On the usual place of burial, the Ceramicus, 'the fairest suburb of Athens,' τὸ κάλλιστον προάστειον τῆς πόλεως, cf. Aristoph. *Aves*, 395 sqq.

κατακεχρῆσθαι.] The simple pf. κεχρῆσθαι is usually transitive; but the compound is passive both in this passage and in a fragment of the comic poet Amphis, the only other instance quoted by Veitch *Gk. verbs*, p. 605. In Plato, *Crat.* 426 E, &c. κατακεχρῆσθαι is trans.

ἐκ τῶν ὑπολοίπων.] Dem. *de Cor.* 312, § 256, ἐκ τῶν ἐόντων.

§§ 75—84. *The excellence and the public spirit of those who held sway in Athens and Sparta before the Persian wars, and schooled their citizens to virtue and valour. The younger generation thus became such brave antagonists of the Barbarians, (82—84) that no praise has ever been found adequate to their merits. They*

ἐπαίνων ἀξίους ἡγοῦμαι γεγενῆσθαι τοὺς τοῖς σώμασιν ὑπὲρ
τῆς Ἑλλάδος προκινδυνεύσαντας· οὐ μὴν οὐδὲ τῶν πρὸ τοῦ
πολέμου τούτου γενομένων καὶ δυναστευσάντων ἐν ἑκατέρᾳ 56
τοῖν πολέοιν δίκαιον ἀμνημονεῖν· ἐκεῖνοι γὰρ ἦσαν οἱ προα-
σκήσαντες τοὺς ἐπιγιγνομένους καὶ τὰ πλήθη προτρέψαντες
ἐπ' ἀρετὴν καὶ χαλεποὺς ἀνταγωνιστὰς τοῖς βαρβάροις
76 ποιήσαντες. οὐ γὰρ ὠλιγώρουν τῶν κοινῶν, οὐδ' ἀπέλαυον
μὲν ὡς ἰδίων, ἠμέλουν δ' ὡς ἀλλοτρίων, ἀλλ' ἐκήδοντο μὲν
ὡς οἰκείων, ἀπείχοντο δ' ὥσπερ χρὴ τῶν μηδὲν προσηκόν-
των· οὐδὲ πρὸς ἀργύριον τὴν εὐδαιμονίαν ἔκρινον, ἀλλ'
οὗτος ἐδόκει πλοῦτον ἀσφαλέστατον κεκτῆσθαι καὶ κάλ- b
λιστον, ὅστις τοιαῦτα τυγχάνοι πράττων, ἐξ ὧν αὐτός τε
μέλλοι μάλιστ' εὐδοκιμήσειν καὶ τοῖς παισὶ μεγίστην δόξαν
77 καταλείψειν. οὐδὲ τὰς θρασύτητας τὰς ἀλλήλων ἐζήλουν,
οὐδὲ τὰς τόλμας τὰς αὑτῶν ἤσκουν, ἀλλὰ δεινότερον μὲν
ἐνόμιζον εἶναι κακῶς ὑπὸ τῶν πολιτῶν ἀκούειν ἢ καλῶς

surpassed the heroes of the Trojan war, and proved themselves worthy of the same immortal memory as the sons of the Gods.

75—81. Dionysius of Halicarnassus devotes a long passage in his *Judicium de Isocrate*, to the dissection of nine or ten sentences quoted from this chapter. His quotations are introduced in words to this effect: 'from the actual diction of Isocrates we shall plainly see that in the rhythm of his periods he is constantly aiming at a polished smoothness, and that the puerility of his figures spends itself on parallelisms of sense, of structure, and of sound: I am not blaming these figures as a class, for many writers and orators have made use of them, in the desire to adorn their diction with the flowers of speech; I blame them only in their excess'...ἐν γ' οὖν τῷ *πανηγυρικῷ*, τῷ περιβοήτῳ λόγῳ, πολύ ἐστιν ἐν τοῖς τοιούτοις. Dionysius then quotes, in § 75, πλείστων —ἡγοῦμαι, in § 76, οὐδ' ἀπέλαυον—προσηκόντων, αὐτός τε—καταλείψειν, in § 77, οὐδὲ τὰς θρασύτητας—ἀποθνή-

σκειν, in § 78, ὅτι τοῖς—ὁμονοήσουσιν, and in § 80, τὰ τῶν ἄλλων—ἐμμένειν ἀξιοῦντες.

75. πλείστων...ἀξίους.] Dionys. Hal. *l.c.*, ἐνταῦθα ..οὐ μόνον τῷ κώλῳ τὸ κῶλον ἴσον, ἀλλὰ καὶ τὰ ὀνόματα τοῖς ὀνόμασι, κ.τ.λ. τοῖν πολέοιν.] § 17. n.

76. οὐ γὰρ ὠλιγώρουν.] 'They despised not the public good; nor did they (while enjoying it as their own) disregard it as another's.' In translation, the clause containing μὲν may be often made subordinate in English to the clause containing δέ. Cf. Dem. *de Cor.* § 179, οὐκ εἶπον μὲν ταῦτα, οὐκ ἔγραψα δέ, οὐδ' ἔγραψα μέν, οὐδ' ἐπρέσβευσα δέ, οὐδ' ἐπρέσβευσα μέν, οὐκ ἔπεισα δὲ Θηβαίους· ἀλλ' ἀπὸ τῆς ἀρχῆς διὰ πάντων ἄχρι τῆς τελευτῆς διεξῆλθον. (v. Brougham's n. on the various ways of translating this climax.)

πρὸς ἀργύριον—ἔκρινον.] § 11. πρὸς τοὺς—σκοποῦσι. n.

77. τὰς θρασύτητας.] For the pl. abstract, v. § 11, μετριότησται. n. κακῶς ὑπὸ τῶν πολιτῶν ἀκούειν.] *Male audire a civibus.* This idiom

ὑπὲρ τῆς πόλεως ἀποθνήσκειν, μᾶλλον δ᾽ ἠσχύνοντ᾽ ἐπὶ τοῖς c
κοινοῖς ἁμαρτήμασιν ἢ νῦν ἐπὶ τοῖς ἰδίοις τοῖς σφετέροις
78 αὐτῶν. τούτων δ᾽ ἦν αἴτιον, ὅτι τοὺς νόμους ἐσκόπουν,
ὅπως ἀκριβῶς καὶ καλῶς ἕξουσιν, οὐχ οὕτω τοὺς περὶ τῶν
ἰδίων συμβολαίων, ὡς τοὺς περὶ τῶν καθ᾽ ἑκάστην τὴν
ἡμέραν ἐπιτηδευμάτων· ἠπίσταντο γὰρ ὅτι τοῖς καλοῖς
κἀγαθοῖς τῶν ἀνθρώπων οὐδὲν δεήσει πολλῶν γραμμάτων,
ἀλλ᾽ ἀπ᾽ ὀλίγων συνθημάτων ῥᾳδίως καὶ περὶ τῶν ἰδίων d
79 καὶ περὶ τῶν κοινῶν ὁμονοήσουσιν. οὕτω δὲ πολιτικῶς
εἶχον, ὥστε καὶ τὰς στάσεις ἐποιοῦντο πρὸς ἀλλήλους, οὐχ
ὁπότεροι τοὺς ἑτέρους ἀπολέσαντες τῶν λοιπῶν ἄρξουσιν,
ἀλλ᾽ ὁπότεραι φθήσονται τὴν πόλιν ἀγαθόν τι ποιήσαντες

is imitated by Spenser, Ben Jonson, and Milton : *e.g.* Milt. *Areopagitica*, p. 51, ed Arber. *What more nationall corruption for which England hears ill abroad, then household gluttony?*

78. τοὺς νόμους—ὁμονοήσουσιν.] Cf. *Areop.* § 39—41.

ἠπίσταντο γὰρ κ.τ.λ.] 'For they were aware, that, for good men and true, there will be no need of many written laws, but that, with the help of a few points of agreement, they will readily be of one mind, with regard both to private and to public interests.'

καλοῖς κἀγαθοῖς.] The expression καλὸς κἀγαθός, should always be written as two words. The form καλοσαγαθός is suspected by Lobeck (*Phryn.* p. 603), and καλὸς καὶ ἀγαθός is condemned by Cobet (*nov. lect.* p. 393), who quotes Photius : καλὸς κἀγαθὸς λέγεται κατὰ συναλοιφήν, οὐχὶ καλὸς καὶ ἀγαθός. From καλὸς κἀγαθὸς we have καλοσαγαθίη and καλοκαγαθία (*ad Dem.* § 6, 51), just as from the parathetic forms ἀνὴρ ἀγαθός, θεοῖς ἐχθρός, ὁ Ἄρειος πάγος, ἡ Μεγάλη πόλις, we obtain the synthetic words ἀνδραγαθία, θεοσεχθρία, Ἀρειοπαγίτης, Μεγαλοπολίτης (Cobet *u. s.* p. 394). For a discussion on the meaning of καλὸς κἀγαθός, v. Donaldson's *New Cratylus*, § 311-8.

γραμμάτων.] 'Legal documents.' Plat. *Politicus*, 293 A, ἐάν τε κατὰ γράμματα, ἐάν τε ἄνευ γραμμάτων, explained immediately afterwards by the equivalent expression ἐάν τε κατὰ νόμους, ἐάν τε ἄνευ νόμων. Isocr. *Areop.* § 41, δεῖν τοὺς ὀρθῶς πολιτευομένους οὐ τὰς στοὰς ἐμπιμπλάναι γραμμάτων ἀλλ᾽ ἐν ταῖς ψυχαῖς ἔχειν τὸ δίκαιον· οὐ γὰρ τοῖς ψηφίσμασιν ἀλλὰ τοῖς ἤθεσι καλῶς οἰκεῖσθαι τὰς πόλεις κ.τ.λ.

79. τὰς στάσεις...τὰς ἑταιρείας.] 'Political parties,' 'political clubs.' This flattering description of the noble ends to which party-spirit was consecrated in the early days of Greece, is evidently meant to be contrasted with the disastrous development of the same spirit in later times. Cf. § 167, πολέμους καὶ στάσεις κ.τ.λ., and the profound analysis of factions in their worst forms, given by Thuc. III. 82 sqq.

τὰς στάσεις ἐποιοῦντο...ὁπότεροι.] Cf. § 85, ὁπότεραι—ποιούμενοι τὴν ἅμιλλαν. For the sense, cf. Herodot. VIII. 179 (Aristides to Themistocles), ἡμέας στασιάζειν χρεόν ἐστι, ἔν τε τῷ ἄλλῳ καιρῷ καὶ ἐν τῷδε, περὶ τοῦ ὁκότερος ἡμέων πλέω ἀγαθὰ τὴν πατρίδα ἐργάσεται. Benseler cites the rivalry between Lycurgus and Alcander, Miltiades and Xanthippus.

καὶ τὰς ἑταιρείας συνῆγον οὐχ ὑπὲρ τῶν ἰδίᾳ συμφερόντων,
80 ἀλλ᾽ ἐπὶ τῇ τοῦ πλήθους ὠφελείᾳ. τὸν αὐτὸν δὲ τρόπον καὶ
τὰ τῶν ἄλλων διῴκουν, θεραπεύοντες ἀλλ᾽ οὐχ ὑβρίζοντες
τοὺς Ἕλληνας, καὶ στρατηγεῖν οἰόμενοι δεῖν ἀλλὰ μὴ τυραννεῖν αὐτῶν, καὶ μᾶλλον ἐπιθυμοῦντες ἡγεμόνες ἢ δεσπόται c
προσαγορεύεσθαι καὶ σωτῆρες ἀλλὰ μὴ λυμεῶνες ἀποκαλεῖσθαι, τῷ ποιεῖν εὖ προσαγόμενοι τὰς πόλεις, ἀλλ᾽ οὐ βίᾳ
81 καταστρεφόμενοι, πιστοτέροις μὲν τοῖς λόγοις ἢ νῦν τοῖς
ὅρκοις χρώμενοι, ταῖς δὲ συνθήκαις ὥσπερ ἀνάγκαις ἐμμέ- 57
νειν ἀξιοῦντες, οὐχ οὕτως ἐπὶ ταῖς δυναστείαις μέγα φρο-

80. ἀλλ᾽ οὐχ.] For this use of
ἀλλά (occurring four times in the
same §), where 'and' is the most
idiomatic rendering, cf. *ad Dem.* § 2 n.
σωτῆρες ἀλλὰ μὴ λυμεῶνες ἀποκαλεῖσθαι.] 'To be called by the
name of saviours and not reviled by
the name of destroyers.' ἀποκαλεῖν
(besides its primary sense, 'to call
aside') = to give a by-name, a nickname, *apart from* (ἀπό) the correct
name; hence, to revile. The word is
omitted in Mitchell's *Index Graec.
Isocraticae*, but may be found in
Sophist. § 4, λέγουσι μὲν (οἱ σοφισταί),
ὡς οὐδὲν δέονται χρημάτων, ἀργυρίδιον
καὶ χρυσίδιον τὸν πλοῦτον ἀποκαλοῦντες and *Hel.* § 57, τοὺς μὲν ὑπ᾽ ἄλλῳ
τινὶ δυνάμει γιγνομένους λοιδορούμεν
καὶ κόλακας ἀποκαλοῦμεν. In both
these passages it is used in a depreciatory sense; and this is the meaning which it almost invariably bears
in early Greek authors. The only
exceptions that have been noticed are
Xen. *de re eq.* X. 17, ἀποκαλοῦσιν
ἐλευθέριον (Jahn's *Jahr. Philol.*
Suppl. 3, p. 571), and Aristot. *Eth.*
II. 97 (quoted by Mr Shilleto on
Dem. *Fals. Leg.* § 274, λογογράφους
καὶ σοφιστὰς ἀποκαλῶν): ταῦτ᾽ χαλε-
παίνοντας ἀνδρώδεις ἀποκαλοῦμεν. In
late Gk. this usage is common, *e.g.*
Plutarch, *vit. Sull.* 34, σωτῆρα καὶ
πατέρα τὸν Σύλλαν ἀποκαλοῦντες and
Moral. I. 776 E (quoted by Lennep
on Phalaris, *Ep.* 65), ἀκούομεν δὴ
Ὁμήρου τὸν Μίνω θεοῦ ὀαριστὴν ἀπο-
καλοῦντος. But in almost every early

instance the bad sense is prominent,
e.g. Plat. *Gorg.* 512 c. ἂν δὲ ὀνείδει
ἀποκαλέσαι ἂν μηχανοποιόν, and (besides the other passages quoted by
L. and S.) Dem. *Fals. Leg.* p. 439 A,
βάρβαρον κ. ἀλάστορα ἀποκαλῶν,
and Antisthenes (the Cynic. fl. 336
B.C.), *Dialam.* B, ἀποκαλεῖ ἱερό-
συλον.

Applying the conclusions gained
from the above passages, and esp.
those from Isocr., we are almost
compelled to translate ἀποκαλεῖσθαι,
'to be reviled;' a rendering which
suits λυμεῶνες, but does not suit
σωτῆρες. We must therefore understand, from ἀποκαλεῖσθαι, a simple
verb like καλεῖσθαι, and accept the
sentence as an instance of *Zeugma*.
v. § 16. n. and cf., for other instances
of this figure, Soph. *Aj.* 1034—5, *El.*
71, Propert. *Eleg. lib. ult.* 1. 17—19.
Also St Paul's *Ep. to Tim.* 1. iv. 3,
Κωλυόντων γαμεῖν; [π. εἰλενότων]
ἀπέχεσθαι βρωμάτων, and Browne's
Vulgar Errors, I. 10, 'some deny-
ing His humanity and (*sc.* saying)
that He was one of the Angels, as
Ebion.'

In the speech *de Pace*, § 141
(written in 357 B.C.), Isocr. expresses
himself more regularly: προσῆκαι
τῇ τῶν Ἑλλήνων ἐλευθερίας, καὶ σω-
τῆρας ἀλλὰ μὴ λυμεῶνας αὐτὸν εἶση-
θῆναι.

81. πιστοτέροις—χρώμενοι.] Cf.
ad Nicocl. § 22.

ἀξιοῦντες...ἀξιοῦντες.] Consider-
ing the pains Isocr. generally takes

νοῦντες ὡς ἐπὶ τῷ σωφρόνως ζῆν φιλοτιμούμενοι, τὴν αὐτὴν
ἀξιοῦντες γνώμην ἔχειν πρὸς τοὺς ἥττους ἥνπερ τοὺς
κρείττους πρὸς σφᾶς αὐτούς, ἴδια μὲν ἄστη τὰς αὐτῶν πόλεις ἡγούμενοι, κοινὴν δὲ πατρίδα τὴν Ἑλλάδα νομίζοντες
εἶναι.

82 (κγ΄.) Τοιαύταις διανοίαις χρώμενοι καὶ τοὺς νεωτέρους
ἐν τοῖς τοιούτοις ἤθεσι παιδεύοντες, οὕτως ἄνδρας ἀγαθοὺς b
ἀπέδειξαν τοὺς πολεμήσαντας πρὸς τοὺς ἐκ τῆς Ἀσίας,
ὥστε μηδένα πώποτε δυνηθῆναι περὶ αὐτῶν μήτε τῶν ποιητῶν μήτε τῶν σοφιστῶν ἀξίας τῶν ἐκείνοις πεπραγμένων
εἰπεῖν. καὶ πολλὴν αὐτοῖς ἔχω συγγνώμην· ὁμοίως γάρ
ἐστι χαλεπὸν ἐπαινεῖν τοὺς ὑπερβεβληκότας τὰς τῶν ἄλλων
ἀρετὰς ὥσπερ τοὺς μηδὲν ἀγαθὸν πεποιηκότας· τοῖς μὲν
γὰρ οὐχ ὕπεισι πράξεις, πρὸς δὲ τοὺς οὐκ εἰσὶν ἁρμόττοντες
83 λόγοι. πῶς γὰρ ἂν γένοιντο σύμμετροι τοιούτοις ἀνδράσιν, c
οἳ τοσοῦτον μὲν τῶν ἐπὶ Τροίαν στρατευσαμένων διήνεγκαν,

to ensure variety of expression, this
recurrence is remarkable. Here, and
occasionally elsewhere (*Phil.* § 132,
προσαγορευομένοιs, *de Perm.* § 128,
συμβέβηκε, and *Paneg.* § 24, ἔχωσει),
he has the good sense to allow a repetition to stand unaltered. Pascal
has an excellent maxim on this point
(*Pensées*, I. 10): 'Quand dans un discours on trouve des mots répétés, et
qu'essayant de les corriger, on les
trouve si propres qu'on gâterait le
discours, il les faut laisser.'

ἄστη...πόλεις] Primarily ἄστυ=
a city regarded as a dwelling-place:
πόλις = a city regarded as an association of individuals. The former
is connected with the Indo-European
root *vâs*, 'to dwell,' whence the
Sanskrit *vâs-tya*, *vâstu*, 'dwelling-
place,' 'house;' the Greek *ἀσ-τία*,
ἑστία; and the Lat. *Vesta* (and
ves-ti-bulum?). The latter with the
Sanskrit *pur*, *pura*, *purî*, a word
which is still constantly found as an
element in the names of Indian cities,
villages, &c., e.g. *Cawnpore*, *Seram-
pore*, *Midnapore*. *Pur* or *purî* (=πό-
λις) and *pura* (=πολίς) are doubt-

less connected, as both sets come
from the root *pâr*, 'to fill.' (Partly
from Fick's *Wörterbuch der Indo-
germ. Grundsprache.*)

'Ἑλλάδα.] The Cod. Urb. in this
passage, and the Cod. Ambros., both
here and in the corresponding passage in the speech *de Perm.* read τὴν
αὐτῶν πόλιν, but the reading adopted
by BS and Bens. is evidently correct.
(See further, Havet, p. 202.)

82. μήτε τῶν ποιητῶν μήτε τῶν
σοφιστῶν.] Cf. *ad Dem.* § 51. n. and
Paneg. § 3. n. Schn. quotes Arist.
Rhet. III. 2. τῷ μὲν σοφῷ †ῇ...τῷ ποι-
ητῇ δέ... The distinction here drawn
resembles that of § 186, τῶν ποιεῖν
δυναμένων...τῶν λέγειν ἐπισταμένων,
Phil. § 109, οὔτε τῶν ποιητῶν οὔτε
τῶν λογοποιῶν, and *ib.* § 144, οὔτε
λόγων εὑρετὴς οὔτε ποιητής.

Among the Sophists here referred
to may be mentioned Gorgias (v.
p. 82, n.); among the poets, Aeschylus (*Persae*), and Choerilus of Samos,
whose chief work was a poem on
the Persian wars, a few fragments of
which are still extant. (v. p. 81. n.)

83. τοσοῦτον τῶν ἐπὶ Τροίαν

ὅσον οἱ μὲν περὶ μίαν πόλιν ἔτη δέκα διέτριψαν, οἱ δὲ τὴν ἐξ
ἁπάσης τῆς Ἀσίας δύναμιν ἐν ὀλίγῳ χρόνῳ κατεπολέμησαν,
οὐ μόνον δὲ τὰς αὑτῶν πατρίδας διέσωσαν, ἀλλὰ καὶ τὴν
σύμπασαν Ἑλλάδα ἠλευθέρωσαν; ποίων δ᾿ ἂν ἔργων ἢ d
πόνων ἢ κινδύνων ἀπέστησαν ὥστε ζῶντες εὐδοκιμεῖν, οἵτινες ὑπὲρ τῆς δόξης ἧς ἔμελλον τελευτήσαντες ἕξειν οὕτως
84 ἑτοίμως ἤθελον ἀποθνήσκειν; οἶμαι δὲ καὶ τὸν πόλεμον
θεῶν τινα συναγαγεῖν ἀγασθέντα τὴν ἀρετὴν αὐτῶν, ἵνα μὴ
τοιοῦτοι γενόμενοι τὴν φύσιν διαλάθοιεν μηδ᾿ ἀκλεῶς τὸν

στρατευσαμένων διήνεγκαν ὅσον
κ.τ.λ] The Grecian heroes of the
Trojan War formed a favourite
standard of comparison, and the
comparison was generally to their
disadvantage. We are told, by Plutarch, *Peric.* c. 28 (cited by Grote,
IV. p. 171, new ed.), that Pericles,
in his speech of the Samian expedition, boasted that, while Agamem-
non had spent ten years in taking
a foreign city, he himself had in
nine months reduced the first and
most powerful of all the Ionic com-
munities. Isocr. (*Phil.* 111-2) praises
Hercules for conquering Troy in a
smaller number of days than the
years spent by the besieging Greeks;
and, lastly, Hyperides, (who is said
to have been a pupil of Isocr.), finely
lays of the welcome destined for
Leosthenes in the under-world:
' Will not the Grecian heroes who
sailed to Troy accost him, and ad-
mire him for the deeds he has done
and the spirit he has shewn? Deeds
like theirs, indeed, but superior; for
they, united with all Greece, took but
one city, but he, depending only on
his own country, humbled the power
of all Europe and Asia.' (From
Prof. C. Babington's *paraphr.*) Cf.
also (Dem.) *Or. Fun.* p. 1392, and
below, §§ 181, 186.
διήνεγκαν § διέτριψαν...διέσωσαν
§ ἠλευθέρωσαν.] Instances of παρομοίωσις.
ἔμελλον.] In Attic poets μέλλω is
used only in pres. and impf. The

augment in η is never found in
Hom. Aesch. Soph. or Eur.; never
in Hdt. (and perhaps Thucyd.); it is
rare in Aristoph. (*Ran.* 1038, τὸν
λόφον ἤμελλ᾿ ἐνιήσειν, and *Eccl.*
597, where, however, Mr Shilleto
proposes, on rhythmical grounds, to
read τουτὶ γὰρ ἔμελλον ἐγὼ λέξειν);
further, it is found twice in Xen. and
(in the impf.) a few times in the Attic
orators. (Chiefly from Veitch, *Gk.
Verbs.*)   In Benseler's edition of
Isocrates the form ἤμελλον is adopted
in every case, but in the present
passage all the MSS. have ἔμελλον.
(v. tab. of var. readings, n.) In Gk.
composition ἔμελλον ought always to
be preferred. Cf. § 102, ἠβουλήθημεν. n.
ἤθελον ἀποθνήσκειν.] On θέλω,
ἐθέλω v. ad *Dem.* § 14. n. ἤθελον is
used as the impf. of both verbs. On
ἀποθνήσκειν v. § 55. n.
84. οἶμαι—ἀποίησαν.] 'I would
even deem that one of the gods
brought about that conflict, in admi-
ration for their valour, that, having
such an inborn spirit, they might
not remain in obscurity, nor end
their lives ingloriously, but be held
worthy of the same honours as those
who are born of the gods, and are
called demigods; for even in *their*
case, while they yielded their bodies
to the doom of nature, they nevertheless made immortal the memory
of their valour.'
This burst of imagination is perhaps one of the finest conceptions
in the whole speech; the expression

βίον τελευτήσαιεν, ἀλλὰ τῶν αὐτῶν τοῖς ἐκ τῶν θεῶν γεγονόσι καὶ καλουμένοις ἡμιθέοις ἀξιωθεῖεν· καὶ γὰρ ἐκείνων
τὰ μὲν σώματα ταῖς τῆς φύσεως ἀνάγκαις ἀπέδοσαν, τῆς ε
δ' ἀρετῆς ἀθάνατον τὴν μνήμην ἐποίησαν.

85   (κδ´.) Ἀεὶ μὲν οὖν οἵ θ' ἡμέτεροι πρόγονοι καὶ Λακεδαιμόνιοι φιλοτίμως πρὸς ἀλλήλους εἶχον, οὐ μὴν ἀλλὰ
περὶ καλλίστων ἐν ἐκείνοις τοῖς χρόνοις ἐφιλονίκησαν, οὐκ 38
ἐχθροὺς ἀλλ' ἀνταγωνιστὰς σφᾶς αὐτοὺς εἶναι νομίζοντες,
οὐδ' ἐπὶ δουλείᾳ τῇ τῶν Ἑλλήνων τὸν βάρβαρον θεραπεύοντες ἀλλὰ περὶ μὲν τῆς κοινῆς σωτηρίας ὁμονοοῦντες, ὁπότεροι δὲ ταύτης αἴτιοι γενήσονται, περὶ τούτου ποιούμενοι
τὴν ἅμιλλαν. ἐπεδείξαντο δὲ τὰς αὐτῶν ἀρετὰς πρῶτον μὲν
86 ἐν τοῖς ὑπὸ Δαρείου πεμφθεῖσιν. ἀποβάντων γὰρ αὐτῶν εἰς
τὴν Ἀττικὴν οἱ μὲν οὐ περιέμειναν τοὺς συμμάχους, ἀλλὰ

καὶ καλουμένοις ἡμιθέοι is not an idle
repetition of τοῖς ἐκ τῶν θεῶν γεγονόσι, but introduces the idea of mortality resulting from the half-human
nature of these sons of the gods; an
idea which leads up to the mention
of the surrender of their bodies to
the debt of nature.

ἐκ τῶν θεῶν.] ἐκ denotes immediate origin; ἀπό generally, remote
origin, Panath. § 81. τοὺς μὲν ἀπὸ
θεῶν, τοὺς δὲ ἐξ αὐτῶν τῶν θεῶν γεγονότας.

ἐκείνων.] Sc. τῶν ἡμιθέων.—ἀπέδοσαν sc. οἱ θεοί. The reading
ἐκείνων.....ἐποίησαν here adopted is
sanctioned by the Codd. Urb. and
Ambr. (followed by Bens. and BS).
Other MSS. have ἐκείνοι (sc. οἱ ἡμί-
θεοι)...κατέλιπον, an alteration which
makes the construction simpler, but
does not improve the sense.

ταῖς τῆς φύσεως ἀνάγκαις.] 'The
necessities, the stern laws, of nature.'
Cf. the Tacitean use of necessitas
suprema, ultima, extrema, in the
sense of 'death.'

§§ 85—98. The noble rivalry of
Athens and Sparta, displayed in the
wars against Darius and Xerxes.
The battles of Marathon, Thermopylae, Artemisium, and Salamis.

85. The expressions in this and the
following section are closely parallel
to those of Lysias (?) Or. Funebr.
§ 23, οὐκ ἀνέμειναν τυθέσθαι οὐδὲ
βοηθῆσαι τοὺς συμμάχους.. μόνοι γὰρ
ὑπὲρ ἁπάσης τῆς Ἑλλάδος πρὸς πολλὰς μυριάδας τῶν βαρβάρων διεκινδύ-
νευσαν. § 24, ἀπήντων ὀλίγοι πρὸς
πολλούς· ἐνόμιζον γάρ...τὰς μὲν ψυχὰς
ἀλλοτρίας διὰ τὸν θάνατον κεκτῆσθαι.
§ 26, οὕτω δὲ διὰ ταχέων τὸν κίνδυνον ἐποιήσαντο, ὥστε οἱ αὐτοὶ τοῖς
ἄλλοις ἀπήγγειλαν τήν τ' ἐνθάδε
ἄφιξιν τῶν βαρβάρων καὶ τὴν τῶν
προγόνων νίκην. v. § 55. n.

οὐ μὴν ἀλλά......] Sc. οὐ μὴν
[περὶ κακῶν] ἀλλὰ περὶ καλλίστων
ἐφιλονίκησαν. Cf. § 172 and ad Dem.
§ 9. n.

ἀλλήλους...σφᾶς αὐτούς.] v. §
34. n.

ἐπὶ δουλείᾳ—θεραπεύοντες.] A
passing thrust at the subsequent
policy of the Lacedaemonians.

τοῖς ὑπὸ Δαρείου πεμφθεῖσιν.]
Under Datis and Artaphernes, 490
B.C. Herodot. VI. 94—120.

86. οὐ περιέμειναν τοὺς συμμάχους.] Hdt. VI. 106. Before the
battle of Marathon the courier Phi-
dippides was sent by the Athenian
generals to summon Sparta to their

τὸν κοινὸν πόλεμον ἴδιον ποιησάμενοι πρὸς τοὺς ἁπάσης b
τῆς Ἑλλάδος καταφρονήσαντας ἀπήντων τὴν οἰκείαν δύναμιν ἔχοντες, ὀλίγοι πρὸς πολλὰς μυριάδας, ὥσπερ ἐν ἀλλοτρίαις ψυχαῖς μέλλοντες κινδυνεύειν, οἱ δ᾽ οὐκ ἔφθησαν
πυθόμενοι τὸν περὶ τὴν Ἀττικὴν πόλεμον καὶ πάντων τῶν
ἄλλων ἀμελήσαντες ἧκον ἡμῖν ἀμυνοῦντες, τοσαύτην ποιησάμενοι σπουδήν, ὅσην περ ἂν τῆς αὑτῶν χώρας πορθου-
87 μένης. σημεῖον δὲ τοῦ τάχους καὶ τῆς ἁμίλλης· τοὺς μὲν c
γὰρ ἡμετέρους προγόνους φασὶ τῆς αὐτῆς ἡμέρας πυθέσθαι
τε τὴν ἀπόβασιν τὴν τῶν βαρβάρων καὶ βοηθήσαντας ἐπὶ
τοὺς ὅρους τῆς χώρας μάχῃ νικήσαντας τρόπαιον στῆσαι τῶν
πολεμίων, τοὺς δ᾽ ἐν τρισὶν ἡμέραις καὶ τοσαύταις νυξὶ
διακόσια καὶ χίλια στάδια διελθεῖν στρατοπέδῳ πορευο- d

ald. 'And the Spartans wished to help the Athenians, but were unable to give them any present succour, as they did not like to break their established law. It was then the ninth day of the first decade; and they could not march out of Sparta on the ninth, when the moon had not reached the full. So they waited for the full of the moon.' (Rawlinson.)

ἀλλοτρίαις κ.τ.λ.] Thuc. I. 70, τοῖς μὲν σώμασιν ἀλλοτριωτάτοις ὑπὲρ τῆς πόλεως χρῶνται.

οἰκείαν δύναμιν.] Isocr. advisedly says nothing of the help given by the Plataeans (Hdt. VI. 108); his argument is confined to a comparison between Athens and Sparta.

ὀλίγοι πρὸς πολλὰς μυριάδας.] The Athenians are commonly reckoned at 10,000, either including or excluding the 1000 Plataeans; the Persians are estimated by Leake (Demi, p. 210) at 177,000, by Rawlinson at 210,000. The numbers slain (according to Hdt. VI. 117) were, on the side of the barbarians, about 6400 men; on that of the Athenians 192.

οὐκ ἔφθησαν πυθόμενοι...καὶ... ἧκον.] 'They no sooner heard...than they came.' Evag. § 53, οὐκ ἔφθασαν ἀλλήλοις πλησιάσαντες καὶ περὶ

πλείονος ἐποιήσαντο σφᾶς αὐτούς. Madv. Synt. § 185 b.

ἔφθησαν.] v. table of var. readings and § 165. n.

87. σημεῖον δὲ...τοὺς μὲν γάρ.] This use of γάρ is very common after such formulae as σημεῖον δέ· τεκμήριον δέ· κεφάλαιον δέ· τὸ δὲ μέγιστον· ὃ δὲ πάντων δεινότατον. Cf. § 149, Phil. § 30, 52, ad Nicocl. § 21, &c. The technical name given to it (by Hoogeveen and others) is γὰρ inchoativum. In English we generally leave out 'for' in such cases; and this omission is not uncommon in Greek; e.g. Phil. § 95, τὸ μὲν τοίνυν μέγιστον... not followed by γάρ, Areop. § 83, Dem. Lept. 503, § 152, Mid. 525, § 35, σημεῖον δέ· ἔθεσθε ἱερὸν νόμον... Madv.Synt. :96 a.

τῆς αὐτῆς ἡμέρας.] 'It is clear that the Greeks were encamped for several days opposite to the Persians, unless we are to set aside altogether the narrative of Hdt.' (Rawlinson on Hdt. VI. 110, Leake's Demi, p. 213, Blakesley's Excursus on the Battle of M.)

διακόσια κ. χίλια στάδια.]=about 150 miles. Hdt. VI. 120, 'After the full of the moon 2000 Lacedaemonians came to Athens. So eager had they been to arrive in time, that

μένους. οὕτω σφόδρ᾽ ἠπείχθησαν οἱ μὲν μετασχεῖν τῶν
κινδύνων, οἱ δὲ φθῆναι συμβαλόντες πρὶν ἐλθεῖν τοὺς βοη-.
88 θήσοντας. (κε´.) Μετὰ δὲ ταῦτα γενομένης τῆς ὕστερον
στρατείας, ἣν αὐτὸς Ξέρξης ἤγαγεν, ἐκλιπὼν μὲν τὰ βασί-
λεια, στρατηγὸς δὲ καταστῆναι τολμήσας, ἅπαντας δὲ τοὺς
ἐκ τῆς Ἀσίας συναγείρας περὶ οὗ τίς οὐχ ὑπερβολὰς
89 προθυμηθεὶς εἰπεῖν ἐλάττω τῶν ὑπαρχόντων εἴρηκεν; ὃς
εἰς τοσοῦτον ἦλθεν ὑπερηφανίας, ὥστε μικρὸν μὲν ἡγησάμενος ἔργον εἶναι τὴν Ἑλλάδα χειρώσασθαι, βουληθεὶς δὲ ε
τοιοῦτον μνημεῖον καταλιπεῖν, ὃ μὴ τῆς ἀνθρωπίνης φύσεώς
ἐστιν, οὐ πρότερον ἐπαύσατο, πρὶν ἐξεῦρε καὶ συνηνάγκασεν,

they took but three days to reach
Attica from Sparta. They came
however too late for the battle.'
(Rawlinson.) Isocr. speaks of 'three
days and as many nights,' and this
is possibly what Herodotus means.

88. **μετὰ δὲ ταῦτα κ.τ.λ.**] Lysias(?)
Or. Funebr. § 27 sqq.—The principal verb of this long sentence is
ἐπαύσατο (in § 90). The mention of
Xerxes suggests a parenthetical description which does not close till the
end of § 89, and the general sense
of the previous clauses is there summed up in the words **πρὸς δὴ τὸν
κ.τ.λ.**, introduced by the resumptive
particle **δή**. Madv. *Synt.* § 216.

τῆς ὕστερον στρατείας κ.τ.λ.]
480 B.C. Herod. VII—IX.

89. **ὃ μὴ...ἐστιν.**] *Quod humanam
naturam excederet.* Wolf. Cf. § 10,
λέγειν περὶ ὧν μηδεὶς πρότερον εἴρηκεν. Madv. *Synt.* § 203.

οὐ πρότερον ἐπαύσατο κ.τ.λ.]
'He ceased not, until he had devised
and by compulsion executed the task
that is on the lips of all men,
so that with his armament he sailed
through the mainland and marched
across the sea, by throwing a bridge
across the Hellespont and digging a
canal through Athos.'

The elaborate parallelism of the
words and clauses of this sentence
is too marked to escape notice.
πλεῦσαι ‖ πεζεῦσαι· ἠπείρου)(θαλάτ-
τῃ· and ζεύξας ‖ διορύξας. Whether

this affectation is worth preserving
in a translation is questionable:
what is barely tolerable in Greek is
in this case insufferable in English.
We might, if necessary, preserve it:
as follows: 'With his hosts he sailed
across the mainland, and marched
across the main, by bridging the
Hellespont and abridging the voyage
round Athos.' Wolf preserves the
parallelism thus: *ut cum exercitu
continentem navigaret, pedibus mare
ambularit, tum Hellesponto ponte
juncto, tum Atho monte perfosso:*
and a similar attempt is made by
Cartelier, the French translator of
the speech *de permutatione,* p. 45.

In Lysias (?) *Or. Funebr.* § 29, we
have ὁδὸν μὲν διὰ τῆς θαλάσσης
ἐποιήσατο, πλοῦν δὲ διὰ τῆς γῆς ἠνά-
γκασε γενέσθαι. It is unnecessary
to suppose either that Isocrates is
plagiarising from the writer of the
Or. Funebris, or the converse; both
may be quoting from the Funeral
Oration of Gorgias, the remains of
which are characterized by a series
of frigid conceits like those of the
present passage; or else both may
be repeating some popular and tra-
ditional sentence, in which the deeds
of Xerxes were commemorated in a
rhythmical and antithetical form.
Lucian, in his bitterly sarcastic
Rhetorum praeceptor, § 20, ironically
commends this topic to the aspirant
after oratory: ἐπὶ πᾶσι δὲ ὁ Μαρα-

ὃ πάντες θρυλοῦσιν, ὥστε τῷ στρατοπέδῳ πλεῦσαι μὲν διὰ
τῆς ἠπείρου, πεζεῦσαι δὲ διὰ τῆς θαλάττης, τὸν μὲν Ἑλλήσ-
90 ποντον ζεύξας, τὸν δ᾽ Ἄθω διορύξας· πρὸς δὴ τὸν οὕτω 39
μέγα φρονήσαντα καὶ τηλικαῦτα διαπραξάμενον καὶ τοσούτων δεσπότην γενόμενον ἀπήντων διελόμενοι τὸν κίνδυνον,
Λακεδαιμόνιοι μὲν εἰς Θερμοπύλας πρὸς τὸ πεζὸν, χιλίους
αὐτῶν ἐπιλέξαντες καὶ τῶν συμμάχων ὀλίγους παραλαβόντες, ὡς ἐν τοῖς στενοῖς κωλύσοντες αὐτοὺς περαιτέρω
προελθεῖν, οἱ δ᾽ ἡμέτεροι πατέρες ἐπ᾽ Ἀρτεμίσιον, ἑξήκοντα b

θίον καὶ ὁ Κυναίγειροε, ὃν οὐκ ἄν τι
ἄνευ γένοιτα. καὶ δεῖ ὁ Ἄθων πλείσθω
καὶ ὁ Ἑλλήσποντοι πεζευέσθω καὶ ὁ
ἥλιοι ὑπὸ τῶν Μήδων βελῶν σκε-
πέσθω καὶ Ξέρξη φυγέτω καὶ ὁ Λεω-
νίδαι θαυμαζέσθω καὶ τὰ Ὀθρυάδου
γράμματα ἀναγινωσκέσθω, καὶ ἡ Σα-
λαμὶς καὶ τὸ Ἀρτεμίσιον καὶ αἱ Πλα-
ταιαί πολλὰ ταῦτα καὶ πυκνά.

. In the four clauses πλεῦσαι—διορύξας observe the *chiasmus*; the first
clause corresponds to the fourth;
the second to the third. v. *ad Dem.*
§ 7. n., *Paneg.* § 54. n.

. On the subject-matter of the sentence v. Hdt. VII. 22·24 (with Rawlinson's n.), 33·36, Aesch. *Pers.*
744·50, Cic. *de Fin.* II. 34, § 112,
and Juv. X. 173 sqq.

ὥστε.] Cf. *Archid.* § 4, ἦν δεδει-
γμένον ὥστε τοὺς πρεσβυτέρους περὶ
ἀπάντων εἰδέναι τὸ βέλτιστον; *ib.* § 40,
γέγονεν ὥστε...ἀρατηθῆναι. Madv.
Synt. § 143, a. 3, and Goodwin's
Gk. Moods and Tenses, § 98, n. 2.

90. χιλίους.] According to Hdt.
VII. 202, the original numbers were
as follows: 300 Spartan hoplites;
1120 Arcadians, from Tegea, Mantinea, and the Arcadian Orchomenus,
and 1000 from other cities in Arca-
dia; from Corinth 400, from Phlius
200, from Mycenae 80. Also, from
Boeotia, 700 Thespians and 400
Thebans. 'There were also doubtless Helots and other light troops, in
undefined number, and probably a
certain number of Lacedaemonian
hoplites, not Spartans.' Grote, *H. G.*
III. 424, new ed.

Subsequently, Leonidas ordered
the allies to depart. The Lacedaemonians (not the Spartans) may have
retired at the same time. Only the
Thespians and the Thebans remained with the 300 Spartans.

These 300 may have been (as Morus
supposes) attended by 2 or 3 Helots
each; by this hypothesis we obtain
an approximation to the number
1000 mentioned by Isocr. In this
passage. The Lacedaemonians are,
in this case, stated to have chosen
from themselves 300 Spartans and
700 Helots. The chief objection to
this view is the importance thereby
assigned to the Helots. I therefore
prefer assuming a confusion of numbers arising from the fact that, after
the desertion of the Theban contingent, the 300 Spartans and the 700
Thespians exactly made up a force
of 1000 men. The number 1000 thus
became associated with the battle;
and was erroneously supposed to be
the number contributed by Lacedaemon.—The numbers given by Diodorus Siculus, XI. 4 (quoted by
Morus, &c.), are, Λακεδαιμονίων χί-
λιοι καὶ σὺν αὐτοῖς Σπαρτιᾶται τρια-
κόσιοι, where the 300 are probably
included in the 1000.

ἐπιλέξαντες.] Cf. Hdt. VII. 205,
ἐπιλεξάμενοι (Λεωνίδη) ἄνδρας τε
τοὺς κατεστεῶτας τριηκοσίους καὶ τοῖσι
ἐτύγχανον παῖδες ἐόντες...

ἑξήκοντα τριήρεσι.] According to
Hdt. VIII. 1, out of the total of 271
Grecian vessels that met at Artemi-
sium, the Athenians furnished 127,

τριήρεις πληρώσαντες πρὸς ἅπαν τὸ τῶν πολεμίων ναυτικόν.
91 ταῦτα δὲ ποιεῖν ἐτόλμων οὐχ οὕτω τῶν πολεμίων καταφρονοῦντες ὡς πρὸς ἀλλήλους ἀγωνιῶντες, Λακεδαιμόνιοι μὲν
ζηλοῦντες τὴν πόλιν τῆς Μαραθῶνι μάχης, καὶ ζητοῦντες
αὐτοὺς ἐξισῶσαι, καὶ δεδιότες μὴ δὶς ἐφεξῆς ἡ πόλις ἡμῶν
αἰτία γένηται τοῖς Ἕλλησι τῆς σωτηρίας, οἱ δ' ἡμέτεροι
μάλιστα μὲν βουλόμενοι διαφυλάξαι τὴν παροῦσαν δόξαν
καὶ πᾶσι ποιῆσαι φανερὸν, ὅτι καὶ τὸ πρότερον δι' ἀρετὴν c
ἀλλ' οὐ διὰ τύχην ἐνίκησαν, ἔπειτα καὶ προαγαγέσθαι τοὺς
Ἕλληνας ἐπὶ τὸ διαναυμαχεῖν, ἐπιδείξαντες αὐτοῖς ὁμοίως
ἐν τοῖς ναυτικοῖς κινδύνοις ὥσπερ ἐν τοῖς πεζοῖς τὴν ἀρετὴν
92 τοῦ πλήθους περιγιγνομένην. (κε'.) Ἴσας δὲ τὰς τόλμας

manned by themselves and the Plataeans; and 20 manned by Chalcideans. These were subsequently
reinforced by 53 ships from Attica.
According to Isocrates the number
of triremes manned by the Athenians is sixty. Coray proposes to
remove the discrepancy by adding
καὶ ἕκαστον. It is safer to suggest
that Isocr. supposes that the Attic
reinforcement of 53 vessels is included in the 127 vessels mentioned
by Hdt. In this case, 74 Athenian
vessels would form the original contingent manned by the Athenians
and Plataeans. Making a rough
allowance for the Plataeans, Isocr.
arrives at his estimate of 60 vessels.
In the above explanation I have
been anticipated by Schneider, and
other suggestions might easily be
made, but it is enough to notice
broadly that throughout this section
the merit of the Lacedaemonians
is slightly depreciated, and that of
the Athenians exaggerated; hence
the empty phrase πρὸς τὸ πεζὸν,
contrasted with the fulness of πρὸς
ἅπαν τὸ τῶν πολεμίων ναυτικόν, and
hence also the adoption of such an
account of the number of triremes
manned by the Athenians, as would
allow the battle of Artemisium to
be plausibly compared with that of
Thermopylae.

91. ἀγωνιῶντα.] Usually ἀγωνιᾶν
has an *intensive* meaning; here,
however, it has no such force. Cf.
Harpocration, ἀγωνιῶντες· ἀντὶ τοῦ
ἀγωνιζόμενοι παρὰ τῷ αὐτῷ (sc.
Ἰσοκράτει) ἐν τῷ πανηγυρικῷ.

ζηλοῦντες ‖ ζητοῦντες.] παρονομασία. Cf. § 45, ῥώμῃ ‖ γνώμῃ, § 186,
φήμη ‖ μνήμη, n. *ad Dem.* § 28, χρήματα ‖ κτήματα, also above, § 89. n.

τῆς Μαραθῶνι μάχης.] This (and
not ἐν Μαραθῶνι μάχῃ) is the almost universal formula, e.g. *Phil.*
§ 147, ἐκ τῆς Μαραθῶνι μάχης and
τῆς ἐν Σαλαμῖνι ναυμαχίας, Dem. *de
Cor.* § 208, μὰ τοὺς Μαραθῶνι προκινδυνεύσαντας κ. τοὺς ἐν Πλαταιαῖς παρα-
ταξαμένους κ. τοὺς ἐν Σαλαμῖνι ναυ-
μαχήσαντας, Dem. *Aristocr.* § 196, 198,
Thuc. I. 73, and Plat. *Menex.* 240,
241. Μαραθῶνι is in all these passages
a quasi-adverb, like Ἐλευσῖνι, Αὐ-
λῶνι, Ἀγροῦντι, Ῥαμνοῦντι, &c. The
form ἐν Μαραθῶνι is sometimes found
(e.g. Hdt. VI. 111·117), Aesch. *Ctesiph.* § 181, Plato, *Gorg.* 516 D, Arist.
Rhet. II. 22). Cobet (*nov. lect.* p.
96) lays down the law, 'nemo unquam veterum ἐν Μαραθῶνι dixit.'

The name of the *demus* is derived,
not from any hero called Marathon
(as Pausanias tells us), but probably
from the growth of μάραθον, or fen-
nel, beside its λειμῶν· ἐρόεντα (Ar.
Av. 246). For similar botanical

παρασχόντες οὐχ ὁμοίαις ἐχρήσαντο ταῖς τύχαις, ἀλλ' οἱ
μὲν διεφθάρησαν καὶ ταῖς ψυχαῖς νικῶντες τοῖς σώμασιν
ἀπεῖπον, (οὐ γὰρ δὴ τοῦτό γε θέμις εἰπεῖν, ὡς ἡττήθησαν·
οὐδεὶς γὰρ αὐτῶν φυγεῖν ἠξίωσεν) οἱ δ' ἡμέτεροι τὰς μὲν d
πρόπλους ἐνίκησαν, ἐπειδὴ δ' ἤκουσαν τῆς παρόδου τοὺς
πολεμίους κρατοῦντας, οἴκαδε καταπλεύσαντες [καὶ κατα-
σκευάσαντες τὰ περὶ τὴν πόλιν] οὕτως ἐβουλεύσαντο περὶ
τῶν λοιπῶν, ὥστε πολλῶν καὶ καλῶν αὐτοῖς προειργασμέ-
νων ἐν τοῖς τελευταίοις τῶν κινδύνων ἔτι πλέον διήνεγκαν.

93 ἀθύμως γὰρ ἁπάντων τῶν συμμάχων διακειμένων, καὶ Πελο-
ποννησίων μὲν διατειχιζόντων τὸν Ἰσθμὸν καὶ ζητούντων c
ἰδίαν αὑτοῖς σωτηρίαν, τῶν δ' ἄλλων πόλεων ὑπὸ τοῖς βαρβάροις γεγενημένων καὶ συστρατευομένων ἐκείνοις, πλὴν εἴ
τις διὰ μικρότητα παρημελήθη, προσπλεουσῶν δὲ τριήρων
διακοσίων καὶ χιλίων καὶ πεζῆς στρατιᾶς ἀναριθμήτου μελλούσης εἰς τὴν Ἀττικὴν εἰσβάλλειν, οὐδεμιᾶς σωτηρίας 60
αὑτοῖς ὑποφαινομένης, ἀλλ' ἔρημοι συμμάχων γεγενημένοι
94 καὶ τῶν ἐλπίδων ἁπασῶν διημαρτηκότες, ἐξὸν αὐτοῖς μὴ
μόνον τοὺς παρόντας κινδύνους διαφυγεῖν ἀλλὰ καὶ τιμὰς

---

names of Attic *demi* cf. Ἀγροῦς,
Ἰατή, Ἐλαιοῦς, Μυρρινοῦς, Οἰνόη,
Πρασίαι, Ῥαμνοῦς, Φηγοῦν.

92. οἱ μὲν—ἠξίωσεν.] Cf. Lysias (?)
Or. Funebr. § 31 and Hyperid. *Or.
Funebr.* col. 23.

τὰς πρόπλους.] The advanced
squadron of 200 vessels mentioned in
Hdt. VIII. 7.

καὶ κατασκευάσαντα — πόλιν.]
These words, though found in all
MSS. of the corresponding passage
(*de Permutatione*), are omitted by all
the MSS. in the present passage, and
therefore enclosed within brackets.

πολλῶν καὶ καλῶν.] In English
we omit the conjunction. A further
extension of the Greek idiom may
be noticed in Plato, *Apol.* p. 28 A,
πολλοὺς καὶ ἄλλους καὶ ἀγαθοὺς
ἄνδρας.

93. διακειμένων ... διατειχιζόντων ... γεγενημένοι ... διημαρτηκότες,
ἐξὸν ... οὐχ ὑπέμειναν κ.τ.λ.] The

sentence begins with a number of
participial constructions, the principal vb. does not appear till the
3rd line of the next p.

τριηρῶν διακοσίων καὶ χιλίων.]
The exact number, according to
Hdt. VII. 89, was 1207. Cf. Aesch.
Pers. 341, Plato, *Legg.* 699 D. Elsewhere (*Panath.* § 49) Isocr. reckons
the fleet of Xerxes at 1300, and the
infantry at five millions, 700,000 of
whom were fighting men. (v. Leake's
Demi, p. 150.)

οὐδεμιᾶς—ὑποφαινομένης.] 'Als
ihnen da nirgends ein Rettungstern
leuchtete' is Benseler's transl. The
metaphor is (as Rauchenstein observes), borrowed from the first gleam
of day-break on the horizon.—Xen.
Anab. IV. 2. 7, ἡμέρα ὑπέφαινεν.
Cf. Aristot. *Probl.* 25. 5, ὑποφωσκού-
σης ἕω, and for the metaphor, Cic.
pro domo, § 75, *lucem salutemque
redditam sibi ac restitutam accipere*.

ἐξαιρέτους λαβεῖν, ἃς αὐτοῖς ἐδίδου βασιλεὺς ἡγούμενος, εἰ
τὸ τῆς πόλεως προσλάβοι ναυτικὸν, παραχρῆμα καὶ Πελο-
ποννήσου κρατήσειν, οὐχ ὑπέμειναν τὰς παρ' ἐκείνου δωρεὰς,
οὐδ' ὀργισθέντες τοῖς Ἕλλησιν, ὅτι προὐδόθησαν, ἀσμένως
95 ἐπὶ τὰς διαλλαγὰς τὰς πρὸς τοὺς βαρβάρους ὥρμησαν, ἀλλ'
αὐτοὶ μὲν ὑπὲρ τῆς ἐλευθερίας πολεμεῖν παρεσκευάζοντο,
τοῖς δ' ἄλλοις τὴν δουλείαν αἱρουμένοις συγγνώμην εἶχον.
ἡγοῦντο γὰρ ταῖς μὲν ταπειναῖς τῶν πόλεων προσήκειν ἐκ
παντὸς τρόπου ζητεῖν τὴν σωτηρίαν, ταῖς δὲ προεστάναι τῆς
Ἑλλάδος ἀξιούσαις οὐχ οἷόν τ' εἶναι διαφεύγειν τοὺς κινδύ- c
νους, ἀλλ' ὥσπερ τῶν ἀνδρῶν τοῖς καλοῖς κἀγαθοῖς αἱρετώ-
τερόν ἐστι καλῶς ἀποθανεῖν ἢ ζῆν αἰσχρῶς, οὕτω καὶ τῶν
πόλεων ταῖς ὑπερεχούσαις λυσιτελεῖν ἐξ ἀνθρώπων ἀφανι-
σθῆναι μᾶλλον ἢ δούλαις ὀφθῆναι γενομέναις. δῆλον δ' ὅτι
96 ταῦτα διενοήθησαν· ἐπειδὴ γὰρ οὐχ οἷοί τ' ἦσαν πρὸς
ἀμφοτέρας ἅμα παρατάξασθαι τὰς δυνάμεις, παραλαβόντες
ἅπαντα τὸν ὄχλον τὸν ἐκ τῆς πόλεως εἰς τὴν ἐχομένην d
νῆσον ἐξέπλευσαν, ἵν' ἐν μέρει πρὸς ἑκατέραν κινδυνεύσω-

---

94. **ἐδίδου.**] The offer was really
made by *Mardonius* in 479 B.C.,
through Alexander, the son of
Amyntas; IIdt. VIII. 136, 140.

βασιλεύς] = 'the Great King.'
The article is in this case nearly
always omitted. v. § 145. n.

95. **ὥσπερ τῶν — γενομέναις.**]
Obs. the aor. and the pres. tenses.
The distinction is carefully pointed
out by Goodwin's translation of this
passage (*Gk. Moods and Tenses*,
§ 23, 1): 'as it is preferable for
honourable men to die (*Aor.*) nobly
rather than to continue living (*Pres.*)
in disgrace, so also they thought
that it was better (*Pres.*) for the pre-
eminent among states to be (*at once*)
made to disappear from the earth,
than to be (*once*) seen to have fallen
into slavery.'

καλῶς ἀποθανεῖν ἢ ζῆν αἰσχρῶς.]
Cf. *Archid.* § 89, Lysias (?) *Or. Funebr.* § 62, and (for the order of
words) v. *ad Dem.* § 7, πλούτου κρείττων, n.—On the constr. of δούλαις,
v. § 124. n.

96. **ἐπειδὴ κ.τ.λ.**] *i.e.* 'For when
they were unable to marshal themselves against both the land and the
sea force at once, they took with
them all the multitude from the city,
and sailed forth to the neighbouring
island, that so they might contend
in turn against the two opposing
forces.'

τὸν ἐκ τῆς πόλεως.] Cf. §§ 174,
187, and Madv. *Synt.* § 79 h.

ἐξέπλευσαν.] *Quanto rectius in
Aeginetico scribitur*, § 31, ἀρῶσα τοὺς
πολίτας τοὺς ἡμετέρους, ὅσοιπερ ἦσαν
ἐν Τροιζῆνι, διαπλέοντας εἰς Αἴγιναν,
ad omnino διαπλεῖν, *διαπορθμεῖσθαι et
sim. in usu sunt de iis, qui in vici-
nam insulam trajiciunt. Saepe apud
Isocratem quoque ἐξ et δι confusa
sunt: quare confidenter rescribe* διά-
πλευσαν. Cobet, *nov. lect.* p. 172.
The word ἐξέπλευσαν is however far
more expressive. 'Ce n'est pas ici
une simple traversée, c'est une émi-
gration.' Havet.

ἐν μέρει.] 'In turns,' first against
the sea force at Salamis, secondly

σιν. (κζ΄.) Καίτοι πῶς ἂν ἐκείνων ἄνδρες ἀμείνους ἢ
μᾶλλον φιλέλληνες ὄντες ἐπιδειχθεῖεν, οἵτινες ἔτλησαν
ἐπιδεῖν, ὥστε μὴ τοῖς λοιποῖς αἴτιοι γενέσθαι τῆς δουλείας,
ἐρήμην μὲν τὴν πόλιν γενομένην, τὴν δὲ χώραν πορθουμένην, ἱερὰ δὲ συλώμενα καὶ νεὼς ἐμπιπραμένους, ἅπαντα
δὲ τὸν πόλεμον περὶ τὴν πατρίδα τὴν αὑτῶν γιγνόμενον; e
97 καὶ οὐδὲ ταῦτ᾽ ἀπέχρησεν αὐτοῖς, ἀλλὰ πρὸς χιλίας καὶ
διακοσίας τριήρεις μόνοι διαναυμαχεῖν ἐμέλλησαν. οὐ μὴν
εἰάθησαν καταισχυνθέντες γὰρ Πελοποννήσιοι τὴν ἀρετὴν

against the land force at Plataea.
It will be observed that Isocr. does
not dwell on the battle of Plataea;
doubtless because, while the Athenians defeated the Thebans, the
Lacedaemonians defeated the Barbarians in that engagement.

ἔτλησαν.] The MSS. have ἐτόλμησαν, but in the twin passage (*de
Permutatione*) the Vulg. has ἔτλησαν,
a reading which is supported by
Dionys. Halic. *de vi Demosth.* 40,
and by Aristot. *Rhet.* III. 7, 10, who
says that uncommon words may be
employed when the orator has gained possession of his audience, and
worked them up to enthusiasm: οἷον
καὶ Ἰσοκράτης ποιεῖ ἐν τῷ πανηγυρικῷ ἐπὶ τέλει, 'φήμη δὲ καὶ γνώμη'
(v. § 186. n.), καὶ 'οἳ τινες ἔτλησαν.'
I have therefore followed BS and
Bens. in reading ἔτλησαν. The word
is rare in Attic *prose:* It occurs, however, in Xen. *Cyrop.* III. 1, 2, οὐκέτι
ἔτλη εἰς χεῖρας ἐλθεῖν.

ὥστε.] Cf. § 83, τοίαν ἀπέστησαν
ὥστε.. εὐδαιμῶν. Madv. *Synt.* § 166 b.

**γενομένην … πορθουμένην … γιγνό-
μενον.**] Obs. the force of the aor.
and the pres. participle. v. Goodwin's *Gk. Moods and Tenses*, § 24.
n. 2.

καὶ οὐδὲ ταῦτ᾽ ἀπέχρησεν.] This
is the MS. reading. Dionys. Halic.
however, in quoting §§ 96—99 (*de
vi Demosth.*), gives us the reading
καὶ μηδὲ, which is actually adopted
by Benseler, mainly because it re-
moves the *hiatus*, and is explained
by him as follows: *Praef.* v. *Et ne*

*hoc quidem iis satis fuisse censuerim,
sed audacius etiam quid conaturi
fuissent, si ceteri id sivissent.* If a
reading that stands on such weak
authority needs explanation, it would
be better to attribute the use of μὴ
to the influence of οἵτινες in the
earlier part of the sentence. But the
MS. reading, which I have retained,
needs no explanation; and, as for
the *hiatus*, it is perfectly admissible.
In *Excursus* XI. to Bremi's ed. more
than 20 instances are quoted to shew
that Isocr. often places καὶ immediately before a vowel; some of these
have, of course, been altered by
Henseler; but in three passages (*de
Pace*, § 14, *Panath.* § 107, 184) καὶ
οὐκ is allowed to remain. I can,
therefore, see no sufficient reason for
printing either καὶ μηδὲ (with Bens.),
or κοὐδὲ (with Dindf.), or simply
οὐδὲ (with Havet).

97. διαναυμαχεῖν ἐμέλλησαν.]
'They *were about to* (*were ready to*)
contend, &c.' There is no necessity
for abandoning ἐμέλλησαν (the reading of Cod. Urb. followed by BS)
in favour of ἐμέλλησαν (Cod. Ambr.
followed by Bens. '*curam in eo po-
suerunt, sese praeparaverunt;*' but
subsequently abandoned by him).
'There seems no foundation for
Buttmann, Kühner, Jelf, &c. con-
fining the aor. to the meaning *have
delayed*, see Thuc. I. 134, III. 55,
92, V. 116, VIII. 23, and Isocr. *Archid.* § 44, αὐτὸς μὲν ἐμέλλησεν
ἐκπλεῖν.' (Veitch, *Gk. Verbs*, s. v.)

· **εἰάθησαν.**] Sc. μόνα διαναυμαχεῖν.

αὐτῶν, καὶ νομίσαντες προδιαφθαρέντων μὲν τῶν ἡμετέρων
οὐδ᾽ αὐτοὶ σωθήσεσθαι, κατορθωσάντων δ᾽ εἰς ἀτιμίαν τὰς
αὐτῶν πόλεις καταστήσειν, ἠναγκάσθησαν μετασχεῖν τῶν δι
κινδύνων. καὶ τοὺς μὲν θορύβους τοὺς ἐν τῷ πράγματι
γενομένους καὶ τὰς κραυγὰς καὶ τὰς παρακελεύσεις, ἃ κοινὰ
πάντων ἐστὶ τῶν ναυμαχούντων οὐκ οἶδ᾽ ὅ τι δεῖ λέγοντα
98 διατρίβειν· ἃ δ᾽ ἐστὶν ἴδια καὶ τῆς ἡγεμονίας ἄξια καὶ τοῖς
προειρημένοις ὁμολογούμενα, ταῦτα δ᾽ ἐμὸν ἔργον ἐστὶν εἰπεῖν. τοσοῦτον γὰρ ἡ πόλις ἡμῶν διέφερεν, ὅτ᾽ ἦν ἀκέραιος,
ὥστ᾽ ἀνάστατος γενομένη πλείους μὲν συνεβάλετο τριήρεις b

The pass. of ἐὰν is far from common;
it occurs however in Dem. *Ol.* 11.
§ 16, ἰώμενα, *Steph.* A, § 22, εἴασθαι.
κατορθωσάντων.] Sc. τῶν ἡμετέρων. Cobet (*nov. lect.* p. 359) finds
an unaccountable difficulty in taking
οἱ Πελοποννήσιοι as the subject of
καταστήσειν, and therefore proposes
κατορθώσαντας. For the general historical allusion cf. Hdt. VIII. 63,
ταῦτα δὲ Θεμιστοκλέους λέγοντος ἀνεδιδάσκετο Εὐρυβιάδης· δοκέειν δέ μοι,
ἀρρωδήσας μάλιστα τοὺς Ἀθηναίους
ἀνεδιδάσκετο. μὴ σφέας ἀπολίπωσι, ἢν
πρὸς τὸν Ἰσθμὸν ἀνάγῃ τὰς ναῦς ἀπο-
λιπόντων γὰρ τῶν Ἀθηναίων, οὐκέτι
ἐγίνοντο ἀξιόμαχοι οἱ λοιποί· ταύτην
δὲ αἱρέεται τὴν γνώμην, αὐτοῦ μένοντας
διαναυμαχεῖν. Isocr. says nothing of
the well-known artifice subsequently
adopted by Themistocles to compel
both Athenians and Peloponnesians
to fight the Persians (Hdt. VIII. 75).

θορύβους... κραυγὰς... παρακελεύσεις.] 'All the uproar...the cries...
and the cheers.' The sentence καὶ
τοὺς—διατρίβειν is repeated almost
verbatim in *Evag.* § 31. Cf. Lys. (?)
Or. Funebr. § 38, ἀκούσντες συμμε-
μιγμένου Ἑλληνικοῦ κ. βαρβαρικοῦ
παιᾶνοι, παρακελευσμοῦ δ᾽ ἀμφοτέρων,
κ. κραυγῆς τῶν διαφθειρομένων (with
the context).

98. ἃ δὲ...ταῦτα δέ...] For δὲ in
apodosis v. Buttmann's *Midias*, exc.
XII, and cf. *Panath.* § 133 (bis), *de
Perm.* § 305, and the passages quoted
on p. 43.

ἀκέραιος...ἀνάστατος.] Cf. Ar-

chid. § 66, quoted above, § 37. n.

πλείους...τριήρεις...ἢ σύμπαντες
οἱ ναυμαχήσαντες.] Isocr. here
states that Athens contributed a
larger number of triremes than all
the rest of the allied combatants put
together. Cf. *Panath.* § 50, Lys. (?)
Or. Funebr. § 42. According to
Herodotus (VIII. 48) the total number of triremes in the fleet was 378
(although the number gained by
adding the various contingents together is 366); of these 180 were furnished by the Athenians (*ib.* 44),
and 198 (or 186) vessels were contributed by the rest.

At first sight this proportion hardly warrants the statement of Isocr.
that the Athenian contingent was
greater than that of the rest of the
allies. We must not always look
for arithmetical accuracy in Isocrates,
παραπλήσιον γὰρ φαίνεται μαθηματι-
κοῦ τε πιθανολογοῦντος ἀποδέχεσθαι
καὶ ῥητορικὸν ἀποδείξεις ἀπαιτεῖν, but
if it is necessary to reconcile the
historian and the rhetorician, I may
draw attention to the fact that, while
only 180 vessels were *manned* by
the Athenians themselves, 20 of the
198 (or 186) triremes of the allies
really *belonged to Athens*, and were
only manned by the Chalcideans
(Hdt. VIII. 1 compared with 46);
and that the number of triremes
belonging to Athens was therefore
200, against the 178 (or 166) belonging to the allies. This view is
confirmed by the speech of Themi-

εἰς τὸν κίνδυνον τὸν ὑπὲρ τῆς Ἑλλάδος ἢ σύμπαντες οἱ
ναυμαχήσαντες, οὐδεὶς δὲ πρὸς ἡμᾶς οὕτως ἔχει δυσμενῶς,
ὅστις οὐκ ἂν ὁμολογήσειε διὰ μὲν τὴν ναυμαχίαν ἡμᾶς τῷ
πολέμῳ κρατῆσαι, ταύτης δὲ τὴν πόλιν αἰτίαν γενέσθαι.

99 (κη΄.) Καίτοι μελλούσης στρατείας ἐπὶ τοὺς βαρβάρους
ἔσεσθαι τίνας χρὴ τὴν ἡγεμονίαν ἔχειν; οὐ τοὺς ἐν τῷ προτέρῳ πολέμῳ μάλιστ᾽ εὐδοκιμήσαντας, καὶ πολλάκις μὲν c
ἰδίᾳ προκινδυνεύσαντας, ἐν δὲ τοῖς κοινοῖς τῶν ἀγώνων ἀριστείων ἀξιωθέντας; οὐ τοὺς τὴν αὐτῶν ἐκλιπόντας ὑπὲρ
τῆς τῶν ἄλλων σωτηρίας, καὶ τό τε παλαιὸν οἰκιστὰς τῶν
πλείστων πόλεων γενομένους, καὶ πάλιν αὐτὰς ἐκ τῶν μεγίστων συμφορῶν διασώσαντας; πῶς δ᾽ οὐκ ἂν δεινὰ πά-
θοιμεν, εἰ τῶν κακῶν πλεῖστον μέρος μετασχόντες ἐν ταῖς
τιμαῖς ἔλαττον ἔχειν ἀξιωθεῖμεν καὶ τότε προταχθέντες
ὑπὲρ ἁπάντων νῦν ἑτέροις ἀκολουθεῖν ἀναγκασθεῖμεν; d

stocles (ap. IIdt. VIII. 61), whose
express statement that Athens contributed 100 vessels has sometimes
been unnecessarily accused of exaggeration.

Lastly, it may be noticed that the
popular tradition affirmed that about
two-thirds of the fleet consisted of
Athenian vessels: cf. the speech of
the Athenians in Thuc. I. 74, ναῦς
μὲν γε ἐς τὰς τετρακοσίας ὀλίγῳ ἐλάσ-
σους τῶν δύο μοιρῶν (παρεσχόμεθα),
Dem. de Corona, § 70, τριακοσίων
οὐσῶν τῶν πασῶν (τριήρων), τὰς διακοσίας ἡ πόλις παρίσχετο. Cf. § 107. n.

σύμπαντες οἱ ναυμαχήσαντες.]
In the corresponding passage (de
Perm.) the Cod. Laur. has συνναυ-
μαχήσαντες, which is adopted by
Coray, Bens., and Rauchenstein.
This view may be supported by
Panath. § 50, πλείους ναῦς παρέσχοντο
κ. μείζω δύναμιν ἐχούσας ἢ σύμπαντες
οἱ συγκινδυνεύσαντες. The reading
in the text is supported by the Cod.
Urb. and is retained by BS, Schneider, and others.—σύμπαντες = σύμπαντες οἱ ἄλλοι. cf. § 107, κεκτημένοι
τριήρεις διπλασίας ἢ σύμπαντες (sc.
οἱ ἄλλοι).

ταύτης…αἰτίαν…] i. e. 'Athens

brought about the battle,' not 'brought
about the victory in the battle' (v.
§ 26. n.). Cf. Panath. § 51, τὸν
Θεμιστοκλέα τὸν ὁμολογουμένως
ἅπασιν αἴτιον εἶναι δόξαντα καὶ τοῦ
τὴν ναυμαχίαν γενέσθαι κατὰ τρόπον
καὶ τῶν ἄλλων ἁπάντων τῶν ἐν ἐκείνῳ
τῷ χρόνῳ κατορθωθέντων.

§ 99. Recapitulation of §§ 15—98.
In the event of an expedition against
the barbarians, Athens deserves the
supremacy, for her prowess in the
former war, for her sacrifices in behalf of the salvation of Greece, for
founding all those cities in old time,
and for rescuing them from disaster. Hers was the greatest share of
suffering, hers should be the greater
honour; she was in the fore-front
then, she cannot deserve the second
place now.

99. τὴν αὐτῶν.] Sc. γῆν. Cf.
§ 41, τοῖς δυστυχοῦσιν ἐν ταῖς αὐτῶν
(sc. πόλεσιν), § 49, 146, 168. Madv.
Synt. § 87 b, R. 1, and Jelf (Kühner),
§ 436.

οἰκιστὰς τῶν πλείστων πόλεων.]
§§ 34—37.

τῶν κακῶν πλεῖστον μέρος μετασχόντες.] Cf. Archid. § 3, τῶν κινδύνων πλεῖστον μέρος μεθέξουσι, and

100   (κθ´.) Μέχρι μὲν οὖν τούτων᾽οἶδ᾽ ὅτι πάντες ἂν ὁμολογήσειαν πλείστων ἀγαθῶν τὴν πόλιν τὴν ἡμετέραν αἰτίαν γεγενῆσθαι καὶ δικαίως ἂν αὐτῆς τὴν ἡγεμονίαν εἶναι, μετὰ δὲ ταῦτ᾽ ἤδη τινὲς ἡμῶν κατηγοροῦσιν, ὡς ἐπειδὴ τὴν ἀρχὴν τῆς θαλάττης παρελάβομεν, πολλῶν κακῶν αἴτιοι τοῖς Ἕλλησι κατέστημεν, καὶ τόν τε Μηλίων ἀνδραποδισμὸν καὶ

101 τὸν Σκιωναίων ὄλεθρον ἐν τούτοις τοῖς λόγοις ἡμῖν προφέ- e ρουσιν. ἐγὼ δ᾽ ἡγοῦμαι πρῶτον μὲν οὐδὲν εἶναι τοῦτο σημεῖον, ὡς κακῶς ἤρχομεν, εἴ τινες τῶν πολεμησάντων ἡμῖν σφόδρα φαίνονται κολασθέντες, ἀλλὰ πολὺ τόδε μεῖζον τεκμήριον, ὡς καλῶς διῳκοῦμεν τὰ τῶν συμμάχων, ὅτι τῶν πό- 62 λεων τῶν ὑφ᾽ ἡμῖν οὐσῶν οὐδεμία ταύταις ταῖς συμφοραῖς

elsewhere in Isocr. 'A person who shares anything with another, takes the whole of the part (μέρος, &c. in accusative), part of the whole (substantive in genitive): Aesch. Ag. 507, μεθέξειν φιλτάτου τάφου μέρος, Ildt. IV. 145, μοῖραν τιμέων μετέχοντες, Eur. Iph. T. 1299, &c.' Jelf (Kühner), § 535, 1.

§§ 100—109. Charges brought against Athens, on the ground of the severity of her empire; especially with regard to her treatment of Melos and Scione. 101—102. These charges answered, and further refuted by an appeal (103) to the prosperity of Greece during the supremacy of Athens and (104—6) to the general equity of her political administration. (107—9) Her disinclination to self-aggrandisement shewn by her abstaining from taking possession of Euboea.

100. τὸν Μηλίων ἀνδραποδισμόν.] The affair of Melos is related by Thuc. V. 84—116: οἱ δὲ Μήλιοι Λακεδαιμονίων μὲν εἰσὶν ἄποικοι (cf. Hdt. VIII. 48), τῶν δ᾽ Ἀθηναίων οὐκ ἤθελον ὑπακούειν ὥσπερ οἱ ἄλλοι νησιῶται. In 416 B.C. the Athenians undertook the conquest of Melos, 'one of the Cyclades, and the only one, except Thera, which was not already included in her empire.' The island refused to surrender, and a private discussion en-

sued between the Athenian envoys and the Executive Council of Melos. This debate is thrown into a dramatic and impressive form by Thucydides, to serve as a culminating instance of the injustice of Athens, and to prepare the reader for the subsequent account of the Sicilian expedition and its disastrous issue. The pleas of the Melians were unavailing; the island was compelled to surrender at discretion: 'the Athenians resolved to put to death all the men of military age, and to sell the women and children as slaves. Five hundred Athenian settlers (ἄποικοι) were subsequently sent thither, to form a new community.' (Grote, H. G. P. II. c. 56, ad fin.)

τὸν Σκιωναίων ὄλεθρον.] Scione, situated in the peninsula of Pallene, (the most western of the three peninsulas of Chalcidice) revolted from Athens to Sparta in March 423 B.C. (Thuc. IV. 120). The Athenians accordingly blockaded Scione (ib. 130—1); and captured it in 421 (ib. V. 32), put to death the male population of military age, sold the women and children into slavery, and made over the territory to the Plataean refugees. (Grote, H. G. P. II. c. 54, 55.)

101. σημεῖον)(τεκμήριον.] 'proof')('convincing argument.' The posi-

102 περιέπεσεν. ἔπειτ᾽ εἰ μὲν ἄλλοι τινὲς τῶν αὐτῶν πραγμάτων πραότερον ἐπεμελήθησαν, εἰκότως ἂν ἡμῖν ἐπιτιμῷεν·
εἰ δὲ μήτε τοῦτο γέγονε μήθ᾽ οἷόν τ᾽ ἐστὶ τοσούτων πόλεων
τὸ πλῆθος κρατεῖν, ἢν μή τις κολάζῃ τοὺς ἐξαμαρτάνοντας,
πῶς οὐκ ἤδη δίκαιόν ἐστιν ἡμᾶς ἐπαινεῖν, οἵτινες ἐλαχίστοις
χαλεπήναντες πλεῖστον χρόνον τὴν ἀρχὴν κατασχεῖν ἠδυ-
103 νήθημεν; (λ΄.) Οἶμαι δὲ πᾶσι δοκεῖν τούτους κρατίστους b
προστάτας γενήσεσθαι τῶν Ἑλλήνων, ἐφ᾽ ὧν οἱ πειθαρχή-
σαντες ἄριστα τυγχάνουσι πράξαντες. ἐπὶ τοίνυν τῆς ἡμετέρας ἡγεμονίας εὑρήσομεν καὶ τοὺς οἴκους τοὺς ἰδίους πρὸς
εὐδαιμονίαν πλεῖστον ἐπιδόντας καὶ τὰς πόλεις μεγίστας γε-
104 νομένας. οὐ γὰρ ἐφθονοῦμεν ταῖς αὐξανομέναις αὐτῶν, οὐδὲ
ταραχὰς ἐνεποιοῦμεν πολιτείας ἐναντίας παρακαθιστάντες,
ἵν᾽ ἀλλήλοις μὲν στασιάζοιεν, ἡμᾶς δ᾽ ἀμφότεροι θεραπεύ- c

tion of the two words is evidently
intentional; the converse order would
produce an anti-climax.

102. **πῶς οὐκ—ἠδυνήθημεν;**] *i.e.*
'Does it not become irresistibly
right for others to praise us, in that
we shewed our resentment in a very
few cases, and were enabled to hold
our dominion for a very great length
of time?'
On **πῶς οὐκ** v. § 6. n.   **οἵτινες**=
quippe qui. Cf. Dem. *adv. Callicl.*
§ 28 (where *οἷ γε* is used in the
immediate context).

πλεῖστον χρόνον.] The exact
duration of the Athenian empire is
variously reckoned : *e.g.* Demosthenes, *Ol.* III. § 24, states it at 45 years
(*i.e.* 477—432, τῶν Ἑλλήνων ἦρξαν
ἐκόντων); elsewhere at 65 years
(terminating with 413 B.C., the date
of the Athenian defeat in Sicily);
and in *Phil.* III. § 23 at 73 years
(477—405 inclusive. προστᾶται μὲν
ὑμεῖς ἑβδομήκοντα ἔτη καὶ τρία τῶν
Ἑλλήνων ἐγένεσθε, προστᾶται δὲ τριάκοντα ἑνὸς δέοντα Λακεδαιμόνιοι, *sc.*
405—376, battle of Naxos). Isocrates
himself, *Panath.* § 56 (quoted by
Morus), reckons the uninterrupted
dominion of Athens at 65 years
(477—413 incl.), the sway of Sparta
at 10 years (404—394, battle of

Cnidus). When the period is expressed in round numbers, it is
generally stated at 70 years, *e.g.* by
Lysias (?) *Or. Fun.* § 55, by Plato (?)
Ep. VII. p. 332 B, and (according to
one interpretation) by Isocr. *Paneg.*
§ 106. For other periods mentioned by various ancient authorities,
see Clinton's *Fasti Hell.* II. app.
6, 7, or Böckh's *Publ. Econ.* Bk. III.
c. 20, n. 591.

ἠδυνήθημεν.] In the inflexions of
δύναμαι, the epic poets never use the
augment in η·, the Attic poets rarely,
and that only when compelled by
metre (Aesch. *P. V.* 206, οὐκ ἠδυνήθην). In Attic prose authors (as
represented by the latest critical
editions) the temporal augment is
losing ground, but, in Isocrates,
BS and Benseler, in accordance with
the MSS. edit ἠδυνάμην, ἠδυνήθην
(*constanter at* η, *uno excepto loco*
Callim. § 27, *ubi vulg.* ἐδύνατο *lege-
batur.* Bens. praef. XXII), *e.g. Phil.*
§ 129. *Nicocl.* § 33. (v. Veitch, *Gk.
Verbs,* s.v.)

104. **οὐδὲ ταραχὰς κ.τ.λ.**] The
whole of this passage is pervaded
by an under-current of insinuation
against Sparta.

στασιάζοιεν.] *sc.* οἱ πολῖται, which
is readily supplied from πόλις: cf.

7—2

οιεν, ἀλλὰ τὴν τῶν συμμάχων ὁμόνοιαν κοινὴν ὠφέλειαν
νομίζοντες τοῖς αὐτοῖς νόμοις ἀπάσας τὰς πόλεις διῳκοῦμεν,
συμμαχικῶς ἀλλ' οὐ δεσποτικῶς βουλευόμενοι περὶ αὐτῶν,
ὅλων μὲν τῶν πραγμάτων ἐπιστατοῦντες, ἰδίᾳ δ' ἑκάστους
105 ἐλευθέρους ἐῶντες εἶναι, καὶ τῷ μὲν πλήθει βοηθοῦντες, ταῖς
δὲ δυναστείαις πολεμοῦντες, δεινὸν οἰόμενοι τοὺς πολλοὺς
ὑπὸ τοῖς ὀλίγοις εἶναι, καὶ τοὺς ταῖς οὐσίαις ἐνδεεστέρους,
τὰ δ' ἄλλα μηδὲν χείρους ὄντας, ἀπελαύνεσθαι τῶν ἀρχῶν, d
ἔτι δὲ κοινῆς τῆς πατρίδος οὔσης τοὺς μὲν τυραννεῖν, τοὺς
δὲ μετοικεῖν, καὶ φύσει πολίτας ὄντας νόμῳ τῆς πολιτείας
106 ἀποστερεῖσθαι.   τοιαῦτ' ἔχοντες ταῖς ὀλιγαρχίαις ἐπιτιμᾶν,
καὶ πλείω τούτων, τὴν αὐτὴν πολιτείαν, ἥπερ παρ' ἡμῖν
αὐτοῖς, καὶ παρὰ τοῖς ἄλλοις κατεστήσαμεν, ἣν οὐκ οἶδ' ὅ
τι δεῖ διὰ μακροτέρων ἐπαινεῖν, ἄλλως τε καὶ συντόμως
ἔχοντα δηλῶσαι περὶ αὐτῆς.   μετὰ γὰρ ταύτης οἰκοῦντες c

Ἀπορ. § 51, οὐ πολέμων ἡ πόλι
ἡγεμών, ἀλλὰ πρὸς ἀλλήλους ἡσυχίαν
εἶχον. (Schn.).

105. τῷ μὲν πλήθει κ.τ.λ.] 'As-
sisting the commons,' i.e. the democratical party.

δεινὸν κ.τ.λ.] 'Deeming it a
shame that the many should be under
the few.'

μετοικεῖν] lit. 'to be a resident
alien (μέτοικος).' v. Dict. Antiq. or
Kennedy's transl. of Dem. Lept.
App. 3. The position of a μέτοικος
at Athens is here used metaphorically
to denote the position of the governed
classes, under an oligarchy. '...die
einen die Herren, die andern die
Schutzverwandten spielten,' is Benseler's expressive transl. of this clause.
For metaphorical words similar
to τυραννεῖν, μετοικεῖν, cf. § 131, ἐλω-
τεύειν and περιοίκους καταστῆσαι.

φύσει)(νόμῳ.] 'By nature or
birth')('by law or convention.' These
two words are frequently contrasted:
e.g. Plato, Protag. 337 C, D (Hippias
loq.) ἡγοῦμαι ἐγὼ ὑμᾶς συγγενεῖς τε
καὶ οἰκείους καὶ πολίτας ἅπαντας
εἶναι φύσει, οὐ νόμῳ· τὸ γὰρ ὅμοιον
τῷ ὁμοίῳ φύσει συγγενές ἐστιν, ὁ δὲ

νόμος τύραννος ὢν τῶν ἀνθρώπων
πολλὰ παρὰ φύσιν βιάζεται (with
Wayte's n.), Menex. 239 A, ἡ ἰσογονία
ἡμᾶς ἡ κατὰ φύσιν ἰσονομίαν ἀναγ-
κάζει ζητεῖν κατὰ νόμον, and Isocr.
ad Dem. § 10, κρεῖττω φύσιν νόμου.
This contrast between φύσις and
νόμος, 'nature' and 'convention,'
was not uncommon among the Sophists, but was by no means confined
to them. (v. further Ritter and
Preller, Hist. Philos. § 183, Mr
Cope's art. in J. of Cl. and Sacr.
Philol. I. 155 sqq., and Sir A.
Grant's ed. of Aristot. Eth. Vol. I.
p. 167 sqq. new ed.)

106. μετὰ ταύτης οἰκοῦντες ἑβδο-
μήκοντ' ἔτη διετέλεσαν κ.τ.λ.] ταύτῃ must refer to πολιτείας, not to
ἡγεμονίας.

The period of 70 years here mentioned has given rise to much dispute.
The various views may be summa-
rized as follows:
(i) Wolf, Corny, Spohn, Dindorf,
Breml, and Rauchenstein refer the
70 years to the period between the
establishment of the Athenian Empire at the end of the Persian war,
and the battle of Aegospotami,

ἐβδομήκοντ' ἔτη διετέλεσαν, ἄπειροι μὲν τυραννίδων, ἐλεύ-

which proved the death-blow to the Athenian supremacy (*i. e.* 477—405 B.C.).

(ii) Wieland (one of the translators of the *Paneg.*) understands the time between the expulsion of the Peisistratidae and the dispute between Corinth and Corcyra, which aided in bringing about the Peloponnesian war in 431 (*i. e.* 510—435 B. C.).

(iii) Morus and Lange explain it of the time between the institution of *annual* archons and Cylon's attempt to make himself master of Athens (*i. e.* 683—612 B.C.).

Each of these explanations has been opposed on various grounds.

(i) Is rendered doubtful by the fact that, between 477 and 405, Athens can hardly be said to have been 'at peace with all the world,' as the Peloponnesian war, with all its feuds at home and battles abroad, occupies the last 17 years of that period. And further, the supporters of this view are constrained to admit that the words ἀστασίαστοι πρὸς σφᾶς αὐτοὺς are not in strict accordance with history, but must be accepted as an exaggerated contrast to the fierce factions of the Spartan supremacy.

A similar objection may be raised to (ii), on the ground that in the period between 510 and 435 Athens was fighting against Boeotia and Chalcis (in 506), against Thebes, Corinth, Aegina, and Epidaurus (in 457), against Sicyon and Acarnania (in 454), against Thebes and Sparta (in 447), and against Samos (in 441), to say nothing of the Great Persian War. (Bens. transl. p. 200 n.)—In fact, the acceptance of either (i) or (ii) involves the grossest misrepresentation on the part of Isocr. He may be guilty of exaggeration, of inconsistency, of rhetorical colouring, but such a glaring inaccuracy is beyond belief.

The third view is, perhaps, less open to objection. One of the strongest points that has been urged against it is the fact that the period in question (683—612) is comparatively obscure and (unlike the 70 years of the first view) seldom mentioned. It is a well-known characteristic of Isocr. to speak in praise of the 'good old times' (witness *Panath.* § 131—148, and *Areop.* passim); but Benseler's attempt to prove by quoting *de Pace*, § 75, *Panath.* § 139, that *this very period* is mentioned elsewhere by Isocr. is far from successful.—Another objection to this view is thus stated by Baiter (with reference to the next section, ὑπὲρ ὧν κ.τ.λ.), 'Quis sanae mentis orator contenderit Atheniensibus deberi magnam gratiam, quod ipsi per tot annos felices fuerint?' To answer this, it may be suggested, in passing, that ὑπὲρ ὧν possibly refers to the general sense of the previous context, and esp. to §§ 103—5, while § 106 is a short parenthetical argument.—This view has been combated at length by Wilh. Vischer in an exhaustive article in Schneidewin's *Philologus* (vol. x. pp. 245—9).

Thus far, the account given of the various explanations of the passage goes on the supposition that διετελέσαμεν (which necessarily refers to the Athenians) is the correct reading. At this point the controversy assumes a new phase: διετελέσαμεν is the MS reading, διετέλεσαν the conjectural emendation of Bekker. This has been adopted by BS, Dindorf, Pinzger, Rauchenstein (ed. 1 and 3), Schneider, and Benseler [in the Teubner series (1851). In a later ed. of part of Isocr. with German Trans. and notes (1854) he returns to the MS reading, and defends the third of the views given above].

The conjecture διετέλεσαν is strongly confirmed by Lys. (?) *Or. Funebr.* § 55, *ἐβδομήκοντα μὲν ἔτη*

θεροι δὲ πρὸς τοὺς βαρβάρους, ἀστασίαστοι δὲ πρὸς σφᾶς
αὐτούς, εἰρήνην δ᾽ ἄγοντες πρὸς πάντας ἀνθρώπους. (λα΄.) 63
107 Ὑπὲρ ὧν προσήκει τοὺς εὖ φρονοῦντας μεγάλην χάριν ἔχειν
πολὺ μᾶλλον ἢ τὰς κληρουχίας ἡμῖν ὀνειδίζειν, ἃς ἡμεῖς εἰς

τῆι θαλάττηι ἄρξαντες, ἀστασίαστοι δὲ παρασχόντες τοὺς συμμάχους, and is ably defended by Vischer (*l.c.*). I shall be content with giving his explanation alone. He understands not 'our ancestors' (v. *Panath.* § 54) but 'our allies,' as the nom. to διετέλεσαν, and this view has the great advantage of suiting the whole of the context. If the passage is fairly measured by a rhetorical standard, all is intelligible. The 70 years refer to the period of the Athenian supremacy, during which the states confederate with Athens enjoyed the advantages of her democratical constitution. During this period, her allies were free from tyrants, although before and after the time of her supremacy it was far otherwise (contrast with Schneider, § 117, αἱ μὲν ὑπὸ τυράννοις εἰσί); they were free from the Persians, although before and after that period they were not so (cf. § 117, τῶν δὲ οἱ βάρβαροι δεσπόται καθεστήκασι); they were, as Isocr. seems to think, less disturbed by faction than during the Spartan supremacy (cf. § 116, ἐντὸς τείχους οἱ πολῖται πρὸς ἀλλήλους μάχονται); they were at peace with the outer world, instead of fighting with the Lydians and Persians, as was the case with the Ionians of the 6th century; and lastly, although they frequently aided Athens in her wars, there was an early inclination to substitute money-payment for personal service (Thuc. I. 97—99) which may partially justify the expression εἰρήνην ἄγοντες πρὸς πάντας ἀνθρώπους (cf. § 115, καταπεπολεμηκότες μὲν τὴν θάλατταν κατέχουσι, τελευταῖοι δὲ τὰς πόλεις καταλαμβάνουσι). After a review of all the above opinions and others unrecorded here, I am compelled to the conclusion that,

whichever view is adopted, something may be said against it; that if the MS reading *must* be retained, the third explanation is the least objectionable; if Bekker's conjecture (which I have ventured to print in the text) is accepted, Vischer's view is most satisfactory.

σφᾶς αὐτούς.] The use of the reflex. pron. of the 3rd person, although most suitable to διετέλεσαν, is not conclusive against διετελέσαμεν. v. *ad Dem.* § 14, ἑαυτοῦ. n.

107. ὑπὲρ ὧν.] If διετελέσαμεν is retained in § 106, this must refer to §§ 103—105 and not to § 106.

τὰς κληρουχίας.] On the *Cleruchi* (Athenian citizens who received allotments, κλῆροι, in conquered territory) v. *Dict. Antiq.*—The summary of instances of κληρουχίαι given in Benseler's n. includes the settlements in Lemnos and Imbros (in 556 and 510), in Euboea (506), in Scyros (476), and (under the influence of Pericles) in Naxos, Andros, Euboea, and Sinope, and lastly (during the Pelop. war), in Aegina, Mytilene, Potidaea, Scione, and Colophon.

ὀνειδίζειν.] 'In respect to *the Kleruchies*, or out-settlements of Athenian citizens on the lands of allies revolted and reconquered—we may remark that they are not noticed as a grievance in the treatise of Xenophon, *de Repub. Athen.*, nor in any of the anti-Athenian orations of Thucydides. They appear, however, as matters of crimination after the extinction of the empire, and at the moment when Athens was again rising into a position such as to inspire the hope of reviving it. For at the close of the Peloponnesian war, which was also the destruction of the empire, all the Kleruchs were

τὰς ἐρημουμένας τῶν πόλεων φυλακῆς ἕνεκα τῶν χωρίων
ἀλλ᾽ οὐ διὰ πλεονεξίαν ἐξεπέμπομεν. σημεῖον δὲ τούτων·
ἔχοντες γὰρ χώραν μὲν ὡς πρὸς τὸ πλῆθος τῶν πολιτῶν ἐλαχίστην, ἀρχὴν δὲ μεγίστην, καὶ κεκτημένοι τριήρεις διπλα-
108 σίας μὲν ἢ σύμπαντες, δυναμένας δὲ πρὸς δὶς τοσαύτας κινδυνεύειν, ὑποκειμένης τῆς Εὐβοίας ὑπὸ τὴν Ἀττικὴν, ἣ καὶ b
πρὸς τὴν ἀρχὴν τὴν τῆς θαλάττης εὐφυῶς εἶχε καὶ τὴν ἄλλην ἀρετὴν ἁπασῶν τῶν νήσων διέφερε, κρατοῦντες αὐτῆς

driven home again, and deprived of their outlying property, which reverted to various insular proprietors. These latter were terrified at the idea that Athens might afterwards try to resume these lost rights: hence the subsequent outcry against the Kleruchies.' Grote, *H. G.* IV. 175, new ed.

σημεῖον δὰ...ἔχοντες γάρ.] For this use of γάρ (*inchoativum*) v. § 86 n.

ἔχοντες κ.τ.λ.] The sentence begins in such a manner as to lead us to expect οὐκ ἐπήρθημεν as the principal verb, instead of which we have an equivalent phrase οὐδὲν τούτων ἡμᾶς ἐπῆρε. This is one of the simplest forms of *Anacoluthon*.

ὡς πρὸς τὸ πλῆθος τῶν πολ. ἐλαχίστην.] 'Very small in comparison to the number of our citizens.' For ὡς cf. Thuc. III. 113, ἄπιστον τὸ πλῆθος λέγεται ἀπολέσθαι ὡς πρὸς τὸ μέγεθος τῆς πόλεως.

The number of full citizens, or those who had votes in the Ἐκκλησία is generally reckoned at 20,000 (Plat. *Critias*, p. 112 D, &c), the total population of Attica (including slaves) at 500,000; and lastly the area at more than 700 square miles. The proportion thus obtained represents a density of population approximating to that of Staffordshire in 1861.

καὶ κεκτημένοι.] v. table of various readings.

τριήρεις διπλασίας κ.τ.λ.] Alluding partly to the 200 vessels which formed the fleet of Athens during the year 480 B.C. At Artemisium

the Athenians manned 127 ships, which including the subsequent reinforcement of 53 vessels and the 20 lent to the Chalcideans make up exactly 200, while the other allies contributed 124. At Salamis the total number of vessels belonging to Athens was also 200, and the popular account of the proportion of vessels contributed by Athens to the allied fleet may explain the present passage. Cf. § 98. n. It may also be noticed that, at the beginning of the Peloponnesian war (as well as in the time of Demosthenes), her fleet consisted of 300 triremes; while the united fleet of the Peloponnesians was never apparently greater than 112 (Thuc. II. 13, VIII. 79, and Dem. *Fals. Leg.* p. 369).

σύμπαντες.] v. table of various readings.

108. ὑποκειμένης κ.τ.λ.] 'Although Euboea lay within reach of Attica,' 'was commanded by Attica.' ὑποκεῖσθαι means more than the ordinary word ἐπικεῖσθαι, which would indicate only the proximity of Euboea to the coast of Attica.—(v. table of various readings.)

ἀρετήν.] 'Excellence :' alluding not only to the excellent pasturage and corn-fields of Euboea (Thuc. VII. 28, ἡ τῶν ἐπιτηδείων παρασκευὴ ἐκ τῆς Εὐβοίας, &c.) but also to the copper and iron mines. (On the famous vine of Euboea, v. Soph. *Fragm.* 239.) For the importance of the island, cf. Hdt. V. 31. Εὔβοιαν, νῆσον μεγάλην τε καὶ εὐδαίμονι, and Thuc. VIII. 96 (quoted by Morus)

μᾶλλον ἢ τῆς ἡμετέρας αὐτῶν, καὶ πρὸς τούτοις εἰδότες καὶ
τῶν Ἑλλήνων καὶ τῶν βαρβάρων τούτους μάλιστ᾽ εὐδοκι-
μοῦντας, ὅσοι τοὺς ὁμόρους ἀναστάτους ποιήσαντες ἄφθονον
καὶ ῥᾴθυμον αὐτοῖς κατεστήσαντο τὸν βίον, ὅμως οὐδὲν τού- c
των ἡμᾶς ἐπῆρε περὶ τοὺς ἔχοντας τὴν νῆσον ἐξαμαρτεῖν,
109 ἀλλὰ μόνοι δὴ τῶν μεγάλην δύναμιν λαβόντων περιείδομεν

τοσαύτη ἡ ξυμφορὰ (the revolt of
Euboea in 411 B.C.) ἐπεγεγένητο,
ἐν ᾗ ναῦς τε καὶ τὸ μέγιστον Εὔβοιαν
ἀπολωλέκεσαν, ἐξ ἧς πλείω ἢ τῆς
Ἀττικῆς ὠφελοῦντο.

κρατοῦντες αὐτῆς κ.τ.λ.] 'Though
we had it in our power more than
our own territory.' Cf. *Phil.* § 6,
λόγῳ παραδαὺς τὴν χώραν ἡμῖν ταύτην
(sc. Ἀμφίπολιν) αὐτὸς ἔργῳ κρατήσειε
αὐτῆς. Isocrates means that Euboea
was virtually in the hands of Athens
owing to the naval power of the
latter; so much so that by a rhetorical
exaggeration (as Wolf, Baiter, and
Bens. have noticed) even Attica is
here said to have been less in the
power of Athens. This explanation
is perhaps simpler than that of
Morus '*obtinentes i. e. obtinere volen-
tes.*'—'*Artificiosa explicatione hic locus minime indiget.*' Baiter.

τῶν Ἑλλήνων.] *e.g.* the Spartans,
in their conquest of Messene.

ὅσοι.] Cf. *Nicocl.* § 4, 37, ἐκείνους...ὅσοι...(v. table of various readings).

οὐδὲν ἐξαμαρτεῖν.] This statement
is on the whole fair, but must be
accepted with some caution: in
the time of Cleisthenes, the Athenians sent 4000 *Cleruchi* to Euboea
(Hdt. v. 77) and, after the revolt in
445 B.C. and the re-conquest by
Pericles, τὴν μὲν ἄλλην ὁμολογίᾳ κατεστήσαντο, Ἑστιαιᾶς δ᾽ ἐξοικίσαντες
αὐτοὶ τὴν γῆν ἔσχον (Thuc. I. 114).

109. μόνοι δὴ...αἰτίαν ἐχόντων.]
'We alone, among those who obtained
great power, allowed ourselves to live
in greater embarrassment than those
who have the reputation of being
slaves.' This translation is in accordance with the most common mean-

ing of αἰτίαν ἔχειν. Cf. *Hel.* § 15, ἀπο-
λογεῖσθαι μὲν προσήκει περὶ τῶν ἀδικεῖν αἰτίαν ἐχόντων, ἐπαινεῖν δὲ τοὺς
ἐπ᾽ ἀγαθῷ τινι διαφέροντας, and this
explanation is adopted by Wolf,
Baiter, Rauchenstein, &c. The fact
that τῶν δουλείαν αἰτίαν ἐχόντων is
parallel to τῶν μεγάλην δύναμιν
λαβόντων suggests the possibility of
the former being a direct ἀντίθετον
to the latter; hence as the latter
refers to 'the powerful' in general,
the former may similarly refer to
'slaves' in general; but the more
popular view makes τῶν δουλείαν
αἰτίαν ἐχόντων mean τῶν Ἑλλήνων,
οὓς φασιν αἰτιώμενοι δουλεύειν τοῖς
Ἀθηναίοις, implying that the allies of
Athens have the imputation of being
the slaves of Athens.

Morus, Wieland, Coray, &c.,
make the phrase mean '*in quibus
causa erat quare servirent; digni
servitute,*' a meaning which is hardly
borne out by the passage quoted in
its favour, *de Pace*, § 138, τούτων
τῶν ἀγαθῶν τὴν αἰτίαν ἕξομεν.

Benseler translates thus: '*Als die,
welche zur Unterjochung Veranlas-
sung gaben.*' He refers τῶν—ἐχόντων directly to the Euboeans, and
explains that 'they prompted and
tempted the Athenians to enslave
them'; lit. 'gave occasion to the
Athenians to enslave them.' This
view is very plausible; but I am
unable to find any instance of αἰτίαν
ἔχειν in this meaning. (For a full
account of all the various render-
ings see Benseler's *Trans.* p. 205).

['As far as I know, αἰτίαν ἔχειν
(with the exception of Plat. *Phaed.*
101 c, where it means 'have you,
do you know, any other cause...?')

ἡμᾶς αὐτοὺς ἀπορωτέρως ζῶντας τῶν δουλεύειν αἰτίαν ἐχόντων. καίτοι βουλόμενοι πλεονεκτεῖν οὐκ ἂν δή που τῆς μὲν
Σκιωναίων γῆς ἐπεθυμήσαμεν, ἣν Πλαταιέων τοῖς ὡς ἡμᾶς
καταφυγοῦσι φαινόμεθα παραδόντες, τοσαύτην δὲ χώραν
παρελίπομεν, ἣ πάντας ἂν ἡμᾶς εὐπορωτέρους ἐποίησεν.   d

110   (λβ΄.) Τοιούτων τοίνυν ἡμῶν γεγενημένων καὶ τοσαύτην
πίστιν δεδωκότων ὑπὲρ τοῦ μὴ τῶν ἀλλοτρίων ἐπιθυμεῖν
τολμῶσι κατηγορεῖν οἱ τῶν δεκαρχιῶν κοινωνήσαντες καὶ τὰς

signifies nearly the same as δοκεῖν, δόξαν ἔχειν, 'to have the reputation, character, i.e. the credit or the imputation of...' the former in de Pace, § 138, the two commingled in Thuc. I. 83, 3, varied by μεγίστην δόξαν οἰόμενοι, II. 11, 10.—Benseler's trans. seems to me, if αἰτίαν ἔχειν can be so distorted, to require δουλῶσαι or -εσθαι.' R.S.]

Σκιωναίων.] Cf. § 100. n.

Πλαταιέων—καταφυγοῦσι.] Allusion to the 212 Plataeans, who escaped to Athens in 427 B.C. At the end of the Peloponnesian war they were forced to leave Scione, and once more found a welcome in Athens. At the peace of Antalcidas (387 B.C.) they were restored to their city (Isocr. Plataic. § 13 sqq.), which was subsequently destroyed by the Thebans in 372. They once more fled to Athens, where their wrongs were set forth by Isocrates himself in the speech called the Plataicus, (probably delivered before the δικλησία by one of the Plataeans), but it was not till after the battle of Chaeronea (in 338 B.C.) that they were at length reinstated by Philip of Macedon.

τοσαύτην.] The length of the island (from Histiaea to Geraestus) is about 100 miles; the breadth varies from 4 to 30 miles.

§§ 110—114. The partisans of Lacedaemon accuse Athens of selfishness and cruelty: Athens can retort by pointing to the conduct of her accusers during the Spartan supremacy. These very partisans committed every kind of injustice, and paid constant court to the lawlessness and treachery of Sparta. They deliberately became the slaves of Lysander, and honoured the murderers of their fellow-citizens; 112—3, they reduced us all to a state of brutal apathy, by involving us in disasters that left us no leisure to feel for one another. And these are the men who are not ashamed to accuse us, these who doomed to death untried a greater number than Athens put on trial during the whole of her supremacy. 114. It would be impossible to dwell at length on all their enormities, I can say thus much, that whereas a single decree would have been enough to put an end to the severities of our administration, nothing could ever remedy all the bloodshed and the lawlessness of theirs.

110. οἱ τῶν δεκαρχιῶν κοινωνήσαντες.] Not 'the Lacedaemonians,' but their partisans.—After the victory of Aegospotami (September or October, 405 B.C.) all Greece at once submitted to Sparta, except Athens and Samos, and even these yielded in the course of a few months. In the greater number of cities Lysander established an oligarchy of ten citizens, or a Decarchy, composed of his personal nominees and confederates: while he at the same time planted in each a Lacedaemonian harmost or governor, with a garrison, to uphold the new oligarchy. Athens surrendered in April 404 B.C.; then followed the nomination of the

αὐτῶν πατρίδας διαλυμηνάμενοι, καὶ μικρὰς μὲν ποιήσαντες
δοκεῖν εἶναι τὰς τῶν προγεγενημένων ἀδικίας, οὐδεμίαν δὲ
λιπόντες ὑπερβολὴν τοῖς αὖθις βουλομένοις γενέσθαι πονηροῖς, ἀλλὰ φάσκοντες μὲν λακωνίζειν, τἀναντία δ' ἐκείνοις ϲ
ἐπιτηδεύοντες, καὶ τὰς μὲν Μηλίων ὀδυρόμενοι συμφορὰς,
περὶ δὲ τοὺς αὑτῶν πολίτας ἀνήκεστα τολμήσαντες ἐξαμαρ-
111 τεῖν. ποῖον γὰρ αὐτοὺς ἀδίκημα διέφυγεν; ἢ τί τῶν αἰσχρῶν

Thirty tyrants, under the dictation of Lysander; after a reign of terror that lasted for 8 months, they were deposed and a fresh oligarchy of Ten, consisting in part of the less violent members of the Thirty, was appointed in their stead. To the oppression of the δεκαρχίαι full allusion is made in the important §§ that follow. (See Grote's *H. G.* P. II. chaps. 65 and 72.)

δεκαρχῶν is the reading of Cod. Ambr. in the present passage and in *Phil.* § 95, *Panath.* § 68. The Cod. Urb. has δεκαδαρχιῶν here, and δεκαρχιῶν in *Panath.* l. c., and the latter form is also found in Cod. Vat. *Phil.* l. c. The text of BS always adopts the longer form, that of Benseler the shorter. The former is supported by Harpocration: δεκα-δαρχία· 'Ισοκράτης· τὰς ὑπὸ Λακεδαι-μονίων καταστάθείσας ἐν ταῖς πόλεσι δεκαδαρχίας συνεχῶς ὀνομάζουσιν οἱ ἱστορικοί, κ.τ.λ., the latter by Suidas, and Xenophon *Hell.* III. 4. 2, τὰς δεκαρχίας τὰς κατασταθείσας ὑπὸ ἐκείνου [sc. Lysander] ἐν ταῖς πόλεσιν. The word δεκάδαρχοι is frequently used by Xenophon in its proper sense, 'an officer in command of a δεκάς,' a *decurio*.

οὐδεμίαν λιπόντες ὑπερβολήν, κ.τ.λ.] 'Leaving no power of surpassing them.' Cf. § 4, and Dem. *Aristocr.* p. 689, § 207, τηλικαῦτα καὶ τοιαῦτα, ὥστε μηδένι τῶν ἐπι-γιγνομένων ὑπερβολὴν λελεῖφθαι.

φάσκοντες.] 'Pretending,' Isocr. almost always uses φάσκειν in a bad sense; e.g. *de Pace*, § 121, τοὺς φιλεῖν μὲν τὸν δῆμον φάσκουσιν, ὅλην δὲ τὴν

πόλιν λυμαινομένους. Cf. Soph. *El.* 319, φησίν γε· φάσκων δ' οὐδὲν ὧν λέγει ποιεῖ.

λακωνίζειν.] 'To laconize,' i.e. either 'to imitate the manners, dress, &c. of the Lacedaemonians' (Plat. *Protag.* 342 B, Dem. *Conon.* § 47, and Aristoph. *Aves*, 128 sqq.), or to favour their policy (cf. Μηδίζειν, 'Αττικίζειν, 'Αργολίζειν, Φιλιππίζειν). Cf. *de Pace*, § 108, οὐχ ἡ μὲν τῶν ἀντι-πολιτευόντων πολυπραγμοσύνη λακωνίζειν τὰς πόλεις ἐποίησεν, ἡ δὲ τῶν λακω-νιζόντων ὕβρις ἀντιατίζειν τὰς αὐτὰς ταύτας ἠνάγκασεν; The members of the oligarchical boards not only favoured the policy of the Laconians, and made that policy a pretext for their enormities, but also pretended to imitate their character; their real conduct (says Isocr.) was the reverse of their profession. v. *Areop.* § 61, *Panath.* § 217.

ἐκείνοις.] sc. τοῖς Λάκωσιν or τοῖς Λακεδαιμονίοις implied in λακω-νίζειν. A species of sense-construction (commonly called constr. κατὰ σύνεσιν or σχῆμα πρὸς τὸ σημαινό-μενον), Jelf (Kühner), § 378 sqq. Madv. *Synt.* § 216 a, 2. In Excurs. X. to Bremi's ed. Balter quotes more than 20 instances from Isocrates: e.g. § 90, πρὸς τὸ πλῆθος, (pl. in sense)...κωλύσοντες αὐτούς, § 134, τὴν 'Ασίαν καρπούσθαι καὶ τῷ μὲν (sc. the king of Asia) οὐδὲν προσγυιαίτερον κ.τ.λ. and *de Permt.* § 195, τοῖς αὑτοῖς λόγοις χρώμενος ἀκριβῶν καὶ παυόμενος αὐτῆς (sc. τῆς ἀκριβῆ). Cf. *ad Dem.* § 21, ἐγράφειαν...τοιοῦτος (= ἐγκρατὴ).

ἢ δεινῶν οὐ διεξῆλθον; οἳ τοὺς μὲν ἀνομωτάτους πιστοτά- 64
τους ἐνόμιζον, τοὺς δὲ προδότας ὥσπερ εὐεργέτας ἐθερά-
πευον, ἡροῦντο δὲ τῶν Εἰλώτων ἑνὶ δουλεύειν ὥστ᾽ εἰς τὰς
αὐτῶν πατρίδας ὑβρίζειν, μᾶλλον δ᾽ ἐτίμων τοὺς αὐτόχειρας

ἢ δεινῶν.] c. codd. Urb. Ambr. (followed by BS and Bens.). καὶ δεινῶν Bekk. Dindf.—*Frequens confusio harum particularum* (Bastii *Comment. Palaeogr.*)

111. ἀνομωτάτους.] The reading of Wolf's ed., ἀνοητοτάτους, has apparently no authority except that of a marginal note in a MS of the 11th cent. (Cod. Vat.) used by Coray (II. p. 46).

Εἰλώτων ἑνί.] sc. Lysander, the Spartan commander. He was born of poor parents, and according to Phylarchus (histor. fl. 3rd cent. B.C.), quoted by Athenaeus *Deipnosoph.* VI. p. 271, belonged to the Μόθακες, who were probably children of Helots, brought up as companions (σύντροφοι) to the richer sort, and finally emancipated (ἐλεύθεροι μὲν, οὐ μὴν Λακεδαιμόνιοι· μετέχουσι δὲ τῆς παιδείας πάσης)·

Εἰλώτων.] On the Helots (the serfs of Laconia) v. *Dict. Antiq.* or Grote's *H. G.* II. p. 139 sqq. new ed. (Cf. Plato, *Legg.* 776 C. and § 131. n.)

ἑνί.] This is the reading of Cod. Urb., followed by Rauchenst. Schn. and Benseler (in Teubner series) : ἐνίοις is the reading of Cod. Ambr. followed by Bekker, Dindf., and dubiously by BS. Benseler (*transl.* p. 107. n.) has on, I think, insufficient grounds deserted his former reading in favour of ἐνίοις.

αὐτόχειρας καὶ φονέας τῶν πολ.] 'The assassins and murderers of their own citizens.' The apparently otiose words καὶ φονέας, placed in brackets by Morus, Coray, Dindorf and Benseler (in the Teubner series), are found in all the MSS. They are possibly added to secure a παρονομασία with φονέας (v. § 45. n.) and to give additional clearness to

the rarer word αὐτόχειρας. Twin expressions like this are very common in Isocr. e.g. *de Perm.* § 130, τὰς ταραχὰς καὶ τὴν τύρβην, *ib.* § 11, συναρμόσαι καὶ συναγαγεῖν, *Epp.* IX. 8, γέμει καὶ μεστός ἐστι (is fraught and filled), *Phil.* § 43, ἀθρήσειε καὶ σκέψαιτο, *Areop.* § 4, συντέτακται καὶ συνακολουθεῖ, *de Pace,* § 41, μαίνεσθαι καὶ παραφρονεῖν, and *Areop.* § 12, διεσκαρίφησάμεθα καὶ διελύσαμεν αὐτάς. In several of the above passages it will be observed that one of the words is less common and more expressive than the other, and that the more ordinary word serves to soften the harshness and to light up the obscurity of the rarer word. The word αὐτόχειρ is in prose seldom used *absolutely* in the sense of murderer, and still more rarely with a gen. of the person murdered. (For an instance, may be quoted Dem. *Mid.* p. 549, αὐτόχειρά μου.) It may therefore well be helped out by the addition of τοὺς φονέας.—Themist. *Or.* IV. p. 67. 26 (quoted by Strange in Jahn's *Jahrb. Philol.* suppl. 3. p. 575) has τὸν αὐθέντην καὶ παλαμναῖον.—The other passages in which Isocr. uses the word are *Plataic.* § 29, τοὺς αὐτόχειρας ἐξείργειν, *Phil.* § 130, οὐ γὰρ αὐτόχειρας οὔτε τῶν ἀγαθῶν οὔτε τῶν κακῶν (οἱ θεοί) γίγνονται, and *Aegin.* § 19, ἀνέκτεινας αὐτόχειρας γενόμενος.

The application of the strong term αὐτόχειρας to Lysander and his partisans may be illustrated by the following passage in Harpocration's lexicon: Αὐθέντης Λυσίας ἐν τῷ πρὸς Ἰσόδημον ἰδίως ἔταξεν ἐπὶ τῶν λ᾽ (= the 30 tyrants), οἱ δι᾽ ἑτέρων εἰργάσαντο τοὺς φόνους· ὁ γὰρ αὐθέντης ἀεὶ τὸν αὐτόχειρα δηλοῖ. Of Lysander in particular Plutarch (*vit. Lys.* 13) uses the words πολλαῖς

112 καὶ φονέας τῶν πολιτῶν ἢ τοὺς γονέας τοὺς αὐτῶν, εἰς τοῦτο δ' ὠμότητος ἅπαντας ἡμᾶς κατέστησαν, ὥστε πρὸ τοῦ μὲν διὰ τὴν παροῦσαν εὐδαιμονίαν καὶ ταῖς μικραῖς ἀτυχίαις πολλοὺς ἕκαστον ἡμῶν ἔχειν τοὺς συμπενθήσοντας, b ἐπὶ δὲ τῆς τούτων ἀρχῆς διὰ τὸ πλῆθος τῶν οἰκείων κακῶν ἐπαυσάμεθ' ἀλλήλοις ἐλεοῦντες. οὐδενὶ γὰρ τοσαύτην σχο-
113 λὴν παρέλιπον ὥσθ' ἑτέρῳ συναχθεσθῆναι. τίνος γὰρ οὐκ ἐφίκοντο; ἢ τίς οὕτω πόρρω τῶν πολιτικῶν ἦν πραγμάτων, ὅστις οὐκ ἐγγὺς ἠναγκάσθη γενέσθαι τῶν συμφορῶν, εἰς ἃς αἱ τοιαῦται φύσεις ἡμᾶς κατέστησαν; εἶτ' οὐκ αἰσχύνονται τὰς αὑτῶν πόλεις οὕτως ἀνόμως διαθέντες καὶ τῆς ἡμετέρας c ἀδίκως κατηγοροῦντες, ἀλλὰ πρὸς τοῖς ἄλλοις καὶ περὶ τῶν δικῶν καὶ τῶν γραφῶν τῶν ποτε παρ' ἡμῖν γενομένων λέγειν τολμῶσιν, αὐτοὶ πλείους ἐν τρισὶ μησὶν ἀκρίτους ἀποκτεί-
114 ναντες ἂν ἡ πόλις ἐπὶ τῆς ἀρχῆς ἁπάσης ἔκρινεν. φυγὰς δὲ καὶ στάσεις καὶ νόμων συγχύσεις καὶ πολιτειῶν μετα- βολὰς, ἔτι δὲ παίδων ὕβρεις καὶ γυναικῶν αἰσχύνας καὶ d χρημάτων ἁρπαγὰς τίς ἂν δύναιτο διεξελθεῖν; πλὴν τοσοῦ-

---

παραγινόμενοι αὐτὸι σφαγαῖς (at Thasos).

113. τίς οὕτω...ὅστις οὐκ ἠναγ- κάσθη.] 'The relative with any tense of the indic. can be used to denote a result, where ὥστε might have been expected. This occurs chiefly after negatives, or interrogatives implying a negative. Cf. § 185, τίς οὕτω... ῥᾴθυμός ἐστιν, ὅστις οὐ μετασκεῖν βουλήσεται ταύτῃ τῆς στρατείας.' Goodwin's *Moods and Tenses*, § 65, n. 5.

δικῶν...γραφῶν.] On the full difference between δίκη (a lawsuit) and γραφή (an Indictment) v. *Dict. Antiq.* s.v. Dikē.

ἐν τρισὶ μησὶν κ. τ. λ.] It is unnecessary to refer this to any sharply defined period in the dura- tion of the oligarchical boards. It is sufficient to notice that the 3 months are doubtless included in the well-known 8 months during which the Thirty were in power.

The number of citizens put to death during those months was 1500, Ac- cording to *Areop.* § 67, and *Lochii.* § 11, αὗται γάρ αἱ φύσεις εἰσὶν αἱ ... κατασφαγάσασαι τὰ τείχη τῆς πατρίδος, τετρακοσίους δὲ καὶ χι- λίους ἀκρίτους ἀποκτείνασαι τῶν πολι- τῶν. Plutarch, after speaking of the atrocities of Lysander at Miletus, says (*vit. Lys.* 19), ἦν δὲ καὶ τῶν ἄλ- λων ἐν ταῖς πόλεσι δημοτικῶν φόνος οὐκ ἀριθμητός.

114. παίδων ὕβρεις κ. γυναικῶν αἰσχύνας.] Cf. the story of Aristo- demus, the harmost of Oreus, who seized a beautiful youth, carried him off, and put him to death. The father went to Sparta, and after an unsuccessful appeal for re- paration, put himself to death. Isocr. is speaking here of the δεκαρχίαι alone. None of these outrages are ever ascribed to the Thirty. Grote, *H. G.* VI. 351—3.

τον εἰπεῖν ἔχω καθ᾽ ἁπάντων, ὅτι τὰ μὲν ἐφ᾽ ἡμῶν δεινὰ
ῥᾳδίως ἄν τις ἑνὶ ψηφίσματι διέλυσε, τὰς δὲ σφαγὰς καὶ

καθ᾽ ἁπάντων.] Not 'against one and all of our opponents,' as *e.g.* in *de Pace*, § 56, and *ad Nicocl.* § 47. λέγω δ᾽ οὐ καθ᾽ ἀπάντων ἀλλὰ κατὰ τῶν ἐτόχων τοῖς εἰρημένοις ὄντων, but 'in general' op. to 'in particular,' as in *Hd.* § 1, *de Perm.* § 107, ἀθρούτατον καὶ μάλιστα καθ᾽ ἀπάντων, and esp. *Panath.* § 56, where we have καθ᾽ ἕκαστον διεξιέναι(ὀλίγα καθ᾽ ἀπάντων εἰπεῖν. (So Rauchenst. Schn. and Bens.)

ἐνὶ ψηφίσματι.] Isocr. here says that 'one decree' would have been enough to put an end to the severities (τὰ δεινά) of the Athenian administration. The interpretation of ἐνὶ ψηφίσματι depends on the exact meaning of τὰ δεινά, and on this point the commentators differ. Wolf refers τὰ δεινά to the atrocities committed by Athens with regard to Mitylene (Thuc. III. 49, in 427 B.C.), Scione (Thuc. V. 32, in 421 B.C.) and Melos (Thuc. V. 116, in 416 B.C.). His actual words are these, '*Diodorus scribit lib.* XIII. *Athenienses ψηφίσματι* Μιτυλήνας, Μῆλον, Σκιώνην ἄρδην ἀνηρηκέναι. *Hoc igitur vult Isocrates; Si quis illi decreto irati populi intercessisset; nullum crudele facinus objici potuisse Atheniensibus.*' Wolf apparently thinks that *one decree* covered all the three cases (a fact which is utterly at variance with the dates), and that therefore one counter-decree would have been sufficient to abolish the atrocities in question. (I may notice in passing that his quotation from Diodorus XIII. which has misled one or two editors, is only a loose abstract of chap. 30 of that book).— Benseler (*trans.* p. 210) approves of the drift of Wolf's explanation, and himself explains the passage thus : 'Athens has wronged certain of her confederates by a decree of the people, and could easily have healed the mischief by another decree, as she actually did in the case of Mitylene.' The immediate context suggests

another explanation of τὰ δεινά. We are there told that the enemies of Athens had the assurance to criticise the legal proceedings that took place before her tribunals in the days of her supremacy. A reference to *Panath.* § 63 (κατηγορεῖν τῆι πόλεωι ...καὶ τὰς τε δίκας καὶ τὰς κρίσεις τὰς ἐνθάδε γιγνόμενας τοῖς συμμάχοις καὶ τὴν τῶν φόρων εἰσπραξιν διαβαλεῖν) shews that one of the main points of accusation was the jurisdiction of the Athenian tribunals over the confederate and dependent states. This jurisdiction, although on the whole fairly carried out (v. Thuc. I. 77. 1 and VIII. 48. 5), was nevertheless the subject of blame with the supporters of Sparta, *e.g.* the philolaconian Xenophon in speaking of this very point, says (*Rep. Ath.* I. 16), τοὺς μὲν τοῦ δήμου σώζουσι, τοὺς δ᾽ ἐναντίους ἀπολλύουσιν ἐν τοῖς δικαστηρίοις. If the words τὰ δεινά refer to the severities of these tribunals, the ἓν ψήφισμα of the text must mean a single decree granting αὐτονομία to the confederates of Athens, and thus abolishing the trials in question. It so happens that in the Archonship of Nausinicus (378 B.C.), two years after the publication of the *Pang.*, such a decree (as observed by Sauppe in Rauchenstein's n.) actually formed part of the terms of the restored confederation.

In this case Isocr. says that the wrongs of the allies under the rule of Athens *might* have been done away by a single decree of this nature, but the lawlessness of the Harmosts and Decarchies (against which there was no appeal to Sparta) would remain irreparable.

This view is in the main identical with that of Rauchenstein and Schneider, it is confirmed by the sequel with its pointed mention of the false αὐτονομία of a compact negociated between Sparta and Persia, it harmonises with the previous context,

τὰς ἀνομίας τὰς ἐπὶ τούτων γενομένας οὐδεὶς ἂν ἰάσασθαι
δύναιτο.

115 (λγ′.) Καὶ μὴν οὐδὲ τὴν παροῦσαν εἰρήνην, οὐδὲ τὴν
αὐτονομίαν τὴν ἐν ταῖς πολιτείαις μὲν οὐκ ἐνοῦσαν, ἐν δὲ e
ταῖς συνθήκαις ἀναγεγραμμένην, ἄξιον ἑλέσθαι μᾶλλον ἢ
τὴν ἀρχὴν τὴν ἡμετέραν. τίς γὰρ ἂν τοιαύτης καταστάσεως
ἐπιθυμήσειεν, ἐν ᾗ καταποντισταὶ μὲν τὴν θάλατταν κατέ

and is, perhaps, more satisfactory
than the view advocated by Wolf
and Benseler.

§§ 115—118. *Even the present state
of peace, which has been brought about
by Sparta, is worthless in comparison
with the times of the supremacy of
Athens. The terms of that peace have
proved a delusion, and the promised
independence has not come. As soon as
the supremacy passed from Athens to
Sparta, the Barbarians obtained the
command of the sea, and by the recent
convention (the terms of which are
very different to those which Athens
in former days imposed on Persia) the
great King (as we now call him) was
made dictator of the destinies of Greece.
122—4. The Ionians were surrendered to him, and are now the victims
of cruel oppression; 125—8. Sparta,
which now claims the supremacy, is
day by day taking the field against the
Greeks, and has entered into an alliance, for all time, with the Barbarians.*

115. τὴν παροῦσαν εἰρήνην.] Alluding to the peace or convention of
Antalcidas (ἡ ἐπ᾽ Ἀνταλκίδου εἰρήνη)
387 B.C. The terms are thus given
in Xenophon, *Hell.* V. 1. 31: 'King
Artaxerxes' [*Mnemon*; reigned 405
—359 B.C.] 'thinks it just that the
cities in Asia and the islands of
Clazomenae and Cyprus shall belong to him. He thinks it just also,
to leave all the other Grecian cities,
both small and great, independent
(αὐτονόμους) except Lemnos, Imbros,
Scyros, which are to belong to
Athens as of old time. Should any
parties refuse to accept this peace,
I will make war upon them, along

with those who are of the same
mind, by land and by sea, with ships
and with money.' On this degrading
convention, on which Isocr. dwells
indignantly in the following §§, cf.
Plat. *Menex.* 245 D, where it is called
an αἰσχρὸν καὶ ἀνόσιον ἔργον, and the
fragm. of Theopompus quoted in
§ 134. n. and v. Grote's *H. G. P.* II.
c. 75 ad fin. and c. 76 *passim*.

In a later speech, *de Pace*, § 16,
Isocr. expresses himself less indig-
nantly: (cf. also F. A. Wolf's n. on
Dem. *Lept.* p. 475. § 60).

τὴν αὐτονομίαν.] Cf. *de Pace*, 68,
ἠθέλησαν Λακεδαιμόνιοι ποιήσασθαι
τὰς συνθήκας τὰς περὶ τῆς αὐτονομίας.

ἀναγεγραμμένην.] § 180. n.

καταποντισταί.] 'Pirates.'—In
Greek there are three names for a
'sea-robber.'

(1) λῃστής, a comprehensive
name, which (in the form λῃστήρ)
occurs as early as the Homeric period
(*e.g. Od.* III. 73), when the occupa-
tion of buccaneering implied no disgrace (Thuc. I. 5. 1).

(2) καταποντιστής, which occurs
first, perhaps, in the present passage.
As later instances we have *Panath.*
§ 226, τοὺς καταποντιστὰς καὶ λῃστάς
(cf. *ib.* § 112, καταποντισμοῦ), and
Dem. *Aristocr.* § 166.

The corresp. vb. however occurs
in Lysias, *Alcib.* A. § 27 (delivered
14 years before).

(3) πειρατής (Lat. *pirata*), which
does not occur except in comparatively late Greek (*e.g.* Polybius).

The word καταποντιστής is strictly
a product of the early part of the
5th cent. B.C., just as the Anglicised
word *buccaneer* (from *boucanier*) and

116 χουσι, πελτασταὶ δὲ τὰς πόλεις καταλαμβάνουσιν, ἀντὶ δὲ
τοῦ πρὸς ἑτέρους περὶ τῆς χώρας πολεμεῖν, ἐντὸς τείχους οἱ
πολῖται πρὸς ἀλλήλους μάχονται, πλείους δὲ πόλεις αἰχμά- 65
λωτοι γεγόνασιν ἢ πρὶν τὴν εἰρήνην ἡμᾶς ποιήσασθαι, διὰ
δὲ τὴν πυκνότητα τῶν μεταβολῶν ἀθυμοτέρως διάγουσιν οἱ
τὰς πόλεις οἰκοῦντες τῶν ταῖς φυγαῖς ἐζημιωμένων. οἱ μὲν
γὰρ τὸ μέλλον δεδίασιν, οἱ δ' ἀεὶ κατιέναι προσδοκῶσιν.
117 τοσοῦτον δ' ἀπέχουσι τῆς ἐλευθερίας καὶ τῆς αὐτονομίας,
ὥσθ' αἱ μὲν ὑπὸ τυράννοις εἰσί, τὰς δ' ἁρμοσταὶ κατέχουσιν,
ἔνιαι δ' ἀνάστατοι γεγόνασι, τῶν δ' οἱ βάρβαροι δεσπόται b
καθεστήκασιν· οὓς ἡμεῖς διαβῆναι τολμήσαντας εἰς τὴν Εὐ-
118 ρώπην καὶ μεῖζον ἢ προσῆκεν αὐτοῖς φρονήσαντας οὕτω διέ-
θεμεν ὥστε μὴ μόνον παύσασθαι στρατείας ἐφ' ἡμᾶς ποιουμένους ἀλλὰ καὶ τὴν αὐτῶν χώραν ἀνέχεσθαι πορθουμένην,
καὶ διακοσίαις καὶ χιλίαις ναυσὶ περιπλέοντας εἰς τοσαύτην

---

the Gallicised word *flibustier* (from *freebooter*, v. Littré and Wedgwood) make their first appearance in connexion with the West Indian adventurers of the 17th cent. of our era. The very existence of the new term betrays the fact that 'the police of the Aegean' was less strictly kept than in the previous century.

Morus and those who follow him are hardly justified in supposing that Isocr. refers to the Persians and Lacedaemonians, *ut eorum crudelitatem in expeditionibus marinis indicet*: the explanation given above is simpler and better, and is, I find, adopted by Wolf, Cor., Rauch., Schn. and Benseler, the last of whom aptly quotes Xen. *Hell.* v. 1. 29, 'Αθηναῖοι...πολιορκούμενοι ἐκ τῆς Αἰγίνης ὑπὸ τῶν λῃστῶν...ἐπεθύμουν τῆς εἰρήνην (in 387 B.C.) and Dem. *Theocr.* § 56.

116. ἐντὸς τείχους κ.τ.λ.] *e.g.* at Mantinea, Phlius, and Thebes, Xen. *Hell.* v. 2.

ἀεὶ κατιέναι προσδοκῶσιν.] Eur. *Phoen.* 396, αἱ δ' ἐλπίδες βόσκουσι φυγάδας, ὡς λόγος. On κατιέναι v. § 61. n.

117. τῆς ἐλευθερίας κ.τ.λ.] 'The promised liberty, &c.' Cf. § 122.

τυράννοις.] Cf. § 125—6.

ἁρμοσταί.] οἱ ὑπὸ τῶν Λακεδαιμονίων εἰς τὰς ὑπηκόους πόλεις ἀρχοντες καὶ φρούραρχοι ἀντεμπόμενοι, παρὰ τὸ ἁρμόζειν καὶ καθιστᾶν τὰς ὑπ' αὐτῶν φυλαττομένας πόλεις. Bekk. *Anecdot.* 445. (Bens. *index.*) The name *Harmost* was not confined to governors appointed by Sparta (v. Xen. *Hell.* iv. 8. 8, 'Αθηναῖον ἁρμοστήν, *Anab.* v. 5. 19, &c.).

ἀνάστατοι.] *e.g.* Mantinea v. also § 37. n.

οἱ βάρβ. δεσπόται καθ.] § 122.

οὓς κ.τ.λ.] This sentence evidently alludes to the relation subsisting between Persia and Greece at different periods. Thus διαβῆναι τολμήσαντας, φρονήσαντας, and the mention of the 1200 ships, belong to the expedition under Xerxes. v. § 93. n. On the other hand, τὴν αὐτῶν χώραν ἀνέχεσθαι πορθουμένην and μακρὸν πλεῖον κ.τ.λ. refer mainly to the actual or supposed results of the double victory of Cimon at the river Eurymedon in Pamphylia (466 B.C.).

118. καὶ διακοσίαις κ.τ.λ.] 'And

ταπεινότητα κατεστήσαμεν ὥστε μακρὸν πλοῖον ἐπὶ τάδε
Φασήλιδος μὴ καθέλκειν ἀλλ' ἡσυχίαν ἄγειν, καὶ τοὺς και- c

although they held the sea with 1300
ships, we reduced them to such a
depth of humiliation that they
launched not a vessel-of-war on this
side of Phaselis, but remained in
quiet; and awaited the times of
crisis, but mistrusted their present
power.'

In the present passage and *Areop.*
§ 80, the fact that Persia ceased
from hostilities is described as a
simple result of the victories of
Athens; elsewhere it is clearly connected with a definite convention
between Athens and Persia. This
convention is mentioned by Isocr.
himself in § 120 and *Panath.* § 59—
61, by Dem. *Fals. Leg.* p. 428,
§ 273; 'Callias, the son of Hipponicus, negociated that peace
which is in the mouths of all men
(ὑπὸ πάντων θρυλουμένην), providing
that the king should not approach
within a day's ride of the sea-coast,
nor sail with a vessel of war within
the Chelidonian islands [S.W. of
Phaselis] and the Cyanean rocks [in
the Euxine]... and no man can say
that the commonwealth has made a
better peace either before or after.'
(From *C.R.K.*); and also by Lycurgus, *Leocr.* § 73, συνθήκας ἐποιήσαντο
μακρῷ μὲν πλοίῳ μὴ πλεῖν ἐντὸς
Κυανέων καὶ Φασήλιδος, τοὺς δ''Ελλη-
νας αὐτονόμους εἶναι.

Plutarch (*vit. Cim.* 13) mentions
the treaty (τὴν περιβόητον εἰρήνην
ἐκείνην), and states that Callisthenes
(the writer of a lost *Hist. of Greece*
from 387—357 B.C.) οὔ φησι ταῦτα
συνθέσθαι τὸν βάρβαρον, ἔργῳ δὲ ποιεῖν
διὰ φόβον τῆς ἥττης ἐκείνης, but that
on the other hand a copy of it was
to be found in the collection com-
piled by Craterus (brother of Anti-
gonus Gonatas and writer of a lost
diplomatic hist. of Attica; fl. c. 250
B.C.). Theopompus, one of the
most distinguished pupils of Isocr.,
in his *Philippica* (quoted by Harpocr.

lex. s.v. 'Αττικοῖς γράμμασιν) argues
that the convention was fabricated
(ἐσκευωρῆσθαι), v. § 120, n. 1.

The reality of this treaty of
Callias (erroneously called the
treaty of Cimon) has been impugned
by Mitford, Thirlwall, Manso and
esp. by Dahlmann; and defended
by Grote, who endeavours to prove
that although neither Thuc. nor
IIdt. expressly mentions the treaty,
it is nevertheless confirmed by several hints in Thuc. (VIII. 5, 6, 56)
and IIdt. (VIII. 151), and that, when
allowance has been made for the exaggeration of the orators of the 4th
cent., a sufficient residuum of historical fact remains to attest to its
existence. (v. Grote, *H. G. P.* II. c.
45 = vol. IV. p. 85—89, new ed. and
Thirlwall, c. 17, p. 474.)

The hypothesis of Dahlmann is
that 'The distinct mention and aver-
ment of such a peace as having
been formally concluded appears to
have first arisen among the schools
of the rhetors at Athens, shortly
after the peace of Antalkidas, and
as an oratorical antithesis to oppose
to that peace.'

μακρὸν πλοῖον.] *i.q. navis longa*,
the long and narrow ship-of-war)(
στρογγύλη ναῦς, ὁλκάς, γαῦλος, *navis
oneraria*, the rounded and roomy
merchant-vessel.

ἐπὶ τάδε.])(ἐπέκεινα, either in
temporal, or, as here, in local sense.
—Cf. *cis* and *citra* (connected with
hic) op. to *uls* and *ultra* (connected with *ille*).

Φασήλιδος.] Phaselis—a maritime town of Lycia, standing on
a headland overlooking the Pam-
phylian gulf.—The light sailing-boat
called the *phaselus* is supposed to
have been invented there, and was
commonly represented on the coins
of the place.

καθέλκειν] = *deducere naves*, 'to
launch.' Cf. Thuc. II. 93, καθελκύ-

ροὺς περιμένειν ἀλλὰ μὴ τῇ παρούσῃ δυνάμει πιστεύειν.
119 καὶ ταῦθ᾽ ὅτι διὰ τὴν τῶν προγόνων τῶν ἡμετέρων ἀρετὴν
οὕτως εἶχεν, αἱ τῆς πόλεως συμφοραὶ σαφῶς ἐπέδειξαν· ἅμα
γὰρ ἡμεῖς τε τῆς ἀρχῆς ἀπεστερούμεθα καὶ τοῖς Ἕλλησιν
ἀρχὴ τῶν κακῶν ἐγίγνετο. μετὰ γὰρ τὴν ἐν Ἑλλησπόντῳ
γενομένην ἀτυχίαν ἑτέρων ἡγεμόνων καταστάντων ἐνίκησαν
μὲν οἱ βάρβαροι ναυμαχοῦντες, ἦρξαν δὲ τῆς θαλάττης, κατ- d
έσχον δὲ τὰς πλείστας τῶν νήσων, ἀπέβησαν δ᾽ εἰς τὴν
Λακωνικήν, Κύθηρα δὲ κατὰ κράτος εἷλον, ἅπασαν δὲ τὴν

σαντας ἐκ Νισαίας, τοῦ νεωρίου αὐτῶν, τεσσαράκοντα ναῦς, and *Antiol.* x. 15. 3, ἄρτι δὲ δουρατέοισιν ἐνωλίσθησε κυλίνδροις | ὁλκὰς ἐπ᾽ ἠϊόνων ἐν βυθῷ ἑλκομένη.

119. τῆς ἀρχῆς ἀπεστερούμεθα... ἀρχὴ τῶν κακῶν.] 'For no sooner were we deprived of our dominion than the beginning of evils came upon the Greeks.' The ὁμωνυμία, or play on the two meanings of ἀρχή may be easily preserved by rendering thus: 'no sooner were we deprived of the first place, than the first disaster came upon the Greeks.' Bens. has: *Denn sobald man uns die Herrschaft nahm, fieng auch bei den Hellenen die Noth zu herrschen an.* This particular play of words is repeated elsewhere in *Phil.* § 61, *de Pace*, § 101, *Nicocl.* § 28, the first or the second of which passages is quoted *memoriter* by Aristot. *Rhet.* III. 11, as an instance of τὰ ἀστεῖα. A full list of similar ὁμωνυμίαι is given in Schneider's note: *e.g.* λόγος (*Panath.* § 22), χάρις (*Epp.* II. 6), αἰτία (*Epp.* VI. 3), and ποιεῖν (*Evag.* § 36).

τὴν ἐν Ἑλλησπόντῳ...ἀτυχίαν.] The defeat of the Athenians by Lysander, off Aegospotami, 405, B.C. Conon was there vanquished, owing, it was said, to the treachery of some of his colleagues (οὐ δι᾽ αὐτὸν ἀλλὰ διὰ τοὺς συνάρχοντας *Phil.* § 62, v. Xen. *Hell.* II. 1. 32), and fled with 12 triremes to Evagoras, king of Cyprus. He was after-

wards made commander of the Persian fleet along with Pharnabazus, and gained a decisive victory at Cnidus over Pisander, the Spartan admiral, in August 394 B.C.

ἑτέρων.] Here in its true sense '*the* others,' *i.e.* the Lacedaemonians.

ἐνίκησαν.] *i.e.* at Cnidus. Cf. § 142, and Xen. *Hell.* IV. 3. 10—14. It will be observed that Isocr. is careful not to dwell upon the fact that this victory of Persia was mainly due to the generalship of an Athenian, as he elsewhere plainly intimates (*Evag.* §§ 52—7). Conon, however, was acting only on a private venture, not as a general of Athens. It was in this private capacity also, that in the following year he sailed with Pharnabazus through the islands of the Aegean to Melos and thence to Laconia, where they ravaged the district round Pherae (in Messenia) and other places on the sea-board, gained possession of the island of Cythera, and finally sailed to the isthmus of Corinth. (Xen. *Hell.* IV. 8. 7, 8. Grote *H. G.* VI. 471, new ed.)

τὰς πλείστας τῶν νήσων.] *i.e.* Cos, Nisyros, Chios, &c. (Diod. Sic. XIV. 84).

Κύθηρα.] neut. pl. as also in Xen. *Hell.* I.c. Ἀθηναῖον ἁρμοστὴν ἐν τοῖς Κυθήροις κατέλιπε, Thuc. IV. 53, τὰ δὲ Κύθηρα νῆσός ἐστιν, ἐπίκειται δὲ τῇ Λακωνικῇ κατὰ Μαλέαν, and Hdt. VII. 235. The form ἡ

120 Πελοπόννησον κακῶς ποιοῦντες περιέπλευσαν. (λδ´.) Μάλιστα δ᾽ ἄν τις συνίδοι τὸ μέγεθος τῆς μεταβολῆς, εἰ παρα-
ναγνοίη τὰς συνθήκας τάς τ᾽ ἐφ᾽ ἡμῶν γενομένας καὶ τὰς
νῦν ἀναγεγραμμένας. τότε μὲν γὰρ ἡμεῖς φανησόμεθα τὴν
ἀρχὴν τὴν βασιλέως ὁρίζοντες καὶ τῶν φόρων ἐνίους τάτ- c
τοντες καὶ κωλύοντες αὐτὸν τῇ θαλάττῃ χρῆσθαι· νῦν δ᾽

Κυθήρα appears to belong to later Gk.

κατὰ κράτος εἷλον.] An exaggeration of the fact, as stated by Xen. *Hell. l.c.* φοβηθέντες, μὴ κατὰ κράτος ἁλῶσι, ἐξέλιπον τὰ τείχη.

ἔπαυσαν τὴν Πελοπόννησον.τ.λ.] Xenoph. *l.c.* says nothing of this circumnavigation. After the account of Cythera, he says: ταῦτα δὲ ποιήσας καὶ εἰς Ἰσθμὸν τῆς Κορινθίας καταπλεύσας κ.τ.λ.

120. τὰς συνθήκας τὰς ἐφ᾽ ἡμῶν γενομένας.] The peace of Callias, v. § 118. n. Isocr. evidently implies the existence of documentary evidence of the terms of that peace. Theopompus (ap. Harpocr.) is still more express, although he declares that the peace was a mere fabrication: Θεόπομπος δ᾽ ἐν τῇ πέ τῶν Φιλιππικῶν ἀπεινωρῆσθαι λέγει τὰς πρὸς τὸν βάρβαρον συνθήκας, ὡς οὐ ταῖς Ἀττικαῖς γράμμασιν ἐστηλιτεῦσθαι (v. § 180. n.), ἀλλὰ τοῖς τῶν Ἰώνων.

The Ionic characters were not introduced in *public* documents until the archonship of Euclides, 403 B.C. (v. Franz. Elementa Epigraphices Gr. p. 148.) We infer from the statement of Theopompus that if (as is probable) the inscription contained the words Ἀθηναῖοι καὶ Ἀρταξέρξης, they were spelt thus:

ΛΘΗΝΑΙΟΙΚΑΙΑΡΤΑΞΕΡΞΗΣ
(in Ionic letters), instead of ΑΘΕ-
ΝΑΙΟΙΚΑΙΑΡΤΑΧϟΕΡΧϟΕϟ
(in Attic letters of the period in question).

ὁρίζοντες.] Cf. Lycurg. *Leocr.* § 73, ὅρους τοῖς βαρβάροις πήξαντες τοὺς εἰς τὴν ἐλευθερίαν τῆς Ἑλλά-

δος, καὶ τούτους κωλύσαντες ὑπερβαίνειν. The geographical boundaries are variously stated, v. § 118. n. Elsewhere (*Arop.* § 80 and *Panath.* § 59) Isocr. states that the land-force of Persia was not allowed to cross the river Halys,—an exaggeration which has been severely criticized by Dahlmann, &c.

τῶν φόρων ἐνίους τάττοντες.] lit. 'Assessing some of their taxes' i.e. 'fixing in several instances the rate of the various tributes to be paid to the king of Persia.' The sense is clear enough, but the historical allusion (if such it be), is difficult to explain. Grote (*H. G.* IV. p. 87. n. new ed.) In speaking of this peace endeavours to shew (from Thuc. VIII. 5, 6, 56) 'that the maritime Asiatic cities, belonging to the Athenian Empire, paid no tribute to Susa from the date of the full organization of the Athenian confederacy down to a period after the Athenian defeat in Sicily.' If this is true, it is hard to see why Isocr. expresses himself in such guarded language: he might have said τῶν φόρων ἐνίους ἀπαλλάττοντες (which Schn. even suggests as a probable reading). The expression is meant to be contrasted with προστάττων ἃ χρὴ ποιεῖν ἑκάστους, and may contain a germ of historical fact.

θαλάττῃ.] This is the reading of Cod. Urb., θαλάσσῃ that of Cod. Ambr. The Cod. Urb. almost always supports the later Attic form θάλαττα; and in one passage alone (*Panath.* § 44) the earlier θάλασσα (where Dind. BS and Bens. read θαλάττης).

ἐκεῖνός ἐστιν ὁ διοικῶν τὰ τῶν Ἑλλήνων, καὶ προστάττων
ἃ χρὴ ποιεῖν ἑκάστους, καὶ μόνον οὐκ ἐπιστάθμους ἐν ταῖς
121 πόλεσι καθιστάς. πλὴν γὰρ τούτου τί τῶν ἄλλων ὑπό-
λοιπόν ἐστιν; οὐ καὶ τοῦ πολέμου κύριος ἐγένετο, καὶ τὴν 66
εἰρήνην ἐπρυτάνευσε, καὶ τῶν παρόντων πραγμάτων ἐπιστάτης καθέστηκεν; οὐχ ὡς ἐκεῖνον πλέομεν ὥσπερ πρὸς
δεσπότην ἀλλήλων κατηγορήσοντες; οὐ βασιλέα τὸν μέγαν
αὐτὸν προσαγορεύομεν ὥσπερ αἰχμάλωτοι γεγονότες; οὐκ
ἐν τοῖς πολέμοις τοῖς πρὸς ἀλλήλους ἐν ἐκείνῳ τὰς ἐλπίδας ἔχομεν τῆς σωτηρίας, ὃς ἀμφοτέρους ἡμᾶς ἡδέως ἂν
ἀπολέσειεν;

122   Ὧν ἄξιον ἐνθυμηθέντας ἀγανακτῆσαι μὲν ἐπὶ τοῖς παρ- b

νῦν δ' ἐκεῖνος κ.τ.λ.] 'But now, it is *he* that controls the destinies of the Greeks, that dictates the duties of the several states, and all but establishes vicegerents in our cities.'

προστάττων.] 'Dictating.' The word is exactly the same as that used by Autocles the Athenian envoy at Sparta, respecting the peace of Antalcidas: βασιλεὺς προστάττων αὐτονόμους τὰς πόλεις εἶναι (Xen. *Hell.* VI. 3. 9). Cf. § 176, προστάγματα καὶ μὴ συνθήκας.

μόνον οὐκ] = ὅσον οὐκ, *tantum non*.

ἐπιστάθμους.] 'Quarter-masters.' οἱ ἄρχοντες καὶ σατράπαι οἱ κατέχοντες βασιλεῖ τὰς ὑπηκόους πόλεις, παρὰ τὸ ἐπὶ τοῖς σταθμοῖς εἶναι· σταθμοὶ δὲ αἱ καταγωγαί (*sc.* quarters). Bekk. *Anecd.* 253, v. § 162.

121. κύριος κ.τ.λ.] 'Sovereign over'......'endowed with authority over.'

οὐ...τὴν εἰρήνην κ.τ.λ.] 'Was he not Controller of the peace, has he not been established President of the existing state of affairs?'

ἐπρυτάνευσε.. ἐπιστάτης.] Metaphorical terms borrowed from the subdivisions of the 'Council of the 500.' For full details on these subdivisions see either *Dict. Antiq.* art. *Boule*, or the valuable, but often puerile, *Hypothesis* to Dem. *Androt.* It will be sufficient here to

state (1) that the 50 members of the presiding tribe were called πρυτάνεις, who, during their 35 days of authority, conducted the whole business of the βουλή, and controlled the proceedings of the ἐκκλησία: (2) that one was chosen by lot from the 50 πρυτάνεις to be chairman for one day in the βουλή and ἐκκλησία, and that during his day of office he kept the public records and seal.

For the word πρυτανεύω in particular cf. Dem. *de Pace*, § 6, τὰ παρ' ὑμῶν διοικοῦντα (cf. ὁ διοικῶν *supr.*) Φιλίππῳ καὶ πρυτανεύοντα.

The meaning of ἐπιστάτης may perhaps be illustrated by the prominence given to the *King's seal* in Xenophon's account of the communication of the peace to the assembled ambassadors: ἐπιδείξας ὁ Τιρίβαζος τὰ βασιλέως σημεῖα ἀνεγίγνωσκε τὰ γεγραμμένα. But the use of the pf. καθέστηκε points to a more general application of the word.

For the double metaphor cf. Plat. *Protag.* p. 338 B, πείθεσθέ μοι ῥαβδοῦχον καὶ ἐπιστάτην καὶ πρόεδρον ἑλέσθαι ὃς ὑμῖν φυλάξει (cf. § 175, φύλαξ τῆς εἰρήνης) τὸ μέτριον μῆκος τῶν λόγων ἑκατέρου.

βασιλέα τὸν μέγαν κ.τ.λ.] Cf. *Phil.* § 132 and *Epp.* II. § 11.

122. ἂν ἄξιον κ.τ.λ.] *i.e.* 'Taking thought of all this, we may well feel

οὖσι, ποθέσαι δὲ τὴν ἡγεμονίαν τὴν ἡμετέραν, μέμψασθαι
δὲ Λακεδαιμονίοις, ὅτι τὴν μὲν ἀρχὴν εἰς τὸν πόλεμον
κατέστησαν ὡς ἐλευθερώσοντες τοὺς Ἕλληνας, ἐπὶ δὲ
τελευτῆς οὕτω πολλοὺς αὐτῶν ἐκδότους ἐποίησαν, καὶ τῆς
μὲν ἡμετέρας πόλεως τοὺς Ἴωνας ἀπέστησαν, ἐξ ἧς ἀπῴκησαν καὶ δι' ἣν πολλάκις ἐσώθησαν, τοῖς δὲ βαρβάροις
αὐτοὺς ἐξέδοσαν, ὧν ἀκόντων τὴν χώραν ἔχουσι καὶ πρός c
123 οὓς οὐδὲ πώποτ' ἐπαύσαντο πολεμοῦντες. καὶ τότε μὲν
ἠγανάκτουν, ὅθ' ἡμεῖς νομίμως ἐπάρχειν τινῶν ἠξιοῦμεν
νῦν δ' εἰς τοιαύτην δουλείαν καθεστώτων οὐδὲν φροντί-
ζουσιν αὐτῶν, οἷς οὐκ ἐξαρκεῖ δασμολογεῖσθαι καὶ τὰς

indignant at our present position;
and yearn for our lost supremacy.'

ποθέσαι.] The same form of the
aor. of ποθῶ is found in *Aegin.* § 7,
but ἐπόθησα is more common in
other prose writers; *e.g.* Xen. *Hell.*
v. 3. 20, ἐδάκρυσε καὶ ἐπόθησε τὴν
συνουσίαν. The fut. mid. is always
ποθέσομαι (Veitch, *Gk. Verbs,* s.v.).
Cf. Eustath. on *Odyss.* II. 375, τὸ δὲ
ποθέσαι ἀντὶ τοῦ ποθῆσαι δοκεῖ
μὲν ποιητικόν, ἔστι δὲ ἀληθῶς Ἀττι-
κόν...λέγεται τοίνυν ἑκατέρως καὶ ποθῆσαι καὶ ποθέσαι.

τὸν πόλεμον κ.τ.λ.] sc. the Peloponnesian war. Thuc. IV. 85 (Bra-
sidas *loq.*), ἀρχόμενοι τοῦ πολέμου
προείπομεν, Ἀθηναίους ἐλευθεροῦν-
τες τὴν Ἑλλάδα πολεμήσειν. v.
fragm. of Theopompus, quoted by
Grote, *H. G.* VI. 358, new ed.

κατέστησαν.] Evidently 2nd aor.
and intrans. (not 1st aor. and trans.
as Battie and Lange take it). Cf.
§ 165, καταστάντες εἰς τοὺς μεγίστους
ἀγῶνας.

πολλοὺς ἐκδότους.] sc. τὰς ἐν τῇ
Ἀσίᾳ πόλεις...καὶ τῶν νήσων Κλαζο-
μένας καὶ Κύπρον (Xen. *Hell.* V. 1.
31), v. § 115. n.

ἀπέστησαν...] 1st aor. trans.
'Detached, severed, the Ionians
from Athens.' Alluding to the convention of Antalcidas, as rightly explained by Morus. Bremi and Benseler refer it to the somewhat earlier
successes of Sparta, in withdrawing

Chios, Lesbos, Ephesus, Clazomenae, &c. from Athens, as recorded
in Thuc. VIII. 14—23; and quote
Panath. § 103, τοὺς συμμάχους τοὺς
ἡμετέρους ἀφίστασαν (impf.) ἐλευθε-
ρώσειν αὐτοὺς ὑπισχνούμενοι... But
the use of the aorist, throughout the
whole of this passage, tells in favour
of understanding ἀπέστησαν of one
definite act, like the peace of Ant.,
in which all the more or less successful attempts culminated.

ἐξ ἧς ἀπῴκησαν...] § 34. n.—
δι' ἣν = *propter quam,* δι' ἧς = *per quam.*
Isocr. does not say that the Ionians
had often owed their preservation
to the *direct* agency of Athens, but
to her existence, influence, and
power. A clear recognition of the
difference between δι' ἣν and δι' ἧς
makes it unnecessary to take πολλάκις (as Schn. does) in the sense of
'more than once,' *i.e.* (1) in their
original colonisation and (2) in the
Persian wars.

123. οἷς οὐκ ἐξαρκεῖ δασμολογεῖσθαι κ.τ.λ.] 'For whom it is not
enough to be subject to tribute and
to see their citadels in possession of
their enemies; but, in addition to
these public disasters, they suffer, in
their own persons also, greater cruel-
ties than purchased slaves among *us.*'

οὐκ ἐξαρκεῖ.] Here with a passive: cf. *Aegin.* § 47, εἰ μὴ μόνον
ἐξαρκέσειεν...στέρεσθαι τῶν παιδίων
ἀλλὰ καὶ τοῦτ' αὐτῇ προσγένοιτο.

ἀκροπόλεις ὁρᾶν ὑπὸ τῶν ἐχθρῶν κατεχομένας, ἀλλὰ πρὸς
ταῖς κοιναῖς συμφοραῖς καὶ τοῖς σώμασι δεινότερα πάσχουσι
τῶν παρ' ἡμῖν ἀργυρωνήτων· οὐδεὶς γὰρ ἡμῶν οὕτως αἰκί- d
ζεται τοὺς οἰκέτας, ὡς ἐκεῖνοι τοὺς ἐλευθέρους κολάζουσιν.
124 μέγιστον δὲ τῶν κακῶν, ὅταν ὑπὲρ αὐτῆς τῆς δουλείας
ἀναγκάζωνται συστρατεύεσθαι, καὶ πολεμεῖν τοῖς ἐλευθέροις ἀξιοῦσιν εἶναι, καὶ τοιούτους κινδύνους ὑπομένειν, ἐν
οἷς ἡττηθέντες μὲν παραχρῆμα διαφθαρήσονται, κατορθώ-
125 σαντες δὲ μᾶλλον εἰς τὸν λοιπὸν χρόνον δουλεύσουσιν. (λε'.)
Ὧν τίνας ἄλλους αἰτίους χρὴ νομίζειν ἢ Λακεδαιμονίους, οἳ
τοσαύτην ἰσχὺν ἔχοντες περιορῶσι τοὺς μὲν αὐτῶν συμ- c
μάχους γενομένους οὕτω δεινὰ πάσχοντας, τὸν δὲ βάρβαρον

ἀργυρωνή(των)] = mancipia argento parata (Liv. XLI. 6). Cf. χρυσώνηται. Greek slaves were either δορίκτητοι (captivi) or ὠνητοί or οἰκότριβες (vernae). The first class became rare as civilisation advanced; and the second increased in proportion. These purchased slaves (ἀναμφισβητήτοι δοῦλοι, Plat. Politic. 289 E) would naturally be treated with less consideration than those born in the house. Cf. Plataic. § 18, τὰς πόλεις δοριαλώτας γενέσθαι... οὐδὲν ἧττον τῶν ἀργυρωνήτων δουλεύουσι.—On the general subject see Becker's Charicles, Exc. to Scene VII.

αἰκίζεται τοὺς οἰκέτας.] On the corporal punishments of slaves at Athens—the brand, the fetter, the clog, the collar, the rod, and the stocks—see Becker's Char. p. 369, 3rd ed.

ὡς ἐκεῖνοι τοὺς ἐλευθέρους κολάζουσι.] Alluding to the Persian punishments of branding, flaying, impaling, mutilation, burying alive, &c. Herodotus has some strange stories about them, e.g. in v. 25 we read that Cambyses slew and flayed Sisamnes (one of the royal judges, who had received a bribe), cut his skin into strips, stretched them across the judgment-seat, and appointed the son of Sisamnes to succeed his father, ἐντειλάμενός οἱ μεμνῆσθαι ἐν τῷ κατί-

ζων θρόνῳ διαδίζει.—v. also IIdt. IV. 43, VII. 38—9, 114—5, and (for the abhorrence with which the Greeks regarded such outrages) cf. ib. IX. 78, 9, τὰ πρέπει μᾶλλον βαρβάροισι ποιεῖν ἤπερ Ἕλλησι καὶ ἑκάτω σι δὲ ἐπιφθονέωμεν. (v. Grote, H. G. I. 481, new ed.). Xenophon (Anab. I. 9. 13) tells that, in the satrapy of Cyrus the younger, πολλάκις ἦν ἰδεῖν παρὰ τὰς στιβομένας ὁδοὺς καὶ ποδῶν καὶ χειρῶν καὶ ὀφθαλμῶν στερομένους ἀνθρώπους. — Cf. Aesch. Eumen. 185—190.

124. μέγιστον δὲ τῶν κακῶν, ὅταν κ.τ.λ.] The constr. is most easily explained by supplying τοῦτ' ἐστίν, or τότ' ἐστίν, after κακῶν. Cf. §§ 87, 107, 118, 149.—Madv. Synt. § 197.

πολεμεῖν τοῖς ἐλευθέροις ἀξιοῦσιν εἶναι.] 'To fight against those who claim to be free,' e.g. against the Cyprians, § 134.

ἐλευθέρους.] For the constr. cf. §§ 3, 71, 95, and 110, τοῖς βουλομένοις γενέσθαι πονηροῖς. Madv. Synt. § 158, 2.

125. ἰσχύν...ῥώμη.] For similar variety of expression cf. Hel. § 16, τῷ μὲν (Hercules) ἰσχὺν ἔδωκεν, ἢ βίᾳ τῶν ἄλλων κρατεῖν δύναται, τῇ δὲ (Helen) κάλλος ἀπένειμεν, ὃ καὶ τῆς ῥώμης αὐτῆς ἄρχειν πέφυκεν.

τῇ τῶν Ἑλλήνων ῥώμῃ τὴν ἀρχὴν τὴν αὑτοῦ κατασκευα-
ζόμενον; καὶ πρότερον μὲν τοὺς τυράννους ἐξέβαλλον,
τῷ δὲ πλήθει τὰς βοηθείας ἐποιοῦντο, νῦν δὲ τοσοῦτον 67
μεταβεβλήκασιν, ὥστε ταῖς μὲν πολιτείαις πολεμοῦσι, τὰς
126 δὲ μοναρχίας συγκαθιστᾶσι. τὴν μέν γε Μαντινέων πόλιν
εἰρήνης ἤδη γεγενημένης ἀνάστατον ἐποίησαν, καὶ τὴν Θη-
βαίων Καδμείαν κατέλαβον, καὶ νῦν Ὀλυνθίους καὶ Φλιασίους πολιορκοῦσιν, Ἀμύντᾳ δὲ τῷ Μακεδόνων βασιλεῖ

τοὺς τυράννους ἐξέβαλλον.] Cf.
Pseudo-Plutarch, *de malignit. Hero-
doti*, p. 859 c, cap. 21 (quoted by
Bens. &c.), πόλιν ἐν τοῖς τότε χρόνοις
οὔτε φιλότιμον οὕτως οὔτε μισο-
τύραννον ἴσμεν ὡς τὴν Λακεδαιμονίων γενομένην. Then follows a list of
instances. They expelled the Cyp-
selidae from Corinth and Ambracia,
Lygdamis from Naxos, the Pisistra-
tidae from Athens, Aeschines from
Sicyon, Symmachus from Thasos,
Aristogenes from Miletus, &c.

πολιτείαις)(μοναρχίας.] The same
contrast is found in *Epp.* IV. 6 and
VI. 11. In Dem. *Ol.* 1. § 5 we have
πολιτεία)(τυραννίς, and in Dem.
Phil. I. § 48, II. § 21, πολιτεία=δη-
μοκρατία.
Cf. esp. Aristot. *Pol.* v. 6 (quoted
by Mr Heslop, Dem. *Ol. l.c.*), τὰς
ἀποκλινούσας μᾶλλον πρὸς τὸ πλῆθος
καλοῦσι πολιτείας.
Harpocr. *Lex.* πολιτεία· ἰδίως εἰώ-
θασι τῷ ὀνόματι τούτῳ χρῆσθαι οἱ
ῥήτορες, ἐπὶ τῆς δημοκρατίας, ὥσπερ
Ἰσοκράτης τε ἐν τῷ πανηγυρικῷ καὶ
Δημοσθένης ἐν Φιλιππικοῖς.

126. Μαντινέων πόλιν...ἀνάστα-
τον.] In 383 B.C. Mantinea was blockaded by Agesipolis. On surrender,
the city was dismantled and the inhabitants redistributed into its 4 (or 5)
constituent villages. *de Pace*, § 100,
Μαντινέας δὲ διῴκισαν, Φλιασίους δ᾿
ἐξεπολιόρκησαν, Xen. *Hell.* v. 2. 7;
διῳκίσθη ἡ Μαντίνεια τετραχῇ, καθάπερ τὸ ἀρχαῖον ᾤκουν. Ephorus (one
of the pupils of Isocr., the writer of
a Hist. in 30 books, from the return
of the Heraclidae to the siege of

Perinthus, 341 B.C.) states that Mantinea was broken up into 5 villages,
fragm. 138, ed. Müller.— On the
historical events mentioned in this
section, see Grote, *H. G.* Part II.
c. 76, or Thirlwall, *H. G.* c. 37.

Καδμείαν κατέλαβον.] In the
summer of 382 B.C. Phoebidas seized
the Cadmea, the citadel of Thebes
(Xen. *Hell.* v. 2. 25—30). In the
winter of 379 B.C. (shortly after the
Phliasian war) the Cadmea was recovered by the Theban exiles (Xen.
l. c. 4. 1—9).

Ὀλυνθίους ... πολιορκοῦσιν.] In
382 B.C. Sparta entered the first
campaign of the war against Olynthus. The war was not finished till
both Teleutias, brother of Agesilaus,
and Agesipolis, king of Sparta, had
fallen: at length, in 379 B.C., the
town was reduced to submission by
Polybiades, and the Olynthian confederation extinguished (Xen. *l. c.*
2. 11—27, 3. 18—26).

Φλιασίους πολιορκοῦσιν.] In 380
B.C. the siege of Phlius (situated
between Sicyon and Argos) was
begun by Agesilaus, while Agesipolis, the other king of Sparta, was
engaged before Olynthus. In 379
B.C. the town surrendered after a
siege of twenty months, almost coincidently with the surrender of
Olynthus (Xen. *l. c.* 2. 8, and 3. 10
—25).

Ἀμύντα ... συμπράττουσιν.] A-
myntas II., father of the famous
Philip of Macedon. In 383 B.C., the
year immediately preceding the birth
of Philip, the future conqueror of

καὶ Διονυσίῳ τῷ Σικελίας τυράννῳ καὶ τῷ βαρβάρῳ τῷ
τῆς Ἀσίας κρατοῦντι συμπράττουσιν, ὅπως ὡς μεγίστην
127 ἀρχὴν ἕξουσιν. καίτοι πῶς οὐκ ἄτοπον τοὺς προεστῶτας
τῶν Ἑλλήνων ἕνα μὲν ἄνδρα τοσούτων ἀνθρώπων καθιστάναι δεσπότην, ὧν οὐδὲ τὸν ἀριθμὸν ἐξευρεῖν ῥᾴδιόν
ἐστι, τὰς δὲ μεγίστας τῶν πόλεων μηδ᾽ αὐτὰς αὑτῶν ἐᾶν
εἶναι κυρίας, ἀλλ᾽ ἀναγκάζειν δουλεύειν ἢ ταῖς μεγίσταις
128 συμφοραῖς περιβάλλειν; ὁ δὲ πάντων δεινότατον, ὅταν τις
ἴδῃ τοὺς τὴν ἡγεμονίαν ἔχειν ἀξιοῦντας ἐπὶ μὲν τοὺς Ἕλλη- c
νας καθ᾽ ἑκάστην τὴν ἡμέραν στρατευομένους, πρὸς δὲ

Olynthus (in 347), Amyntas sent
envoys to Sparta to ask for aid
against the Olynthians, who had
refused to restore to him certain
cities of Macedonia and Chalcidice,
which had passed over to their
confederacy. His request (coupled
with that of the Acanthians) was
answered by the siege of Olynthus
(*Archid.* § 46, Xen. *l.c.* 2. 12, 13,
38; 3. 9, and Diodor. XIV. 92,
XV. 19).

Cf. the *Philippus* of Isocr., § 106,
ὁ πατήρ σου πρὸς τὰς πόλεις ταύτας
(Argos, Thebes, Lacedaemon, A-
thens), αἳ σοὶ παραινῶ προσέχειν τὸν
νοῦν, πρὸς ἁπάσαι οἰκείαι εἶχεν.

Διονυσίῳ ...... συμπράττουσιν.]
Dionysius I., tyrant of Syracuse,
405—367 B.C. v. *Phil.* § 63. We
have no mention in extant histories
of definite co-operation between
Sparta and Dionysius the Elder, at
the time of the publication of this
speech (380 B. C.). In 404 B. C. a
Spartan envoy, named Aristus, aided
him in establishing his dominion,
and in 396 B.C. a Spartan captain,
Pharacidas, declared, at a public
meeting in Syracuse, that he had
been sent to aid the Syracusans and
Dionysius against the Carthaginians.
Again, at a later period (374 B.C.),
Timotheus, the Athenian general,
captured a fleet of 9 triremes, ἃς
Διονύσιος ἦν ἀπεσταλκὼς Λακεδαιμονίοις ἐπὶ συμμαχίαν. (Diodor. XIV.

10, 70 and XV. 47.)

These facts are enough to esta-
blish a presumption that in the year
380 some unrecorded event may
have given additional force to the
allusion in the text, or else the allusion may be merely general; cf. *de
Pace*, § 99.—In any case it may be
interesting to notice (with Grote,
H. G. Pt. II. c. 82) the coincidence
between the dates of the establishing
of the supremacy of Sparta and the
despotism of Dionysius: 'the new
position and policy wherein Sparta
now became involved, imparted to
her a sympathy with Dionysius such
as in earlier times she probably
would not have felt' (Vol. VII. p.
404, new ed.). On the sympathy
between Dionys. II. and Sparta v.
Archid. § 63.

τῷ βαρβάρῳ κ.τ.λ.] Alluding to
peace of Antalcidas, § 115. n.

ἕξουσιν.] sc. Amyntas, Dionysius,
and Artaxerxes Mnemon.

127. ἄνδρα...ἀνθρώπων.] 'man'...
'human beings.' '*mann...menschen.*'
Bens. *transl.*

128. ὃ δὲ πάντων δεινότατον,
ὅταν...] Cf. § 176, *Archid.* § 36,
ὃ δὲ πάντων σχετλιώτατον, εἰ κ.τ.λ.,
Callim. § 18, Plat. *Apol.* 18 c, ὃ δὲ
πάντων [sc. ἐστὶ] ἀλογώτατον [sc.
ἐστὶ τοῦτο], ὅτι οὐδὲ τὰ ὀνόματα οἷόν
τε αὐτῶν εἰδέναι (Riddell's *Digest
of Plat. Idioms,* § 247) v. § 124. n.—
Madv. *Synt.* § 197.

τοὺς βαρβάρους εἰς ἅπαντα τὸν χρόνον συμμαχίαν πεποιημένους.

129   (λς΄.) Καὶ μηδεὶς ὑπολάβῃ με δυσκόλως ἔχειν, ὅτι
τραχύτερον τούτων ἐμνήσθην, προειπών, ὡς περὶ διαλλα-
γῶν ποιήσομαι τοὺς λόγους· οὐ γὰρ ἵνα πρὸς τοὺς ἄλλους
διαβάλω τὴν πόλιν τὴν Λακεδαιμονίων οὕτως εἴρηκα περὶ
αὐτῶν, ἀλλ᾽ ἵν᾽ αὐτοὺς ἐκείνους παύσω, καθ᾽ ὅσον ὁ λόγος
130 δύναται, τοιαύτην ἔχοντας τὴν γνώμην. ἔστι δ᾽ οὐχ οἷόν
τ᾽ ἀποτρέπειν τῶν ἁμαρτημάτων, οὐδ᾽ ἑτέρων πράξεων d
πείθειν ἐπιθυμεῖν, ἢν μή τις ἐρρωμένως ἐπιτιμήσῃ τοῖς
παροῦσιν· χρὴ δὲ κατηγορεῖν μὲν ἡγεῖσθαι τοὺς ἐπὶ βλάβῃ
τοιαῦτα λέγοντας, νουθετεῖν δὲ τοὺς ἐπ᾽ ὠφελείᾳ λοιδοροῦν-
τας· τὸν γὰρ αὐτὸν λόγον οὐχ ὁμοίως ὑπολαμβάνειν δεῖ,
131 μὴ μετὰ τῆς αὐτῆς διανοίας λεγόμενον. ἐπεὶ καὶ τοῦτ᾽
ἔχομεν αὐτοῖς ἐπιτιμᾶν, ὅτι τῇ μὲν αὐτῶν πόλει τοὺς ὁμόρους εἱλωτεύειν ἀναγκάζουσι, τῷ δὲ κοινῷ τῷ τῶν συμ- c
μάχων οὐδὲν τοιοῦτον κατασκευάζουσιν, ἐξὸν αὐτοῖς τὰ
πρὸς ἡμᾶς διαλυσαμένοις ἅπαντας τοὺς βαρβάρους περιοί-

---

§§ 129—131. *The harsh terms,
which I have applied to the Lacedaemonians, are prompted by a spirit of
friendly admonition. Their present
attitude calls for vigorous rebuke;
they are oppressing their neighbours
and exacting tribute from the islands
of the Aegean, instead of subduing the
Barbarians and winning the broad
territories of Asia.*
προειπών κ.τ.λ.] In §§ 16—19.
129. δυσκόλως ἔχειν.] 'To be
fretful, petulant, ill-tempered.' v.
Aristot. *Eth.* II. 7. 13, ὁ...ἐν πᾶσιν
ἀηδὴς δύσερίς τις καὶ δύσκολος, and
ib. IV. 6. 2. Cf. further (as a 'study'
in synonyms) *ad Dem.* § 31, δύσερις
...δυσάρεστοι and *Panath.* § 8, τὸ
γῆράς ἐστι δυσάρεστον καὶ μικρόλογον
καὶ μεμψίμοιρον.
130. ἐρρωμένως.] These adverbs
formed from participles (esp.pf. pass.)
are common in Isocr.; *e.g. de Perm.*
§ 144, τεταγμένως, *ib.* § 245, τετα-
ραγμένως, *ib.* § 305, καταβεβλημέ-

νως, *de Pace*, § 62, ἀποκεκαλυμμένως,
ib. § 96, πεφιλαγμένως, *Panath.*
§ 218, οὐκ ἀπαιδεύτως ἀλλὰ νοῦν
ἐχόντως, &c.
κατηγορεῖν)(νουθετεῖν.] 'To accuse')('to admonish.' For a similar
distinction cf. Thuc. I. 69, καὶ μηδεὶς
ὑμῶν ἐπ᾽ ἔχθρᾳ πλέον ἢ αἰτίᾳ νομίσῃ
τάδε λέγεσθαι· αἰτία (expostulation)
μὲν γὰρ φίλων ἀνδρῶν ἐστιν ἁμαρτα-
νόντων, κατηγορία δὲ ἐχθρῶν ἀδικη-
σάντων.—For the sense and. the
phraseology of the whole context v.
de Pace, § 71—2.
131. εἱλωτεύειν.] 'to be Helots'
(metaphorically), *i.e.* 'to live in serf-
dom *like* that of the Helots.' For a
similar use of the word cf. *Epp.* III. 5
(to Philip), ἡγοῦ τόθ᾽ ἕξειν ἀνυπέρβλητον δόξαν, ὅταν τοὺς βαρβάρους
ἀναγκάσῃς εἱλωτεύειν τοῖς Ἕλλησι.
Harpocr. εἱλωτεύειν· δουλεύειν· Ἰσοκράτης ἐν τῷ πανηγυρικῷ. Cf. μετα-
κεῖν, § 105. n., § 111. n.
περιοίκους.] On the περίοικοι (the

132 κοις ὅλης τῆς Ἑλλάδος καταστῆσαι. καίτοι χρὴ τοὺς φύσει
καὶ μὴ διὰ τύχην μέγα φρονοῦντας τοιούτοις ἔργοις ἐπιχειρεῖν πολὺ μᾶλλον ἢ τοὺς νησιώτας δασμολογεῖν, οὓς 68
ἄξιόν ἐστιν ἐλεεῖν, ὁρῶντας τούτους μὲν διὰ σπανιότητα τῆς
γῆς ὄρη γεωργεῖν ἀναγκαζομένους, τοὺς δ' ἠπειρώτας δι'
ἀφθονίαν τῆς χώρας τὴν μὲν πλείστην αὐτῆς ἀργὸν περι-
ορῶντας, ἐξ ἧς δὲ καρποῦνται τοσοῦτον πλοῦτον κεκτημένους.

133 (λζ.) Ἡγοῦμαι δ' εἴ τινες ἄλλοθεν ἐπελθόντες θεαταὶ
γένοιντο τῶν παρόντων πραγμάτων, πολλὴν ἂν αὐτοῖς
καταγνῶναι μανίαν ἀμφοτέρων ἡμῶν, οἵτινες οὕτω περὶ b
μικρῶν κινδυνεύομεν, ἐξὸν ἀδεῶς πολλὰ κεκτῆσθαι, καὶ τὴν
ἡμετέραν αὐτῶν χώραν διαφθείρομεν, ἀμελήσαντες τὴν

134 Ἀσίαν καρποῦσθαι. καὶ τῷ μὲν οὐδὲν προὐργιαίτερόν
ἐστιν ἢ σκοπεῖν ἐξ ὧν μηδέποτε παυσόμεθα πρὸς ἀλλήλους πολεμοῦντες· ἡμεῖς δὲ τοσούτου δέομεν συγκρούειν τι
τῶν ἐκείνου πραγμάτων ἢ ποιεῖν στασιάζειν, ὥστε καὶ τὰς

---

provincials or free inhabitants of the
100 Laconian townships, inferior to
the Spartans but superior to the
Helots) see *Dict. Antiq.*, Thirlwall's
H. G. 1. 307 sqq., or Grote, *H. G.*
Pt. II. c. 6 = Vol II. 132 sqq. (where
the statement of Isocr. *Panath.*
§§ 177—181 on their origin is combated).

131. νησιῶτας.] The inhabitants
of the Cyclades.

ὄρη γεωργεῖν.] *de Pace*, § 117,
Μεγαρεῖς…γῆν μὲν οὐκ ἔχοντες,…πέ-
τρας δὲ γεωργοῦντες.

ἠπειρώτας.] 'The inhabitants of
the continent,' the subjects of Persia. Harpocr. Ἤπειρον· συνήθες
ἐστι τῷ Ἰσοκράτει, τὴν ὑπὸ τῷ βασιλεῖ τῶν Περσῶν γῆν οὕτω καλεῖν.
§§ 163, 174, 187, *Phil.* § 112, *Archid.*
§ 73, and Aesch. *Pers.* 42, ἠπειρογενὲς
ἔθνος.

πλείστην αὐτῆς.] § 34. n.

§§ 133—159. *While the Greeks
are spending their strength on trifles,
the king of Persia is aggrandising
himself at their expense.* 138—143.

*His real weakness illustrated especial-
ly with regard to the revolt of Egypt,
the war with Evagoras, and the battle
of Cnidus; and also proved* (144) *by
the successful raids of Spartan commanders, and lastly* (145—149) *by
the ignominious battle of Cunaxa.*
150—151. *The weakness of the Barbarians results from the cowardice,
luxury, insolence, and servility fos-
tered by their political institutions.*
152—3. *The character of the so-called
Satraps.* 154. *The cases of Themistocles and Conon.* 155—156. *The
enduring feud between the Barbarians
and the Greeks in general; illustrated* (157—9) *by special reference to
the Athenians.*

133. καταγνῶναι μανίαν ἀμφοτέρων.] v. § 157. n. and Madv. *Synt.*
§ 59 a.

134. τῷ μὲν.] sc. τῆς Ἀσίας βασιλεῖ. τῷ refers to the idea of the king
involved in the mention of his kingdom. § 110, ἐκείνοις. n.

ἐξ ὧν μηδέποτε.] § 89, ὃ μὴ…
ἐστιν. Madv. *Synt.* § 204 2.

διὰ τύχην αὐτῷ γεγενημένας ταραχὰς συνδιαλύειν ἐπιχειροῦμεν, οἵτινες καὶ τοῖν στρατοπέδοιν τοῖν περὶ Κύπρον c
ἐῶμεν αὐτὸν τῷ μὲν χρῆσθαι, τὸ δὲ πολιορκεῖν, ἀμφοτέροιν
135 αὐτοῖν τῆς Ἑλλάδος ὄντοιν. οἵ τε γὰρ ἀφεστῶτες πρὸς

τοῖν στρατοπέδοιν τοῖν περὶ Κύπρον...] Allusion to the Cyprian
war between Artaxerxes Mnemon
and Evagoras. It lasted 10 years
(*Evag.* § 64, Εὐαγόρᾳ πολεμῆσαι
ἔτη δέκα, τῶν αὐτῶν κύριον αὐτὸν
κατέλιπεν, ὥσπερ ἦν καὶ πρὶν εἰς πόλεμον εἰσελθεῖν). The first operations appear to have taken place in
390 B.C., when an Athenian fleet
was sent to the assistance of Evagoras (Xen. *Hell.* IV. 8. 24); in 388
Chabrias sailed to Cyprus with the
same object (*ib.* V. 1. 10); in 387
Cyprus was abandoned to Persia by
the peace of Antalcidas; in 385 a
great naval engagement occurred,
in which Evag. was defeated, and,
after a vigorous resistance on the
part of the king of Salamis, the war
was concluded, according to Grote,
in 380 or 379 (soon after the publication of the *Paneg.*) on the terms
that Evag. should remain in full possession of Salamis, and pay a fixed
tribute to Persia.

The dates of the transactions of
this war have been the subject of
some dispute. Diodorus (fl. 30 B.C.),
who makes the war last from 394—
385 B.C., contradicts himself in several points, but appears to be right
in assigning the naval engagement
to the year 38⅘ B.C.—Fynes-Clinton
(*Fasti Hell.* Appendix on the Cyprian
War) takes 385—376 as the dates,
owing mainly to a conclusion drawn
from *Paneg.* § 141 (vid. προδεδυστό-
χηκεν. n.). (v. Grote, Pt. II. c. 76).

The lost histories of Callisthenes
would doubtless have thrown the
fullest light upon the events of this
war. It so happens however that
an abstract of an account of it, by
Theopompus, was made by Photius
(the learned patriarch of Constanti-
nople in cent. 9 A.D.), *Bibl. cod.* 176,

p. 120 Bekker. This abstract proves
that the war was begun before the
peace of Antalcidas, was not vigorously waged till after that peace,
and was apparently not concluded
until the accession of Nectanebis I.
to the throne of Egypt,—an event
which cannot be fixed with certainty.
I transcribe the passage at length,
as it is often cited in these notes:

Theopomp. *fragm.* 111 ed. Müller (part of a summary of the
twelfth book of his *Philippica*),
Ὅπως τε ὁ βασιλεὺς Εὐαγόρᾳ συν-
πείσθη πολεμῆσαι, στρατηγὸν ἐπι-
στῆσαι Αὐτοφραδάτην τὸν Λυδίας
σατράπην (v. § 157. n.), ναύαρχον δὲ
Ἑκατόμνων (cf. § 162). Καὶ περὶ τῆς
εἰρήνης, ἣν αὐτοὶ τοῖς Ἕλλησιν ἐβρά-
βευσαν (§§ 120, 121, 176)· ὅπως τε
πρὸς Εὐαγόραν ἐπικρατέστερον ἐπο-
λέμει, καὶ περὶ τῆς ἐν Κύπρῳ ναυμαχίας (§ 141). Καὶ ὡς Ἀθηναίων
ἡ πόλις ταῖς πρὸς βασιλέα συνθήκαις
ἐπειρᾶτο ἐμμένειν, Λακεδαιμόνιοι δὲ
ὑπέρογκα φρονοῦντες παρέβαινον τὰς
συνθήκας. Τίνα τε τρόπον τὴν ἐπὶ
Ἀνταλκίδου ἔθεντο εἰρήνην (§ 115
sqq.), καὶ ὡς Τιρίβαζον ἐτόλμησεν
(§ 135)· ὅπως τε Εὐαγόρᾳ ἐπεβού-
λευσεν· ὅπως τε αὐτὸν Εὐαγόρας πρὸς
βασιλέα διαβαλών, συνέβαλε μετ'
Ὀρόντου, καὶ ὡς Νεκτασίβιος παρει-
ληφότος τὴν Αἰγύπτου βασιλείαν, πρὸς
Λακεδαιμονίους πρέσβεις ἀπέστειλεν
Εὐαγόρας· τίνα τε τρόπον ὁ περὶ
Κύπρον αὐτῷ πόλεμος διελύθη.

τῷ μέν.] *sc.* the land force of Tiribazus and Orontes; and the sea
force of Gaos, both of which contained Greek contingents from Ionia.

τὸ δέ.] *sc.* the armament of Evagoras.

135. πρὸς ἡμᾶς οἰκείως ἔχ.]
The earliest link between Attica
and Cyprus appears to have been
the legendary foundation of Salamis

ἡμᾶς τ' οἰκείως ἔχουσι καὶ Λακεδαιμονίοις σφᾶς αὐτοὺς
ἐνδιδόασιν, τῶν τε μετὰ Τειριβάζου στρατευομένων καὶ τοῦ
πεζοῦ τὸ χρησιμώτατον ἐκ τῶνδε τῶν τόπων ἤθροισται,
καὶ τοῦ ναυτικοῦ τὸ πλεῖστον ἀπ' Ἰωνίας συμπέπλευκεν,
οἳ πολὺ ἂν ἥδιον κοινῇ τὴν Ἀσίαν ἐπόρθουν ἢ πρὸς ἀλλή- d
136 λους ἕνεκα μικρῶν ἐκινδύνευον. ὧν ἡμεῖς οὐδεμίαν ποιούμεθα πρόνοιαν, ἀλλὰ περὶ μὲν τῶν Κυκλάδων νήσων ἀμ-
φισβητοῦμεν, τοσαύτας δὲ τὸ πλῆθος πόλεις καὶ τηλικαύτας
τὰ μέγεθος δυνάμεις οὕτως εἰκῇ τῷ βαρβάρῳ παραδεδώκα-
μεν. τοιγαροῦν τὰ μὲν ἔχει, τὰ δὲ μέλλει, τοῖς δ' ἐπιβου-
137 λεύει, δικαίως ἁπάντων ἡμῶν καταπεφρονηκώς. διαπέ- e
πρακται γάρ, ὃ τῶν ἐκείνου προγόνων οὐδεὶς πώποτε· τήν
τε γὰρ Ἀσίαν διωμολόγηται καὶ παρ' ἡμῶν καὶ παρὰ
Λακεδαιμονίων βασιλέως εἶναι, τάς τε πόλεις τὰς Ἑλλη-
νίδας οὕτω κυρίως παρείληφεν, ὥστε τὰς μὲν αὐτῶν κατα-
σκάπτειν, ἐν δὲ ταῖς ἀκροπόλεις ἐντειχίζειν. καὶ ταῦτα
πάντα γέγονε διὰ τὴν ἡμετέραν ἄνοιαν ἀλλ' οὐ διὰ τὴν
ἐκείνου δύναμιν.

138   (λη'.) Καίτοι τινὲς θαυμάζουσι τὸ μέγεθος τῶν βασι- 69
λέως πραγμάτων καὶ φασὶν αὐτὸν εἶναι δυσπολέμητον,
διεξιόντες, ὡς πολλὰς τὰς μεταβολὰς τοῖς Ἕλλησι πεποίηκεν. ἐγὼ δ' ἡγοῦμαι μὲν τοὺς ταῦτα λέγοντας οὐκ
ἀποτρέπειν ἀλλ' ἐπισπεύδειν τὴν στρατείαν· εἰ γὰρ ἡμῶν

by Teucer (*Evag.* § 18, &c.). The
connexion is exemplified by the visit
of Solon (from whom Soli received
its name).—Conon, the famous general, and other Athenians, were
harboured in Cyprus during the rule
of Evagoras (*ib.* §§ 49—53).—The
king himself was presented with the
citizenship of Athens (*ib.* § 54), and
his statue was afterwards set up,
with that of Conon, in the Athenian
Cerameicus (*ib.* § 57, and Dem. *Lept.*
§ 70).

Λακεδαιμονίοις—ἐνδιδόασιν.] Cf.
Theopomp. *fragm.* ad fin. (quoted
in § 134. n.)

ἐκ τῶνδε τῶν τόπων.] Not Cyprus
and Cilicia, but Greece itself (cf.
§ 168), and the Greek settlements in
Ionia, esp. Phocaea and Cumae (cf.
§ 124, *Phil.* § 125—6, and Diod.
xv. 5).

136. τοσαύτας κ.τ.λ.] Cf. § 16. n.
τὰ μὲν ἔχει κ.τ.λ.] A scholium on
this passage states that Demosthenes
in the *Philippics* expresses the same
idea in similar words: the passage
alluded to is probably *Phil.* 3. § 27,
18. Cf. *Hel.* § 16, τὰς μὲν ὑπέρ-
θουν, τὰς δ' ἥμιλλον (*sic omn. codd.*
v. § 83. n.), ταῖς δ' ἠπείλουν τῶν πόλεων.

137. ἐν δὲ ταῖς.] ἐν ταῖς δὲ would
have been more regular, but ἐν δὲ
ταῖς is more rhythmical. This order
is common in Isocr. *e.g.* § 89 *fin.*
151.—Madv. *Synt.* § 188, R. 1.

138. στρατείαν.] v. § 15. n.

ὁμονοησάντων αὐτὸς ἐν ταραχαῖς ὢν χαλεπὸς ἔσται προσπολεμεῖν, ἤ που σφόδρα χρὴ δεδιέναι τὸν καιρὸν ἐκεῖνον,
ὅταν τὰ μὲν τῶν βαρβάρων καταστῇ καὶ διὰ μιᾶς γένηται
γνώμης, ἡμεῖς δὲ πρὸς ἀλλήλους ὥσπερ νῦν πολεμικῶς b
139 ἔχωμεν. οὐ μὴν οὐδ᾽ εἰ συναγορεύουσι τοῖς ὑπ᾽ ἐμοῦ λεγομένοις, οὐδ᾽ ὡς ὀρθῶς περὶ τῆς ἐκείνου δυνάμεως γιγνώ-
σκουσιν. εἰ μὲν γὰρ ἀπέφαινον αὐτὸν ἅμα τοῖν πολέοιν
ἀμφοτέροιν πρότερόν ποτε περιγεγενημένον, εἰκότως ἂν ἡμᾶς
καὶ νῦν ἐκφοβεῖν ἐπεχείρουν· εἰ δὲ τοῦτο μὲν μὴ γέγονεν,
ἀντιπάλων δ᾽ ὄντων ἡμῶν καὶ Λακεδαιμονίων προσθέμενος
τοῖς ἑτέροις ἐπικυδέστερα τὰ πράγματα θάτερ᾽ ἐποίησεν, c

χαλεπὸς προσπολεμεῖν.] 'Difficult to fight against.' ' Schwer zu
bekriegen,' Bens. The German and
English idioms are in this case the
same as the Gk. In Lat. we should
have the supine, oppugnatu. Cf. (with
Schn.) Thuc. VII. 51, χαλεπώτερον
εἶναι προσπολεμεῖν, ib. 14, χαλεπαὶ
αἱ ὑμέτεραι φύσεις ἄρξαι, Dem. Ol.
II. § 22, φοβερὸς προσπολεμῆσαι, and
Plat. Menex. 239 B, ὁ χρόνος βραχὺς
ἀξίως διηγήσασθαι. The passive in
such cases is rare; cf., however, de
Perm. § 115 and § 136, ποιήσομεν δὲ
τὴν ἀρχὴν τῶν λεχθησομένων ἀκοῦσαι
μὲν ἴσως τισὶν ἀηδῆ, ῥηθῆναι δ᾽ οὐκ
ἀσύμφορον. Madv. Synt. § 150, or
Goodwin's Gk. Moods and Tenses,
§ 93, 2.
ἢ που.] v. ad Dem. § 49. n.
καταστῇ])(ἐν ταραχαῖς ὤν. Plat.
Legg. VII. 798 A, τὸ κατ᾽ ἀρχὰς συν-
ταραχθεὶς ὑπὸ νόσων, μόγις ποτὲ κατέστη, Lysias, Andoc. § 36, ἐτάραξε
μὲν οὗτοι τὴν πόλιν, κατεστήσατε δ᾽
ὑμεῖς. The corresponding subst. is
κατάστασις, Eur. Rhes. 111, νυκτὸς
ἐν καταστάσει ('in the stillness of
night'), Med. 1197, ὀμμάτων κατάστασις ('her staid and quiet eyes'),
both of which passages have been,
I think, misinterpreted in L. and
S.
διὰ μιᾶς γένηται γνώμης.] For
this use of διά cf. Thuc. I. 40. 4,
Κερκυραίοις οὐδὲ δι᾽ ἀνακωχῆς πώποτ᾽

ἐγένεσθε, ib. 73. 2, δι᾽ ὄχλου ἔσται,
&c.
πολεμικῶς.] ' Periit lepor loci ex
quo aliena manus polemikos inse-
ruit.' Cobet, var. lect. p. 292. It
is unnecessary to strike out πολεμικῶς, as the construction is ὥσπερ-
νῦν ἔχομεν-πολεμικῶς.
139. ὡς...] 'Thus,'=οὕτως. In
Attic prose writers seldom used except in the phrases καὶ ὥς, μηδ᾽ ὥς,
and (as here) οὐδ᾽ ὥς.
For the less common use cf.
Thuc. III. 37. 5, ὡς οὖν χρὴ καὶ ὑμᾶς
κ.τ.λ., Plat. Rep. 530 D, ὣν πρὸς
ἀστρονομίαν...ὡς πρὸς ἐναρμόνιον φο-
ρὰν, Protag. 326 D, ὥσπερ...ὡς δεῖ...
and ib. 338 A, ὡς οὖν ποιήσετε.
(Kroschel's n. to Protag. l.c.).—As
instances in Attic verse we have
Eur. Iph. T. 603, ἀλλ᾽ ὡς γενέσθω,
El. 155, and Bacch. 1069.
εἰ μὲν κ.τ.λ.] i.e. 'For if they had
shewn that on some previous occasion he had been victorious over
both the cities at once, they might
reasonably have attempted to alarm
us on the present occasion; if however (so far from this having happened) it is only because the Lac.
and ourselves are at variance, that
he was often able, by attaching
himself to one of those sides, to
render the exploits of that side more
brilliant, this is no proof of his
strength.'

οὐδέν ἐστι τοῦτο σημεῖον τῆς ἐκείνου ῥώμης. ἐν γὰρ τοῖς
τοιούτοις καιροῖς πολλάκις μικραὶ δυνάμεις μεγάλας τὰς
ῥοπὰς ἐποίησαν, ἐπεὶ καὶ περὶ Χίων ἔχοιμ' ἂν τοῦτον τὸν
λόγον εἰπεῖν, ὡς ὁποτέροις ἐκεῖνοι προσθέσθαι βουληθεῖεν,
140 οὗτοι κατὰ θάλατταν κρείττους ἦσαν. (λθ.) Ἀλλὰ γὰρ
οὐκ ἐκ τούτων δίκαιόν ἐστι σκοπεῖν τὴν βασιλέως δύναμιν,
ἐξ ὧν μεθ' ἑκατέρων γέγονεν, ἀλλ' ἐξ ὧν αὐτὸς ὑπὲρ αὑτοῦ d
πεπολέμηκεν. καὶ πρῶτον μὲν ἀποστάσης Αἰγύπτου τί
διαπέπρακται πρὸς τοὺς ἔχοντας αὐτήν; οὐκ ἐκεῖνος μὲν
ἐπὶ τὸν πόλεμον τοῦτον κατέπεμψε τοὺς εὐδοκιμωτάτους
Περσῶν, Ἀβροκόμαν καὶ Τιθραύστην καὶ Φαρνάβαζον,

ἐν γὰρ τοῖς κ.τ.λ.] 'For in
such times of crisis, small forces
have often had great influence on
the balance of power; for even of
the Chians I can say this, that to
whatever side they chose to attach
themselves, that side was superior
at sea.'—Strictly speaking μεγάλας
has here the force of a predicate, v.
§ 171, τὰς εὐνοίας, n.

μικραὶ δυνάμεις κ.τ.λ.] Cf. Dem.
Ol. II. § 14, ἡ Μακεδονικὴ δύναμις...
ἐν μὲν προσθήκης μέρει ἐστί τις οὐ
μικρά...καὶ ὅσοι τις ἂν, οἶμαι, προσ-
θῇ κἂν μικρὰν δύναμιν, πάντ'
ὠφελεῖ.

ῥοπάς.] A metaphor taken from
the turn of the scale, cf. esp. Soph.
El. 119, μούνη γὰρ ἄγειν οὐκέτι σωκῶ |
λύπης ἀντίρροπον ἄχθος. ('For I am
no longer able by myself to draw up
the weight of grief which is in the
opposite scale.' Porson's transl.)

Χίων.] After the failure of the
Sicilian expedition Chios revolted
from Athens and strengthened the
sea-force of Sparta (Thuc. VIII. 7,
14, 22, 106). After the battle of
Cnidus it revolted from Sparta and
sent contingents to the navy of
Athens (Diodor. XIV. 84, 94). Schn.

βουληθεῖεν...ἦσαν.] Madv. Synt.
§ 133.

κατὰ θάλατταν.] de Pace, § 97,
Χίων... προθυμότατα πάντων τῶν
συμμάχων τῷ ναυτικῷ συγκινδυνευ-
σάντων.

140. ἀλλὰ γάρ.] At enim. The
phrase has two uses: (1) when it introduces an objection (as in the present passage), and answers to the
Demosthenic ἀλλὰ νὴ Δία; (2) when
it means, 'but be that as it may,'
or 'but the truth is.' As an instance
of (1), which is very common, we
have Plat. Rep. 365 C, D, ἀλλὰ γάρ,
φησί τις, οὐ ῥᾴδιον ἀεὶ λανθάνειν κακὸν
ὄντα followed by ἀλλὰ δὴ θεοὺς οὔτε
λανθάνειν οὔτε βιάσασθαι δυνατόν.
As instances of (2), Plat. Symp.
180 A, Αἰσχύλος δὲ φλυαρεῖ κ.τ.λ....
ἀλλὰ γὰρ τῷ ὄντι κ.τ.λ., Apol. 19 C,
and other passages quoted by Riddell, Digest of Pl. Idioms, § 147.

ἀποστάσης Αἰγύπτου κ. τ. λ.]
The details of this section are not
easily illustrated from extant histories. For obvious reasons, they
cannot be referred to the revolt of
Nectanebis I. in 374 B.C. (Diodor.
XV. 41 sqq.), although Pharnabazus
was employed in repressing that
revolt. The expedition of Persia
against Egypt either preceded the
first preparations for the Cyprian
war or was coincident with its earlier
years before vigorous operations had
been commenced, i.e. it lasted either
from 392—390 B.C. or from 390—
388 B.C. (cf. Diodor. XV. 2—4, and
v. Grote, H. G. VII. p. 12, new ed.).

Ἀβροκόμαν...Τιθραύστην...Φαρ-

οὗτοι δὲ τρί᾽ ἔτη μείναντες καὶ πλείω κακὰ παθόντες ἢ ποιήσαντες, τελευτῶντες οὕτως αἰσχρῶς ἀπηλλάγησαν, ὥστε τοὺς
ἀφεστῶτας μηκέτι τὴν ἐλευθερίαν ἀγαπᾶν, ἀλλ᾽ ἤδη καὶ e
141 τῶν ὁμόρων ζητεῖν ἐπάρχειν; μετὰ δὲ ταῦτ᾽ ἐπ᾽ Εὐαγόραν
στρατεύσας, ὃς ἄρχει μὲν μιᾶς πόλεως, ἐν δὲ ταῖς συνθήκαις
ἔκδοτός ἐστιν, οἰκῶν δὲ νῆσον κατὰ μὲν θάλατταν προδεδυστύχηκεν, ὑπὲρ δὲ τῆς χώρας τρισχιλίους ἔχει μόνον
πελταστάς, ἀλλ᾽ ὅμως οὕτω ταπεινῆς δυνάμεως οὐ δύναται 70
περιγενέσθαι βασιλεὺς πολεμῶν, ἀλλ᾽ ἤδη μὲν ἓξ ἔτη διατέ-

νδβαξον.] Satraps of Syria, Ionia,
and the Hellespontine province respectively.

οὗτοι δὲ κ.τ.λ.] 'And these, after
remaining for three years and suffering more disasters than they inflicted, at length came off with such
disgrace that the rebels are no longer
content with their liberty, but are
already seeking to extend their sway
over their neighbours also.'
On τελευτῶντες v. Madv. *Synt.*
§ 176 C, R.

τὴν ἐλευθερίαν ἀγαπᾶν.] Ἀγαπᾶν
in the sense, 'to be content with,'
'to acquiesce in,' is used either with
the acc. as here, or with the partic.
as in *Panath.* § 8, οὐκ ἀγαπῶ ξῶν
ἐπὶ τούτοις, or with the inf., as in
Callim. § 50, οὐκ ἀγαπᾷ τῶν ἴσων
τυγχάνειν τοῖς ἄλλοις, ἀλλὰ ζητεῖ
πλέον ἔχειν ἡμῶν, or, lastly, with εἰ
or ἤν, e.g. *Argin.* § 20, οὐδ᾽ ἐν τούτοις ταῖς κακοῖς ἠγάπησα, εἰ...δυνη-
θείην, and *Epp.* I. 6, ἀγαπᾶν, ἢν τὴν
χώραν ἔχωσι. (Bens. *Areop.* § 34,
ἀγαπᾶν εἰ μηδὲν ἔτι κακὸν πάσχοιεν.
n. p. 300.)

141. μιᾶς πόλεως.] sc. the Cyprian
Salamis. *Evag.* § 47, χώραν πολλὴν
προσεκτήσατο, and *ib.* § 61, ὅτε...γὰρ
αὐτὸν (sc. Evag.) εἷλον (sc. the Persians) εἰρήνην ἄγειν, τὴν αὐτοῦ
πόλιν μόνην εἶχεν· ἐπειδὴ δ᾽ ἐπραγ-
ώσθη πολεμεῖν, τοιοῦτοι ἦν...ὥστε
μικροῦ μὲν ἐδέησε Κύπρον ἅπασαν κατασχεῖν, Φοινίκην δ᾽ ἐπόρθησε,
Τύρον δὲ κατὰ κράτος εἷλε, Κιλικίαν
δὲ βασιλέως ἀπέστησε, κ.τ.λ.

ἐν ταῖς συνθήκαις ἔκδοτος.] v. the
terms of the peace of Antalcidas, in
§ 115. n.

οἰκῶν νῆσον κ.τ.λ.] i.e. Evag.
having an insular dominion, needed
a land-force and a sea-force as well.
The latter had already been defeated, and the former was but feeble
(consisting of only 3000 peltasts):
his condition was therefore desperate.
(Sauppe, Benseler, *transl.* p. 227 n.
and Rauchenst. ed. 3.)

προδεδυστύχηκεν.] 'Has already
sustained a defeat,' alluding to the
great naval action described by Diodorus (XV. 2—4), and (perhaps cor-
rectly) referred by him to the year
of the Archonship of Mystichides
(i.e. 38⅚ B.C.). προδεδυστύχηκεν does
not necessarily imply that this engagement was the 'first action of
the war' (as Fynes-Clinton, *F. H.*
App. 12, explains it).

ἓξ ἔτη διατέτριφεν.] This note of
time is probably to be explained in
connection with the words προδεδυστύχηκεν and οὕτω ταπεινῇ δυνάμεως, and denotes the period between
the more vigorous operations of
Persia, which resulted in the great
naval defeat of Evag., and the date
of the publication of the *Paneg.* i.e.
385—380 B.C. Fynes-Clinton uses
the words ἓξ ἔτη διατέτριφεν to prove
that the war could not have actually
begun until 385 B.C. Grote thinks
that 'Isocrates does not make it
quite clear from what point he reckons the 6 years.'

τρίφεν, εἰ δὲ δεῖ τὰ μέλλοντα τοῖς γεγενημένοις τεκμαίρεσθαι, πολὺ πλείων ἐλπίς ἐστιν ἕτερον ἀποστῆναι πρὶν ἐκεῖνον ἐκπολιορκηθῆναι· τοιαῦται βραδυτῆτες ἐν ταῖς 142 πράξεσι ταῖς βασιλέως ἔνεισιν. ἐν δὲ τῷ πολέμῳ τῷ περὶ Ῥόδον ἔχων μὲν τοὺς Λακεδαιμονίων συμμάχους εὔνους διὰ τὴν χαλεπότητα τῶν πολιτειῶν, χρώμενος δὲ ταῖς ὑπηρε- b σίαις ταῖς παρ' ἡμῶν, στρατηγοῦντος δ' αὐτῷ Κόνωνος, ὃς ἦν ἐπιμελέστατος μὲν τῶν στρατηγῶν, πιστότατος δὲ τοῖς Ἕλλησιν, ἐμπειρότατος δὲ τῶν πρὸς τὸν πόλεμον κινδύνων, τοιοῦτον λαβὼν συναγωνιστὴν τρία μὲν ἔτη περιεῖδε τὸ ναυτικὸν τὸ προκινδυνεῦον ὑπὲρ τῆς Ἀσίας ὑπὸ τριήρων ἑκατὸν μόνων πολιορκούμενον, πεντεκαίδεκα δὲ μηνῶν τοὺς στρατιώτας τὸν μισθὸν ἀπεστέρησεν, ὥστε τὸ μὲν ἐπ' ἐκείνῳ πολλάκις ἂν διελύθησαν, διὰ δὲ τὸν ἐφεστῶτα κίνδυνον καὶ τὴν συμμαχίαν τὴν περὶ Κόρινθον συστᾶσαν c

εἰ δὲ δεῖ κ.τ.λ.] ad Dem. § 34. and Andoc. de Pace (delivered 391 B.C.), § 2, χρὴ γάρ, ὦ Ἀθηναῖοι, τεκμηρίοις χρῆσθαι τοῖς πρότερον γενομένοις περὶ τῶν μελλόντων ἔσεσθαι. Clement of Alex. Strom. VI. 747 (quoted by Coray), accuses Andocides of plagiarism from Isocrates! Although this is impossible, it does not follow that the converse is true, as the sentiment is too common-place to belong to one man more than another. Sophocles has already said the same thing in Oed. Tyr. 915, ἀνὴρ ἔννουν τὰ καινὰ τοῖς πάλαι τεκμαίρεται (Cor. Isocr. II. p. 51).

ἐλπίς ἐστιν ἀποστῆναι.] For the aor. after ἐλπίζω, ἐλπίς ἐστιν, &c. cf. Euthyn. § 15, ἐλπίζειν πράξασθαι, ad Dem. § 24, ἐλπίζε...γενέσθαι, Paneg. § 59, βιάσασθαι προσδοκήσας, &c. v. Madv. Synt. § 172 a, R. or Goodwin's Gk. Moods and Tenses, § 23. 2. n. 2.

βραδυτῆτες.] Dem. de Cor. § 246, τὰς ἑκασταχοῦ βραδυτῆτας δεινοὺς ἀγγελίας φιλοτιμίας.—v. p. 50, col. 2. n.

142. τῷ πολέμῳ τῷ περὶ Ῥόδον.] The war between Persia and Sparta

that ended in the battle of Cnidus, 394 B.C. Phil. § 63, συντάττοι γὰρ αὐτῷ ναυτικοῦ περὶ Ῥόδον καὶ νικήσας (sc. Conon) τῇ ναυμαχίᾳ Λακεδαιμονίους μὲν ἐξέβαλεν ἐκ τῆς ἀρχῆς, τοὺς δ' Ἕλληνας ἠλευθέρωσεν κ.τ.λ. and Evag. §§ 53—6. Also Xen. Hdl. IV. 3. 6.

τὴν χαλεπότητα κ.τ.λ.] v. §§ 110 —114.

Κόνωνος.] Cf. § 135, πρὸς ἡμᾶς. n., Epp. VIII. 8, Areop. §§ 12, 61, Panath. § 105, Dem. Lept. p. 477, §§ 68—70. [The cod. Ambr. alone has Κόνωνος, the cod. Urb. Κόνωσι, and the rest Κίμωνι!]

Isocr. frequently mentions Conon; and Timotheus, the son of Conon, himself a distinguished general, was one of the pupils of Isocr. A long parenthetical eulogy of the son is contained in de Perm. §§ 107—139. Photius preserves a tradition that Isocr. attended Timotheus on his military expeditions, and received a talent (£243) for writing his despatches.

τρία...ἔτη.] 396—394 B.C.

τὴν συμμαχίαν τὴν περὶ Κόρινθον.] The alliance of Argos, Athens,

143 μόλις ναυμαχοῦντες ἐνίκησαν. καὶ ταῦτ᾽ ἐστὶ τὰ βασιλι-
κώτατα καὶ σεμνότατα τῶν ἐκείνῳ πεπραγμένων, καὶ περὶ
ὧν οὐδέποτε παύονται λέγοντες οἱ βουλόμενοι τὰ τῶν βαρβάρων μεγάλα ποιεῖν. (μʹ.) Ὥστ᾽ οὐδεὶς ἂν ἔχοι τοῦτ᾽
εἰπεῖν, ὡς οὐ δικαίως χρῶμαι τοῖς παραδείγμασιν, οὐδ᾽ ὡς
ἐπὶ μικροῖς διατρίβω τὰς μεγίστας τῶν πράξεων παραλεί-
144 πων· φεύγων γὰρ ταύτην τὴν αἰτίαν τὰ κάλλιστα τῶν d
ἔργων διῆλθον, οὐκ ἀμνημονῶν οὐδ᾽ ἐκείνων, ὅτι Δερκυλίδας
μὲν χιλίους ἔχων ὁπλίτας τῆς Αἰολίδος ἐπῆρξε, Δράκων δ᾽
Ἀταρνέα καταλαβὼν καὶ τρισχιλίους πελταστὰς συλλέξας
τὸ Μύσιον πεδίον ἀνάστατον ἐποίησε, Θίβρων δ᾽ ὀλίγῳ

Thebes, and Euboea with Corinth, against Sparta. Corinth was the σύνδρομον of the allies. (Xen. *Hell.* IV. 4. 1 and Diodor. XIV. 82.)

μόλις...ἐνίκησαν.] This depreciatory statement is not borne out by Xen. *l.c.* 3. 12, and is only partially supported by Diodor. *l.c.* 83 *ad fin.*

143. περὶ ὧν.] Dionysius Halic. (*Judicium de Isocrate*) tells us that Isocr. avoids *hiatus* as far as possible. His actual words are these. τῶν φωνηέντων τὰς παραλλήλους θέσεις, ὡς λυπούσας τὰς ἁρμονίας τῶν ἤχων καὶ τὴν λειότητα τῶν φθόγγων λυμαινομένας, παραιτεῖται. The word παραιτεῖται (*lit.* 'deprecates') is enough in itself to prepare us for the fact that Isocr. does not *always* avoid *hiatus*.

The present instance is one of those in question: and the cases in which περὶ is found before a vowel in Isocr. are very numerous.

The following list contains most of the admissible collocations:
1. τί ἂν ὅτι ἂν· τί οὖν· ὅτι οὐδέν· and (§ 45) εἴ τι ἄν.
(2) καὶ οὗ· καὶ εἰρήνης· καὶ ἐξήκοντα, &c. (v. § 96. n.)
(3) Indic. in -αι, *e.g.* βούλομαι οὖν· δέομαι οὖν· (In such cases Bens. prints δ᾽ οὖν instead of the MS reading.)
(4) ὁπότεροι ἄν.
II. πολὺ ἄν· πολλοῦ ἄν· III. ὦ

ἄνδρες· ὦ Ἀρχίδαμε· IV. πρὸ, not seldom before a, ε, η, *e.g.* πρὸ αὐτῶν. πρὸ ἐμοῦ· πρὸ ἡμῶν.

In all the above instances, except I. (3), care has been taken to avoid all passages in which Benseler has removed the *hiatus*. The fact that there are many passages in which alteration is impossible raises considerable doubts as to the propriety of altering the MS reading where such alteration is possible.

η seldom forms a *hiatus* which cannot easily be explained by *crasis* or *prodelision*, *e.g.* μὴ οὐ· ἢ ᾽γώ.

ο in the terminations of verbs and in τοῦτο· ἐκεῖνο· ὑπὸ· and ἄ as in πολλά· ταῦτα· ποιούμεθα and especially ε, may almost always be elided. (v. Bremi's Isocr. *exc.* XI.)

διατρίβω.] § 41, διατρίβῃς. n.

144. Δερκυλίδας κ.τ.λ.] Successor of Thimbron in 399 B.C. Described by Xen. *Hell.* III. 1, 8 as μάλα μηχανητικός, ἐπεκαλεῖτο δὲ Σίσυφος. *ib.* 3, 1, λαβὼν ἐν ὀκτὼ ἡμέραις ἐννέα πόλεις. v. Xen. *Hell.* III. IV. passim.

Δράκων κ.τ.λ.] 398 B.C. Xen. *l.c.* III. 2, 11. Dercylidas captured Atarneus (in Mysia), and appointed Dracon harmost (καταστήσας Δράκοντα Πελληνέα ἐπιμελήτην).

Θίβρων.] 400 B.C. Xen. *l.c.* III. 1, 4. The name Θίβρων is sometimes spelt Θίμβρων. Cf. ἄβροτος and ἄμ-

πλείους τούτων διαβιβάσας τὴν Λυδίαν ἄπασαν ἐπόρθησεν.
Ἀγησίλαος δὲ τῷ Κυρείῳ στρατεύματι χρώμενος μικροῦ
145 δεῖν τῆς ἐντὸς Ἅλυος χώρας ἐκράτησεν. καὶ μὴν οὐδὲ τὴν e
στρατιὰν τὴν μετὰ τοῦ βασιλέως περιπολοῦσαν, οὐδὲ τὴν
Περσῶν ἀνδρίαν ἄξιον φοβηθῆναι· καὶ γὰρ ἐκεῖνοι φανερῶς ἐπεδείχθησαν ὑπὸ τῶν Κύρῳ συναναβάντων οὐδὲν
βελτίους ὄντες τῶν ἐπὶ θαλάττῃ. τὰς μὲν γὰρ ἄλλας μάχας 71
ὅσας ἡττήθησαν ἐῶ, καὶ τίθημι στασιάζειν αὐτοὺς καὶ μὴ
βούλεσθαι προθύμως πρὸς τὸν ἀδελφὸν τὸν βασιλέως δια-
146 κινδυνεύειν. ἀλλ᾽ ἐπειδὴ Κύρου τελευτήσαντος συνῆλθον
ἅπαντες οἱ τὴν Ἀσίαν κατοικοῦντες, ἐν τούτοις τοῖς καιροῖς
οὕτως αἰσχρῶς ἐπολέμησαν ὥστε μηδένα λόγον ὑπολιπεῖν
τοῖς εἰθισμένοις τὴν Περσῶν ἀνδρίαν ἐπαινεῖν. λαβόντες
γὰρ ἑξακισχιλίους τῶν Ἑλλήνων οὐκ ἀριστίνδην ἐπειλεγ- b

βρωτοι, λαβεῖν, and λαμβάνω, λάβδα
and λάμβδα.

Ἀγησίλαος.] 395 B.C. Xen. l. c.
III. 4. 20.

μικροῦ δεῖν.] Madv. Synt. § 168 b.

Ἅλυος.] The river Halys is often
mentioned as a geographical boundary; e.g. (Oracle ap. Diodor. IX.
41), Κροῖσος Ἅλυν διαβὰς μεγάλην
ἀ. χὴν καταλύσει. (Cf. Strabo, XII.
534, XVII. 840.)

145. μετὰ τοῦ βασιλέως.] This is
the reading of Codd. Urb. and Ambr.
The following is Benseler's canon
with regard to the omission or insertion of the article before βασιλεύς,
when the king of Persia is meant:
Βασιλεὺς ab Isocrate et sine articulo
scriptum, ubi rex Persarum in uni-
versum, non certus certoque nomine
appellatus intelligitur, ut eodem jure
ibi regnum Persicum scribi possit.
Hic est de eo Persarum exercitu
sermo, qui ipsum Persicum regem,
non solum Persicum regnum tuetur.

τὸν Κύρῳ συναναβάντων.] The
Ten Thousand Greeks. Their march
up-country (ἀνάβασις) began before
midsummer, 401 B.C.; the battle of
Cunaxa (in which Cyrus himself was
slain, although his army was victorious) took place in the autumn of

ISOC.

the same year; and after an admirably conducted retreat, through Ar-
menia, &c., they took shipping at
Cotyora, on the Euxine, 8 months
after the battle, and finally, in the
spring of 399, the remnant of the
army of Cyrus was incorporated in
the forces of Thimbron.

τίθημι στασιάζειν κ.τ.λ] i.e. 'I
assume that it was a mere party-
question, and that they were unwilling to fight it out with spirit
against the brother of the great
king.'

τίθημι] = I suppose, put the case;
cf. de Pern. § 94, πρὸς οὒς οὕτως
βούλεσθε θεῖτε με διακεῖσθαι, Dem.
Lept. § 21, &c. Similarly pono in
Lat.; e.g. Ter. Ph. 4. 3. 23, verum
pone esse victum eum.

στασιάζειν.] (a quasi-impf. infin.)
v. Goodwin, Gk. Moods and Tenses,
§ 15. 3.

τὸν ἀδελφὸν τὸν βασιλέως.] Xen.
Anab. init. Δαρείου καὶ Παρυσάτιδος
γίγνονται παῖδες δύο· πρεσβύτερος
μὲν Ἀρταξέρξης, νεώτερος δὲ Κῦρος.

146. τελευτήσαντος.] Xen. Anab.
I. 8. 19.

ἑξακισχιλίους.] The number of
hoplites and peltasts reviewed at
Cerasus was 8600 (Xen. l.c. V. 3. 3),

9

μένους, ἀλλ' οἳ διὰ φαυλότητας ἐν ταῖς αὑτῶν οὐχ οἷοί τ'
ἦσαν ζῆν, ἀπείρους μὲν τῆς χώρας ὄντας, ἐρήμους δὲ συμμάχων γεγενημένους, προδεδομένους δ' ὑπὸ τῶν συναναβάντων, ἀπεστερημένους δὲ τοῦ στρατηγοῦ, μεθ' οὗ συνηκο-
147 λούθησαν, τοσοῦτον αὐτῶν ἥττους ἦσαν, ὥσθ' ὁ βασιλεὺς
ἀπορήσας τοῖς παροῦσι πράγμασι καὶ καταφρονήσας τῆς
περὶ αὐτὸν δυνάμεως τοὺς ἄρχοντας τοὺς τῶν ἐπικούρων
ὑποσπόνδους συλλαβεῖν ἐτόλμησεν, ὡς εἰ τοῦτο παρανο- c
μήσειε συνταράξων τὸ στρατόπεδον, καὶ μᾶλλον εἵλετο

the number at Heraclea (ib. VI. 3.
16) was 8140; at the time which
Isocr. is describing the number must
have been greater, nevertheless he
mentions only 6000. The discrepancy may be explained, I think,
by supposing that Isocr. is confound-
ing the remnant of 6000 that served
under Seuthes (ib. VII. 7. 23) with
the original remnant immediately
after the battle of Cunaxa.

ἀριστίνδην.] 'According to worth.'
For similar adverbs in -δην v. § 39. n.

ἐπαλεγμένους.] The reading of
Cod. Ambr. is ἐπιλελεγμένους; that
of Cod. Urb. ἐπειλεγμένους. The
latter is called by Veitch (Gk. Vbs.
s. v. λέγω) the 'more Attic' form,
and has better MS authority.

φαυλότητας.] 'Humble condition,' their poverty and debased
position. (v. Phil. § 120.) Benseler
(trans. p. 233) condemns the version
'propter nequitiam' (Battie &c.).

προδεδομένους ὑπὸ τῶν συνανα-
βάντων.] i. e. Betrayed by Ariaeus
and his Persian troops. Xen. Anab.
I. 8. 5, II. 2. 8, 4. 1, 2, and esp. III.
I. 2, προὐδεδώκεισαν αὐτοὺς καὶ οἱ σὺν
Κύρῳ ἀναβάντες βάρβαροι.

ἀπεστερημένους κ.τ.λ.] 'Deprived
of the general, with whom they had
marched,' i.e. not Clearchus, but
Cyrus.

For the phraseology cf. Plat. Rep.
464 A, μετὰ τούτου...ξυνακολου-
θεῖν τὰς τε ἡδονὰς καὶ τὰς λύπας
ἁπάσῃ, Isocr. Plataic. § 15, and Dem.
Androt. p. 608, § 49. Phrynichus
(fl. 180 A.D.), p. 353, ed. Lobeck,

criticises Lysias for using the construction τὸν παῖδα τὸν ἀκολουθοῦντα
μετ' αὐτοῦ, and says that Lysias
ought to have used the simple dative
αὐτῷ. Coray's note on the dictum
of this late lexicographer is worth
quoting: πότερον οὖν, ὦ φίλα μειρα-
κύλλια, ὅσοι περὶ τὴν Ἑλλάδα πο-
τεῖσθε φωνῆς, Λυσίαν τε καὶ Ἰσοκρά-
την ἁμαρτάνειν ὑπολήπτέον, ἢ Φρύνιχον; ἐγὼ μὲν οἶμαι Φρύνιχον, εἰ μὴ
μαίνομαί γε.

συνακολουθεῖν μετά τινος contains
the idea of union repeated thrice
over, first in μετά, secondly in συν-,
and lastly in the prefix of ἀ-κολουθεῖν.
(From ἀκόλουθον, a copulativum and
κέλευθος, cf., for the vowel-change,
εἰλήλουθα and ἐλεύσομαι.)

Plato (Cratylus, 405 C, D) gives an
unusually correct account of the
derivation of the word, τὸ ἄλφα ση-
μαίνει πολλαχοῦ τὸ ὁμοῦ...τὸν ὁμοκέ-
λευθον καὶ ὁμόκοιτιν ἀκόλουθον καὶ
ἄκοιτιν ἐκαλέσαμεν, but it was reserved for modern Philology to
connect the prefix in ἀδελφός, ἄκοι-
τις, and ἀκόλουθος, with the Sanskrit
prefix sa- in words like satirtha (a
school-fellow), sagara (a brother),
&c.

147. τοὺς ἄρχοντας.] sc. 'Πρό-
ξενοι Βοιώτιοι, Μένων Θετταλός,
Ἀγίας Ἀρκάς, Κλέαρχος Λάκων,
Σωκράτης Ἀχαιός.' (Anab. II. 5. 31).
οἱ μὲν δὴ στρατηγοὶ οὕτω ληφθέντες
ἀνήχθησαν ὡς βασιλέα καὶ ἀποτμη-
θέντες τὰς κεφαλὰς ἐτελεύτησαν. (ib.
6. 1.)

καὶ μᾶλλον—διαγωνίσασθαι.] In

περὶ τοὺς θεοὺς ἐξαμαρτεῖν ἢ πρὸς ἐκείνους ἐκ τοῦ φανεροῦ
148 διαγωνίσασθαι. διαμαρτὼν δὲ τῆς ἐπιβουλῆς καὶ τῶν στρα-
τιωτῶν συμμεινάντων καὶ καλῶς ἐνεγκόντων τὴν συμφοράν,
ἀπιοῦσιν αὐτοῖς Τισσαφέρνην καὶ τοὺς ἱππέας συνέπεμψεν,
ὑφ' ὧν ἐκεῖνοι παρὰ πᾶσαν ἐπιβουλευόμενοι τὴν ὁδὸν ὁμοίως
διεπορεύθησαν ὥσπερ ἂν εἰ προπεμπόμενοι, μάλιστα μὲν
φοβούμενοι τὴν ἀοίκητον τῆς χώρας, μέγιστον δὲ τῶν ἀγα- d
θῶν νομίζοντες, εἰ τῶν πολεμίων ὡς πλείστοις ἐντύχοιεν.
149 κεφάλαιον δὲ τῶν εἰρημένων ἐκεῖνοι γὰρ οὐκ ἐπὶ λείαν
ἐλθόντες, οὐδὲ κώμην καταλαβόντες ἀλλ' ἐπ' αὐτὸν τὸν
βασιλέα στρατεύσαντες, ἀσφαλέστερον κατέβησαν τῶν
περὶ φιλίας ὡς αὐτὸν πρεσβευόντων. ὥστε μοι δοκοῦσιν
ἐν ἅπασι τοῖς τόποις σαφῶς ἐπιδεδεῖχθαι τὴν αὐτῶν μαλα-
κίαν· καὶ γὰρ ἐν τῇ παραλίᾳ τῆς Ἀσίας πολλὰς μάχας c
ἥττηνται, καὶ διαβάντες εἰς τὴν Εὐρώπην δίκην ἔδοσαν, οἱ
μὲν γὰρ αὐτῶν κακῶς ὑπώλοντο, οἱ δ' αἰσχρῶς ἐσώθησαν,

a similar summary of the Ἀνάβασις
(*Phil.* §§ 90—93) Isocr. repeats these
words almost *verbatim*. The quotation is followed by a curious
apology, which concludes with these
words: τοῖς μὲν οὖν οἰκείοις τυχὸν ἂν
χρησαίμην, ἣν σφόδρα κατεπείγῃ καὶ
πρέπῃ, τῶν δ' ἀλλοτρίων οὐδὲν ἂν
προσδεξαίμην, ὥσπερ οὐδ' ἐν τῷ παρ-
ελθόντι χρόνῳ. (v. § 158. n.)

ἐκ τοῦ φανεροῦ.] Cf. § 13, ἐξ
ὑπογυίου. n.

148. ἐπιβουλῆς.] 'Design.' This is
the reading of most of the MSS, the
Cod. Urb. alone has ἐπιβολῆς, 'attack.' The sense is greatly in favour
of the other MSS. It is not true
that Artaxerxes has failed in his
attack; thanks to treachery, he had
been singularly successful; he had
failed in his object, design, ἐπιβουλή.
The use of ἐπιβολὴ in almost the
same sense as ἐπιβουλὴ is confined
to late authors; Polybius, Plutarch,
and Diodorus : *e.g.* in Diodor. XIII.
47, τοὺς ἐξ ἐπιβολῆς ἀδικήσαντας)(τοὺς
ἀκουσίως ἐξαμαρτάνοντας. In Thuc.
III. 45. 5, τὴν ἐπιβολὴν ἀφροντίζων
means '*planning the attack.*'

Τισσαφέρνην κ. τ. λ.] v. Xen.
Anab. II. 4. 9 (even *before* the capture of the generals) Τισσαφέρνους
ἡγουμένου...ἐπορεύοντο.

ὥσπερ ἄν.] sc. διεπορεύθησαν,
§ 69. n.

τὴν ἀοίκητον τῆς χώρας.] § 34,
τὴν πλείστην τῆς χώρας. n.

149. ἐκεῖνοι γάρ.] § 87, σημεῖον
δὲ...τοὺς μὲν γάρ. n.

ἐπὶ λείαν.] Codd. Urb. and Ambr.
ἐπὶ λείαν, Vict. ἐπὶ λίαν, other MSS
ἐπιμελείαν. Wolf and Lange have
ἐπὶ μὲν λείαν, and Coray conjectures
ἐπὶ Μυσῶν λείαν. The reading
adopted in the text forms the nearest approach to that of the two best
MSS, and is accepted by BS and
Bens.

δοκοῦσιν.] sc. οἱ Πέρσαι.

ἐν τῇ παραλίᾳ—ἥττηνται.] §§
140—144.

διαβάντες—ἔδοσαν.] §§ 85—98,
§ 117.

οἱ μὲν γὰρ—ἐσώθησαν.] Quoted
by Ar. *Rhet.* III. 9 as an instance of
ἀντικειμένη λέξις. v. § 35, ἀμφοτέρους—ἐπόρισαν. n.

καὶ τελευτῶντες ὑπ' αὐτοῖς τοῖς βασιλείοις καταγέλαστοι
γεγόνασιν.

150   (μα'.) Καὶ τούτων οὐδὲν ἀλόγως γέγονεν, ἀλλὰ πάντ' 71
εἰκότως ἀποβέβηκεν· οὐ γὰρ οἷόν τε τοὺς οὕτω τρεφομένους καὶ πολιτευομένους οὔτε τῆς ἄλλης ἀρετῆς μετέχειν
οὔτ' ἐν ταῖς μάχαις τρόπαιον ἱστάναι τῶν πολεμίων. πῶς
γὰρ ἐν τοῖς ἐκείνων ἐπιτηδεύμασιν ἐγγενέσθαι δύναιτ' ἂν
ἢ στρατηγὸς δεινὸς ἢ στρατιώτης ἀγαθός, ὧν τὸ μὲν πλεῖ-
στόν ἐστιν ὄχλος ἄτακτος καὶ κινδύνων ἄπειρος, πρὸς μὲν
τὸν πόλεμον ἐκλελυμένος, πρὸς δὲ τὴν δουλείαν ἄμεινον τῶν b
παρ' ἡμῖν οἰκετῶν πεπαιδευμένος. οἱ δ' ἐν ταῖς μεγίσταις
151   δόξαις ὄντες αὐτῶν ὁμαλῶς μὲν οὐδὲ κοινῶς οὐδὲ πολιτικῶς

τελευτῶντε.] 'Lastly, *i.e.* as a climax.' (§ 140, τελευτῶντες n.) In the present passage the idea of *time* must be carefully excluded, as the battle of Cunaxa, to which reference is here made, took place *before* the events recorded in §§ 140—141.

ὑπ' αὐτοῖς τοῖς βασιλείοις κ.τ.λ.] Cf. *Evag.* § 58, and Xen. *Anab.* II. 4. 4, οὐ γὰρ ποτε ἐκεῖ γε βουλήσεται (*sc.* βασιλεύς), ἡμᾶς ἐλθόντας εἰς τὴν Ἑλλάδα ἀπαγγεῖλαι ὡς ἡμεῖς τοσαῖδε ὄντες ἐνικῶμεν βασιλέα ἐπὶ ταῖς θύραις αὐτοῦ καὶ καταγελάσαντες ἀπήλθομεν.

Xenophon (who does not mention the name Cunaxa) was informed that the field of battle lay 360 *stadia* (about 41 miles) from Babylon. Plutarch (to whom we owe the name of the battle) states (*vit. Artax.* 8) that Cunaxa was 500 *stadia* (about 58 miles) distant.

καταγέλαστοι γγγ.] lit. 'Have become ridiculous.' Obs. the distinction between καταγέλαστος (the butt of wit, the laughing-stock) and ὁ γελοῖος (the humorist). Plat. *Symp.* 189 B, φοβοῦμαι οὖ τι μὴ γελοῖα ἀλλὰ μὴ καταγέλαστα εἴπω. Both the ideas are combined in the Lat. 'ridiculus,' which is applicable not only to one who is 'witty himself,' but also to one who is 'the cause of wit in others.' When Cicero, in the speech *pro Murena*, was bantering Cato, the

latter made to the bye-standers the double-edged remark, 'Quam ridiculum consulem habemus,' for such must have been the original form of the sentence that appears in Plut. *Cat.* 21, ὡς γελοῖον ὕπατον ἔχομεν.

150. δεινόs.] 'Able,' 'skilful,' &c.; the idea of terror (δέος) is here, as often, entirely lost. In Plat. *Protag.* 341 A, B, we find that Prodicus protested against the use of the word in this secondary meaning. περὶ τοῦ δεινοῦ Πρόδικός με οὑτοσὶ νουθετεῖ ἑκάστοτε, ὅταν ἐπαινῶν ἐγὼ ἢ σὲ ἢ ἄλλον τινὰ λέγω, ὅτι Πρωταγόρας σοφὸς καὶ δεινός ἐστιν ἀνήρ, ἐρωτᾷ, εἰ οὐκ αἰσχύνομαι τἀγαθὰ δεινὰ καλῶν, τὸ γὰρ δεινόν, φησί, κακόν ἐστιν· οὐδεὶς γοῦν λέγει ἑκάστοτε δεινοῦ πλούτου οὐδὲ δεινῆς εἰρήνης οὐδὲ δεινῆς ὑγιείας, ἀλλὰ δεινῆς νόσου καὶ δεινοῦ πολέμου καὶ δεινῆς πενίας, ὡς τοῦ δεινοῦ κακοῦ ὄντος.

151. αὐτῶν.] The insertion of this word is not necessary as ὧν has already been used at the beginning of the former clause, but it adds to the perspicuity of the sentence. This addition of the demonstrative or personal pron. is most common when a *different* case to that of the relative pron. is required (v. Madv. *Synt.* § 104 B), but is also found when the two cases are identical, as here. Cf. Weber's n. on Dem. *Aristocr.* § 111, ᾧ ἔλυσιτέλει...καὶ...αἱρετώτερον

οὐδεπώποτ' ἐβίωσαν, ἅπαντα δὲ τὸν χρόνον διάγουσιν εἰς
μὲν τοὺς ὑβρίζοντες, τοῖς δὲ δουλεύοντες, ὡς ἂν ἄνθρωποι
μάλιστα τὰς φύσεις διαφθαρεῖεν, καὶ τὰ μὲν σώματα διὰ
τοὺς πλούτους τρυφῶντες, τὰς δὲ ψυχὰς διὰ τὰς μοναρχίας

ἦν αὐτῷ, 'A pronomine relativo de-
flectit constructio alterius membri ad
demonstrativum. Proprin est enim
Graecorum indoles liberius loquendi
et ad directam orationem transcundi
&c.' This constr. must not be confounded with the Hebraisms of the
Septuagint and Gk. Test. e.g. Joshua
iii. 4, τὴν ὁδὸν ἣν πορεύεσθε αὐτήν,
and Mark vii. 25, where the demonstrative is repeated in the same clause
as the rel. (v. Winer's N. T. Gram.
P. III. § 22, 4); a constr. which has
perhaps no examples in Classical Gk.
['Soph. Phil. 316, οἷς...αὐτοῖς is not
an instance. αὐτοῖς must there mean
ipsis, in spite of Hermann's objections. v. ib. 275.' R. S.]

ὁμαλῶς—ἐβίωσαν.] The negative
οὐδεπώποτε influences ὁμαλῶς, and
also intensifies the negatives οὐδὲ κοινῶς οὐδὲ πολιτικῶς. Cf. Dem. Androt.
§ 4, οὗτοι ἁπλοῦν μὲν οὐδὲ δίκαιον
οὐδὲν ἂν εἰπεῖν ἔχοι, Thuc. VI. 55. 2,
στήλη..., ἐν ᾗ Θεσσαλοῦ μὲν οὐδ' Ἱπ-
πάρχου οὐδεὶς ταῖς γέγραπται, Hdt.
I. 215, σιδήρῳ δὲ οὐδ' ἀργύρῳ χρέωνται
οὐδέν, and ib. II. 52, ἐπωνυμίην δ' οὐδὲ
οὔνομα ἐποιεῦντο οὐδενὶ αὐτέων (quoted
by Rauchenst. and Schneider).

ὁμαλῶς.] 'Evenly,' 'equably.'
The meaning is exactly explained
by the immediate context: εἰς τοὺς
μὲν ὑβρίζοντες, τοῖς δὲ δουλεύοντες, and
(in § 152) τὰ μὲν ταπεινῶς, τὰ δὲ
ὑπερηφάνως ζῶντες. Throughout the
passage there is an evident contrast
intended between Athenian democracy and Oriental despotism, the
equality of rights, enjoyed under the
former, and the inequality that resulted from the various gradations
of rank in the latter. Under the
dominion of Persia, while the majority (τὸ πλεῖστον) were levelled to
an abject slavery, the higher classes
were at once the victims and the
agents of oppression, and had never

experienced the equality, the social
feeling, the loyalty of the Athenian
citizen.—A confirmation of this view
of the meaning of ὁμαλῶς κ.τ.λ. may
be found in the Menexenus of Plato
238 E (which Isocr. may have actually read during the composition of the
Paneg.)—Αἰτία δὲ ἡμῖν τῆς πολιτείας
ταύτης ἡ ἐξ ἴσου γένεσις. Αἱ μὲν γὰρ
ἄλλαι πόλεις ἐκ παντοδαπῶν κατε-
σκευασμέναι ἀνθρώπων εἰσὶ καὶ ἀνω-
μάλων, ὥστε αὐτῶν ἀνώμαλοι καὶ αἱ
πολιτεῖαι, τυραννίδες τε καὶ ὀλιγαρ-
χίαι.

The meaning 'contentedly' given
to ὁμαλῶς in this passage by Lidd.
and Scott is somewhat unsatisfactory.

Ilenseler refuses to allow οὐδέποτε
to influence ὁμαλῶς, and holds that
if Isocr. had intended that meaning,
he would have written οὐδ' or οὐχ
ὁμαλῶς. He takes ὁμαλῶς as a contrast to ὄχλοι ἄτακτοι and translates
thus: und da die, welche bei ihnen
in dem grössten Ansehen stehen, zwar
in einer gewissen Gleichmässigkeit,
aber nie voll eines gemeinschaftlichen
Strebens oder patriotischen Sinnes
gelebt haben. But this sense would
almost require ὁμαλῶς μὲν ἀλλ' οὐ
κοινῶς κ.τ.λ.

ἐβίωσαν.] This is the second aor.
of a somewhat rare present βιόω,
formed on the model of the ordinary
verbs in -μι, with this difference that
βίθωμι has ἔβωσαν with a short penult., but βιόω has ἐβίωσαν (cf. ἔγνω-
σαν· ἑάλωσαν) with a long penult.
ἐβίω occurs in Evag. § 71. The first
aor. ἐβίωσα is extremely rare. (v.
Veitch, Gk. Verbs, s. v. βιόω and ζάω,
and Cobet, nov. lect. 576).

τὰ μὲν σώματα κ.τ.λ.] In Phil.
§ 124 the βάρβαροι are spoken of as
μαλακοὶ καὶ πολέμων ἄπειροι καὶ δια-
φθαρμένοι ὑπὸ τῆς τρυφῆς.

πλούτους.] This pl. is not very
common; it occurs however in § 182,

ταπεινὰς καὶ περιδεεῖς ἔχοντες, ἐξεταζόμενοι πρὸς αὐτοῖς
τοῖς βασιλείοις καὶ προκαλινδούμενοι καὶ πάντα τρόπον c
μικρὸν φρονεῖν μελετῶντες, θνητὸν μὲν ἄνδρα προσκυνοῦντες καὶ δαίμονα προσαγορεύοντες, τῶν δὲ θεῶν μᾶλλον ἢ
152 τῶν ἀνθρώπων ὀλιγωροῦντες. τοιγαροῦν οἱ καταβαίνοντες
αὑτῶν ἐπὶ θάλατταν, οὓς καλοῦσι σατράπας, οὐ καταισχύ-

a:l *Nicocl.* § 5, *de Pace*, § 6, 117,
Panath. § 196. The blunder which
has made the word 'riches' (*richesse*)
plural in English, enables us to
render it adequately in every case.

ἐξεταζόμενοι.] lit. 'being exa-
mined,' 'appearing on muster or
parade, being drilled and reviewed.'
The word is here used to express
the stiff formalities of attendance on
the King's court. v. Xen. *Cyrop.*
VIII. 1. 6.—For the corresponding
subst. ἐξέτασις, cf. *Areop.* § 82, τῶν
περὶ τὸν πόλεμον οὕτω πατημμελήκαμεν,
ὥστ᾽ οὐδ᾽ εἰς ἐξετάσεις ἰέναι τολμῶ-
μεν, ἢν μὴ λαμβάνωμεν ἀργύριον.

In Dobree's *Adversaria* we have
this n. '*utcunque intelligas,* drilled,
trained (to servitude), *sed vide an
haec transponenda* (71 E), καὶ τελευτῶντες ἐξεταζόμενοι πρὸ αὐτοῖς ταῖς
βασιλείοις, καταγέλαστα γεγόνασιν,
*ut pugnam ad Cunaxam pompam
fuisse meram dicat:*' and Dobree's
transl., whatever may be said of the
rest of his n., is certainly better than
the tame rendering '*ante palatium
inveniuntur i. e. versantur*' given by
Morus at the end of a long note on
the meaning of ἐξετάζεσθαι.

προκαλινδούμενοι.] 'Προσκυλίνδομαι
et προκαλινδοῦμαι *sic differunt, ut hoc
adulantis sit et adorantis, illud sup-
plicis.*'—*Attici aut* κυλίνδω *et* κυλίν-
δομαι *aut* καλινδοῦμαι *disissevidentur:
sequiores* κυλινδῶ *et* κυλινδοῦμαι *usurpabant.*' Cobet, *nov. lect.* pp. 639,
637.
Cf. Xen. *Cyrop.* VIII. 3. 14. On
the etiquette observed between different ranks in Persia, v. Hdt. I. 134,
ἢν δὲ πολλῷ ᾖ οὕτεροι ἀγεννέστεροι,
προσείπων προσκυνέει τὸν ἕτερον.
πάντα τρόπον—μελετῶντες.] Quo-

ted by Ar. *Rhet.* III. 10 *fin.* as an
instance of metaphor: τὸ γὰρ μελετᾶν αὔξειν τί ἐστιν
προσκυνοῦντες.] Cf. Nepos, *Co-
non.* 111. 3, *Necesse est, si in conspec-
tum veneris, venerari te regem (quod*
προσκυνεῖν *illi vocant).* Schn.
δαίμονα προσαγορεύοντες.] In
Aesch. *Persae,* 156, the *Chorus* addresses Atossa: μῆτερ ἡ Ξέρξου γε-
ραιά, χαῖρε Δαρείου γύναι· θεοῦ μὲν
εὐνάτειρα Περσῶν, θεοῦ δὲ καὶ μήτηρ
ἔφυς, and Gorgias (quoted by the
author of the treatise περὶ ὕψους,
3. § 2) uses the expr., Ξέρξης ὁ τῶν
Περσῶν Ζεύς.
A fragment of Theopompus (preserved by Athenaeus, *Deipn.* VI. 252,
§ 60) tells us the following story of
the Argive Nicostratus—καθ᾽ ἑκάστην
ἡμέραν, ὁπότε μέλλοι δειπνεῖν, τρά-
πεζαν παρετίθει χωρίς, ὀνομάζων τῷ
δαίμονι τῷ βασιλέως, ἐμπλήσας σίτου
καὶ τῶν ἄλλων ἐπιτηδείων, ἀκούων
μὲν τοῦτο ποιεῖν καὶ τῶν Περσῶν τοὺς
περὶ τὰς θύρας διατρίβοντας, οἰόμενος
δὲ διὰ τῆι θεραπείας ταύτη χρημα-
τιεῖσθαι μᾶλλον παρὰ τοῦ βασιλέως.
προσαγορεύοντες.] v. § 24, προσειπεῖν. n.

151. σατράπας.] *Phil.* § 104, τῶν
ἄλλων σατραπῶν. The derivation of
the word σατράπης has been disputed: Hesychius in his *lex.* s. v.
defines the σατράπαι, as = ἀρχηγοί,
στρατηλάται, and adds Περσικὴ δὲ
ἡ λέξις. He elsewhere records the
form ξατράπης, and there are other
forms besides. In Gesenius (*Thes.
Ling. Hebr.* s. v. אֲחַשְׁדַּרְפְּנִים) and
in Lidd. and Scott it is stated that
the form ἐξατράπης is used by the
historian Theopompus. This state-

νουσι τὴν ἐκεῖ παίδευσιν, ἀλλ' ἐν τοῖς ἤθεσι τοῖς αὐτοῖς
διαμένουσι, πρὸς μὲν τοὺς φίλους ἀπίστως, πρὸς δὲ τοὺς c
ἐχθροὺς ἀνάνδρως ἔχοντες, καὶ τὰ μὲν ταπεινῶς, τὰ δ' ὑπερηφάνως ζῶντες, τῶν μὲν συμμάχων καταφρονοῦντες, τοὺς
153 δὲ πολεμίους θεραπεύοντες. τὴν μέν γε μετ' Ἀγησιλάου
στρατιὰν ὀκτὼ μῆνας ταῖς αὑτῶν δαπάναις διέθρεψαν, τοὺς
δ' ὑπὲρ αὐτῶν κινδυνεύοντας ἑτέρου τοσούτου χρόνου τὸν

ment requires a slight modification : the word 'satrap' occurs once only, as far as I am aware, in the fragments of Theopompus, and that in the summary drawn up by Photius from one of the 180 books read by him on his embassy to Assyria. The passage has been already quoted in § 134. n. One of three MSS of Photius has ἐξατράπην (which is the reading of the old ed. of Stephens), two have σατράπην (which is adopted by Bekker). We cannot therefore be perfectly certain that Photius used the word, much less that he actually found it in Theopompus. It is worth noticing however that the very same MSS that agree in writing σατράπην, also agree elsewhere in an abstract of Arrian (Phot. *Bibl. Cod.* 92. p. 71, 25 Bekker) in the reading τῶν δὲ ἄνω ξατραπειῶν. The existence of the form in ξ is also attested by the safer evidence of ancient inscriptions, (1) An inscr. found at Tralles (in Caria, the hereditary Satrapy of the Hecatomnos mentioned in § 162) which has the words

ΑΡΤΑΣΕΣΣΕΩΒΑΣΙΛΕΥΟΝ
ΤΟΣΕΞΣΑΤΡΑΠΕΥΟΝΤΟΣ
ͰΙΔΡΙΕΩΣ *i. e.* in Attic Gk. Ἀρ-
ταξέρξου βασιλεύοντος, σατραπεύοντος
Ἰδριέως : and (2) three inscriptions (belonging to the years 367, 361 and 355 B.C.) discovered at Mylasa in the same satrapy, which have

ΑΡΤΑΞΕΡΞΕΥΣΒΑΣΙΛΕΥ
ΟΝΤΟΣΜΑΥΣΣΩΛΛΟΥΕΞ
ΑΙΘΡΑΠΕΥΟΝΤΟΣ (The pre-
fixed vowel in ἐξσατραπεύσσοι and

ἐξαθραπεύοντος may be also noticed in the Hebrew form which occurs in *Esther* iii. 12, viii. 9, ix. 3 and *Ezra* viii. 36.)

The form in ξ, the evidence for which has now been stated at length, is important, because it gives us the key to the derivation of the word : ξ corresponds to the Sanskrit *ksh* (cf. δεξιός and *dakshina*, ξυρόν and *kshura* &c.); hence σατράπην or ξατράπην must be *kshatrapa* = *kshatra* (from '*ksh*', 'to govern') + *pa*, 'one who upholds or rather guards the empire.'—The word *kshatrapa* occurs twice in the celebrated Behistun inscription (the record of the exploits of Darius the Great), and *kshatram* is constantly found in the same inscr. in the sense of 'empire.' (Partly from Stephens' *Thesaurus*, new ed. s.v. Böckh's *Corpus Inscr. Gr.* vol. II. p. 584, n. 2919 and p. 470, n. 2691, and Rawlinson's n. on Hdt. I. 192. For the Sanskrit details in this n. I am indebted to Prof. Cowell).

οὐ καταισχύνουσι κ.τ.λ.] *i.e.* Do not disgrace their court-education. For a similarly ironical use, Rauchenst. quotes Dem. *de Cor.* § 261, οὐ κατήσχυνας μὰ Δι' οὐδὲν τῶν προϋπηργμένων τῷ μετὰ ταῦτα βίῳ ('you disgraced not your antecedents by your subsequent life.' *C. R. K.*).

153. Ἀγησιλάου κ.τ.λ.] Xen. *Hell.* III. 4. 26, Τιθραύστης δίδωσι [*sc.* τῷ Ἀγησιλάῳ] τριάκοντα τάλαντα, ὃ δὲ λαβὼν ᾔει ἐπὶ τὴν Φαρναβάζου Φρυγίαν. Plut. *Ages.* 10.

τοὺς...κινδυνεύοντας.] § 142.
ἑτέρου τοσούτου χρόνου.] 'Twice that length of time' or (according to

μισθὸν ἀπεστέρησαν· καὶ τοῖς μὲν Κισθήνην καταλαβοῦσιν
ἑκατὸν τάλαντα διένειμαν, τοὺς δὲ μεθ᾽ αὑτῶν εἰς Κύπρον
154 στρατευσαμένους μᾶλλον ἢ τοὺς αἰχμαλώτους ὕβριζον. ὡς c
δ᾽ ἁπλῶς εἰπεῖν καὶ μὴ καθ᾽ ἓν ἕκαστον ἀλλ᾽ ὡς ἐπὶ τὸ
πολύ, τίς ἢ τῶν πολεμησάντων αὐτοῖς οὐκ εὐδαιμονήσας
ἀπῆλθεν, ἢ τῶν ὑπ᾽ ἐκείνοις γενομένων οὐκ αἰκισθεὶς τὸν
βίον ἐτελεύτησεν; οὐ Κόνωνα μὲν ὃς ὑπὲρ τῆς Ἀσίας 73
στρατηγήσας τὴν ἀρχὴν τὴν Λακεδαιμονίων κατέλυσεν, ἐπὶ
θανάτῳ συλλαβεῖν ἐτόλμησαν, Θεμιστοκλέα δ᾽ ὃς ὑπὲρ τῆς
Ἑλλάδος αὐτοὺς κατεναυμάχησε, τῶν μεγίστων δωρεῶν

§ 142) 15 months. The phrase in itself is ambiguous, and may either mean (1) ' for another space of time equally long' or (2) as here, 'for twice the space of time.' For ἕτερον τοσοῦτον in the first sense, cf. Hdt. II. 149, where we are told of two pyramids standing in the midst of lake Moeris, each, as the context tells us, 100 ὀργυιαί in entire height, τοῦ ὕδατος ὑπερέχουσαι πεντήκοντα ὀργυιὰς ἑκατέρη, καὶ τὸ κατ᾽ ὕδατος οἰκοδόμηται ἕτερον τοσοῦτο.—There is the same ambiguity in Latin. *Alterum tantum* and *majus altero tanto* may be used in the same sense. Cic. *Orat.* 56, § 188, *Omnis (sc. numerus) talis est ut unus sit e tribus. Pes enim, qui adhibetur ad numeros, partitur in tria, ut necesse sit, partem pedis aut aequalem alteri parti, aut altero tanto aut sesqui esse majorem. Inde fit aequalis dactylus, duplex iambas, sesquiplex paean:* (the long syllable of an iambus is *altero tanto major,* twice as long as the short syllable), and Liv. X. 46, *militibus ex praeda centenos binos asses, et* alterum tantum *centurionibus atque equitibus divisit.*

Κισθήνην.] Κισθήνη· Ἰσοκράτης Πανηγυρικῷ. ὄρος τῆς Θρᾴκης. Κρατῖνος ' ξανθὴν δ᾽ ἐπὶ τέρματα γῆς ἥξεις καὶ Κισθήνη ὄρος ὄψει.' Harpocration. (Cf. Aesch. *P. V.* 793, Dindf, Γοργόνεια πεδία Κισθήνης, with Paley's n.) This explanation does not help us much; as the Gorgon-haunted boundary of the world

(which the lexicographer apparently identifies with an unknown mountain of Thrace) is little likely to have been captured by any of the Spartan commanders. Henseler maintains that the place in question may have been in *Bithynian* Thrace, where Dercylidas passed the winter of 399 B.C. (ἀσφαλῶς φέρων καὶ ἄγων τὴν Βιθυνίδα, Xen. *Hell.* III. 2), but it appears equally reasonable to identify it with a town in Aeolis, on the sea-coast of Mysia, north of Atarneus. In Strabo's time the town was deserted (XIII. p. 606), and this fact may account for Harpocration's apparent ignorance of its existence. The capture of Cisthene possibly formed one of the unrecorded exploits of Agesilaus in 395 B.C.

154. ἐπὶ θανάτῳ συλλαβεῖν.] Isocr. only says that Conon was captured with a view to being put to death: Cornel. Nepos, *Con.* 5, 3, tells us that Tiribazus treacherously put Conon into chains, *in quibus aliquamdiu fuit. Inde nonnulli eum ad regem abductum ibique eum periisse scriptum reliquerunt. Contra Dinon Historicus, cui nos plurimum de Persicis rebus credimus,* [fl. c. 360 B.C.] *effugisse scribit.*—Diodor. XV. 43, ὑποπτεύσας ὁ Ἰφικράτης μὴ συλληφθῇ καὶ τιμωρίας τύχῃ καθάπερ Κόνων ἔπαθεν ὁ Ἀθηναῖος.—For the phraseology cf. Hdt. III. 119, συλλαβὼν δὲ σφέας ἔδησε τὴν ἐπὶ θανάτῳ.

κατεναυμάχησε.] *sc.* at Salamis,

155 ἠξίωσαν; καίτοι πῶς χρὴ τὴν τούτων φιλίαν ἀγαπᾶν, οἳ τοὺς
μὲν εὐεργέτας τιμωροῦνται, τοὺς δὲ κακῶς ποιοῦντας οὕτως
ἐπιφανῶς κολακεύουσιν; περὶ τίνας δ' ἡμῶν οὐκ ἐξημαρ-
τήκασιν; ποῖον δὲ χρόνον διαλελοίπασιν ἐπιβουλεύοντες b
τοῖς Ἕλλησιν; τί δ' οὐκ ἐχθρὸν αὐτοῖς ἐστὶ τῶν παρ' ἡμῖν,
οἳ καὶ τὰ τῶν θεῶν ἕδη καὶ τοὺς νεὼς συλᾶν ἐν τῷ προτέρῳ
156 πολέμῳ καὶ κατακάειν ἐτόλμησαν; διὸ καὶ τοὺς Ἴωνας

cf. IIdt. VIII. 75 sqq. and § 98.
ταύτη... αἰτίας, n.

μεγ. δωρεὰν ἠξίωσαν.] sc. the
revenues of Magnesia, Lampsacus,
and Myus, Thuc. I. 138.

155. τοὺς μὲν εὐεργέτας — κολακεύουσιν.] Cf. Panath. § 160.
τὰ τῶν θεῶν ἕδη καὶ τοὺς νεώς.]
'The images and the temples of
the Gods.' ἕδος in Gk. prose means
either (1) 'a statue' or (2) 'a temple.' Timael lex. ἕδος τὸ ἄγαλμα
καὶ ὁ τόπος ἐν ᾧ ἵδρυται. As an
instance of (1) we have Xen. Hell.
I. 4. 5, and Lycurg. Leocr. § 1, τοὺς
νεὼς καὶ τὰ ἕδη καὶ τὰ τεμένη καὶ
τὰς...θυσίας, cf. (1) Plat. Phaedo, III.
B, καὶ δὴ καὶ θεῶν ἕδη τε καὶ ἱερὰ
αὑτοῖς εἶναι ἐν οἷς τῷ ὄντι οἰκηταὶ
θεοὶ εἶναι. In the present passage
(1) is the right meaning. Cf. de
Perm. § 2, τὸ τῆς Ἀθηνᾶς ἕδος where
the context (quoted at length on p.
49) shews that simulacrum is meant.
There is no great objection to (2),
except the fact that this meaning is
not found elsewhere in Isocr. and
the sense gained thereby is slightly
tautological and not very forcible.
(v. however p. 107, col. 2. n.) The
passing suggestion thrown out by
Morus, 'hanc periphrasin templorum
τὰ τῶν θεῶν ἕδη, ad indignationem
augendam facere,' would be pertinent
if the words in question came after
τοὺς νεών.
For the historical fact, cf. Hdt.
VIII. 53 (on the capture of Athens),
τὸ ἱερὸν συλήσαντες, ἐνέπρησαν πᾶσαν
καὶ ἀκρόπολιν, and ib. 144, πολλά τε
γὰρ καὶ μεγάλα ἐστὶ τὰ διακωλύοντα
ταῦτα μὴ ποιεῖν (sc. μηδίσανται κατα-

βουλῶσαι τὴν Ἑλλάδα), μηδ' ἢν ἐθέ-
λωμεν· πρῶτα μὲν καὶ μέγιστα, τῶν
θεῶν τὰ ἀγάλματα καὶ τὰ οἰκή-
ματα ἐμπεπρησμένα τε καὶ συγ-
κεχωσμένα. Aesch. Persae, 809—
812, οὐ θεῶν βρέτη ᾐδοῦντο συλᾶν,
οὐδὲ πιμπράναι νεώς, κ.τ.λ. Also
Panez. § 96.

156. Ἴωνας κ.τ.λ.] The historical allusion to the Ionians presents
some difficulty. After the capture
of Miletus (494 B.C.) the Persians
burnt the great temple of Apollo in
Branchidae, Hdt. VI. 19, ἱρὸν τὸ ἐν
Διδύμοισι, ὁ νηός τε καὶ τὸ χρηστήριον,
συληθέντα ἐνεπίμπρατο. Similarly in
the case of Naxos (ib. 96).—But
neither Herodotus nor Diodorus
nor indeed any one of the historians mentions the imprecation of
which Isocr. speaks. However, in
the speech of Lycurgus in Leocr. §§
80, 81 we read of an oath taken by
the collective allies (Οἱ Ἕλληνες) before the battle of Plataea. The actual words of the oath are recited as
follows: Οὐ ποιήσομαι περὶ πλείονος
τὸ ζῆν τῆς ἐλευθερίας, οὐδὲ κατα-
λείψω τοὺς ἡγεμόνας οὔτε ζῶντας οὔτε
ἀποθανόντας, ἀλλὰ τοὺς ἐν τῇ μάχῃ
τελευτήσαντας τῶν συμμάχων ἅπαντας θάψω· καὶ κρατήσας τῷ πολέμῳ
τοὺς βαρβάρους τῶν μὲν μαχεσαμένων
ὑπὲρ τῆς Ἑλλάδος πόλεων οὐδεμίαν
ἀνάστατον ποιήσω, τὰς δὲ τὰ τοῦ
βαρβάρου προελομένας ἁπάσας δεκα-
τεύσω· καὶ τῶν ἱερῶν τῶν ἐμπρησθέντων καὶ καταβληθέντων ὑπὸ
τῶν βαρβάρων οὐδὲν ἀνοικοδομή-
σω παντάπασιν, ἀλλ' ὑπόμνημα
τοῖς ἐπιγινομένοις ἐάσω κατα-
λείπεσθαι τῆς τῶν βαρβάρων

ἄξιον ἐπαινεῖν, ὅτι τῶν ἐμπρησθέντων ἱερῶν ἐπηράσαντ'
εἴ τινες κινήσειαν ἢ πάλιν εἰς τἀρχαῖα καταστῆσαι βουληθεῖεν, οὐκ ἀποροῦντες, πόθεν ἐπισκευάσωσιν, ἀλλ' ἵν'
ὑπόμνημα τοῖς ἐπιγιγνομένοις ᾖ τῆς τῶν βαρβάρων ἀσε- c
βείας, καὶ μηδεὶς πιστεύῃ τοῖς τοιαῦτ' εἰς τὰ τῶν θεῶν
ἐξαμαρτεῖν τολμῶσιν, ἀλλὰ καὶ φυλάττωνται καὶ δεδίωσιν,

ἀσεβείας. This formula is quoted with a few trifling variations by Diodorus (IX. 29), who states further that the scene of the solemn rehearsal was the isthmus of Corinth. Immediately before quoting the oath, Lycurgus tells us that the oath was framed on the model of the customary Athenian oath (οὐ παρ' αὑτῶν εὑρόντες ἀλλὰ μιμησάμενοι τὸν παρ' ὑμῖν εἰθισμένον ὅρκιν). It will be observed that part of the formula above quoted presents a remarkable parallel to the passage before us. The questions arise: (1) whether the Ionians really uttered the formal Imprecation mentioned in the text, (2) whether the Athenians ever had any customary oath of this nature, (3) whether the collective allies took that oath. While we may answer (1) by a doubtful affirmative, we are almost compelled to answer (2) and (3) in the negative. The oath is probably a mere subsequent development of the short and sensible resolution mentioned in Hdt. VII. 132; and it is a relief to know that Theopompus the pupil of Isocrates, whom we have already (§ 110 n.) quoted as a denouncer of fabrication, asserts that the oath is an Athenian fiction. *Fragm.* 167 (ed. Müller), 'Ελληνικὸν ὅρκον καταψεύδεται, ὃν Ἀθηναῖοί φασιν ὁμόσαι τοὺς Ἕλληνας πρὸ τῆς μάχης τῆς ἐν Πλαταίαις. Pausanias X. (*Phocica*) 35. 2, simply tells us that the Greeks resolved not to set up the temples burnt by the barbarians, but to allow them to remain for all time as τοῦ ἔχθους ὑπομνήματα. He then goes on to say that this was the reason that in

his own time the temples in Haliartus, the temple of Hera on the road from Athens to Phalerum, and the temple of Demeter at Phalerum remained half-burnt.

τῶν ἐμπρησθέντων ἱερῶν.] Lange actually translates these words as *Gen. absol.* This would, of course, require ἐμπρησθέντων τῶν ἱερῶν. We may explain the construction either (1) as gen. after ἐπηράσαντο 'sware by the temples' (L. and S.), or (2) as a *partitive gen.* ('any of, or any part of, the burnt temples'), or (3) as gen. after εὑεῖν, in a sense cognate to that of ψαύειν, θιγγάνειν. (2) and (3), which are nearly identical, are preferable to (1). For a similar use of εὑεῖν c. gen. cf. Thuc. I. 143. 1. Plato, *Rep.* IV. *ad fin.*, οὔτε γὰρ ἂν πλείονι οὔτε εἰς ἐγγενόμενος κινήσειεν ἂν τῶν ἀξίων λόγου νόμων τῆς πόλεως (where Stallb. reads ἂν τι against the best MSS). To account for this gen. Valckenaer proposed εἴ τι τινες for εἴ τινες (which is the reading of all the MSS). This conjecture is accepted by Auger, Cor., Spohn, and Dind., but appears unnecessary.

κινήσειαν.] εὑεῖν especially used of 'meddling' with things sacred.

ἐπισκευάσωσιν.] 'Repair,' 're store,' = *reficere*. Cf. Xen. *Anab.* V. 3. 13, ἐκ δὲ τοῦ περιττοῦ (the surplus) τὸν ναὸν ἐπισκευάζειν. Hdt. II. 174, τῶν ἱερῶν...ἃ ἐπισκευῆ.

τὰ τῶν θεῶν.] After these words the cod. Ambr. inserts ἔδη, the cod. Urb. does not. In *Nicol.* both these MSS unite in the reading τὰ τῶν θεῶν against τὰ τῶν θεῶν ἔδη of inferior MSS.

ὁρῶντες αὐτοὺς οὐ μόνον τοῖς σώμασιν ἡμῶν ἀλλὰ καὶ τοῖς
ἀναθήμασι πολεμήσαντας.

157   (μβ΄.) Ἔχω δὲ καὶ περὶ τῶν πολιτῶν τῶν ἡμετέρων
τοιαῦτα διελθεῖν. καὶ γὰρ οὗτοι πρὸς μὲν τοὺς ἄλλους,
ὅσοις πεπολεμήκασιν, ἅμα διαλλάττονται καὶ τῆς ἔχθρας
τῆς γεγενημένης ἐπιλανθάνονται, τοῖς δ' ἠπειρώταις οὐδ' d
ὅταν εὖ πάσχωσι χάριν ἴσασιν· οὕτως ἀείμνηστον τὴν
ὀργὴν πρὸς αὐτοὺς ἔχουσιν. καὶ πολλῶν μὲν οἱ πατέρες

σώμασιν … ἀναθήμασι] ὁμοιοτέλευτα.
157. καὶ γὰρ—ἔχουσιν.] Cf.
Liv. XXXI. 29, *Aetolos, Acarnanas,
Macedonas, ejusdem linguae homines,
leves ad tempus ortae causae disjun-
gunt conjunguntque: cum alienigenis,
cum barbaris aeternum omnibus Grae-
cis bellum est eritque.* Natura enim,
quae perpetua est, non mutabilibus in
diem causis, hostes sunt, and Plat.
Rep. 470 C.
ἐπιλανθάνονται.] 'They forget.'
The parts in use in Attic prose are
λανθάνω, ἐλάνθανον, λήσω, ἔλαθον,
λέληθα, ἐλελήθειν· ἐπιλανθάνομαι,
ἐπελανθανόμην, ἐπιλήσομαι, ἐπελα-
θόμην, ἐπιλέλησμαι (I have forgotten),
ἐπελελήσμην. In short as a general
rule λανθάνω, &c., and ἐπιλανθάνομαι, &c., are used in Attic prose;
not ἐπιλανθάνω, &c., nor λανθάνομαι,
&c. (for full details see Veitch, *Gk.
Vbs.* s. v. λανθάνω).
πολλῶν…μηδισμοῦ θάνατον κατέ-
γνωσαν] '*Multos capitis damnarunt,
quod Medis studere viderentur.*' Wolf.
—The construction of καταγιγνώσκειν is extremely varied: it takes
either a gen. of the person condemned and the acc. of the charge,
e.g. § 133, καταγνῶναι μανίαν ἀμφοτέρων, ad *Nicocl.* § 12, *Archid.*
§ 13, *de Pace,* §§ 17, 66, *Panath.* § 23,
Callim. § 65, τοσαύτην πονηρίαν ἡμῶν
καταγνώσεσθε, *Lochit.* § 6, ὅταν τοῦ
καταγνῶσι ἱεροσυλίαν ἢ κλοπήν, οὐ
πρὸς τὸ μέγεθος ὧν ἂν λάβωσι, τὴν
τιμωρίαν ποιεῖσθε, ἀλλ' ὁμοίως ἀπάντων θάνατον κατακρίνετε, or (2) a
double gen. (of the person and of

the legal charge), *e. g.* Dem. *Aristo-
git.* I. § 7, παρανόμων αὐτοῦ κατέγνωτε,
Lysias, *Agorat.* (XIII) § 65, συκοφαν-
τίας αὐτοῦ κατέγνωτε, or (3) (rarely)
a double acc. Xen. *Hdl.* I. 7. 33,
προδοσίαν καταγνόντες…οὐχ ἱκανοὺς
γενομένους κ.τ.λ., Lobeck, *Aj.* p. 351,
ed. 2, or (4) (very rarely, if ever)
acc. of the person and gen. of the
crime, Lysias *de caede Eratosth.* § 30,
τούτου μὴ καταγιγνώσκειν φόνου
(which Reiske and Frohberger rightly alter into τούτου…φόνον). Besides
these constructions we have simple
forms like that in Dem. *Aristocr.*
§ 203, μηδισμὸν κατέγνωσαν.
   In the present passage we have
the gen. of the person (πολλῶν)
governed directly by κατά in κατα-
γιγν., the gen. of the charge (μηδισμοῦ), the acc. of the penalty
(θάνατον),
   To illustrate the historical allusion, we may refer to the story of
Lycidas told in Hdt. IX. 5. In 479
B.C. Mardonius, after an unsuccessful appeal to Athens made through
Alexander (§ 94. n.), resolved on a
further attempt, through one Mury-
chides, to induce the Athenians to
come to terms: he met with a
refusal which was all but unani-
mous. One senator, Lycidas, ventured to propose acceptance of the
overtures; and the senate and the
people stoned him to death, and
the Athenian women in Salamis
inflicted the same vengeance on his
wife and children. (Cf. Lycurg.
Leocr. § 122, ἄξιον τοίνυν ἀκοῦσαι
περὶ τοῦ ἐν Σαλαμῖνι τελευτήσαντος

ἡμῶν μηδισμοῦ θάνατον κατέγνωσαν, ἐν δὲ τοῖς συλλόγοις
ἔτι καὶ νῦν ἀρὰς ποιοῦνται, πρὶν ἄλλό τι χρηματίζειν, εἴ
τις ἐπικηρυκεύεται Πέρσαις τῶν πολιτῶν· Εὐμολπίδαι δὲ
καὶ Κήρυκες ἐν τῇ τελετῇ τῶν μυστηρίων διὰ τὸ τούτων
μῖσος καὶ τοῖς ἄλλοις βαρβάροις εἴργεσθαι τῶν ἱερῶν, ὥσπερ e

γενομένου ψηφίσματος, ὃν ἡ βουλὴ
ὅτι λόγῳ μόνον ἐπιχειρεῖ προδίδοσθαι
τὴν πόλιν, περιελομένη τοὺς στεφά-
νους, αὐτοχειρὶ ἀπεκτείνεν, and Grote,
H. G. III. 493 n.)—v. also Demosthenes (*Fals. Leg.* p. 427. § 270),
where the stories of the Medism of
Arthmius and of Callias are introduced with the words ἐπὶ τοῖς τοιούτοις ἔργοις ῥαθυμεῖτε, ὧν θάνατον
κατεγνώκασιν οἱ πρόγονοι.

τοῖς συλλόγοις.] 'Public assemblies.' σύλλογος is here a generic
term; the existence of the specific
word ἐκκλησία leads to an occasional use of σύλλογος for any public
assembly differing from the ἐκκλησία (*e.g.* Dem. *Fals. Leg.* p. 378,
§ 122), but in this passage it is
not so. σύλλογος here includes the
ἐκκλησία, as well as the βουλή.
At the commencement of these
assemblies, a long form of blended prayer and imprecation was recited, and one of the clauses was
devoted to a special curse against
all who entered into negociations
with the Persians. According to
Plutarch, this anathema was introduced into the existing formula by
Aristides, shortly after the battle of
Salamis: *vit. Arist.* 10, ὅτι δὲ ἄρα
θέσθαι τοὺς ἱερεῖς ἔγραψεν, εἴ τις
ἐπικηρυκεύσαιτο Μήδοις ἢ τὴν συμμαχίαν ἀπολίποι τῶν Ἑλλήνων. The
whole of the formula is parodied by
Aristophanes, *Thesmophor.* 295 sqq.
cf. esp. 355, εἴ τις ἐπιβουλεύει τι τῷ
δήμῳ κακὸν | τῷ τῶν γυναικῶν, ἢ
'πικηρυκεύεται | Εὐριπίδῃ Μή-
δοις τ' ἐπὶ βλάβῃ τινι | τῇ τῶν γυναι-
κῶν κ.τ.λ....| κατῶς ἀπολέσθαι τοῦτον
αὐτὸν κ.τ.λ.—Dem. *Fals.
Leg.* p. 363, § 70, (after the 'Αρὰ
has been recited in court) ταῦτα...
καθ' ἑκάστην τὴν ἐκκλησίαν ὁ κῆρυξ

εὔχεται...καὶ ὅταν ἡ βουλὴ καθῆται
παρ' ἐκείνῃ πάλιν, and *Aristocr.* § 97.
(See further Schömann *de comitiis
Ath.* c. VIII.)

χρηματίζειν.] 'To transact business.' Cf. esp. Aeschin. *Timarch.*
§ 23, πῶς κελεύει τοὺς προέδρους
χρηματίζειν; ἐπειδὰν τὸ καθάρσιον
περιενεχθῇ καὶ ὁ κῆρυξ τὰς πατρίους
εὐχὰς εὔξηται. Also Aristoph.
Thesm. 378.

εἴ τις ἐπικηρυκεύεται.] Goodwin's
Gk. Moods and Tenses, § 53, n. 2.

Εὐμολπίδαι.] 'Eumolpus of Eleusis was the son of Poseidon (v.
§ 18) and the Eponymous hero of
the sacred gens called the Eumol-
pids, in whom the principal func-
tions, appertaining to the myste-
rious rites of Demeter at Eleusis,
were vested by hereditary privilege.'
v. Grote, *H. G.* I. 168–9, new ed.
and especially Lobeck's *Aglaoph.* I.
pp. 211–215.

Κήρυκες.] The priestly house of
Eleusinian heralds, descended from
a legendary Ceryx, (according to
Pausan. I. 38) son of Eumolpus, or
(according to Pollux, VII. 103) son of
Hermes and Pandrosus daughter of
Cecrops. Cf. Xen. *Hell.* II. 4. 20,
(after the battle in the Peiraeeus
between Thrasybulus and the Thirty)
Κλεόκριτος ὁ τῶν μυστῶν κῆρυξ
μάλ' εὔφωνος ὢν κατασιωπησάμενος
ἔλεξε κ.τ.λ. Andoc. *de mysteriis,*
p. 15, § 116, ἐξηγῇ Κηρύκων ὤν, οὐχ
ὅσιόν σοι ἐξηγεῖσθαι ('this was apparently reserved to the Eumolpidae or
Eubutadae.' Sluiter's n. *ad loc.*); their
hereditary nature is proved by *ib.*
p. 16, § 127, τὸν παῖδα ἤδη μέγαν
ὄντα εἰσάγει εἰς Κήρυκας, φάσκειν
εἶναι υἱὸν αὐτοῦ.

ἐν τῇ τελετῇ.] v. p. 58–9. n.
βαρβάροις εἴργεσθαι κ.τ.λ.] Hdt.

158 τοῖς ἀνδροφόνοις, προαγορεύουσιν. οὕτω δὲ φύσει πολεμικῶς πρὸς αὐτοὺς ἔχομεν, ὥστε καὶ τῶν μύθων ἥδιστα συνδιατρίβομεν τοῖς Τρωϊκοῖς καὶ Περσικοῖς, δι' ὧν ἔστι πυνθάνεσθαι τὰς ἐκείνων συμφοράς. εὕροι δ' ἄν τις ἐκ μὲν τοῦ 74

VIII. 63, αὐτέων (sc. 'Αθηναίων) ὁ βουλόμενος καὶ τῶν ἄλλων Ἑλλήνων
μνεῖται, Lysias, Andoc. p. 198, § 8,
and Libanius, Or. Corinth. p. 356.
t. IV. (quoted by Lobeck, Agl. i. p.
15), οὗτοι (sc. οἱ μυσταγωγοί)...κα-
θαροὺς εἶναι τοὺς μύσταις ἐν καιρῷ
προαγορεύουσιν, οἷον τὰς χεῖρας, τὴν
ψυχήν, τὴν φωνὴν Ἑλληνας εἶναι.
ἀνδροφόνοις.] Liv. XLV. 5, and
for more general passages Dem.
Lept. p. 505, § 158, ὁ Δράκων φοβερὸν
κατασκευάζων καὶ δεινὸν τό τινα αὐτόχειρα ἄλλου ἄλλου γίγνεσθαι καὶ γράφων χέρνιβος εἴργεσθαι τὸν ἀνδρο-
φόνον, σπονδῶν, κρατήρων, ἱερῶν,
ἀγοράς κ.τ.λ., and Soph. O. T. 236—
241.
158. τῶν μύθων...τοῖς Τρωϊκοῖς.]
For the constr. cf. ad Dem. § 50,
τοὺς φαύλους τῶν ἀνθρώπων. D.
τῶν μύθων—Περσικοῖς.] i. e.
'So that even in the case of legends,
we spend our time most pleasantly
on those that tell of the Trojan
and the Persian wars.' Cf. Evag. § 6,
τοὺς περὶ τὰ Τρωϊκὰ ὑμνουμένους καὶ
τραγῳδουμένους. The 'tale of Troy
divine' with its accessory events
formed the staple of a vast number
of Athenian tragedies : e. g. the
Μυρμιδόνες, the "Οπλων κρίσις, and
the extant Orestean trilogy of Aeschylus ; the Φρύγες (or "Εκτορος λύτρα),
the extant Ajax of Sophocles ; the
Ἑκάβη and the extant Hecuba and
Troades of Euripides. Besides these
may be mentioned the 'Ιλίου πέρσις
of Iophon, Agathon, Cleophon and
Nicomachus.
The Persian war was celebrated
by Aeschylus in the Persae.
These μύθοι were also rehearsed
in festal hymns like those of Pindar,
and were doubtless favorite subjects
with a humbler class of men, of
whom Philepsius may be an example.

(Ar. Plut. 177, Φιλέψιος δ' οὐχ ἕνεκα
σοῦ μύθους λέγει ; Schol. οὗτος πένης
ὢν λόγων ἱστορίας ἐτρέφετο).
The words ἥδιστα συνδιατρίβομεν
(jucundissime immoramur Baiter)
include reading as well as hearing.
συνδιατρίβομεν...δι' ὧν.] Rauchenstein prints ἐνδιατρίβομεν...ἐξ ὧν,
the conjectural readings of Mehler
and Cobet respectively.
ἐκείνων] = τῶν βαρβάρων, and
refers with strong emphasis to the
preceding αὐτούς. Cf. Panath. § 41,
φαινόμεθα .... πλέον ἀπολελακότες
αὐτοὺς ἢ 'κεῖνοι τοὺς ἄλλους. Thuc.
i. 132. 5, αὐτοῦ...ἐκείνῳ, IV. 29. 3,
αὐτούς...ἐκείνων, VI. 61. 6, θάνατον
κατέγνωσαν αὐτοῦ (Alcibiades) τε καὶ
τῶν μετ' ἐκείνου, and Plat. Cratyl.
430 E, προσελθόντα ἀνδρί...δεῖξαι αὐτῷ, ἂν μὲν τύχῃ, ἐκείνου εἰκόνα, ἂν
δὲ τύχῃ, γυναικός.
εὕροι δ' ἄν τις—μεμιμημένους.]
This sentence is partly borrowed
from the λόγος ἐπιτάφιος of Gorgias
(p. 82. n.). Philostr. vit. Soph. p. 493,
ἐνδιέτριψε τοῖς τῶν Μηδικῶν τροπαίων
ἐπαίνοις, ἐνδεικνύμενος, ὅτι τὰ μὲν
κατὰ τῶν βαρβάρων τρόπαια
ὕμνους ἀπαιτεῖ, τὰ δὲ κατὰ τῶν
Ἑλλήνων θρήνους. The immediate context of these words has not
been preserved ; otherwise we might
find a still closer resemblance between the diction of Gorgias and his
pupil. The sentence before us is pervaded by the same rhetorical artifices
of ἀντίθεσις, παρίσωσις and παρομοίωσις, as those which are crowded into the long fragment of the λόγος ἐπιτάφιος, which may be found in Baiter
and Sauppe's Oratores Att. II. p. 130,
with the comment of Dionys. Halic.
or Maximus Planudes, to this effect :
' Here Gorgias has heaped together
a number of pompous phrases to con-
vey somewhat superficial (ἐπιπολαιο-

πολέμου τοῦ πρὸς τοὺς βαρβάρους ὕμνους πεποιημένους, ἐκ
δὲ τοῦ πρὸς τοὺς Ἕλληνας θρήνους ἡμῖν γεγενημένους, καὶ
τοὺς μὲν ἐν ταῖς ἑορταῖς ᾀδομένους, τοὺς δ᾽ ἐπὶ ταῖς συμ-
159 φοραῖς ἡμᾶς μεμνημένους. οἶμαι δὲ καὶ τὴν Ὁμήρου ποίησιν
μείζω λαβεῖν δόξαν, ὅτι καλῶς τοὺς πολεμήσαντας τοῖς
βαρβάροις ἐνεκωμίασε, καὶ διὰ τοῦτο βουληθῆναι τοὺς προγόνους ἡμῶν ἔντιμον αὐτοῦ ποιῆσαι τὴν τέχνην ἔν τε τοῖς
τῆς μουσικῆς ἄθλοις καὶ τῇ παιδεύσει τῶν νεωτέρων, ἵνα b

τέρας) ideas, whilst he embellishes his
speech all through with πάρισα and
ὁμοιοτέλευτα, and ὁμοιοκάταρκτα to
a nauseous excess.' (I cite the words
by preference from Mr Cope's *transl.*
in his art. in *Journ. of Cl. and S.
Philol.* vol. III. no. 7. p. 67, 8, q. v.).

For a sentence framed on the
same model, as that before us, cf.
Phil. § 117—8.

ὕμνους.] *e. g.* the famous *fragm.*
of Pindar (46), αἱ τε λιπαραὶ καὶ
ἰοστέφανοι καὶ ἀοίδιμοι, Ἑλλάδος
ἔρεισμα, κλειναὶ Ἀθᾶναι, where
Athens is praised as 'bulwark of
Hellas,' doubtless with reference to
the Persian wars. (Cf. *de Perm.* § 166,
where Isocr. institutes a calm comparison between himself and Pindar
with reference to their respective
praises of Athens).—In Pindar *Isth.*
IV.(= v) 50 (=64) we read of the
heroism of Aegina in the 'ruinous
rain and deathful battle-storm of
Salamis.'

θρήνους.] v. Becker's *Charicles,*
Exc. on the Burials, especially p.
387—8. Thuc. II. 46 (at the funeral
of those who had fallen in fighting
πρὸς Ἕλληνας) νῦν δὲ ἀπολοφυράμενοι
ὃν προσήκει ἑκάστῳ, ἀποχωρεῖτε. The
'dirges' may also (as Ikens. suggests)
have formed part of the ἀγῶνες μου-
σικῇ πᾶσῃ which Plato (*Menex.*
249 B) mentions among the acces-
sories of a public funeral.

τοὺς δ᾽...ἡμᾶς μεμνημένους.] Observe the sudden change from the
passive participles πεποιημένους &c.
to μεμνημένους which, though passive
in form, is middle in sense. ἡμᾶς is

the subject, τοὺς the object of μεμνημένους. For the rare acc. after
μέμνημαι cf. Aesch. *Choeph.* 491,
μέμνησο λουτρῶν, followed in the
next line by μέμνησο δ᾽ ἀμφίβληστρον.
(Madv. *Synt.* § 58 R 3). The reading adopted in the text is sanctioned
by codd. Urb. and Ambr. The
reading of Bekker and BS (τῶν δ᾽)
has nothing but simplicity to recom-
mend it.

159. Ὁμήρου ποίησιν...ἐν τοῖς τῆς
μουσικῆς ἄθλοις.] Cf. Plato, *Hip-
parch.* 228 B and Lycurgus, *Leocr.*
p. 161, § 102, οὕτω ὑπέλαβον ὑμῶν
οἱ πατέρες σπουδαῖον εἶναι ποιητὴν
(sc. τὸν Ὅμηρον) ὥστε νόμον ἔθεντο
καθ᾽ ἑκάστην πεντετηρίδα τῶν Πα-
ναθηναίων μόνον τῶν ἄλλων ποιητῶν
ῥαψῳδεῖσθαι τὰ ἔπη. (Grote, *H. G.*
P. I. c. XXI. = vol. I. p. 524, new
ed.) Cf. also Plat. *Ion,* passim.

τῇ παιδεύσει τῶν νεωτέρων.] 'The
poems of Homer were thought to
contain, by precept and example,
everything calculated to awaken
national spirit and to instruct a man
how to be καλὸς κἀγαθός.' In Plat.
Rep. X. 606 E we hear of certain eu-
logists of Homer who asserted that
he had educated Greece. In Xen.
Symp. 35, Niceratos says of himself:
ὁ πατὴρ ἐπιμελούμενος ὅπως ἀνὴρ
ἀγαθὸς γενοίμην, ἠνάγκασέ με πάντα
τὰ Ὁμήρου ἔπη μαθεῖν. (v. Becker's
Charicles, Exc. Scene I. p. 233,
3rd. ed.) Plutarch, *Alcib.* VII. Τὴν
δὲ παιδικὴν ἡλικίαν παραλλάσσων
ἐπίστη γραμματοδιδασκάλῳ καὶ βι-
βλίον ᾔτησεν Ὁμηρικόν. Εἰπόντος δὲ
τοῦ διδασκάλου μηδὲν ἔχειν Ὁμήρου,

πολλάκις ἀκούοντες τῶν ἐπῶν ἐκμανθάνωμεν τὴν ἔχθραν
τὴν ὑπάρχουσαν πρὸς αὐτοὺς, καὶ ζηλοῦντες τὰς ἀρετὰς τῶν
στρατευσαμένων, τῶν αὐτῶν ἔργων ἐκείνοις ἐπιθυμῶμεν.
160 (μγ́.) "Ωστε μοι δοκεῖ πολλὰ λίαν εἶναι τὰ παρακελευόμενα
πολεμεῖν αὐτοῖς, μάλιστα δ᾽ ὁ παρὼν καιρός, οὗ σαφέστερον
οὐδέν. ὃν οὐκ ἀφετέον· καὶ γὰρ αἰσχρὸν παρόντι μὲν μὴ c
χρῆσθαι, παρελθόντος δ᾽ αὐτοῦ μεμνῆσθαι. τί γὰρ ἂν καὶ
βουληθεῖμεν ἡμῖν προσγενέσθαι, μέλλοντες βασιλεῖ πολε-
161 μεῖν, ἔξω τῶν νῦν ὑπαρχόντων; οὐκ Αἴγυπτος μὲν αὐτοῦ
καὶ Κύπρος ἀφέστηκε, Φοινίκη δὲ καὶ Συρία διὰ τὸν πόλεμον ἀνάστατοι γεγόνασι, Τύρος δ᾽ ἐφ᾽ ᾗ μέγ᾽ ἐφρόνησεν,
ὑπὸ τῶν ἐχθρῶν τῶν ἐκείνου κατείληπται; τῶν δ᾽ ἐν Κι-
λικίᾳ πόλεων τὰς μὲν πλείστας οἱ μεθ᾽ ἡμῶν ὄντες ἔχουσι, d
τὰς δ᾽ οὐ χαλεπόν ἐστι κτήσασθαι. Λυκίας δ᾽ οὐδεὶς
162 πώποτε Περσῶν ἐκράτησεν. Ἑκατόμνως δ᾽ ὁ Καρίας

πανδήλῳ καθικόμενοι αὐτοῦ παρῆλθεν.
Ἑτέρου δὲ φήσαντος ἔχειν Ὅμηρον
ὑφ᾽ αὐτοῦ δωρθωμένον· 'Εἶτ'' ἔφη
'γράμματα διδάσκεις, Ὅμηρον ἐπαν-
ορθοῦν ἱκανὸς ὤν; οὐχὶ τοὺς νέους
παιδεύεις;' See also Ar. *Ranae*, 1035.
§§ 160—169. *We are summoned
to war by the critical position of Persia, and we must grasp our opportu-
nity before it is too late. We are also
summoned by the present deplorable
condition of Greece, which is the result
of our internal feuds and factions.*
160. πολλὰ λίαν.] The adv.
λίαν often comes after the word
which it qualifies. *e. g.* § 73, μὴ ταχὺ
λίαν παραδραμεῖν, *de Perm.* § 215,
and *Areop.* § 77. (Contrast λίαν ἀκριβῶν in § 162). Cf. adv. πάνυ, Thuc.
VIII. 56, Plat. *Hip. Maj.* 282, Dem.
Conon. init. πολὺ χρόνον πάνυ. (v.
also Strange ap. Jahn's *Jahrb. Philol.* suppl. 3, p. 585—6.)
καιρός.] v. *ad Dem.* § 3. n.
ὃν οὐκ ἀφετέον.] Madv. *Synt.*
§ 84 c or Goodwin's *Gk. moods and
tenses*, § 114. 2.
161. Αἴγυπτος... καὶ Κύπρος.]
v. §§ 140. 141.
Φοινίκη καὶ Συρία κ.τ.λ.] Cf.

Evag. § 62, μικροῦ μὲν ἐδέησε Κύπρον
ἅπασαν κατασχεῖν, Φοινίκην δ᾽ ἐπόρθησε Τύρον δὲ κατὰ κράτος εἷλε, Κιλικίαν δὲ βασιλέως ἀπέστησεν, and
Diodor. XV. 2, 'Εκρίνευ (sc. Evagoras) κατὰ τὴν Φοινίκην Τύρου καὶ
τινῶν ἑτέρων.
ἀνάστατοι.] 'devastated.' v. §
37. n.
Λυκίας—ἐκράτησεν.] Lycia was
conquered by Harpagus, general of
the elder Cyrus, after a desperate
resistance on the part of the Xan-
thians (Hdt. I. 176), it was included
in the satrapies of Darius (*id.* III.
90), and contributed fifty ships to
the navy of Xerxes (*id.* VII. 92).
But it is probable that the Lycians
were so far defended by mount
Cragus, Massicytus, and other spurs
of the range of Taurus as to render
the allegiance to Persia little more
than nominal.
162. Ἑκατόμνως κ.τ.λ.] Cf. Diodor. XV. 2, Εὐαγόρας παρ' Ἑκατόμνου
τοῦ Καρίας δυνάστου λάθρα συμπράτ-
τοντος αὐτῷ χρημάτων ἔλαβε πλῆθος
εἰς διατροφὴν ξενικῶν δυνάμεων. v.
fragm. of Theopompus quoted § 134
n., where Hecatomnos appears as

ἐπίσταθμος τῇ μὲν ἀληθείᾳ πολὺν ἤδη χρόνον ἀφέστηκεν,
ὁμολογήσει δ' ὅταν ἡμεῖς βουληθῶμεν. ἀπὸ δὲ Κνίδου μέχρι
Σινώπης Ἕλληνες τὴν Ἀσίαν παροικοῦσιν, οὓς οὐ δεῖ πείθειν
ἀλλὰ μὴ κωλύειν πολεμεῖν. καίτοι τοιούτων ὁρμητηρίων
ὑπαρξάντων καὶ τοσούτου πολέμου τὴν Ἀσίαν περιστάντος,
τί δεῖ τὰ συμβησόμενα λίαν ἀκριβῶς ἐξετάζειν; ὅπου γὰρ c

admiral of the Persian fleet at the
beginning of the war with Evagoras.
ἐπίσταθμος.] Harpocr. *lex.* ' Ἑκατόμνως ὁ Καρίας ἐπίσταθμος,' ὅτι οὐδὲν
ἕτερον ἦν ἢ κατὰ σατραπείαν Καρίας κύριος. Strictly speaking, Hecatomnos was hereditary prince of
Caria : he was probably descended
from the Artemisia (of Halicarnassus) who distinguished herself at
Salamis. He was succeeded by his
three sons Maussolus, Hidrieus (v.
§ 152. n. or Idrieus, *Phil.* § 103) and
Pidoxarus in turn, and by his two
daughters, Artemisia, the consort of
Maussolus, and Ada, the consort of
Hidrieus. (On the famous Mauso-
leum v. Newton's *Travels and Discoveries in the Levant*, letters 36
sqq. The prize of oratory at the
contest instituted by Artemisia, in
honour of her husband, was won by
Theopompus. Suidas, s. v. Ἰσοκράτης Ἀμύκλα.)
Κνίδου μέχρι Σινώπης.] From
Cnidus (in Caria) to Sinope (in
Paphlagonia).
τὴν Ἀσίαν παροικοῦσιν.] 'Dwell
along the coasts of Asia.' *Epp.* 9. 8,
οἱ τὴν Ἀσίας τὴν παραλίαν οἰκοῦντες.
Cic. *de rep.* II. 4, § 9, (speaking
of the Gk. colonies in Asia, Thrace,
Italy, Sicily and Africa) *barbarorum
agris quasi* attexta *quaedam vittetur
ora esse Graeciae* (a *fringe*, as it were,
upon the robe of Barbarism). Schneider understands βασιλεῖ after παρα-
κοῦσιν and translates ' are his neighbours in Asia,' but the explanation
given above appears simpler.
οὓς οὐ δεῖ πείθειν ἀλλὰ μὴ κωλύειν
πολεμεῖν.] 'Whom we need not
persuade to declare war, so much
as abstain from checking them :' *i.e.*

so far from their requiring to be
prompted, they are ready enough to
go to war, if we do not prevent
them.
μὴ κωλύειν πολεμεῖν.] The following points may be noticed in the
usage of κωλύω :—
(1) τοῦτο κωλύει αὐτοὺς μὴ πολεμεῖν
is the Greek for ' This prevents them
from going to war.'
(2) οὐδὲν κωλύει αὐτοὺς πολεμεῖν =
' nothing prevents them from going
to war.'
(3) οὐδὲν κωλύει αὐτοὺς μὴ πολεμεῖν
=' nothing prevents them from *not*-
going-to-war' (i.e. they are allowed
to remain at peace).
(3) is rather an awkward form of
expression but is sometimes necessary. It may be seen in Aristot.
Eth. III. 9. 6, στρατιώτας δ' οὐδὲν
ἴσως κωλύει μὴ τοὺς τοιούτους κρατίστους εἶναι, ἀλλὰ τοὺς ἥττον μὲν ἀν-
δρείους, ἄλλο δ' ἀγαθὸν μηδὲν ἔχοντας
(i.e. ' Perhaps there is no reason why
not such men as I have described
should make the best soldiers, but
those who &c.') ; Plato, *Phaedo*, 106 B,
τί κωλύει...μὴ γίγνεσθαι ; (=οὐδὲν
κωλύει μὴ γίγνεσθαι): and *Phaedr.*
268 E, οὐδὲν κωλύει μηδὲ σμικρὸν
ἁρμονίας ἐπαΐειν κ.τ.λ.
ὁρμητηρίων.] The context shews
that this means ' starting-points,'
i.e. ' bases of operation.' Cf. § 163,
ἐπὶ τοῖς ἐντεῦθεν ὁρμωμένοις. Henseler is right in condemning as less
satisfactory such translations as ' *op-
portunitates*,' and '*Anreizungen*,'—a
condemnation which includes the explanation given by L. and S. who
doubtless borrowed their translation
' incentives' from the *incitamentum*
of Mitchell's *Lex. Graec. Isocr.*

μικρῶν μερῶν ἥττους εἰσίν, οὐκ ἄδηλον, ὡς ἂν διατεθεῖεν,
163 εἰ πᾶσιν ἡμῖν πολεμεῖν ἀναγκασθεῖεν. ἔχει δ᾽ οὕτως. ἐὰν
μὲν ὁ βάρβαρος ἐρρωμενεστέρως κατάσχῃ τὰς πόλεις τὰς
ἐπὶ θαλάττῃ, φρουρὰς μείζους ἐν αὐταῖς ἢ νῦν ἐγκαταστήσας, 73
τάχ᾽ ἂν καὶ τῶν νήσων αἱ περὶ τὴν ἤπειρον, οἷον Ῥόδος
καὶ Σάμος καὶ Χίος, ἐπὶ τὰς ἐκείνου τύχας ἀποκλίναιεν·
ἢν δ᾽ ἡμεῖς αὐτὰς πρότεροι καταλάβωμεν, εἰκὸς τοὺς τὴν
Λυδίαν καὶ Φρυγίαν καὶ τὴν ἄλλην τὴν ὑπερκειμένην χώραν
164 οἰκοῦντας ἐπὶ τοῖς ἐντεῦθεν ὁρμωμένοις εἶναι. διὸ δεῖ σπεύ-
δειν καὶ μηδεμίαν ποιεῖσθαι διατριβήν, ἵνα μὴ πάθωμεν,
ὅπερ οἱ πατέρες ἡμῶν. ἐκεῖνοι γὰρ ὑστερίσαντες τῶν βαρ- b
βάρων καὶ προέμενοί τινας τῶν συμμάχων ἠναγκάσθησαν
ὀλίγοι πρὸς πολλοὺς κινδυνεύειν, ἐξὸν αὐτοῖς προτέροις
διαβᾶσιν εἰς τὴν ἤπειρον μετὰ πάσης τῆς τῶν Ἑλλήνων
165 δυνάμεως ἐν μέρει τῶν ἐθνῶν ἕκαστον χειροῦσθαι. δέδεικται
γάρ, ὅταν τις πολεμῇ πρὸς ἀνθρώπους ἐκ πολλῶν τόπων
συλλεγομένους, ὅτι δεῖ μὴ περιμένειν, ἕως ἂν ἐπιστῶσιν,

---

163. ἐρρωμενεστέρως.] Also found
in § 172, de Perm. § 278, and ad
Nicol. § 14. For similar compar.
adverbs in -ων, cf. § 43, τιμιωτέρως,
§ 109, ἀπορωτέρως, § 116, ἀθυμοτέρως, de Pace, § 60, βεβαιοτέρως, de
Bigis, § 29, εὐδοκιμωτέρως. Also ἀνειρω-
τέρως, σωφρωτέρως, φιλοτιμοτέρως.—
We also find (but less frequently)
the forms in -ον, e.g. Archid. § 101,
and de Perm. § 72 ἐρρωμενεστερον,
Archid. § 14, and Evag. § 34, συντομώτερον. (Partly from Exc. II.
of Bremi's Isocr.) On adverbs derived from pf. pass. part. v. § 130. n.

οἷον Ῥόδος καὶ Σάμος καὶ Χίος.]
'An dé?' Dobree (Adversaria ad
loc.).—Cod. Ambr. has Ῥόδος Σάμος
Χίος.

αὐτάς.] sc. τὰς πόλεις τὰς ἐπὶ
θαλάττῃ.

τὴν ὑπερκειμένην χώραν.] 'The
rest of the up-country.' Similarly
we speak of 'Upper Carolina,'
'Upper Canada,' &c.

ἐντεῦθεν.] Refers to the Greek
cities on the sea-coast, not to the
Islands.

164. διατριβήν.] v. § 41 n.
προέμενοί τινας.] The abandoned allies were the Ionians. Hdt.
v. 103. μετὰ δὲ (sc. after the defeat
of the Ionians at Ephesus) 'Αθηναῖοι
τὸ παράπαν ἀπολιπόντες τοὺς Ἴωνας,
ἐπικαλεομένου σφέας πολλὰ δι᾽ ἀγγέ-
λων 'Αρισταγόρεω, οὐκ ἔφασαν τι-
μωρήσειν σφίσι. κ.τ.λ. 'It is perhaps not going too far to say that if
Athens and the other maritime states
of Greece had given a hearty and
resolute support to the Ionian cause,
the great invasions of Darius and
Xerxes might have been prevented.'
Rawlinson, n. on Hdt. l. c.

ἐν μέρει κ.τ.λ.] The construction
is χειροῦσθαι ἐν μέρει ἕκαστον τῶν
ἐθνῶν. Cf. § 96, ἐν μέρει πρὸς ἑκατέρας.

165. ἕως ἂν ἐπιστῶσιν.] 'Until
they are upon one.' ἐπιστῶσιν ought
not to be translated as=συστῶσιν.
The idea of collective attack is only
implied by the context.—It was a desire to bring out this implied force
that led the old editors to print ἐφορ-
μηθῶσιν which is found in a similar

ἀλλ' ἔτι διεσπαρμένοις αὐτοῖς ἐπιχειρεῖν. ἐκεῖνοι μὲν οὖν c
προεξαμαρτόντες ἅπαντα ταῦτ' ἐπηνωρθώσαντο, καταστάντες εἰς τοὺς μεγίστους ἀγῶνας· ἡμεῖς δ' ἂν σωφρονῶμεν, ἐξ
ἀρχῆς φυλαξόμεθα, καὶ πειρασόμεθα φθῆναι περὶ τὴν Λυ-
166 δίαν καὶ τὴν Ἰωνίαν στρατόπεδον ἐγκαταστήσαντες, εἰδότες
ὅτι καὶ βασιλεὺς οὐχ ἑκόντων ἄρχει τῶν ἠπειρωτῶν, ἀλλὰ
μείζω δύναμιν περὶ αὐτὸν ἑκάστων αὐτῶν ποιησάμενος·
ἧς ἡμεῖς ὅταν κρείττω διαβιβάσωμεν, ὃ βουληθέντες ῥᾳδίως d
ἂν ποιήσαιμεν, ἀσφαλῶς ἅπασαν τὴν Ἀσίαν καρπωσόμεθα.
πολὺ δὲ κάλλιον ἐκείνῳ περὶ τῆς βασιλείας πολεμεῖν, ἢ πρὸς
ἡμᾶς αὐτοὺς περὶ τῆς ἡγεμονίας ἀμφισβητεῖν.

167   (μδ'.) Ἄξιον δ' ἐπὶ τῆς νῦν ἡλικίας ποιήσασθαι τὴν
στρατείαν, ἵν' οἱ τῶν συμφορῶν κοινωνήσαντες, οὗτοι καὶ
τῶν ἀγαθῶν ἀπολαύσωσι καὶ μὴ πάντα τὸν χρόνον δυστυ-
χοῦντες διαγάγωσιν. ἱκανὸς γὰρ ὁ παρεληλυθώς, ἐν ᾧ τί e

---

passage, *Lochit.* § 13, μὴ τριμμεί-
νηθ' ἕως ἂν ἀθροισθέντες κ.τ.λ. and
also in Thuc. III. 97, μὴ μένειν ἕως ἂν
ξύμπαντες ἀθροισθέντι ἀντιτάξωνται.
This passage has been discussed by
Strange (Jahn's *Jahrb. Philol.* Sup.
III. p. 588), who points out that
ἐπισῶσιν forms a parallelism with
ἐπιχειρεῖν and is therefore preferred
to συστῶσαι.

ἐπηνωρθώσαντο.] v. *ad Dem.* § 3,
ἐπανορθῶ, n. and *Archid.* § 48, τὰς
τοιαύτας συμφορὰς αἱ πόλεις ἐπανορ-
θοῦνται. (v. Lobeck, *Phrynichus*,
250, 1).

φθῆναι.] The *second* aor. inf.
of φθάνω is also found in § 87.
The *first* aor. inf. φθάσαι does not
occur in Isocr. but the opt. φθάσειε
is used in *de Pace*, § 120. We have
ἐφθησαν in *Paneg.* § 86, and *de Bigis*,
§ 37, and ἐφθασαν in *de Pace*, § 98,
Phil. § 53, and *Evag.* § 53. In
the 3rd pers. sing. and in the 1st
and 2nd pl. the *second* aor. form
alone is used, *Trapez.* § 23, ἔφθη,
Aegin. § 22, ἐφθημεν, and *Phil.* § 7,
ἔφθητε. (*Exc.* 1. to Bremi's *Isocr.*)
For the usage of other authors v.
Veitch, *Gk. verbs.*

166. ἧς—καρπωσόμεθα.] 'And
when we have transported a stronger
force than *this* (which we could easily
do, if we pleased), we shall securely
reap the revenues of the whole of
Asia.' βουληθέντες is = εἰ βουληθεῖμεν. 'The participle often stands
for the *protasis* of a conditional sentence and its tenses represent the
various forms of *protasis* expressed by
the Indic., the Subjunct., or (as here)
the Optative. Cf. Eur. *Phoen.* 504,
ἄστρων ἂν ἔλθοιμ' αἰθέρος πρὸς
ἀντολὰς | καὶ γῆς ἔνερθε, δυνατὸς ὢν
(= εἰ δυνατὸς εἴην) δρᾶσαι τάδε,'
Goodwin's *Gk. moods and tenses*,
§ 109, 6.

167. ἱκανὸς γὰρ, κ.τ.λ.] 'For the
time past is sufficient,—a time that
has been filled with every horror.'
A literal transl. (*e.g.* in which what
horror &c.?) would be at variance
with Eng. idiom; τί τῶν δεινῶν οὐ
γέγονεν;=is there a single horror
that has not happened? *i. e.* every
horror *has* happened.

ὁ παρεληλυθώς.] κ. χρόνος (which
is actually added in cod. Ambr.).
v. Madv. *Synt.* § 87, h. R.

τῶν δεινῶν οὐ γέγονεν; πολλῶν γὰρ κακῶν τῇ φύσει τῇ
τῶν ἀνθρώπων ὑπαρχόντων, αὐτοὶ πλείω τῶν ἀναγκαίων
168 προσεξευρήκαμεν, πολέμους καὶ στάσεις ἡμῖν αὐτοῖς ἐμ-
ποιήσαντες, ὥστε τοὺς μὲν ἐν ταῖς αὐτῶν ἀνόμως ἀπόλ-
λυσθαι, τοῖς δ᾽ ἐπὶ ξένης μετὰ παίδων καὶ γυναικῶν ἀλᾶ- 76
σθαι, πολλοὺς δὲ δι᾽ ἔνδειαν τῶν καθ᾽ ἡμέραν ἐπικουρεῖν
ἀναγκαζομένους, ὑπὲρ τῶν ἐχθρῶν τοῖς φίλοις μαχομένους
ἀποθνήσκειν. ὑπὲρ ὧν οὐδεὶς πώποτ᾽ ἠγανάκτησεν, ἀλλ᾽
ἐπὶ μὲν ταῖς συμφοραῖς ταῖς ὑπὸ τῶν ποιητῶν συγκειμέναις
δακρύειν ἀξιοῦσιν, ἀληθινὰ δὲ πάθη πολλὰ καὶ δεινὰ γιγνόμενα διὰ τὸν πόλεμον ἐφορῶντες, τοσούτου δέουσιν ἐλεεῖν,
ὥστε καὶ μᾶλλον χαίρουσιν ἐπὶ τοῖς ἀλλήλων κακοῖς ἢ b
169 τοῖς αὐτῶν ἰδίοις ἀγαθοῖς. ἴσως δ᾽ ἂν καὶ τῆς ἐμῆς εὐη-

---

168. ὑπὲρ τῶν ἐχθρῶν κ.τ.λ.] 'To die, fighting with their friends on behalf of their enemies.'

ἐπὶ μὲν κ.τ.λ.] A similar contrast may be observed in Andoc. *Alcib.* § 23 (quoted by Bens.), ἀλλ᾽ ὑμεῖς ἐν μὲν ταῖς τραγῳδίαις τοιαῦτα θεωροῦντες δεινὰ νομίζετε, γιγνόμενα δ᾽ ἐν τῇ πόλει ὁρῶντες οὐδὲν φροντίζετε. καίτοι ἐκεῖνα μὲν οὐκ ἐπίστασθε πότερον οὕτω γεγένηται ἢ πέπλασται ὑπὸ τῶν ποιητῶν· ταῦτα δὲ σαφῶς εἰδότες οὕτω πεπραγμένα παρανόμως ῥᾳθύμως φέρετε.

ὑπὸ τῶν ποιητῶν συγκειμέναις.] For the constr. cf. *ad Dem.* § 36. n. The active of συγκείμενος is συντίθημι. Cf. *Evag.* § 36 (Schn.), οὐ μόνον τῶν γεγενημένων τὰς καλλίστας ἀπαγγέλλουσιν (οἱ ποιηταί), ἀλλὰ καὶ παρ᾽ αὑτῶν καινὰς συντιθέασιν. The poets in the text are doubtless the tragedians.

δακρύειν.] In Xen. *Symp.* III. 11, we hear of Callippides the actor, ὃς ὑπερσεμνύνεται, ὅτι δύναται πολλοὺς κλαίοντας καθίζειν. The impressible nature of an Athenian audience may be further illustrated by the story in Herodotus, VI. 21, where we are told that the whole theatre fell into tears (ἐς δάκρυα ἔπεσε τὸ θέητρον) at the representa-

tion of the *Capture of Miletus* by Phrynichus (although *that* was an instance of ἀληθινὸν πάθος). Plutarch, more than once, tells of the effect produced on the brutal Alexander of Pherae as he listened to a pathetic drama of Euripides. He hurried from the theatre, lest the audience should see the murderer of many citizens 'weeping for Hecuba.' (Plut. *Pelop.* 29). On the effect produced by the recitation of Homer on the Rhapsodist and his audience (a kindred subject to that in the text) v. the interesting passage in Plato where Ion describes himself (like the player in Hamlet, *'tears in his eyes, distraction in his aspect'*) as influenced by the pathos and the horror of his theme, and his audience κλαίοντάς τε καὶ δεινὸν ἐμβλέποντας καὶ συνθαμβοῦντας τοῖς λεγομένοις. (*Ion,* 535 C, D.)

ἐφορῶντες.] 'Gazing upon.' The context alone implies that it is a careless and indifferent gaze. Soph. *Trach.* 1269, θεοὶς ἀγνωμοσύνην | εἰδότες... | οἱ φύσαντες καὶ κληρόμενοι | πατέρες τοιαῦτ᾽ ἐφορῶσι πάθη. | τὰ μὲν οὖν μέλλοντ᾽ οὐδεὶς ἐφορᾷ.

169. εὐηθείας.] εὐήθης and its subst. εὐήθεια have a double meaning, (1) 'well-disposed,' 'good dispo-

θείας πολλοὶ καταγελάσειαν, εἰ δυστυχίας ἀνδρῶν ὀδυροί-
μην ἐν τοῖς τοιούτοις καιροῖς, ἐν οἷς Ἰταλία μὲν ἀνάστατος
γέγονε, Σικελία δὲ καταδεδούλωται, τοσαῦται δὲ πόλεις τοῖς
βαρβάροις ἐκδέδονται, τὰ δὲ λοιπὰ μέρη τῶν Ἑλλήνων ἐν
τοῖς μεγίστοις κινδύνοις ἐστίν.

170 (μέ.) Θαυμάζω δὲ τῶν δυναστευόντων ἐν ταῖς πόλεσιν,

sition,' (2) from a supposed connexion between good-nature and feebleness of intellect, 'simple' or 'silly,'
'simplicity' or 'silliness.' (v. Thuc.
III. 83. 1.)
For εὐήθεια in the good sense, cf.
Plato, *Rep.* III. 400 E, εὐλογία ἄρα
καὶ εὐαρμοστία καὶ εὐσχημοσύνη καὶ
εὐρυθμία εὐηθείᾳ ξυνακολουθεῖ, οὐχ
ἣν ἄνοιαν οὖσαν ὑποκοριζόμενοι καλοῦμεν ὡς εὐήθειαν, ἀλλὰ τὴν ὡς ἀληθῶς εὖ τε καὶ καλῶς τὸ ἦθος κατε-
σκευασμένην διάνοιαν.
Of the secondary sense the present passage is one instance out of
many. Cf. ἡδύ (='εὐήθη· ἐκάλουν
δὲ οὕτω τοὺς ὑπομώρους' Suidas)
γλυκύ, &c.
An exact parallel to the history
of the word εὐήθη may be noticed
in the word 'simple' (cf. 'simple-
ton'). Thus also the word 'silly'
has lost the connexion it once had
with the Germ. *selig* (blessed, holy),
in the time when Fletcher spoke
of the Infant Saviour as 'the harm-
less silly babe.' Cf. Latimer's and
sermon of the card, 'Who made thee
so bold to meddle with my silly beasts
whom I bought so dearly with my
precious blood?' and Bp. Andrewes'
Sermons, p. 655, ed. 1611, 'the silly
innocent babe.' (The last reference
is due to Mr Mayor).
'Ἰταλία...ἀνάστατος.] Alluding
to the devastation of part of Italy by
Dionysius I. In 389 B.C. (according to Diodorus, XIV. 106, 107, 111)
he captured Caulon, removed its
inhabitants to Syracuse, destroyed
(κατασκάψας) the city, and gave the
territory to others; in the next year
did the same to Hipponium; and
in 387, after reducing Rhegium to

great straits by famine, he took the
place, doomed the commander Phy-
ton to a tragical death, and sold
into slavery many of the citizens.
(v. Bens. *transl.* n.)
Σικελία...καταδεδούλωται.] Dionysius I. had, by a disgraceful peace,
surrendered Selinus, Acragas and
Himera to Carthage (Diodor. XIII.
114); had subdued many of the states
of Sicily (*e.g.* Syracuse, Naxos,
Leontini, *id.* XIV. 14 sqq.); had more
recently (in 396 B.C.) captured Messene, Solus, Henna and other places,
and entered into terms with the
tyrant of Agyris and the prince of
Centuripae (*ib.* 78. v. Bens. *transl.* n.).
πόλεις.] *sc.* in Asia.
τὰ λοιπὰ μέρη.] *sc.* Greece
proper. Cf. § 126 (on Mantinea,
Thebes and Phlius).
§§ 170—186. *The leading states-
men of Greece ought to have long
since endeavoured to bring about an
expedition against Persia, instead of
leaving the question to others.* 173—4.
*Nothing short of such an expedition
can heal our dissensions and place
our goodwill upon a firm foundation.*
175—8. *The convention of Antalcidas is no hindrance to the proposal
expedition. That disgraceful compact has been already broken: Its
terms were unjustly negociated, in accordance with the dictates of the king
of Persia, who has thereby* (179) *obtained half the world for his dominion;*
(180) *and these terms, to the dishonour
of all Greece, remain engraved in our
public temples,—a nobler trophy than
Persia ever raised upon the field of
battle.* 181—4. *We are loudly called
to war by every plea of Justice, Expediency, Revenge and Glory.* 185. *No*

εἰ προσήκειν αὐτοῖς ἡγοῦνται μέγα φρονεῖν, μηδὲν πώποθ'
ἱπὲρ τηλικούτων πραγμάτων μήτ' εἰπεῖν μήτ' ἐνθυμηθῆναι
δυνηθέντες. ἐχρῆν γὰρ αὐτούς, εἴπερ ἦσαν ἄξιοι τῆς παρούσης δόξης, ἁπάντων ἀφεμένους τῶν ἄλλων περὶ τοῦ
πολέμου τοῦ πρὸς τοὺς βαρβάρους εἰσηγεῖσθαι καὶ συμβου-
171 λεύειν. τυχὸν μὲν γὰρ ἄν τι συνεπέραναν· εἰ δὲ καὶ προαπεῖπον, ἀλλ' οὖν τούς γε λόγους ὥσπερ χρησμοὺς εἰς τὸν

*one will refuse to join an enterprise
that has Athens and Sparta for its
generals and the infliction of vengeance
on the Barbarians for its end.* 186.
*The heroes of this enterprise will out-
rival the heroes that fought against
Troy; and every poet and every orator
will celebrate their valour.*

170. θαυμάζω τῶν δυναστευόντων...εἰ...] Cf. § 1, ἐθαύμασα τῶν
συναγαγόντων...ὅτι. D.

ἐχρῆν γὰρ αὐτούς, εἴπερ ἦσαν
ἄξιοι.] An iambic line. Cf. *Panath.*
init. νεώτεροι μὲν ὦν προηρούμην γράφειν. (Cic. *Orat.* § 190, *elegit ex multis Isocrati libris, xxx fortasse versus
Hieronymus, plerosque senarios, sed
etiam anapaestos* cet. q. v.) Similar
lines have been found in Dem. *Ol.* I.
§ 5, δῆλον γάρ ἐστι τοῖς 'Ολυνθίοις
ὅτι, *Mid.* § 165, ὁ πανταπασιν ἀσθενὴς
τῷ σώματι, and *Lacr.* § 22, τοιαῦτα
τούτων ἐστὶ τὰ κακουργήματα (Mr
Heslop's n. on *Ol. I.s.*). As an instance of a trochaic line we have
Dem. *Androt.* § 54, τοὺς ταλαιπώρους
μετοίκους οἳς ὑβριστικώτερον.—In the
summary of the lost τέχνη of Isocr.
(preserved by Maximus Planudes
and Joannes Sicel.) we have these
maxims: ὅλως δὲ ὁ λόγος μὴ λόγος
ἔστω· ξηρὸν γάρ. μηδὲ ἔμμετρον·
καταφανὲς γάρ· ἀλλὰ μεμίχθω παντὶ
ῥυθμῷ, μάλιστα ἰαμβικῷ καὶ τρο-
χαϊκῷ. Isocr. here recommends a
blending of various rhythms, especially the iambic and trochaic. An
iambic or trochaic rhythm may be
produced without resulting in an
iambic or trochaic line, by giving
merely a general preponderance to
the *iambus* or *trochee*; but in the
present passage the limit has been

passed, and the result is unmistakeable *metre*,—a violation of the rule
above quoted. (Cic. *Brut.* § 32.) On
this subject, cf. Aristot. *Rhet.* III. 8,
ῥυθμὸν δεῖ ἔχειν τὸν λόγον, μέτρον δὲ
μή· ποίημα γὰρ ἔσται. ῥυθμὸν δὲ μὴ
ἀκριβῶν...ὁ δ' ἴαμβος αὐτή ἐστιν ἡ λέξις
ἡ τῶν πολλῶν...διὸ μάλιστα πάντων
ἰαμβεῖα φθέγγονται λέγοντες. Aristo-
tol. then proceeds to disapprove of
the trochaic rhythm, as being too
lively and tripping, of which disap-
proval Spengel says 'Aristotelem..
hic tecte Isocratis doctrinam impug-
nare certum [?] est.'—Also Cic. *Orat.*
§ 189. *versus saepe in oratione per
imprudentiam dicimus; quod est ve-
hementer vitiosum: sed non attendi-
mus neque exaudimus nosmetipsos:
Senarios vero et Hipponacteos effu-
gere vix possumus; magnam enim
partem ex iambis constat nostra oratio;* and Quintil. 9. 4. 72. (v. Spengel's
n. on Arist. *Rhet. l.c.* and Mr Cope's
Introd. pp. 303 sqq. 379 sqq.)

εἰσηγεῖσθαι.] 'To introduce, or
propose a subject,' *Phil.* § 13 and
Epp. 1. 7, εἰσηγούμην...συμβουλεύειν.

171. τυχόν.] 'Perhaps.' *Phil.*
§ 94. τοῖς...οἰκείοις τυχὸν ἂν χρησαίμην. Madv. *Synt.* § 181.

εἰ καὶ προαπεῖπον.] sc. πρὸ τοῦ
συμπεράναι τι. καὶ emphasizes προαπεῖπον. 'If they had even *failed*,
they might at any rate have be-
queathed us their counsels as oracles
for the time to come.'

ἀλλ' οὖν...γε.] 'Yet at any rate.'
ad *Dem.* § 39. Soph. *Phil.* 1306,
ἀλλ' οὖν τοσοῦτόν γ' ἴσθι.

χρησμούς.] 'Solemn, oracular
utterances.' Cf. Lycurg. *Leocr.* § 92
(quoted by Schn.), καί μοι δοκοῦσι

ἐπιόντα χρόνον ἂν κατέλιπον. νῦν δ' οἱ μὲν ἐν ταῖς μεγίσταις δόξαις ὄντες ἐπὶ μικροῖς σπουδάζουσιν, ἡμῖν δὲ τοῖς d
τῶν πολιτικῶν ἐξεστηκόσι περὶ τηλικούτων πραγμάτων
συμβουλεύειν παραλελοίπασιν.

172   Οὐ μὴν ἀλλ' ἴσῳ μικροψυχότεροι τυγχάνουσιν ὄντες οἱ
προεστῶτες ἡμῶν, τοσούτῳ τοὺς ἄλλους ἐρρωμενεστέρως δεῖ
σκοπεῖν, ὅπως ἀπαλλαγησόμεθα τῆς παρούσης ἔχθρας. νῦν
μὲν γὰρ μάτην ποιούμεθα τὰς περὶ τῆς εἰρήνης συνθήκας·
οὐ γὰρ διαλυόμεθα τοὺς πολέμους ἀλλ' ἀναβαλλόμεθα, καὶ
περιμένομεν τοὺς καιρούς, ἐν οἷς ἀνήκεστόν τι κακὸν ἀλλή- c
173 λους ἐργάσασθαι δυνησόμεθα.   (μγ'.) Δεῖ δὲ ταύτας τὰς
ἐπιβουλὰς ἐκποδὼν ποιησαμένους ἐκείνοις τοῖς ἔργοις ἐπιχειρεῖν, ἐξ ὧν τάς τε πόλεις ἀσφαλέστερον οἰκήσομεν καὶ
πιστότερον διακεισόμεθα πρὸς ἡμᾶς αὐτούς. ἔστι δ' ἁπλοῦς
καὶ ῥάδιος ὁ λόγος ὁ περὶ τούτων· οὔτε γὰρ εἰρήνην οἷόν τε
βεβαίαν ἀγαγεῖν, ἢν μὴ κοινῇ τοῖς βαρβάροις πολεμήσωμεν, 77
οὔθ' ὁμονοῆσαι τοὺς Ἕλληνας, πρὶν ἂν καὶ τὰς ὠφελείας ἐκ
τῶν αὐτῶν καὶ τοὺς κινδύνους πρὸς τοὺς αὐτοὺς ποιησώμεθα.
174 τούτων δὲ γενομένων καὶ τῆς ἀπορίας τῆς περὶ τὸν βίον
ἡμῶν ἀφαιρεθείσης, ἢ καὶ τὰς ἑταιρίας διαλύει καὶ τὰς

τῶν ἀρχαίων τινὲς ποιητῶν ὥσπερ
χρησμοὺς γράψαντες τοῖς ἐπιγενο-
μένοις τάδε τὰ ἰαμβεῖα καταλιπεῖν,
Aesch. *Ctesiph.* § 136 (after quoting
some verses of Hesiod), οἶμαι ὑμῖν
δόξειν οὐ ποιήματα Ἡσιόδου εἶναι
ἀλλὰ χρησμὸν εἰς Δημοσθένους πολιτείαν, and Plat. *Apol.* p. 79 c, ἐπι-
θυμῶ ὑμῖν χρησμῳδῆσαι...καὶ γάρ εἰμι
ἤδη ἐνταῦθα, ἐν ᾧ μάλιστ' ἄνθρωποι
χρησμῳδοῦσιν, ὅταν μέλλωσιν ἀποθα-
νεῖσθαι.
τοῖς τῶν πολιτικῶν ἐξεστηκόσι.]
Isocr. was prevented from public
speaking by weakness of voice and
nerve. *Panath.* § 9, 10, *Epp.* i. 9
and 8. 7, *Phil.* § 81. 2, πρὶν μὲν τὸ
πολιτεύεσθαι πάντων ἀφυέστατος ἐγε-
νόμην τῶν πολιτῶν· οὔτε γὰρ φωνὴν
ἔσχον ἱκανὴν οὔτε τόλμαν δυναμένην
ὄχλῳ χρῆσθαι καὶ μολύνεσθαι καὶ
λοιδορεῖσθαι τοῖς ἐπὶ τοῦ βήματος
καλινδουμένοις κ.τ.λ. *q. v.* v. Plin. *Ep.*

VI. 29. 6.
ἐξεστηκόσι.] In the very next §,
we have a *syncopated* form προεστῶτες. (v. table of various readings.)
172. οὐ μὴν ἀλλ'.] *ad Dem.* § 9,
Paneg. § 85.
ἐρρωμενεστέρως.] v. § 163. n.
νῦν μὲν γὰρ...οὐ γάρ.] For this
double γάρ cf. § 92, 145, 185, 186.
For three in succession, v. *Phil.*
§ 141, for five Plato, *Apol.* p. 40 A
(Schn.).—v. also Porson's n. on Eur.
Med. 139.
173. πρὸς ἡμᾶς αὐτούς.] Almost
= πρὸς ἀλλήλους. v. § 34, σφίσιν
αὐτοῖς. n.
ἐκ τῶν αὐτῶν.] sc. ἐκ τῶν βαρβάρων.
174. ἑταιρίας.] Not 'political
clubs,' as in § 79, but 'companion-
ships,' 'friendships.' Cf. *ad Dem.* § 10,
(Dem.) XXIX. *adv. Aphob.* §§ 22,
23, ἔχθρα}(ἑταιρία.

συγγενείας εἰς ἔχθραν προάγει καὶ πάντας ἀνθρώπους εἰς
πολέμους καὶ στάσεις καθίστησιν, οὐκ ἔστιν ὅπως οὐχ
ὁμονοήσομεν καὶ τὰς εὐνοίας ἀληθινὰς πρὸς ἡμᾶς αὐτοὺς
ἕξομεν. ὧν ἕνεκα περὶ παντὸς ποιητέον, ὅπως ὡς τάχιστα b
τὸν ἐνθένδε πόλεμον εἰς τὴν ἤπειρον διοριοῦμεν, ὡς μόνον
ἂν τοῦτ' ἀγαθὸν ἀπολαύσαιμεν τῶν κινδύνων τῶν πρὸς
ἡμᾶς αὐτούς, εἰ ταῖς ἐμπειρίαις ταῖς ἐκ τούτων γεγενημέναις
πρὸς τὸν βάρβαρον καταχρήσασθαι δόξειεν ἡμῖν.

175 (μζ΄.) Ἀλλὰ γὰρ ἴσως διὰ τὰς συνθήκας ἄξιον ἐπισχεῖν,
ἀλλ' οὐκ ἐπειχθῆναι καὶ θᾶττον ποιήσασθαι τὴν στρατείαν; c
δι' ἃς αἱ μὲν ἠλευθερωμέναι τῶν πόλεων βασιλεῖ χάριν ἴσα-
σιν, ὡς δι' ἐκεῖνον τυχοῦσαι τῆς αὐτονομίας ταύτης, αἱ δ'

προάγει.] 'Perverts,' here, as often, = in rem malam ducere. Dem. Aristocr. § 1, προάγειν εἰς ἀνέχθειαν, Lept. p. 468, § 36, πρὸς κακίας ὑπερβολήν, Xen. Hell. III. 5. 2, εἰς μῖσος.

οὐχ ἔστιν—ἕξομεν.] i. e. 'We cannot fail to be at harmony, and the good-will that we shall have towards one another cannot fail to be genuine.' On οὐκ ἔστιν ὅπως οὐχ.. v. Madv. Synt. § 102 b. R. 2.

τὰς εὐνοίας ἀληθινὰς ἕξομεν.] The art. shews that εὐνοίας is to be translated as a subject, ἀληθινὰς as a predicate. Cf. Soph. Aj. 1111, οὐ γάρ βάναυσον τὴν τέχνην ἐκτησάμην, and § 166, οὐχ ἱκάνων ἀρχεὶ τῶν ἠπειρωτῶν.—v. Donaldson Gk. Gr. § 489—498, 'On the Tertiary Predicate.'

τὸν ἐνθένδε πόλεμον κ.τ.λ.] For the form of expression cf. §§ 88, 96, and esp. 187, τὴν ἐκ τῆς Ἀσίας εὐδαιμονίαν εἰς τὴν Εὐρώπην διακομίσαιμεν. τὸν ἐνθένδε πόλεμον instead of τὸν ἐνθάδε πόλεμον is due to the influence of διοριοῦμεν. v. Madv. Synt. § 79 b.

ἤπειρον.] v. § 137, ἠπείρωτας. n.

διοριοῦμεν.] The Attic form of διορίσομεν. This contraction is very rarely used, except with futures in -έσω, -άσω, and -ίσω, from verbs of more than two syllables (which have a short antepenult), in -εω, -αζω, and -ιζω, e.g. τελῶ, βιβῶ, κομιῶ, from

τελέω, βιβάζω, κομίζω. (v. Donaldson, Gk. Gr. § 302, Obs. 3). As an exception may be quoted Ar. Eq. 891, προσαμφιῶ, fut. act. of προσαμφιέννυμι, which has no existing form ending in -ίω, and, as a verb of varied usage, ἐξετάζω, which generally has ἐξετάσω, and in one passage only (Isocr. Evag. § 34) has ἐξετῶ. (v. Mr Jebb's n. on Soph. Aj. 1027, ἀποφθείω, and Cobet, nov. lect. p. 65.) On the fut. of verbs in -ίω, cf. ad Dem. § 45. n.

The exact meaning of διορίζω ('transfer') is 'remove across the boundary (ὅροι),' = Lat. exterminare, 'to banish.' Cf. Plat. Legg. 873 e, τὸ δὲ ὀφλὸν ἔξω τῶν ὅρων τῆς χώρας ἀποκτείναντας διορίσαι, and ib. 874 A, τὸ ὀφλὸν ἐξορίζειν (v. Dem. Aristocr. § 76, and Kennedy's Lysines, &c. App. p. 329), and lastly, Plato, Rep. 560 D, ὠθοῦσιν ἔξω … ἐκβάλλουσι … ὑπερορίζουσι.

175. τὰς συνθήκας.] § 115. n.

ὡς δι' ἐκεῖνον κ.τ.λ.] "'Because (as they believe) they have obtained this independence through him.' ὡς is often prefixed to a participle denoting a cause or a purpose. It shows that the participle expresses the idea of the subject of the leading verb, or that of some other person prominently mentioned in the sentence; without implying that it is also the

ἐκδεδομέναι τοῖς βαρβάροις μάλιστα μὲν Λακεδαιμονίοις
ἐπικαλοῦσιν, ἔπειτα δὲ καὶ τοῖς ἄλλοις τοῖς μετασχοῦσι
τῆς εἰρήνης, ὡς ὑπὸ τούτων δουλεύειν ἠναγκασμέναι. καίτοι
πῶς οὐ χρὴ διαλύειν ταύτας τὰς ὁμολογίας, ἐξ ὧν τοιαύτη
δόξα γέγονεν, ὡς ὁ μὲν βάρβαρος κήδεται τῆς Ἑλλάδος καὶ
φύλαξ τῆς εἰρήνης ἐστὶν, ἡμῶν δέ τινές εἰσιν οἱ λυμαινό-
176 μενοι καὶ κακῶς ποιοῦντες αὐτήν; ὁ δὲ πάντων καταγε-
λαστότατον, ὅτι τῶν γεγραμμένων ἐν ταῖς ὁμολογίαις τὰ
χείριστα τυγχάνομεν διαφυλάττοντες. ἃ μὲν γὰρ αὐτονόμους ἀφίησι τάς τε νήσους καὶ τὰς πόλεις τὰς ἐπὶ τῆς
Εὐρώπης, πάλαι λέλυται καὶ μάτην ἐν ταῖς στήλαις ἐστίν·
ἃ δ' αἰσχύνην ἡμῖν φέρει καὶ πολλοὺς τῶν συμμάχων ἐκ-
δέδωκε, ταῦτα δὲ κατὰ χώραν μένει καὶ πάντες αὐτὰ κύρια c
ποιοῦμεν, ἃ χρῆν ἀναιρεῖν καὶ μηδὲ μίαν ἐᾶν ἡμέραν, νομί-
ζοντας προστάγματα καὶ μὴ συνθήκας εἶναι. τίς γὰρ οὐκ
οἶδεν, ὅτι συνθῆκαι μέν εἰσιν, αἵτινες ἂν ἴσως καὶ κοινῶς
ἀμφοτέροις ἔχωσι, προστάγματα δὲ τὰ τοὺς ἑτέρους ἐλατ- 78
177 τοῦντα παρὰ τὸ δίκαιον; διὸ καὶ τῶν πρεσβευσάντων ταύτην τὴν εἰρήνην δικαίως ἂν κατηγοροῖμεν, ὅτι πεμφθέντες
ὑπὸ τῶν Ἑλλήνων, ὑπὲρ τῶν βαρβάρων ἐποιήσαντο τὰς

---

idea of the speaker or writer." Goodwin's *Moods and Tenses*, § 109. n. 4,
Madv. *Synt.* § 176 d.

πῶς οὐ χρή :] § 6. n.

κήδεται—ἐστίν.] 'Cares tenderly
for Hellas, and is guardian of her
peace;' *i.e.* watches over the various
States to prevent them from going
to war with one another. The allusion is particularly (but, as Bens.
observes, not exclusively) to the
peace of Antalcidas. v. Plato, quoted
in § 121. n.

**οἱ λυμαινόμενοι καὶ κακῶς ποι-
οῦντες αὐτήν.**] 'Those who outrage
and maltreat her.' For the double
expression, v. § 111, αὐτόχειρας καὶ
φονέας. n.

176. **ὁ δὲ πάντων καταγελαστό-
τατον.**] (*sc.* τοῦτ' ἐστὶν) ὅτι. v. §
118. n.

λέλυται.] *sc.* by the Spartans. Cf.

§§ 132, 135, and fragm. of Theopompus, quoted in § 134. n.

στήλαις.] v. § 180, ἐν στήλαις
λιθίναις ἀναγράψαντες. n.

ἃ δὴ...ταῦτα δέ.] Δέ in *apodosis.*
v. §§ 1, 98. n.

χρῆν) = ἐχρῆν. v. § 19. n.

προστάγματα καὶ μὴ συνθῆκαι.]
'Dictates and not compacts.' v. § 120,
προστάττων. n. and cf. *Archid.* § 51,
τὰς ἐκ τῶν ἐπιταγμάτων συνθήκας.

ἴσως καὶ κοινῶς.] ' Equally and
impartially.' Similar twin expressions are very common; *e.g.* in the
same sense as the present pair,
Thuc. IV. 105, &c. ἴσοι καὶ ὅμοιοι,
and Hdt. VI. 52, Ar. *Pol.* III. 11. 10,
ὅμοιος καὶ ἴσος; and, in a different
sense, *Antiop.* § 78, ὁμοίας καὶ παρα-
πλησίας. Thuc. VII. 52, ἴσοι καὶ
παραπλήσιοι. (v. Lobeck, *Paralip.*
p. 61, 2).

συνθήκας. ἐχρῆν γὰρ αὐτοὺς, εἴτ᾽ ἐδόκει τὴν αὑτῶν ἔχειν
ἑκάστους, εἴτε καὶ τῶν δοριαλώτων ἐπάρχειν, εἴτε τούτων
κρατεῖν ὧν ὑπὸ τὴν εἰρήνην ἐτυγχάνομεν ἔχοντες, ἕν τι
τούτων ὁρισαμένους καὶ κοινὸν τὸ δίκαιον ποιησαμένους, b
178 οὕτω συγγράφεσθαι περὶ αὐτῶν. νῦν δὲ τῇ μὲν ἡμετέρᾳ
πόλει καὶ τῇ Λακεδαιμονίων οὐδεμίαν τιμὴν ἀπένειμαν, τὸν
δὲ βάρβαρον ἁπάσης τῆς Ἀσίας δεσπότην κατέστησαν,
ὥσπερ ὑπὲρ ἐκείνου πολεμησάντων ἡμῶν, ἢ τῆς μὲν Περσῶν
ἀρχῆς πάλαι καθεστηκυίας, ἡμῶν δ᾽ ἄρτι τὰς πόλεις κατοι-
κούντων, ἀλλ᾽ οὐκ ἐκείνων μὲν νεωστὶ ταύτην τὴν τιμὴν
ἐχόντων, ἡμῶν δὲ τὸν ἅπαντα χρόνον ἐν τοῖς Ἕλλησι δυ- c
179 ναστευόντων. (μη΄.) Οἶμαι δ᾽ ἐκείνως εἰπὼν μᾶλλον δηλά-
σειν τήν τε περὶ ἡμᾶς ἀτιμίαν γεγενημένην καὶ τὴν τοῦ
βασιλέως πλεονεξίαν. τῆς γὰρ γῆς ἁπάσης τῆς ὑπὸ τῷ
κόσμῳ κειμένης δίχα τετμημένης, καὶ τῆς μὲν Ἀσίας, τῆς

ἐχρῆν γὰρ κ.τ.λ.] Isocr. says that three definite and equitable courses were open to those who negotiated the peace: viz. that each state should either keep its own original territory; or extend its rule over all the territories it had from time to time acquired by right of war (e.g. Cynuria in the case of Sparta; Aegina, Scione, Mitylene, &c. in that of Athens; Cyprus, Clazomenae, &c. in that of Persia); or, lastly, remain in possession of all that it actually had immediately before the peace (in which case Thebes would have kept her Boeotian cities, Persia her continental territory, but not Cyprus). Instead of deciding on one of these courses they had paid no deference to Athens and Sparta, and had made the Persian king lord of all Asia. (v. Bens. *transl.* n.)

τὴν αὑτῶν.] v. § 99. n.

συγγράφεσθαι.] *Panath.* § 158, εἰρήνην...συνεγράψαντο.

ὥσπερ...ἀλλ᾽ οὐκ.] v. § 11, ὥσπερ. n.

179. τὴν περὶ ἡμᾶς ἀτιμίαν γε-
γενημένην.] On this position of the substantive between the article and participle v. Madv. *Synt.* § 9. R. 1. Cf. § 174, τὰς εὐνοίας ἀληθινάς, n. and esp. Dem. *Aristocr.* § 133, ἐκ τῆς τῷ Χαριδήμῳ νῦν ἀδείας κατασκευαζομέ-
νης, with Weber's n. p. 395—7.

ὑπὸ τῷ κόσμῳ.] 'Beneath the heavens.' For this meaning of κόσμος cf. Plat. *Timae.* p. 28 B ὁ δὴ πᾶς οὐρανὸς ἢ κόσμος ἢ καὶ ἄλλο ὅ τι ποτε ὀνομαζόμενος μάλιστ᾽ ἂν δέχοιτο, τοῦθ᾽ ἡμῖν ὠνομάσθω. Philolaus (?), the Pythagorean (ap. Stob. *Ecl. Physic.* I. p. 488), gives the name of κόσμος to the region of the 5 planets with the sun and the moon, bounded above by Ὄλυμπος and beneath by Οὐρανός.

δίχα τετμημένης.] In ancient Greek geography it was a common tenet, that the earth was divided into two parts, Asia and Europe. Africa was reckoned as a mere appendage to one or the other. (v. *Geographi Graeci minores*, II. 495 ed. Müller, Sallust, *Jug.* 17, and Lucan IX. 411.)

δ' Εὐρώπης καλουμένης, τὴν ἡμίσειαν ἐκ τῶν συνθηκῶν
εἴληφεν ὥσπερ πρὸς τὸν Δία τὴν χώραν νεμόμενος, ἀλλ' d
180 οὐ πρὸς τοὺς ἀνθρώπους τὰς συνθήκας ποιούμενος. καὶ
ταύτας ἡμᾶς ἠνάγκασεν ἐν στήλαις λιθίναις ἀναγράψαντας
ἐν τοῖς κοινοῖς τῶν ἱερῶν καταθεῖναι, πολὺ κάλλιον τρό-
παιων τῶν ἐν ταῖς μάχαις γιγνομένων· τὰ μὲν γὰρ ὑπὲρ
μικρῶν ἔργων καὶ μιᾶς τύχης ἐστίν, αὗται δ' ὑπὲρ ἅπαντος
τοῦ πολέμου καὶ καθ' ὅλης τῆς Ἑλλάδος ἐστήκασιν.

τὴν ἡμίσειαν.] sc. τῆι γῆι. v. §
34. τὴν πλείστην τῆς χώρας. n.

ὥσπερ — ποιούμενος.] i. e. 'As
though he were dividing the territory with Zeus, and not entering
into a compact with mortal men.'
Isocr. may be alluding (as Wolf
suggests) to the well-known division
of empire between Zeus, Poseidon,
and Pluto; who took respectively
the heaven, the sea, and the under
world, the earth remaining common
to all; but we are told that the
Great King has one-half, not one-
third of the dominion. The expression therefore appears to mean
little more than, ' As though Zeus
and he had the world between them,
Zeus might have one-half if he
pleased, he would take the other.'
Isocr. may have been thinking of a
passage in Hdt. vii. 8, where Xerxes
vauntingly declares, τὴν γῆν Περσίδα
ἀποδέξομεν τῷ Διὸς αἰθέρι ὁμουρέου-
σαν· οὐ γὰρ δὴ χώρην γε οὐδεμίαν
κατόψεται ὁ ἥλιος ὅμουρον ἐούσαν τῇ
ἡμετέρῃ, and the Scholiast on Ari-
stid. Panath. 128 (quoted by Dindf.
&c.) appears to have understood it
in some such fashion. His words are
ὥσπερ πρὸς τὸν Δία τὰ ὄντα διανεμό-
μενοι, τῷ μὲν τοῦ Ὀλύμπου ταραχω-
ρῶν, ἑαυτῷ δὲ τὴν γῆν ἔχειν.

180. ἐν στήλαις λιθίναις κ.τ.λ.]
At Athens, nearly all important
public documents were inscribed on
pillars: it was in this manner e.g.
that those who were disfranchised
(ἄτιμοι) were 'posted' in the Acro-
polis (Arist. Rhet. II. 23. 25, στηλί-

τη γεγονὼς ἐν τῇ Ἀκροπόλει. Isocr.
de Bigis, § 9, στήλιτην ἀναγράφειν,
Dem. Phil. III. 121, § 41, Fals.
Leg. 428, § 271—2, and Lycurg.
Locr. 220, § 117 sqq.). Treaties
were generally engraved on such
pillars and placed either inside the
public temples, or in their immediate precincts, Thuc. v. 18. 10,
στήλας δὲ στῆσαι Ὀλυμπίασι καὶ
Πυθοῖ καὶ Ἰσθμοῖ καὶ ἐν Ἀθήναις ἐν
πόλει καὶ ἐν Λακεδαίμονι ἐν Ἀμυ-
κλαίῳ, Thuc. v. 47, τὰς δὲ ξυνθήκας
...ἀναγράψαι ἐν στήλῃ λιθίνῃ Ἀθηναίους μὲν ἐν πόλει, Ἀργείους δὲ ἐν ἀγο-
ρᾷ ἐν τοῦ Ἀπόλλωνος τῷ ἱερῷ, Μαντινέας δὲ ἐν τοῦ Διὸς τῷ ἱερῷ ἐν τῇ
ἀγορᾷ· καταθέντων δὲ καὶ Ὀλυμπίασι στήλην χαλκῆν, Dem. Lept. 468,
§ 36 (speaking of the decrees of
Athens in favour of Leuco king of
Bosporus), τούτων ἀπάντων στήλας
ἀντιγράφους ἐστήσαθ' ὑμεῖς ἐκείνοι
(at Bosporus, Piraeus and Hieron).
Cf. §§ 115, 176. (v. Franz Elementa
Epigraphices graecae, p. 313 sqq.)

ἐν τοῖς κοινοῖς τῶν ἱερῶν.] The
public temples of Hellas, e.g. at
Olympia, Delphi, &c. Thuc. v. 18,
ἱερὰ κοινὰ (of the temple at Delphi).
The terms of the peace of Antalcidas were also inscribed in the
temples of Sparta and her allies,
as Isocr. expressly tells us (Panath.
§ 107).

πολὺ—πολέμου.] Quoted me-
moriter by Arist. Rhet. III. 10 (on
metaphors).

μιᾶς τύχης.] De Perm. § 128.

181 Ὑπὲρ ὧν ἄξιον ὀργίζεσθαι, καὶ σκοπεῖν ὅπως τῶν τε γεγενημένων δίκην ληψόμεθα καὶ τὰ μέλλοντα διορθωσόμεθα. καὶ γὰρ αἰσχρὸν ἰδίᾳ μὲν τοῖς βαρβάροις οἰκέταις c ἀξιοῦν χρῆσθαι, δημοσίᾳ δὲ τοσούτους τῶν συμμάχων περιορᾶν αὐτοῖς δουλεύοντας, καὶ τοὺς μὲν περὶ τὰ Τρωικὰ γενομένους μιᾶς γυναικὸς ἁρπασθείσης οὕτως ἅπαντας συνοργισθῆναι τοῖς ἀδικηθεῖσιν, ὥστε μὴ πρότερον παύσασθαι πολεμοῦντας, πρὶν τὴν πόλιν ἀνάστατον ἐποίησαν τοῦ τολ- 79

182 μήσαντος ἐξαμαρτεῖν, ἡμᾶς δ' ὅλης τῆς Ἑλλάδος ὑβριζομένης μηδεμίαν ποιήσασθαι κοινὴν τιμωρίαν, ἐξὸν ἡμῖν εὐχῆς ἄξια διαπράξασθαι. μόνος γὰρ οὗτος ὁ πόλεμος εἰρήνης κρείττων ἐστί, θεωρίᾳ μὲν μᾶλλον ἢ στρατείᾳ προσεοικώς, ἀμφοτέροις δὲ συμφέρων, καὶ τοῖς ἡσυχίαν ἄγειν καὶ τοῖς πολεμεῖν ἐπιθυμοῦσιν. εἴη γὰρ ἂν τοῖς μὲν ἀδεῶς b τὰ σφέτερ' αὐτῶν καρποῦσθαι, τοῖς δ' ἐκ τῶν ἀλλοτρίων μεγάλους πλούτους κατακτήσασθαι.

183 (μθ΄.) Πολλαχῇ δ' ἄν τις λογιζόμενος εὕροι ταύτας τὰς πράξεις μάλιστα λυσιτελούσας ἡμῖν. φέρε γάρ, πρὸς

181. ἰδίᾳ μὲν—δουλεύοντας.] Quoted *memoriter* by Arist. *Rhet.* III. 9, omitting ἀξιοῦν and αὑτοῖς, and substituting πολλοὺς for τοσούτους.

τοῖς βαρβάροις οἰκέταις...χρῆσθαι.] *e.g.* Phrygians, Paphlagonians, Scythians.—v. Becker's *Charicles*, Exc. sc. vii. p. 364, 3rd ed.

ἀνάστατον.) § 37. n.

182. εὐχῆς ἄξια.] 'Worthy of our prayers,' 'worth praying for.' *Phil.* § 19, οὐκ ἐλάττω τῆς βασιλείας πεποίηκεν, ἀλλ' εὐχῆς ἄξια διαπέπρακται. Slightly different to this is the phrase εὐχῇ ὅμοιος used in *Phil.* § 118, περιβάλλεσθαι τῇ διανοίᾳ τὰς πράξεις δυνατὰς μέν, εὐχῇ δ' ὁμοίας, ἐξεργάζεσθαι δὲ ζητεῖν αὐτάς, ὅπως ἂν οἱ καιροὶ παραδιδῶσιν, and Plat. *Rep.* VIII. 540 D, εὐχαῖς ὅμοια λέγοντες.

θεωρίᾳ.] '*Legationi solenni, sacrorum et splendoris causae profecturae.*' Morus. v. *Dict. Antiq.* s.v. Isocr. says that the proposed expedition against Persia would less resemble a warlike invasion than the peaceful pomp of a sacred embassy to the great Panhellenic games and temples. v. *de Bigis*, § 34, where Isocr. speaks of the splendour of the Olympic θεωρία of Alcibiades.

The above explanation is adopted by Wolf, Bens., Rauchenst., and in the main by all the other commentators except Schneider, whose translation is '*Vergnügungsreise*' (a pleasure-tour). He quotes Hdt. I. 30, *Τυραν.* § 4, κατ' ἐμπορίαν καὶ κατὰ θεωρίαν, and Plat. *Rep.* 556 c, ἢ κατὰ θεωρίας ἢ κατὰ στρατείας, ἢ ξύμπλοι ἢ συστρατιῶται.

στρατείᾳ.] v. § 15. n.

κατακτήσασθαι.] '*Solus Urbinas, ut solet, oratoris manum servat* κατακτήσασθαι.' [cet. κατακτήσασθαι.] Cobet. *Var. lect.* p. 125.

183. φέρε γάρ—σκοπούντας.] *i.e.* 'Against whom, I ask, is it right for *those* to make war who are eager for no self-aggrandisement but are looking to the claims of justice *alone?*'

τίνας χρὴ πολεμεῖν τοὺς μηδεμιᾶς πλεονεξίας ἐπιθυμοῦντας
ἀλλ' αὐτὸ τὸ δίκαιον σκοποῦντας; οὐ πρὸς τοὺς καὶ πρότερον κακῶς τὴν Ἑλλάδα ποιήσαντας καὶ νῦν ἐπιβουλεύ-
οντας καὶ πάντα τὸν χρόνον οὕτω πρὸς ἡμᾶς διακειμένους; c
184 τίσι δὲ φθονεῖν εἰκός ἐστι τοὺς μὴ παντάπασιν ἀνάνδρως

The imperative φέρε ('come! tell me!' Cf. ἄγε) gives additional animation to the sentence, and is one of the few oratorical touches that rescue the *Paneg.* from being merely a written pamphlet. This imper. is used by Isocr. only in the speech *de Perm.* § 251. As might be expected, it occurs frequently in the speeches of Demosthenes and in the dialogues of Plato.

αὐτὸ τὸ δίκαιον.] 'Justice by itself, alone.' Cf. *Areop.* § 67, αὐτοὺς τοὺς αἰτιωτάτους (and Schneider's n.) Dem. *de Cor.* § 126, αὐτὰ τἀναγκαιότατα &c. μόνοι is often coupled with αὐτός in this sense. In a *philosophical* passage, the expr. αὐτὸ τὸ δίκαιον would be properly translated by 'Justice in the abstract,' but in the present instance such a rendering would be too formal and technical.

184 τίσι δὲ—χρωμένους;] The exact meaning of τούτῳ τῷ πράγματι is open to dispute. It will be observed, that in the present and the preceding section Isocrates asks three distinctly different questions. He begins by stating that there are many points of view (πολλαχῇ κ.τ.λ.) in which the expedition against Persia would be found *advantageous* to the Greeks. The word λυσιτελούσαν is the key to the three questions that follow. In those questions the Greeks are divided into three classes; the first question takes the case of those who look to the claims of justice alone, without regard to personal advantage; the last refers to those who desire to satisfy the call of expediency and of justice; the second must therefore, naturally, refer to those who are mainly influenced by the motives of expediency. The characteristic of this class is φθόνος, and their courage in asserting their claims to the objects of their envy is of a lower order than the surpassing boldness of those who fight from the purest motives (αὐτὸ τὸ δίκαιον). The courage of those who fight for their own advantage is μέτριον, neither too great nor too little.

If this view of the general drift of the passage be correct, τούτῳ τῷ πράγματι must refer to ἀνδρία, which is implied in the word ἀνάνδρως, and the present passage will be one of the many instances of sense-constructions in Isocrates (v. § 110. n.). The meaning will in this case be as follows: 'Against whom is it right that *those* should direct their envy, who are not altogether destitute of courage, but who employ that faculty (*sc.* courage) in accordance with the true mean?' This explanation is supported on various grounds by Battie, Cor., Spohn, Breml, Baiter, Rauchenst., and Schneider. It only remains to state that according to Wolf and Morus τούτῳ τῷ πράγματι = φθόνῳ, according to Auger and Lange (in *transl.*) = ἀνανδρίᾳ, and lastly, according to Benseler = πλεονεξίᾳ. All of these opinions illustrate the sense of the passage, but fall short, I think, of a satisfactory explanation. For the phraseology cf. *Archid.* § 7, ἐλευθερίας, ὑπὲρ ἧς οὐδὲν ὅ τι τῶν δεινῶν οὐχ ὑπομενετέον, οὐ μόνον ἡμῖν ἀλλὰ καὶ τοῖς ἄλλοις τοῖς μὴ λίαν ἀνάνδρως διακειμένοις ἀλλὰ καὶ κατὰ μικρὸν ἀρετῆς ἀντιποιουμένοις. (To explain μετρίων as = καὶ κατὰ μικρόν, would require the insertion of καὶ before μετρίως).

διακειμένους ἀλλὰ μετρίως τούτῳ τῷ πράγματι χρωμένους;
οὐ τοῖς μείζους μὲν τὰς δυναστείας ἢ κατ' ἀνθρώπους περι-
βεβλημένοις, ἐλάττονος δ' ἀξίοις τῶν παρ' ἡμῖν δυστυχούν-
των; ἐπὶ τίνας δὲ στρατεύειν προσήκει τοὺς ἅμα μὲν εὐσε-
βεῖν βουλομένους, ἅμα δὲ τοῦ συμφέροντος ἐνθυμουμένους;
οὐκ ἐπὶ τοὺς καὶ φύσει πολεμίους καὶ πατρικοὺς ἐχθροὺς, d
καὶ πλεῖστα μὲν ἀγαθὰ κεκτημένους, ἥκιστα δ' ὑπὲρ αὐτῶν
ἀμύνεσθαι δυναμένους; οὐκοῦν ἐκεῖνοι πᾶσι τούτοις ἔνοχοι
185 τυγχάνουσιν ὄντες.　(ν'.) Καὶ μὴν οὐδὲ τὰς πόλεις λυπή-
σομεν στρατιώτας ἐξ αὐτῶν καταλέγοντες, ὃ νῦν ἐν τῷ
πολέμῳ τῷ πρὸς ἀλλήλους ὀχληρότατόν ἐστιν αὐταῖς· πολὺ
γὰρ οἶμαι σπανιωτέρους ἔσεσθαι τοὺς μένειν ἐθελήσοντας
τῶν συνακολουθεῖν ἐπιθυμησάντων. τίς γὰρ οὕτως ἢ νέος
ἢ παλαιὸς ῥάθυμός ἐστιν, ὅστις οὐ μετασχεῖν βουλήσεται c
ταύτης τῆς στρατιᾶς τῆς ὑπ' Ἀθηναίων μὲν καὶ Λακεδαιμονίων στρατηγουμένης, ὑπὲρ δὲ τῆς τῶν συμμάχων ἐλευθερίας ἀθροιζομένης, ὑπὸ δὲ τῆς Ἑλλάδος ἁπάσης ἐκπεμπομένης, ἐπὶ δὲ τὴν τῶν βαρβάρων τιμωρίαν πορευομένης;

μείζους ἢ κατ' ἀνθρώπους κ.τ.λ.]
Cf. § 179, ὥσπερ πρὸς τὸν Δία κ.τ.λ.
— The dominion of the Persians
was excessively great, their strength
excessively small. They were παντάπασιν ἀνθρώπων διακείμενοι. Hence
the appropriateness of the appeal to
those amongst the Greeks whose
courage was μέτριον.

εὐσεβεῖν] Resembles αὐτὸ τὸ δίκαιον σκοπεῖν in § 183. The word
must be explained in immediate reference to φύσει πολεμίους καὶ πατρικοὺς ἐχθρούς, just as τοῦ συμφέροντος refers to the clauses πλεῖστα
μὲν—δυναμένους.

185. καταλέγοντες.] 'Enrolling.'
Cf. κατάλογοι.

μένειν...συνακολουθεῖν] Cf. § 35.
ἀκολουθήσαντας)(ὑπομείναντας and
§ 147. n.

τίς κ.τ.λ.] sc. τίς γὰρ ἢ νέος ἢ
παλαιὸς οὕτω-ῥάθυμός ἐστιν. In
Isocrates, the adverb οὕτως is more
frequently placed before than after
the word qualified by it. Here it

stands several places before ῥάθυμος,
cf. Phil. § 12, οὕτως ἐπὶ γήρᾳ γέγονα
φιλότιμος. Callim. § 44, οὕτω...σφό-
δρα, and elsewhere. As an instance
of closer connexion we have Εὐαγ.
§ 37, οὐδεὶς γὰρ οὕτω ῥάθυμος
κ.τ.λ.

ἢ νέος ἢ παλαιός.] The use of the
somewhat poetical word παλαιὸς instead of γέρων or πρεσβύτερος has
led to a suspicion that παλαιὸς is not
the right reading. The same collocation occurs however in Plat. Symp.
181 B. οὐκ ἂν τις εἴποι οὔτε νέος οὔτε
παλαιός (which may be a quotation).
(Cf. Legg. 717 C). The use of the
poetical word may be justified by
the principle mentioned in Ar. Rhet.
III. 7. 10 (quoted in § 96. n.).

οὕτως...ὅστις] Cf. 113. n.—This
sentence as far as ἐκπεμπομένης (with
the slight alteration τίς γὰρ οὐκ ἂν
ἡδέως μετάσχοι στρατείας) is quoted
by Alexander (Walz. Rhet. Gr. IX.
461) as an instance of περίοδος τετράκωλος.

186 φήμην δὲ καὶ μνήμην καὶ δόξαν πόσην τινὰ χρὴ νομίζειν ἢ
ζῶντας ἕξειν ἢ τελευτήσαντας καταλείψειν τοὺς ἐν τοῖς 80
τοιούτοις ἔργοις ἀριστεύσαντας; ὅπου γὰρ οἱ πρὸς Ἀλέξανδρον πολεμήσαντες καὶ μίαν πόλιν ἑλόντες τοιούτων ἐπαίνων
ἠξιώθησαν, ποίων τινῶν χρὴ προσδοκᾶν ἐγκωμίων τεύξεσθαι
τοὺς ὅλης τῆς Ἀσίας κρατήσαντας; τίς γὰρ ἡ τῶν ποιεῖν

186. **φήμην–ἀριστεύσαντας.**] *i.e.*
'And how great must we deem the
fame and the name (*lit.* memory)
and the glory which *those* will either
have in their lives or bequeath in
their deaths, who have been fore-
most in such exploits as these?'

φήμην ll μνήμην.] The same παρονομασία may be found in *Phil.* § 134,
τὴν εὐλογίαν καὶ τοὺς ἐπαίνους καὶ τὴν
φήμην καὶ τὴν μνήμην and in Lysias
(?) *Or. Funebr.* § 3, μνήμην παρὰ τῆς
φήμης λαβών. The collocation of
these two words appears to have
been a common formula, not unlike
such collocations as μέλη καὶ μέρη,
ὥρα καὶ χώρα, χρήματα, καὶ κτήματα,
and others which have been collected by Lobeck (*Paralip.* 54 sqq.).
In the English Poets we have
'*name and fame,*' '*chance and
change,*' and many similar forms
of expression. Aristotle doubtless
alludes to this passage in *Rhet.* III.
7. 10 (quoted in § 96. n.), although
the MSS there give us the inexpli-
cable reading γνώμη instead of
μνήμη.

τοὺς...ἀριστεύσαντας.] Past with
ref. to ἕξειν...καταλείψειν.

ὅπου γὰρ κ. τ. λ.] v. § 83. n.

Ἀλέξανδρον] According to Apol-
lodorus (*Bibl. Myth.* III. 12. 5)
Paris was the name given to the infant son of Priam and Hecuba, by
the servant who found him on
mount Ida, and Alexander was a
subsequent name. γενόμενος νεανί-
σκος...Ἀλέξανδρος προσωνομάσθη, λῃ-
στὰς ἀμυνόμενος καὶ τοῖς ποιμνίοις
ἀλεξήσας, ὅπερ ἐστι βοηθήσας· καὶ
μετ' οὐ πολὺ τοὺς γονέας ἀνεῦρε.

ἐπαίνων...ἐγκωμίων] v. § 51. n.

τίς γὰρ—καταλιπεῖν;] *i.e.* ' For

is there a single one of those who
have either the power of poetry or
the knowledge of oratory, who will
refuse to toil earnestly in the desire
to leave behind him for all time a
memorial at once of his own intellect and of their valour?'

**τῶν ποιεῖν δυναμένων...τῶν λέγειν
ἐπισταμένων.**] Cf. Lysias (?) *Or.
Funebr.* § 2, καὶ τοῖς ποιεῖν δυναμένοις καὶ τοῖς εἰπεῖν βουληθεῖσιν. This
use of ποιεῖν is extremely common,
e.g. Hel. § 65, Ὁμήρῳ προσέταξε
ποιεῖν, and esp. Plato, *Ion,* 534 B,
κοῦφον γὰρ χρῆμα ποιητής ἐστι καὶ
πτηνὸν καὶ ἱερόν, καὶ οὐ πρότερον οἷός
τε ποιεῖν, πρὶν ἂν ἔνθεός τε γένηται
καὶ ἔκφρων καὶ ὁ νοῦς μηκέτι ἐν αὐτῷ
ἐνῇ· ἕως δ' ἂν τουτὶ ἔχῃ τὸ κτῆμα,
ἀδύνατος πᾶς ποιεῖν ἐστιν ἄνθρωπος καὶ
χρησμῳδεῖν. Sometimes the word is
used both in its generic and specific
sense in the very same passage, *e.g.
Evag.* § 36, φοβερούς ποιησάμενοι
τοὺς κινδύνους... followed by οἱ μὲν
πλεῖστοι πεποίηνται διὰ τύχην λαβόντες τὰς βασιλείας. (Cf. Plat.
Lysis, 206 B, σκόπει...ὅπως μὴ πᾶσι
τούτοις ἔνοχον σαυτὸν ποιήσῃς διὰ τὴν
ποίησιν, and Ben Jonson's Transl. of
the *Ars Poetica* of Horace, l. 317,
*And I shall bid the learned maker
looke On life and manners and make
these his booke.*)

From this meaning of ποιεῖν we
have the common Greek words
which have become familiar in their
English forms,—*poesy, poem,* and
poet. Poets are to the Greek mind
(as Sir William Temple puts it)
'*makers or creators,—such as raise
admirable frames and fabrics out of
nothing.*'

In modern English we are unable

δυναμένων ἢ τῶν λέγειν ἐπισταμένων οὐ πονήσει καὶ φιλοσοφήσει βουλόμενος ἅμα τῆς θ' αὐτοῦ διανοίας καὶ τῆς b
ἐκείνων ἀρετῆς μνημεῖον εἰς ἅπαντα τὸν χρόνον καταλιπεῖν;

187   (να'.) Οὐ τὴν αὐτὴν δὲ τυγχάνω γνώμην ἔχων ἔν τε
τῷ παρόντι καὶ περὶ τὰς ἀρχὰς τοῦ λόγου. τότε μὲν
γὰρ ᾤμην ἀξίως δυνήσεσθαι τῶν πραγμάτων εἰπεῖν νῦν
δ' οὐκ ἐφικνοῦμαι τοῦ μεγέθους αὐτῶν, ἀλλὰ πολλά με
διαπέφευγεν ὧν διενοήθην. αὐτοὺς οὖν χρὴ συνδιορᾶν, ὅσης
ἂν εὐδαιμονίας τύχοιμεν, εἰ τὸν μὲν πόλεμον τὸν νῦν ὄντα
περὶ ἡμᾶς πρὸς τοὺς ἠπειρώτας ποιησαίμεθα, τὴν δ' εὐδαι- c
μονίαν τὴν ἐκ τῆς Ἀσίας εἰς τὴν Εὐρώπην διακομίσαιμεν,

188 καὶ μὴ μόνον ἀκροατὰς γενομένους ἀπελθεῖν, ἀλλὰ τοὺς μὲν
πράττειν δυναμένους παρακαλοῦντας ἀλλήλους πειρᾶσθαι

to translate ποιεῖν literally; but there was a time when '*to make*,' with its derivatives '*maker*' and '*making*,' was commonly applied to poetry; *e. g.* Spenser's *Aeglaga*, VI. 82, *The God of shepheards, Tityrus is dead, Who taught me humbly as I can to make*, and Sir Philip Sidney's *Apologie for Poetrie* (printed 1595 A.D.), p. 24, ed. Arber, *The Greekes called him a Poet, which name, hath as the most excellent, gone thorough other Languages. It commeth of this word Poiein, which is, to make: wherein I know not, whether by lucke or wise-dome, wee Englishmen haue mette with the Greekes, in calling him a maker.*

The contrast in the text between ποιεῖν and λέγειν must not be confounded with that of § 188, between πράττειν δυναμένους and λόγων ἀμφισβητοῦνται.

δυναμένων...ἐπισταμένων.] v. § 11, *ad fin.* n.

πονήσει καὶ φιλοσοφήσει.] Cf. *Evag.* § 78, φιλοσοφεῖν καὶ ποιεῖν, and esp. § 6, σκοπεῖν καὶ φιλοσοφεῖν. n.

§§ 187—189. *The Peroration. I have fallen short of the hopes which I entertained at the beginning of my speech and have failed to reach the full grandeur of my theme. I therefore appeal for aid to my audience. The men of practical power must endeavour to reconcile Athens and Sparta; and those who contend for the palm of rhetoric must cease to write on trifling subjects, but must attempt to outrival this oration. Thus shall they be released from their present penury, and be seen by the world to be the causes of abundant blessing.*

187. οὐ τὴν—λόγου.] Obs. the blended iambic and trochaic rhythm and v. § 170. n.

ἔν τε τῷ παρόντι.] Benseler's text adds καιρῷ (against the authority of the best MSS). In such cases Isocr. generally omits καιρῷ, *e. g. Archid.* § 15, 104, *Trapez.* § 9, and esp. *Evag.* § 80, ἐν τῷ παρόντι καὶ τὸν λοιπὸν χρόνον, *de Pace*, § 121, and 14 other passages quoted by Schn. on *Areop.* § 78, where Isocr. adopts the fuller form ἐν τε τῷ παρόντι καιρῷ καὶ τοῖς παρεληλυθόσι χρόνοις.

πολλά με διαπέφευγεν.] Contrast § 14.

τὴν ἐκ τῆς Ἀσίας κ.τ.λ.] v. § 174, τὸν ἐνθένδε πόλεμον... n.

διαλλάττειν τήν τε πόλιν τὴν ἡμετέραν καὶ τὴν Λακεδαιμονίων, τοὺς δὲ τῶν λόγων ἀμφισβητοῦντας πρὸς μὲν τὴν
παρακαταθήκην καὶ περὶ τῶν ἄλλων ὧν νῦν φλυαροῦσι d
παύεσθαι γράφοντας, πρὸς δὲ τοῦτον τὸν λόγον ποιεῖσθαι
189 τὴν ἅμιλλαν καὶ σκοπεῖν, ὅπως ἄμεινον ἐμοῦ περὶ τῶν αὐτῶν πραγμάτων ἐροῦσιν, ἐνθυμουμένους, ὅτι τοῖς μεγάλα

188. τοὺς—ἀμφισβητοῦντας.] lit.
'Those who lay claim to oratory,'
i.e. 'are rival claimants for the prize
of rhetoric.' Cf. Hel. § 9, τοὺς ἀμφισβητοῦνται τοῦ φρονεῖν καὶ φάσκον-
ται εἶναι σοφισταὶ οὐκ ἐν τοῖς ἡμελη-
μένοις ὑπὸ τῶν ἄλλων, ἀλλ' ἐν οἷς
ἅπαντές εἰσιν ἀνταγωνισταί, προσήκει διαφέρειν καὶ κρείττους εἶναι τῶν
ἰδιωτῶν.

Benseler rightly condemns Battie's
transl. 'qui de verbis disputant.'

πρὸς μὲν τὴν παρακαταθήκην
κ.τ.λ.] One of the forensic speeches
of Isocr. (πρὸς Εὐθύνουν ἀμάρτυρος),
relates to a deposit of 3 talents
placed by one Nicias in the hands of
Euthynus. The latter (the defendant)
had paid two talents to Nicias (the
plaintiff), and Isocr. contends on
behalf of Nicias that another talent
was still due from Euthynus. As
no witnesses were present on the
occasion of the alleged deposit, the
case has to be argued on a priori
grounds. Isocr. states the case for
his client with considerable ingenuity. Lysias was probably retained
on the side of the defendant (v.
Baiter and Sauppe, Orat. Att. II.
199), and a rival speech was also
written by Antisthenes, (the Cynic),
a pupil of Gorgias, as we are told
by Diog. Laert. VI. 9, 15, who
states that the first volume of the
writings of Antisthenes contained
the Aias and 'Οδυσσεὺς (v. Orat.
Att. II. 167), and also a composition, πρὸς τὸν Ἰσοκράτους ἀμάρτυ-
ρον. To this writing of Antisthenes
allusion is probably made in the
present passage. (It may be noticed
in passing that in the Helenae Enc.
§ 1 sqq. we have a pointed attack

on Antisthenes, Plato and Euclides.
Their names are not mentioned, but
the allusion cannot be disputed. It
was partially discerned by Wolf,
who however expresses himself still
more clearly on the well-known anti-
Platonic allusion in Phil. § 12.—
v. Dr Thompson's ed. of Plat.
Phaedr. p. 175 and 179. n.)

This expl. was first proposed by
Wolf, and has been accepted by
all the best commentators, except
Benseler, who concludes his note
with words to this effect: 'It is far
more probable that Isocrates refers
to such subjects as those which an
Alcidamas, Antisthenes, or Polycrates chose for themselves mainly
from the world of legend, frequently in reference to modern political
circumstances. Thus the question
whether Hercules had entrusted the
kingdom of Argos to Tyndareus, or
Messene to Nestor (v. esp. Pausan.
II. 18. 6), had a political colouring.
inasmuch as it touched upon the
claims of Sparta to those territories,
but, nevertheless, it could by no
means lead to a political result.'
Benselcr, it must be remembered,
does not believe in the genuineness
of the πρὸς Εὐθύνουν; hence his artificial explanation.

φλυαροῦσι.] Cf. Soph. § 11.

πρὸς δὲ τοῦτον τὸν λόγον κ.τ.λ.]
This challenge was actually taken
up by one Aristoteles, who is described by Diog. Laert. vit. phil.
V. 1, § 35 as Σικελιώτης ῥήτωρ, πρὸς
τὸν Ἰσοκράτους Πανηγυρικὸν ἀντιγε-
γραφώς.

189. τοῖς μεγάλα ὑπισχν.] Alluding esp. to the vaunting profes-
sions of some of the Sophists. v.

ὑπισχνουμένοις οὐ πρέπει περὶ μικρὰ διατρίβειν, οὐδὲ τοιαῦτα λέγειν, ἐξ ὧν ὁ βίος μηδὲν ἐπιδώσει τῶν πεισθέντων,
ἀλλ᾽ ὧν ἐπιτελεσθέντων, αὐτοί τ᾽ ἀπαλλαγήσονται τῆς ε
παρούσης ἀπορίας καὶ τοῖς ἄλλοις μεγάλων ἀγαθῶν αἴτιοι
δόξουσιν εἶναι.

Soph. passim, esp. § 1, μείζους
ποιεῖσθαι τὰς ὑποσχέσεις...οἱ τολμῶν-
τες λίαν ἀπερισκέπτως ἀλαζονεύεσθαι,
and § 10, τὰς ὑπερβολὰς τῶν ἐπαγ-
γελμάτων.

περὶ μικρὰ διατρίβειν.] Alluding
partly to πρὸς μὲν—γράφοντας.—
Some of these trifling subjects have
been recorded; *e. g.* humble-bees and
salt. (*Hel.* § 12, τῶν τοὺς βομβυλιοὺς
καὶ τοὺς ἅλας καὶ τὰ τοιαῦτα βουληθέν-
των ἐπαινεῖν. Cf. Plat. *Symp.* 177 B).
Polycrates, a Sophist, whose decla-
mation, in defence of the monster
Busiris, is attacked by Isocr. in a
special treatise, was particularly famous for these compositions. We
are told that he wrote in praise of
mice, and pots, and pebbles. Cf.
Arist. *Rhet.* II. 24, and Alexander's
Ῥητορικαὶ ἀφορμαί ('Rhetorical ma-
gazine'), *Rhet. Gr.* ed Walz. IX. 334,
ὅταν χύτρας ἐγκωμιάζωμεν ἢ ψήφους,
ὡς Πολυκράτης, οὐ πάντως καὶ τεθαυ-
μασότες τὴν χύτραν ἢ τὰς ψήφους
ἐπαινοῦμεν, ἀλλὰ γυμνάζοντες ἑαυτοὺς
πιθανοῖς τισι λόγοις. These *tours de
force* doubtless resembled the extant
μυῖας ἐγκώμιον of Lucian, which contains all that ingenuity can suggest
in praise of the *musca domestica.*

ἀπορίας.] Not τῶν λόγων, but τῆς
οὐσίας (*Pecuniary* embarrassment),
as the context clearly shews. *Vi-
dentur enim,* says Wolf, (from personal experience) *ut nunc, ita olim
etiam paupertatis clientes fuisse ludi-
magistri.* Cf. the peroration of the
speech *de Pace,* and esp. the words,
ἐν ταῖς τῆς Ἑλλάδος εὐπραγίαις συμ-
βαίνει καὶ τὰ τῶν φιλοσόφων πράγματα πολὺ βελτίω γίγνεσθαι. Isocrates frequently speaks of the penury of his rivals, *e.g. Soph.* § 4,
λέγουσι μὲν, ὡς οὐδὲν δέονται χρημά-

των...μικροῦ δὲ κέρδους ὀρεγόμενοι
μόνον οὐκ ἀθανάτους ὑπισχνοῦνται
τοὺς συνόντας ποιήσειν, *ib.* § 7, τοὺς
τὴν εὐδαιμονίαν παραδιδόντας...αὐ-
τοὺς πολλῶν δεομένους καὶ τοὺς μαθη-
τὰς μικρὸν πραττομένους. The fee
demanded by these rivals was 3 or 4
minae (£12—16). Isocr. himself
charged (according to an anonymous
writer of his life) as much as 10 minae (£40), apparently for the whole
course (Cf. Dem. *Lacr.* § 15, οὑτοσὶ
Λάκριτος Φασηλίτης, μέγα πρᾶγμα,
Ἰσοκράτους μαθητής, and *ib.* § 42, ταῖς
χιλίαις δραχμαῖς ἃς δέδωκε τῷ διδα-
σκάλῳ). We know of one at least of
his pupils (the historian Ephorus of
Cymae), who passed through the
course with such poor success that
his father was compelled to send
him again, and pay a second fee,
which led the master to give his
pupil the nickname of Δίφορος. He
had as many as 100 pupils in all
(Phot. *Bibl.* cod. 176.); Hermippus
(ὁ Καλλιμάχειος) wrote a book a-
bout these pupils: amongst them, as
we learn from various sources, were
the orators Isaeus, Hyperides, Lycurgus, the historians Theopompus
and Ephorus, and the tragedians
Astydamas, Theodectes and Ascle-
piades. The vast sums he accumu-
lated, from these and similar sources,
exposed him to envy (*de Perm.* §§ 4,
146, 154), but in the speech *de Permutatione* he defends himself on
the ground that all these sums were
obtained not from Athenians but
from foreigners (*ib.* §§ 39, 40); many
of these pupils stayed with him for
3 or 4 years, and at the conclusion
of the course parted from him with
tears of regret (*ib.* § 88, μετὰ πόθου
καὶ δακρύων ἀπηλλάγησαν).

GREEK INDEX.

The numerals in general refer to the *pages* of this edition and to the notes on those pages, but when preceded by §§, they refer only to the *sections* of the *Panegyricus*.

166   GREEK INDEX.

ENGLISH INDEX.

October, 1868.

New Works

IN COURSE OF PUBLICATION

BY

Messrs. RIVINGTON,

WATERLOO PLACE, LONDON;

HIGH STREET, OXFORD; TRINITY STREET, CAMBRIDGE.

Newman's (J. H.) Parochial and Plain
Sermons.
Edited by the Rev. W. J. Copeland, Rector of Farnham,
Essex. From the Text of the last Editions published by
Messrs. Rivington.
8 vols. Crown 8vo. 5s. each. (Vols. I. to VI. just pub-
lished.)

The Witness of the Old Testament to
Christ. The Doyle Lectures for the Year 1868.
By the Rev. Stanley Leathes, M.A., Preacher at St. James's,
Westminster, and Professor of Hebrew in King's College,
London. 8vo. 9s.

London, Oxford, and Cambridge

A

The Reformation of the Church of

England; its History, Principles, and Results. A.D. 1514—1547.
By **John Henry Blunt**, M.A.

8vo. (*Nearly ready.*)

The Divinity of our Lord and Saviour

Jesus Christ ; being the Bampton Lectures for 1866.

By **Henry Parry Liddon**, M.A., Student of Christ Church,
Prebendary of Salisbury, and Examining Chaplain to the Bishop
of Salisbury.

Third Edition. Crown 8vo. 5*s*.

Preparation for Death.

Translated from the Italian : forming the Advent Volume of
the " Ascetic Library."

Square Crown 8vo. (*Nearly ready.*)

Five Years' Church Work in the King-

dom of Hawaii.

By the **Bishop of Honolulu.**

With Map and Illustrations. Crown 8vo. 5*s*.

From Morning to Evening :

a Book for Invalids.

From the French of M. L'Abbé Henri Perreyve. Translated
and adapted by an Associate of the Sisterhood of S. John
Baptist, Clewer.

Small 8vo. 5*s*.

The Virgin's Lamp:

Prayers and Devout Exercises for English Sisters, chiefly composed and selected by the late Rev. J. M. Neale, D.D., Founder of St. Margaret's, East Grinstead.

Small 8vo. 3s. 6d.

Perranzabuloe, the Lost Church Found;

or, The Church of England not a new Church, but Ancient, Apostolical, and Independent, and a Protesting Church Nine Hundred Years before the Reformation.

By the Rev. C. Collins Trelawny, M.A., formerly Rector of Timsbury, Somerset, and late Fellow of Balliol College, Oxford. With Illustrations.

New Edition. Crown 8vo. 3s. 6d.

Spiritual Life.

By John James, D.D., Canon of Peterborough, Author of a "Comment on the Collects of the Church of England."

12mo. (*Nearly ready.*)

Bible Readings for Family Prayer.

By the Rev. W. H. Ridley, M.A., Rector of Hambleden.
Old Testament—Genesis and Exodus.
New Testament—St. Luke and St. John.
In 2 Parts. Crown 8vo. (*Nearly ready.*)

The Doctrine of the Church of Eng-

land, as stated in Ecclesiastical Documents set forth by Authority of Church and State, in the Reformation Period between 1536 and 1662.

8vo. (*Nearly ready.*)

London, Oxford, and Cambridge

A 2

Selections from Modern French Authors.
With English Notes.
By Henri Van Laun, French Master at Cheltenham College.
Part 1.—Honoré de Balzac.
Crown 8vo.   3s. 6d.   (*Nearly ready.*)

Miscellaneous Poems.
By Henry Francis Lyte, M.A., Late Vicar of Lower Brixham, Devon.
New Edition.   Small 8vo.   5s.

A Key to the Knowledge and Use of the Holy Bible.
By John Henry Blunt, M.A.
Small 8vo.   2s. 6d.

Vox Ecclesiæ Anglicanæ : on the
Church Ministry and Sacraments. A Selection of Passages from the Writings of the Chief Divines of the Church of England. With short Introductions and Notices of the Writers.
By George G. Perry, M.A., Prebendary of Lincoln, Rector of Waddington, Rural Dean, and Proctor for the Diocese of Lincoln.
Crown 8vo.   6s.

England v. Rome : a Brief Handbook of the Roman Catholic Controversy, for the use of Members of the English Church.
By H. B. Swete, M.A., Fellow of Gonville and Caius College, Cambridge.
16mo.   (*Nearly ready.*)

Manual of Family Devotions, arranged

from the Book of Common Prayer.
By the Hon. Augustus Duncombe, D.D., Dean of York.
Printed in red and black. Small 8vo. 3s. 6d.

Sketches of the Rites and Customs of

the Greco-Russian Church.
By H. C. Romanoff. With an Introductory Notice by the
Author of "The Heir of Redclyffe."
Crown 8vo. 7s. 6d.

Annals of the Bodleian Library, Ox-

ford, from its Foundation to A.D. 1867; containing an Account
of the various collections of printed books and MSS. there preserved; with a brief Preliminary Sketch of the earlier Library
of the University.
By W. D. Macray, M.A., Assistant in the Library, Chaplain
of Magdalen and New Colleges.
8vo. 12s.

A Key to the Knowledge and Use of

the Book of Common Prayer.
By John Henry Blunt, M.A.
Small 8vo. 2s. 6d.

The Mysteries of Mount Calvary.

By Antonio de Guevara.
Being the First Volume of the "Ascetic Library," a Series of
Translations of Spiritual Works for Devotional Reading from
Catholic Sources. Edited by the Rev. Orby Shipley, M.A.
Square crown 8vo. 3s. 6d.

London, Oxford, and Cambridge

Vestiarivm Christianvm : the Origin

and Gradual Development of the Dress of the Holy Ministry in
the Church, as evidenced by Monuments both of Literature
and of Art, from the Apostolic Age to the present time.

By the Rev. **Wharton B. Marriott**, M.A., F.S.A. (sometime
Fellow of Exeter College, Oxford, and Assistant-Master at
Eton), Select Preacher in the University, and Preacher, by
licence from the Bishop, in the Diocese of Oxford.

Royal 8vo.   38s.

The Annotated Book of Common

Prayer; being an Historical, Ritual, and Theological Commentary on the Devotional System of the Church of England.

Edited by **John Henry Blunt**, M.A.

Third Edition. Imperial 8vo, 36s. Large paper Edition,
royal 4to, with large margin for Notes, 3l. 3s.

The Prayer Book Interleaved ;

with Historical Illustrations and Explanatory Notes arranged
parallel to the Text, by the Rev. **W. M. Campion**, B.D., Fellow
and Tutor of Queens' College and Rector of St. Botolph's,
and the Rev. **W. J. Beamont**, M.A., Fellow of Trinity College,
Cambridge, and Incumbent of St. Michael's, Cambridge. With
a Preface by the **Lord Bishop of Ely**.

Fourth Edition. Small 8vo.   7s. 6d.

Flowers and Festivals ; or, Directions

for the Floral Decorations of Churches.   With coloured Illustrations.

By **W. A. Barrett**, of S. Paul's Cathedral, late Clerk of
Magdalen College, and Commoner of S. Mary Hall, Oxford.

Square crown 8vo.   5s.

Proceedings at the laying of the First

Stone of Keble College, Oxford, on St. Mark's Day, April 25th, 1868.

Small 4to. 3s. 6d.

Selections from Aristotle's Organon.

Edited by John R. Magrath, M.A., Fellow and Tutor of Queen's College, Oxford.

Crown 8vo. 3s. 6d.

Curious Myths of the Middle Ages.

By S. Baring-Gould, M.A., Author of "Post-Mediæval Preachers," &c. With Illustrations.

First Series. *Second Edition.* Crown 8vo. 7s. 6d.
Second Series. *Second Edition.* Crown 8vo. 9s. 6d.

Household Theology: a Handbook of

Religious Information respecting the Holy Bible, the Prayer Book, the Church, the Ministry, Divine Worship, the Creeds, &c. &c.

By J. H. Blunt, M.A.

Third Edition. Small 8vo. 3s. 6d.

Consoling Thoughts in Sickness.

Edited by Henry Bailey, B.D., Warden of St. Augustine's College, Canterbury.

Large type. Small 8vo. 2s. 6d.

London, Oxford, and Cambridge

Scripture Acrostics.

By the Author of "The Last Sleep of the Christian Child."
With Key. Square 16mo. 2s.

The Sacraments and Sacramental Or-

dinances of the Church ; being a Plain Exposition of their
History, Meaning, and Effects.
By John Henry Blunt, M.A.
Small 8vo. 4s. 6d.

Queen Bertha and her Times.

By E. H. Hudson.
Small 8vo. 5s.

Catechesis ; or, Christian Instruction

preparatory to Confirmation and First Communion.
By Charles Wordsworth, D.C.L., Bishop of St. Andrew's.
New and cheaper Edition. Small 8vo. 2s.

The Life and Times of S. Gregory the

Illuminator, Patron Saint and Founder of the Armenian
Church.
By S. C. Malan, M.A., Vicar of Broadwindsor.
8vo. 10s. 6d.

The Annual Register: a Review of

Public Events at Home and Abroad, for the Year 1867 ; being
the Fifth Volume of an improved Series.

8vo. 18s.

₀ *The Volumes for 1863, 1864, 1865, and 1866 may be had,
price 18s. each.*

Thomas à Kempis, Of the Imitation of

Christ : a carefully revised translation, elegantly printed with
red borders.

16mo. 2s. 6d.

Also a cheap Edition, without the red borders, 1s., or in Wrapper, 6d.

The Rule and Exercises of Holy Living.

By **Jeremy Taylor**, D.D., Bishop of Down, and Connor, and
Dromore.

A New Edition, elegantly printed with red borders. 16mo.
3s. 6d. (*Just ready.*)

A Short and Plain Instruction for the

better Understanding of the Lord's Supper ; to which is an-
nexed, the Office of the Holy Communion, with proper Helps
and Directions.

By **Thomas Wilson**, D.D., late Lord Bishop of Sodor and
Man.

New and complete Edition, elegantly printed with rubrics and
borders in red. 16mo. (*Nearly ready.*)

Aids to Prayer: a Course of Lectures

delivered at Holy Trinity Church, Paddington, on the Sunday
mornings in Lent, 1868.

By **Daniel Moore**, M.A., Honorary Chaplain to the Queen,
&c.

Crown 8vo. 4s. 6d.

The Greek Testament.

With English Notes, intended for the Upper Forms of
Schools, and for Pass-men at the Universities. Abridged from
the larger work of the Dean of Canterbury.

In one Volume, Crown 8vo.   10s. 6d.   (*Nearly ready.*)

Thoughts on Personal Religion; being

a Treatise on the Christian Life in its Two Chief Elements,
Devotion and Practice.

By Edward Meyrick Goulburn, D.D., Dean of Norwich.

New Edition.   Small 8vo.   6s. 6d.

An edition for presentation, Two Volumes, small 8vo.   10s. 6d.

Also, a Cheap Edition.   3s. 6d.

Six Short Sermons on Sin. Lent Lectures

at S. Alban the Martyr, Holborn.

By the Rev. Orby Shipley, M.A.

Fourth Edition.   Small 8vo.   1s.

Daily Devotions; or, Short Morning

and Evening Services for the use of a Churchman's Household.

By the Ven. Charles C. Clarke, Archdeacon of Oxford.

18mo.   1s.

A Fourth Series of Parochial Sermons,

preached in a Village Church.

By the Rev. Charles A. Heurtley, D.D., Rector of Fenny
Compton, Warwickshire, Margaret Professor of Divinity, and
Canon of Christ Church, Oxford.

Small 8vo.   5s. 6d.

London, Oxford, and Cambridge

Popular Objections to the Book of

Common Prayer considered, in Four Sermons on the Sunday
Lessons in Lent, the Commination Service, and the Athanasian
Creed, with a Preface on the existing Lectionary.
By **Edward Meyrick Goulburn**, D.D., Dean of Norwich.
Small 8vo. 2s. 6d.

Sickness; its Trials and Blessings.

Fine Edition. Small 8vo. 3s. 6d.
Also, a Cheap Edition, 1s. 6d., or in Paper Wrapper, 1s.

Devotional Commentary on the Gospel

according to S. Matthew.
Translated from **Pasquier Quesnel**.
Crown 8vo. (*In the Press.*)

Flosculi Cheltonienses: a Selection

from the Cheltenham College Prize Poems, 1846—1866.
Edited by **C. S. Jerram**, M.A., Trinity College, Oxford, and
Theodore W. James, M.A., Pembroke College, Oxford.
Crown 8vo. 9s.

The Dogmatic Faith: an Inquiry

into the Relation subsisting between Revelation and Dogma.
Being the Bampton Lectures for 1867.
By **Edward Garbett**, M.A., Incumbent of Christ Church,
Surbiton.
Second Edition. Crown 8vo. 5s.

London, Oxford, and Cambridge

London Ordination, Advent, 1867;

being Seven Addresses to the Candidates for Holy Orders, in December, 1867.

By **Archibald Campbell, Lord Bishop of London,** and his **Chaplains.**

Together with the Examination Papers.

8vo. 4*s.*

Family Prayers: compiled from various

sources (chiefly from Bishop Hamilton's Manual), and arranged on the Liturgical Principle.

By **Edward Meyrick Goulburn,** D.D., Dean of Norwich.

New Edition. Crown 8vo, large type, 3*s.* 6*d.* 16mo, 1*s.*

Cheap Edition.

Eastern Orthodoxy in the Eighteenth

Century; being a Correspondence between the Greek Patriarchs and the Nonjurors.

Edited, with an Introduction, by the Rev. **George Williams,** B.D., Senior Fellow of King's College, Cambridge.

8vo. (*Nearly ready.*)

Catechetical Notes and Class Questions,

Literal and Mystical; chiefly on the Earlier Books of Holy Scripture.

By the late Rev. **J. M. Neale,** D.D., Warden of Sackville College, East Grinstead.

Crown 8vo. (*In the Press.*)

The Treasury of Devotion: a Manual

of Prayers for daily use.

Edited by the Rev. **T. T. Carter,** Rector of Clewer.

16mo. (*In preparation.*)

London, Oxford, and Cambridge

Liber Precum Publicarum Ecclesiæ

Anglicanæ.

À **Guilelmo Bright**, A.M., et **Petro Goldsmith Medd**, A.M., Presbyteris, Collegii Universitatis in Acad. Oxon. Sociis, Latine redditus.

In an elegant pocket volume, with all the Rubrics in red.
New Edition. Small 8vo. (*Nearly ready.*)

The Voice of the Good Shepherd to His

Lost Sheep ; being an Exposition of the former part of the Parable of the Prodigal Son.

By **Robert G. Swayne**, M.A., Rector of St. Edmund's, Salisbury.

Small 8vo. 2s. 6d.

Counsels upon Holiness of Life.

Translated from the Spanish of "The Sinner's Guide" by **Luis de Granada**; forming a volume of the "Ascetic Library."

Crown 8vo. (*In preparation.*)

A Glossary of Ecclesiastical Terms ;

containing Explanations of Terms used in Architecture, Ecclesiology, Hymnology, Law, Ritualism, Theology, Heresies, and Miscellaneous Subjects.

By Various Writers. Edited by the Rev. **Orby Shipley**, M.A.

8vo. (*In preparation.*)

Reflections on the Revolution in France,

and on the Proceedings in certain Societies in London relative to that Event. In a Letter intended to have been sent to a Gentleman in Paris, 1790.

By the Right Hon. **Edmund Burke**, M.P.

New Edition. With a short Biographical Notice. Crown 8vo.

3s. 6d.

London, Oxford, and Cambridge

Apostolical Succession in the Church
of England.

By the Rev. **Arthur W. Haddan**, B.D., Rector of Barton-on-the-Heath, and late Fellow of Trinity College, Oxford.

8vo.   (*In preparation.*)

The Holy Bible.

With Notes and Introductions.

By **Chr. Wordsworth**, D.D., Archdeacon of Westminster.

				£	s.	d.
Vol. I.	38*s.*	I.	Genesis and Exodus. *Second Edit.*	1	1	0
		II.	Leviticus, Numbers, Deuteronomy. *Second Edition*	0	18	0
Vol. II.	21*s.*	III.	Joshua, Judges, Ruth. *Second Edit.*	0	12	0
		IV.	The Books of Samuel. *Second Edit.*	0	10	0
Vol. III.	21*s.*	V.	The Books of Kings, Chronicles, Ezra, Nehemiah, Esther. *Second Edition*	1	1	0
Vol. IV.	34*s.*	VI.	The Book of Job. *Second Edition.*	0	9	0
		VII.	The Book of Psalms. *Second Edit.*	0	15	0
		VIII.	Proverbs, Ecclesiastes, Song of Solomon	0	12	0
Vol. V.		IX.	Isaiah	0	12	6

Sermons preached before the University
of Oxford, chiefly during the years 1863—1865.

By **Henry Parry Liddon**, M.A., Student of Christ Church, Prebendary of Salisbury, Examining Chaplain to the Lord Bishop of Salisbury, and lately Select Preacher.

Second Edition. 8vo. 8*s.*

Stones of the Temple: a familiar

Explanation of the Fabric and Furniture of the Church, with Illustrations, engraved by O. Jewitt.

By the Rev. **Walter Field**, M.A., Vicar of Godmersham.

Post 8vo. (*In preparation.*)

A Summary of Theology and Ecclesiastical

History: a Series of Original Works on all the principal subjects of Theology and Ecclesiastical History.

By Various Writers.

In 8 Vols., 8vo. (*In preparation.*)

Parish Musings; or, Devotional Poems.

By **John S. B. Monsell**, LL.D., Vicar of Egham, Surrey, and Rural Dean.

Tenth Edition. 18mo, 1s., or, in limp cloth, 1s. 6d.
A superior Edition may be had, in small 8vo, 2s. 6d.

Standing and Stumbling.

Part I.—Seven Common Faults.
Part II.—Your Duty and Mine.
Part III.—Things Rarely Met With.

By **James Erasmus Philipps**, M.A., Vicar of Warminster.

Small 8vo. 2s. 6d.

(*The Parts may be had separately, 1s. each.*)

An Outline of Logic,

for the use of Teachers and Students.

By **Francis Garden**, M.A., Trinity College, Cambridge, Sub-Dean of Her Majesty's Chapels Royal ; Chaplain to the Household in St. James' Palace ; Professor of Mental and Moral Science, Queen's College, London.

Small 8vo. 4s.

London, Oxford, and Cambridge.

An Introduction to the Devotional

Study of the Holy Scriptures.
By **Edward Meyrick Goulburn**, D.D., Dean of Norwich.

Ninth Edition. Small 8vo. 3*s*. 6*d*.

The London Diocese Book for 1868

(fourth year of issue), under the sanction of the Lord Bishop of London.

Crown 8vo. In wrapper, 1*s*.

On Miracles; being the Bampton

Lectures for 1865.
By **J. B. Mozley**, B.D., Vicar of Old Shoreham, late Fellow of Magdalen College, Oxford.

Second Edition. 8vo. 10*s*. 6*d*.

Sermons on Unity; with an Essay on

Religious Societies, and a Lecture on the Life and Times of Wesley.
By **F. C. Massingberd**, M.A., Chancellor of Lincoln.

Crown 8vo. 3*s*. 6*d*.

Songs of Joy for the Age of Joy.

By the Rev. **John P. Wright**, B.A.

18mo. 6*d*.

Semele; or, The Spirit of Beauty:

a Venetian Tale.
By **J. D. Mereweather**, B.A. Oxon., English Chaplain at Venice.

Small 8vo. 3*s*. 6*d*.

London, Oxford, and Cambridge

Warnings of the Holy Week, &c.;

being a Course of Parochial Lectures for the Week before
Easter and the Easter Festivals.

By the Rev. **W. Adams**, M.A., late Vicar of St. Peter's-in-
the-East, Oxford, and Fellow of Merton College.

Sixth Edition. Small 8vo. 4*s.* 6*d.*

Farewell Counsels of a Pastor to his

Flock, on Topics of the Day: Nine Sermons preached at
St. John's, Paddington.

By **Edward Meyrick Goulburn**, D.D., Dean of Norwich.

Third Edition. Small 8vo. 4*s.*

An Illuminated Edition of the Book of

Common Prayer, printed in Red and Black, on fine toned Paper;
with Borders and Titles, designed after the manner of the 14th
Century, by **R. R. Holmes**, F.S.A., and engraved by **O. Jewitt**.
Crown 8vo. White vellum cloth illuminated. 16*s.*

This Edition of the PRAYER BOOK *may be had in various
Bindings for presentation.*

Yesterday, To-day, and For Ever: a

Poem in Twelve Books.

By **Edward Henry Bickersteth**, M.A., Incumbent of Christ
Church, Hampstead, and Chaplain to the Bishop of Ripon.

Second and Cheaper Edition. Small 8vo. 6*s.*

The Gate of Paradise: a Dream of

Easter Eve. With Frontispiece.

Square crown 8vo. 6*d.*

The Greek Testament.

With Notes and Introductions.
By Chr. Wordsworth, D.D., Archdeacon of Westminster.
2 Vols. Impl. 8vo. 4*l.*

The Parts may be had separately, as follows :—

The Gospels, 6*th Edition*, 21*s.*
The Acts, 5*th Edition*, 10*s.* 6*d.*
St. Paul's Epistles, 5*th Edition*, 31*s.* 6*d.*
General Epistles, Revelation, and Indexes, 3*rd Edition*, 21*s.*

The Acts of the Deacons ; being a

Course of Lectures, Critical and Practical, upon the Notices
of St. Stephen and St. Philip the Evangelist, contained in the
Acts of the Apostles.
By Edward Meyrick Goulburn, D.D., Dean of Norwich.
Second Edition. Small 8vo. 6*s.*

Sermons for Children ; being Twenty-

eight short Readings, addressed to the Children of St. Mar-
garet's Home, East Grinstead.
By the late Rev. J. M. Neale, D.D., Warden of Sackville
College.
Small 8vo. 3*s.*

Our Lord Jesus Christ Teaching on

the Lake of Gennesaret : Six Discourses suitable for Family
Reading.
By Charles Baker, M.A., Oxon, Vicar of Appleshaw,
Hants.
Small 8vo. 1*s.* 6*d.*

London, Oxford, and Cambridge

The Greek Testament.

With a Critically revised Text ; a Digest of Various Readings ; Marginal References to Verbal and Idiomatic Usage ; Prolegomena ; and a Critical and Exegetical Commentary. For the use of Theological Students and Ministers. By **Henry Alford**, D.D., Dean of Canterbury.

4 Vols. 8vo. 102s.

The Volumes are sold separately as follows :—

Vol. I.—The Four Gospels. *Sixth Edition.* 28s.
Vol. II.—Acts to II. Corinthians. *Fifth Edition.* 24s.
Vol. III.—Galatians to Philemon. *Fourth Edition.* 18s.
Vol. IV.—Hebrews to Revelation. *Third Edition.* 32s.

The New Testament for English

Readers ; containing the Authorized Version, with a revised English Text ; Marginal References ; and a Critical and Explanatory Commentary. By **Henry Alford**, D.D., Dean of Canterbury.

Now complete in 2 Vols. or 4 Parts, price 54s. 6d.

Separately,

Vol. 1, Part I.—The three first Gospels, with a Map. *Second Edition.* 12s.
Vol. 1, Part II.—St. John and the Acts. 10s. 6d.
Vol. 2, Part I.—The Epistles of St. Paul, with a Map. 16s.
Vol. 2, Part II.—Hebrews to Revelation. 8vo. 16s.

The Beatitudes of Our Blessed Lord,

considered in Eight Practical Discourses.

By the Rev. **John Peat**, M.A., of St. Peter's College, Cambridge, Vicar of East Grinstead, Sussex.

Small 8vo. 3s. 6d.

Arithmetic for the Use of Schools;

with a numerous collection of Examples.

By **R. D. Beasley**, M.A., Head Master of Grantham Grammar School, and formerly Fellow of St. John's College, Cambridge; Author of "Elements of Plane Trigonometry."

12mo. 3s.

The Examples are also sold separately:—Part I., Elementary Rules, 8d. Part II., Higher Rules, 1s. 6d.

The Formation of Tenses in the Greek

Verb; showing the Rules by which every Tense is Formed from the pure stem of the Verb, and the necessary changes before each Termination. By **C. S. Jerram**, M.A., late Scholar of Trinity College, Oxon.

Crown 8vo. 1s. 6d.

Professor Inman's Nautical Tables,

for the use of British Seamen. *New Edition*, by the Rev. **J. W. Inman**, late Fellow of St. John's College, Cambridge, and Head Master of Chudleigh Grammar School. Revised, and enlarged by the introduction of Tables of ½ log. haversines, log. differences, &c.; with a more compendious method of Working a Lunar, and a Catalogue of Latitudes and Longitudes of Places on the Seaboard.

Royal 8vo. 21s.

Arithmetic, Theoretical and Practical;

adapted for the use of Colleges and Schools.

By **W. H. Girdlestone**, M.A., of Christ's College, Cambridge.

Crown 8vo. 6s. 6d.

A Greek Primer for the use of Schools.

By the Rev. **Charles H. Hole**, M.A., Scholar of Worcester College, Oxford; late Assistant Master at King Edward's School, Bromsgrove.

Crown 8vo. 4s.

Sacred Allegories :

The Shadow of the Cross—The Distant Hills—The Old Man's Home—The King's Messengers.

By the Rev. **W. Adams**, M.A., late Fellow of Merton College, Oxford. With Illustrations.

New Edition. Small 8vo. 5s.

The Four Allegories are also published separately in 18mo., 1s. each in limp cloth.

Priest and Parish.

By the Rev. **Harry Jones**, M.A., Incumbent of St. Luke's, Berwick Street, Soho ; Author of "Life in the World."

Square crown 8vo. 6s. 6d.

Private Devotions for School-boys ;

together with some Rules of Conduct given by a Father to his Son, on his going to School.

By **William Henry**, third **Lord Lyttelton**; revised and corrected by his Son, fourth **Lord Lyttelton**.

Fifth Edition. 32mo. 6d.

The Office of the Most Holy Name :

Devotional Help for Young Persons.

By the Editor of "The Churchman's Guide to Faith," &c.

18mo. 2s. 6d.

Henry's First Latin Book.

By **Thomas Kerchever Arnold**, M.A., late Rector of Lyndon, and formerly Fellow of Trinity College, Cambridge.

Twentieth Edition. 12mo. 3s.

London, Oxford, and Cambridge

Hymns and Poems for the Sick and

Suffering ; in connexion with the Service for the Visitation of the Sick. Selected from various Authors.

Edited by **T. V. Fosbery**, M.A., Vicar of St. Giles's, Reading.

This Volume contains 233 separate pieces ; of which about 90 are by writers who lived prior to the 18th Century ; the rest are Modern, and some of these original. Amongst the names of the writers (between 70 and 80 in number) occur those of Sir J. Beaumont, Sir T. Browne, Elizabeth of Bohemia, Phineas Fletcher, George Herbert, Dean Hickes, Bishop Ken, Francis Quarles, George Sandys, Jeremy Taylor, Henry Vaughan, Sir H. Wotton ; and of modern writers, Mrs. Barrett Browning, Bishop Wilberforce, Samuel Taylor Coleridge, William Wordsworth, Archbishop Trench. Rev. J. Chandler, Rev. J. Keble, Rev. H. F. Lyte, Rev. J. S. Monsell, Rev. J. Moultrie.

New and cheaper Edition. Small 8vo. 3s. 6d.

Döderlein's Handbook of Latin Synonymes.

Translated from the German, by **H. H. Arnold**, B.A.

Third Edition. 12mo. 4s.

The Church Builder : a Quarterly

Journal of Church Extension in England and Wales. Published in connexion with "The Incorporated Church Building Society." Volume for 1868.

With Illustrations. Crown 8vo. 1s. 6d.

A Christian View of Christian His-

tory, from Apostolic to Mediæval Times.

By **John Henry Blunt**, M.A.

Crown 8vo. 7s.

A Practical Introduction to Latin

Prose Composition : Part I.

By **Thomas Kerchever Arnold**, M.A., late Rector of Lyndon,
and formerly Fellow of Trinity College, Cambridge.
Fourteenth Edition. 8vo. 6s. 6d.

A Practical Introduction to English

Prose Composition. An English Grammar for Classical
Schools; with Questions, and a Course of Exercises.

By **Thomas Kerchever Arnold**, M.A., late Rector of Lyndon,
and formerly Fellow of Trinity College, Cambridge.
Eighth Edition. 12mo. 4s. 6d.

A Plain and Short History of England

for Children : In Letters from a Father to his Son. With a Set
of Questions at the end of each Letter.

By **George Davys**, D.D., late Bishop of Peterborough.
New Edition. 1s. 6d.

A Manual of Confirmation, comprising

—1. A General Account of the Ordinance. 2. The Baptismal
Vow, and the English Order of Confirmation, with Short Notes,
Critical and Devotional. 3. Meditations and Prayers on Passages of Holy Scripture, in connexion with the Ordinance. With
a Pastoral Letter instructing Catechumens how to prepare themselves for their first Communion.

By **Edward Meyrick Goulburn**, D.D., Dean of Norwich.
Seventh Edition. Small 8vo. 1s. 6d.

London, Oxford, and Cambridge

Latin via English;

being the Second Part of Spelling turned Etymology.

By **Thomas Kerchever Arnold**, M.A., late Rector of Lyndon, and formerly Fellow of Trinity College, Cambridge.

Third Edition. 12mo. 4s. 6d.

A Collection of English Exercises,

translated from the writings of Cicero, for Schoolboys to re-translate into Latin.

By **William Ellis**, M.A.; re-arranged and adapted to the Rules of the Public School Latin Primer, by **John T. White**, D.D., joint Author of White and Riddle's Latin-English Dictionary.

12mo. 3s. 6d.

A complete Greek and English Lexicon

for the Poems of Homer, and the Homeridæ; illustrating the domestic, religious, political, and military condition of the Heroic Age, and explaining the most difficult passages.

By **G. Ch. Crusius**. Translated from the German, with corrections and additions, by **Henry Smith**, Professor of Languages in Marietta College. Revised and edited by **Thomas Kerchever Arnold**, M.A., late Rector of Lyndon, and formerly Fellow of Trinity College, Cambridge.

Third Edition. 12mo. 9s.

A copious Phraseological English-

Greek Lexicon; founded on a work prepared by **J. W. Frieders-dorff**, Ph. Dr., late Professor of Modern Languages, Queen's College, Belfast.

Revised, Enlarged, and Improved by the late **Thomas Kerchever Arnold**, M.A., formerly Fellow of Trinity College, Cambridge, and **Henry Browne**, M.A., Vicar of Pevensey, and Prebendary of Chichester.

Fourth Edition. 8vo. 21s.

London, Oxford, and Cambridge

NEW PAMPHLETS

ON THE IRISH CHURCH QUESTION.

BY THE BISHOP OF OSSORY.

The Case of the Established Church in Ireland. By
JAMES THOMAS O'BRIEN, D.D., Bishop of Ossory, Ferns, and Leighlin.
Third Edition. With Appendix. 8vo. 2s. 6d.
The Appendix may also be had separately, 1s.

BY LORD MAYO.

Speech delivered in the House of Commons, 10th
March, 1868, upon Mr. Maguire's Motion as to the State of Ireland. By the
Earl of MAYO. 8vo. 1s.

BY LORD REDESDALE.

Speech in the House of Lords on Friday, 17th July,
1868, on moving for a copy of the Coronation Oath; with a Reply to an
Article in the "Saturday Review." 8vo. 6d.

BY JOHN JEBB, D.D.

The Rights of the Irish Branch of the United
Church of England and Ireland Considered on Fundamental Principles,
Human and Divine. By JOHN JEBB, D.D., Rector of Peterstow, Prebendary
and Prælector of Hereford Cathedral, and one of the Proctors for the Clergy
of Hereford in the Convocation of Canterbury. *Second Edition.* 8vo. 1s.

BY THE REV. LORD O'NEILL AND THE REV. DR. LEE.

The Church in Ireland. 1. *The Difficulties of her*
Present Position Considered. By the Rev. Lord O'NEILL, of Shane's
Castle, formerly Prebendary of S. Michael's, Dublin. II. The Duty of
Churchmen in England and Ireland at this Crisis towards Her. By the
Rev. ALFRED T. LEE, LL.D., Rector of Ahoghill, and Chaplain to his
Excellency the Lord Lieutenant. Two Sermons, lately preached in the
Parish Church of Ahoghill, Diocese of Connor. *Second Edition.* 8vo. 6d.

The Irish Difficulty. 1. *The Church Question.*
2. The Land Question. 3. The Education Question. Being a Review of the
Debate in the House of Commons on Mr. Maguire's Motion (March 10,
1868). By an OBSERVER. *Fifth Edition.* 8vo. 6d.

The Church, the Land, and the Constitution; or,
Mr. Gladstone in the newly-reformed Parliament. *Second Edition.* 8vo. 6d.

NEW PAMPHLETS.

BY THE BISHOP OF WORCESTER.

A Charge delivered to the Clergy and Churchwardens
of the Diocese of Worcester. By HENRY, Lord Bishop of WORCESTER,
at his Visitation in June, 1868. 8vo. 1s. 6d.

BY THE BISHOP OF PERTH.

Christ's Spiritual Presence with His Worshippers
the True Glory of His House: a Sermon preached in the New Parish
Church of Stroud, Gloucestershire, on Wednesday, August 5, 1868 (the
Morrow of the Consecration). By the Right Rev. MATTHEW HALE, D.D.,
Bishop of Perth. 12mo. 3d.

BY ARCHDEACON WORDSWORTH.

On the Proposed Council at Rome: an Address, at
the Ordination of Priests and Deacons in the Diocese of Oxford, Sept. 20,
1868. By CHR. WORDSWORTH, D.D., Canon of Westminster, and Archdeacon. 8vo. 1s.

Sacred Music: a Sermon preached at the Anni-
versary of the Choral Association of the Diocese of Llandaff, in the Cathedral Church of Llandaff, Sept. 2, 1868. By CHR. WORDSWORTH, D.D.,
Archdeacon of Westminster. 8vo. 6d.

BY ARCHDEACON BICKERSTETH.

A Charge delivered at his Tenth Visitation of the
Archdeaconry of Buckingham, in June, 1868. By EDWARD BICKERSTETH,
D.D., Prolocutor of the Lower House of Convocation of the Province
of Canterbury, Archdeacon of Buckingham, Honorary Canon of Christ
Church, and Vicar of Aylesbury. 8vo. 1s.

BY ARCHDEACON DENISON.

The Churches of England and Ireland one Church
by identity of Divine Trust: a Paper read at a Special Meeting of the Irish
Church Society, Dublin, Wednesday, September 30, 1868. By GEORGE
ANTHONY DENISON, M.A., Vicar of East Brent, Archdeacon of Taunton.
8vo. 6d.

BY ARCHDEACON ROSE.

The Position of the Church of England as a National
Church Historically Considered; being the Primary Charge of HENRY
JOHN ROSE, B.D., Archdeacon of Bedford. 8vo. 1s.

BY THE REV. F. PIGOU.

The Power of Unostentatious Piety: a Sermon
preached in St. Philip's Chapel, Regent Street, Sunday, June 14, and before
the Queen and Royal Family, in the Private Chapel, Windsor Castle,
Sunday, June 21. By FRANCIS PIGOU, M.A., F.R.G.S., Incumbent of
St. Philip's. 8vo. 6d.

BY THE REV. JOHN MARTIN.

Bribery: a Sermon. By JOHN MARTIN, M.A., of Sidney Sussex
College, and Vicar of St. Andrew the Great, Cambridge. 8vo. 6d.

CATENA CLASSICORUM,

A SERIES OF CLASSICAL AUTHORS,

EDITED BY MEMBERS OF BOTH UNIVERSITIES UNDER
THE DIRECTION OF

THE REV. ARTHUR HOLMES, M.A.

FELLOW AND LECTURER OF CLARE COLLEGE, CAMBRIDGE, LECTURER AND LATE
FELLOW OF ST. JOHN'S COLLEGE,

AND

THE REV. CHARLES BIGG, M.A.

LATE SENIOR STUDENT AND TUTOR OF CHRIST CHURCH, OXFORD, SECOND
CLASSICAL MASTER OF CHELTENHAM COLLEGE.

The following Parts have been already published:—

SOPHOCLIS TRAGOEDIAE,

Edited by R. C. JEBB, M.A. Fellow and Assistant Tutor of Trinity
College, Cambridge.
 [Part I. The Electra. 3s. 6d.   Part II. The Ajax. 3s. 6d.

JUVENALIS SATIRAE,

Edited by G. A. SIMCOX, M.A. Fellow and Classical Lecturer of
Queen's College, Oxford.   . [Thirteen Satires. 3s. 6d.

THUCYDIDIS HISTORIA,

Edited by CHARLES BIGG, M.A. late Senior Student and Tutor of
Christ Church, Oxford. Second Classical Master of Chelten-
ham College.
 [Vol. I. Books I. and II. with Introductions. 6s.

DEMOSTHENIS ORATIONES PUBLICAE,

Edited by G. H. HESLOP, M.A. late Fellow and Assistant Tutor
of Queen's College, Oxford. Head Master of St. Bees.
 [Parts I. & II. The Olynthiacs and the Philippics. 4s. 6d.

ARISTOPHANIS COMOEDIAE,

Edited by W. C. GREEN, M.A. late Fellow of King's College,
Cambridge. Classical Lecturer at Queens' College.
 [Part I. The Acharnians and the Knights. 4s.
 [Part II. The Clouds. 3s. 6d.
 [Part III. The Wasps. (*Just ready.*)

ISOCRATIS ORATIONES,

Edited by JOHN EDWIN SANDYS, B.A. Fellow and Lecturer of
St. John's College, and Lecturer at Jesus College, Cambridge.
 [Part I. Ad Demonicum et Panegyricus. 4s. 6d.

London, Oxford, and Cambridge

CATENA CLASSICORUM—Opinions of the Press.

Mr. Jebb's Sophocles.

"Of Mr. Jebb's scholarly edition of the 'Electra' of Sophocles we cannot speak too highly. The whole Play bears evidence of the taste, learning, and fine scholarship of its able editor. Illustrations drawn from the literature of the Continent as well as of England, and the researches of the highest classical authorities are embodied in the notes, which are brief, clear, and always to the point."—*London Review, March 16, 1867.*

"The editorship of the work before us is of a very high order, displaying at once ripe scholarship, sound judgment, and conscientious care. An excellent Introduction gives an account of the various forms assumed in Greek literature by the legend upon which 'The Electra' is founded, and institutes a comparison between it and the 'Choephorae' of Æschylus. The text is mainly that of Dindorf. In the notes, which are admirable in every respect, is to be found exactly what is wanted, and yet they rather suggest and direct further inquiry than supersede exertion on the part of the student."—*Athenæum.*

"The Introduction proves that Mr. Jebb is something more than a mere scholar,—a man of real taste and feeling. His criticism upon Schlegel's remarks on the Electra are, we believe, new, and certainly just. As we have often had occasion to say in this Review, it is impossible to pass any reliable criticism upon school-books until they have been tested by experience. The notes, however, in this case appear to be clear and sensible, and direct attention to the points where attention is most needed."—*Westminster Review.*

"We have no hesitation in saying that in style and manner Mr. Jebb's notes are admirably suited for their purpose. The explanations of grammatical points are singularly lucid, the parallel passages generally well chosen, the translations bright and graceful, the analysis of arguments terse and luminous. Mr. Jebb has clearly shown that he possesses some of the qualities most essential for a commentator."—*Spectator*

"The notes appear to us exactly suited to assist boys of the Upper Forms at Schools, and University students; they give sufficient help without over-doing explanations. . . . . His critical remarks show acute and exact scholarship, and a very useful addition to ordinary notes is the scheme of metres in the choruses."—*Guardian.*

"If, as we are fain to believe, the editors of the *Catena Classicorum* have got together such a pick of scholars as have no need to play their best card first, there is a bright promise of success to their series in the first sample of it which has come to hand —Mr. Jebb's 'Electra.' We have seen it suggested that it is unsafe to pronounce on the merits of a Greek Play edited for educational purposes until it has been tested in the hands of pupils and tutors. But our examination of the instalment of, we hope, a complete 'Sophocles,' which Mr. Jebb has put forth, has assured us that this is a needless suspension of judgment, and prompted us to commit the justifiable rashness of pronouncing upon its contents, and of asserting after due perusal that it is calculated to be admirably serviceable to every class of scholars and learners. And this assertion is based upon the fact that it is a by no means one-sided edition, and that it looks as with the hundred eyes of Argus, here, there, and everywhere, to keep the reader from straying. In a

CATENA CLASSICORUM—Opinions of the Press.

concise and succinct style of English annotation, forming the best substitute for the time-honoured Latin notes which had so much to do with making good scholars in days of yore, Mr. Jebb keeps a steady eye for all questions of grammar, construction, scholarship, and philology, and handles these as they arise with a helpful and sufficient precision. In matters of grammar and syntax his practice for the most part is to refer his reader to the proper section of Madvig's 'Manual of Greek Syntax;' nor does he ever waste space and time in explaining a construction, unless it be such an one as is not satisfactorily dealt with in the grammars of Madvig or Jelf. Experience as a pupil and a teacher has probably taught him the value of the wholesome task of hunting out a grammar reference for oneself, instead of finding it, handy for slurring over, amidst the hundred and one pieces of information in a voluminous foot-note. But whenever there occurs any peculiarity of construction, which is hard to reconcile to the accepted usage, it is Mr. Jebb's general practice to be ready at hand with manful assistance."—*Contemporary Review*.

"Mr. Jebb has produced a work which will be read with interest and profit by the most advanced scholar, as it contains, in a compact form, not only a careful summary of the labours of preceding editors, but also many acute and ingenious original remarks. We do not know whether the matter or the manner of this excellent commentary is deserving of the higher praise: the skill with which Mr. Jebb has avoided, on the one hand, the wearisome prolixity of the Germans, and on the other the jejune brevity of the Porsonian critics, or the versatility which has enabled him in turn to elucidate the plots, to explain the verbal difficulties, and to illustrate the idioms of his author. All this, by a studious economy of space and a remarkable precision of expression, he has done for the 'Ajax' in a volume of some 500 pages."—*Athenæum*.

Mr. Simcox's Juvenal.

"Of Mr. Simcox's 'Juvenal' we can only speak in terms of the highest commendation, as a simple, unpretending work, admirably adapted to the wants of the school-boy or of a college passman. It is clear, concise, and scrupulously honest in shirking no real difficulty. The pointed epigrammatic hits of the satirist are every where well brought out, and the notes really are what they profess to be, explanatory in the best sense of the term."—*London Review*.

"This is a link in the *Catena Classicorum* to which the attention of our readers has been more than once directed as a good Series of Classical works for School and College purposes. The Introduction is a very comprehensive and able account of Juvenal, his satires, and the manuscripts."—*Athenæum*.

"This is a very original and enjoyable Edition of one of our favourite classics."—*Spectator*.

"Every class of readers—those who use Mr. Simcox as their sole interpreter, and those who supplement larger editions by his concise matter—will alike find interest and careful research in his able Preface. This indeed we should call the great feature of his book. The three facts which sum up Juvenal's history so far as we know it are soon despatched; but the internal evidence both as to the dates of his writing and publishing his Satires, and as to his character as a writer, occupy some fifteen or twenty pages, which will repay methodical study."—*Churchman*.

CATENA CLASSICORUM—Opinions of the Press.

Mr. Bigg's Thucydides.

"Mr. Bigg in his 'Thucydides' prefixes an analysis to each book, and an admirable introduction to the whole work, containing full information as to all that is known or related of Thucydides, and the date at which he wrote, followed by a very masterly critique on some of his characteristics as a writer."—*Athenæum.*

"While disclaiming absolute originality in his book, Mr. Bigg has so thoroughly digested the works of so many eminent predecessors in the same field, and is evidently on terms of such intimacy with his author as perforce to inspire confidence. A well-pondered and well-written introduction has formed a part of each link in the 'Catena' hitherto published, and Mr. Bigg, in addition to a general introduction, has given us an essay on 'Some Characteristics of Thucydides,' which no one can read without being impressed with the learning and judgment brought to bear on the subject."—*Standard.*

"We need hardly say that these books are carefully edited : the reputation of the editor is an assurance on this point. If the rest of the history is edited with equal care, it must become the standard book for school and college purposes."—*John Bull.*

"Mr. Bigg first discusses the facts of the life of Thucydides, then passes to an examination into the date at which Thucydides wrote ; and in the third section expatiates on some characteristics of Thucydides. These essays are remarkably well written, are judicious in their opinions, and are calculated to give the student much insight into the work of Thucydides, and its relation to his own times, and to the works of subsequent historians."—*Museum.*

Mr. Heslop's Demosthenes.

"The usual introduction has in this case been dispensed with. The reader is referred to the works of Grote and Thirlwall for information on such points of history as arise out of these famous orations, and on points of critical scholarship to 'Madvig's Grammar,' where that is available, while copious acknowledgments are made to those commentators on whose works Mr. Heslop has based his own. Mr. Heslop's editions are, however, no mere compilations. That the points required in an oratorical style differ materially from those in an historical style, will scarcely be questioned, and accordingly we find that Mr. Heslop has given special care to these characteristics of style as well as of language, which constitute Demosthenes the very first of classic orators."—*Standard.*

"We must call attention to New Editions of various classics, in the excellent 'Catena Classicorum' series. The reputation and high standing of the editors are the best guarantees for the accuracy and scholarship of the notes."—*Westminster Review.*

"The notes are thoroughly good, so far as they go. Mr. Heslop has carefully digested the best foreign commentaries, and his notes are for the most part judicious extracts from them."—*Museum.*

"The annotations are scarcely less to be commended for the exclusion of superfluous matter than for the excellence of what is supplied. Well-known works are not quoted, but simply referred to, and information which ought to have been previously acquired is omitted."—*Athenæum.*

London, Oxford, and Cambridge

CATENA CLASSICORUM—Opinions of the Press.

Mr. Green's Aristophanes.

"The Editors of this Series have undertaken the task of issuing texts of all the authors commonly read, and illustrating them with an English Commentary, compendious as well as clear. If the future volumes fulfil the promise of the Prospectus as well as those already published, the result will be a very valuable work. The excellence of the print, and the care and pains bestowed upon the general getting up, form a marked contrast to the school-books of our own day. Who does not remember the miserable German editions of classical authors in paper covers, execrably printed on detestable paper, which were thought amply good enough for the school-boys of the last generation? A greater contrast to these can hardly be imagined than is presented by the *Catena Classicorum*. Nor is the improvement only external: the careful revision of the text, and the notes, not too lengthy and confused, but well and judiciously selected, which are to be found in every page, add considerably to the value of this Edition, which we may safely predict will soon be an established favourite, not only among Schoolmasters, but at the Universities. The volume before us contains the first part of an Edition of Aristophanes which comprises the Acharnians and the Knights, the one first in order, and the other the most famous of the plays of the great Athenian Satirist."—*Churchman.*

"The utmost care has been taken with this Edition of the most sarcastic and clever of the old Greek dramatists, facilitating the means of understanding both the text and intention of that biting sarcasm which will never lose either point or interest, and is as well adapted to the present age as it was to the times when first put forward."—*Bell's Weekly Messenger.*

"The advantages conferred on the learner by these compendious aids can only be properly estimated by those who had experience of the mode of study years ago. The translated passages and the notes, while sufficient to assist the willing learner, cannot be regarded in any sense as a *cram*."—*Clerical Journal.*

"Mr. Green has discharged his part of the work with uncommon skill and ability. The notes show a thorough study of the two Plays, an independent judgment in the interpretation of the poet, and a wealth of illustration, from which the Editor draws whenever it is necessary."—*Museum.*

"Mr. Green presumes the existence of a fair amount of scholarship in all who read Aristophanes, as a study of his works generally succeeds to some considerable knowledge of the tragic poets. The notes he has appended are therefore brief, perhaps a little too brief. We should say the tendency of most modern editors is rather the other way; but Mr. Green no doubt knows the class for which he writes, and has been careful to supply their wants."—*Spectator.*

"Mr. Green's admirable Introduction to 'The Clouds' of the celebrated comic poet deserves a careful perusal, as it contains an accurate analysis and many original comments on this remarkable play. The text is prefaced by a table of readings of Dindorf and Meineke, which will be of great service to students who wish to indulge in verbal criticism. The notes are copious and lucid, and the volume will be found useful for school and college purposes, and admirably adapted for private reading."—*Examiner.*

"Mr. Green furnishes an excellent Introduction to 'The Clouds' of Aristophanes, explaining the circumstances under which it was produced, and ably discussing the probable object of the author in writing it, which he considers to have been to put down the Sophists, a class whom Aristophanes thought dangerous to the morals of the community, and therefore caricatured in the person of Socrates,—not unnaturally, though irreverently, choosing him as their representative."—*Athenæum.*

London, Oxford, and Cambridge

CATENA CLASSICORUM.

The following Parts are in course of preparation:—

PLATONIS PHAEDO,

Edited by ALFRED BARRY, D.D. late Fellow of Trinity College, Cambridge, Principal of King's College, London.

DEMOSTHENIS ORATIONES PUBLICAE,

Edited by G. H. HESLOP, M.A. late Fellow and Assistant Tutor of Queen's College, Oxford.   Head Master of St. Bees.
[Part II. De Falsâ Legatione.

MARTIALIS EPIGRAMMATA,

Edited by GEORGE BUTLER, M.A. Principal of Liverpool College ; late Fellow of Exeter College, Oxford.

DEMOSTHENIS ORATIONES PRIVATAE,

Edited by ARTHUR HOLMES, M.A. Fellow and Lecturer of Clare College, Cambridge.   [Part I.   De Coronâ.

HOMERI ILIAS,

Edited by S. H. REYNOLDS, M.A. Fellow and Tutor of Brasenose College, Oxford.   [Vol. I. Books I. to XII.

HORATI OPERA,

Edited by J. M. MARSHALL, M.A. Fellow and late Lecturer of Brasenose College, Oxford.   One of the Masters in Clifton College.

TERENTI COMOEDIAE,

Edited by T. L. PAPILLON, M.A. Fellow and Classical Lecturer of Merton College, Oxford.

HERODOTI HISTORIA,

Edited by H. G. WOODS, M.A. Fellow and Tutor of Trinity College, Oxford.

TACITI HISTORIAE,

Edited by W. H. SIMCOX, M.A. Fellow and Lecturer of Queen's College, Oxford.

PERSII SATIRAE,

Edited by A. PRETOR, M.A., of Trinity College, Cambridge, Classical Lecturer of Trinity Hall, Composition Lecturer to Perse Grammar School, Cambridge.

www.ingramcontent.com/pod-product-compliance
Lightning Source LLC
Chambersburg PA
CBHW020106030726
47498CB00006B/1980